VENICE

LIA HALE

To Luke

Who always listened

ONE

I stomp outside, the anger vented towards my mother fading with each step I take. It is one thing to announce we're moving, but another not to tell us until a week before we are supposed to leave. A *week*. What on Earth is Mom thinking? We can't pack up and move in one week, especially since we haven't even started cleaning up the house or giving away the stuff we can't take with us or telling our friends that we're moving. It's all so frustrating. I want to scream and yell and argue with my mom, but I know it's no use. She has her mind set on a tiny little town in the middle of nowhere, a.k.a. central Virginia, and there is no changing her decision.

She says that she wants to go to Virginia because it's green and peaceful and not too cramped with city life, but I know she wants to get out of California, away from my grandparents, her in-laws, and memories of my dad, her ex-husband. In normal circumstances, I would understand, but to run away from the sweet *old* couple that despite the divorce have always treated her like their own daughter makes me know this isn't normal. What kind of woman runs from the people who have proven the least likely to judge her?

My mom and dad split up nearly six years ago. They were always getting in fights, and we all knew their relationship wasn't going to last much longer. Dad was constantly complaining about my mom and how crazy she was with her ideas on how to save the planet and go green; that she was starving him with all the organic food she bought from the supermarket; that she was always nagging him to install solar panels on our roof and to buy a Hybrid so we wouldn't pollute the air as much. I admit that my mom *is* rather strong with her opinions, and she sometimes goes over the top, like when she turned off the water so my twin sister couldn't take a ten-minute shower. Or the time when Mom threw a party and refused to use paper and plastic plates, cups, and utensils, instead buying over three dozen of those things in stainless steel.

Mom does excel at being a tree hugger. And I love her for it. She doesn't shy away from people who disagree with her beliefs. She has never escaped an argument except for now, when she can barely face us. She knows she's made all of us mad. My twin sister, Florence, threw a big fit about how Mom can shout down someone pouring motor oil into a local lagoon—long story—but she couldn't even stand to be in the same gigantic city as her ex-husband? I partly agree with Florence, but also with Mom. Maybe we should leave. Each time we visit Grandma and Grandpa Ferrari, it gets quiet and uncomfortable. And Dad is never around—he comes up with excuses not to see his kids. I don't even know where he is.

I reach my mailbox and yank it open, not as angry as when I'd stomped out of the house. I extract a handful of junk mail that will make Mom mad if she sees it, and she'll break into a lecture about how many trees were cut up to produce that junk mail, and all we use it for is to throw it away.

At the back of the mailbox is a thin, light blue envelope that is so familiar I groan.

"Florence!" I yell back at the house.

Half a second later, the front door bangs open and my twin sister comes running out. "What?" She knows why I called her.

I hand her the envelope. "Kent wrote to you again. Better not let Mom see that letter. She's in a bad enough mood, and I doubt she won't take the time to scold you about paper and letters and trees and things like that."

Florence snorts. "It's her fault we're moving." Whirling around, she starts to head back inside, and then calls over her shoulder, "Thanks, Venice! I'm glad you didn't snoop."

I roll my eyes. "I am *not* like Roman."

She giggles, and it's the last thing I hear before she goes inside the house. I shake my head, returning to the junk mail. She's so like me, yet at the same time we're different. People have a hard time telling us apart, they say, but my siblings and Mom know how to. Florence dresses much differently than I do. She wears leather and tank tops and the shortest shorts Mom will let her wear. I dress in naturally-dyed jeans, hand-me-down cotton T-shirts I can buy at the thrift store for less than five dollars, and pretty much anything that can be recycled.

Florence puts on plenty of make-up. She spends an hour each morning in the bathroom, carefully dashing eye-shadow on her eyelids or making sure her mascara hasn't clotted on her lashes or brushing her rose-tinted blush across her cheeks or whatever else she does. She curls her hair, too, into tiny ringlets that stick in all day, but that might be because of how much hair spray she uses. Her lipstick, in a stroke of rebellion, is the very kind Mom heartily disapproves of—the stuff made with wax and pigment. Mom is constantly telling Florence to use plant-based lipstick, but Florence ignores her.

I don't wear any make-up. Mom hates it except for the plant-based lipstick she bought for Florence that my twin refused to put on. Florence gave it to me, and I'm fine with that, I guess. The color is a bright red that reminds me of blood. I still wear it whenever I want; I like the shade of red.

Florence owns plenty of jewelry. She has baskets overflowing with bracelets, small hooks holding necklaces, tiny cushions covered in rings, and rack after rack of earrings. She changes her jewelry every day; today she is wearing a beaded bracelet her boyfriend, Kent, gave her, a big necklace that falls down to her belly button, and dangly earrings that look so heavy they must be weighing down her ears.

The only jewelry I own is a ring my dad sent me on my fifteenth birthday a year ago. I also have two pairs of earrings: the ones my ears were pierced in and some Grandma Ferrari gave me, purple teardrops. I have worn my ring every single day since my birthday— it's the only present I've gotten from Dad since he divorced Mom. It's a simple gold ring with a clear blue stone set in the middle. Two tiny stones were once next to the blue one, but they were gone when I got it. The ring is just barely too small for my fingers, so I slip it on my pinky and it fits almost perfectly. It isn't loose, which I'm glad for. I hate rings that slide around or fall off and get lost.

Flo can't stand Mom's opinions. She thinks it's embarrassing to be so obsessed in conserving energy and using recyclable things. She argues with Mom about pretty much everything, doing her best to persuade Mom otherwise, but Mom just shakes her aside. Left to her own devices, Florence decided to be the complete opposite from Mom. She takes long showers and leaves the water on when she brushes her teeth. She rides the bus to school instead of walking and buys her lunches from either the vending machines or the cafeteria. She keeps her phone plugged in even after it's charged and writes letters on paper rather than email. She wears clothing made from animal skin and other materials besides organic cotton or naturally dyed cloth. She decorates her face with every type of make-up that contains ingredients that are harmful to the environment and herself, though she doesn't know it. She won't listen to me or to Mom when we tell her that.

On the other hand, I faithfully go along with Mom's crazy ideas, never telling her that her judgment is quite strange and slightly over the top. I don't want Mom to leave us, too. I'm fine with walking to school. I'm fine with drinking tap water and wearing second-hand clothes bought at thrift stores. I'm fine with using a refillable pen and unplugging my phone halfway through the night when it's finished charging. I'm fine with wiping down counters with rags instead of paper towels.

Yes, Mom might be a little psychotic with her views, but I love her, and I never complain as long as she doesn't leave us like Dad did, because that would break my heart. It would hurt our family even more than it is.

I walk back inside the house, releasing a sigh as I smell the sharp tang of the chlorine-free chemicals Mom is using to wipe down every surface. She's attacking the coffee table in the living room when I walk in. She looks up at me and smiles.

"Hey, Venice," she says. "Care to join me?"

I grab a rag and crouch next to her, holding my breath as I begin to wipe off the nearest table leg. "Do you think we'll be able to finish up the house in one week?"

Mom pauses to stare long and hard at me. "Yes," she says finally. "And I've already sold the house to someone. They'll be here in six days."

"You've already sold the house?" I repeat, shocked.

She nods, returning to the table. "I'm sorry I didn't tell you earlier. But I knew Florence wouldn't take it well, so I kept putting off the news for a day when she was in a good mood."

"Mom, why are we moving?"

She hesitates, her rag dangling in one hand. "Because," she says after the silence between us has stretched so long it becomes uncomfortable. "I want to get out of city life. Don't you?"

I shrug. "I like California."

"Eh, it's too crowded for me." Mom steps back from the coffee table and starts spraying the end table with her chlorine-free chemicals. "And there is too much pollution. Why, if those stupid celebrities stopped flying all over the place in their fancy private jets, the air would be loads cleaner." She drags her rag along the top of the end table. "You'll like Virginia, Venice. It's green and rains a lot there and you'll make plenty of friends."

"I have friends here," I point out, walking over to her.

She snorts. "Yes, the kids who can't tell the difference between you and Florence."

I flinch, and Mom immediately blushes and corrects herself. "You have lots of friends," she says quickly. "Jenna and Hailey and Emma."

"Yeah." I scrub at a milk spot on the end table, but what Mom said is stuck in my head. Most of Flo's shallow friends mistake me for her sometimes. I've given up correcting them. It makes me both annoyed and depressed. I'm annoyed because they can't even tell which twin is their actual friend, and I'm depressed because I don't have any good friends. I try to fit in, but it seems like everyone in my school is the complete opposite of me. Will Virginia be any better? Or is it just going to be like California?

"VENICE! Tell Roman he has to give me my phone back! He took it and now he's reading all my texts!"

I groan and pull my pillow over my face, not wanting to hear another word out of Florence's mouth. Apparently Roman, our younger brother, has stolen her phone from the charging rack and is currently snooping on her thousands of texts to Kent.

My bedroom door bursts open and Florence, decked out in a pink tank top and ripped jeans, runs inside. "Venice!" she yells. "Get your lazy bum out of bed and come *help* me!" She drags the pillow off my face. "Come on! Hurry up! You're so slow!"

Giving up any hope of falling asleep again, I swing my legs off the bed and squint up at her, one hand reaching for my glasses. "Why do I have to get your phone back? Can't you?"

"You're the oldest!"

My eyes focus the instant I put my glasses on. I see her face is red. "I'm older by eight minutes. That's not a lot."

"Whatever." Flo tosses her hair over her shoulder. "Come on!"

She leads me into Roman's room, the one he shares with our

other younger, dear, annoying brother, Pompeii. Both boys are on Roman's bed, scrolling through something on a phone I recognize as Florence's by the glittery pink case. The boys look up at me when I enter the room. I have to choke back a gag as the near-fatal fumes of *boy* greet my nose. Their stinky clothes are draped over every available surface, including the lamp and the bookshelf that holds nothing close to a book. It has Roman's failed rocket experiments on it instead, like rockets are more important than books. The only window is blocked by the shade, which is pulled down, since Mom is constantly telling us it will save money on air conditioning and heating to keep the blinds shut.

Their room is a complete mess, even though we're supposed to be leaving for Virginia tomorrow.

"Will you please give Flo her phone back?" I ask politely, hoping they will ignore the fact that I obviously just rolled out of bed.

Roman snorts. "Why would we do that?"

"I don't have to get Mom, do I?" I threaten.

Suddenly, a pajama-clad figure appears at my elbow, tugging on my shirt sleeve. "Venice, can you help me pour the milk? I can't lift the heavy jug high enough for any milk to come out, and Mom said she is too busy getting the house ready and can't pour my milk."

"Sure, Siena," I say, resisting the urge to rub my forehead. "I just need to help Florence first. Alright?"

Siena nods. "Okay."

I turn my attention to Roman. "You're fourteen, Roman. Don't you think it might be time to grow up?"

"Growing up is for losers," spits Roman. His gaze is fixed resolutely on the glowing screen in his hand. He's clearly doing this to get a reaction from our sister and cause a fight.

Pompeii chortles and points to something. "Look! Kent said he thought Flo was hot! How gross is that?"

I give in to my anger. Stomping across the room, I snatch the phone out of Roman's hand, then whirl around and shove it towards my twin, who takes it, sticks her tongue out at Roman, and flaunts away. Roman snarls at me, his curly hair somehow making him look like the adorable little boy I remember from childhood.

"Why do you ruin everything, Venice?" he snaps. "I was having bonding time with Pompeii, and you just came in here and wrecked it all!"

I lift an eyebrow. "You might have been bonding with Pompeii, but you're not bonding with Florence."

He frowns. "Why would I want to bond with her? She's so annoying about her boyfriend and she hates Mom and she refuses to do what Mom says or asks her to do."

"That's rich," I say, "coming from you."

Tired of arguing, I take Siena's hand and tug her downstairs and into the empty, clean kitchen. The only thing in the fridge is a jug of organic milk and the mini cooler we'll take when driving to Virginia. The cabinets are bare; it's both saddening and relieving. We don't have any more cleaning to do.

Siena's bran cereal is on the table. I pour the milk for her, and her smile of gratitude is almost enough to make me feel cheery again. I sit down next to her and pour myself a bowl of cereal.

"So," I say, twirling my spoon around in my bowl, "what are you most excited about moving?"

The ten year-old shrugs. "Mom says the school is too far from our house to walk, so she'll have to drive me there. I won't be able to walk with any friends I make."

"You're already planning on befriending the entire school and neighborhood?" I tease, knowing it'll probably happen. Siena is such a cute little girl; it's hard to resist her charms. I think more people are sad to see her go than the rest of us. Her elementary school even threw her a goodbye party. My high school didn't do that for me or Florence or Roman. Not that I had wanted them to. If they had, I would've stayed as far away from them as possible. I'm not social, and too much attention makes me uncomfortable. That's probably why I have so few friends.

"If they give me some cookies, I'll be friends with anyone," Siena is saying, and I pull myself back into the conversation.

"Just make sure that person is mindful of the environment," I warn. "Mom might forbid you to talk to them if not."

Siena rolls her eyes, spooning in a mouthful of cereal. She takes a minute to swallow before saying, "Mom sometimes goes over the top. But I still love her for it."

I grin and take another bite of my cereal so I don't have to answer. We finish and clean off our things, placing them in a box full of other dishes and silverware, and I close the flaps with some melancholy. I'll miss California.

Mom suddenly comes rushing into the kitchen, her face flushed with excitement.

"We're leaving!" she announces. "The buyers are here and need us to get out!"

TWO

The second we pull away from our house-that-isn't-ours-any-more, Mom is yelling at me to find the map to Virginia so we won't get lost. I don't bother pointing out that we haven't even left our neighborhood and fish my phone from my back pocket. Turning it on, I find the map she'd shared with me. Our way to Virginia. It's going to be so weird, tromping around the countryside with my siblings, not knowing anyone besides ourselves. I know Florence will make friends with kids at school, but unless I accidentally crash into someone at the library or something like that, I'm going to be left alone this year.

The drive is boring and uneventful. The most exciting thing that happens is Pompeii throwing up all over Roman as the boys try to see how many jelly beans they can eat. Mom isn't very happy, but after the mess is cleaned up, we're back on the road. I'm Mom's navigator—she is truly terrible at it, and she *is* driving, so I pretty much stay up all night helping her not fall asleep or telling her that she's missed the only vegan restaurant for miles and miles and we should either turn around or go to a burger joint. Mom isn't vegan; in fact, she loves meat and cheese, along with milk and butter. She just really likes vegan food. She says it tastes like fresh times. I don't quite agree with her—just between you and me, grass drizzled with ranch dressing tastes better than the wilted greens salads served at vegan restaurants. The only person in our family of six with different eating habits is Roman, who decided two years ago that he hates soup, so he refuses to eat it.

Speaking of Roman...I twist my head around to stare at his sleeping form in the glowing orange of the streetlights that pass above us. Roman looks a bit like my dad—he inherited his temper and brown eyes. Other than that, he's like Mom—dark auburn curls; a sharp, pointed nose; a strong jaw; and thick eyelashes. Roman, named after Rome, is the most peculiar, troublesome fourteen year-old I have ever known. He gets in trouble, but he manages to persuade Mom otherwise, getting out of the deepest pits and escaping the harshest punishments. Personally, I think Mom has a weakness for his wide eyes and brilliant smile.

My gaze shifts to Pompeii, who is asleep next to Roman, his head on his brother's shoulder. I feel closer to Pompeii than Roman, partly because the kid is twelve and deserves an older sister who cares for him—Florence does *not* put up with his daydreaming—and partly because he is so like me. We are both socially awkward. We both would rather spend an afternoon in a local library than hanging out at the mall with hoards of friends. Pompeii looks similar to Roman, just younger and less wild. His curly hair isn't as curly as Roman's; his eyes are from Mom—deep, dark green; and unlike his other siblings, he doesn't have to wear glasses. Florence, Roman, Siena, and I all received Mom's terrible eyesight.

Siena is squished against Pompeii, her glasses slipped down her nose. She looks so calm and peaceful there, asleep. You'd never guess how capable she is of fighting with Pompeii. It's kind of like a routine of theirs: wake up, find something to fight about, throw a huge fit loud enough to rouse the entire neighborhood, then walk away with nothing accomplished, nothing gained, except for Mom's annoyance and frustration. Siena acts so charming to each person she meets, it's as if the true demon inside is buried beneath an angel. She looks like Mom and me, with curly auburn hair and the green eyes. Her jaw is strong—she could bite off a finger if one wanted to let her—and her chin is sharp. Her tongue is faster than a trained politician's. She could make any man cry by simply, sincerely, pointing out something about him. Every word that comes out of her mouth is so believable that it's hard to tell when she's joking and when she's not.

Way in the backseat is Florence, hidden in the shadows. I can't see her, but I don't need to know what she looks like. I have each of her features memorized. The way her curly auburn hair falls softly to her shoulders. Her small, delicate nose. Her high cheekbones. Even without make-up, my sister is naturally beautiful. Florence fits right in with the other girls, gossiping about the poor souls at school, swapping different eye-shadow colors, and flirting with every boy that walks by. As for me, I dislike gossip. I don't care at all for eye-shadow, and there will never be a time when I flirt with a boy. I would just make a fool out of myself, and totally embarrass the boy.

Mom sighs, and I return my attention to her, belatedly remembering I am supposed to be keeping her awake. Mom looks like all of us. Curly auburn hair. Dark green eyes. Sharp nose and jaw. That horrible eyesight. Oh, and she's got the signature thick eyelashes we are all cursed with. It may sound silly, but being poked in the eye with a thick eyelash is more painful than being poked by a thin one.

I reach over and switch on the radio, turning down the volume so it won't wake up any of the kids. Mom looks at me briefly, gives me a smile, and goes back to driving. Her glasses are slipping down her nose, and I lean across the seat to fix them for her.

"Do you want me to drive for a bit?" I ask quietly.

Mom shakes her head. "No, I've got this. There is a rest stop in about ten miles. We can sleep there for a few hours, and then maybe you can take a turn at the wheel."

I nod slowly. "Okay."

I'm fine with staying up late. I'm better at it than any of my siblings. Siena falls asleep after an hour in the car; Pompeii gets carsick easily and his last escape is sleep; Roman is constantly napping, or just pretending to so he doesn't have to do certain things; and Florence goes to bed early in the evening so the next morning she can wake up without feeling groggy and can spend the first hour after waking up doing her make-up. I enjoy sleeping in. It isn't exactly healthy for you, and I hate rolling out of bed on a cold or hot day and having to suffer through a freezing shower—Florence uses up all the hot water—so I should probably get up earlier.

I twist the ring on my finger, thinking about how different Virginia is going to be from California. It'll be colder, and more wet. But at least there will be plenty of trees and grass and plants. That's one thing I'm looking forward to. Hopefully our new house is right near a forest, so Pompeii and I can climb the trees whenever we want. The sycamores that grew near our house were difficult to climb. Florence often teases me about doing "boy" things like climbing trees and rollerblading instead of hanging out at the mall shopping for clothes I'll use once in my life then forget about. Florence and I don't necessarily get along—she's Florence and I'm Venice—but it would make me grateful if she wouldn't tease me in public.

Once, when we were in eighth grade, we attended a school dance. Flo, of course, attracted boys left and right, while I sat against the wall and refused to meet anyone's gaze in fear that someone would talk to me. After an hour or two, Florence brought over a large group of boys and tried to talk any of them into asking me to dance. I suppose she thought she was helping me, but all she succeeded in doing was making things really awkward for me. I got up and left after a minute of her coaxing the boys.

From then on, I didn't go to any more dances or parties. I stayed home and read or played with Siena and Pompeii. As much as Flo tried to convince me to go shopping and partying with her, I turned her down. I know she'll have a better time without having to worry about me and how I'm doing, unless she doesn't really care and just acts like she does so people don't think she's a bad sister. She's not—she's only different from me. She is a fun person to talk with and confide secrets in—though normally it's her who tells me secrets, like which boy she now has a crush on—and I love her for who she is.

I sigh and settle back in my seat, eyes on the dark road. The radio is faintly playing something that sounds like classical music—Mozart, maybe?—and I switch the channel to a heavy metal station. Anyone can fall asleep during Mozart, and we need to stay awake.

Still, the rocking car lulls me to sleep before I can stop myself. Before my eyes slide shut, I see the sign promoting a rest area in fifteen miles.

I wake to Siena shaking me. She is standing outside the car, a big grin on her face. Her hair glints dark red in the sunlight. She sees I'm awake and squeals, "Mom said she'll buy us ice cream if we behaved, and we did, so now we're getting some!"

I smile drowsily. "Good for you," I say, my voice slurred. Have I mentioned I am not a morning person?

"Do you want some?" asks Siena. She's so darn cute I can't help but feel excited for ice cream. Her eagerness is so easy to catch onto.

"What kinds of ice cream are there?" I say, stretching an arm over my head.

Siena shrugs. "Delicious kinds. Are you going to come?"

I shake my head. "Nah. I need to wake up fully. Could you get me some vanilla?"

"That is the most boring type," she says, scowling. "Come on, Venice. Why don't you want to get ice cream with us? I'll let you have a bit of mine. Mom said I could have a cone, so we don't use the plastic cups the ice cream comes in."

"Alright, I'll come," I say, unbuckling and sliding out of the car. We're in a parking lot for a small ice cream shop. It's a tiny thing, with a red-and-white striped canopy hung across the top of the shop. A bright sign nailed to the roof reads: *Milo's Ice Cream.* A few traffic cones are set out along the front of the ice cream parlor, resembling something like a line, but the only people here are our family. I look up and see the sun is high in the sky, so it has to be at least ten in the morning. Have I really slept that long?

Roman and Pompeii are already in line. Florence is examining the menu; probably trying to decide which ice cream flavor is the one Mom would hate the most. Mom herself is on her phone across the parking lot, talking quietly with someone. As I watch, she grows more and more animated, waving her arms around, pacing, looking out at distant spots on the horizon, once even stomping her foot.

Siena closes the car door behind me and takes my hand, tugging me into line next to Roman and Pompeii. No one else is around, so I wonder why the boys aren't moving until I spot a tall blonde girl standing behind the parlor's counter, picking at a piece of imaginary lint on her uniform.

"She's the most beautiful girl I've ever seen," whispers Roman. He can't be thinking clearly.

I choke on a suppressed snort. Realizing the boys are too scared to order their ice cream, I approach the counter. The blonde girl looks up, her pretty face twisted into a sneer. Her lip curls.

"Good morning," I say, aiming for pleasantries.

The blonde girl scoffs, her perfect red lipstick twitching as she moves her lips to reply to me. "Is it a good morning, or are you just saying that?"

I take a step back, surprised at the girl's bluntness. "Um…" As I have said, I am socially awkward. I'm okay at ordering things and shopping by myself at the grocery store, but when someone confronts me, my mind goes blank and I forget what to say.

Thank the trees, Siena saves me. She pipes up, "Hey, can I

order a triple-chocolate fudge sundae? I've been *dying* to try one!"
She sounds so cute, so excited, just for ice cream. I remind myself to give her a hug once this is all over and we're far away from this barista.

The blonde girl, whose name tag reads *Pearl,* flicks her gaze down to my little sister, and I recognize that look immediately. She's been captivated by Siena's big, dark green eyes.

"Sure," says Pearl, smiling at Siena. "Is that all?"

I'm not in the mood for ice cream anymore, so I say, "Yes. How much does a triple-chocolate fudge sundae cost?"

"Read the sign," Pearl says brusquely, turning to go make Siena's order at the other side of the shop.

I frown at her retreating form. "She wasn't very nice."

"But she's amazing," says someone by my elbow, and I look down at my love-struck brother, Roman. He obviously ignored how rude Pearl was. He has a dopey grin on his face, and next to him, so does Pompeii. I groan and turn away from the counter, searching for Florence, needing her to save me from the boys' stupidity. Florence isn't in sight. She was by the menu sign a few minutes ago, but now where is she? I widen my search range and spot Flo by Mom, talking. Mom isn't on her phone; she must have finished her call.

A while later, Pearl returns and slaps a bowl down on the counter. It's filled with chocolate ice cream, drizzled with chocolate sauce, and sprinkled with chocolate chips. I almost throw up looking at it. I can't stomach chocolate when it's in the extreme like that.

"Could I have it in a cone?" Siena asks sweetly.

Pearl melts. "Of course." She grabs a plastic spoon and a waffle cone, then begins to shovel the ice cream into the cone.

I'm just starting to think that *I* will have to pay for Siena's ice cream when Mom and Flo come over, Mom eyeing the sundae with distaste. She isn't a big fan of chocolate, either. Once, she heard rumors that her favorite chocolate was being made by child labor, so she refused to touch chocolate again, and even organized a protest against the manufacturing company. Her protest was shut down due to overexcited protestors that showed up buck-naked with *Save the children!* painted across their bodies, but she's never touched a chocolate bar since.

Mom sheds a couple bucks for Siena's ice cream, and we all go back to the car. She frowns at us when we climb in.

"How come Siena was the only one who got ice cream?"

I claim the driver's seat. Mom should take a break for a while. "I decided not to get any. The barista was plenty rude."

"And beautiful," Roman says dreamily.

Florence moans. "Ugh! You're disgusting!" She reaches over her seat and smacks him on the head.

It seems to snap Roman out of whatever daze Pearl has put him in. He yells in pain and twists around to hit Flo back, but Mom sharply tells them to stop, and he obeys, though reluctantly.

I start the car and pull out of the parking lot. "Where to?"

"Um…hold on a minute, I've got to find the map…" Mom turns on her phone and spends less than ten seconds scrolling through things before she looks up and says, "Continue down that road for half a mile, then you'll see the ramp to the freeway."

I follow her instructions carefully, ignoring the little voice in my head that always comes up when I'm driving: the voice that tells me I'll crash and kill all my family. I hate driving, but I have my permit, and Mom needs a break. Florence often complains about how she isn't allowed to get her permit—Mom doesn't trust her driving— and it's a pretty sore spot with Flo, driving a deeper wedge between them, and giving her another reason to resent me.

The day drags by. Since I haven't eaten any food, I'm starving, and since I am the one driving, I can't reach back and grab a granola bar, so I am stuck in the front seat, sweating in the hot sun that filters through the window. Each time I turn on the air conditioning, Mom stops me, saying we should roll down the windows instead. I roll down the windows, but we're going over sixty miles and Roman yells that I'm messing up his hair. The windows go back up, and I'm left melting into the seat.

I drive for five hours, then Mom has me stop at this tiny Greek restaurant for late, late, lunch/early dinner. I eat a huge salad, with Florence saying the amount of dressing I'm using is making my salad not healthy at all. She eats a tray of deep-fried something I can't pronounce, and the stuff couldn't be any less healthy than my salad drowned in dressing. I don't say anything, though. I know better than to argue with my twin. She can beat me. Her tongue is quicker and she doesn't shy away from insults that might actually hurt really badly. I'm always frightened I'll hurt her, so I back away from a fight. Call me a coward, but I'm fine with not causing her to be mad at me for an entire week and completely ignore me. She's done it before, once when I asked if her snake-skin purse was artificial, and once when I accidentally stepped on a starched white shirt and got mud all over it. Apparently, it was her favorite shirt, but she had three others that looked exactly like it.

Mom drives again, and I help her navigate through a tiny, stinky town in northern New Mexico, a crowded city at the edge of Oklahoma, and a blocked intersection barely a mile into Arkansas. Roman and Pompeii think it's hilarious to yell at every car we drive past, and after two minutes, Mom screams for them to stop, and we spend the next hour in silence. The only noise is from the radio, which is playing classical music again, though I think it is Beethoven this time, not Mozart. It's so faint and quiet, yet it fills the car with haunting melodies that make me want to curl up and fall asleep.

Tonight, we stop at a huge hotel. The moving van behind us, faithfully following in our footsteps, can't find a parking spot and has to park across the street at a dingy motel that looks to be out of business. After seeing it, I'm glad we aren't staying there. It seems like an unstable place that houses unstable people.

Our hotel is nice: five floors, a pool and hot tub, a fitness center, snack bar, and vending machines on each floor. Roman and Pompeii gleefully examine the contents of the vending machine, ogling over the different kinds of treats and candy inside, and it isn't until Mom reminds them that the stuff has probably been in there for years that they come to their senses and help carry their suitcases up to our room.

The room is small but comfortable. There are two beds and a couch that can turn into a bed, a TV, a narrow bathroom with barely any space for the shower, and a balcony overlooking the shady area. Mom immediately goes to the shower and is in there for approximately three minutes before coming back out, her hair wet. Florence moves to claim the shower next; Mom stops her and says, "Three minutes. No longer."

Florence snorts and enters the bathroom, slamming the door shut. I hear the lock click, and a second later the rush of the water. Then all those sounds are drowned out by Pompeii and Siena as they beg Mom to let them swim in the hotel pool.

"Venice, can you take them?" asks Mom, already punching in a number on her phone. "I need to call the moving van people."

I'm about to face them when I remember something. "Mom," I say, stopping her finger from pressing the dial button. "Earlier, at that ice cream shop, you were having a very animated conversation with someone. Who was it, if you don't mind my asking?"

She hesitates. "It was Grandma Ferrari," she admits quietly. "She's still upset about our move. She doesn't think I should have moved us just to avoid all those memories of your dad."

"Is that why you moved?" I'm startled she confessed that. I had had a sneaking suspicion that Dad was the reason, but I didn't know for sure.

"Not entirely," Mom says, glancing nervously at my younger siblings, who are standing behind me. I don't think they're paying attention to us. "I have lived in California for nearly sixteen years. I want to move somewhere closer to my parents, who are in Florida."

"The Popes are great," I say. "But I'll miss the Ferraris."

Mom nods slowly, eyes back on her phone. "So will I. But it's getting harder and harder talking to them."

Curious, I ask, "Why?"

She waves me away. "Venice, I need to call the moving van. Please go take the kids to the pool."

I sigh in defeat and turn to my siblings. "Are you ready to go?"

To my surprise, they have changed into their swimsuits. I am stunned they were able to find their swimsuits deep in the mess of packages and suitcases and bags and any other things we use to hold our stuff. I know *my* swimming suit is lost somewhere amid the confusion that is my backpack, or maybe it's stuffed far back in the moving truck…

I lead my little siblings down to the swimming pool, grimacing as the sharp smell of chlorine greats my sensitive nose. I've always hated chlorine, and so has Mom. She's not going to be excessively happy when we return.

Pompeii and Siena immediately jump in the water; Siena forgetting she still has her glasses on, and she has to climb out of the pool to give them to me to hold them for her. She gets back in, and she and Pompeii start up a game of splashing me. I move to the far side of the indoor pool and sit down on a plastic chair that looks like it might collapse any minute; the legs tremble the moment I sit.

I watch my siblings swim around, having to break up three fights Pompeii started and two attacks Siena made on him. As I watch them, my thoughts wander to Virginia. What is it going to be like? Am I going to actually be able to talk to kids and make friends? Or is it going to be California all over again, where I only meet with different kids at school during lunch, and we rarely speak because it's too loud in the cafeteria? I had a couple of friends, but we weren't close enough to be best friends. And they kept mistaking me for my twin sister.

I kick at a puddle of water on the concrete floor. "Hey, Siena."

My littlest sister swims up to the side of the pool and yells back at me, "Yeah?"

I climb to my feet and walk up to her. "Do you think we'll like Virginia, or do you think it'll be boring?"

"It's certainly gonna be cold," says Pompeii, swimming up next to Siena. I can't believe she doesn't punch him for being so close to her. "I heard they get snow sometimes."

"Sometimes isn't a lot." She pouts, pulling herself onto her elbows. "I'm not happy moving to a cold state. I liked California. I liked how we could go to the beach whenever we wanted, because it was only a few miles away. I liked hanging out with my friends. I liked having Christmas and New Year's and Thanksgiving at Grandma and Grandpa Ferrari's house."

"So did I," says Pompeii.

I raise my eyebrows. When Pompeii and Siena both agree on something, then it's *serious.*

"It was warm," Siena continues. "And sunny."

"And there were tons of people in our neighborhood," says Pompeii. "I got rich off of walking people's dogs."

I hide a smirk. Dogs are pretty much the only living thing he isn't afraid of. He's scared of talking to humans. He's scared of cats, saying they scratch too much; he's scared of fish, saying they are too slimy; he's scared of crabs, saying their pinching hurts; and he's scared of seagulls, saying they are too loud and scary and have sharp beaks.

"All of our memories of Dad were there," I say, and my siblings both look at me with interest. They don't remember him as well as I do, and even then that's not very much. I only have a few memories of him.

"Yeah, but Dad doesn't live in California anymore," Pompeii puts in. "He moved somewhere far away a few years ago."

"To get away from us?" Siena snorts in disgust. "What a terrible dad."

I feel a pang of sympathy for her. She knows the least about Dad out of all of us. She had just turned four a month before he divorced Mom.

"Do you ever think we'll see him again, Venice?" she asks.

The question is a painful one. I have always feared Dad was gone for good, that he was never going to stop by our house in California to say hello, that we wouldn't meet up with him ever again. But I can't tell Siena that. "I don't know," I say instead. "Dad might not know we're moving. He might not visit for a few years."

Siena is quiet for a minute. Pompeii is sticking his hand in the pool's filter, and I don't bother telling him that that is incredibly gross. He probably won't listen to me, anyway.

"If Dad ever comes back," Siena says slowly, "then I'll want him to explain why he left."

"He'll say it was Mom's fault," Pompeii replies absentmindedly.

She frowns at him. "I don't think so. I mean, that's a really pathetic excuse to abandon us."

I stare at my little siblings. I've never heard Siena talk like this before. She's usually childish and acts like the ten year-old she is.

"So that's why I'm not very happy with leaving," she concludes. "Because of Dad." Then she smiles, a little sheepishly. "And there was Kent."

The moment between us all is broken as Pompeii groans while I laugh.

"Siena," I say, "I think you love Kent more than Florence does."

"Kent is awesome," says Siena. She doesn't sound disappointed any longer. "And dreamy. And hot. And everything a girl could want and more."

Pompeii groans again. "Ugh! You're disgusting!" He flicks water at Siena. "You realize you're hitting on a dude seven years older than you, right? Do you know how gross that is?"

"*You* are gross," Siena retorts, ducking under the water.

A second later, Pompeii is pulled down as she grabs his ankle and yanks on him. They have an underwater fight, then I find someone's arm that is waving above water, and pull on it until Siena surfaces. I stand and drag her through the water all the way to the concrete steps leading out of the pool, where I release her.

"Don't pull him under," I chide. "You could have drowned your brother."

Siena rubs her arm where I'd grasped her. "Good! I *want* him to drown! He is the most annoying boy in the whole world!"

"I am not!" Pompeii yells from the center of the pool. "Roman is way more annoying than me!"

Siena yells back how Roman doesn't deserve to drown as much as Pompeii does. There is another fight, and I can handle it until the point when one of the kids brings in me, asking me who is more annoying, and I just shake my head and say nothing. Then Siena gets mad—she believes that I was going to say *her*—and she starts to complain about how I love Pompeii and not her, and I always side with Pompeii, no matter the circumstance. That's when I sigh, return to my seat, and gather up Siena's glasses and the towels I brought to dry off the kids.

"Time to go," I say, checking the time on the clock hanging above the pool. "Holy Mother Earth. It's eight ten. I am *starving*. Let's go get some food."

After much grumbling, Siena and Pompeii climb out of the pool and accept a towel from me. They wrap them around themselves and, teeth chattering in the cold, follow me back up to our room. Florence is sitting on one of the beds, eating a carton of Chinese food and watching a serial killer TV show currently streaming. Mom is nowhere to be seen.

"Where's Mom?" I ask Florence above the pounding noise Siena is making.

Roman is now in the shower, or maybe just the bathroom, doing whatever personal hygiene stuff he does, like shaving, and he won't get out so Siena can change into her clothes.

Florence tosses her hair. "Don't know. Probably across the street talking to the moving van guys."

I cross the room and peer out the window. The motel is hidden in the dark that has crept up so suddenly. I can't see the moving van or Mom or really anything. I shiver involuntarily, hoping Mom hasn't met any foul business or that she wasn't stupid enough to go outside at night in the first place. I strain my eyes, trying to see into the black, but there's nothing.

"Roman!" Siena slams her fist against the bathroom door. "Open up! I'm freezing out here! I need to change my clothes!"

There's a muffled response, probably Roman saying something rude and mean, because Siena turns to me and yells, "Venice! Make Roman get out of the bathroom!"

I exchange an annoyed look with Florence. She rolls her eyes. "You've got to go save the day," she says dryly.

I give a snort of laughter. "By earning Siena access to the bathroom, I will have gained Roman's anger and annoyance. Should I even do anything?"

"Why ask me?" Florence scoops some noodles into her mouth.

I frown. She sounds...sardonic.

Shaking myself free of everything plaguing me, I walk over to Siena and lightly rap on the bathroom door with my knuckles.

"Hey, Roman, will you please let Siena use the bathroom for a quick minute? You can have it back when she's done, which won't be very long."

There's a moment of silence. Then, "Fine." The door opens and Roman comes out, his hair damp. So he *had* taken a shower. He looks at me and says, "All it takes is someone asking politely. If Siena hadn't thumped on the door and yelled at me, I would have gotten out ages ago."

Siena growls low in the back of her throat. "One day, Roman, you won't wake up." She grabs her clothes and shoves past him into the bathroom, slamming the door shut behind her.

Roman cocks his head at me. "Was that a threat? It sounded like one to me."

"Watch out," I warn. "Siena is known for carrying out her threats."

We both laugh, because it's the complete truth, and for a second I feel that maybe Roman and I could get along if he acted like this all the time.

Of course, he has to ruin it.

"She's such an annoying sister," says Roman, pushing me aside as he goes into the bedroom. "Kinda like you, Venice. But your threats are much more practical."

I scowl at his back. I open my mouth to tell him that insulting people isn't polite, and he just lectured Siena on being polite, but at that moment the hotel room door opens and Mom comes in. I forget all about Roman and go up to Mom, questions bubbling in my mind.

"Where were you?" I ask, noting her pink cheeks and red nose and wind-blown hair. She doesn't seem downcast about Grandma Ferrari and Dad and whatever her conversation had been any more. I want to know why she isn't telling me what Grandma Ferrari said, but I can accept the fact that Mom doesn't want to talk to her because of Dad.

Mom stomps her shoes on the foot rug by the door, a habit she hasn't been able to break. She always makes sure to knock off any dirt or mud on her shoes before coming inside. I notice she's carrying a take-out bag that smells rather heavenly to me—I'm *starving*—and my stomach rumbles. She grins, lifting up the brown-paper bag.

"There's a restaurant just down the road," she says. "Italian. My favorite."

She follows me deeper into the room, and her smile fades slightly when she sees Florence sitting on one of the beds, her legs folded beneath her, the big carton of Chinese noodles in her lap, watching TV. Mom freezes, counting how many kids are in the room, and she looks back at me after a quick second and asks, "Where is Siena?"

I point to the bathroom. "Changing out of her swimsuit."

"I just changed in the closet," pipes up Pompeii, emerging from the closet with his wet swimsuit in one hand. He's now wearing a clean T-shirt and naturally-dyed jeans. His hair has already dried, and we got back from the pool only a few minutes ago. He's so lucky his hair dries so fast—mine takes longer than four hours, and by then it's still slightly damp. That's the problem of having long, thick hair.

Mom dumps the bag of food onto a corner table. "I'm not sure Siena is as comfortable changing in a closet. Pompeii, make sure you hang that soaking wet swimsuit up so it will dry."

Roman jumps off the bed he is sitting on and comes over to the table, as if he is going to claim all the food before anyone else can. "Mom, how much food can I have? Am I allowed to eat Florence's, since she ordered Chinese?"

Mom gives Florence a sharp look. "I told you I was going out to buy food. I said wait a half an hour or so, but you still bought your own dinner?"

"Wait, hold on," I cut in. "You told Flo you were getting food?"

After a second, Mom nods. "Yes."

I turn to Florence, who is looking bored at what's happening. Her TV show is too quiet for anyone to hear what they're saying, but the flashing lights make one thing obvious: a murder was just committed. I'm not paying any attention to the TV, however. I'm staring at my twin. "You *knew* where Mom was," I say, irritated. "But you told me that you didn't know, and that made me worried. Couldn't you think of someone else's feelings for once?"

"It's not that important, Venice. I wasn't paying attention," says Florence, exasperated. "I said Mom was out. I just didn't say where she went. What's the big deal?"

"If you're not going to help at all you might at least not make things harder," I say. I'm angry, but I don't let my voice rise higher than normal pitch. I don't want to look like I can't control myself. I don't want to be like Roman and Pompeii and Siena when they lose their composure.

"Okay, girls." Mom looks from Florence to me, then back to Flo. "We're all tired and stressed from a long day on the road. Let's get some food and try to relax a bit, okay?"

Florence sighs long and loud, exaggerating the noise to make it seem like she's bored with this confrontation, and I know she is. "Fine, that's what I was trying to do. It's Venice that overreacted."

Mom shakes her head. "Alright, well maybe you can take a turn with the younger kids sometime, Florence."

My twin narrows her eyes. "Of course," she says icily.

"Can I have the lasagna?" Roman says loudly, digging through the bag. "I saw it first, so I get it."

The bathroom door clicks open, and Siena walks out, dressed in the same clothes she wore earlier today. "No," she says. "*I* get the lasagna. Everyone knows lasagna is my favorite."

"Really?" says Mom, nudging Roman away from the bag.

"Yup." Siena proudly raises her chin in the air.

Mom glances up at me. "Venice, could you get the plates and forks from the black sack over by Flo's suitcase?"

I duck into the entryway and search through a mesh bag for the things she wants, hearing Mom comment on how, luckily, she bought *two* pieces of lasagna. Hiding a smirk, I return and give Mom the plates and utensils.

"Thanks, Venice," says Mom, smiling. She, too, has a glint of humor in her eyes as she dishes out the lasagna to Roman and Siena, who decides she has a craving for ravioli instead. I take her lasagna, and she and Pompeii fight over the ravioli while Mom chides Roman for eating his food so fast he burns his mouth.

"Water!" he yells. "I need water!"

"Get it yourself!" Mom says good-naturedly.

Florence laughs sarcastically. "He deserves to have his mouth burned. And water won't help him. It's his fault he ate his food so fast. He shouldn't have gobbled it up without waiting for it to cool down. That's what happens to impatient people."

Mom glares at Flo with irritation. "You're not helping, Flo," she says, giving Roman a glass of cold water.

"My pleasure," says Florence. She tosses her empty carton of Chinese food onto the floor, then leans back on the bed, throwing an arm over her face. A second later, she says, "Turn out the lights. I'm trying to sleep."

"Turn them off yourself," retorts Siena.

"Let's all quiet down," Mom says, breaking up a budding fight, "and let Flo sleep. We have a big day tomorrow."

Flo scoffs. "You mean staring at the road for ten hours?"

"Yes," Mom says coldly. She picks at a piece of her breadstick. "We'll reach Virginia soon. We only have three more days of driving." She smiles tersely at me and leaves the bedroom to hide in the bathroom, away from Flo and her churlish comments.

THREE

Mom anxiously taps the steering wheel with her fingers. "Well," she finally says after two whole minutes of silence, "we're here."

I peer out the car window at the house that's ours now. It's a cute thing, a mixture of modern and old-fashioned. The siding is a bright white color, like it was recently power-washed, and the side garage barely looks big enough to hold our car. The front door, painted dark blue, has a glass screen door we will probably break. The outside of the house is clean; all windows reflecting the mid-afternoon sunlight. The porch is small with no roof overhead or any space for a lawn chair, which Florence finds disappointing. She told me that she wants to sit on the porch all day, watching the neighborhood and spying on the boys that walk by or live around here. Our new house isn't surrounded by tons of other houses— each is built at least fifty feet away from the other. This also makes Florence disappointed, because she wanted to have hot boy neighbors for every square inch in our backyard.

The lawn of our new house is green, but there are several brown spots in the lush yard, where the grass has died in the morning frosts. There are pots of wilted flowers on the porch, and some shrubs grouped around the north side of the house. The shingles on the roof are light colored, and that makes Mom pleased—light colored roofs somehow lower the heat effect inside during the summer. I wonder if the materials used to cover the roof are recyclable. That might cheer Mom up even more. I almost voice the question out loud, but I stop myself. Maybe later.

We're based in a large neighborhood in a town on the small side. We passed lots of farmland on the way in, but Mom said if we had kept going we would have reached a bigger part of the county where there are more people. The portion we're in seems perfect; I noticed the quaint shops and the scattered houses here and there on the drive here, and this town is a great size, Mom thinks. Not too big and not too small, not completely isolated and not too close to an enormous city. Washington, D.C. is about an hour away, which I find interesting, seeing as Mom didn't want to be near a metropolis.

Deciding to make the first move, I open the car door and step out onto the asphalt road. I grab my backpack and swing it over my shoulders, surprised at how heavy it feels. My water bottle must be filled. It weighs down my bag by a lot.

I close the car door without a sound, then start to trek up the lawn to the front door, though I don't have the key to unlock the house and I probably should have asked Mom for it before exiting the car. Laughing internally, I step up onto the porch and peer inside the window next to the door. I see polished hardwood floors, blank walls painted boring, neutral colors, and a hardwood staircase leading up to carpeted floors. The banister along the staircase looks rather rickety. I hope Roman and Pompeii don't accidentally rip it out.

A car door closes. I glance back and spot Mom walking up the driveway, her purse in her hand, a nervous smile on her face. Siena is next to her, practically skipping with excitement. As they come within earshot, she says, "Oh, isn't this a pretty little house?"

"Wait until you see inside," says Mom, visibly pleased that someone actually seems hyped up. Florence and the boys are still in the car—they either refuse to come out or they're too lazy.

Probably the second one.

Mom rummages around in her purse for the key, emerging

victorious as she holds up a tiny metal key. "A-ha! You ready to enter, girls?"

"Yes!" shouts Siena, bouncing on the tips of her toes. "Can I have my own room, Mom? Can I live in the attic? Can you make Pompeii sleep outside in the garage? Am I going to get my own bathroom? Florence always takes the bathroom for *hours*, and I can't ever use it!"

"Slow down," laughs Mom, handing the key to me. "Venice, would you do the honors?"

Touched she wants me to do it, I take the key and stick it in the doorknob. I twist it, feeling the lock click, and turn the doorknob, opening up the house. Siena bounds inside instantly, laughing and shrieking with delight at every little thing she sees. Mom follows, calling, "Take off your shoes, or you'll get dirt all over the place!"

I hesitate, glancing back at the car before entering our new house, ready to discover how different it is from our old home in California. For one thing, the air is cleaner, colder, sharper. To make Mom happy, and partly out of habit, I slip off my shoes, leaving them by the front door, and wander deeper into the house, noting the polished bamboo floors and the shiny windows. The living room is big and spacious and empty—our furniture hasn't come yet. The moving van guys are a couple of days behind us, back in Kentucky. I think they ran into bad traffic during a sudden and surprising snowstorm that sprung out of nowhere.

I peek around a corner and find Mom in the kitchen, opening cupboards and examining the dishwasher, her purse on one of the counters. There's an indent in the wall, probably where the refrigerator is supposed to go. I don't know why, but for a random reason Mom chose to pack up our refrigerator and bring it with us. I hope it comes soon, otherwise we'll have to use our coolers for the cold stuff we buy, and coolers aren't the best at keeping food cold or frozen. Also, our cooler has a crack in it.

Thumping overhead announces that Siena has found the

bedrooms. I exit the kitchen and dart up the staircase by the front door, my socks sliding on the slippery hardwood stairs. I come out on tan carpet and open the first door to my immediate right. It's a bathroom, but the door next to it reveals a big, empty bedroom, the walls painted white. What a boring color. If Flo gets this room, she'll convince Mom to repaint the walls bright pink, or maybe yellow.

Ugh. I shiver. I'm probably going to have to share a room with Flo, since we are closest in age—by eight minutes—and having bright yellow walls is not going to enlighten the punishment. It's not that I hate the color yellow or sharing a room with Florence—I don't, not to either of those things—it's the prospect of having my room filled with the stuff Florence likes. We're in a new house, in a new state, and I kind of want a fresh start at finding space for myself and to be myself.

But Flo might also want space. Or maybe she needs me to be there for her in this strange environment. I should be kind to her, more than I already try.

I turn in a full circle in the room, liking the curtains over the windows and the big walk-in closet that Florence will easily fill. If I'm allowed to pick my own bedroom, this one will definitely be it.

"Venice!" Siena appears in the doorway, her eyes shining. "Hey, Venice, come here! I found the *best* room ever!"

Energized by her simple exclamation, I follow Siena across the hall and down a bit to another room. This one is smaller than the one I was just in, but it's the perfect size for a ten year-old girl who is excellent at keeping tidy. I examine the windows—double-paned—and check out the closet; it's tiny compared to the one I was just in. The carpeted floor will stain easily, but if Siena keeps Roman and Pompeii out, this will probably be the cleanest room in the house.

"Are you going to claim this as yours?" I ask, watching Siena dump out her backpack's contents onto the floor.

Siena nods, sorting through a pile of knickknacks. "Yep. This is mine now. If Roman tries to take it from me, then I'll..." she holds up a shoehorn. "I'll change his mind."

I hide a smile. She might get offended and attack *me* if I laugh at her. "Is it okay if I warn him first?" I say. "Just so he knows what he's up against?"

"Nah," she says, setting down the shoehorn with tender care. "He already knows."

"Ah." I grin. "If he's smart, he'll leave you alone."

Siena glares up at me. "Roman is *never* smart. It's what makes him him. You should know that."

Holding my insides with laughter, I manage a nod. "You're right. I do know that. But Roman might not."

"Roman doesn't know one plus one," retorts Siena, returning to her pile of stuff. "He shouldn't even go to school. He's too dumb. And so is Pompeii. I can't believe they got accepted into school. They're so stupid."

By now, I can't take it anymore. I clap a hand over my mouth and duck out of the room, returning to the bedroom I might share with Florence. She's in there, critically examining it, and when I burst in, unable to control my laughter, she whirls around, instantly annoyed.

"What's your problem?" she yells. "Why are you laughing? Can't you just leave me alone?"

"Sorry!" I say, truly meaning it. I try to stop the giggles, but they bubble out anyway. "Flo, you should have heard what Siena was saying about Roman and Pompeii..."

"Why should I have?" Flo asks irritably. "I don't care."

That shocks the laughter away. I straighten and study her, my head listed to one side. Florence sounds like she's frustrated, yet at the same time, her voice holds a hint of...melancholy. The shade of sorrow isn't there when she speaks again.

"So, what do you think?" she says brusquely. "I was hoping the two of us could have this room. I love the closet, and the windows give me a great view of the neighborhood."

I'm momentarily stunned. Flo wants to share with me? She already plans on us sharing? She instantly assumed that because we shared a room back in California, we'll do the same here? I'm touched; I thought she didn't like me. I suddenly feel a little guilty for dreading having our room overrun by too much of her.

"Well?" Flo glares at me. "Hey, Venice! You still in there?"

I shake my head to clear myself of those thoughts. "Um, yeah. I, uh, really want to share a room with you, too. And the closet *is* pretty nice. You could probably stash Roman and Siena and Pompeii in there with room leftover for a TV and mini fridge. And the two windows *do* show a good view of the houses. You could spy on all the boys from up here."

"I know, right?" Flo beams. "I *love* this room. It's bigger and better than the one back in California."

"Sure is bigger," I agree softly.

Flo claps her hands together. "Alright! Now that we've claimed this room, I need to unload all my stuff from the car. Venice, will you help me?"

"Um, yeah," I say, surprised at her question. "Of course."

"Thanks." She smiles. "I have two suitcases, four carry-on bags, and my ugly backpack. The rest of my belongings are in the moving van. You know, they'd better hurry up. There is *no* way I can survive without knowing all my stuff is safely put away in our room."

I nod in agreement, though my mind is whirling. I'd known she had packed a ton of bags, managing to shove half of them into the car, but two whole suitcases? Four carry-on bags? And even her backpack? The only luggage I have with me is *my* backpack. Nothing more, nothing less. I'll probably have to wear the same clothes for a few days until the moving van arrives. Hopefully, it will come soon.

I follow Flo out of the house and back to the car. Pompeii is still in there, complaining to himself about books, dogs, and overgrown hedges, and when he sees me, he yells, "Venice! Can you unbuckle my seat? It's stuck! And Roman wouldn't help me!"

"Have you been in here for the past fifteen minutes, just sitting in your seat?" I ask, horrified. I crawl into the backseat and examine his buckle, my eyebrows inching upwards when I see how Pompeii has somehow gotten the seatbelt twisted around in knots. I yank at it a few times, ending up having to pick out a knot, squirm him under the seatbelt, and untie the rest before it straightens out. I hear Flo rummaging around in the trunk as I turn back to Pompeii and say, "How on Holy Mother Earth did you get stuck?"

He shrugs. He's standing just outside of the car, watching me.

"Did Roman tie you up?" Flo calls from the trunk. "That's something dumb he would do."

"Nah," says Pompeii. "I fell asleep and got twisted up. Thanks, Venice. I'd still be stuck if you hadn't saved me."

I climb out of the car and give him a hug, ruffling his thick auburn hair. "Of course, Pompeii," I say. "Any time."

Flo snorts, peering around the car at us. "Of course," she says, her voice mocking. "Of course, Pompeii. Because I'm the best sister in the world, and I'm so much better than Florence, so don't ever ask her for help. You can just ignore her."

Then, posture stiff, she whirls and stalks towards the house, a small pink bag in her hand.

"Um..." Pompeii blinks after her. "Is it just me, or does Flo seem spiteful these days?"

"It's not just you," I say sadly. "She's mad at everyone. She did *not* want to move here, and for some reason she's taking it out on me."

"So," says Pompeii, shaking me from my thoughts, "when we were driving here, we passed a library..."

I perk up. "Really? Where was it?"

"Not too far from here," he says, closing the car door. "About a mile down the road. Two miles at most."

"Want to check it out?" I ask, helping him unload luggage from the trunk. I find his dark blue suitcase and drag it out from under a pile of Flo's carry-on bags. "Here."

Pompeii takes the suitcase from me. "Thanks, Venice."

We walk up to the house, me carrying one of Flo's bags so I can show her that I don't only help the littler kids.

"We totally should go to the library," Pompeii agrees. "I could spend hours there. And so could you."

Florence, storming outside at just the right moment to catch what Pompeii has said, snaps angrily, "Why would you go to the library? Hot boys *never* hang out there. You need to stop by skate parks or arcades."

I step to the side so she can pass me. She sneers at me as she stomps down the porch.

"Venice, you know you're only going to become friends with old people if you spend all your time at the library. And even if a hot boy comes by for some random reason, you're too awkward to be able to talk to him. And he'll only notice you if you slam into him."

"Same goes for you, Flo," Pompeii says matter-of-factly.

Flo turns her sneer on him, then flaunts off towards the car, hair swinging wildly.

I try not to let her words hurt. I tell myself that she's just annoyed Pompeii returned my kindness with kindness. But it still stings a little that she is poking me in a sore spot.

"Hey, Venice." Pompeii peers up at me. "You're not seriously considering what Flo told you, are you?"

I shake my head, somewhat sadly. "No. Why would I? She's only saying those things to pick a fight with me, a fight I don't want to participate in. Anyway, let's get inside. You should grab a room before Mom turns all the spare bedrooms into offices or indoor gardens."

FOUR

I **empty the contents of my** last bag onto my bed. I toss the bag over my shoulder onto a pile of other unloaded luggage, then pick through the stuff on my bed. Most of the things are trinkets and such I couldn't bear to part with, so I packed it, despite Mom's subtle hints that I should donate them. I snatch up a magnet in the shape of Italy. It's one Grandma Ferrari had given me for Christmas a few years ago. There are five words on the magnet, in five different spots—Venice, Florence, Rome, Pompeii, and Siena. Grandma, at first not really approving of the names Mom had chosen for us, quickly decided she liked our Italian names, and she created small things for us each year that were Italy-themed. I have a tiny gondola she'd carved out of wood, with the help of a carpenter, of course. I also have a painting of the canals at sunset, the dark outline of a man on his gondola, gently padding a happy couple through the water.

It all suddenly makes me miss Grandma and Grandpa Ferrari. I wish we hadn't left so abruptly. We hadn't been able to have a proper farewell. Mom didn't even tell them until the day before we left. Grandma had given me a floppy hat, saying I probably wouldn't use it, but it was better safe than sorry in a whole new state. Grandpa, not one for sticking around, just hugged me and told me not to be tempted to leave Roman behind at a rest stop along the way to Virginia. I'd replied that I would *never* be tempted to, but I lied. I had almost done it twice in Tennessee, when Roman was taking forever to examine the paper maps and wouldn't get in the car so we could leave.

I stand up and cross the room, holding the Italy-shaped magnet in my fist, having to step around three piles of Florence's stuff before reaching the door leading out into the hallway. I skip down the stairs, my socks slipping on the bamboo. It's one of the reasons Mom bought the house—everything is bamboo, and she prefers it over wood.

I enter the kitchen, amazed at how fast the cabinets have been filled with foods and the healthy snacks that Roman complains taste like grass. I make a beeline towards the fridge, sticking my magnet somewhere near the top so it won't get knocked off and break. Deciding I'm hungry, I open the fridge door and peer inside. Milk, cheese, butter, leftovers from yesterday's caprese, a half-eaten slice of pizza that is probably Roman's, and several other things are in there that change my mind about eating right now.

Turning on my heel, I head back upstairs, taking the stairs two at a time. I return to my room, crashing into Florence when I enter.

"Sorry!" I say, instinctively grabbing onto her arm so she won't fall over.

Flo regains her footing, ripping herself free. "Watch where you're going, Venice." She sounds tired and bored.

"Sorry," I say again. "Are you all right?"

"Yeah." She sighs, scratching her head, and that's when I notice she isn't wearing any make-up. Her hair is naturally curly, not curled by her iron. She's dressed in faded jeans and a plain, solid-color T-shirt she most likely stole from me. I frown. Why has she not gotten ready for the day? It's ten in the morning. She should be prepared to tackle the day.

"Flo?" I look at her anxiously. "How are you...doing?"

She rolls out her neck, glancing around the hallway. She grabs my hand and pulls me into our room. "I'm not doing great," she admits, closing the door behind me. She locks it, then turns and flops down on her bed, pressing her face into the pillow, not bothering to take off her glasses.

I hesitate awkwardly. "What's wrong?" I ask gently.

"Remember Kent?" Flo mumbles, her voice muffled by the pillow. "When we moved, I knew there was no way we could keep up our relationship, so I sort of broke up with him, but not officially. Anyway, today I learned that my best friend, Carla, had secretly been dating Kent behind my back, and now I feel betrayed. To be cheated on by your boyfriend is hard enough, but for him to be cheating on me with my *best friend*...it's just a huge betrayal."

I sit on the edge of her bed and stroke her hair. "I understand."

"No, you don't." Flo pulls away from me, shifting her body so we're inches apart. "Venice, you've never had a boyfriend. Or a best friend, for that matter. You don't know how it feels to be left alone. To be abandoned, betrayed, discarded, by your boyfriend or best friend. Both Kent *and* Carla have stopped texting me. They deleted my contact off their phones."

"That's horrible," I say, dread filling me. Poor Flo. I had always liked Kent and Carla. I had always thought they were loyal to my sister.

Flo groans and looks up at me. "I know, Venice. I'm just so *ugh* right now. I don't think I'll ever be happy again."

Twisting my lips to one side, I slide my ring off my finger and take Flo's hand. I put the ring on her pinky finger, surprised at how her finger is smaller than mine. She jerks at the sudden contact, but I hold onto her tighter, refusing to let go.

"What?" she says. "Why did you—I don't want to wear your stupid dumpy ring."

I ignore her. "You remember how on our tenth birthday, Dad announced that he was divorcing Mom?"

Confused at the question, Flo only nods.

"Well," I say, "after Dad left, he never sent me something for my birthday. The only things he sent were for you. It seemed to me that he'd forgotten I existed. Anyway, last year, on our fifteenth birthday, we got that package from him that contained something for you and surprisingly, something for me. It was this ring." I turn it over on her finger. "Every time I see it, I am reminded of that birthday. It's become my favorite thing I have ever received from Dad."

"Oh." Flo looks down at it. She curls her fingers around mine. "Thank you, Venice. You're a great sister."

"I try," I say, smiling softly.

We sit still for the next few minutes, saying nothing, simply soaking up each other's company. I'm glad I can talk to Flo, to bond with her, because this won't happen often. She won't be this vulnerable all the time. She's too strong for that. And she won't turn to me for comfort unless it's really bad. I hope she knows that, despite the cutting remarks she makes about me, I still love her.

Flo sniffles, breaking the silence. "Thanks, Venice," she repeats in a soft voice. She sounds...meek.

I squeeze her hand, then she pulls away. "I'm tired of being depressed and moody," she says, now robust. "Is there anything fun you'd like to do?"

I think hard. "Um, Pompeii wants to visit the library. We've been here for nearly two weeks, and he's dying to see the books. I was hoping we could go today. Would you like to come with us?"

Flo groans. "Seriously?" She sits up. "Go to a dusty old library? What hot boy goes to a library?"

"It's Saturday," I say. "There might be some."

She lets out a long sigh. "Alright. But I can't go looking like this. Will you wait a couple minutes for me to patch up my face?"

"Of course." I get off her bed, pleased I was able to cheer her up. "I'll just go find Pompeii and tell him we're leaving soon. Maybe Siena might want to come, too."

"Hurry up with it, will you?" Flo snaps, though she's teasing. "You're taking longer telling me this than I take when I'm in the shower."

"I doubt that," I say. I unlock the bedroom door and open it. "We'll leave in ten minutes, okay?"

She rolls her eyes. "Five."

"Fine." I exit the room, closing the door behind me. I know she's feeling much better now, and that makes *me* feel good, too. At least Florence will occasionally accept my compassion.

"Here, Venice, can you hold this for me? Thanks!" Siena tips a stack of books and coloring pages and bookmarks into my waiting hands, the heavy weight causing me to stagger briefly before regaining my balance.

"Siena!" I groan. "Can't you moderate yourself? You don't need to check out the entire library. We live just down the street and can come here anytime we want."

"I know." Siena whirls around, crouching in front of a packed bookshelf. "But we're not coming back tomorrow since the library is closed, and I have to get a ton of books to help me survive the weekend. And school starts on Monday, so I need to read a ton of books to prepare myself for that. I can't sit in boring school all day long with nothing to think about! These will give me something to ponder on and imagine better endings."

I shift the books onto my left arm. "Whatever you say." I know it's pretty much pointless talking to Siena. When she's made up her mind, she sticks with it. She is rarely persuaded otherwise.

Glancing across the row of books, I spot Pompeii by the nonfiction section, his nose buried in a huge biography about one of the presidents. I can't tell who it is from this far away, and I silently laugh to myself, wondering what twelve year-old boy reads biographies in his spare time. I twist my head and look for Florence, finding her examining the stack of magazines over by the front doors of the library. She seems more energetic now, and I notice that she's still wearing my ring on her pinky.

Smiling to myself, I turn a sharp corner in the maze of bookshelves, making my glasses slip down my nose. Not having any free limbs to push them back up, I raise the books and gently nudge my glasses, hoping to get them up my nose. It works a little. I manage to poke myself in the eye with a corner of a book and have to blink back the reflexive tears that spring up, then my glasses slip off and land on my arm. I'm hesitating in the middle of the aisle, and Siena comes up to me—at least, I *think* it's her; I can't see—and says, "Here, Venice. I've got more books for you to hold."

She dumps the books on top of the ones I'm already holding, then turns to find even more.

"Wait—Siena!" I call, but she ignores me.

Perfect.

The books start to slide. One falls onto the floor, the sound causing my heart to wince. I hope I haven't damaged the binding. I adjust my grip, still blind, and drop more books. My glasses are dangling somewhere on my arm, and I desperately shift around the books, trying to prevent any others from tumbling down while not seeing anything. I manage to stack three on top of each other, but then Siena's papers flutter to the ground, followed by yet another book. How many has she given me? And why can't she carry them? She has hands, too!

Someone takes several books out of my arms. I blink, not being able to see what's going on, and I hear a voice saying, "You sure have a lot of books."

The voice is friendly and humorous and obviously masculine. I fumble for my glasses so I can see who he is, but there are still too many books in my arms and I can't reach my glasses.

"Venice, what's going on?" It's Florence. She must have seen me making a fool of myself.

I feel the person who helped me take more of the books,

relieving my sore arms. I finally snatch up my glasses and slide them on, blinking at the boy holding Siena's books. He's grinning, like he finds this whole exchange the most hilarious thing he has ever seen. Flo is standing across from him, arms folded tightly, glaring at me. I clear my throat.

"Sorry," I tell Florence. "Siena thought I could carry all these…" I gesture limply at the books on the floor and at the ones being held by the boy.

Flo scoffs. "You obviously couldn't."

"Siena doesn't know that," I mutter as my little sister comes up again, carrying yet another pile of books.

She hands them to me, and I take them awkwardly, not having the heart to refuse them. "Thanks, Venice," she says, whirling around to go build up her stack for the fourth time.

I shove the books towards Flo, forcing her to take them, then I crouch and start gathering up the fallen books and papers. I've totally forgotten about the boy who had helped me, so when he speaks, I jerk upwards.

"Are you all sisters?" he asks.

Noticing him for the first time, Florence turns her attention to my helper, a small smile playing at the corners of her mouth. "Yes," she says, adopting her flirty voice. "We just moved in a few weeks ago, and Venice was begging me to come to the library to check out a hundred books for the longest time ever, so today I gave in and we came here. I wasn't expecting *this* to happen." She gestures flippantly to my distress, as if I'm an inconvenience.

A pink flush creeps up my cheeks at the way she's talking about me, like I am a four year-old kid. *Begging?* I only suggested that she come with us and I did it to cheer her up, too.

Flo tosses her hair, setting her books on a nearby shelf with a dull *thud.* "I'm Florence Ferrari," she says. "What's your name?"

The boy shifts the books he's holding onto his other arm. "Nate. It's nice to meet someone who likes reading."

For a second I think he means Flo, and I almost snort, then I realize Nate means *me*. I keep my eyes on the hard carpet, stacking the books and papers together so I don't have to look at my twin's surprised expression.

"What, do you?" asks Flo, trying to keep her composure.

"Yes. This library is my favorite place in town," says Nate.

I collect the books and papers and slowly straighten, placing the items on top of Flo's on the bookshelf.

Nate cocks his head at us. "You've got to be twins," he says, his grin still on his face.

Flo seems to be reconsidering whether or not to continue flirting. She makes her decision. "Yes, we're twins, but I do *not* look like Venice," she says, her voice aloof and offended. "We have very different styles. Now, if you'll excuse me?" She turns on her heel and marches away, leaving me humiliated by her behavior.

"Um…" Nate hesitates awkwardly.

I push up my glasses again and reach for the books he's holding. He hands them to me, and I stack them up without looking at his face. I'm mortified at how Flo acted. One moment, she's happy and has a meaningful conversation with me, but then twenty minutes later, she decides to embarrass me in front of a stranger.

"Thank you," I say quietly, gathering together the books and papers and picking them up, this time getting a much better grip.

Nate smiles. It's obviously something he does all the time; I can tell by the ease it forms. "You're welcome," he says. "And—did I hear correctly? Is your name Venice?"

I nod slowly, staring at a something over his shoulder. "Yes. And Florence really *is* my twin sister. She's not usually like…that." It's a total lie. Flo is often like that. It's how her personality works.

"Do you like having a twin?" asks Nate, making no move to leave me be.

I shrug. "Sometimes, yeah."

"Do you ever trick people into thinking you're each other?"

Surprised at his questions, I nod again. "Every once in a while. Flo doesn't really like it, but occasionally she'll do it with me."

"And do people actually fall for it?"

"Yep." I switch my gaze from a far-distant end table to an old man reading near the back of the library. "The only person that can always tell us apart is our mom. She knows which of us is which."

Nate's smile widens. "That seems like fun."

I nervously clutch the books tighter to me, amazed I'm actually talking to a stranger. A *boy* stranger. I've never talked to someone at the library, unless I count Pompeii or the librarians who know me. I hope I'm not being supremely awkward.

Florence comes flaunting up right before the silence between us can become uncomfortable. She purses her lips, ignoring Nate and addressing only me. "Venice, we need to get home soon. Mom won't want you out this long. You know how she is."

I blush at how condescending her words are. She's treating me like I'm a kid that can't be on their own without supervision.

"Are Pompeii and Siena ready to go?" I ask, regaining control of my blush.

Flo makes the facial expression equivalent to a shrug. "I don't know. I'm sure you'll be able to round them up?" She whirls around and stalks away again, posture stiff and jerky. She's miffed at me.

"Pompeii?"

My head whips up. I squint at Nate while trying to interpret his question. What about Pompeii?

"You have a brother named Pompeii?" he clarifies.

"Oh." I almost smack myself on the forehead for being so thick. "Um, yes, I do."

Nate looks thoughtful. "Are all of you named after cities in Italy? Because you're Venice, you've got a twin sister, Florence, and a brother, Pompeii, and another sister named Siena, which I'm guessing is an Italian city."

"My mom is kind of obsessed with Italy," I mumble. "She's

always wanted to go, but never had enough time or money or stuff, so she just named us all places from…there. I have a second brother, Roman, but he didn't want to come here with us. He's not a big fan of the library."

Nate's grin returns. It's the most he's got me to say since meeting him. If he keeps this up any longer, I might actually start to ramble. I *never* ramble. I always speak quickly so I don't have to waste more time with the attention on me. I hate it when I'm the center of attention.

"Your sister, Florence, said you moved here a few weeks ago," says Nate.

I tuck a strand of hair behind my ear. "We did. My mom's a realtor, so we moved pretty fast. We're just down the road from this library." I gesture to nothing in particular. The bookshelves. The old people reading quietly in the cozy armchairs. The librarian putting away returned books. The hard carpet floor. Nate himself.

"Cool," he says. "Do you like Virginia so far?"

I nod, surprised our conversation has survived this long. He asks a lot of questions, which makes me wonder if he does this a lot. "Virginia is nice. But it's cold compared to California."

"It's only January," Nate says. "Just you wait until next month. That's when the ice comes. And March is really windy. And it rains a lot in April."

I glance at him uneasily. "Are you trying to scare me away?"

He laughs, the sound effortless and smooth, as if he laughs all the time. "I would hate to be the reason for you moving again," he says. "Especially since I'm supposed to show neighborly kindness, not chase you out of here."

This time, I'm the one that laughs. *Neighborly kindness?* Is that something they do in Virginia? Sure, a few families that live near us brought over gifts and freezer dinners and introduced themselves— does that count as kindness, or was it just an excuse to learn who we are?

Glancing at my phone, I notice it's been two hours since we'd come to the library. We should probably head back home before Mom bans us from ever leaving the house for too long. She gets paranoid that we're somewhere on the side of the road, dead, when we don't return after a few hours.

"I've got to go," I say. I correct myself as I spot Siena stumbling toward me, a fourth stack of books, taller than the others, balanced precariously in her arms. "*We've* got to go. Oh, it's going to take forever to check out all these books."

Nate's quiet smile comes back. "Sure will."

I risk a quick look at him. "Thanks again for helping me."

"Of course."

I gather together all the books and papers Siena has given me, then turn around and make my way over to Siena, who is taking a break from carrying her things, flopped down on a comfortable-looking armchair.

"You ready to go?" I ask.

She groans weakly. "How on Holy Mother Earth are we going to be able to carry all these books home? And Pompeii hasn't even picked out all of the ones he wants."

"I think the librarian might give us some bags," I say, glancing back at the front of the library, where I see Flo talking to a boy, her hand pressed gently against her mouth. She's flirting. As I watch, she titters, softly slapping her hand on his arm. The boy straightens his stance, obviously pleased that he made her laugh.

"Ugh," grunts Siena. "Flo is so gross when she flirts."

Pompeii appears at my elbow, holding his biography on some president that I now realize is William Howard Taft, the twenty-seventh president of the United States. "Hey, Venice," he says, scratching his nose. "Are we going home soon? The heat is too high in here, and I want to get back home where it's cooler."

"Yeah, we'll leave as soon as Siena gets her books checked out," I reply. I quickly look at Florence. "And once Flo stops flirting."

"Ew," Pompeii says. "That's disgusting."

I lead my siblings over to the front desk, where the librarian lady smiles at us and asks, "How may I help you?"

I go to tell her my library card number, then realize it's the one for some of California's libraries. I'll need a new one.

After filling out a pile of paperwork, I'm given a plastic card and am able to check out the books—finally. Siena has only grabbed thirty-six, where I had thought she'd gotten over a hundred.

Flo wanders up to us as we're shoving the books into brown-paper bags, and her face is shining brightly. She isn't mad at me for whatever I'd done earlier; instead, she squeals with excitement and whispers in my ear, "Guess what. I was asked out on a *date*. And this is only the fifteenth day that we're here in Virginia!"

"Wow," I say dryly, hoping she won't hear my sarcasm. "I'm surprised the boys took that long to ask you."

Flo scoffs, twisting my ring on her finger. She's moved it to her fourth; her hands are smaller than mine and she can fit it on a different finger. "Venice, are you jealous?"

"Not in the slightest," I admit cheerfully and truthfully. I really don't care if she's asked out after two weeks here and I'm not.

Turning to face her, I hold out a brown-paper bag full of books. "Can you carry these home?"

Her jaw drops. "Do you think I'm some kind of *servant*?"

"What?" I blink at her. "What—no! I just—"

Flo tosses her hair over her shoulder. "Fine. Whatever. I don't care." She grabs the bag from my astonished hands, then turns on her heel and skips out of the library, leaving me behind, my mind whirling with what has just happened.

FIVE

The weekend passes much too fast for my taste. The books we checked out at the library are all read by everyone except Roman and Florence, who say they have better things to do than reading—in Roman's case, he tells me he is busy trying to swindle the next-door neighbor out of two hundred or so dollars—and in Flo's case, she says she's too busy texting her newest crush, the boy she met at the library. I don't even know his name.

Mom seems cheerful and happy, here in Virginia. She isn't weighed down any more by our dad, and I catch her sneaking bites of ice cream when she thinks we aren't looking. It's how I know she's all right. She always snitches in something sugary when she's not depressed. I try not to let the start of the week make me miserable, but knowing I'm going to a new school in the middle of the school year is intimidating. That, and the fact that the only two kids I'll know are Florence and Roman, and *they* aren't going to hang around with me. Flo will fit in nicely. She's already charmed all the neighbors and convinced them she can babysit their kids, though she mostly just texts her friends instead of making sure the kids are still alive.

Siena and Pompeii are starting school this week, too. They both go to the same place, a middle school/elementary school on the other side of town. Whereas my high school is half a mile away from our house, Mom will have to drive Siena and Pompeii to theirs, or have them take the bus, which she will *not* do. She hates school buses. She tells me all the time about how they pollute the air too much. Naturally, since Mom is against them, Flo rides to school in one, just to rile Mom up. Roman, who doesn't really care for any of Mom's opinions and decided he didn't want to walk, is taking the bus with my twin. I think I'm the only one walking, and the only one who would walk, just because Mom prefers it if we do.

Monday morning dawns cold, the sun hidden behind stormy grey clouds. I have noticed that it's cloudy a lot here. It also rains. We've gotten three rain storms that flooded our tiny backyard, and Siena went outside with Pompeii in their swimsuits and jumped around in the puddles until Mom yelled at them to come back inside before they caught cold.

I think that, so far, I prefer California.

Flo is fixing her lipstick in our bedroom mirror when I roll out of bed, sliding on my glasses so I won't be blind. She glances at my reflection and grimaces. "Please tell me you're not going to school like *that*, Venice." She looks horrified.

I pat the top of my head, feeling how tangled my hair is. "Um, no. It'd be embarrassing for you and for me."

"I know." She puckers her lips, then smacks them together a few times. At last, satisfied that her lipstick isn't smeared, she steps back and looks me over. "I can help you," she offers. "So you don't look like a total geek."

"No thanks," I reply, moving to leave the room.

Flo stops me by putting a hand on my arm. "Venice, you know you're the new kid, so people are going to stare at you, right?"

"Uh, no."

She rolls her eyes. "What I'm saying, Venice, is please consider what you are about to dress up in. Don't go to school looking like my exact opposite. It will ruin my reputation."

"What reputation?" I ask.

She snorts. "You don't pay attention to how I operate, do you?"

I shrug, exiting our room, and wander down the hallway. Siena is outside the bathroom, banging on the door. "Roman!" she yells. "Get *out!*"

"No!" Roman yells back. "Go to a different bathroom! We *have* four of them for a reason!"

"This is *my* bathroom, dumbhead!" screams Siena. "It's mine, not yours! You can't just hang out inside for the entire day while I *actually* need to use it for *actual* things!"

"Siena," I say gently, interrupting Roman's rude response, "can't you just leave him alone? You know he purposely does this to make you mad."

She snorts. "So what? He's succeeding."

Shaking my head, I slip softly down the stairs, hearing Siena and Roman continue their argument above. I walk into the kitchen, first realizing that Mom isn't here by the pile of dirty dishes in the sink, and second seeing the note she's left on the counter. I pick it up and read:

Dear children,
Duty calls! I'm sorry I won't be able to be here for you—I am
investigating a house that a Mister Goldbeck might want. I hope
school goes well for you today. Venice, please don't trip again.
Florence, just...be nice to everyone. And, Roman, if your little sister
wants to use the bathroom, and you're taking a long time just to
shave your non-existent facial hair, then let her in.
Thank you. I love you all.
Mom

I laugh. I can't help it. She's totally guessed what would happen with Roman and Siena about the bathroom. And—she told me not to trip again? What does that mean? She can't be talking about the time I slipped on some water in the cafeteria and ended up shoving my sandwich up someone's nose. Why would she remind me of that horrible time? I hadn't been able to face anyone after that. I avoided the kid I'd smashed into with my lunch; I avoided everyone who laughed about the whole episode; I avoided the people who knew me so I wouldn't have to see them and have them tease and mock me because of the incident.

I dig through the cabinets for something edible. Finding several pieces of non-moldy bread, I spread peanut butter and drizzle honey over them and squish them into each other to form a sort-of sandwich, bringing back even more memories of that dreadful lunch experience. I pull out a Tupperware, shove the bread inside, and hunt around for something else to pack. I check the fridge, decide not to eat that random rotten apple, and extract myself from the cold appliance.

Flo meets up with me as I'm mixing together a bag of different nuts for my snack. She wrinkles her nose. "Ew," she says. "Why do you like gross stuff like nuts?"

"They have nutrients." I add a handful of sugarless craisins to the trail mix.

"Who cares about nutrients?" Flo snorts, sitting down at the counter. She quickly reads Mom's note, then groans and sits back, rubbing a hand over her eyes. "Ugh! She *had* to tell me to be nice! Like I'm not nice. Venice, do you think I'm nice?"

I hesitate awkwardly, not wanting to say anything. Truthfully, I don't think Florence is nice. If I lie, then she'll know I'm lying. I'm a terrible liar.

"Ye-es," I say slowly. "Sometimes."

She huffs, offended. "That's rich," she says mockingly—I say that a lot—"coming from you."

It hurts me more than I let on, though she kind of just proved my point. I fill up my water bottle, hiding my face from her, and quickly pack up my lunch, then shove it into my backpack and rush out of the kitchen.

Once in the seclusion of my bedroom, I angrily yank open the closet door and search for some clothes I can wear to school that won't embarrass Flo. She asks me if I think she's nice, and when I reply in the most polite way possible, she *still* gets offended and mocks me, which proves my point that she's only sometimes nice. Why can't she understand that, no matter how kind I am to her, she's mean back to me? Ugh, she's so frustrating!

I pull on a faded plain-colored T-shirt and a pair of naturally-dyed jeans. I drag a brush through my hair, not caring about the pain it causes as I pick at the snarls. Blinking back sudden tears, I bend over my shoes and quickly lace them up, tying them as tightly as I can, then straighten and snatch up my backpack. I sling it over my shoulder, march back downstairs, crash into Flo on my way to the front door. My stomach grumbles at her plate of fried eggs. I haven't eaten breakfast. I don't have *time* to eat breakfast, or I'll be late to school.

Flo gives me a hard look. "You're leaving?"

"I'm walking," I correct.

She heaves a sigh. "Perfect little Venice, doing whatever Mom says. I can't believe you're going to walk to school. What if you time it incorrectly and end up half an hour after school starts?"

"Then I'll explain it to the teachers," I say, going around her.

Flo pushes something at me. "Here," she says. "Take your lame ring back. I don't want to wear it anymore."

I slip it onto my pinky, glad to have it on again. I'd missed it.

"See you later," I mutter, stomping out of the house. I stare at the sidewalk the entire time I walk, only looking up when I'm checking to make sure I am actually going in the right direction. Why is Flo so annoyed at me? I'm just listening to Mom. If she suggests that I walk to school instead of taking the bus, then I'll walk! It's not a hard thing to do, and it'll wake me up so I'm not drooping during class.

Class…In all of the drama earlier today, I'd totally forgotten that

I'm going to be in a new school with new students and new teachers. I won't know any kids there. I'll be by myself, unless I'm desperate enough to make friends with the rejects, the kids who sit alone at cafeteria tables, not making eye contact with anyone. Normally, they turn me away, but once I managed to talk to one for an entire lunch break. The next day, she ignored me and acted like I didn't exist.

Please, I whisper to myself as I near the school. *Please, Mother Earth, let me not make a complete fool out of myself today.*

A yellow school bus rumbles past me, full of kids all excited— well, maybe not *excited*—for a new week of school. I wonder if Flo and Roman are on the bus, pretending they don't know me.

The high school looms in front of me. I feel my palms start to sweat as I merge with a group of chattering kids, heading towards the front doors. My heart is hammering in my throat, and I unobtrusively wipe my hands on my jeans, telling myself not to shake anyone's hand. That'd be gross for them and for me. The flow of kids pushes me into the school, into packed hallways full of even more happily nattering teenagers. A pang of sorrow touches my heart, and I look around for Roman or Flo so I'm not loitering in the hallway doing nothing, but I don't see them.

Remembering I'm supposed to be in class, I spend the next few minutes hunting down which homeroom I'm assigned to. No one pays attention to me as I slip in and take an empty seat.

Class goes well. That is to say, I'm ignored. Which is fine.

The morning passes in a blur. I don't remember much, except that I see Roman flirting with a cheerleader who's probably years older than him, and I also see Flo laughing with a group of chic girls. It all serves to make me even more depressed. We're new here, and they don't want to stick with me, just for the first day of school, to lend strength and security? And how on Holy Mother Earth am I going to work up the courage to talk to someone if I'll just be awkward and nervous and fidgety? I'm best left alone. I can keep myself company. I don't need anyone else to talk to or hang out with. I'm perfectly fine on my own. I've always been that way, too. Don't need any one besides myself.

I enter the cafeteria, whispering quietly under my breath, over and over again, "Don't trip. Don't trip." I get a tight grip on my backpack, as if my sandwich will suddenly spring out and lodge itself up someone's nose. That'd be fun. I can embarrass Flo *and* Mom *and* my own self in one fell swoop.

The tables are all crowded. I search for an empty one, where I can sit alone and friendless, but there aren't any. Sighing, I head towards the back of the room where the tables aren't as packed.

"Venice! Hey, Venice!"

I pause, unsure who is calling my name and how on Mother Earth I can hear the person above the swelling chatter around me.

"Venice!"

I turn slowly towards the source of the sound. Three tables away from me is a slightly familiar boy. I list my head, trying to remember, when it strikes me. Nate. The kid who helped me at the library the other day. He comes to this school? It makes sense, if he lives near or in the same neighborhood as us.

He beckons me over, and I hesitantly step closer to the table. Two other kids are sitting there, a broad-shouldered boy with light blond hair and the beginnings of a moustache, and a short girl with dark black hair cut to her shoulders. She eyes me curiously as I stop by the table, my hand wrapped so tightly around my backpack strap that I start to lose feeling in my hand. I'm surprised I haven't fainted yet from the waves of uneasy sensations crashing through me.

Nate is grinning, as usual. I wonder if he ever stops. "Hey, Venice," he says, motioning for me to sit down across the table from him, next to the short-haired girl. "Why don't you join us?"

I hesitate even longer, long enough for the girl to huff and twist around to glare at me. "Are you going to sit down?" she asks in a no-nonsense voice, but I have the feeling she isn't normally like this.

I have experience with people who pretend to be what they aren't, and she's clearly acting.

Quickly deciding this is the best thing to do, I sit down, swinging my backpack off my shoulder and onto the floor. I have to make myself meet their gazes briefly before I hide in the safety of my bag as I search for my lunch.

The girl leans towards me. She sniffs my arm, making me freeze. "Are you a geek?" she asks, and I resist the urge to pump a fist at how right I was.

Instead, my back stiffens. "Um…"

"Looks like one," says the boy, picking at his sandwich.

Somewhat against my will, I glance over at Nate. He grins in response, and I decide that yes, he never stops.

"I'm Amanda Price," the girl says, her attention pinned firmly on me. "But don't call me that. It sounds too formal. I'm Mandy to my friends and a few acquaintances."

"Er, nice to meet you, Mandy," I say. "I'm Venice Ferrari."

The blond kid leans forward. "Ferrari? Like, the car?"

I blink, my gaze sliding over to him. "Um, sure. It's also an Italian name. Like Venice."

"Cool," says the boy. "My name's Elijah Jenkins. I'm not named after no one or nothing. Just boring Elijah." Then he brightens. "Oh, but I'm a geek, like you. That's a cool thing, right?"

My eyes flick back over to Nate before I look down into my backpack again. "I don't know," I say. "Being a cool geek is a matter of opinion."

Elijah laughs. He reaches over and slaps me on the shoulder. "I like you!" he exclaims loudly.

I gulp. I seriously doubt this is how Florence makes friends. Then again, she doesn't talk to *geeks*.

"So," says Mandy, picking at her salad, "are you a geek or not?"

I shrug. "Sure."

"Do you like rocks?" asks Elijah.

Taking in a deep breath of air to calm my nerves, I nod. "Yeah. Rocks are pretty cool."

"Do you like cars?"

I shrug again. "Depends on the car. I like Ferraris."

"What about math?" Elijah asks, grinning.

I pull a face and everyone laughs, Elijah the loudest. He's just taken a bite of his sandwich so, unfortunately, we all see a glob of bread and meat fall out of his mouth and onto his knee. I grimace as Mandy hands him a napkin, rolling her eyes while she does.

"Chew and swallow before you laugh," Mandy scolds.

Elijah grins at me. "She's like my mom," he stage-whispers, purposely loud enough so we all hear it. "She's always telling me what I should and should not do." He winks at me. "Secretly, it's because she's in love with me."

He laughs again as Mandy goes purple and smacks him on the arm. Nate, still smiling at nothing and no one, says, "They're always like this." I assume he's talking to me—Elijah and Mandy are arguing about some random thing—and I'm the only one not engaged besides Nate.

"Is this your first day here?" he asks me.

"Yeah." I finally extract my lunch. "The last two weeks we were too busy to come." I glance around the cafeteria, spotting Flo far off to my right, flirting with a group of boys sitting at her table. "I'm sure my sister wouldn't have minded, though."

Nate follows my line of sight. "Ah, yes," he says. "Your twin. What's her name again?"

I stare at him, curious to know why he wants a confirmation. Nearly every person that comes in contact with Flo remembers her name. I've never had someone ask me to certify her name.

Realizing he's waiting for my answer, I quickly collect myself and say, "Florence."

"Florence Nightingale?" asks Mandy, breaking away from her argument.

"No." I point in the direction of my sister. "That's my twin."

Elijah looks over at her. He lets out a low whistle. "Woah!" he says. "She is one *babe*."

I blush as both Nate and Mandy smack him, though I notice Nate is a whole lot softer than she is.

"What?" Elijah demands, facing me again. "Venice, are you offended that I was objectifying your sister?"

"Not at all," I mumble, pulling my sandwich out. "Florence just has a ton of admirers, and personally, I think you should find a girl who knows you better than she does."

I swear his eyes flick over to Mandy for just one second before he replies, "Whatever you say, Venice. You know best."

Mandy, bored with this conversation, holds out a hand to me. "Can I see your schedule?"

Startled, I instinctively give her my schedule—I had printed it out despite Mom not wanting me to use paper—then turn to my sandwich with the intent of eating it before I somehow accidentally shove it up Elijah's nose. That would be embarrassing.

"Hey, Nate," Mandy says, waving my schedule at him. "She has biology with you later today."

Nate grins. "Nice."

Feeling self-conscious, I quickly start eating so I don't have to look at him or anyone. Elijah is nursing his wounds, moaning and complaining about the unfair circumstances, how Mandy and Nate had teamed up against him. He slops his lunch all over the table, making Mandy raise my schedule above her head in case some food might hit it.

"Stop being immature!" she snaps.

He freezes. "Oh really? Are you sure *I'm* the immature one?"

Mandy shoves my schedule at me, and I immediately place it back in my bag, worried it'll get dirty. Mandy pushes herself up, hands on the table, her body leaning towards Elijah. Her short hair falls around her face, giving her a terrifyingly dark aura. "I am *not* immature," she snarls, her tone harsh. "You're the one who filled my locker with ripped-up valentines last year!"

I snort with refrained laughter. Elijah and Mandy ignore me, but Nate meets my eye and winks.

"So what?" Elijah yells, though I notice he keeps his voice down; his large stance makes up for the noise and pressure. "You deserved it! You tricked me into eating that disgusting chocolate-covered grasshopper!"

Mandy tosses her hair. "I *told* you it might not taste good."

"I got a leg stuck between my teeth!" Elijah jabs a finger at his mouth. "Do you know how long it took to get it out?"

"Ten minutes!" retorts Mandy. "It was *all* you could talk about for the next eight weeks!"

Elijah sucks in a deep breath. "I wouldn't have talked for *eight weeks* if you hadn't convinced me to eat it! Think of how that backfired!"

This time, I can't help it. A giggle slips out.

Elijah and Mandy freeze. They slowly turn to look at me, both shocked to be interrupted. Across from me, Nate is holding back his own laughter, but when I break down laughing, not being able to stop it, he joins in.

"Why are you laughing?" demands Elijah.

Mandy sinks down onto her chair next to me and erupts into laughter herself, her face flushed red. I wipe my eyes, control my laughter. I don't usually laugh for very long. It draws attention to me, and I always try not to be in the spotlight.

I turn to Mandy, noting her blue T-shirt with white words on the front and, hoping to change the subject, I say, "Mandy, are you vegan?"

She startles. Looking down at her shirt, she lets out another bark of laughter. "No," she says.

"Then why does your shirt say *Go Vegan!* on it?" I ask.

Mandy rolls her eyes. "It was a gag gift from my vegan cousin.

She is constantly telling me I need to go vegan, but I can't live without bacon."

Elijah pushes away his food. "Ugh," he groans. "Girls."

"What's wrong with girls?" Nate asks, humoring him.

Elijah points at Mandy and me. "Them. They're so weird. They have the strangest conversations."

"Chocolate-covered grasshoppers aren't a strange topic?" I put in, and this time all three of them laugh. They sure laugh a lot. I'd love to hang out with them more, to joke around and laugh with them. They're fun. It's weird to be here, making them laugh, acting like we're friends from the instant I sat down at this table.

A shrill alarm sounds on Mandy's phone, announcing lunch is almost over and we have five minutes to get to class before we're late. She switches it off as Elijah sighs, shoving his food into his backpack without wrapping it up first. I grimace, trying not to imagine what homework and papers and such he is soiling with his lunch.

I look down at my own lunch, surprised to see I've eaten it all. I stand up and after making sure I've got everything, I sneak a quick peek at my schedule to determine which class I have next.

"Biology," says Nate, and I jump. He's standing close to me. I hadn't heard him come over. "We have biology next," he says, pointing at my schedule. "Come on. I'll show you how to get to the classroom."

I wave goodbye to Mandy and Elijah, who both wave back, then I follow Nate out of the cafeteria. I pass Flo right as we're about to leave, and she gapes at me, no doubt recognizing Nate. I flash her a nervous smile, making her eyes narrow. I'm relieved when she disappears from my sight. I'm not as anxious for her any more. I don't need to have her with me to boost my courage. She can go off with her friends, and I'll manage without her. She'd probably just ignore me anyway if I trailed after her like a puppy, along with all her other admirers.

Nate seems to know everyone. He calls out greetings to nearly every kid we pass on our way to biology. Nate's a friendly guy, I realize, as he stops briefly to compliment someone on their brand new shoes.

The classroom for biology is, unlike my other classrooms, dark. The chairs are set up in a circle with one chair in the middle. Several kids are fighting over that chair, joking loudly and pushing each other around. I don't know how they can see with the blinds closed—the only light is coming from the faint outline of the windows where the blinds can't reach.

Nate enters the room, looks around, and points to two empty chairs side-by-side near one of the blocked windows. "We can sit there," he says, "unless you'd rather sit with someone else."

"No, no," I say quickly, worried I'll be on my own again. "No, it's fine. We can sit there."

Grinning in the dark lighting, Nate leads me over to the chairs, flopping down gracefully and pulling his backpack off his shoulder at the same time. I take a little longer, first checking to make sure there isn't anything on the chair before carefully sitting down.

The kid next to me immediately turns to me and says, "You got a cigarette?"

Nate stiffens, but I beat him to it. "Do I look like I carry cigarettes?" I say, offended, but trying not to be rude.

The kid shrugs. "Sure."

"Well, I don't," I reply, maybe a little too stiffly. "Do you know how much they pollute the air? And they destroy your lungs. And they're the most littered item worldwide."

The kid gawks at me. Then—"Who cares?" he asks.

"Plenty of people!" I say, shocked.

He eyes me warily, then gets up and moves to a different seat, to which I'm grateful.

"That went well," I note.

Nate isn't grinning when I look over at him. In the dim light, I see he's glaring in the direction of the smoker boy. I frown. "Nate? What's wrong?"

He shakes himself slightly. "Uh, nothing. Just—that kid, Keller Jacobs—he used to be my best friend. Last year, he started to get into smoking, so I told him I wasn't going to socialize with him if all he was doing was hanging out in the parking lot with his pack of cigarettes." Nate scowls at Keller Jacobs, the look so strange that it occurs to me that I haven't seen him scowl in the short time I've known him. He always seems to be smiling.

"Oh. That's sad." I wait for him to continue, because he seems like he has something else to say, but at that moment a tall man wearing a fedora walks into the classroom, whistling to a song that's faintly familiar. The chatter falls silent, and I know this must be the teacher.

"Hey, kids," he says, closing the door behind him. Now the only light is coming from the dim outline of the windows. "How are you all doing today? Did anyone break a bone?" The man drops his briefcase near the chair in the middle of the room. That must be his, I guess.

"Joshua fractured his wrist," yells one girl.

The teacher—I forgot his name; it's on my schedule—looks around him and snorts with restrained laughter. "Again? Isn't this the fourth time?"

"Yeah," says the same girl. "Mom's real pissed."

He passes out papers, saying, "I'd be, too, if my son continued to be an idiot." He hands me one of the papers, then pauses. "Who are you?" he asks. "I've never seen you before."

"Um." I wonder how he could tell the difference between me and another of his students in this dark lighting. "I'm new," I say, growing red because of all the attention I'm getting. The kids are all staring at me, along with the teacher. "I'm, uh, Venice Ferrari."

"Ah." The teacher nods a few times. I almost don't catch it. "Ferrari. I had your brother earlier today."

"Roman?"

He nods again. "Yep. That's the one."

I grimace. "I'm so sorry." I really mean it. The poor man.

Laughter ripples through the listening kids. Even the teacher grins at me, his white teeth even brighter in the dim light. "Venice, you sound like the exact opposite of your brother."

"I try to," I reply, and the kids laugh for the second time. I'm having a good day—a better one than I thought I would. I've made Mandy and Elijah and Nate laugh; I've made the teacher and his students laugh; and I'm not really feeling embarrassed or awkward or anything. In fact, I feel warm inside, and I wonder if this is what Flo feels like when she's surrounded by people who laugh at anything she says, even if it isn't funny, just so they'll be allowed to stay.

"I'm Mr. Castro," he says moving on from me. "So, class, today we welcome Venice Ferrari into our midst. Say welcome."

"Welcome," chorus the kids.

I shrink down in my chair, suddenly shy.

Thank the trees, Mr. Castro saves me. "Today," he says, distributing the last of his papers, "we will be talking about animals. Yes, I know you all want to learn about Kingdom Protista—"

Everyone groans except for Nate and me.

"So, today, I thought we could take a break from that." Mr. Castro sits in the empty seat, confirming it's his. "Switching over to Kingdom Animalia. And for those who don't know which one that is, it's basically animals. They are such interesting creatures. We have some as pets. We kill some for food. We watch some in cages behind glass and protective barriers. They are majestic, intriguing, *weird*, and in some cases, dangerous." Mr. Castro taps his temples and it's hard to see in this scant lighting. "But...and here's the big question...*But,* are they really beneficial to humankind?"

It hits me hard. I've never asked that before. I've never even *considered* it.

Do we need animals?

Sure, they are one-of-a-kind, and it's always sad to see a species become extinct, but what is their purpose here? Why *are* they here? We just gawk at some, stay away from others, totally ignore different ones, keep some for pets, use others to hunt and earn a wealthy profit off of...The list goes on and on. But in the end, they're just animals. Creatures of the night, creatures of the day; creatures of the earth, creatures of the sky; creatures of the sea, creatures of the trees...Do we really need them?

"So..." Mr. Castor points to our papers. "Look at what I just gave you."

There is a rustle as everyone looks down. Mine is blank. I glance over at Nate and see his is, too. He catches me looking and grins, whispering, "This means we're going to have to write a report and do a presentation on something. Probably an animal."

"You're going to write a report," says Mr. Castro, and I match Nate's grin. "I want it to be a team project, though. Last time it was all singles, only ten of you turned them in."

Another collective groan arises, and again Nate and I are the only kids that don't join in. It's obviously a thing that happens in this class.

"Hey, hey!" Mr. Castro shouts, and they all go quiet. "Team up," he says, at a more normal level, "and create a presentation on any animal you want. It has to be at least five minutes long, and your report will be ten or more pages."

I look down at my paper again. The pale white color seems brighter, here in the dim light.

"And," continues Mr. Castro, "the topic is: *How are [insert animal species here] Beneficial to the Human Race?* And, because I know you've got plenty of homework from your other teachers— plus I'm really nice—I'll give you two months."

A third groan, but this time of relief. I can't help but smirk to myself.

"Two months," repeats Mr. Castro. "At least five minutes long. At least ten pages. And you gotta team up. If your partner dumps this whole assignment on you, come tell me and I'll give them a talking to about working together and all the comrade crap like that." He claps his hands, the loud and sudden noise startling me. "Alright, kids? Can I trust you on this, or am I gonna have to call your parents and make sure you'll actually do it?"

Someone scoffs. "You can trust us, Castro!" the kid yells.

He slowly nods. "Okay. Now that we've got that underway, who is your partner going to be, and what animal will you write your beneficiary report on?"

SIX

The moment he finishes talking, everyone jumps to their feet and starts to hunt for whoever will be their partner. I have a feeling that Mr. Castro has them do reports a lot, because he has to break up some teams, telling them to pick a different associate. I see the dark outlines of two kids far to my left, conversing quietly about elephants, and I decide, by the way they've quickly established what they're doing, that they *have* done dozens of reports like this one before.

"So," Nate says, drawing my attention to him. "Tanya is pretty nice. She'll be a great partner, but she takes so many extra classes you might not get to meet up with her a lot. Brenda's also nice—"

"What about you?" I ask, interrupting him.

He stops and stares at me in the dim light. "Um...Well, I thought you'd probably want to be teamed up with a girl..."

"Not really," I say, and I mean it. I don't want to have to find someone I don't know. "But I can team up with one if you've already got a partner you normally work with for these things."

"No, no," he says quickly. "I just—I usually wait around until everyone has been picked except the remaining person, and then I team with them. It's always a kid who isn't interested in finishing this assignment, and I end up doing the report for them so they don't get bad marks." I make a face at his words, and am surprised he sees it. He hastens to explain. "They help me," he says. "Not as much as Mr. Castro would like, but they still help out with the project. I do the research and write the paper, and they present it to the class."

"That's an intriguing way of helping someone," I comment, resting my chin on my fist.

Nate shrugs. "I don't want them to fail." He looks around the room, noting how nearly everyone has a teammate, then turns back to me. "We can be partners," he says.

His careless tone makes me blush. "Alright," I agree.

"What animal are we going to do?"

"I don't know." I think hard. "Do you have any ideas?"

"Nope."

"You don't have any favorite animals?" I press, embarrassed at how forward I was in this endeavor.

"Nope."

I start to doubt my decision in becoming his partner. "Um, what about the red panda?"

"Whatever you want to do."

I scroll through my mental list of animals I like. Sharks. Are they even considered animals though? Boa constrictors. Eh, those are reptiles. Giraffes. Those are cool.

Orangutans. I've always liked them. Mom used to take us to the zoo on nearly every holiday, and I could watch the orangutans swing on the ropes stretching between their habitats all day. They're fascinating creatures, especially since they are born with the ability to reason and think. They're smart, fascinating, and very, very ugly. I sometimes feel sorry for them. They are one of the most hideous mammals I've ever seen.

"What about orangutans?" I ask.

Nate thinks for a minute then says, "Okay. Apes are cool. And orangutans are even more special."

"How?" I'm humoring him.

He grins at me. His teeth are really, really white. And even nicer than Flo's. I flush pink at the thought. "They're orange," he says, and I lean back in my seat, laughing, but it's a quiet laugh. I don't want to draw attention to myself.

Mr. Castro comes up to us, a clipboard in one hand, a pen in the other. He squints at us. "You two a team?"

"Yep," answers Nate.

He quickly scribbles something on his clipboard. "And what's your beneficiary animal? Please don't say aardvark—I've gotten that three times."

"Don't worry," I put in. "We're doing the orangutan."

"Yes!" Mr. Castro writes something else on his paper. "Thank you, Venice. And Nate, of course. Orangutans are one of my favorite mammals. They're such an interesting species."

He moves to continue on to the next team, but I stop him by saying, "If I may ask, why do you keep the lights off and the blinds closed?"

"Conserves energy," he replies, then turns away.

I stare at his dark figure, trying to decide if he's serious or not. I voice the thought out loud, and Nate says, "That's what he tells us every single time we ask."

"Oh." I return to my blank sheet of paper, wondering what I should write on it. "Two months is a long time to prepare a presentation and write a ten-page report."

Nate taps my paper with a finger. "We have tons of homework from the other teachers. We came back from winter break and, as a special treat, we were loaded up with tons of assignments and essays and tests and quizzes and the sort." He flashes me another of his typical grins, the one that makes me want to smile back at him. "Great Christmas/New Year's present, right?"

My Christmas/New Year's present was moving here. "That *is* sad," I say. "Do you still have homework left to do?"

He hesitates, and I imagine he's looking for an answer that won't make him seem like a braggart or a failure. "Um," he begins,

"I have a lot of free time, so I fill my weekends and after-school afternoons with finishing up the, uh, assignments I'd gotten that day. So, no, I don't have any homework left from last week." He gestures at my paper. "And this is the first presentation/homework assignment that I've gotten today. This is the only schoolwork I have currently."

"Ah." I click my tongue. "Cool. Does anyone ever get jealous that you can complete your work in a day?"

Nate gives me a strange look. "*Anyone* can finish their stuff if they really want to get it over with," he says. "I'm willing to bet that you're like me. You do your homework immediately so you aren't tempted to procrastinate and have to hurry up and do it the night before it's due."

"Good guess," I say, surprised.

His quiet smile returns. "So," he says, looking at his own blank paper, "are you anxious to get started on this project?"

"Finish it, more likely," I reply, picking at a spot on my shirt so I don't have to look at him.

"Are you doing anything today after school?"

I'm startled by the question. I have to take a moment to compose myself before responding. "I don't know. I'll need to ask Florence. She always seems to know what's going on."

"Okay." Nate shifts in his chair. "If you're free, we could meet at the library. I'm sure they have plenty of information there on orangutans. *And*, they have free Wi-Fi." He grins at me as I snort with restrained laughter.

"The library isn't far from here, right?" I ask.

He nods. "Correct. It's actually only some ways back. About a two-minute walk away."

"I didn't see it when I walked here," I say, my brow creasing into a frown. Oh, I'd been staring at the sidewalk. No wonder I'd missed it.

"You walk to school?"

My head snaps up. I find Nate is staring at me. At least, his face is turned towards mine. He can have his eyes closed for all I know. "Uh, yeah," I say, a little surprised by the question. "My mom doesn't like the school buses, so I walk instead of ride."

"That's..." he stalls, searching for a word. "Interesting," he says finally. "So do I."

Before I ask why, however, Mr. Castro claps his hands together loudly, drawing all attention to him. "Now that you've all got partners and an animal picked out," he says, "we have no need to continue class. Spend the next few minutes thinking about what you're going to do to research your animal." He holds up his hands as some kids begin to stand up. "Hey, hey, sit back down! I'm not finished yet."

The kids sit down impatiently. I squint and see one fidgeting.

"Remember," says Mr. Castro, waggling a stack of paper in the air, "that this report is for finding out why we shouldn't just kill off these species. Why are they important to us? What is their value? *How are they beneficial to us?* Don't forget to answer all those questions. I'm not looking for a report on their eating habits. I want to know why I shouldn't go shoot all the sea otters and Asian elephants and giant pandas. Got it?"

"Yeah!" yells someone, and several other kids chorus their agreement. I'm quiet, trying to imagine Mr. Castro with a shotgun going around and killing all the endangered animals. It makes me want to giggle, but I hold it back for the sake of not drawing attention to myself. *Hush your thoughts*, I tell myself. *You don't even know what Mr. Castro looks like and if he owns a shotgun or has enough money to go to Africa and kill all the elephants.*

I choke on a laugh that bubbles up my throat. I'm lucky no one notices.

The rest of the day goes well. I still don't have my schedule memorized, and I have to keep checking to make sure I'm going to the right places. I'm pretty sure Mandy remembered my entire schedule from just one look, because after nearly every class, she's waiting in the hallway for me. She talks a lot, but it's nice chatter, and I doubt I'll ever grow bored of it. She isn't in any of my classes, unfortunately, though Nate is in math with me and I sit next to Elijah during Spanish. I quickly learn why no one else wants to sit by him; he is constantly wiggling and squirming in his seat, disrupting any quiet moment in class.

I spot Roman and Florence a few times in the hallways, but I don't have any classes with my twin. I'd been hoping we could be together, even though I know she is taking much different classes than I am. The only ones she takes that I do are math and language arts, but the times and teachers are dissimilar.

When school ends, Mandy instantly appears. She loops her arm through mine and drags me down the packed hallway, her friendliness rather foreign to me. No one has ever done this before. I wonder if her only friends are Elijah and Nate, and I immediately feel sympathy for her. She's like me in several ways. I'm surprised she wants to be my friend so soon after meeting me, but I'm definitely grateful. Today worked out better than I'd hoped.

"So, how was your first day at a new school?" she asks while we're gradually pushed towards the front doors by the flow of kids heading outside.

"Fun," I answer, having to speak louder than normal, otherwise she won't hear me above the swell of chatter around us.

"How so?" Mandy shoves open the door, and we stumble out of the high school.

I blink furiously in the bright light. It'd been cloudy when I left home this morning. "Well, I barely got any homework. Just an essay and a report. And some review questions for whatever the heck my history class is about."

Mandy snorts, leading me over to a line of yellow school buses. "It said on your schedule that you have US Government."

71

"Huh. That makes sense now."

She laughs. "What did you think you had?"

"Um, it just seemed like a lecture on someone's political opinions," I say. "I didn't even think it was a class for the longest time ever. Until you told me what it was, really."

Mandy looks at me strangely. "You know what," she says, making it sound like a declaration, not a question, "I honestly like you, Venice. I think everything is going to be a whole lot different with you around."

Then, before I can ask if that's a good thing or a bad thing, she lets go of me and climbs onto the nearest school bus.

I'm left staring after her. Several kids jostle past me, and once one mutters about being in the way, I turn on my heel and march away in the direction of home. I've totally forgotten about Flo, so when she thrusts her way through the crowd and stops me in my tracks, knocking my glasses down, I stumble back and hurriedly push them up. I don't want to be blind for this.

"So," Florence drawls, crossing her arms over her chest in a threatening sort-of gesture, "you've got a *friend*. Finally."

My heart plummets. Why is my *twin* so mean to me?

"Three, actually," I correct, and Flo's eyes narrow.

"How on Earth did you manage that?" she asks, incredulous. "Did you pay them?"

I flush angrily. Dozens of come-backs rise to the tip of my tongue, but I don't want to hurt Florence. I want to become her friend. I want her to, at long last, realize I'm trying to be kind to her. "Flo," I say patiently, keeping my temper in check, "is it wrong of me to talk to people? Can't you be happy for me?"

She tosses a long curl of hair over her shoulder. "No," she says, waggling her pink-painted fingernails at me. "But when you're obnoxious about it, then I'm left thinking you're spiteful about me having so many friends. I have four boys who worship the ground I walk on. More than you, I must say."

I'm growing tired of this. I wish she'd get it past her thick head that *she* is the one acting spiteful. And she knows I don't care for being worshipped.

"And," Flo continues, dragging a fingernail down the side of my face, and I am suddenly glad I'm taller than her, "you're associating with *geeks*. Those are the dirt of high school, you know. The idiots, the outcasts." She smirks. "I hope you come to your senses and reject them. You can join my friends. I've taken over the popular group, because I'm obviously the prettiest and most delicious to look at and talk to."

"You want me to join your clan?" I ask dubiously.

Flo smiles prettily. "Yes, if you learn how to dress properly and stop talking to geeks."

I bristle. "No, thanks," I say, moving to push past her.

She grabs my arm, her nails digging into my arm through my thin jacket. "I am giving you one chance," she whispers. "I won't extend the offer a second time. Think hard, Venice. Do you want to be popular, or do you want to be a nobody?"

I look over her shoulder and spot Nate and Elijah talking by the front doors of the school. "I think I'd rather be a nobody," I tell Flo. "And I'll continue to be one. Thanks for the offer, but no thanks." I flash her a brief, tight-lipped smile, then bow my head and brush past her right into a large group of kids who hopefully hadn't heard what my twin said to me.

I emerge on the other side with my glasses dangling off my nose. After fixing them, I make my way over to Nate and Elijah, wanting to recover from what Flo just said to me.

The boys both grin at me as I come closer. "Hey, Venice," says Elijah, lifting up his hand for a fist-bump.

I return the greeting. "Hey, Elijah. Do you walk home, too?"

"Nah," he says. "I take the bus with Mandy. We live in the same neighborhood." He wrinkles his nose. "Which reminds me...I should hurry or the bus will leave without me. It's happened before. A lot."

He winks at me, grinning, and steps away. "We'll see ya tomorrow, right?"

"Right," I confirm.

Elijah salutes us, whirls around, and disappears into a crowd of chattering kids all headed for the school buses.

"Where do you live?"

I jerk in shock and glance up at Nate, surprised he would be interested in knowing. "Um, about half a mile past the library."

I haven't ever really *looked* at him before, examined him that carefully. Mostly, I've been unable to meet his gaze, so I haven't exactly seen his features. But standing here in the sunlight, I find myself studying him. He's tall—really tall—but he isn't thin as a toothpick like some tall people I know or have seen. His hair, dark brown, is ragged and uneven and incredibly messy; it keeps falling over his eyes, which are a clear blue color like the cloudless sky. He's wearing a jacket and fingerless gloves despite the warm sun. He must get cold easily.

I realize he's talking and hurriedly pull myself back down to Earth.

"...just forty minutes," he is saying.

"Sorry," I say, truly meaning it, "but could you repeat what you just said? I was...distracted."

Nate grins at me, and that's when I notice he has dimples. The discovery makes my cheeks tinge pink.

"I was saying," he says, "that I have to walk three miles to get here, and it's about a forty minute walk, though sometimes I can get here faster, especially if I know it's an important day." His grin widens, turning somewhat sheepish. "Like today," he adds after a brief moment.

I frown. "What was important about today?"

Nate dips his head at me. "You."

I blink, not comprehending what he means. "Um, what?"

"Ever since that day at the library, I've been wondering if you and your siblings would show up here," he explains. "And sure enough, you did."

Slightly baffled, I say, "Um." Regular smooth-talker, am I not?

He jerks his head. "Come on. I'll walk you home. We can talk about our report on the way."

"Oh...okay." I grip my backpack strap and lead the way to the sidewalk, still trying to think through what he'd said. Important? Me? He's got to be teasing.

"I saw your sister was talking to you," Nate says lightly, and I quickly glance over at him before respectfully returning my gaze to the sidewalk.

"Uh, yeah." I push my glasses up my nose. "She wanted me to join her posse on the condition that I stopped hanging out with you and Elijah and Mandy. Naturally, I refused, and she got rather offended, I think."

Nate frowns. "Why would she not want you to talk to us?"

"One word," I say, smiling grimly. "Geeks."

His muddled confusion clears. "Ah," he says, nodding his head knowingly a few times. He's an understanding kid. "She's worried that we'll ruin her reputation."

"Exactly."

Nate sounds slightly embarrassed when he says, "I'm sorry. I know you just told me earlier, but I keep forgetting her name. I remember Roman and Pompeii and Siena, but I can't remember hers. I know it isn't Sardinia or Naples..."

I laugh at the idea of being named Sardinia. "It's Florence," I say, suspicious that he has forgotten again.

"Yes!" Nate snaps his fingers. "That's what it is. Man, why can I not remember that? Florence is a big city! And it's popular."

"Just like my sister," I say, somewhat sadly. It's true. Well, not the *city* part, but the popular.

He recognizes I'm becoming depressed. "So," he says. "Why did you pick orangutans for our report?"

"I've always liked them," I reply, grateful for the change of subject. "I can't help but feel bad for them since they're so ugly."

Nate snorts with laughter. "Seriously."

"All apes are hideous," I continue sincerely, hoping to maintain my streak of making him laugh, "but orangutans are top of the list. Along with gorillas."

He doesn't disappoint. He laughs again, this time the sound sending a thrill of some unfamiliar emotion running down my spine.

"Why do you think they're beneficial, then?" he asks. "To make us feel like we aren't ugly compared to them?"

"Yes," I say firmly. "Definitely. Though, seriously, why *are* they beneficial? I've never really been asked that question—I've just thought they were really cool. I liked watching them swing on those special lines at the zoo."

"Did any fall down?"

I cast a frown on him, not amused. He laughs in reply.

Reaching the end of the street, I pause at the stop sign, making sure there aren't any cars about to run me over before crossing to the other side, Nate trailing after me. Once back on the sidewalk, I continue to head for my house, wondering if Flo will be looking out the bus window and gritting her teeth when she passes me. I wonder if she's going to give me a real talk-to the instant I get back home. Will she tell Mom lies about me to prevent me from ever talking to Nate or Mandy or Elijah again? I don't doubt Flo will give up easily. Sometimes, it seems she's determined to destroy my life, and she won't admit defeat, and it's quite strange why she's so self-centered but spends so much time and energy bullying me.

"Venice? Venice, are you on auto-pilot?"

I blink back my thoughts, releasing a deep sigh at the same time. "Uh, sorry. I was...thinking, I guess."

"You guess?"

I cough into my fist. "Yeah." I'm quiet for a long time, and so is he. The school bus Flo and Roman ride on eventually catches up to us, turning onto our street before circling back and passing us again. We walk in silence for the next few minutes, and when I see the familiar sign of my street up ahead, I realize we've barely talked about our report. We're lucky we have two months.

Nate and I are almost to the street sign when a huge, shiny black SUV comes roaring around the bend, zooming past us. Nate is on my right, blocking me from seeing who is driving the car, so I can't sneak a quick glimpse of whoever is ignoring the speed limit. The SUV lets out a loud rumble, smoke trailing out of the exhaust. I bury my face in my elbow to prevent myself from inhaling the fumes, watching the car turn sharply and disappear down a different street, leaving us staring after it.

SEVEN

"That was weird," says Nate, a slight frown on his face. "The people who live in this area normally have big expensive cars like that one, but I've never seen that car before."

"It smells bad," I choke out, my eyes watering. I *hate* the smell of exhaust. Why does it have to stink so badly?

Nate smiles at me—it has a hint of a smirk, something I haven't seen in him yet. "Most cars smell bad," he says, his tone humorous. "Just wait until you smell the garbage trucks that collect trash every Wednesday and Saturday. Those are even worse."

"I'll bet."

We wander down the street with Nate leading now; I think he knows the house my family and I moved into—he's obviously familiar with this area and neighborhood. He must live near here or walk past or through this place often to be able to know where everything is and what cars people own.

"Have you lived in Virginia your entire life?"

He looks over at me. "Uh, no, not technically. I was born in D.C."

"But you've lived around here for most of your life, then?"

"Yeah." He doesn't say anything else, so the conversation dies. I wonder if there's something about him that he doesn't want me to know. I'm getting that vibe from him every now and then. During biology class, about that kid, Keller Jacobs, Nate had told me they used to be friends, but he hadn't gone into detail why. And now, he's not very talkative about his childhood. I wonder why he seems evasive about his past. It's a completely different side of him from the cheerful, friendly, grinning Nate. I make a mental note to ask him about it later, when we're maybe better friends.

My house appears in the distance. I spot Mom's car in the driveway, which means she must be back from work.

I suddenly stop walking. Nate pauses uncertainly and looks back at me. "What's wrong?" he asks.

My eyes narrow. "What on Holy Mother Earth is *that*?"

Nate follows my line of sight. Sitting in my driveway, parked next to Mom's car, is a rusty red pick-up truck, the exact kind of car Mom hates. Why is one at my house? Who owns it?

"What?" Nate glances over at me again. "What's what?"

"That truck," I say, stalking toward my house. "Why is it at my house?"

Nate hurries to catch up with me. "I've never seen it before around here. Have you?"

"No." I hurry up to the driveway, confusion tumbling through me; what is going on here?

"Well…"

I peer back at Nate, realizing he's stopped at the mailbox, looking rather uncomfortable. "Yeah?" I prompt.

"Um, I guess I'll see you tomorrow at school," he says, shoving a hand into his pocket. "Maybe we can meet afterwards at the library or some other place to actually start on our report."

"Oh, yeah, sure," I say, my thoughts all on the red pick-up and not Nate. "I-I'll see you then, Nate." Without waiting for a response, I head up the driveway, intending on extracting an explanation from Mom about why that truck is at our house and who owns it and if she's convinced them to switch to a greener fuel yet.

I open the front door and walk in, closing it as loudly as I can. Happy chatter from somewhere deeper into the house, probably the kitchen or dining room, ceases immediately. A second later, I hear the faint patter of slippered footsteps on the floor, and Mom arrives in the doorway leading to the kitchen.

"Hey, Venice," she says. She's still wearing her work clothes—a plain white blouse, a short skirt falling to her knees, and black tights—but her high heels are gone, replaced with the fluffy pink slippers Roman bought her for Christmas last year.

"Hey, Mom," I say, swinging my backpack off my shoulder. I hadn't realized how heavy it was until I drop it to the floor. "Whose car is that?"

She turns slightly pink, instantly making me nervous. Oh no. No, no, no, no. She can't...

A tall man steps out of the kitchen, a small smile playing at the corners of his mouth. He's unfamiliar—I'm sure I've never seen him before. He has long blond hair falling to his shoulders, a smooth, clean-shaven face, and dull, dark blue eyes. His nose is crooked, like he broke it a long time ago and it healed incorrectly. He has a dark aura about him; I can sense it. There's something wrong with him.

"Venice, this is Marc Tyron," says Mom, gesturing between the two of us. "Marc, this is my oldest daughter, Venice."

"Nice to meet you, Venice." His voice is level. Even. Smooth like his face.

I stare at him in response, not saying anything.

"Linda told me you and Florence are twins," Marc continues, ignorant of the wary look I'm giving him. "I didn't believe her until I saw you." He grins, displaying brilliantly white teeth. There's no way that's natural. He must've paid thousands for those. "You look just like Florence," he says, then turns to Mom, who is awkwardly wringing her hands. "They're both such beautiful girls," he says. "I can see where they got their good looks."

Mom smiles, her cheeks still quite pink. "Thanks, Marc. You're a regular silver-tongued charmer." She nervously glances over at me, swallows hard. I can tell she's anxious for me to say something.

"What's the deal with your truck?" I blurt out.

Marc startles, returning his attention to me. "What? Oh, my truck. It sure looks like it's gonna die soon, huh?"

He's drastically misinterpreted what I'd said. And his response confirms to me that he doesn't know Mom well at all. Shaking my head, I grip my backpack and move to go upstairs, to get away from him and Mom, but Flo suddenly shows up, smiling brightly.

"Venice! You're finally home!" She loops her arm through mine. "Come into the kitchen! You *have to* try this really delicious stuff that Marc brought over. It is so *good!*" She drags me away from the stairs, away from my safe haven of a bedroom, and leads me into the kitchen. Roman, Pompeii, and Siena are all sitting at the counter, eating something orange. Bright candy wrappers litter the counter and floor.

"It's called Sperlari," explains Flo, shoving one of the candies into my hand.

I examine it. It's an orange hard candy, the kind of stuff Mom tends to avoid. She hates individually-wrapped items.

"It's an Italian candy," Marc says from somewhere behind me.

Clenching the hard candy in my fist, I turn to face him, letting go of Flo as I do. "Who *are* you?" I demand. I know it sounds rude; I just feel so uneasy about him that it comes out as an accusation.

He grins again, but it feels threatening. Predatory. "I just moved here from New York," he says. "Your mom helped me find a good house to buy."

My frown deepens. "What brings you to rural Virginia from a metropolis like New York?"

"I've been waiting for a good opportunity." Marc shrugs. "You should try the Sperlari, Venice. It's one of my favorite candies. I get it straight from Italy, too."

I squeeze the candy harder. "Then why are you sharing your expensive candy with us?"

"Your mom mentioned how she likes Italy," he says, surprised and by now slightly irritated by all my questions. "She told me she had her own little Italy. All you kids, she said. So I thought I could repay her kindness by giving you guys a treat they love in Italy." He studies me thoughtfully, his brow creased in a frown to match mine. "Was that wrong of me?"

Mom, standing by his shoulder, glares at me. She seems rather shocked that I'm not being polite like usual. The thing is, I don't trust Marc. He's too nice, his voice too calming, his smile too forced. And there's something really off about him.

"No, no," Mom says quickly. "Venice is just wary of strangers." She shoots me a look that, quite plainly, says: *Either behave yourself or leave.*

I uncurl my fist, feeling the hard candy against my skin. "You said you came from New York," I say conversationally. "What sort of work do you do?"

Marc's lips curve back into the sickening smile. "I hunt down law breakers and petty thieves," he says, his serene voice flowing over me.

It doesn't do anything to sway my opinion of him.

"So, you're an FBI agent?" asks Florence, munching on another Sperlari candy.

Marc tips his head in her direction. "Not exactly. I work for the government, doing pretty much what the FBI does, but I'm just a special operative. I'm not on the police force, either."

"What, did you fail training?" Roman puts in bluntly. He has a dozen wrappers littered around him: on the counter, on the floor...

Slob.

"Not exactly," Marc says again. It's followed by a short bark of laughter, which sharply increases my dislike of him. "I showed traits of a different type of officer."

"Do you know how to use a gun?" Pompeii says.

Marc nods energetically. "Oh, yeah. You wanna learn? I can teach you."

"No, silly." Mom rolls her eyes. "Why would you teach a twelve year-old kid how to shoot a gun? I'd never forgive you."

He grins at her, the look so disgusting I'm tempted to shove all the Sperlari candies up his nose. "We can't have that happening, then," he says, his smirk of a smile growing with each word he says.

I can't take it anymore. I step past him and go back to the entryway, away from his glittery smile and foul aura. I snatch up my bag, then stomp up to my bedroom, hoping to get some peace and quiet so I can think through all that has happened to me today. My mood keeps swinging wildly from nervous to happy to shocked to humored to angry.

I dump my backpack on the floor and flop down on my bed. I stare up at the ceiling, wondering how on Mother Earth I'm going to process all of this. Mom truly seems to like him. And coming from my mother, it's kinda gross. I have never considered that she might find someone else after Dad. I have always thought that it's going to be the six of us for until we grow up and leave and start our own families. I try to be objective. If it had been any other man, would I like him? Am I just being protective of Mom? Am I jealous? But none of those explanations sit right with me. Marc is...strange. He has done all the right things, flattering us with his charm and Italian candies and interesting facts about his career. Why am I so utterly repulsed by him?

Also, if Mom hasn't lectured him about his truck, that means she doesn't care anymore. She's been distracted. She never gave up the chance to correct Dad about something like Marc's truck and switching to a greener alternative. Maybe she's trying not to come on too strong with her environmental obsessions, but that's such an important part of her. Why is she suddenly interested in him? She can't have known Marc for very long. Only two weeks. Maybe less than that. I hope she isn't rushing into a relationship, especially one where she can't be herself. I wish she'd let him have it about his truck already. With luck, that might scare Marc off so he'll leave us alone. But that thought doesn't feel right, either. Something tells me even that wouldn't keep him away.

I unclench my fist, letting the orange Sperlari candy drop to the floor. It falls into my backpack, getting buried by all my stuff inside.

Another thing. Florence. She changes her mood even more than I do. She's so confusing and irate and cheerful and pleasant and furious and annoyed. I don't understand. One moment she's mocking me—the next she's joyfully explaining something to me, seemingly forgetting all about how mean she was to me just twenty or so minutes ago. Is she going to be like this our entire lives? Will she always taunt me at school, out in the open where people can overhear? How am I going to survive if she does? It's only the first day of school, and I'm ready to avoid her for life. And why is she so concerned that I'd talked with some people? Sure, they aren't in the popular crowd, and some might consider them weird, but Elijah and Mandy are hilarious and friendly. I had definitely *not* expected to meet anyone like them. And Nate. Just landing my thoughts on him begins to calm me and soften my critical thoughts.

I smile at the idea, and just like that, my bad mood is gone. I sit up, reach into my backpack, pull out the blank sheet of paper from Mr. Castro before I sink onto my pillow again. What are we going to write? Not eating habits, that's for sure.

Laughing to myself, I grab my phone and look up pictures of orangutans, ready to feel bad for how ugly they are, ready to focus on much more pleasant and much less difficult topics.

EIGHT

TO: Sleepy Gumption
FROM: Hubris Jargon
SUBJECT: Attempt 1.0
TIME: 4:29 p.m.
DATE: Tuesday, January 21

Failure. Could not get close enough to determine if she suspects anything or if she has it. Will try again. Get closer. Actually scare her? Maybe threaten if not able to ascertain identity.

Note—Seen with companion. Associate unknown.

NINE

I wake up late the next morning. I hadn't meant to sleep in so much, but I'd been kept awake half the night by Flo yammering to someone on her cell phone. Apparently, after I'd stormed upstairs yesterday, Marc had left, saying he felt embarrassed. Mom invited him over for dinner tomorrow, so I have a feeling I'll either be up in my room all evening, or I'll go meet up with Mandy somewhere. Mom hasn't spoken to me once this morning—she's hiding in her office and refuses to come out. I don't know what she's doing in there, and I really hope she isn't calling Marc. She's talking to someone, I know—I can hear her faint voice through the walls. It's not like her not to confront me. Then again, it's not like me to cause trouble for her.

When I arrive in the kitchen, fully dressed and not fully awake, I find Siena yelling at Roman about something random, as always. I catch the word *toaster*, but it's all I manage to untangle from her mess of screams. Pompeii is reading at the dining room table, shoveling cereal into his mouth at the same time. Florence is pouting by the microwave, holding a frozen bagel in one hand and a butter knife in the other.

"The microwave is broken," she complains.

I peer at it. "Um, it's unplugged."

Roman laughs caustically above Siena's rampage. "You are *such* an idiot, Flo. Of course it's unplugged! Can't you tell?"

Flo goes red. "Yeah, I can," she snaps. "Thanks for the obvious."

"Still an idiot," mutters Roman.

"At least I didn't shove someone's slippers into the toaster," she retorts, her back to him as she searches for an outlet to plug in the microwave.

I groan, facing Roman. "Did you seriously?"

"Seriously what?" he asks, pushing Siena away from him. She growls, then stomps off to yell at Pompeii.

I sigh deeply, folding my arms over my chest. "Did you seriously put Siena's slippers in the toaster?"

"Who says they were Siena's?" Roman rolls his eyes, turning to the fridge to search for something to eat. "They could've been yours. And I just wanted to see if they would catch fire. They did. And the toaster's broken now. Mom will have to buy a new one. I'm not paying for it."

Groaning again, I snatch up a loaf of bread and begin to make myself a sandwich. "I have the most insane siblings ever," I murmur to the slices of bread, spreading peanut butter and honey on them. I smash the pieces together, slam it into a container, and toss it into my backpack. I have two minutes to leave or I'll be late.

I've just packed a bag of trail mix when someone knocks on the front door. Crinkling my nose, I sling my backpack over my shoulder and stalk out of the kitchen, irritated that no one else feels the need to answer the door. Flo is now in an argument with Roman about the differences between a conventional and a convection microwave. Siena and Pompeii are throwing cereal at each other. Pompeii's book, I notice, is safely stored on top of the fridge.

I yank open the front door, cringing as I hear a crashing noise behind me, followed by the tinkling of broken glass.

Nate is standing on the porch, working hard not to smile. "Hi, Venice," he says. "I was walking past your house and remembered you didn't take the bus, and I was wondering if maybe we could walk to school together, get started on that report."

"Great idea," I say, meaning it. I glance over my shoulder in the direction of the kitchen and my crazy siblings, then return my attention to Nate. "Should I grab a jacket?"

He shrugs. "I guess. It's kind of cold out."

I turn to the rack of coats and jackets hanging from the wall next to the door, searching for mine. Once I find it, I slip it on, slide my backpack over my shoulder, and gratefully leave the house, closing the door softly behind me. There's no way any of my siblings would've heard me. They're still in the kitchen, yelling at each other.

It's windy outside. The wind is harsh and unrelenting, battering me from all sides and never dropping or slowing. Nate seems used to it—he's wearing what must be the world's thinnest jacket—and he's acting like his normal, cheerful self.

"You don't have to answer," he says, "but what was going on back there, at your house?"

I instinctively look over my shoulder at my house before returning my gaze to the sidewalk. "Oh, it's just a typical day at the Ferrari household," I say. "It happens every day. Siena gets in fights with Pompeii and Roman, Florence is busy with her stuff but won't give up an opportunity to argue..." I shrug. "I try to stay out of it. Thanks for giving me a chance to get out of there. I don't last long in arguments."

"How come?"

I hide a grin. "Um, because I always back down. They call me a coward, but I think *not* bickering shows maturity."

"And bickering shows immaturity?"

"Exactly."

Nate laughs. "How old are Pompeii and Siena?"

"Twelve and ten. You'd think they'd stop being childish, yet they choose to keep it up." I glance quickly at him, then look back at the street. "Nate, do you have any siblings?"

"Nah," he says, but he stiffens and doesn't offer up any other information. After a minute, I anxiously look up at him, but his face is devoid of expression. Wondering what I've done to make him retreat to silence like yesterday, I embarrassingly switch my gaze to my feet, uncomfortable silence stretching between us just going on and on without anyone breaking it. We don't say anything as we cross the street. We don't say anything as a yellow school bus rumbles past us. We don't even say anything as we approach the high school, where crowds of kids are gathered, all talking excitedly and greeting friends.

Spotting a currently friendlier individual, I leave Nate behind and hurry to meet up with Mandy.

She actually *squeals* with delight and rushes up to greet me, engulfing me in a hug.

"Venice!" she says loudly, squeezing me around the middle. She's several inches shorter than me, her forehead reaching my jaw. "It's great to see you! How was your night? Have you already written your report for biology with Nate?"

I frown. "Um, how do you know about that?"

"What goes around comes around," replies Mandy, dragging me over to Elijah. "Hurry. School starts in a few minutes."

I wave hi to Elijah, who grins brightly at me. "It's great to see you!" he says, squealing just like Mandy. "How was your night? Have you already written your report for biology with Nate?"

"Hardy har har," Mandy says, dry with sarcasm, punching him on the shoulder.

I smile at them both as Mandy's five-minute alarm rings. "See you all later," I say, heading inside and out of the wind. The heat slashes through the cold, clashing together to start fogging up my glasses. I take them off and wipe them on the corner of my shirt, then put them back on, blinking, glad to see again. I notice Florence hanging out by some lockers with a group of boys all vying for her attention. I watch as she leans against one, slipping her hand into his. He's obviously pleased, and he gives the other boys a smug look. He glances around, searching for more kids to smirk at, and spots me. He jerks back in surprise, looking between Flo and me, then back at Flo. His brow is creased in a frown as he compares us. I smile to myself and continue on to my homeroom, thinking that sometimes, it's tricky being identified if you've got someone who looks just like you.

Lunch is by far the most exciting, most interesting thing about the school day. I spend the time listening to Mandy and Elijah argue good-naturedly about random things; from socks to frozen fruit to recyclable dishwashers and if they even can *be* recyclable. I try to engage in the conversation but I am very aware that Nate has yet to join in—I'm still confused why he became silent when I asked if he has any siblings, and why he hasn't talked to me yet. I can't think of what I might have done wrong, but I wish I hadn't done whatever it was. I want to make it right so that he'll go back to the Nate I met at the library and on my first day of school.

His friends don't seem to notice that he's quiet, but they mostly talked the day before, and I get the feeling Nate often just listens to them unknowingly flirt with each other. Plus, it's hard to squeeze in even one word when Mandy is in a chatty mood.

So far, that's been every time I've interacted with her.

She's such a great person, great friend, and I'm glad I was introduced to her and Elijah, and my life is already so much better here than it was back in California, where I was too shy to approach anyone and talk to them. Here in Virginia I feel like I have been given a free pass to friends simply because I met a genuine, kind boy at the library who was willing to welcome me into his social group.

As the lunch hour passes without Nate saying a word, I start to panic that maybe I've blown all that with a careless question.

I'm sad and slightly nervous when lunch ends and I have to go to biology with Nate. I slowly get to my feet, not wanting to leave

Mandy and Elijah for Nate, and trudge out of the cafeteria without waiting for him. He catches up with me when I exit the bubbling cafeteria—he's got a smile back on his face, making me wonder if I've been stressing over nothing.

"Are you doing anything after school?" he asks.

My heartbeat surprisingly speeds up. "I don't know." I say, tense.

His smile vanishes. "Hey, are you mad at me?"

"I don't know. I was worried you were mad at me. Did I say something wrong? I'm really sorry if I did."

We walk in silence for a minute, pushing past kids crowding the hallways and generally getting in the way. Finally, Nate says, "I'm sorry for going mute on the trip here. I just—I don't really like talking about my family."

I clutch my backpack tighter to my side. "Oh. I see. Why?"

He's not amused. "Nice try," he says dryly, but with humor.

"Sorry." I manage a smile back.

"So. Are you free after school?"

I really do want to spend time with Nate—well, the friendly Nate. I relax my grip on my backpack strap and decide I should be a good friend and respect his privacy. "Sure. I'll just need to let my mom know where I'll be going, though."

"The library, of course, for our report," Nate responds instantly.

"Oh, okay." I look up and recognize we're almost to our biology classroom. "Because the library has free Wi-Fi, right?"

He laughs, and the sound breaks apart any remaining tension. "Bingo."

Feeling lighter now, I grin and prepare myself for being stuck in a dark room for the next hour.

TEN

"**This is disgusting**," **I comment**, shoving away the laptop. "Ugh, how are we going to write a report about *this*?"

Nate grins at me. "Defecating is the most important thing an orangutan can do."

I groan and bury my face in my arms. "Why on Mother Earth did I choose orangutans? Our presentation is going to be so gross!"

"Hey, this website uses the word *disposal*," Nate points out. "That's better than defecate, right?"

"Never say that word again," I mumble.

I swear he's smirking at me as he asks, "Which one?"

Groaning again, I raise my head, look him straight in the eye. "You know. Now, can we please move on to how they're critically endangered and stuff like that? There's got to be something else about them that's a good reason for them to not be wiped out."

"They maintain the health of the forest ecosystem," says Nate, scrolling through the web page on his laptop.

"How?"

He's trying hard not to smile. "Um, I just said one reason how."

At my hard glare, Nate hurries to come up with another. "Let's see…You know how they sleep up in trees? They have these sweet nests up there. Pretty cool, right? Anyway, they apparently build a new nest every evening, and that breaks up the branches and allows the sunlight to filter through the thick canopy onto the forest floor, which helps plants grow and not starve without the proper nutrients from the sun."

I grumble something under my breath, raise my voice. "That's a whole lot better than the other...thing."

"And...that's pretty much it." Nate closes his laptop with a flourish of his hand. "Boom! It's over. We're done."

"Great." I move to stand up. "I can go eat dinner now."

He's still grinning. "Are you sure you can eat after learning this stuff about orangutans?"

"Probably not." I sink back down on my chair, resting my chin on my palms, and stare at the laptop, trying to forget what I had just learned. "Eating a bunch of fruit and...uh, *disposing* of the fruit's seeds apparently helps keep the exotic fruit trees from going extinct, and I do like to eat fruit, although I'll never look at exotic fruit the same way."

"What kinds of fruit are, um, nourished by orangutan, uh...by orangutans?" Nate is trying desperately to keep a straight face.

I flip open the laptop again. "Let's see...durians."

He frowns. "What the heck is a durian?"

"See for yourself." I push the laptop towards him, and he spends a quiet moment reading through something. He suddenly laughs, leaning back in his chair.

"They smell bad!" he says. "Oh, look what this one guy wrote about how bad durians smell."

I pull a face. "No, thanks. I'm good."

"They're banned from some places," he goes on. "Hm...Maybe I should get a couple for Elijah."

I give him a horrified look. "What! Why would you do that?"

"He's always looking for ways to get out of school," says Nate, shrugging. "If he takes one in, we can have a day or two off while they have to air out the school." He says it like it's a great idea, and I can't help imagining Elijah being presented with a durian and its developmental history. I'm fairly certain he'd love the attention eating it would get him. When I burst out laughing, Nate loses it too and we can't stop until one of the librarians gives us the stink eye, which actually makes us start laughing all over again, just quieter.

I dry my eyes from the laughing spell and run a hand through my hair, gathering some in my fist. "Nate, how will we manage to write a ten-page report about durians and how bad they smell?"

Nate nods and pretends to think deeply. "I think we're going to have to be very descriptive. And you're going to have to get over your fear of the word--"

"Don't say it!" I whisper-shout, putting my hands over my ears.

Laughing, he gently pulls my hands from my ears. "It's safe. I won't say it," he says.

Rolling my eyes to escape, I extract my hands from his and reach for the laptop. "First off, we should write how orangutans are endangered, so if Mr. Castro wants to go shoot them all, there aren't many. Second, we'll say how they build nests in the trees and that stuff. Lastly, *you* can write about the seed dispersal."

"Wait..." Nate taps his fingers on the table we're sitting at. "I thought Mr. Castro didn't want to hear about their eating habits."

I brighten, only to become glum once more. "Yeah, but this isn't really a *habit*. It's...how they save the economy. How they're beneficial. Because they keep fruit trees from going extinct."

"Huh. Well, I guess you're right." Nate glances at his phone. "It's ten till. Do you have to get back soon?"

I shrug. "I'm not sure. My phone died before I could call my mom but I told Florence that I'd be here for a while."

"Okay." He reaches over and closes his laptop, sliding it off the table. "We should maybe call it quits for today. The sun sets in a little bit, and it isn't a smart idea to be wandering around in the dark." He grins at me, teasing. He leans closer to me and whispers, "That's when the bears come out and eat people on their way home from the library."

I snort. "At least the bears recognize that they can't eat anyone unless the person is leaving the library."

"Bears are smart," Nate says philosophically.

Shaking my head, I stand up and stretch out the cramps I'd gotten from sitting down for the past hour and a half. "Are we going to meet here again tomorrow?"

He stares off into the distance for a moment, then slowly says, "No, I can't. Elijah has been bugging me to go over to his house and play video games with him for a long time. I think he'll be mad if I refuse again." Nate's expression is annoyed when he looks back at me. "The thing is, I end up sitting on his couch reading a book while he jumps around killing virtual people."

"That's...interesting. And, actually, I don't think I'd be able to come here, either. My mom invited this guy over for dinner, and as much as I'd love to skive off, I'm pretty sure I have to be there."

"Oh." Nate packs up his laptop, sliding it into a slim bag. "You don't like the guy?"

I press my mouth into a thin line. "That's an understatement," I reply finally. "There's just something *off* about him." Then I laugh sarcastically. "Maybe I misjudged him. I'm not used to men paying attention to my mom, so maybe I got protective of her and didn't want her to get mixed up with anyone else."

Nate leads me out of the library. "Are your parents divorced?"

"Yeah." I shiver in the cold air, amazed that it's dark outside. "For the past six years. Well, it'll be six soon, on my birthday."

"Your birthday?" He frowns. "They divorced on your birthday?"

I manage a small nod. "Yeah. Great present, huh?"

The silence stretches on forever until he finally says, "That's really sad."

"It's hardest on my—well, *our* birthday—Florence and I have the same birthday, of course. Anyway, it's hardest then. I'm always reminded of that...time."

We're quiet again. I keep thinking Nate is going to say

something—something about his parents or an event equally as sad as divorce—but he doesn't speak at all. The sky is now streaked with dark blue and grey—it'll be cloudy tonight and might rain in the early morning. The air is cold; I tell myself to be grateful it isn't windy. My jacket won't protect me from the wind if it starts up.

I've just spotted my street when Nate, a touch too lightly, suddenly says, "I preferred talking about orangutans."

"Not me," I reply, though I don't mean it at all. "Especially after learning why they're beneficial."

He laughs, but it sounds slightly forced. "We should adopt an orangutan and present it in two months so our presentation will be the best."

"We'd have to keep it away from fruit," I put in seriously, and Nate laughs a second time, sounding smoother than the first.

"Why?" he asks, teasing. "Aren't we supposed to show—"

"No," I interrupt. "We don't have to *show* anything. Plus, I think we'd get the orangutan confiscated the instant we entered school."

"Just dress it up in human clothing."

I peer up at him, frowning. "Have you *seen* what they look like? There's no way one would pass for a normal human being. They're hairy and big and their arms are super long—"

"And they're orange," Nate cuts in.

"Yes," I agree. "They're orange. And they're more squat than humans, and they have flat faces and look nothing like us."

"All the more reason to adopt one."

I playfully bump his shoulder with mine, making him grimace. "We'd totally get an A, though."

"We should look into it," he suggests, his voice laced with barely-concealed pain. I narrow my eyes. There's no way I hit him hard enough for it to hurt that badly. "Mr. Castro might give us full marks for imagination and presentation. Bringing an orangutan to class...I doubt anyone has ever done that before. Hmm...what if we just borrow one?"

"How do you borrow an orangutan?" I say carefully, listening intently to his voice. Did I really hurt him?

Nate rubs the back of his neck. "BorrowAnOrangutan.com?"

I groan. "Seriously?"

"What?" He gives me a curious look. "Did you actually think we were having a contemplative conversation?"

"No, I guess not." I laugh. "Just...BorrowAnOrangutan.com?"

He shrugs. "Maybe it's a thing. I think I saw something similar on the Internet, just with llamas. Or maybe it was goats."

We're almost to my house. The sun has sunk behind the houses lining the street, casting long shadows of the tips of roofs and tops of trees. I feel bad for Nate, who has to walk even farther to get home, and I'm about to ask if he wants a ride back when the front door flies open, releasing Florence. She storms down the driveway, yelling something over her shoulder at someone hesitating in the doorframe. Flo's words are jumbled together, unintelligible, and I instinctively shrink closer to Nate, not wanting to be yelled at also. Flo completely ignores us, though we're only twenty or so feet away from the driveway.

"No!" she screams back at the figure in the doorway. "I said no! Now leave me alone!"

A slight tremble flashes down my spine, triggering an almost-unpreventable shiver. I quickly duck behind the car belonging to our neighbor-across-the-street, hoping Flo won't see me. Nate is frowning, his head cocked to one side, most likely wondering what I'm hiding from and why. I motion for him to join me, and when he does, I twist around and peer through the car's window back at my brightly-lit house. Mom hates it when we leave on all the lights.

Florence is angrily sorting through the mail, muttering under her breath as she does. The figure from the doorway has retreated back inside before I can recognize who it is, but judging from their height, I guess it was Roman. Or maybe Mom. I feel bad for her.

Shaking her head, and still muttering, Flo storms back up the driveway, leaving the mailbox open in her wake with most of the contents spilling out. She's clutching a letter in her hand, which makes me blink in shock—I notice it's light blue. She can't still be writing to Kent? I thought they broke up. They live on the opposite sides of the United States, and Kent cheated on Flo.

The front door slams shut, announcing that she is back inside. I sigh in relief and sag against the car, forgetting I have company.

"What was that all about?"

I jump. Pushing up the bridge of my glasses, I squint at Nate in the steadily darkening light. "Um, it's just Florence."

Nate nods slowly. "Yeah. Why are you—actually, this is none of my business." He straightens on the sidewalk, towering taller than the car. I scramble to my feet so I don't seem as pathetically short compared to him. "I should head home," he says, looking over his shoulder in a random direction. "If I hurry, I can get home before nightfall." He glances back at me. "See you at school tomorrow. Hopefully we can meet at the library again. That was a lot of fun."

"Okay," I mumble, resisting the urge to follow him home so I don't have to face Florence. "See you then."

He gives me a slight smile in return. Tightening his grip on his computer bag, Nate turns and walks away, deeper into the neighborhood. I watch him reach a corner, wait for a car to pass, then disappear from sight down the street. That's when I heave another sigh and make my way across the road to my own house. I don't want to suffer the wrath of Flo. She'll tear me down, especially since she's in such a bad mood right now. I don't know how she became so angry—I cross my fingers and fervently wish that it isn't because of something I've done.

I close our mailbox after scooping out the remaining mail, then head up the driveway, sorting through what we've gotten today. All junk except for one, which is some important business letter Mom is going to freak out about, yelling that we have email now and don't need to use paper. Stepping up onto the porch, I hesitate for a second before opening the front door and slipping inside. The lights are all on, blinding me. I blink a few times to clear my vision, eyes adjusting to the brilliant light compared to the outside.

I shut the door silently, toss the mail on the floor by my shoes, and listen to what's going on. Stomping sounds above me. Clattering in the kitchen. Muted yells coming from the direction of Mom's bedroom upstairs. A distant timer beeping repeatedly, saying that it's time for something to be taken out of the oven. Pompeii singing along to whatever song playing either on his headphones or ear-buds.

The chaos is familiar and somehow soothing because of it.

Swallowing hard, I decide going upstairs to my room is a bad idea, so I go into the kitchen. Pompeii is the only one in there, screaming along to the song blasting out of his headphones; he's also washing dishes in the sink, his sleeves rolled up to his elbows. He whirls around, flinging soapy water all over the kitchen, and notices me standing in the doorway, staring at him and trying not to laugh hysterically.

Pompeii slides down his headphones. "Venice!" he yells. "Hey, where did you go? Mom was worried!"

My fears confirmed, I flop down at the dining room table. Flo had forgotten to tell Mom where I'd gone. I know Flo isn't the best person to tell things to—she forgets most of the time—but I'd hoped...Looking back, I realize I should've told Roman that I was going to be at the library, not Florence.

"Venice!" A flick of soapy water lands on my wrist. I look up. Pompeii is right next to me, eyebrows raised, a dripping pot in his hand. "Where were you?" he asks.

"At the library," I mutter, sinking my chin onto my palms. "I *told* Flo where I was going, but I guess she forgot."

Pompeii sighs. "Yeah," he says, still shouting. Faint rock music streams out of his headphones. "What were you doing at the library? How come you didn't bring back any books?"

"I was doing schoolwork."

Pompeii nods in understanding. "Ah. Cool."

I grab his arm to stop him from going back to the dishes. "Pompeii, what was Flo yelling about?"

"Oh, yeah." He gives me a funny look. "You. Dad. Moving. Dinner. Toilet paper. There might have been more, but I put on my headphones after the toilet paper fight. Mom kept asking Flo if she knew when you'd be back, and Flo kept yelling at Mom that she didn't and to stop asking."

I'm suddenly very tired. "But...I *told* Florence that I was at the library. Repeatedly. Over ten times. I guess I didn't really tell her when I'd be back."

Pompeii shrugs one shoulder, not saying anything. He starts to hum along to the song playing, a sign that he's bored with our conversation. I let go of his arm, but before he slips his headphones back on he gives me a playful push.

"Hey, it's not your fault. You're allowed to take some time for yourself even if it means the family falls apart because of it. Look, I'm being responsible." He winks and returns to the kitchen sink, already singing to the music. The oven timer is still going off.

I watch him for a moment, amused and touched at Pompeii's attempt to comfort me. I really am impressed and grateful that he's doing to dishes so cheerfully. A sudden rush of affection makes me grab him from behind in a quick embrace that startles and embarrasses him. I'm rewarded with retaliatory soap suds spilling down my head and shoulders. Happy chaos ensues until Mom suddenly appears in the kitchen doorway, arms folded tightly across her chest. She's giving us a non-nonsense glare, the sight of it instantly sobering our silliness and making me involuntarily shiver.

"Venice," she says, her voice low and stern, "would you please explain yourself."

I swallow. "I'm so sorry. I was at the library doing schoolwork. I told Florence to tell you. Did she forget? My phone died and I couldn't call or text. I thought you'd all be fine for a couple of hours. Did I miss something big?"

Mom takes a breath and sighs. "No, you didn't miss anything. I wonder why Flo didn't tell me where you were. I guess she isn't to be trusted with messages like that." She sounds defeated. "Why were you doing schoolwork at the library? Can't you do it here?"

"You see…" I struggle for words. "I'm doing a team project," I finally say. "And, well, we concentrate better at the library." I wave a hand at the kitchen, the upstairs, everything. "Less distractions."

Mom sighs. "True. I just needed you today."

I narrow my eyes, studying her thoughtfully. Her hair is a mess, like she hasn't brushed it all day. She's wearing half pajamas, half work clothes—slippers and fluffy red pajama pants, a plain blouse and a thin, stylish black jacket. There are bags under her eyes; she looks like she just rolled out of bed. I don't know much sleep she's been getting.

"Mom, are you okay?" I ask.

She rubs her forehead. "Yes. Maybe. No. Of course not."

"What?"

"No." She looks me straight in the eye. "No, I'm not okay. Your twin sister has been yelling at me ever since she got back from school two hours ago about the most random of things. It seems she *wants* to pick a fight with me. I was able to hold on for half an hour, knowing you'd come home soon and rescue me, but you decided that today was the day to run off and do something without asking for my permission or even telling me where you were going and when you would come back." Mom groans. "Just bad timing, Venice."

I'm frozen where I stand, my feet cemented to the tile floor. I can barely understand what Mom is saying. She needed me to rescue her from Flo? What does that even mean? How does everything always add up to be *my* fault? It's exhausting, really.

"I'm sorry, Mom," I say truthfully. "I'm sorry I wasn't here to stop Flo from whatever she was doing. But I can't always be acting like the policeman while you're working. I've got things of my own that I have to do—I can't constantly be keeping my siblings in line."

Mom sighs again. "I know. I just—I'm having a really bad day. Tomorrow will be so much better—Marc is coming over for dinner."

I tense. My shoulders roll back, my spine stiffens, my glare turns icy. *Marc.* He just adds to my problems.

Mom seems to register that I'm not pleased, even in her bad mood. "Come on, Venice," she says, her voice turning from anger and frustration to pleading. "Can you promise not to be rude to him? Yesterday, you were a little cold, and it was awkward because of it. Can you please not do that at dinner tomorrow?"

"I'll try," I say. And I will try, for Mom's sake, but I know that I will also follow my instincts. I cannot trust Marc just yet. Not until I find out for sure that he's genuine about everything, that he's just a normal, friendly guy. Not until I can sincerely know he doesn't have bad intentions.

Mom bites her lip. "Alright." She looks around the kitchen, thinking. Finally she turns back to me and says, "I'm glad you're home." She blinks furiously, making me realize that she's close to tears, which sends sparks of guilt flooding through me. Mom's bottom lip trembles, then she says, "Turn off that timer, Pompeii," and she's dashing away back up to her bedroom before we can see her begin to sob.

ELEVEN

The day passes too quickly. One moment I'm enjoying lunch with Mandy and Elijah and Nate—the next I'm walking home in the freezing rain and trying not to think about what's happening tonight. I've already had a fun time at school, and don't want it to be ruined by Marc's presence. At lunch I'd asked Mandy if she was free tonight, but unfortunately she wasn't, which killed my last hope of escaping dinner. I walk home by myself; Nate left with Elijah to go play video games—and in Nate's case, read—and I'm far more miserable because of it. I take longer to arrive home, purposely dragging my feet though Marc isn't coming until six, in three hours.

I tell myself that I should be nice to him. He seems like a really great guy. I'm just protective of my mom and assume that every man she meets isn't a good person. I tell myself that I can't say anything rude or ask rude questions or be rude in general. I need to cheer up Mom, make her proud that *one* of her kids is polite.

I really don't want to do this, but I have to.

Regrettably.

Turning onto my street, I squint through the misty rain in the direction of my house. Mom, no doubt, is probably storming around inside, scrubbing down every surface and raising a ruckus that can be heard on the other side of the world, though I can't hear it yet. I will soon, that I know. We so rarely have company over for dinner, and Mom always goes a little crazy with the cleaning jobs. Once, she'd made me clean the windows, which didn't make any sense, as we were eating outside, not inside. I wonder what is for dinner. Italian, most likely, since Mom knows Marc likes that kind of food. Personally, though, I think he only likes it because Mom does. Marc seems like a person who seeks to please.

I stumble on something and have to catch my balance on the street sign. I peer down at my feet, confused why I tripped, and notice my shoelaces are untied. Sighing, I bend down and start to lace them back up.

A roar splits the air. Startled, I look up and notice a huge black car rushing down the street, splashing through puddles and kicking up spray all along the road. I frown as the car comes closer. Why are they driving so fast and so close to the side of the road? Realizing I'm going to get soaked by the spray the car is spewing up, I hurriedly cover my head with my arms, tucking my hands into my hair so my ring won't get wet, a pointless action since I'm sure it already is.

The car zooms by, followed by a fountain of dirty water that crashes on top of me, soaking into my clothes. I sputter at how cold it is, then lift my head and watch the car disappear into the mist.

"Idiot," I mutter to myself. It's almost like that person sprayed me on purpose.

Finishing tying my shoes, I straighten and wipe the water off my face with my sopping coat sleeve. I think I end up spreading more water across my face than I wipe off. Shaking my head, I continue to walk home, gagging on the exhaust let out by the car. Doubly punished. Maybe it's a sign, getting me back for being mean to Marc when I first met him. Today I need to be nice to him, otherwise something worse might happen to me. That car might come back and throw mud on me. Or slush. Or snow, if it ever snows here. It hasn't yet; it disappoints Siena. She wants to shove some in Pompeii's face.

I'm dripping when I walk inside, stomping my feet on the welcome mat. I hear Mom yelling at Roman to clean the bathroom, hear Siena complaining that her arms are tired, hear Flo pacing in our bedroom upstairs. I pull off my shoes, laughing at myself for lacing them up if I was just going to take them off a minute later. I toss my shoes into the bin in the closet—the door is wide open, which means Roman or Pompeii must've been forced to clean it out—and wander deeper into the house, finding Siena grumbling about how unfair things are.

"What's unfair?" I ask.

She startles. Whirling around, she gapes at me, taking in how water keeps dripping off my coat and onto the bamboo floor. "What happened to *you*?"

"A stupid car splashed me," I answer.

Siena rolls her eyes, turning back to wiping down the counter. "I'm glad you're finally here. Now you can help clean up. Mom's in the hallway, telling Roman to work his lazy butt off."

"When does he ever?" I leave the kitchen to go find Mom. Sure enough, by following her voice, I discover her lecturing Roman on the proper way to scrub a bathroom sink. Roman is yelling back that he *knows how to so stop bothering me*, and I startle both of them as I walk up. My glasses are fogging up, and I have to wipe them on my slightly-damp shirt before putting them back on and catching Mom's horrified look.

"Venice!" she protests. "You're getting water all over the floor!"

I lift up my arms, releasing another storm of raindrops. "Would you like me to mop?"

"With your coat?" Roman shouts from inside the bathroom.

I ignore him, waiting for Mom's response. She's still frowning, but it has taken on a humorous tinge. "Alright," she says finally. "Not with your coat, though."

"Wasn't planning on using it," I say cheerfully, shrugging out of my coat. I continue down the hallway to the utility room, where I hang my coat up on a hook, placing a bucket underneath it to catch any other water droplets that decide to fall. I grab the mop, close the utility room door behind me, and go back to the kitchen to begin cleaning the floor. Siena can't be complaining about unfairness now, I think to myself; almost immediately, I have to bury my face in my wet sleeve to smother a laugh that threatens to burst out of my throat.

Siena can always find something unfair about a situation.

Before I know it, dinner is ready, the table is set, and Marc has arrived. Mom is wearing her typical work clothes—minus the fluffy pink slippers—and she encourages us to dress nicely, too, though no one does except Flo, and even then she's just wearing a silk top and jeans. Roman is dressed as usual in a T-shirt and sweatpants. Pompeii has his headphones around his neck. Siena's shirt is stained with paint and mud. My pants and shirt are still damp from three hours ago when I'd gotten splashed. I had time to change, but really I just didn't want to dress up for Marc.

Marc is the complete opposite from us. He's in a dress shirt and nice pants and an informal jacket. It's still raining outside, so his hair is wet, and Siena jokes about letting him use her hair dryer—which is actually Flo's—to dry off his shoulder-length hair. Marc brings more Italian candy and I'm the only one who refuses it, though my excuse isn't rude; I simply say I don't want anything sweet right before dinner.

We all sit down at the table, and I'm glad Mom has Marc sit at the head of the table, meaning I sit farthest away from him, next to Roman and Pompeii. The boys badger Marc with questions during the entire meal, forcing me to learn more about him than I want. He likes hiking the nearby mountain trails and watching the wildlife. I doubt that part, because seconds later he tells my brothers about the time he'd shot a running deer. Once Siena and Flo chime in with the questions, I learn more practical things, like his favorite color, (blue) and how old he is, (forty-six). The revelation of his age strikes me the most—he's two years older than Mom. It makes me feel sick inside, because it reminds me that my mom is interested in this man. I try not to show disapproval in my expression, so I busy myself with eating the spaghetti Mom cooked for dinner.

When Marc starts complimenting every little thing about our house and my siblings and me and Mom, things start to get very uncomfortable for me. I don't like Marc. I tried to. I really did. I wish he would leave us alone and that he'd never met our mom. Yet here he is, laughing and joking around with my family. He praises Siena on her paintings of the trees on our kitchen wall. He thanks Flo for making the breadsticks, which is pretty much the only thing she can bake, and they are *seriously* delicious. Marc makes Pompeii proud by sharing his favorite songs—amazingly and suspiciously, both he and Marc like the same songs. Marc intrigues Roman by telling stories about all his crazy, unbelievable experiences hunting down criminals.

He starts on Mom, saying how he loved her meal, it was the best spaghetti he has *ever* tasted, she could make a living by selling it, on and on until I'm actually physically trembling.

I squeeze my fork harder and take a quick drink of water to soothe myself. It doesn't work or help. Instead, I concentrate on remembering what happened at school earlier today. Classes had been fine. Lunch had been awesome. I'd noticed that Nate hadn't eaten anything, but it isn't until now that the memory comes back. Why hadn't he eaten lunch? I mentally shrug. It's none of my concern. I'd also noticed that he wore gloves the entire day, and had moved slowly, as if exhausted. I feel guilty for making him walk home during dusk last night, but he hadn't complained once.

Then again, he's not one to complain.

Folding my hands into my lap, I look down at the ring on my pinky finger. I twist it around and around, staring into the light blue stone. Oh, how I wish Dad was here. I wish he and Mom were still married. I wish we could become a happy family again.

The meal finally ends. I stand up and clear away my plate, washing it off in the sink and placing it on the counter to dry. As I'm doing so, Marc comes up behind me, holding his own plate. He's suddenly much too close. My heart starts thumping loudly in my chest as I scoot out of the way, putting as much distance between the two of us as I can.

He smiles at me, the look making my palms sweat. "Hey, how are you doing, Venice?" he asks, cleaning off his plate.

"F-fine," I stutter out, not daring to meet his gaze. I press my palm against my leg, the action drawing his attention down.

"That's a nice ring," he says casually. "Are you like, engaged or something?"

My eyebrows rise. This is clearly not a wedding ring. It's on my pinky, anyway. And plenty of girls wear rings these days; he must not know that. Also, why did he say that in front of Mom and Flo?

Sure enough, Mom comes marching over, her face pinched. "What?" she says. "What ring?"

I lift up my wrist. "The one Dad gave me. I'm not engaged. This isn't a wedding ring."

"Oh!" A sad smile breaks across her face. "For a second, you got me, Marc." She turns her smile on him. "You're such a tease."

"I wouldn't be surprised if Venice was engaged," he replies, winking at me. "I'll bet plenty of boys are throwing themselves at her feet and begging for her attention."

His words stun me into silence. I want to laugh and tell him that it's the complete opposite, but Florence doesn't give me the chance. She stalks up to us, her expression furious. No doubt she heard what Marc said and now she's jealous.

Before she can spew insults about me, I duck past Mom and Marc, go back to the table and begin collecting the plates. I keep my head down as I carry the plates to the sink and begin cleaning them, not looking at anyone. I'm not sure I can face Florence or Marc right now.

But Flo won't give up an open opportunity to criticize me.

"I've never seen a boy throw himself at Venice," she says, twirling a finger around a lock of her auburn hair. "But there is that hot one she keeps talking to."

Mom looks up from the spaghetti she's cramming into a container. "What boy?" she asks, interested.

"Oh, just this boy," says Flo, drifting off to the living room, her face buried in her phone, leaving me to deal with Mom, who is waiting for a detailed description.

I ignore the look she's giving me. Turning my back on her, I scrub furiously at the silverware, washing all the spaghetti sauce into the sink. Marc starts up a conversation about teenagers and their secrets, and I catch him staring at my hands while I work. It makes me really self-conscious, so I shift my body so he can't see them as I angrily wash the plates. Leave it up to Florence to put me in a tight spot.

The adults soon follow Flo into the living room; I stay behind to clean up with Siena, Pompeii, and Roman, though Roman deserts us quickly after, running down to his bedroom in the basement so he won't have to wipe down the table. Siena complains about unfairness for what seems like hours until I tiredly ask her to stop.

She doesn't, of course.

Finally not able to take it anymore, I dry my hands on a dish towel and go to the living room to listen in on the conversation. It's boring—all about their different opinions on politics—and I find myself slipping off to sleep. I hurriedly give myself a shake before opening my eyes and noticing that Flo is staring at me, her glare hard. She sees me looking at her and mouths, *Go away* before jumping back into the conversation.

I'm groggy and uncomprehending. Flo wants me to go away? Why? Did I mess up again somehow? My brain is working so slowly it's as if she suddenly announced she's moving to Antarctica to practice her cosmetology skills on the seals and polar bears and penguins. I don't have the emotional energy to figure it all out so I stand up and slowly head out of the room, up the stairs, and into our bedroom. I close the door softly, not wanting to disturb anyone or reveal how confused I feel. Taking a deep breath, I glance around my room, trying to find something that will distract me. I cross the room to the window and stare out into the darkness, feeling the cold seeping through the panes to touch me.

Leaning against the sill, I stand there for a long time, not moving, not doing anything. I'm there long enough to watch Marc leave, his horrible red pick-up truck sputter down the street, go around a bend, and whisk out of sight. I'm still by the window when someone softly knocks on the bedroom door, the sound familiar.

"Come in," I call, not exactly wanting to talk to Mom.

Mom enters the room and flicks on the lamp, engulfing us in bright yellow light. "Hey," she says. "Are you all right?"

I don't move. "I'm fine."

"You...you don't act like you are."

"I'm fine, Mom. Really."

She walks over to me and sits on the end of Flo's bed, about two feet away from me. "Well, *I* feel like a terrible mom. I'm sorry, I've been so busy over the past three days, I totally forgot to ask how your first day of school went. Did you make any friends?"

I lift my shoulders in an almost-shrug. "Sure."

"You did?"

Sighing, I turn around and sit next to her. "Yeah."

"Like that boy Florence mentioned?"

I scowl at Mom, not amused. She holds up her hands in front of her in a non-threatening gesture, saying, "What? I'm your mom! I'm allowed to ask you questions like these! Questions about boys."

"I don't have to answer them."

"No, you don't," she agrees. "But it'd be nice if you did."

110

I play with my ring, twisting it over on my finger. "If you want to talk to someone about boys, go to Flo. She's got plenty of stories. I'm pretty sure every Friday night and Saturday on her calendar for the next *year* is packed with dates from different boys."

"Unfortunately, Flo can't talk to me without saying something negative." Mom sighs. "Roman can't, either. Pompeii just talks nonsense, and Siena is constantly yelling—I have a bad feeling she's going to turn out just like Flo. You see, Venice, you're the only one I can talk to. You're always so nice and quick to compliment, and you never pick a fight for whatever reason. That's why I'm concerned about you right now. You're acting strange."

"It was only tonight," I say, eyes on my ring.

"Oh." Mom's voice takes on a shade of vulnerability. "I know you don't like Marc, Venice, but can't you please at least give him a chance? At least you weren't as rude as before. I guess I should be grateful for that. But you barely said a word the whole time at dinner."

"The others kept him busy," I murmur.

She sighs again. "I hope you aren't like that every time he comes over."

My head snaps up. "Every time?" I repeat, incredulous. "What do you mean, every time? How often are you planning on having him over for dinner?"

"Often. I think I like him," she admits, not meeting my gaze.

I gape at her, unsure of what to say. I manage, "Uh, are you guys serious?"

She hesitates so long I have a feeling my heart will burst before she can reply. Thankfully, she finally says, "I don't know, Venice. He came to see me today when I was looking through another house, and he bought me lunch at this really cute restaurant called the Rainy Afternoon. It's not far from here, actually. Just behind your school. He makes me laugh and compliments me. And he's trying so hard to like all of you. That's got to be worth something."

My mouth has fallen open, and I'm gawping at her like an idiot.

"I should take you to that restaurant one day," Mom continues. "You would like it. Though, it's more of a café than a restaurant. They have this really good hot chocolate that is *extremely* addictive. One of the topping options is candy cane pieces, and I had some of them sprinkled in...Mmm."

I blink at her. "But, Mom, you can't get into a relationship. You—you can't! You just can't! And, wait, you got hot chocolate? You hate chocolate. What's going on?"

She purses her lips. "I came here to talk to *you* about *you*, not me. Now, I want you to tell me about school and friends and maybe the boy. No changing the subject anymore."

"Fine." She wants to talk to me about me? Then that's what she'll get. I stand up and begin pacing in my room, back and forth, back and forth. Stepping over piles of Flo's stuff. Looking anywhere except at Mom. "I met some kids, talked to them, and I really like them and they like me. Only thing is Florence is worried about people mistaking me for her and she doesn't want to be seen with those kinds of kids. What did she refer to us as? Ah, yes. The dirt of high school. The idiots, the outcasts."

Mom's the one gawping now.

"I really like these people, Mom. Mandy is genuine and smart and funny, and Elijah is such a kind-hearted tease. And Nate...Well, anyway, they like me, Mom, without me even giving them a reason to. It's only been a few days and it's like we've been friends forever. But Florence just sees my friendship with them as a drag on her reputation."

Mom goes to speak, but I cut across her. "To make things worse, Florence changes her mind about me too often. One day, we're having a *moment* together, and I share something that helps me get through hard times, and then half an hour later, she's making me look like an immature kid in front of this one person—who, might I add, she flirted with first.

"I'm constantly trying to be nice to her so she'll change her mind and decide she should be nice to *me*. But that's never going to happen." I shake my head angrily. "Every time I attempt to do something kind, whether it's for Flo or the other kids, she gets mad. And I don't even know why!" Spreading my hands out in front of me to show my frustration, I continue, "No matter how hard I try, she still hates me."

I turn on my heel and resume my pacing. "I don't know *why*. I've no *idea* why she hates me." Sighing deeply, I bury my face in my hands. "Whatever. It doesn't—It's not important."

"Yes, it is." Her ragged voice breaks through my subconscious. "I'm sorry," she says, as she takes my hands from my face and cups it inside of both of hers. "I'm so sorry. I didn't realize how badly Flo treats you. I've been so caught up in my work, I haven't taken the time to really connect with you all like I should. I'm your mom. I should be there for you more. We have problems because I'm not fulfilling my duty as a parent."

"It's not your fault," I mutter. "It's ours. We're the ones who determine how we act. You can't mold us into perfect kids, you can only teach us and help us along the way."

Mom extends her arms, and I go to her, hugging her tightly. "I'll try to be better," she mumbles into my hair. "I'll try."

"So will I."

It's a little awkward hugging a person sitting down, so after a minute I step back and say, "You're a great mom. And I'm really glad we moved here. Sure, I miss Grandma and Grandpa Ferrari, but this is a great place."

Mom smiles, a tinge sadly. "Yeah. I like Virginia, too, and I'm so pleased that you've found some people you consider friends." She stands up, first stretching before crossing the room to grasp the doorknob. "I've got to go make sure the kids haven't set the house on fire while I was up here talking to you."

I manage a dry laugh. "Siena would *love* to start a fire."

"She has threatened to do it," Mom says seriously, opening the door. She waves at me, then slips out, leaving me alone.

I sigh and sit down on my bed, thinking through what I'd just said during my tirade about Flo. How can I treat her better? What can I do to help rebuild the connection between us?

I fall asleep before I can come up with any answers.

TWELVE

TO: Sleepy Gumption
FROM: Hubris Jargon
SUBJECT: Attempt 2.0
TIME: 9:03 p.m.
DATE: Wednesday, January 22

Failure. Went up close. Still couldn't see. Will try again.

THIRTEEN

TO: Sleepy Gumption
FROM: Malaise Tone
SUBJECT:
TIME: 9:51 p.m.
DATE: Wednesday, January 22

She has it.

FOURTEEN

The week speeds by. Thursday is unmemorable. So is Friday. By Saturday, I still haven't met up with Nate to work on our report, and I desperately need the distraction. I'm unsure, though, if I should initiate meeting up or wait for him to bring it up. The weather is terrible—it rains all day every day, and soon I'm tired of Siena complaining and Roman yelling at Siena for complaining and Flo telling Roman that yelling is worse than complaining. I need to get out of the house—preferably without my siblings. Mom seems even more distant, even though she told me she wanted to be better about having family time, and I have a faint suspicion that she's meeting up with Marc every day for lunch or any other kind of date. And Saturday comes and goes with no word from Nate.

Sunday morning, I wake up to Florence chattering on her phone to one of her friends. I fumble for my glasses, slide them on, and realize that sunlight is streaming through the two windows. Suddenly energized, I roll out of bed and look out the nearest window. The rain is gone. The only sign that the past four days were rainy are the puddles grouped in the dips of the road. The sky is a brilliant blue, with not a cloud in sight. I instantly decide today is going to be great.

I wait until Flo hangs up her phone and leaves the room before changing into my casual clothes and heading downstairs to eat breakfast in the warm sunlight. Siena and Pompeii are in the kitchen, fighting over the different types of cereal stashed in our pantry. I am feeling generous so I add my opinion to the mix, Gordon Ramsey-style, and we all try to out-do each other as food critics of the organic, vegan, gluten-free, sugar-free offerings Mom has stocked for us.

Roman comes storming up seconds later, his expression dark and moody. He yells at Siena and Pompeii to shut up, which they do, to their credit. I think the compliance throws Roman off because he actually apologizes to us all and makes some excuse about being hangry. Pompeii and Siena decide they need to convince Roman to partake of the gourmet cereal they've been critiquing, and he astonishingly plays along. I knew today was going to be great.

By the time Flo comes in the kitchen we're all talking and laughing like a functional family and it feels so good. I think we're all waiting to see how Florence's entrance will change things because conversation starts to quiet down as she rummages around for something to eat.

"Good morning, Flo," I say, bracing myself for a come-back.

"Good morning," she responds, but it's muffled because she has practically climbed into the pantry digging for something way back. When she emerges she has in hand a huge family-size box of sugar cereal.

Everyone lets out their personalized exclamations of disbelief, wonder, and jealousy. Flo smiles and waves the box at us.

"Want some?" she asks.

I'm surprised she's willing to share with us, but I won't pass up the opportunity and neither will anyone else. Pompeii already has a bowl in his hand, and Roman reaches into the fridge for the almond milk. Siena hastens to fetch the spoons, and me, I'm just soaking in the moment.

"Where did you get this gift from heaven?" asks Pompeii.

Flo's grin widens. "I don't just spend my money on clothes."

We group around the kitchen table, and she ceremoniously pours out equal amounts of cereal into each bowl. Pompeii and Siena are far too excited to argue that they got less than someone else. The next few minutes are filled with appreciative sighs as we eat a cereal full of flavor for the first time in months. Mom hates sugary cereals, which is why we generally eat bran, but it tastes like crunchy cardboard, and having something that has actual *taste* is literally sensational.

"Thank you," I mumble through a mouthful of deliciousness.

Florence nods back, but she's clearly pleased. She's even more so when the others add their gratitude. We haven't had a moment like this in forever, and I want to have these types of fun times every day.

"Let's agree not to tell Mom," says Florence, pouring seconds for Pompeii and Roman, who have vacuumed down their portions. I notice Siena begins eating faster after that, like she's determined to get the same as our brothers, and I have to laugh out loud. I love my family.

"I promise," Pompeii says after swallowing. "Florence, could you bring cereals like this every morning?"

"Mom might catch us then," she says, though she's beaming. A warm yellow has lightened around her aura, revealing how happy she is right now.

"I don't care," says Roman. "Oh, man, this is so good."

We all laugh. This day has so far turned out even better than I had hoped.

I get up and gather everyone's bowls and spoons, taking them over to the sink to clean. We've polished off the entire box of cereal and Flo isn't exasperated at all; in fact, she's grinning like mad, and I know she's enjoying the positive attention. She says something that makes the younger kids bust up laughing, and I smile to myself. She needs to have good interactions with them. It'll help her and help them, and we'll be a lot happier and more loyal to each other.

Conversation starts up again, and I'm putting the clean bowls and spoons back in their places when a knock sounds on the door, making everyone look up in surprise.

Drying my hands off, I exchange a brief look with Flo, then walk out of the kitchen cautiously, wondering who would be here this early in the morning.

I open the door, wary, and find Nate standing on the porch holding his computer bag in one hand and trying hard not to smile, but it blossoms once he sees me.

"Nate. Oh, thank the trees." I run a hand through my tangled hair. "I thought some police officer would be here, telling me my little sister robbed a bank or killed an old lady or something."

"Nope." His grin widens, as usual. "Just me. And I don't have the authority to arrest anyone, so your little sister is safe."

Glancing back over my shoulder, I notice Siena and Pompeii loitering in the doorway to the kitchen, staring at me and sizing up Nate. I snap my attention back to him, wondering why he'd come over to my house today. Not complaining at all, though.

"I didn't think anyone was home at first," he says. "There's no car. But when I heard voices, I knew you guys were here."

"No car?" I repeat. I step out to scan the front of the house. Sure enough, Mom's car isn't at the curb. She doesn't have work today. That must mean one thing—she's out with Marc.

I retreat inside. "Would you like to come in for a moment?" I invite Nate. "I've got to talk to Florence about something."

He gives me a suspicious look. "Will I come out in one piece?"

"I make no promises," I reply, moving to the side so he can enter. I close the door behind him, then make my way into the kitchen, where Roman and Flo have also stood up, curious. She has flattened the cardboard box, and Roman appears to be searching for matches to burn the evidence of our decadence.

"Hey, Florence," I call.

She lifts an eyebrow. "Who's at the door?"

I hesitate. Is she in a good enough mood to hear the answer? "A friend of mine. Nate."

Flo just grins. "Cool. What did you need?"

"Um." I push the bridge of my glasses up. "Did you know Mom was gone?"

She shakes her head, surprised. "No. I thought she was doing work stuff up in her bedroom."

"Oh." I frown. "Well, the car's not here."

"She's probably off with her *boyfriend*," sniggers Roman, the book of matches in his hand. "If you ask me, I think Marc's a cool guy and all, but they have definitely rushed this relationship."

Flo nods her agreement. "Yeah. I miss old Mom."

It's nice to have my own thoughts validated. "Well, you guys know how I feel about him."

Roman chortles and Flo snickers, "Yeah, you haven't been shy about that, have you?" She bursts out laughing.

"Anyway," I say, gently smirking, "Mom's probably showing a house or something. You know how weekends can get."

Remembering Nate is waiting for me, I add, "I'm heading out now. Text me if she contacts you. I should be back in a few hours."

"Okay. We'll be fine here. But I'm leaving this afternoon so be back before then. Have fun!" Flo chirps.

I hesitate only because this is the most normal exchange I've had with Florence in weeks. "Thanks," I say, giving her a quick hug. Before she can react I've turned away and fled the kitchen.

It's cold but sunny outside. There's no wind, which cheers me up even more. Nate tells me the library isn't open on Sundays, so he's planned for us to work together at a little café he likes that's just past the school. He says he likes the atmosphere there and that the Wi-Fi there is almost as good as the library's.

"Wait." I pause. "Is the café called the Rainy Afternoon?"

He's surprised. "Yeah, have you already been there?"

"No, but my mom has. She told me all about it and even said she wanted to take me."

"It's a good café."

I nod absentmindedly. "Are you a regular?"

He shakes his head. "No. I haven't been there in a while. I used to go often when I was a kid. Now I tend to avoid it. I don't want to run into someone I used to know and have to field these awkward questions."

"I can't imagine you not wanting to talk to anyone," I say. "You're always talking to people."

Nate laughs. "Oh sure, I'm pretty friendly, but I usually do the listening not the talking. I'm much less comfortable when others are doing the asking."

"If you avoid this place would you rather we go somewhere else?" I offer.

He hesitates, then says, "Nah, it'll be fine. It's just up there."

"Good," I say. "I'm about to freeze to death out here."

Nate glances over at me. I expect him to say something teasing about how it's not really that cold, but instead he says, "Can't have that happen. Then I'd have to write the entire report by myself and present it."

I frown humorously.

"And," he continues, "Mandy would probably kill me for letting you die. She's really happy that you moved in. You're one of the first girls to hang out with her."

"Is that why she keeps acting like I'm going to disappear if I get out of her sight?"

He laughs. "Yeah."

After making sure there aren't any cars rushing towards us, Nate and I travel to the other side of the road. That's when I say, "What's the deal with her and Elijah?"

"Um." He shrugs. "I don't really know. I'm pretty sure they like each other, but they are both too scared to admit it."

I twist my lips to one side, thinking hard. "Elijah is constantly teasing her, right?"

"Yeah. About her being in love with him."

"And you think that might be true."

Nate shrugs again. "Maybe. Yeah, definitely. You've seen how Elijah looks at her."

We've stopped in front of a tiny restaurant cramped between a salon and a dry cleaner's. A lit-up sign above the door announces that it's the Rainy Afternoon Café. The outside sure is uninspiring.

Nate holds open the door for me. "How does Elijah look at Mandy?" I murmur to Nate as I pass beside him.

"Like she's his shining star," he mutters back, closing the door.

We duck into the café, a wave of hot air crashing over me. I'm instantly really, really warm.

I glance around the café, noting how every other table is taken, which means this place isn't super popular, but it manages pretty well. The tables are mostly all for two, though nearly everyone is sitting by themselves, on their phones or laptops or reading a book. The café is brightly lit with neon lights strung up around the tops of the walls. Jazzy music streams out of hidden speakers. I decide that no matter if Marc and Mom like this café, it's now my second-favorite place in Virginia.

Nate leads me towards the back of the shop to an empty table surrounded by other empty tables. No one looks up from their work as we pass them—I see an old man doing a crossword puzzle accidentally drip some of his coffee on the very last word he's looking for.

"I prefer the library," Nate whispers as we sit down at the table. "There are too many people here."

I take a deep breath, inhaling the smell of hot chocolate and coffee and freshly baked pastries. "It smells better here." Suddenly even hotter than before, I shrug out of my coat and drape it over my chair.

Nate pulls his laptop out of the bag and places it on the table, flipping it open. I watch him as he signs into the network. Without warning, he leans back in his chair and says, "Alright, what are we planning on doing today? Learning about how many bullets an orangutan can stand before dying?"

I stare at him, horrified. "You're just teasing, right?"

He grins in response. "Only sort of. Don't you think Mr. Castro would really appreciate it if we told him the details for wiping out the orangutans? He'd probably give us full marks."

"You said the same thing about borrowing an orangutan and bringing it to our presentation," I say, resisting the urge to bury my face in my hands. I am, yet again, seriously doubting having Nate as my biology partner.

"I know," says Nate. "I come up with great ideas."

Thank the trees, a waitress wanders over to us, saving me from having to reply to Nate. The waitress twirls a lock of her black hair with a finger as she says in a nasally voice, "How can I help y'all?"

I order the hot chocolate Mom liked, and Nate doesn't get anything. When I ask why, he just shrugs and says he isn't hungry. The waitress leaves to get my drink, and I scoot my chair closer to Nate's so I can see his laptop screen and make sure he isn't watching funny cat videos instead of researching orangutans like we're supposed to.

"Should we write out an outline?" he suggests. "I took notes on all the stuff we read about last time, so we just need to figure out the structure."

"Sure." I wait for him to start, but instead he pushes the laptop towards me.

"You should do the outline," he says. "You're faster at typing than I am."

My eyes roll. "You've never seen me type before. How can you know if I'm faster?"

"No clue." Nate's grin returns. "I'm just guessing."

Shaking my head, I pull the laptop closer. "Whatever." I rip off my gloves and shove them in my coat pocket, then turn back to the laptop. Tapping on one of the keys, I say, "What am I supposed to start with? Their eating habits that aren't habits but a critical point in the fruit trees' survival?"

"Mr. Castro is going to love this."

"I'm already hating this." I've only typed two sentences when the waitress returns with my drink, and I quickly use that as an excuse to make Nate take over on the laptop while I slowly sip the hot chocolate. I can't help but agree with Mom. Candy canes in hot chocolate makes it much better. Except...she hates chocolate, and I didn't understand why she would make an exception until now. This stuff is delicious.

I watch Nate stare at his laptop, not doing anything. Weird. His hands are in his lap, nowhere near the keyboard, and I don't get why he isn't typing. We sit in silence, Nate not moving; I'm drinking my hot chocolate and trying to figure him out. For someone so friendly and full of smiles, he can be really quiet and overlooked. The only noise in the café is the faint jazzy music that for some reason reminds me of rainy days, and I have to quickly look outside to make sure that it's still sunny.

When I finish my drink, I set the Styrofoam cup on the table and pull the laptop towards me again, reading through the notes Nate took the last time we'd met, at the library. I can't concentrate very well, because I keep stealing brief glances at him, wondering too many things to pay attention to the orangutans. It seems like he isn't really focused on the report anyway. I start to get more hot, amazed at how boiling the temperature is in here and that Nate is immune to it. He's still wearing his jacket and fingerless gloves, but they have *got* to be suffocating.

I finally can't take it anymore. Closing the laptop, I push it back across the table to Nate, who slides it into his bag, his expression one of confusion. I lean forward in my seat, propping my elbows on the table, resting my chin on my palms. "Nate," I say carefully, "is everything okay? You seem distracted. I'm a pretty decent listener if you want to talk about it."

He goes tense. His expression darkens, but there seems to be a bit of a struggle going on between the cheerful, friendly Nate and the closed, moody Nate. He doesn't say anything, not that I'd expected him to, but I have experience with stubborn people. I wait patiently for him, staring right into his light blue eyes, trying to communicate my sincerity. He doesn't shift his gaze from mine, either, though I notice he blinks a lot more than I do.

After a while my elbows begin to ache from being pressed on the hard table. I consciously relax my arms and allow the sensation to pass through my chest, up my neck, and into my facial features. The softening seems to pass from me to Nate because I notice there is a release in the tension he's holding in his own face. Suddenly it's not a contest anymore because I find I'm not really waiting for an answer, I'm just looking at him. My breath catches and I glance away. How long have we been staring at each other? I exhale and am about to change the subject when he surprises me.

With a big sigh, Nate finally gives in. "Fine," he mutters, leaning back in his chair. "Fine. Sure." He becomes interested in his gloved hands, not meeting my sharp gaze. "I don't like talking about my family because they're all jerks."

I blink. "What?"

"They're jerks," Nate repeats. "I don't know my mom. My dad doesn't care about me, so he dropped me off to live with my grandpa, who hates having to look after me."

I watch him carefully. He still won't meet my gaze.

"And I don't know if I have any siblings, since no one in my extended family knows I even exist." Nate tugs at one of his gloves, grimaces, and stops. "That's why I hate talking about them. They don't care about me, so I don't want to spend time moping over it." He finally looks up at me, his expression distraught. "Please, Venice, don't ask again. Don't…don't bring up the subject. There's nothing I can do about it so I've got to get past it, and not talking about it is how I'm trying to do that."

I nod slowly, feeling the weight of his confession settle in my heart and conscience. "I understand, Nate. I'm sorry. I won't ask again. I didn't realize…" I trail away, and I'm the one who looks down. I feel awful for asking.

Nate shrugs. "You didn't know. It's fine. You don't need to pity me. Now, are we going to be able to focus on the report, or should we call it quits?"

Before I can respond, a low vibrating noise sounds. He sighs and reaches into his pocket, pulling out his phone. "Guess we'll have to call it quits," he says, then answers the call. "Hey, Elijah."

I can't help but feel extremely relieved at the interruption. I'm still smarting a little from the pity jab. Is it wrong to feel compassion for his situation? Thank the trees for Elijah's timing.

A minute later, Nate hangs up. He looks at me. "Elijah made a pretty compelling case for needing my presence at his house right now."

"Video game spectator support?" I ask, teasing, grateful that he seems to have forgiven the awkwardness, and I'm so glad that he is such a kindhearted person.

He scoffs. "Yep. Some master tournament is about to begin. He needs me over for motivation and morale."

"You should have Mandy go over with you," I say, grinning.

Nate assumes a thoughtful look. "Good idea. I'll call her and extend the invitation. Hey, would you like to come, too?"

I stare at him, amused at the suggestion, and truly flattered. For a minute I think I'm going to accept, but then I answer, "Uh, I can't this time. I should get back home. Flo said she wanted to go out and I need to see if my mom has returned. Somebody's got to be there to make sure my siblings haven't burned down the house or taped each other to the ceiling."

"They seem capable of doing those things," says Nate.

I roll my eyes. "You wouldn't believe how capable."

Standing up, he slings his computer bag over his shoulder. "I'd walk you home, but Elijah lives opposite you. You'll be okay?"

"Of course I'll be okay. We'll get back to orangutans later."

"Sure." He hesitates, like he wants to say something else, but he just turns around, and with a wave of his hands, walks out of the café, leaving me behind wondering about too many things to count.

FIFTEEN

When I get home, Mom isn't back and Flo has left on a date with one of her many boyfriends. Roman and Pompeii are watching TV in the living room, the volume turned up so loudly I can hear it from outside. Siena is in the kitchen, painting more trees all over the blank walls. I ask her if she's allowed to do that, and she shrugs. I'll let Mom deal with that one. The trees actually look really good.

The afternoon speeds by and still Mom hasn't returned. I'm concerned enough to send a text asking her when she is coming home, but she doesn't respond. By the time the sun is setting, casting a pink glow across the sky, Siena bursts into my room, screaming something about Pompeii spilling her paint. I have to go back downstairs to solve the problem, and once it's sorted out, I start pacing, trying to convince myself that everything is fine with Mom. Roman yells at me to relax—I'm somehow disturbing his movie.

I flop down on the couch, not really paying attention to what's happening in the movie. There are lots of guns and shoot-outs and blood and death, so when it finally ends I grab the remote and switch to a different show, this weird cartoon about a unicorn that accidentally misplaced his horn and has to go on a mission to get it back. Siena comes in to watch, and starts laughing that Roman is watching, too. She teases him, but instead of freaking out like usual, he playfully tackles her to the rug. She screeches and yells for my help, but they are both laughing now and I can tell Sienna is thrilled with the attention.

We watch TV for another two hours, following the unicorn around on all his different missions to exotic places in the magical realm. Pompeii joins us, soon becoming engrossed just like Roman and Siena. I can't concentrate on it; I'm too occupied. My neck hurts from twisting around when I look out the bay window at the empty driveway.

Where is Mom?

Six o'clock, I peel myself off the couch and heat up leftovers for dinner, bringing the plates back into the living room to distribute among my siblings.

We eat in silence, all eyes on the TV, where Chuck the Unicorn is contorting in what is supposed to be a ceremonial dance with some butterflies. My siblings laugh hysterically and shout at him to break-dance and whatnot.

Seven o'clock, I take the dishes into the kitchen and wash them, glad to be doing something with my hands. The dishes don't take long, and all too soon I'm in the living room again, listening to Chuck sing a fairy to sleep.

Eight o'clock, Siena falls asleep on Roman and starts snoring. Roman pokes her until she wakes up, and she's in a bad mood that she missed Chuck's adventured into the Shadow Lands to find a forgotten witch to help with a special spell to reverse the curse that turned Unicornia monochromatic.

Nine o'clock, we finish the entire season of Chuck the Unicorn episodes and have to search for another show to watch. Pompeii chooses a mystery one, and it's boring to everyone except him. I don't have the heart to switch to a more interesting show. Roman and Siena complain most of the time, but I ignore them. We have bigger problems.

Where is Mom? I've called and texted a dozen times by now.

Ten o'clock, I'm frantic. Mom has been out for the entire day.

Where on Holy Mother Earth is she? Could she really be showing houses this late? Maybe she's—*ugh*—watching a super long movie with Marc. Maybe she's on her way home. Maybe she's pulling up right now...I twist around to stare out the window. Nope. The driveway remains empty. Pompeii notices me fidgeting anxiously, and he says, "Mom'll be home soon."

I give him a tight-lipped smile. "I hope so."

"She's fine," snaps Roman. "And I'm trying to listen to this stupid show."

Eleven o'clock, everyone has fallen asleep except for me. I turn down the volume on the TV and change to a movie about a runaway kid escaping an orphanage. It makes me want to yell, *Seriously? Yet another movie about an orphan running away from the Institution?* I don't say or yell anything because I know it's not really the show that's stressing me out.

I'm just drifting off to sleep myself when I hear a car door slam. I jump to my feet and bolt to the front door, yanking it open. Flo is standing out of the porch, startled at the sight of me.

"Venice, what—"

I clench my fists. "Flo, Mom isn't home yet."

She goes white in the light spilling out of the house. "She's not? Why?"

"I don't know but I'm really worried." I tiredly step back so my twin can come inside. "How was your date?"

Flo closes the door behind her. "Fun. We went to the bowling alley, then out for a really late dinner. How was your date?"

"What?"

She rolls her eyes. Bending over, she starts to unlace her shoes. "You left earlier today, at eleven. With that kid. The one from the library."

"Oh." I frown. "It wasn't a *date*. It was an educational—"

"Was it just the two of you?"

My frown deepens. Florence laughs. "It was a date," she says, heading into the living room. She stops as she takes in the fact that our siblings are asleep on the couch. "Um, why is everyone here?"

"We're waiting for Mom." I sit down next to the sleeping Roman, messing with the remote, turning it over in my hands.

Flo sits on the chaise, pulling her phone from her purse. "She hasn't sent me a text, or tried to call me," she mumbles. "I wonder where she is. She's not still with Marc, is she?"

"I don't know. She hasn't responded to me either," I say worriedly, changing the channel on the TV.

"Here. I'll wait up with you." Flo leans over and pats my knee. "Mom will come home soon."

I study my sister critically. It really has been a good day for the Ferrari siblings.

"Now," says Flo, grabbing the remote from me, "if these kids are going to sleep here, then I'm not gonna respect them. What would you like to watch? Chick-flick? Action? A documentary for the geek in you?"

I smile weakly at her attempts to cheer me up. "You would die watching a long, boring documentary."

"Hey, you're doing a report on something for biology, right?"

I eye her seriously, wondering if this is all a set-up to tease me. "Um, yeah. On orangutans."

"Then let's see if there's a documentary about them." Flo flips through the different shows, searching for an interesting one that isn't very long. She says, "It can't be long, because after this, I'm choosing. We'll watch something romantic."

I try to pay attention. I really do try. But I'm too occupied with my whirling thoughts of Florence and Mom. Where is Mom? Why hasn't she come back yet? Why is Flo acting so weirdly? She has *never* looked at what I'm currently doing and helped me with it, like she's doing now. Learning all about the orangutan probably isn't on her life-schedule. And she's doing it for *me*. What has happened to the Florence Ferrari I know? Is she only helping me out because

Mom is off gallivanting with Marc or something? Has Flo finally come to her senses? Is this only temporary, or will she—hopefully—be like this forever?

I find myself immune to sleep. Each time I think I'm going to pass out, a quiet noise shakes me completely awake. Florence also seems alert—she's always shifting around in her seat, changing her position on the chaise, checking the driveway for Mom's car. She's mirroring my actions from earlier, when I was in that space.

The documentary ends without me learning anything. Flo lets out a groan of pleasure and spends the next few minutes searching for a romance that she hasn't already seen. It's more interesting than watching apes swinging in the treetops, but I still can't concentrate. I can't see the window from my spot on the couch—Roman is blocking everything with his massive head—and I'm more anxious than ever. Tapping my toes on the floor. Frequently glancing over at Flo to make sure she's looking out the window every few minutes. Fidgeting with my ring, turning it over on my finger, trying to calm myself down.

I end up pacing again. I hesitate long enough to take off Roman and Siena's glasses, putting them on the short coffee table before resuming my agitated pacing around the living room. Flo briefly meets my gaze, smiles, then returns to the movie.

Something happens during the movie where the music gets loud and dramatic and there's some shouting, and Roman suddenly wakes up with a snort, yelling, "I hate lobster bisque!"

Flo bursts out laughing. Siena grumbles under her breath, rolling off the couch and bringing Pompeii down with her. The two snap awake, starting to punch each other instinctively. I have to pull them apart while Flo laughs her head off and Roman fumbles for his glasses and the couple in the movie make out in celebration of their victory.

"EW!" Roman exclaims, pointing at the TV, his glasses roughly in place.

"Wha…?" Siena blindly extends her hand, smacking me in the face. She steals my glasses, putting them on and leaving *me* almost blind. "Ugh, your eyesight is better than mine, Venice."

I reach for my glasses. "Siena, give them back!"

They are pressed into my hand, and I quickly slide them on, blinking at the confusion reigning in the room. Roman is wrestling the remote away from Flo, trying to fast-forward the kissing scene. Pompeii is mumbling something about a book while crawling around the living room, looking under people's feet and under the couches. Siena is on my lap, hands wildly swinging in the air as she fruitlessly searches for her glasses. I pluck them off the coffee table and give them to her; she puts them on and yells, "I can see! Blessed Hallelujah!"

The volume on the TV rises higher and higher, increasing the noises of the man and woman smooching. Roman groans, letting go of the remote and stumbling back, covering his ears protectively.

"I LOVE YOU, JOHN!" the woman on TV says loudly.

The man replies a second later, just as loud as her. "I LOVE YOU TOO, MY DARLING AMELIA!"

"Turn it down!" Roman shouts.

John and Amelia resume their love fest, making my brothers start yelling, trying to block out the sounds. Flo is laughing hysterically, doubled over and clutching the remote in her hand. Siena leans against me and after a short moment begins to snore softly, the noise almost blotted out by the racket fit to raise the dead going on in our house.

Flo finally lowers the volume, but not after the scene has changed, and the two lovebirds are getting married. "This is amazing!" cries Flo. "Oh, you should have seen…Hahaha!"

"I'm gonna murder you, Florence!" screams Roman, tackling her onto the rug. "Ugh, why do you have to be so gross?"

Florence is still giggling, giving me proof that Roman isn't *actually* killing her like he said he would. My twin chucks the remote control at me, and I awkwardly catch it one-handed. "The movie's boring now!" Flo yells. "You can change it!"

Instead, I stand up and switch off the TV, which has the effect of settling down the ruckus. Turning around, I face my siblings, who are all sitting down somewhere in the living room. Siena looks asleep, so I decide not to disturb her.

"Guys," I say, "Mom isn't back yet, and it's..." I check the time on my phone. "Eleven forty-six. That means she's either dead on the side of the road, or she's enjoying herself too much."

"Dramatic are we?" Roman raises his hand, acting sarcastic. "Oh, what will we do about this, wise Teacher Venice?"

I shoot him a pleading look. "Roman, this is serious. Mom has *never* been out this late. Isn't she always telling us to be back at ten-thirty? And she's always leaving notes and texting. She's done none of these things today!"

Flo nods. She of all people should know. She doesn't obey the curfew, though, and I suddenly find that funny. In the midst of this chaos, it's *funny*.

"I'm really worried about Mom," I continue. "She's awesome and a great mom and I love her very much." I anxiously scan their faces. "I know we're not the best kids. We fight a lot, argue a lot, get mad at each other a lot. Yet in the end, we're still siblings."

Sienna has awakened, and my words must have started to trouble her because she rushes up to me and looks earnestly into my eyes, asking desperately, "You don't think Mom has left us, do you? Like Dad did?"

Everyone gets really still, and the *quiet* is thick and palpable. Is everyone is waiting for me to respond?

"Oh, Siena, Mom would never leave us," I say, and hug her.

Flo comes up and pats her on the head. "Exactly. She loves us."

Roman snorts. "I agree with Florence. Look, there are dozens of other explanations that don't involve death or abandonment. Let's give Mom the benefit of the doubt."

We're momentarily stunned by Roman's maturity and rational thought process, and we let his words reassure us.

Feeling like he's on a roll, he continues. "Siena is our sister, no matter how annoying she is." Okay, this is more like the Roman we know. "Pompeii is still our brother, no matter how frustrating he can be. Flo is still our sister, no matter how caught up she is in her friends and dates and boyfriends." We're just letting him finish at this point. I guess backhanded compliments are still compliments? "And Venice is still our sister, no matter how bossy she is."

Siena runs to hug Roman now. "And Roman is still our brother, no matter how often he shoves our slippers in the toaster and ends up frying the appliance. I love you, Roman."

I can tell he's not comfortable with this display of affection, but he doesn't push her away.

"So what do we do about Mom?" asks Pompeii.

I share a sad smile with Florence and Roman and I say, "I guess we wait. If we don't hear from her by the morning we'll need to get some other people involved. Let's all try to get some sleep."

Still feeling the love, Siena goes around hugging each of us, telling us how much she loves us. She asks if we can all sleep together in the living room, so we gather blankets and pillows and find comfortable spots, finally turning out the lights.

Before she drifts off to sleep, Siena adds happily, "When Mom comes back, I'm going to be the best daughter and sister in the world so she doesn't have any reason to stay away from us." She says it in all sincerity and with enthusiasm, but her pledge casts a shadow of uncertainty over the rest of us.

SIXTEEN

I wake to a familiar-sounding, gas-guzzling engine. Jumping to my feet, I fumble for my glasses, and slide them on. I blink repeatedly in the bright light spilling into the living room, illuminating my sleeping siblings. Siena is on top of Pompeii, her chest rising and falling with even breaths. Florence is asleep on the chaise, eyes closed. Roman is next to me on the couch, a trail of drool leaking out of the corner of his mouth. I grimace and quickly move to the window, throwing back the curtains.

Roaring down our street is Marc's horrible red pick-up truck, going in the direction opposite to us. I cock my head, confused as to why he's leaving. He hadn't rung the doorbell, or banged on the door to wake us up. Maybe…Maybe Mom is back!

I turn away from the window, heading for the front door. It's still unlocked from the night before when I was too anxious to lock it. I yank open the door, expecting to see Mom standing on the porch, a perfectly understandable excuse ready to burst out of her. She will apologize for not responding to our texts and making us so worried. She will promise not to leave without telling us where she went or when she'd be back. I suddenly realize this must be how *she* felt when I was off at the library with Nate and she didn't know where I was. At least I came back before nightfall, and most certainly not early the next morning. I'm going to have a long talk with Mom after this. There is no way I'm letting her off easy.

I abruptly change my mind when I see her. She's curled into a fetal position on the porch, deathly still. Her auburn hair is a tangled mess, fanned out underneath her across the doormat and onto one of the steps leading to the walkway. Her eyes are closed—for one terrible moment I think she's dead, but then she draws in a shuddering breath and mutters to no one, "I only eat organic."

I almost laugh with relief. Glancing back over my shoulder, I yell, "Roman! Florence! Mom's home!"

My siblings stir on their temporary beds. No one gets up except Flo, who is used to waking early, and she stumbles over to me, her curly hair a mess just like Mom's.

"What is *wrong* with her?" Flo exclaims, looking down at Mom with barely-restrained horror.

"I don't know, but she's..." I gesture limply at her. "Let's get her inside."

We step out onto the porch. Flo hooks her arms under Mom's, pulling her up to a sitting position. I grab Mom's legs, and together we carry her into the living room, placing her on the couch I had so recently vacated. Roman is asleep still, his glasses dangling off his nose. I shake him gently after putting Mom down next to him.

"Roman," I say, shaking him harder when he doesn't respond. "Roman! Wake up!"

He groans and shoves me. "Ugh, Venice, you're so annoying." He yawns widely, stretching an arm over his head. Fixing his glasses, he notices Mom on the couch by him. "Mom!" he yells. "She's here! What *happened* to her, Venice?"

"I don't know," I admit, closing the front door. "But I woke up to Marc's red truck driving away down our street. The two of them must have been together last night."

"And..." Flo puts her hands on the sides of Mom's face, turning her to look up at us. Mom's eyes are still closed. "There's something really wrong with her. Why isn't she waking?"

I kneel on the rug, brushing away Mom's knotted hair. I feel her pulse, find she's breathing heavily and her heart rate is slower than usual. Suddenly more worried than before, I grab a pillow from under Pompeii and use it to elevate Mom's head. She mutters something, the words slurred together, impossible to discern. I lean closer to her and catch a whiff of a familiar scent. Shoving back from the couch, I stand up, disgusted. "She's drunk," I say bitterly.

"Drunk?" Flo repeats, sounding as disgusted as me.

I nod. "Yes. Why, though, I don't understand. She hates alcohol. She hates it! Why would she go and drink too much?"

"She *was* with Marc," says Roman. "Maybe it's his fault."

I clench my fists. "If this *is* Marc's doing, then I am never going to let Mom near him again."

"Hear, hear," agrees Flo.

I sigh, exhausted. I haven't slept very well. "Roman, could you go get some water for Mom? Flo, can you get a few blankets and pillows? Mom's going to have to sleep here. She's too heavy to carry all the way upstairs."

Flo and Roman hurry off to do as I'd asked, their concern for Mom overcoming their normal defiance. I push up the bridge of my glasses and bend over her once more, trying to figure out what to do next. Mom hasn't ever come home drunk before. She is philosophically opposed to any drink that makes her falsely feel emotions like energy and excitement and euphoria. She doesn't drink coffee or caffeinated soda because she thinks they're bad for her system. So why has she chosen now to decide against her beliefs? I've only seen her drink alcohol once, and it was just a sip, not even enough to become tipsy. Yet here she is, full-out *drunk*. I hope this is the sole time she'll be drunk. I don't ever want to see her like this again. Passed out on the couch. Having her kids take care of her while they're freaking out that she's incapacitated.

"Here." Flo shoves a pile of blankets at me, pulling me from my thoughts. I wearily smile my thanks, begin to drape the blankets over Mom. She lets out a moan, mumbling incoherently.

Roman appears at my elbow, holding a glass of water. I take it from him, quickly suck in a breath, then throw the water on Mom's peaceful face. She splutters as Flo and Roman both gape at me, seemingly not having expected me to do that to Mom. I shrug. "It's what they do in movies," I say carelessly, handing the empty glass to Roman. "Go fill that up again. Mom isn't fully awake yet."

He leaves without a word, a grin playing around the corners of his mouth. I bet he's enjoying this. If he's having a good time, I don't understand how. I'm so angry and so worried and so anxious and so—so—*everything*.

"What's going on?" murmurs a sleepy voice.

I turn around. Siena and Pompeii have finally woken up and are confused about all the excitement currently happening. "Mom's back," I tell them, and they brighten.

Jumping up, Siena approaches the couch. "Eesh, she looks terrible," she comments.

"That's because she's indisposed," says Flo.

Roman returns, a jug filled to the brim with water. He grins at me. "Can I have the honors?" he asks.

"No!" I take the jug from him. "You can't toss this much water on her! We are trying to *help* her, not drown her. Anyway, it'd ruin the couch. Mom'd be extra mad when she wakes."

Roman sighs heavily. "Fine." He flops down on the floor, arms crossed over his chest. "You ruin all my fun."

Shaking my head, I flick a little of the water at her. She stirs but doesn't wake. Disappointed, I tip the jug until a stream of crystal-clear tap water falls onto Mom's face, making her splutter again. She weakly raises a hand, trying to block the water, and I shove the jug at Florence. Crouching in front of Mom, I take her hand and say softly, "Mom?"

She mumbles something.

"Mom?" I shake her shoulders roughly. "Mom, wake up!"

She sucks in a shuddering breath. Her mouth opens, releasing a whisper of alcohol that causes me to gag. She says something, so quiet that I can't hear it above the dim *thud* of my heart.

"What?" I put my ear next to her lips, listening hard.

Mom breathes in deeply. She repeats what she'd said.

I straighten, my face white. I look down at the floor, expression distraught and confused and astonished.

"What'd she say?"

I glance up at Flo, working hard not to laugh or cry. "She said...Mom said *Angelo*."

Florence starts to laugh in shock. It soon turns into pathetic wheezing as she doubles over, clutching the jug to her chest. "Angelo," she echoes. "Of all the things to say. *Angelo*."

"I wonder why she said Dad's name," I murmur.

Roman scoffs from where he sits on the floor. "Better than Marc," he says in a disgruntled tone. He's disappointed about the water. Wow.

"True," I acknowledge, looking down at Mom again. "She isn't waking up. I might need the jug, Flo."

My twin holds out the jug. "At your service."

"Thanks." I accept it, undecided what I should do. I can pour all the water onto Mom, or I can sprinkle it, or I can just wait for her to wake. I don't know which is the best option, so I move the jug over Mom's face and continue to drip water onto her. She gasps, suddenly sitting up on the couch. Her hand shoots out, grabbing the jug from me. I flinch at the unexpected movement and release it, letting Mom take it and do whatever she wants, as long as she stays awake. Instead, she drops the glass jug onto the floor, spilling some water on her as she does so. The jug shatters, sending shards of glass spinning dangerously close to my bare feet. I skip away from the couch, Flo copying me. Siena and Pompeii are standing by Roman in the doorway to the kitchen, safely out of harm's way.

"Water," Mom pants, sinking back down onto the cushions. "Ah, water."

I exchanged glances with Flo. We're both thinking the same thing—what is happening to our mom, and how do we prevent it from getting worse? Moving at the same time, Flo and I approach Mom again, group around the couch, try to decide what to do next.

"She said more water," Flo suggests, gesturing to Mom. "She wants more water."

"Or she wants us to stop," I reply. Chewing on a fingernail, I quickly review our options. "Alright," I say eventually, taking my fingernail out of my mouth. "I don't really know what to do, but water seems to be helping Mom wake up. Let's get her into the backyard and pour a bucket of water onto her. Roman, could you carry her?"

Roman stands up, careful not to get impaled by the broken glass around us. He scoops Mom into his arms and carries her out of the room, towards the kitchen and, ultimately, the backyard.

"Pompeii," I call, and my younger brother looks up at me. "Will you clean up the glass, please? Oh, and Siena, will you help him?"

Siena gives me a nasty look but hurries off to grab some towels from the utility room. Pompeii starts to pick up the glass pieces, humming softly to himself as he does. Flo is still standing by me, waiting for her instructions on how she can help Mom.

"Would you like to fill up the bucket?" I ask her.

Flo grins wickedly. "Of course."

"Thanks."

She pats my arm, then disappears deeper into the house, searching for a big enough bucket to satisfy her needs. I'm about to follow Roman into the backyard when someone knocks on the front door. I groan, spinning around. After a quick check to make sure I'm not wearing my pajamas, I open the door, resisting a yawn.

Nate is there, standing on almost the exact spot I found Mom. I'd forgotten all about school. Nate isn't smiling like usual—in fact, his expression is serious, the most serious I have ever seen. "What's wrong?" he immediately asks.

I blink at him in sleepy confusion. "Sorry?"

"What's wrong?" he repeats. "There's something wrong going on with you guys right now."

I scratch my nose in the most undignified way possible. "How can you tell?"

"Your house is deathly quiet," he says. He *sounds* serious, too. "Plus, you look really stressed out right now. Is everything okay?"

"My mom," I say, playing with the doorknob so I don't have to look Nate in the eye. "She came home this morning. Like twenty minutes ago."

Nate moves, trying to force me to meet his gaze. I avoid his attempts for less than ten seconds. When he has my full attention, he says, "She was gone all day yesterday and all night?"

"Yeah. And she came back..." my voice wavers. I'm not really sure I should share this with Nate. "She's really tired," I say instead. "So I don't think we'll be able to go to school today. Could you be so nice as to spread the word to our teachers?"

"Of course." Nate smiles sadly. "Mandy will be disappointed."

"I know. Tell her I wanted to come, but I had more pressing matters. I'll be back tomorrow or...I don't know. Soon."

Nate nods. "Okay. I hope your mom—I hope everything is solved, and that tomorrow when I walk past your house, I hear the muffled voices of your arguing siblings."

I smile at his effort to make me laugh. "Yeah. Thanks, Nate." I watch him leave, feeling somehow even more dispirited than before. After a moment, I close the door and walk slowly to the backyard, my thoughts a jumbled mess inside my head. I feel bad for making Nate go to school by himself, but today I really have to take care of Mom. I need to learn why she's drunk, why she got drunk, and how Marc was involved.

Roman, Flo, and Mom are in the backyard when I slip outside; I shiver in the slight chill. A large red bucket is balanced on Flo's hip. She waves at me as I come out. "Are you ready?" she calls.

I walk up to them. Roman has carefully set Mom on the grass, making sure nothing is poking into her.

"Go ahead," I say, waving my hand.

Flo doesn't hesitate. She tips the bucket, throwing a gallon of freezing water onto Mom's face. Mom lets out a gargled scream, sitting up reflexively and reaching for the source of her watery punishment. Not to my surprise, Flo quickly backs away.

"Wha' was that for?" Mom asks, her voice slurred.

A sudden wave of relief crashes over me. I laugh loudly, the sound partly forced, but I don't care. At least Mom's fully awake now. I kneel down on the grass next to Mom, fixing her glasses so she can see us clearly. "Hey, Mom," I say gently.

She squints up at me. "Who're you?"

Behind me, Flo scoffs and mutters to Roman, "No doubt she's got brain damage and can't recognize her own kids."

"Mom, it's me," I say, ignoring Flo. "Venice. Your daughter."

"Venice?" Mom crinkles her nose. "Always wanted a girl named Venice. It reminds me of...of..."

"Italy?" I offer.

She frowns. "Nah. What's Italy?"

"Um." I think hard for a moment. "You don't know what Italy is? What about Florence? Or Roman?"

Mom mumbles again. "No, no. Italy. Where's Angelo?"

I recoil. Looking up at my siblings, I say, "She's delusional. Roman, can you carry her back inside so we can warm her up? Then she's going to need a nice, long nap to clear her mind. Hopefully, that'll help her and us. I think today we're on our own."

144

SEVENTEEN

We take care of Mom all day and the next. She seems more like her usual self—stronger and more capable of speech. When she's sober enough, she explains that she stayed up all night talking with Marc and he tempted her with too much drink. I'm still mad at Marc—I doubt I'll ever change my opinions about him now. He has crossed the line. The flattery I can pardon, but the drinking and keeping Mom out late and making us worried, I will *never* forgive him for.

And he dumped her on the doorstep! How utterly rude of him!

At least he had towed her car back, leaving it parked by the mailbox as always, but I'm burning with fury.

Mom apologizes profusely over and over for being such a high matter of concern to us. She promises she won't leave the house without telling us where she's going and how long she thinks she'll be out, and if she has to stay longer wherever, she'll call us to explain. Her sincerity soothes me only a little; I notice she doesn't make any promises about staying away from both Marc and alcohol. When I approach the subject, she sighs and tells me, rather sullenly, that she won't touch another drink for the rest of eternity unless she *has to*, but she says nothing of the sort about Marc. It all serves to increase my discomfort. She can at least limit her time with him—I catch her talking on the phone to him, texting him, planning outings that she claims are work related but are probably excuses to see him. To me, it looks like my forty-four year-old mom is acting like a schoolgirl with a schoolgirl's crush. Is this what happens in a mid-life crisis? She can't *bear* to be apart from him for too long before she's moody and downcast. It reminds me of all of Flo's crushes and her past boyfriends and her devastation when they broke up or she found one cheating on her. Mom is old enough to judge who is right for her, but she is not using her best judgment during these times.

I'm really beginning to worry about her. It's unhealthy the way she is constantly talking to him. I hope they aren't seriously considering taking their relationship further. I mean, Mom has five kids, the oldest two fifteen and fifty-one weeks old. Marc doesn't have *any* kids, and I don't know if he has been married before. He clearly doesn't know how to work with women. Anyway, he is portraying a teenage boy hitting on a girl he likes, and I don't want him to see Mom any more.

Especially after Sunday night.

When I bug her about him leaving her on the porch, she says he knew she wouldn't want him bursting into our house carrying our drunk mom, and the excuse is so flimsy and frail I want to tell her, but I feel like I'm being too harsh and confrontational. So though this whole shebang is unacceptable, I decide to back off and let her come to realize that she did wrong and should never do it again.

Except I fear she'll never realize that.

Wednesday morning dawns bright and early. I lay on my bed, drowsy in the warm sun, mulling through things in my head. Mom. Marc. Orangutans. Mom. Marc. I can't come up with anything else to think about, so I probably should get out of bed and prepare for the school day, but I'm too lazy. The sun is really, really, nice. It's been cloudy for the past few days, and I missed the warm sun—I love how cheerful the day seems when the sun is shining like this.

A pounding on the bathroom door startles me. I look up from my pillow, a hand fumbling blindly for my glasses. I find them and, sliding them on, spot Flo's empty, tidy bed.

"Florence!" yells a muffled voice, one I recognize. "Florence, get out of the shower! You have been in there for much longer than fifteen minutes!"

A pause while Flo responds.

"Fifteen minutes was plenty of time to shampoo your hair!" Mom says, pounding on the door again. "You're wasting water! Get out now before I come in and turn it off myself!"

I smile, my depression and stress momentarily dispersing like I had so fervently hoped, and drop my head onto my pillow, not caring about my glasses digging into my nose. I know Mom is perfectly fine now. She's all right. She is definitely back to normal if she's yelling at Flo to stop using up the water and being greedy about the time she takes in the shower.

Apparently in Virginia, if it's towards the end of January and the sun is bright and warm outside, it's still cold. Freezing. And the sunnier it is, the windier it is. I learn this while walking to school with wet hair and wearing a thin jacket and no gloves. The wind is brutal. It nearly pulls my glasses off my face, and I end up holding onto them with one frozen hand during the walk, turning my hand into an ice block by the time Nate and I reach the school building.

"This is terrible weather," I grumble. "Who would walk to school in the cold, windy outside?"

"You, obviously," says Nate. He's cheerful this morning for some reason. It is a horribly cold morning, not warm enough for me to be happy, but I enjoy the bright sunlight. "And me."

"Stupid sun," I mutter, shielding myself from the harsh wind. My cold hand feels like it's about to fall off when we approach the front doors of the high school and merge with the flow of other teenagers entering the building. I spot Mandy and wave at her—she lets out a shriek of delight and shoves her way through the crowd towards me, Elijah trailing after her.

"Venice!" She throws her arms around me, nearly tackling me

to the hard pavement. I reach for something to help keep my balance and end up falling awkwardly against Nate while trying with some difficulty not to fall against him.

He just laughs even harder, grabbing my shoulders to help me stand up straighter. "Watch out for Mandy's bear hugs," he warns.

I disengage from Mandy, a pink flush rising up my cheeks, though it has nothing to do with the cold. "Hey, Mandy," I say, rubbing my sore ribs. She has some serious arm strength.

"You're back! Finally!" She beams. "Do you know how *boring* our conversations were at lunch? All Elijah could talk about was his annoying boy cousin that's coming over to visit in two weeks, and all Nate could talk about was..." she frowns, thinking hard.

"Whatever books he was reading," Elijah supplies, and Mandy nods her agreement.

"Yes," she says. "Books. Got *very* uninteresting after a while."

I turn to Nate and raise an eyebrow, wanting to know his opinion on the matter. He just shrugs and says, "Books were a whole lot more exciting when I read them, not when I explained them out loud to two kids who prefer playing video games."

I half-smile, half-smirk. "Alright then."

Flo suddenly appears at my elbow, her posse nowhere in sight. She grabs my arm and drags me away, whispering in my ear as she does so, "Venice, can you help me with something?"

"Um..." I glance over my shoulder, back at my friends who are gawking after me in confusion. "What do you need help with, Flo?"

She looks back at my friends, too. "Venice," she says quietly. "Can you not have...*them* freak out when you arrive? I mean, that one girl screamed your name and drew a lot of attention to you and them..."

I stop in my tracks, whirling around to face her. "Florence! Are you trying to control my social life? Why?"

"I'm not *trying*," she says disgustedly. "I want you to stop causing a scene. You're embarrassing yourself and me."

Speechless, I just gape at her.

"The popular kids can't tell us apart," says Flo. "They mistake you for me, and me for you. I've already lost popularity among the some of the kids, and having you parade around with your loud and awkward friends isn't exactly helping."

I start to feel angry that my selfish younger sister can't handle me having different friends from her, but I force down the fury, taking several deep breaths. "Flo," I say, putting my hands on her shoulders, "I'm sorry if the more popular kids aren't smart enough to tell us apart, but I'm not going to make my friends behave differently. And I have *never* tried to draw everyone's attention away from you to me. I hate having people stare at me." I wave a hand towards where Mandy and Elijah and Nate are talking. "Now, I don't know about them, but I'm pretty sure they don't really want to attract attention either, just like me. Seriously, Flo. We're not striving to make you less popular."

She eyes me carefully. "Huh."

I wait for her to say something else. She doesn't.

Shaking my head in wonder, I turn away from her, intent on returning to the school building before the bell rings and I'm late for class. Flo stops me by grabbing my hand. "Venice!" she says quietly.

I face her again. "Yeah?"

"I don't care if I'm messing up your social life," she says harshly. "But you'd better not ruin mine."

EIGHTEEN

"Peanut butter and honey? What kind of sandwich is *that*? Are you trying to poison yourself?"

I shake my head. "Nope. It's just the easiest kind of sandwich to make while my siblings are fighting and breaking stuff in the kitchen. It's hard to even microwave oatmeal in there."

"How many siblings do you have?" asks Mandy.

I switch my gaze from Elijah to her. "Four. Two brothers, two sisters. I have an identical twin sister, Florence—" I jerk my thumb over my shoulder in the direction of where she is sitting in the cafeteria, surrounded by her friends, and Mandy twists in her seat to spot Flo. Elijah has already seen her, I know, but I guess Mandy hasn't paid much attention.

"She doesn't really look like you," says Mandy, returning to her food. "She gets plenty of attention from all the popular people."

I examine my lunch that Elijah made fun of, annoyed that the honey has soaked into my top slice of bread, making it all squishy and sticky and crystallized.

Mandy reaches across the table, grabbing a protein bar that is sitting in front of Elijah. "Can I have this?"

Elijah shrugs. "It's not mine. I stole it from Nate."

She turns to Nate, who is watching the whole exchange with a great deal of amusement. "Can I have this?" she repeats, shaking the protein bar so that the plastic wrapping crinkles.

Nate mirrors Elijah's shrug. "Sure."

"Thanks." Mandy sits back in her seat, unwrapping the bar. "Continue, Venice. You were telling me about your siblings."

"They're all pretty uninteresting," I say, though that's probably false. "Why don't you tell me about your siblings, Mandy?"

She takes a bite of the protein bar, rolling her eyes at me. After swallowing, she says, "They're more boring than yours, I'll bet. I've just got two older brothers who are absolute *trash*."

"How come?" I ask as Elijah laughs.

Mandy groans. "Ugh. They're just terrible. They're Mom and Dad's favorite kids, too. Mom is *always* reminding me of the things they've done, and then she says that I should be like them and act all goody-goody and other gross things like that. Dylan—he's the oldest—is this really tall guy who wanted to become a lawyer, so he did, and Mom kept fawning over him for that. And Zac—my other brother—wanted to become an architect, so he did all this math and equally lame stuff just to get the job."

"Serious perseverance," I comment. "Wait, Mandy, since when do you think math is boring?"

She scoffs, taking another bite of the protein bar. "Actually, you're right. I do admire their initiative, and drive. They're both brilliant, to be honest. It just that they're so dang obnoxious about it. They're constantly rubbing it in my face. That's why whenever they're visiting, I go to Elijah's house and watch him play video games. He sometimes lets me play."

"Are you any good?" I ask her, slamming my sandwich back together and sliding it into my container. I think I'll eat it when I have an appetite for that kind of messed-up sandwich.

"I don't know," says Mandy. "I mean, I'm awesome at shooting people and I can dodge bullets, but I suck at the controls."

Elijah cuts in, "Stop being modest, Mandy." He leans closer to me and says softly but loud enough for her to hear, "She's better than me."

I laugh while Mandy's cheeks tinge pink at Elijah's compliment. She goes quiet all of a sudden, as if she's mulling over the fact that Elijah has just said something nice about her. In all the time I've known them, neither of them has said anything kind to each other.

"You should see her bad-mouth the other players," Elijah says, sounding like he's enjoying making her speechless. "She's caused several to quit just by telling them how bad they are."

"And..." I hesitate. "*Bad-mouthing* other players is...good?"

Elijah gives me a look that quite plainly says, *Are you an idiot or what?* I have to force myself not to laugh again.

"Venice, you should come over sometime and see how good Mandy is," Elijah continues. "She's epic. Once, there was this guy hiding in a run-down building, and Mandy came bursting in and they had a big fight. Mandy almost lost, but in the end she managed to shoot him." Elijah mimes firing a gun. "I was so proud of her."

"I think I was there," says Nate.

I look across the table at him. "You were?"

He nods. "It was that day..." he stutters to a halt, thinking hard.

Before he can remember what happened that day, Mandy suddenly says, "Um, Elijah, when is your cousin coming again?"

Elijah frowns at her. "I've told you like, a million times. He'll be here in two weeks. And if you ever see my mom, tell her it was *not* my idea to have Sam over."

"Do you not like Sam?" I put in.

Elijah rolls his eyes. "That's an understatement. Yeah, I don't like him. He's kinda like your sister, uh, what's-her-face Florence."

"Popular?" I suggest.

He switches his attention to me. "*Hot*," he says.

Both Nate and I snort. "Hot?" I repeat. "Seriously, Elijah? How am I going to determine what kind of person he is if all you can say about him is that he is *hot*?"

"Well, you can determine that he's hot," says Elijah.

I resist the urge to bury my face in my hands right as Mandy's alarm rings. Climbing to my feet, I grab my backpack and swing it onto my shoulder, the strap digging into my skin. It's a rather heavy backpack. I probably should put some of the books in my locker, but I can't help it.

Nate suddenly appears at my side, towering over me as always. I wish he wasn't as tall—I feel short next to him.

I follow him out of the loud cafeteria and into the crowded hallways. We don't talk, and it occurs to me that he has barely said anything during the short lunch break. I look at him out of the corner of my eye, watching him twist out of the way of kids that push past him. He seems to be moving slowly and carefully, like something is hurting him.

"What's wrong?" he asks, catching my thoughtful frown.

I chew my bottom lip, not bothering to reply. He'd most likely clam up and refuse to answer my questions. He won't appreciate them, either, since he doesn't want me to ask too much about him.

When he turns down a different hallway than the one we usually use to reach biology class, I hesitantly go after him.

"Um, Nate, where are you going?"

He startles. "Oh! Didn't you get the email that we're in the actual classroom for biology today? The other room Mr. Castro uses for days when we don't need to study our actual biological matter. Like last week, we just needed a classroom to talk about our—" He stops abruptly. He lifts his head and peers behind us.

I glance over my shoulder, not really sure what I'm supposed to be looking at. The crowded hallways. The chattering kids. The tall man in a striped suit talking loudly to several of the kids.

"Oh, great."

I look back at Nate. He's frowning. "What?"

He gestures to the man. "He's one of the guidance counselors, Mr. Hennessey. He's constantly asking me bothersome questions about...my family."

"And you try to avoid him?"

His frown turns into a smile. "Definitely. Shoot, he's heading this way."

I'm about to confirm what Nate said when he suddenly steps behind a row of lockers, grabs me by the shoulders, and wheels me around to hide him from view of the counselor, which is pointless because he's a head taller than me. He's got these lockers, though, and he's mostly hidden. But I'm rather unsettled by the unexpected contact and can't move as Nate anxiously scans the hallway for a way to escape.

Frozen where I stand, I notice the sleeve of his jacket has risen higher than the cuff of his glove on his right arm. There's barely an inch of skin showing, but I find myself staring at it. I've always wondered why Nate often wears a jacket and his fingerless gloves all day—now that I think of it, I have rarely seen him *not* wearing them. Is he self-conscious of how his hands look? Or is he just cold all the time and has to bundle up otherwise he freezes to death? I guess I just figured it was his own personal fashion statement.

My eyes dart up to his face. He isn't paying any attention to me; he's too busy making sure the counselor is heading in a different direction. I detect a tightness in Nate's expression, one of deeply hidden pain. He really must not like that counselor.

"Thanks, Venice. He's moving on, just a few more..." His eyes are following Mr. Hennessey's movement through the hallway. Returning my gaze to his wrist, I study the skin thoughtfully. There is a faint white line running over the curve of his wrist, down to the other side, where it disappears. It's an interesting scar. Maybe he wears gloves to hide his scars.

I open my mouth to ask him about it, then stop myself. That's one thing that makes him irritating to me. He's hiding things, not just family issues. I wish he trusted me enough to tell me. I suppose he did open up that one time at the café, but he also made me promise not to ask any more. I can sometimes read people by how they act and speak, but Nate is one very bewildering person.

He shifts, causing his sleeve to move up even more, revealing another spot of skin. However, this time it doesn't have a white scar but a long, fresh cut that's still bleeding. A drop of blood trails down his arm, and unable to stop myself, I lift a finger to brush it away.

Nate, of course, chooses this moment to finally look back at me. "Venice, what are you doing?"

I pause uncertainly, a light blush rising to my cheeks as I realize his hands are still on my shoulders. "I might ask you the same thing," I say, my voice quivering slightly.

"What? Oh, sorry." He steps back, dropping his hands. His sleeve covers up his cut.

I point to his arm. "You're bleeding."

Nate shrugs one shoulder. "It happens all the time. I cut myself easily. You would think that with protection, though somewhat thin protection"—he pats his jacket—"I'd be able to prevent cuts."

I just stare at him, saying nothing. I don't really believe that's the reason why he wears a jacket and gloves. Who cuts himself, even by accident, and doesn't bandage it? The blood is going to soak into the fabric of his jacket, maybe leak through and stain his desk or something.

"Come on." He jerks his head. "Mr. Hennessey has moved on. We need to get to class soon, or Mr. Castro will count us tardy."

I numbly follow Nate to the new biology classroom, thinking all the while. I can't get the image of that blood dripping down Nate's arm out of my head. Not for a second do I accept his explanation. Why won't he tell me the truth? And why hasn't he put a bandage around the cut yet?

I know better than to ask him. He'd become quiet again, and I don't want that to happen. Cheerful Nate is much better company. But I *do* want to help him, and my desire is stronger than my discomfort. I just need to find the right way to either earn his trust or convince him to tell me.

NINETEEN

Two days later I don't remember it's my birthday until I come home from school and find Mom has decorated the house with blue-and-green streamers, balloons, and glitter to top it off. Flo is in the kitchen, snitching in the frosting on a giant pink cake while Pompeii complains how unfair it is that she's allowed to but he can't.

"It's my birthday," Flo replies, licking her fingers clean. She spots me in the kitchen doorway and pauses. "Hey, Venice. You're finally home. How was walking with that one guy?"

I frown at her. "That one guy?" I repeat.

"Yeah." Flo steals the bowl of extra frosting from Pompeii and starts to lick it before he can get it back.

I don't answer her. I don't really want to. She'd just tease me forever and ever; she's like that. Plus, she doesn't care about my response—she only wants to bring up the subject of Nate to make Mom and our siblings curious and badger me with questions, a tactic she's used plenty of times before.

Deciding the best thing to do is go up to my bedroom, I exit the kitchen and climb the stairs, my backpack weighing me down. I need to clean it out sometime. Today, though, all I want to do is flop onto my bed and get away from everyone. The only problem about my birthday is that everyone in my family—except for Flo—loves swarming me—and Flo—and yelling a happy birthday to my face. It gets old quick. *Really* quick.

Reaching the top of the staircase, I wearily turn down the hallway, ready to crash.

Instead, I slam into Siena when she is leaving the bathroom. She sees me, lets out a scream, and hugs me around the middle.

"Happy birthday, Venice!" she shouts.

I pat her head and disengage from her hug. "Hey, Siena. How was your day at school?"

She rolls her eyes. "Boring and stupid like always. Pompeii dropped his macaroni on the ground, though, and I ate it. Then the principal made me go to the nurse's office to make sure I didn't eat any bad stuff on accident."

"Ah." I can't help but smile. "Did you?"

"Nope." Siena shakes her head. "The nurse lady said I was as healthy as a horse, but I don't know if that is a good way to say it. I mean, what if that one random horse I was compared to was sick? Then would I also be sick, not healthy?"

"Um, sure."

Siena grins crazily at me. "Cool." Leaning around me, she yells to no one in particular, "I'm a sick horse!"

I laugh fondly. She has cheered me up considerably. "Good work, Siena. Being a sick horse is something to be proud of."

"I know!" She hugs me again, then skips away, humming to herself. I watch her trip down the stairs, all the while muttering about sick horses under her breath.

Shaking myself, I enter my bedroom and dump my backpack on my bed, then sit next to it. I'm exhausted, though nothing exciting happened today. I think the most interesting thing was Elijah purposely shoving a straw up his nose during lunch. All in all, it had been a normal day. I walked to school with Nate. I went to all my classes. I ate lunch with Mandy, Elijah, and Nate, the latter who, I noticed, didn't eat anything again. I wonder if he's starving himself or if he just doesn't have any food.

After class, I'd walked home, this time alone; Nate had been forced to go over to Elijah's house to play video games/read. I'd come into the house and remembered that it's my birthday.

So why do I feel drained?

I roll onto my stomach and unzip my backpack, beginning to sort through the things it contains. Books. Textbooks. Notebooks. Papers. A lone pencil. A handful of mechanical pencils. My empty lunchbox. A wrinkled slip of purple paper with Mandy's phone number written on it. She'd shoved it into my hand the day after I met her, and since then we'd texted a few times. She's more of a talk-to-in-person girl than a text girl. Still, it's nice to have her on my list of contacts so I can say I actually *have* a contact list whenever Flo scornfully asks me.

Picking through my books, I decide some can stay in my bedroom and a few others can stay in my backpack. Only a *few*, though. I might become stronger than Roman if I carry this many books to school every weekday for a year.

Suddenly wanting to fall asleep, I bury my face in my pillow and sigh, long and loud. The pillow is soft and cold, just how I like it, and gradually I feel myself drifting off to sleep. I haven't taken off my shoes—I'm too tired—and I hope Mom doesn't come in, find me like this, and demand I put my shoes in my closet, no matter if it's my birthday. Shoes are *not* allowed on the bed. Mom has made that clear before.

The front door slams shut, startling me awake. I groan and ease onto my back, annoyed that I'd been so close to falling asleep just to be woken up. I know there's no way I'll be able to drift off again, so I crawl out of bed and begin to unlace my shoes, my drowsy fingers picking at the knots to no avail. I'm too tired. How am I going to stay conscious for dinner and cake and the other stuff Mom has planned? I'd better not face-plant into that giant pink cake Mom made, otherwise Florence and Roman and Pompeii and Siena will be greatly displeased.

Giving up on my shoes, I peer out the window, searching for

the person who had slammed the door and ultimately prevented me from sleeping. I spot Flo by the mailbox, sifting through whatever mail we've gotten today. No doubt she's expecting a package from Dad containing the usual stuff he gets her. I don't think he'll send me anything, but he did last year, so maybe he actually remembered I exist.

Flo emerges from the mailbox triumphant. There is a light blue envelope clutched in her hand—but before I can determine if it really *is* blue she pushes it into her back pocket and it disappears from sight. She can't still be writing her ex-boyfriend Kent, can she? I thought she hated him for cheating on her with Carla, her best friend.

A moment later, Florence comes back inside the house, not bothering to bring in the rest of the mail. She's also left the mailbox door open. Smirking, I quit on attempting to nap and stomp back downstairs, intending on asking Flo who she's writing letters to and if it's Kent and if she's forgiven him. It's not like her to forgive someone, especially someone who hurt her as much as Kent had.

Roman intercepts me in the entryway. "Hey!" he yells. "It's the birthday girl! Well, one of them." He slaps me on the shoulder. "You get sixteen slaps, right? Because you're sixteen now?"

"I can legally strangle you," I reply matter-of-factly.

His smirk withers slightly. "Really?"

"No." I roll my eyes, a smile teasing at the corners of my mouth. "I'm just messing with you. Though I wouldn't mind if it became an actual law...great way to dispose of annoying younger brothers."

"I'm not sure I'm biodegradable," he says as we walk into the kitchen. The others are waiting for us.

"I'm sure you are, Roman," I mutter. "I'll just throw your body into the compost and let you decompose. Mom would probably like that better than cremation."

Roman responds with a snort of laughter.

"Hurry up!" Flo calls. "The waffles are getting cold."

I sit down at the table, examining the food set out. "Waffles for dinner?"

"Yeah." Flo flips her hair over her shoulder. "Waffles are my favorite, so Mom made some for our birthday."

I look up at Mom. She's smiling at me, the lines around her eyes more pronounced than ever. She must not be getting much sleep. "Thanks, Mom," I say, though I'd rather have a number of other dinners tonight than waffles. I love waffles, yes, but I feel like they should be eaten for breakfast and not the evening meal, especially since we're having sugary cake afterwards. Does Flo *want* me to drop dead from sugar overdose?

"Pass the jam," says Pompeii. "I'm starving."

Nobody moves. There are nearly half a dozen jars of jam out on the table, and no one knows which kind Pompeii wants. He releases a heavy sigh and says, "Venice, can you pass the strawberry jam?"

I toss him the jar—luckily, he catches it, and the small action triggers the rest of my family to start eating. Flo talks the entire time, either about all her friends or what parties she's been invited to recently. There are plenty of Valentine's Day parties coming up that she's decided to go to; it makes me roll my eyes that kids are already planning parties for a sort-of holiday. She must really be popular. I see her talking with all the "cool" kids at school, and I've sometimes been mistaken for her, but I have never stopped to think about how many people know her name or what she looks like.

A month. We've lived here for a month, and my twin is famous. I'll bet that plenty of kids her age that have been in Virginia their entire lives aren't anywhere as close in popularity as Flo is. She's just really good at talking to kids and making shallow friends, whereas I'm hanging out with a bookworm from the library—not that I'm complaining—and two video game addicts.

I chuckle into my waffle. Last week, when Elijah complimented Mandy on her excellent killing skills, she'd texted me after school and screamed over the Internet how she was freaking out that he'd done that. I wish those two would get to their senses and realize they both like each other and hurry up and get together.

How did Nate even become friends with them? Elijah and Mandy are the weirdest kids I've met—which isn't saying much—and they're the complete opposite from Nate, who is quiet and enjoys reading. Elijah and Mandy are loud, crazy, and plain *odd* in their own way. I have a suspicion that they met because of whatever video game they like to play, and since then they've been friends. Maybe. I don't really know. I'm only guessing, but that idea seems like the most realistic one. I'll have to ask them the next time I see them.

Roman jabs his elbow into my ribs, painfully shaking me from my thoughts about my contrasting friends.

"What was that for?" I ask, rubbing my side.

He nods at Mom. "I had to kick you out of La-La Land. Mom wants to tell you something."

I wearily look over at her. "Yeah?"

"Just wanted to say…" Mom bends down and pulls a plastic bag onto the table. My frown deepens. Plastic? Mom *hates* plastic. "A few days ago," she says, "I was talking with Marc and happened to mention that you and Flo were having a birthday—"

"Wait," I interrupt, my siblings going still. Their happy chatter ceases. The clatter of forks and knives on plates silences. They all turn to glare at Mom, who is acting confused.

"What?" she asks, her voice full of bewilderment.

I give her the death stare. "You're still talking to Marc?"

"Of course," says Mom. "Why wouldn't I? We're good friends. He comes to see me at work whenever I'm checking out a house near him—"

"Hold on." I lift my hand. "You're still hanging out with Marc? The guy who made you…you drink all that *stuff* and come back here like *that*?"

Mom slowly nods her head. "Yes, Venice."

The atmosphere has turned from happy celebratory to icy hostility. Flo has a hard look on her face. My brothers are scowling at Mom. Siena is stabbing her waffle repeatedly with her fork like she's imagining it's Marc's face.

"Even after last week?" I press.

Mom raises her hands in front of her. "Listen, kids, I didn't mean for...*that* to happen. I just drank a little too much—but I promise that I won't ever do it again. Okay?"

No one moves.

Mom sighs. "As I was saying, a few days ago I was talking with Marc and told him that you, Venice, and Flo had a birthday today, so he sent me several things..."

Flo brightens considerably. A small part of me caves in when I realize how she is so easily swayed by the mention of gifts.

"He bought this for you, Flo," says Mom, pulling a jewelry case out of the bag and handing it to my twin. Mom digs around in the bag for a moment, and then gives Flo a box of fancily-packaged candies and a stylish jean jacket. I'm impressed—slightly—at how Marc has guessed what Flo likes. He must pay close attention and remember every boring thing she tells him.

"Aww," Flo coos, sliding into the jacket. "It fits perfectly! Hey, next time you see Marc, tell him thanks." She pops the lid on the candy box, already sorting through it.

My jaw tightens. Flo gave in so quickly. This is proof that she is a shallow, manipulated girl with no true feelings for anyone besides herself. I know I'm being harsh, but I feel betrayed.

"Here, Venice." Mom holds out another box of candy. "This one is for you. And so is this."

I don't move as she adds a hard-backed book. I don't take the things from her outstretched hand. I refuse. Roman ends up having to accept them from Mom and set them down next to my plate, where I pointedly look everywhere except there and at Florence.

How *could* she do that to me?

"Can we hurry up?" my twin says, clearing her plate off the table. "I've got a date with an *incredibly* hot guy in an hour, and I want to have some cake before I leave."

Her words strike me.

Hard.

"You're going out on our birthday?" I ask incredulously, shoving back from my chair.

Florence nods, looking supremely bored. "Yeah. With a mega-hot guy. So, let's hurry and eat cake and watch me open all my presents. Venice, if you want, you can scurry upstairs and spend the evening alone. It's not like anyone is wanting to hang out with you."

I recoil, my face heating up. Ashamed and embarrassed, I blink furiously to dispel the surprising tears that have formed, wishing Flo hadn't said that in front of our family.

"Whoa," Mom starts.

"Hey!" Siena shouts, standing up roughly. "*I* like hanging out with Venice! She's a whole lot nicer than you, Flo!"

"Yeah," Pompeii agrees. "Venice actually talks to me. All you do is say how annoying I am and that you think I should grow up, but really, *you're* the one that needs to grow up!"

Flo glares at them both. "Nobody asked you!" she scoffs. "I was talking to Venice, not you two."

"I don't think that was *talking*," Roman cuts in. "It was more criticizing."

"You're all acting like idiots," says Flo. "Shut up and let me enjoy *my* birthday without being bothered by my little siblings."

"It's not just your birthday," says Roman. "It's also Venice's. So why don't *you* shut up and let her enjoy her birthday without being bothered by her little sister?"

Flo's eyes widen angrily. She swells up, ready to burst out with even more criticism, but Mom suddenly gets to her feet and says in a strict tone, "That's enough. Florence, you can apologize to your older sister"—she puts extra stress on *older*—"or you can tell your date that you won't be able to make it tonight."

My twin shoots me a furious look. "Fine," she snaps, slamming her plate down on the counter. "I'm sorry, Venice," she says in a sickly sweet voice.

She doesn't mean it.

"I'm sorry, too," I say quietly. "I'm sorry for not being the sister you want me to be."

Turning on my heel, I march out of the kitchen with my head held high, my heart aching, and an indescribable feeling of pain weighing me down.

TWENTY

Mom knocks on my bedroom door nearly a dozen times over the next hour and a half. I ignore her, not wanting to talk to her or any of my siblings, even the ones who had defended me. That's the only thing keeping me from being able to wallow in unadulterated self-pity—not Flo tearing me down, but how Roman and Pompeii and Siena had rushed to my defense, telling Flo off for being the terrible sister she is. It makes me feel warm inside, that at least three of my siblings love me; yet at the same time I want to curl up into a ball and cry my eyes out into my pillow. I also want to forget everything Flo said about me. Most of what she says just goes over my head, but today it really stuck. Maybe it is because today is our birthday. Maybe it's because she's my *twin* sister and we're supposed to have a special connection that others don't.

What's *wrong* with us? I want so badly to have that connection.

I yank my blanket up to my ears, not caring when my glasses dig into my nose. I'm hiding in my bed, trying to escape all the criticism and attacks swirling around in my mind to no avail. The way Flo had said *watch me open all my presents* made it sound like no one had given me anything. If they haven't, it's totally fine with me. I'm perfectly used to not receiving gifts; to me, it's just more stuff I can add to my overflowing hoard of tchotchkes decorating the shelves around our walls. And with Dad not remembering that I exist, it's not like I'm depressed when he doesn't give me anything for my birthday, even though I'm his oldest child and I *should* be easily remembered.

Especially on my birthday.

I frown at my thoughts. I'm only succeeding in making myself feel even worse.

Throwing back the blanket, I crawl out of bed, pausing to fix my glasses more firmly on my nose before searching in the darkness for my phone. To cheer me up, I'll call Mandy. Spending just one minute talking with her will most definitely make me feel better.

She doesn't answer, which instantly sparks disappointment and misery inside of me. Can't *someone* talk to me?

I sink onto the ground, soaking up the darkness that fills my room. This is *not* how I'd imagined my birthday to go three weeks ago. I'd thought maybe I could have some quality time with Flo up here in our room, just like we used to in California. We'd stay up for hours, talking and swapping funny stories to make each other laugh and generally having a great time. But now...by the time I'm ready for bed, she's asleep. When I'm awake, she's fixing her make-up or is eating breakfast downstairs in the cramped, loud kitchen or she's yelling at our younger siblings. I can never catch her alone and spare the time to talk with her.

I had hoped that tonight after dinner we could have a nice conversation. I shouldn't have hoped. And now she's out on a date with whatever boy who easily fell for her. Even though it's *our* birthday. She hadn't stopped for a second to think for someone else.

A harsh thought strikes me. What If *I'm* being the selfish one?

I'm always pointing out Florence's flaws—only to myself of course, but I'm still recognizing what she's doing wrong and how her actions are negative to those around her. I haven't looked for the *good* things about her. I've been too fed up with all the sass she gives me to notice the times when she was actually kind to me. Like the night Mom didn't come back. Florence offered consolation, right up to the point where she chose to turn on that documentary about orangutans just for me. And when she'd opened up to me, telling me how Kent had been cheating on her with her best friend.

There are plenty of moments in my life where Flo and I got along. Right now isn't one of those precious moments, but I tell myself I need to focus more on those.

My phone vibrates, startling me so badly I nearly fall over. I pick up the device and see Mandy is calling. I quickly answer.

"Hello?" asks a voice that is most definitely *not* Mandy's.

"Nate, what are you doing with Mandy's phone?" I say, resting against my bed, racing heart calming down.

He laughs. "Stole it. She's too busy beating Elijah's high score. Oh, she just did. Can you hear them?"

Loud cheering and yelling greets my ear. I grimace. "Yep. I can hear them. Is Elijah mad she beat his high score, or is he proud?"

"Proud. I think. I can't tell."

Nate's voice disappears, cut off by Mandy's as she screams into the phone. "Hi, Venice! I just totally whipped Elijah!"

"I heard," I say, resisting the urge to add *literally*.

She squeals with excitement. "It took him three years to get that score, and I just beat it! Oh man, I feel so *good*! But at the same time sympathetic. I should go apologize."

"No need!" yells Elijah's voice. "I'll just beat the score you made after you beat mine!"

Mandy gasps. "The villain."

"You can just wreck his score again," I say.

"True, true." She giggles. "Venice, you should come over and watch me destroy him. It's amazing. And I think Nate is getting bored. Hey, do you play video games?"

"Nope," I say, stretching an arm over my head. "I prefer reading. It's a lot more educational."

She groans. "Ugh, you sound like Nate. Did you know he enjoys reading Shakespearian plays? This is for *fun*, not for homework or any of his classes. He reads those ridiculously hard to understand plays when he's *bored*."

"Don't blame a guy for having good taste!" Nate calls from somewhere in the background.

I laugh as Mandy tells him reading Shakespeare doesn't count as having good taste in entertainment.

"You seriously need to come over," says Mandy, returning to me. "Save us from Nate. He might start quoting lines soon..."

"Sorry," I say. "I can't. Tonight is a little busy for me." Which is a total lie.

Mandy sighs sadly. "That's too bad. Here, I'm going to put you on speaker-phone. Elijah wants to talk to you."

His voice suddenly cuts in, the volume making me flinch. "Hey, Venice!" he yells. "I'm killing a bunch of players in my round! I'm like, the best dude in the game. No one can kill me!"

"Except for this one guy," says Mandy's voice. "He's killed you twice."

"And then you got him the next time," replies Elijah.

I hear automatic guns firing and artificial grunts and footsteps running back and forth. Elijah is yelling loudly, and after a moment I hear Mandy join in. I suddenly feel really sorry for Elijah's family. I wonder how they can stand his rampage.

Listening to your friends yell at a video game for two minutes isn't exactly my idea of hanging out with them, and I think Nate realizes that, too. Mandy and Elijah are muffled as he switches off speakerphone and says, "I can't get them to stop."

"They're almost as loud as my siblings," I say, laughing both internally and externally.

"Maybe," says Nate. His voice crackles over what he says next, and I nearly miss it. "I feel bad for his mom, Mrs. Jenkins. She has a newborn, and it takes forever for him to fall asleep, especially with Elijah yelling downstairs. She's had to tell Elijah to shut up countless times."

"And he ignores her each time?"

Nate laughs, the sound wavering. "Nah, he just forgets. See, when he gets excited, Elijah forgets to keep quiet."

"Somehow, I'm not surprised." I glance down at my ring, which is glinting gold in the dim light of my phone. A sudden sharp pang of sorrow strikes my heart as I remember Dad and how I haven't seen him in over six years. I have always hoped that he might come back and visit us, even just for a few minutes. I really miss him. Where is he right now? Has he gotten remarried, or is he dating someone like Mom is? Does he regret leaving us? Does *he* ever wish he could visit us?

"Venice? Did you hang up?"

I jolt. "What? Oh, sorry, I spaced out for a minute. Sorry, Nate. I forgot I'm still on the phone."

"Did something happen today?"

I reel back in shock, bumping against my bed frame. "Excuse me?"

"Did something bad happen to you today?" Nate asks again. "You don't sound like you normally do."

"What do I sound like normally?"

He makes a short, disagreeing noise. "Venice, you're changing the subject. What happened?"

"Nothing." I stubbornly refuse to tell him anything. If he can keep things from me, then I'll do the same to him. "I'm just tired. Seriously, Nate. I'm just exhausted from the school day. I'm looking forward to the weekend, when I can sleep in."

"Hm." He isn't convinced, but when am I satisfied with his unbelievable replies to the questions I ask him?

Silence stretches between us. I can faintly hear Mandy and Elijah yelling in the background; something about a hidden player in the abandoned house up ahead. I open my mouth to say I'd better hang up when Nate says, "Hey, are you doing anything tomorrow?"

"Uh, no," I say, intrigued why he would ask.

"Cool. Think we can meet and get some of that report done? We only have six weeks left to finish it."

I smother a snort of laughter. "Okay, okay. Are we going to the library or that café like last time? Wait, wasn't that a week ago?"

"Yeah. On Sunday."

I stare off into the darkness of my bedroom, thinking. Six days. It has been six days since Mom...since she...

"Did you fall asleep?"

I sigh, bringing myself back to the present. "No. Just thinking. So, where do you have in mind for our report?"

"That café was great. Nice Wi-Fi." Nate's voice implies that he's grinning, and he probably is.

"Sometimes," I say, "it seems that fast and free Wi-Fi is all that matters to you."

He's quiet again. Then he says, "Don't worry, Venice. I care about plenty of other things. They matter a lot to me. It's not just free Wi-Fi, though that *is* pretty nice..."

I let my laughter slip out this time. "Alright, I get it. What time tomorrow?"

"Whenever you're ready. I'll be waiting."

TWENTY-ONE

I avoid Florence the next morning. I have no desire to talk to her, especially after last night, and she doesn't deserve a *minute* of my time. All she'd do is criticize me, anyway.

I leave my room early in the morning, finding the things Marc has given me stacked against the wall in the hallway, along with several gift bags that hold what my family gave me. Seeing them there fills me with guilt. I wish I hadn't let Florence get me so upset last night. The others were trying so hard to help me feel good on my birthday and I had to sulk in my bedroom all night. I'm ashamed that I didn't allow them to help make my birthday better, even with the Flo fiasco.

In my mind I start rehearsing an apology and a gratitude speech but I find that no one is in the kitchen, surprisingly. It's empty and sparkling clean, also surprising. I fish leftover waffles out of the freezer, then microwave them and eat quickly. I want to leave this house as soon as possible. For all my resolve, I don't really want to face my family right now.

Once my waffles are gone, I write a quick note detailing where I am and what I'm doing and that I'll be back in a few hours, so don't worry. After sticking the note to the fridge, I exit the kitchen and slip into the entryway. I grab my coat from the closet and put it on while opening the front door and quitting the warm house for the chilly outside. It's barely eight in the morning, and I wonder if Nate has even left his place to come here. Maybe, maybe not. He had told me that he'd be waiting for when I was ready, and right now I'm ready. Did he know I was going to get up early?

I spot a distant figure walking towards me along the sidewalk, and a small smile tugs at the corners of my mouth. I watch as Nate comes closer, hands in his pockets.

He doesn't seem surprised to see me. "Thought you'd be up early," he says when he's closer.

"How?" I ask.

Nate shrugs. "Just a feeling." He studies me seriously. "Are you all right?"

I frown. "Yes, of course. Why?"

"Last night you sounded...off. Something happened to you and you won't tell me what."

"I don't need to." I begin walking, and he follows me. "It's none of your concern, Nate. But thanks all the same. Most people don't recognize when I am having a bad day."

He swings his computer bag onto his other shoulder. "Fridays are normally great for me. What caused—"

"I'm fine now," I interrupt. "You don't need to ask. Really."

We walk in silence for a minute until Nate speaks again. "So, what did you spend your time doing yesterday? You know I was at Elijah's, watching him and Mandy win their video game."

"Yesterday was really tiring for me, but I don't know why." That's all I'll let him learn. I'm not going to spill how Florence treats me and how just the mention of Marc's name spoiled my birthday and that I can't face Mom since she's still meeting up with Marc despite the tragedy last week, where she had freaked all of us by not showing up until the morning. Drunk.

There is no way I'll tell Nate these things. He doesn't share personal things like these to me, so why should I have to?

I feel Nate's eyes on me, like he's trying to read my thoughts and figure out what is bothering me, and I ignore him. Quickly digging around in my mind for something to change the subject, I say, "Do you walk everywhere? Don't you have a bike or car or something?"

"Oh." Nate looks away from me. "Yeah, I walk everywhere. Pretty much. I don't have my driver's license yet—I'm old enough to but there's no car for me to drive, so why would I get my license?" He grins down at me, and I roll my eyes. "My bike was destroyed," he continues. "I was riding it to school, and this really annoying kid pushed me over. The bike's handlebars twisted, making the bike useless."

I fight a smile. "Who was the annoying kid who pushed you?"

Nate narrows his eyes, calculating. I'm immediately wary.

"I'll tell you," he says slowly, "if you tell me why your day was miserable."

Anger boils inside of me. Can't he drop it? I don't want to tell him, and I don't have to, either.

Is this how he feels when I ask about his family? I understand now why he is so guarded. But I also realize that maybe he's asking out of genuine concern, like I am when I ask him.

"That's a no, then," Nate says after the silence between us has stretched too thin.

As much as I want to learn who pushed him over—the kid is obviously one Nate knows—I'm not going to let him know how Flo verbally abuses me. It's none of his business.

But...I *do* have something I can share.

"Yesterday was miserable for me because..." I kick at a small rock near my toe and successfully move it onto the road. "Because it was my birthday, and that meant it was also Florence's. You won't believe how hard it is to have your birthday be the same as someone else's. Flo kind of just sucked away all the excitement."

"Wait." Nate stops, whirling around to face me. I blink at him, resisting the urge to clean my glasses. A spot of something is stuck to the bottom of the lens, and it is annoying me a lot. It's like having

173

a piece of dandruff stuck to your eyelash that you can't find to brush away.

"Yesterday was your birthday?"

I startle out of my thoughts. Looking up at Nate, I collect myself and nod. "Yes. It was very...long."

He has a peculiar look in his eyes. "Why didn't you tell us? Mandy would have made cupcakes and brought them to school, and Elijah probably would have started to sing really loudly in front of everyone in the cafeteria, and I would have..." he stops, frowns at me, and doesn't finish.

"I totally forgot," I say, surprised by his sudden hesitation to not complete his sentence. "I didn't remember it was my birthday until I got back from school and found my mom decorating the house."

Nate twists his lips to one side. "You didn't remember your birthday that you share with your twin sister? And when I called you back on Mandy's phone, you didn't say anything."

"I was in a bad mood," I say dismissively.

He suddenly grabs both my wrists in his gloved hands. "Why?"

"Um..." I gulp, the unexpected touch making my heartbeat speed up. I've never had a boy touch me like this before. Though, Nate's action was a bit rough. "I-I, uh. Too much sugar?"

He doesn't move. He's still studying me thoughtfully. His hands tighten around my wrists ever so slightly, and I'm instantly aware of the fact that his blue eyes are the same color as the stone set into my ring on my pinky. The revelation flushes my cheeks pink.

Nate abruptly steps away, shaking his head in amusement. "Too much sugar?" he repeats.

"We had waffles for dinner," I whisper, watching him carefully.

"And cake for dessert?" He's back to his regular, teasing self, and for some reason I want to see more of the other side of him— that unfaltering, steady gaze that makes me want to stare right back at him until a hidden discovery becomes known.

Instead, we both turn and, walking in tandem, continue on to the Rainy Afternoon. Nothing else is said about yesterday or what has just happened only a moment ago; we talk on the subject of our report and placing bets on how long we think it will take to finish it. Nate says if today goes well, he has a feeling we'll be done after the *next* meeting. I argue that we usually get distracted or something comes up that interrupts our discussion. It'll take longer than two meetings.

Finally, our conversation turns to whatever random things we bring up. I want to know more about Nate—of course, he won't share anything with me—but he asks plenty of questions about *me*.

"Did you ever visit Hollywood?"

I shake my head. "Never. Mom would have grounded me for all eternity if I went near that place."

"How come?"

"She disagrees with them. She doesn't like how celebrities are constantly flying to different places in their private jets and ruining the environment with all the fuel the jets burn."

"So where did you live?"

"Oakland."

"Do you prefer Oakland to Virginia, or do you like the greenery around here?" Nate waves a hand at the trees surrounding the neighborhood, at the brown-spotted grass, at the vegetation deep into the woods.

I think hard. "I love California," I say after a while. "It's warm there and my grandparents—Mom's in-laws—live there, too, so we got to see them all the time. We also would go down to the beach nearly every weekend and hang out, whether with friends or just each other. And we lived in this gigantic neighborhood; there were plenty of kids our ages barely a hundred feet away from us.

"But..." I glance up at the cloudy sky. "We never saw the stars. They were always hidden by all the lights around us. And there was barely any green. So I think I prefer Virginia. We're far away from our grandparents; there aren't as many people living next to us; we're nowhere close to my dad..." I shrug. "And I have better friends here, too."

I expect Nate to be grinning—he constantly is—but when I risk a quick peek at him, he has a thoughtful frown settled across his face. His dimples aren't anywhere in sight, and I feel annoyed with myself for wanting to see them. No one in my family has dimples. Plus, Nate is just...Nate.

"If you were given the choice," he says finally, "would you move back to Oakland, or would you stay here in Virginia?"

"Stay here," I answer immediately.

He turns, surprised at my quick and heartfelt response. "Even if you could be with your dad?"

Anger flares inside of me again, this time not at Nate. "My dad rarely remembers I exist," I say, scowling at my feet as I walk and talk at the same time. "He never calls me anymore. He doesn't remember my birthday or Christmas or any other occasion. I last spoke to him face-to-face two weeks after my tenth birthday. I haven't seen him in person since. He used to call every month for a few minutes, but now he doesn't at all. He used to send me emails, but now he doesn't. I don't know if he has forgotten about me, or if he's just a lousy dad who can't spare a second of his life for his oldest daughter."

"I don't think he forgot who you are," Nate says quietly, startling me somewhat. "You're too memorable."

I laugh, though it's forced. "You really don't know me too well."

"You're right," he agrees. "I've known you for less than a month, and that isn't a long time. But if you were to move again, I wouldn't forget you. Not even for a day."

I shiver, though it has nothing to do with the cold. I glance back up at him, finding him staring right at me. I don't really know what to reply to what he has just said, so I decide on, "Um, thanks."

His lips twitch; he's trying to hide a smile at my awkwardness. I have a sudden wish to see him smile—it seems to brighten up any gloomy atmosphere—but I instead return my gaze to the sidewalk. We've just passed the library, which means we still have five more minutes until we reach the Rainy Afternoon. Hopefully those five minutes won't be supremely uncomfortable; the tension between us is growing with each step we take in silence. Nate appears to be carefully ignoring the thick cloud of discomfort that has fallen over us, and after a moment, he starts to whistle the same tune Mr. Castro does when he walks into class. I feel like his whistling is only making things worse, but I don't say anything. That would be rude.

A minute has slowly trickled by when I say, "Who was the annoying boy that pushed you over when you were riding your bike to school? You never told me."

Nate stops whistling. "Keller Jacobs."

"Really?" I'm not exactly surprised; I'd had a sneaking suspicion who it might be, but it still comes as a shock to me that Nate actually admitted it.

"Yeah. He's hated me ever since..." Nate hesitates, getting an annoyingly familiar look in his eyes. He doesn't plan on continuing his explanation.

I almost huff with irritation. "You said Keller Jacobs started smoking, and that's why you stopped being friends."

"True. That's only one of the reasons, though."

I wait expectantly, wanting to learn the other reasons why, too. However, Nate doesn't say anything else on the subject.

"Why did your parents divorce?"

I stiffen, annoyed that he can get answers out of me yet I can barely get a single answer from him. "I'll tell you if you tell me another reason why Keller Jacobs hates you," I reply, using his own design against him.

Nate frowns, but it's laced with humor. "Alright. Keller saw something he wasn't supposed to see—he was spying on me—so I confronted him and we have never liked each other since."

"What did he see? And why was he spying on you?"

He shakes his head. "I don't have to tell you. That wasn't part of the deal."

I clench my fists. Talking to Nate is near impossible. "Why don't you ever tell me? You always go mute and refuse to give me an acceptable answer for my questions."

"Because." His voice has gone cold. "It's personal."

My scowl deepens. "Then how come you manage to get me to gush out all *my* personal information?"

To my annoyance, he laughs. "You're easy to talk to," he says, swinging his computer bag onto his other shoulder. "I'd much rather listen to you speak than talk myself."

"And I'm the opposite," I say, exasperation leaking into my words. "Why do you rarely talk when we're around Elijah and Mandy? They're the ones who have to keep up the conversation at lunch. You just sit in silence and only speak when you have to."

"I'm not needed." Nate shrugs. "Plus, Elijah and Mandy and I have been friends for years. We know almost everything about each other."

That strikes a chord.

"Do they know how you're incredibly clumsy and accidentally stab yourself sometimes?" I ask sarcastically.

Nate stops suddenly, eyes boring into mine. "What?"

"Oh, come on," I say, giving a caustic laugh. "I saw your arm last week, in the hallway when you were trying to avoid your counselor. There's no way you could have been able to gouge such a deep cut in your arm by accident. And even if you had, you would have bandaged it up, first thing." I step closer to him; he flinches back. "And you have plenty of scars. I only noticed one, but there's no doubt you have more. Especially if you *accidentally* impale yourself all the time."

Nate watches me carefully, his face revealing nothing. His jaw clenches; his eyes shift slightly to stare over my shoulder at some distant thing. "Venice," he says quietly, "I don't want you to spend any more time thinking through this. Forget it. And you can *never* bring up the subject again." His eyes meet mine for barely a second before he looks away. "*Ever.*"

By now, my scowl is so fierce it hurts to hold for very long. "Why." My voice is harsh—I've only sounded this mad once when Roman ripped the cover off my favorite book.

Nate blinks at me in surprise—he probably thought I'd give up.

I hold his gaze, my facial muscles trembling as I force myself to scowl for even longer. He and I have a silent battle, neither refusing to back down; I am *done* with him keeping secrets, and it's even worse with how he's hurt and bleeding.

He suddenly laughs again, the sound slightly forced. He leans closer to me, so close my knees start to quake, and whispers, "Venice, you know you are *really* terrifying when you're mad." Then he straightens, turns around, and resumes walking towards the Rainy Afternoon.

I'm left on the sidewalk, shaking internally. Shaking with both anger and nerves.

He had been too close. I don't like having people that close, and definitely not a boy I keep getting mad at because he's tight-lipped and won't let me help him with whatever is going on.

So what if it's personal? He was bleeding and doing nothing about it! Why won't he tell me what's happening?

I glare after him, not moving. He is growing farther and farther away with each step he takes, but right now I'm considering returning home. If the rest of the day is going to be like this, then I don't want to be anywhere near him.

Especially if he won't tell me anything.

Especially if he'll get that close again.

Especially if he doggedly ignores my questions that will *help*.

With a resigned sigh, I go after him instead of away from him. I shouldn't be so pushy. I should stop asking about him and can pretend I didn't see the cut on his arm. I should do what he told me to do.

I should never bring up the subject again.

I catch up, falling into step with him. "Sorry," I say finally, resisting the urge to grab him by the shoulders and demand an answer from him, despite him being almost a foot taller than me. "I didn't mean to be so..."

"Scary?" Nate suggests. "Intimidating? Ambitious?"

I stare at him. He has switched personalities for the third time in seconds. How can he change from aggravated to cheerful and teasing? Well, I *think* he's teasing. He had better be.

"Whatever." I look away from him so he doesn't notice my eye-roll. I've calmed down considerably.

We walk in silence, but this time it's more comfortable. Just slightly more comfortable, though. It's still tense, painful. Not as much as before, however, and I'm suddenly grateful Nate forgives easily. If I had been him, I would have gone home in a rage.

Since Nate seems to be looking anywhere but me, I watch him out of the corner of my eye, noting how he walks and how he holds his computer bag and how his hands are clenched into fists. His posture is stiff and relaxed at the same time.

So what is wrong with him?

There's no way he'll tell me.

Not after what happened barely a minute ago.

I wonder if Mandy or Elijah know anything that can help me figure out why Nate is like this. I make a mental note to ask Mandy about this the next time I see her.

We pass the school, and I'm relieved that we're almost to the Rainy Afternoon. There we can finally start on our report and forget all that went on during the walk. At least, I'll try to forget. Nate acts like he already has, and it makes me both annoyed and thankful.

"You didn't answer my question," he says suddenly, breaking the silence and startling me. I hadn't expected him to talk.

"What question?"

Nate's eyes flick over to me for a brief second. "Why did your parents get divorced?"

"Oh." I squeeze my hands together. I don't like talking about it—the very reason is so *ridiculous*—but I grudgingly admit to myself that I need to keep my end of the bargain and tell him. It might open him up more. "My dad and mom had very different opinions from the start," I say, pushing my glasses up my nose. "My mom is a nature conservationist, and Dad thought that was stupid and bothersome and pointless. Even after having five kids, he still up and left us because of Mom's immoveable stances on saving the planet and going green and things like that."

I stop talking, but Nate waves me on.

"Dad complained that Mom was starving him by forcing him to eat organic food. He argued that he shouldn't have to do the stuff she does. That they have opposite beliefs and she can't force hers on him."

Nate frowns thoughtfully. "And after ten years he just decided to quit on all you guys?"

"Yeah. Pretty much. Though, on our birthday he sometimes sends Florence something."

"Your dad sends Florence things but not you? Why would he do that?"

"I don't know," I say irritably. "Why don't you ask him?"

Nate sighs softly to himself. He most likely finds me immature and childish, how I'm acting like a little kid. "Where does your dad live?" he asks.

"Nebraska?" I grimace. "I can't remember. Nevada?"

"Somewhere out west?"

I nod. "Yeah. Somewhere." My voice is tinged with melancholy.

"Do you ever wish they hadn't divorced?"

My eyes narrow. I almost don't want to let him know. "Yes," I admit. "All the time. Like..." I hesitate, then plunge on. "Like last week. When my mom was...*sick*, she kept saying Dad's name. It made me think that maybe, she also misses him. I know my siblings do. Roman wishes that Dad would help him with boy stuff like shaving. Pompeii wishes that Dad would share all his favorite books. Siena wishes that Dad would laugh at her terrible jokes and not mind her complaining. And Flo..." I hesitate again. I'm not sure I want to keep talking.

"I don't know about Flo," I admit. "She's a confusing person. But I *do* know that I would appreciate Dad coming back. At least, I think we do. Maybe we just want things to be better and we've tagged that with Dad coming back."

It's the truth. I'm still sore from his abrupt departure that tore apart my life, but I desperately want our family to be together again. We used to have so much fun with each other. Dad made us all laugh with *his* terrible jokes. He helped us figure out problems. He turned every uncomfortable, hard time in our lives into a ridiculous scenario, lightening some of the strain.

So why isn't he here now when we need him?

"I'm making you depressed again, aren't I?"

I give myself a shake and return my attention to Nate, who looks guilty and concerned. "No," I say after a moment. "Not really. I'm wondering why you're so interested in my family. Specifically my parents. You're asking a lot of personal questions."

He holds my gaze for an entire minute, which is when I realize we have stopped in the middle of the sidewalk again. I seriously doubt we'll get to the Rainy Afternoon anytime soon if we keep pausing to hold little stand-offs.

"I'm curious," Nate says after another minute has passed. "You have a mom who may or may not still love your dad. And you have a dad who has neglected his kids for the past ten years, his reasons either not understandable or idiotic."

I study Nate carefully, my expression guarded. "Yes. And what does that have to do with you?"

He doesn't reply for a long time. I've just about given up when he mutters, "I don't exactly have parents."

My jaw drops. He'd told me that he doesn't know his mom, and that his dad sent him to live with his grandpa, but this is the first time he has brought up his parents without my asking.

"You're lucky you even *have* one parent," Nate whispers, suddenly not able to look me in the eye. "I've never met my mom. And I don't really remember what my dad is like."

I wait for him to go on. Because I want to know more. I want to learn why his dad doesn't care for him—the jerk—and why he doesn't know his mom. Is she dead? Or did she just desert him, like his dad did? They both must regret not knowing Nate.

Do they? They should.

"At least you get to see your mom every day," Nate says, still not meeting my gaze. "I don't even know what my mom looks like."

I inch closer to him. "Why don't you go searching for her?"

"What, leave Virginia and my grandpa and you and Mandy and Elijah to find someone who gave up on me when I was an *infant*?"

"Yeah." I manage a small nod. "Find your dad. And your mom. Figure out why and how everything went wrong between you all."

Nate turns away from me. "No." He sounds harsh and cold— nothing like the friendly, cheerful Nate I know. "I'm not going to hunt down my parents. If they regret leaving me, then *they* can find me. For now, I'm staying here and I'm not going anywhere."

Shivering from both the chilly morning and the glare he is giving me, I pull my coat tighter around my shoulders, and brush past him. I want to get to the Rainy Afternoon before we have any more tense conversations that result in him furious at me or me furious at him.

I don't hear him following me, but he has such a soft tread I can't tell if he is behind me or not. And I don't risk looking back.

The sidewalk curves sharply at the corner of the crossroads. I stop by the street sign, waiting for any cars to pass before I attempt to walk across the road. Several cars speed by, taking no notice of the stop sign posted right next to me, and it flares up my irritation. Why can't drivers obey the laws and stop when they have to?

I don't mind waiting. I was born into an impatient family, so tolerance is something I've developed. I won't say I'm excellent at being patient, because I'm not, but I can bear a minute or two of watching the cars flash by without tapping my foot.

However, it's the matter of Nate that makes the back of my neck itch. I want to enter the café as soon as possible, as quickly as possible. And I can't while I'm standing on the curb, waiting for the ignorant drivers to speed by me.

I'm lucky they're going fast. And there aren't many. This strip mall isn't very popular—it attracts a decent amount of customers—and the roads aren't super busy.

When the last car has gone by, I start across the street, nearing the Rainy Afternoon. I need to welcome the faint jazzy music and the delicious smells and the quietness that fills the shop. Hopefully Nate will also calm enough for us to resume the slow progress of our report. We haven't even started on the presentation. Yes, yes, we have six weeks to do this, but if we don't get *some* done, I'll begin to worry and stress about not finishing it in time.

A low rumble splits the air, startling me from my thoughts. I pause in the middle of the street—a terrible idea, but I'm stuck to the asphalt where I stand.

The sound is slightly familiar. I list my head, trying to determine when I've heard it before. It's obviously an engine. A car engine.

Someone yells my name.

I turn slowly towards the source, first spotting Nate running towards me, then the huge black SUV roaring down the street, coming closer to me by the second.

It looks *and* sounds familiar. Where have I seen and heard it?

I suddenly realize it's about to hit me. I probably shouldn't have stopped in the street. Now that I think of it, it's incredibly stupid.

Why would you freeze in the middle of the road with a car rushing at you? Chances are, you will be flattened.

Only one thought flits through my mind as I brace myself for impact.

Why hasn't the car slowed down?

Then something hits me and I'm flung back, landing awkwardly half on the sidewalk and half on the road, pain racing jolting through my entire body. I smack my head on the curb and my vision goes black.

TWENTY-TWO

The first thing I register is the horrible smell. The twisting, stinking smell of exhaust. It fills my head, drifting through all my senses until I realize another thing that makes me forget the exhaust.

I'm not dead.

A startled laugh bursts out of me, triggering a sharp throb in my head. I turn the laugh into a grunt. One hand moves to reach up and touch my head, but I can't. My hands refuse to cooperate. Nothing in my body is cooperating right now.

The third realization is that people are talking. Worried voices overlapping each other, words blending together so I can't understand what the people are saying. Not that I really care. All I care about is that I'm not dead and my head hurts and the lingering exhaust is doing nothing to decrease the discomfort.

The fourth thing I discover is that I can't see. My sight is blocked by a dark red-and-black curtain. Panic speeds up my heartbeat, and I almost start to hyperventilate when I find out my eyes are closed.

Oh. How stupid of me.

Maybe I hit my head too hard.

I crack open my eyelids, bright light temporarily blinding me. Blurry shapes begin to appear, though they remain blurry. I can see the figures, just not in detail. My glasses aren't on my face, which explains my horrible eyesight, why I can't focus.

A fifth thing makes itself known. I'm still half on the hard, gritty road and half on the smooth, cold curb. My head is using the curb as the world's most uncomfortable pillow. A headache is throbbing in my skull, a dim reminder of what just happened.

The car. Coming closer and closer.

Me. Frozen to the street.

Nate. Running towards me.

His name sends a shiver of fear racing down my spine, which in fact, hurts a lot, too.

Nate. Where is he? He hasn't been hit by the car, has he? How did he *not* get hit? He probably wasn't in the way enough. Last time I'd seen him, he was at the stop sign, on the other side of the road.

Could he have…

I snap my thoughts shut. I won't think about it. Right now, I have to…have to see. I need my glasses.

I force my hands to move, and thankfully they do. My fingers dance over the rough, bumpy asphalt, searching for my glasses. I can't find them, and after several fruitless attempts, I give up. I'll just ask the people above me if they have seen them.

Trying to sit up is a bad idea. My headache flares even worse, and with a barely-stifled groan, I relax against the curb.

The chattering is ceased as someone else speaks.

"Venice. Venice, what were you *thinking*?"

I nearly laugh, but remembering the pain that was caused earlier for doing that, I settle for trying to sit up again.

Nate grabs my hand, helping me, and I press my fingers to my head as a wave of nausea washes over me. I hurt all over. My back and my spine and my neck and especially my head and pretty much every bit of me aches. I want to rest back on the curb, but I tell myself I *have to* sit up. I have to let Nate know I'm not about to pass out again.

"Can I have my glasses?" I ask, my voice slurred. Talking doesn't lessen the pain at all. If anything, it makes it worse.

"Your glasses?" Nate repeats.

I tighten my grip on his hand. "Yes. My glasses. Where are they? I can't see a thing."

Cold metal is pressed into my other hand. I recognize just by feeling them that one of the lenses is cracked. With a sigh, I slide them on, blinking as my eyes finally focus.

My gaze sharpens on Nate, who is crouching on the road inches away from me, his face white. His eyes are anxious and hold a glint of exasperation—he must be annoyed at me for freezing in the middle of the street instead of darting to the safety of the sidewalk.

"Hi," I say, unsure of what else I should say.

Nate groans and gently pulls me to my feet. Too much pain for that small movement swirls through me, making my vision dim again. I latch onto his other arm, squeezing so hard he winces.

"Take it easy," he mutters, his mouth right next to my ear.

I have to suppress a shiver at how close he is. "Yeah, yeah. I got it, thanks." All the same, I relax my grip on his arm.

A group of concerned people are surrounding us, asking questions and offering rides to the hospital or if they need to call the police or call my mom or someone who can help. I sway on my feet. Nate is the only thing keeping me standing. I want to sit down on a plushy seat. I want my racing heart to calm down and for that too-familiar SUV never to come back.

I've seen it before. It zoomed past me on my first day of school when I was walking home with Nate. And it splashed me with muddy water on that day when Marc came over for dinner. The exhaust gives it away. Otherwise I'd just think it was another car that had the misfortune of almost running me over, turning me into a pancake flattened to the road.

"Are you all right, Venice? What hurts?"

I look up at Nate, my cracked lens distorting his face. "Um, yeah. I'm fine, Nate. I nearly got hit by a car and my entire body hurts and I have a serious craving for chocolate."

He doesn't laugh. The corners of his mouth twitch, however, and I feel like I've earned something.

Leaning closer to him, I mutter, "Can you get rid of all these people? They are doing wonders to my head. And I'm thoroughly embarrassed."

"But are you sure you don't need to go to the hospital? Did you break anything? You hit your head pretty hard. You might have a concussion."

"I'm just really sore, I think. And, yeah, my head hurts. Can we go some place and sit down?"

Nate helps me walk, step by step, towards the Rainy Afternoon just barely twenty feet from us. The crowd of people follow us, still asking questions and increasing the throbbing sensation in my body. I ache and I really do have a craving for chocolate. Maybe a cup of hot chocolate from the café will fix me up.

We're at the door when I realize something. I turn to my friend and say, "Nate, where's your laptop?"

"On the other side of the street." He opens the door and ushers me in, closing the door behind us on the concerned people.

I frown, looking around the café. It's more empty than usual— some of the customers must be part of the group of people outside. It warms me to see how they had left their stuff behind to check on me. Yet I had turned away from them.

I tell Nate I want to go back out. Pressing a hand against the door, I push it open and say to the people, "Thank you for your concern. I'm doing a lot better now. No need to call the police or take me to the hospital. I think I'll be perfectly fine."

Nate holds the door with one arm and me with another, and that's also rather embarrassing, but I feel comforted by his concern.

"That car came out of nowhere," says a woman near me. "You are a lucky thing that you weren't hit."

"I know." I smile grimly, my facial muscles screeching in aching protest. "It was stupid of me to stop in the middle of the road. But I was paralyzed. I hadn't expected that car to come rushing around the corner."

Several heads bob in agreement.

"Didn't even slow," says a tall man standing next to the woman who had spoken earlier. "The driver saw you, yet he didn't make any attempt to slow down."

"Must not have been paying attention," says another woman. "Or he just wanted to hit you." She gives me an indescribable look.

I blink. "Who would want to hit me?"

"That's not something I know!" she says, laughing. "It's only a theory, dear. More likely the driver didn't have his eyes on the road. Dangerous business, driving." She grimaces, facing the other adults. "Did any of you see what he looked like?"

"He was definitely a he," says a third woman. "Had red hair."

"Or orange," says the young man at her side. He meets my gaze. "His car windows were tinted dark, hiding most of his features. But he had reddish orange hair."

I nod slowly. I haven't seen him before. Unless we somehow accidentally walked past each other on some random occasion.

"Alright." I shift my weight to my other foot, the small action sending more pain shooting through me. I flinch. "Thanks," I say again. "Thanks for all your help."

"Of course," the woman closest to me says fondly, patting my wrist. She leans even closer to me and whispers, "Don't forget to thank *him*." And, to my absolute shock, she winks.

I'm left stunned as Nate and I slowly return to the café where he's picked out a secluded space with a cushy armchair that I slowly sink into. Nate is very solicitous and doesn't let go of me until I'm safely ensconced in the deep cushions. I can't feel his hands—they are covered in the thin material of his gloves—but I imagine they are warm and soft and I have the most undesirable urge to take off his gloves.

He'll get mad at me if I do.

I still want to.

"Venice." Nate pulls a chair up close to me. "Are you really fine? Or are you saying that so someone won't call the ambulance?"

I swallow hard. "Um…" I can't put together a sentence.

He frowns, cocking his head to one side. "Venice?"

"Can I…" my mouth dries. "Can I just get some water and maybe just close my eyes for a minute? Then I'll answer. I need to just breathe a bit before I…"

The same waitress as before appears instantly, handing me a glass of crystal-clear water. I accept it and thank her warmly, and she smiles and scurries off to fill another order. I take a sip of the cold beverage, the ice clinking merrily, and allow it to flow through my aching body and relieve some of the pounding pain.

Finally, I set down the glass and relax against the back of my chair. Nate hasn't moved. "I'm so tired," I mumble. I definitely had *not* expected the day to go like this. "And, Nate, I'm terrified. That car nearly hit me. I would have been crushed if you hadn't saved me." I gulp and risk a look up. He's leaning in, an intense look of concern on his face. It does nothing to soothe my nerves.

"So…" I clear my throat. "Thank you. A lot."

He doesn't reply.

I'm growing more nervous than ever. My fingers twitch, and I unconsciously twist the ring on my pinky finger.

But it isn't there.

Panicked, I hold up my hands, finding no ring. Where is it? I'm sure I was wearing it when I left this morning. It's the only thing I have from Dad except for memories, and some of those are hazy and half-forgotten.

Nate notices my agitation. "What's wrong? Venice?"

"My ring." I sit up, searching my pockets, my coat, wearily, painfully. I start to get down on the floor, but Nate stops me and I don't have the strength anyway. "Nate, did you see a small gold ring with a blue stone anywhere?"

He hesitates. "Gold with a blue stone? I've noticed you wear it before. Is it special to you?"

"Yes, very!" I nearly shout, attracting the attention of the few remaining customers. "My dad gave it to me. It's the only thing he's sent me since the divorce. Do you know where it is?" I start to get up—well, I try, anyway.

"Venice, sit down." Nate gently forces me back onto my chair.

I'm still shaking. I have to find it. That ring is one of the most precious things I own.

After a quick glance around, Nate leans forwards and whispers, "I have your ring. Just hold tight a moment. I'm going to go across the street and get my laptop before someone steals it. Can you wait for me here? Promise not to chase after me and almost get hit?"

"Fine." I spit out the word. "Hurry up."

He smiles, though it's nothing like his usual smile, and quickly leaves the café. I watch him through the window, wondering why he won't give me my ring back and why I have to wait for him and why he didn't tell me he had it until I brought up the subject.

I'm bursting with impatience when he finally returns, computer bag on one shoulder. He slides into his seat, placing the bag in his lap. I open my mouth to demand my ring, only to be stopped as he raises a hand and softly says, "Wait."

Snapping my mouth shut, I obey him and wait. My anger at him has flared considerably.

"Venice." Nate places the ring on our table, out of my reach. "Just listen to me for a second. Please."

I fidget with my fingers. "Hurry."

He sighs. "I am." Flipping open his laptop, he spends a long time typing on the keyboard, longer than I would have taken. Maybe he *is* slower than I am. He told me that once.

"This is pointless," he mutters, closing the laptop. He meets me gaze and continues. "When that car sped by, I was the closest to it. I saw the license plate and the driver and what he wanted."

"What? He wanted something?"

Nate motions to my ring. "That."

I give a caustic laugh. "Don't be ridiculous. Who would want a dumpy ring like mine?"

"You don't think it's dumpy."

I wave a hand. "Whatever. It's just a word Florence used to describe it."

Nate studies my face intently. "Venice, when that car came roaring around the corner, the driver had plenty of time to slow down. Why didn't he? And he could have easily swerved to the side to avoid you."

"He—"

Nate shuts me up with just a look. "Please. Just listen. We've seen that car before. It drove past us that first day of school. Remember?" He doesn't let me answer, which makes me think how that *remember* was useless. "The driver is looking for something. And I think it's your ring. I don't know why, and what for, but this is the second—"

"Third," I interrupt. "The car drove right by me another time. A week and a half ago, this same car splashed me. He could have gone by without doing it. It confused me why he did, and that was the day Marc..." I freeze in my chair as I recall that evening.

Marc had come to dinner.

He had made everything uncomfortable and awkward and I had ended up in my room to escape him.

Oh, and to escape Florence, too.

"Marc?" Nate repeats.

I blink at him, pulling myself back to Earth. "Yeah. Marc Tyron. He's kinda like my mom's...boyfriend." I gag over the word. Nate pretends not to notice and I thank him for it.

"Was he the man over on the first day of school?" Nate leans forward, the café table suddenly too small for both of us. I fight the urge to back away as he continues. "When we stopped at your house," he says, "there was a red pick-up in your driveway. It was unfamiliar to you. Was that Marc Tyron's truck?"

I slowly nod, dumbfounded that he remembered about the truck. "Yeah. Two days later—"

"You said we couldn't meet and work on the report because a visitor was coming for dinner," Nate cuts in, pointing a gloved finger at me. "And when I asked if you didn't like him, you said how that was an understatement. But also that maybe you judged him too fast."

My jaw is dropping farther and farther down with each word he says. How can he, word for word, recite our conversation from nearly two weeks ago? *I don't even remember it all!*

"I'm guessing you still don't like him," says Nate. He is watching me carefully.

"Nope," I cough out. "Especially not after—" I stop abruptly.

Something flashes in Nate's blue eyes. Something that looks slightly like triumph?

"After what?" he asks, coming even closer.

"I don't want to talk about it," I whisper. I look down at my lap, tugging at my pinky finger. It usually has my ring on it, and seeing it bare sends a shiver running through me. When will Nate give me my ring back? Why does he think that driver wanted it? This is all so confusing and bizarre and dangerous. I've had my share of action. Almost getting hit by a car is enough to last a lifetime for me.

"Venice, it was so weird after I pulled you out of the road."

I don't meet his gaze.

"You were unconscious for a few minutes. It all happened so fast, I practically tackled you to get you out of the way. But the driver skidded to a halt. I thought he was going to get out and make sure you were okay. Instead, he turned his head and glared at me so badly it made me worried he would come after me next."

He leans in closer and brings his voice lower, so low I have to strain to hear him. "But he searched the ground for something—

your ring—and he spotted it right next to my shoe. If I could have seen his face better, I'm positive I would have recognized greed. He made as if to go for the ring, but I reached for it and put it in my pocket. Instantly he took off. By then people had started to gather anyway."

"Why would he want my ring?" I whisper, almost breathlessly. We're so close I'm worried to breathe too much.

Nate shrugs, sitting back in his chair. "I was hoping you could tell me?"

"Nope." I inhale deeply to soothe my nerves. Somehow, he being that close was more frightening than the oncoming car. I don't bother wondering why.

"You were telling me about what happened with Marc," he says. He doesn't seem to want to give up on that.

I glare at him.

"Look, maybe there's a connection with today's event and Marc. You said your mom was really tired," Nate continues. "The day after she was gone for an entire night. Does that have to do with Marc and why you dislike him so much?"

"Yes." I force the word past my numb lips. "That's why. Now, can you take me home?

Nate stares at me for a long time. I try not to notice that his eyes remind me of my ring's stone. Or that the way he's looking at me makes me want to straighten in my seat and gaze right back at him. An unwanted, unexpected thought wiggles into my mind, starling me so badly I drop my gaze and look at my lap again.

It's no wonder Flo flirted with him. He is naturally handsome.

My cheeks go bright red at the realization.

He groans in embarrassment. "I'm such a jerk. Of course I'll take you home. You're probably so tired. Can I call your mom to come get you? She may want to take you to the hospital just to make sure you didn't really damage anything."

I lift my head quickly—bad idea—and stare at him in horror.

"No. I can't. I don't want to stress her more than she is. I'm fine, really, but I do think I should get home."

He is silent for a moment. Then he says, "But you almost got hit by a car. Don't you think your mom would want to know?"

"Of course I'll tell her, but I don't need to go to the hospital. I just want to go home. Please understand, Nate. I nearly got run over by a car and my head hurts and I want to go home and pretend I only tripped and got hurt, not something completely different." I drop my eyes to my lap, to my pinky that is ring-free.

When he doesn't reply, I risk a glance up and see his expression is full of concern for me and my decision. It also holds a hint of distress. I wish he would stop looking at me like that. It makes me want to do whatever he wants.

He's a little like Siena—able to twist your insides and make you feel guilty for letting him down.

I really need to stop getting into conversations with him that lead to this.

Nate doesn't say anything for another whole minute. Finally, he turns his head and stares pointedly out the window. "All right," he concedes. "But we should walk slowly. For your sake."

"Okay."

I nab my ring off the table-and slide it on my pinky as I get to my feet. I have to close my eyes for a second before I'm ready to walk, but aside from the pounding in my head, I feel steadier.

"And I'd appreciate it if you told me about Marc sometime," he adds, opening the café door for me. I frown to myself as I exit, thinking he didn't need to say that. Then again, he isn't telling Mom about the near-fatal accident today just because I don't want him to, and he isn't making me go to the hospital.

The crowd of people outside the café has disappeared. No one is on the sidewalk except for an old man slowly hobbling towards a cell phone repair shop down the street. The chilly morning air still lingers, but the sun has forced its way out of the clouds, washing the area in yellow light. Any other time, I'd love to see the sun out and shining; this very moment, however, it does nothing to cheer me up.

I cross the road with Nate at my side, and though I constantly twist around to make sure there aren't any cars, we arrive at the other side safely, if in heavy silence.

We wander in the direction of my house, not saying a thing. My headache doesn't go away—it increases with every step I take—and my broken glasses cut up my view of the sidewalk. I know I shouldn't have my eye so close to broken glass, but I need them on to see. I don't want to be walking around blind, and that'll happen if I take them off. That's one thing I really hate about myself: I have to wear glasses or my eyes are pretty much useless. I wonder how Mom gave her terrible eyesight to all of us except Pompeii—it might be because he loves reading and needs good eyes to see the tiny print in those biographies he enjoys.

I hadn't thought my pain could get worse, but I'm wrong. I feel something burning on my elbow and look down to see a dark spot has leached into my coat sleeve. I shrug out of my coat, still walking, and flip it over one arm while I examine my elbow.

It's scraped raw, blood spilling down my arm.

It also stings. A lot.

Huffing, I check my other elbow.

Not bleeding, but my forearm has a nasty scrape.

I'm lucky my coat protected my skin like this. I might have had little bits of asphalt embedded in my flesh if I hadn't worn a coat. Or long sleeves, at least.

A drop of blood falls onto the sidewalk. And that's when Nate notices my condition.

He stops, staring at my arms. "You're hurt."

"Not too badly," I say stiffly, not having completely forgiven him. But why I got mad at him is now lost in my mind. I can't remember the reason. I know there's a reason.

Nate gently takes my arm in his gloved hand, turning it over to inspect my bleeding elbow. "You're right," he says. "It's not too bad. You'll survive."

I roll my eyes.

"Can I see your other arm?"

I turn, offering him my left arm, where the patch of scratched skin is oozing crimson-red blood. Nate spends more time studying it than my elbow, and after a long, hard minute, he nods and steps away from me, releasing my arm.

"It's more banged-up than your elbow," he says. "But it's not critical."

"Really?" I peer at it. "I won't have to get it amputated?"

Nate grins at me, all our past anger gone. "No," he says. "No amputation. Unless you want to."

"Cut off my arm?" I snort. "That sounds like something Elijah would do. For fun."

"Amputate your arm or his?"

I roll my eyes, resuming my steady pace towards home. "His, obviously. The only person who would let Elijah cut off their arm is Mandy. Because she will do *anything* for him."

"I've observed them for the past few years," he says, hovering closer than necessary; he must be expecting me to faint. "They are pretty much meant for each other."

"I know!" I spread out my hands, the action stretching my sore skin and sending pain racing down my arms. I wince. "From the moment I met the two of them, I knew they're destined to be together. Mandy is interested in video games like Elijah, and Elijah is flattered that she likes the same games. One of these days, we need to knock their heads together and make them realize how perfectly matched they are."

"Elijah's cousin is coming next week," says Nate. "We could do something then."

I twist my lips to the side. "And what would we do?"

198

"Talk to Mandy first," Nate suggests. "She's more hopelessly in love with Elijah than he is with her. I mean, he still likes her, but she lets it show more."

I nod slowly. "Ah. Got it."

"You should talk to Mandy. You're better at girl stuff than me."

I stare at him wide-eyed as he laughs. "If you're suggesting that I'm good at being a matchmaker," I say, "then you are wrong."

"Dang it. It's always embarrassing when you're wrong. I guess I just thought you'd be interested."

My humorous stare falters. I have absolutely no experience with romance, either my own or my friends'. I've only watched Flo at work and listened on the occasion when she needed to talk, but when it comes to Flo I make a conscious effort to stay completely out of it if I can. Personally, I don't approve of teen-age romance, mostly because of Flo's experiences.

"...blanked out again," Nate is saying, shaking me from my thoughts. He's also grinning at me. "You did it again."

"Did what?" I ask with a slight hint of weariness. I need to rest. Heal. My head is pounding, worse than ever before. The scratches on my forearm and elbow are raw and chafing and painful. I think I have some on the back of my shoulders too because I've started to notice a stinging sensation there.

"This is the second time you've zoned out," says Nate. "I'm really concerned you have a concussion."

"Actually, I zone out kind of often. Roman calls it La-La Land," I reply dully. My pain is quickly turning into exhaustion. "But I am having a hard time concentrating right now."

Nate draws closer, studying me intently, expression suddenly serious. My palms begin to sweat, much to my confusion. Why are my palms sweating?

Then his gaze slides off my face and over to the row of houses we walk past to get to mine, and I take in a deep breath of air. I hadn't realized I was neglecting the vital duty of inhaling oxygen.

Nate stiffens. He gently grabs my arm, careful of my bleeding patch of skin, and softly says, "Don't be rash."

"What?" I blink at him, my heartbeat picking up speed.

"Marc is at your house," he whispers.

I snap around, yanking my arm out of his grip and the sudden movement sends needle sharp pains through my aching head. Maybe I am going to faint. But the adrenaline surge is on.

Sure enough, a red pick-up is innocently sitting in my driveway, nearly hidden by the enormous full-sized van belonging to our next-door neighbor that is parked near our mailbox. All my focus is on the pick-up, though. I'm seething with anger and blind rage and my irrational, concussed brain nearly misses what Nate tells me next.

"Venice, please don't be impulsive," he says. "I know you want to storm over there and sock him in the eye—"

"Thanks for the idea," I growl, stomping across the street.

He hurries to catch up with me. "Wait! Please!" He slips his hand into mine, tugging me to a stop on the sidewalk in front of my house. "Please, wait a few seconds. Someone else is here, too. It's not just Marc. There is another car besides his."

TWENTY-THREE

As soon as he says that, I spot a white Prius pulled up against the curb in front of Mom's hybrid. I frown. Who else is here?

The door to our house is flung open. "Venice!"

I jolt. Whipping my head up, and instantly regretting the violent movement, I squint painfully at the figure in the doorway. I can't recognize her face with my broken lens and my pounding headache and the fury swelling through me and—oh. Nate is still holding my hand, too. That is really not helping. But the voice is familiar.

"I'll see you later," I say bluntly, snatching my hand out of his grasp. I hope none of my family saw us like this.

Nate nods. "Okay. Good luck." He turns and starts walking away in the direction he always goes, and immediately I have the strange impulse to run after him and not have to deal with Marc and the owner of the white Prius. It isn't the first time I've wanted to drop everything and follow Nate. I doubt I ever will, though.

The thought is somewhat unfortunate to me.

"Venice!" the woman calls again.

Returning my attention to her, I make my way up the lawn to the door. As I come closer, I see she is heartbreakingly recognizable.

"Grandma Pope!" I hug her tightly. "What are you doing here?"

Mom's mom pats my back. "My dear Venice! You have grown six inches since I last saw you!"

"What are you doing here?" I repeat.

"Happy late birthday!" She hugs me again. "Your grandfather and I wanted to surprise you and Florence, so we drove up from Florida yesterday and arrived here only twenty minutes ago. Linda—sorry, your mother—told me you were out and about, and we didn't expect you back this early." She winks at me. "Who was that you were with?"

"Just a friend," I say, sliding past her. I'm super glad to see her, but my heart is still pounding because of that truck outside. I need to face Marc.

Grandma is chattering kindly, but I'm so distracted with what I'm going to say to Marc that I don't pay much attention. So when I bump into Grandpa Pope in the entryway, I do a double take. "Grandpa Pope! Hey, how are you doing? Is your garden still alive?"

He chuckles and hugs me. "It died a year ago, unfortunately. But your grandma and I won't give up!"

"Good." I peer over his shoulder—he's pretty short—and spot motion in the living room.

I duck under Grandpa's arm and enter the living room, stopping when I see Marc on the couch with Mom, laughing brightly at something she just said. My teeth grind.

Mom looks up, cheeks pink. Her gaze falls on me. Her jaw drops. "Venice? What? Why are your glasses broken? Why are you *bleeding*? What happened? Are you all right?"

My shoulders are trembling. I throw my coat into the hallway closet and, not caring that we have guests over, march up to Marc.

"What are *you* doing here?" I snap, crossing my arms tightly.

He assumes a surprised look. "Am I not allowed to visit Linda?"

"Of course not!" I snarl. "Not after last week! How *dare* you even talk to her after what you did!"

Marc gapes at me.

"Venice," says Mom, her tone stiff. "That is not how you treat our guests. Please apologize. And have you seen that Grandma and Grandpa Pope have arrived? And what happened to you?"

"I'm not going to apologize to him!" I shout, pointing a finger at Marc. "He is the one who should have to apologize."

Mom stands up. "That is enough, young lady. I think it's best that you go take care of those scratches right *now*."

I shove my cracked glasses up my nose. I turn on my heel and leave the living room, annoyed at myself for backing down so easily. I should have fought back. I should have…

Pushing past my gawking grandparents, I storm upstairs. With each stomp up the steps I remember how tired, hurt, and scared I am from everything that's happened today. My anger is suddenly gone and I allow myself to feel the gamut of emotions I've been trying to hold back. I should have listened to Nate. Instead, I was impulsively rude to my grandparents and confrontational with Marc, and now Mom is mad at me when I could really use her love and concern.

Siena is sitting on the top of the staircase, chin on her palms, struggling to hide a smile that is desperate to blossom. She shakes with uncontrollable laughter, trying to force it deep inside of her.

"Venice," she says, "that was amazing. None of us had the guts to do that to Marc. You are our hero."

"Then why don't I feel like one?" I mutter, stepping around her, surprised to find myself fighting back tears.

I notice a hard-backed book resting against the wall by my door. It's the one Marc gave me, the one I refused to take. The box of candies I had also gotten isn't there—I have a sneaking suspicion that Pompeii or Siena or maybe Roman has eaten them. And my other presents are there, too, clearly snooped in.

Snatching up the book and the few bags, I roughly shove open the bedroom door, startling Flo, who is sitting on her bed. She looks up from her phone as I stomp in, her bright red lipstick perfectly smeared across her mouth.

"Where have you been?" she asks.

I kick the door shut with my heel. "Out."

"Your glasses are broken."

"I know." I toss the stuff onto my bed. "I fell over. They cracked. It wasn't my fault."

Flo raises an elegant eyebrow. "You were out with that one boy again."

"Yeah." I flop down on the floor, snatch up my phone from my bedside table. Turning it on, I see Mandy has texted me. She wants to know if I can come hang out with her later today for lunch and video games. I'm not in the mood, so I decline.

"What's his name again?" Flo asks innocently.

I glare at her. After a moment, I mutter, "Nate."

Flo switches off her phone, placing it next to her on the bed. She studies me. "How did you fall over? He push you into the road or something? It sure does look like it."

I stare at her. She doesn't know how close to the truth she is.

I'm not ready to tell her what happened. Why, I don't know. Maybe because it all sounds so very ridiculous. Almost getting hit by a car...the driver wanting—according to Nate's theory—a worthless ring that I'd gotten from Dad on my fifteenth birthday...

"You're bleeding," says Flo.

I hold up my arms, checking on the raw skin. "I know. I should probably go clean them up, but I don't want to."

"Because of Marc?" she guesses.

I nod. "Yes. Why is he here, anyway? I thought Mom..."

"He showed up minutes after you left," says Flo, twisting a lock of her hair around her finger. "And he and Mom sat in the living room and talked for a bit, and then Grandma and Grandpa Pope arrived, which was a birthday surprise for us."

I rub my forehead. "And our grandparents are okay with Marc being over here?"

Flo shrugs. "I don't know. She's a grown woman, Venice, and has been for years. I think they're long past the point of trying to manage her life decisions. Besides." my twin says. "It was Mom's fault she drank too much. She is to blame, not Marc." Flo swings her legs off the bed and stands, only to sit by my side. She's grabbed a little alcohol swab and indicates to me that she wants to help clean my elbow. "What book did he give you?"

Florence's tenderness is just enough to make my emotions start to spill out. To keep the tears at bay, I reach up and drag the book off my blankets. I flip open the cover and read the title. "He gave me *The Merchant of Venice* by William Shakespeare."

"What a play on your name, eh?" Flo nudges my ribs with her elbow. "But isn't that boring poetry?"

"Shakespeare's plays aren't boring," I say. "Though he did write a couple of rather dull sonnets. His plays are written in interesting English, and it's quite hard to understand." I tap a finger against the spine. "I don't want this book. But I know someone who might."

Marc stays all day. He leaves only after dinner, and that's when I finally breathe a sigh of relief. Grandma and Grandpa Pope seem to like him, having fallen for his charming smile, amusing stories, and flattering words. I work hard to pointedly look everywhere but at him. My feelings towards him are not concealed at all.

As soon as Marc finally leaves, Mom turns to me. "What was *that*?" she demands.

I raise my chin, broken glasses distorting her angry face. "I don't like him," I say proudly. "He is a terrible, horrible person who doesn't deserve to be in your presence. I don't know *how* you tolerate his presence when it's clear he's not a moral man."

"Did you hit your head or something?" snaps Mom. "Why are you acting so strangely?"

"Of course I hit my head," I say, resisting the urge to scoff. "But that did nothing to change my mind about Marc. He's *bad*, Mom. I can sense it. He's a rotten man."

Mom yanks my glasses off. I see her blurry form fingering the lens. "And how did you break these?"

"Fell over."

"Did Marc push you?" she asks sarcastically.

I narrow my eyes and slowly shake my head. What is she up to?

"Was it the boy you walk to school with?"

I hesitate. Technically, Nate *had* been the reason my glasses broke, but he was preventing me from becoming road-kill. I'm not completely sure why I don't want to tell my family about my dance with death today, so I just shake my head again and say, "No. It wasn't him."

"Did *anyone* push you over?"

"Myself."

She isn't amused. "If Marc didn't push you, then you can't claim that he is a terrible, horrible man. And I know him best. Better than you do, better than your siblings do."

"Can I have my glasses back?"

Mom hesitates. Finally, she slides them on my face, allowing me to see the angry expression she is wearing. "When did you become so judgmental, Venice?" she whispers. "You used to be my perfect little girl. You used to tell me everything and act politely, but now you won't tell me about your friends and you don't even disguise your hatred towards Marc."

"I don't *hate* him," I say harshly, crossing my arms over my chest. "I dislike him intensely. There's a difference, Mom."

She opens her mouth to say something, but I continue.

"And for my friends, if you want to use something against me, just talk to Flo. She'll be happy to supply false information about them and me that makes me look bad."

Mom's expression changes slightly. She isn't angry any more—sympathy has taken over the fury. "Is this all because of Flo?" she asks softly. We're alone in the kitchen—everyone else is downstairs watching a movie—so it's not like anyone can hear what we're saying. "Is your new attitude because of how your sister treats you at school and at home?"

"What?" My arms unravel. "No, why would you think—"

"You're acting like her," Mom says worriedly, scanning my face with a hint of desperation in her gaze. "You're acting like Florence. All your secretive meetings with that boy; yelling at people; ignoring your grandparents when they drove this far to visit with you—"

"Woah!" I hold up my hands, stopping her. "*Secretive*? I'm not meeting with Nate *secretively*. I told you, Mom, we're working on a report for biology. On orangutans."

Mom chews on her bottom lip. "Oh. I thought you were doing other...stuff. Not school stuff."

I stare at her in horror, my cheeks flaming. "No! That's gross!"

"Hey." She gives me a serious look. "You came back scraped and bleeding and your glasses broken today. My first thought was that you were in some sort of gang, and you were plotting world domination—"

Mom says it with such a straight face that at first I think she's serious. Then the absurdity of it all makes me burst out laughing. Soon Mom is laughing with me and it's like we can't stop. When the tears start flowing I let them come, grateful for the safety of laughter to hide them.

Finally, Mom calms. "You say you just fell over and you were doing *school stuff*," she says, looking deeply into my eyes. "Tell me, Venice. How does one who is working on a report suddenly fall over and break her glasses and scrape her arms?"

"I—" I hesitate, then quickly say, "I tripped. My glasses dropped off my nose and I accidentally fell on them. And I skinned my forearm and elbow in the process." I feel bad lying to her, but I'm sure she'd take me to the hospital and I'm just so tired.

Mom glares at me, not completely believing my story. It's no wonder. I'm a terrible liar. She says that's a good thing, but there are times—like right now—I wish I was convincing.

"Fine." She shrugs. "You tripped. We're going to have to buy you new glasses, and I haven't contacted any eye doctors around here, so you'll have to sit tight before I can get you another pair. You don't have a spare, do you?"

I shake my head. She rolls her eyes.

"Okay," she says. "Now, tell me why you hate—sorry, *dislike*—Marc so much."

I scrunch up my nose. "Beside the fact that he brought you home drunk and didn't even bring you in the house, but just drove off? His aura is off."

Mom's jaw drops. "His *aura*? What are you even talking about, Venice?"

"Everyone has an aura," I say stubbornly. I know what I'm saying is slightly childish, but I don't really care. "Of all people, Mom, you should understand these kinds of things. It's not too different from your belief that all living things have a vital energy. You have an aura, Mom. Yours is light green with shades of blue twisted in-between. One moment you're energetic and bouncy and *alive*, and the next you're depressed and escaping us to hang out with Marc."

Mom's jaw drops even lower. I keep going.

"Like whenever you're with Marc," I say, "your aura is flickering back and forth from blue to green. You're happy, but you're sad. I'm guessing Marc reminds you of the time you were dating Dad."

Her face goes pale.

"Marc's aura is..." I search for an appropriate word and settle for: "wicked. It's silvery but dark at the same time. Like you, they alternate according to his mood. When I'm around, he acts silvery, but he's dark. When you're with him, it's silver. He's happy to see you—he is *not* happy to see me. For some reason, he doesn't like me."

"Maybe it's because you don't like him?" Mom suggests, her voice lilting towards sarcasm once more.

I sigh. Rubbing my forehead with a cold hand, I say, "Maybe. But there's something else, too. Something he has against me.

There's more than just my dislike for him that makes *him* dislike *me*."

"What on Holy Mother Earth would Marc have against you, Venice?"

I wearily shake my head. "I don't know. It started ever since that day we first met. He immediately knew I disliked him. He knew I felt his aura was off. I wasn't very discreet about showing how I felt towards him. Yet he hasn't done anything *bad*, except for bringing you home drunk after an entire night. And Marc hasn't harmed any of us or been creepy to me or Flo—he bought us birthday presents—but I still don't like him."

Mom huffs. "Please tell me it's not because of your dad."

"I don't know if I like Dad, either," I say, jutting my chin out. "He seems to have forgotten I exist."

Her sharp gaze softens somewhat. "I know," she says. "He didn't even give Florence anything this year like he usually does, and she was pretty bummed out."

"About not receiving a gift or not receiving a gift from Dad?"

"No clue." Mom tucks a curl behind my ear. "You don't like Marc," she concludes. "That much is clear. But your reason why is not clear. Could you try to be at least a little kind to him when he visits? Or ignore him, if you want. Just don't confront him and make him feel uncomfortable that you're accusing him of things and embarrassing me in one fell swoop."

I exhale slowly. "Alright," I say finally. "I'll try."

"Thank you." Mom touches my cheek fondly. "And, another thing. Please don't turn into Flo. I already have one too many. I love her no doubt, but I don't think I could stand it if you became rude and impolite and mean to the younger kids. Flo doesn't treat me with respect. She disregards my simple instructions, and she won't obey my rules. She criticizes me for my opinions and beliefs. She thinks ill of my point in life. And if the chance arises, she'll humiliate me, kind of like what you did back there with Marc earlier today."

"I'm sorry," I say sincerely. "I didn't mean to embarrass you. I was only concentrating on Marc and I was mad he was here, especially after last week which was entirely his fault, no matter how much you try to convince me otherwise."

Mom groans. "Not this again, Venice! Just—just go downstairs and hang out with your grandparents before they decide they're bored and want to return to Florida."

"Alright, alright!" I scamper past her, my socks slipping on the polished bamboo floor. I open the basement door and jump down the stairs, entering the cold atmosphere of the lower level that hits me like a sharp gust of wind. I wrap my arms around myself, shivering, and sit on the squishy couch next to Grandma Pope, who pretty much radiates heat. The movie we're watching is one I'm not familiar with, and I soon find myself bored. I let my gaze wander to the people around me, noticing Flo isn't here. Leaning closer to Grandma Pope, I mutter, "Where's Florence?"

"She went upstairs just a few minutes before you came down," replies my grandma. "Her phone was ringing."

"Ah." It's a perfectly understandable excuse to dismiss her. She gets calls twenty-four-seven from her admirers and boyfriends and simple-minded chic girls who probably don't know how to read.

I try to focus on the movie, but my attention hasn't been snagged. I end up returning to the kitchen, and from there to my bedroom, where Florence is on her bed, sniffing. I freeze in the doorway, bewildered and concerned why she's crying, and she spots me. Her cheeks flush an angry red. Her aura hits me like a freight train—blinding white and deep scarlet. She's beautiful and angry. Both a good and a bad combination.

"What do you want?" she mumbles, her voice pathetically attempting a snarl.

"Are you..." I let my voice trail away.

Flo swipes at her cheeks. "I'm fine. Just leave me alone."

Instead, I shut the door, then climb onto Flo's bed and put my arms around her. She stiffens at first, soon giving in and sobbing into my shirt. I stroke her curly hair, wondering what has stoked her emotions up enough to make her sob like this. It can't have been a boy, can it? She's too strong to be broken down over a boy so soon after starting school here.

"What's wrong?" I ask, squeezing her slightly.

Flo draws in a shuddering breath. "I don't know," she says, hiccupping. "I'm just under the weather. Emotionally. But nothing bad happened. It was only a sudden...predicament."

"Oh." I hold her closer against me. "Want to tell me about it?"

She shakes her head. "N-no."

"Alright." I rest my chin on her head, and we sit there for minutes or for hours, I don't know—just comforting silence as I hold her. She occasionally trembles, and during those times I hug her tighter, showing how I love her despite how she treats me. I doubt this small act of solace will help her with her actions towards me later, but right now I'll appreciate it. She isn't pushing me away. She isn't yelling at me to go away. So I'll take it.

After a long time, Flo stops quivering, her body goes slack in my embrace, and she starts to breathe deeply. I gently lay her on her pillows, pulling her blanket around her, and slide off the bed. I move towards the window, eyes staring up at the twinkling stars. It's dark outside. The porch lights on several houses illuminate the small parts of the neighborhood. They are the only source of light other than the irregular car that drives by.

As another car passes underneath my window, I'm reminded of what had happened to me earlier today. What day it's been. Did that really happen? And was it really just this morning? It feels like it was forever ago.

That SUV had almost run me over.

I had almost died.

The memory speeds my heart up. I almost died. Almost. And I'd gotten up and walked around, seemingly unconcerned about my near escape. What had I been *thinking*? How embarrassing that I froze in the middle of the road! And what if Nate hadn't shoved me out of the way?

I owe it all to him.

My knees start to tremble and soon my entire body is shaking, just like Flo had been only minutes ago. I sink to the ground next to my bed, desperately trying to forget those horrifying seconds in which I'd thought I was going to die.

TWENTY-FOUR

TO: Sleepy Gumption
FROM: Hubris Jargon
SUBJECT: Attempt 3.0
TIME: 8:40 a.m.
DATE: Sunday, February 2

Almost succeeded. Unknown associate foiled plan. Ruined everything. But I saw it. I saw it.

Will get it for you. Will try again.

Will succeed.

Did so on other mission. Am coming back now.

TWENTY-FIVE

I sleep in late the next morning. When I finally get up, Florence is gone, her bed tucked in neatly. She may be a total slob when it comes to throwing her clothes on the floor, but she's excellent at keeping her bed tidy. I don't see a point in making my bed if I'm just going to wreck my beautiful job the next day, so I don't bother with that simple act of hygiene.

Everyone is in the kitchen. Grandpa Pope has made delicious pancakes that rival Mom's stellar waffles, and I manage to grab one before the rest are gobbled up by my family members. Rolling my eyes at their moderation, I listen in on Mom's conversation with Grandma Pope about the recent ninety-degree weather in Florida. Then I scoff to myself, wondering why I'm eavesdropping on a talk about *weather*, and I turn to my twin.

"Hey, Florence," I say. "Could you pass the blackberry jam?"

She shoves it in my direction without looking at me. She doesn't say a word.

I give her a look of concern she ignores, and my heart sinks.

I don't know what's wrong with her. Is she embarrassed about last night and suddenly can't look me in the eye?

I drop my gaze to my plate, the forgotten jar of blackberry jam sitting by my fork.

One step forward, one step back, I suppose.

"Venice, are you going to eat that?"

I peer over at Pompeii, who is eyeing my pancake with hunger. "Yes," I say. "I'm going to eat it. And no, you can't have it."

He pouts. "Why not?"

"Because it's my breakfast. Look, Grandpa just made some more. Get one off the stack."

Pompeii turns to accept a fresh, hot pancake from Grandpa, and in doing so Roman catches my eye.

"Did you watch the movie last night?"

I shake my head. "No. I was upstairs with Flo."

"Agh!" Roman leans back in his chair. "That movie was epic! It's too bad you missed it. There was this really hot woman who was the main character, and she was sick. I mean, she shot that one guy in the *nose* with a bullet! His nose went spinning across the room!"

I pretend to be shocked. "Mom, you let them watch that?"

"Hm?"

Resisting the urge to bury my face in my hands, I busy myself with eating my pancake before it cools down too much. The blackberry jam is a great choice, and I use it as my topping for the other three pancakes I eat for my breakfast.

"Mom, look!"

I move my attention from my plate to Siena, who has written on her pancake in Sharpie. I squint at it. Does the word really spell *wimps*?

"I eat wimps for breakfast!" she yells, taking a large bite of the pancake.

I can't help it—I laugh. Everyone else joins in, and we sound like a happy family until Flo slams down her plate, shattering it.

The whole kitchen quiets. The only noise is the sizzle of the uncooked pancakes on the griddle.

Florence gets to her feet. "Can't you shut up?" she yells. "I have a massive headache, and all your screaming isn't helping at all! Ugh! You guys don't care for other people's problems!"

She whirls around and storms away, leaving us shocked and

confused. I'm trying to guess what's bothering her when Siena says, "I think she's mad because I read one of her letters from Kent."

"I thought she burned those," says Roman.

Grandma Pope gasps. "She *burned* them? Not recycled?"

If anything, the Popes are more obsessed with going green and saving the environment than Mom is. I think that's where Mom got it, though. All her crazy, amusing ideas come from her parents.

"Nah," says Siena, and I have to pull myself back into the conversation. "I found the letters stashed somewhere in her room. And I read one. It was weird. He used a different name, and the letter was from North Dakota. But he used the same blue stationary he always uses, and he said a couple times that he loves her and misses her."

"Gross," says Pompeii.

"What was the name Kent used?" asks Mom.

Siena thinks for a moment. "I can't remember. Something like Michael Bubble."

Grandpa frowns. "Bubble? Do you mean Bublé?"

"Yeah, sure." Siena shrugs. "Who is he?"

"A singer and songwriter," Grandpa Pope says. "I wonder why Florence and this Kent-keister-guy write about him.

I hold back a sort of laughter. "Kent-*keister*-guy?"

He goes to reply, but Mom's frightened expression stops him from going on. "Linda?" He puts a comforting hand on her shoulder. "Linda? What's wrong?"

"Angelo's favorite singer was Michael Bublé," Mom mumbles.

My blood freezes over. Mom resists talking about Dad as much as possible.

The silence is thick and heavy. Grandma and Grandpa exchange a long look. Siena jabs at her pancake with a finger. Roman is trying to put a piece of whipped cream in Pompeii's ear, who is oblivious to the attempts. I drop my gaze to the table, where Flo's cracked plate is oozing maple syrup across the polished wood. I pick out the shards, my fingers collecting sticky syrup as I do so. I carry the broken plate over to the recycling bin and carefully set it inside the brown paper bag. I then clean off my fingers in the sink, wiping my wet hands on my jeans.

Everyone is still quiet when I return to the table. Roman hasn't succeeded in lodging the whipped cream in Pompeii's ear yet, but I'm positive he won't give up. Mom is pale, staring off into the distance, and my grandparents are having a wordless battle, trying to decide what they should do next. I feel bad for them.

I clear my throat, bringing all attention to me. "I'm going to go check on Florence," I say, edging towards the entryway. "Save a few pancakes for me, Grandpa."

He nods.

I slip out of the suffocating room, heading for the upstairs. I need to figure out what's bothering Flo. Is Kent making her mean and snappy and short-tempered? At least more than usual.

Our bedroom door is closed, so I knock softly before entering. The blinds are put down—strange for her. She loves the sunshine and light. She says it helps with her complexion.

My twin is on her bed, facing away from me. "What do you want?" she mutters when I enter.

"I just—wanted to know if I can help you with anything," I say, nervously shifting my weight to my other leg. She hasn't sent me away yet, which is also strange, but maybe she's vulnerable at this moment. If so, she won't be vulnerable for very long.

She's too strong for that.

"No one can help me except one person," Flo whispers.

I swallow hard. "Who?"

Flo scoffs. "Why should I tell you?"

"Because I want to help."

She scoffs again, rolling over to face me. "Venice," she says in a sassy voice, "you are the most annoying, do-gooder I know and hope to ever come in contact with."

217

My cheeks flush pink at her harsh words. I don't know if she meant them to be harsh, but they are in my ears. "Thank you, Flo."

"You're welcome," she says, turning her back on me. "Now, go away or, I don't know, save a baby from a burning building."

"Excuse me?"

Flo sniggers. "You're eager enough to please that you'd risk your life just to save another."

I am speechless. What is she *talking* about? And why is she being so mean?

"Are you still here?"

I close the door, fully entering the room. "Flo, what's going on with you? You're snappy and quick to anger. Something's upset you and you're taking it out on me. Why?"

"Because you're my sister."

I brush aside the insult. "I know, but that isn't an acceptable excuse. I'm not the one who determines *your* actions and emotions and feelings and all that!"

Flo swings off the bed, standing chest-to-chest with me. "I heard what you and Mom were saying last night in the kitchen. I heard how Mom doesn't like me. She said I was rude and impolite and mean and I disrespect people and she doesn't want *Perfect Little Venice* to turn into *Nasty Florence*, the disappointment of the family!"

I stumble backwards, holding up my hands. "Hey, hey, slow down. What are you talking about?"

"I heard Mom telling you I'm a humiliation!" she yells. "And how I'm secretive and I yell at people and ignore our grandparents and all this other stuff about me, and—"

"Florence." I put my hands on her shoulders, stopping her rampage. "Flo, listen to yourself. You're contradicting yourself right here, right now. You're *yelling* at me."

She draws in a huge breath, about to start screaming more, but Mom's voice suddenly rings out.

"Venice! Florence! Come talk to your grandparents! They're leaving in two days!"

My sister and I lock gazes for a moment. Then I step back, dropping my hands. "We'll resume this chat another time," I say, moving towards the door. "I'm curious to see how you have been looking at your life and mine over the past years."

She doesn't reply. By the time she moves, I'm downstairs and out of ear-shot.

Grandma and Grandpa Pope are sitting on the couch, chatting with Siena and Pompeii, who are miraculously working together on an old puzzle. While they look pleasant, I notice Pompeii keeps knocking aside Siena's hand when she reaches for the puzzle box, and occasionally she will steal a piece that he is searching for. Mom and Roman are arguing quietly in the hallway, and when I pass by them, they stop.

"Where's Flo?" Mom asks.

I gesture upstairs. "In our room. She's…confused."

Mom nods. She isn't pale any more, but her aura is sparking. There is no trace of green. It's all blue. Deep, depressing blue.

She's sorrowing. That mention of Dad? Florence's scene at breakfast? Roman's attitude? Me confronting Marc? Poor Mom.

I arrive in the living room, sitting on the chaise near my grandparents. They look politely bored, and I suddenly feel bad for not being a gracious host or even talking to them after their long, hard trip up here to visit us for Flo and my birthday.

"So," I say, by way of starting a conversation. "What do you do in Florida in your spare time?"

Grandma giggles like a little girl. "I hang out on the beach and check out the guys."

I gape at her, only faintly amused. "Grandma!"

"What?" The corners of her mouth are twisted up. "Oh, Venice, you should see this one lifeguard…" she claps her hands to her chest. "He is a *dream*! I always go on days when he's out there."

Grandpa grunts, a disagreeing noise rather than the impression of a pig. "I am shocked to learn you flirt with men forty years your junior," he says.

Grandma gasps, slapping his arm. "Forty? That's an insult!"

"And you're the one sitting here talking about boys with poor Venice," Grandpa replies, winking at me.

His wife pouts. "Fine. Venice, dear, why don't you tell us about the boys around here that you have your eye on? What about the one you were with yesterday?"

I give both of my grandparents a horrified look. "Um, I don't…"

"Come on, dear," says Grandma. "Don't be shy."

Thank the trees, Pompeii saves me. He jumps to his feet and yells, "Siena! You're doing it wrong! You have to do the border first, not the inside! Give me that piece!"

"No!" She throws a puzzle piece across the room. "If you want it, then go get it."

Pompeii skitters over to search for the piece as Mom and Roman come in, closely followed by Flo. My twin sister is wearing a frown and doesn't look happy to be here. She must have been dragged out of our room when she hadn't shown up after a minute.

"Venice." Grandma leans forward. "Go on."

I freeze. "Um…" Desperately needing someone to help me, I give Florence a wide-eyed message for assistance. She sighs and comes up to us, her face dark.

"What?" she grumbles.

"I…" I clear my throat. "Grandma is in a romantic mood and wishes to hear stories about the very subject I have nothing to say."

Flo rolls her eyes. "Boys." It isn't a question.

"Yeah." I pull a strained expression. "You're the informer when it comes to boys. I don't have *anything* to share."

She cocks an eyebrow only I see, and by the time she turns to Grandma and Grandpa, her face is smooth as glass. So is her voice. "What do you want to hear about, Grandma?" she asks sweetly.

"The most romantic dates, the cutest guy I've ever kissed, my favorite boyfriend…"

"All of it!" Grandma is thrilled, Grandpa less so. He meets my eye and draws a finger across his neck. I have to stifle a laugh.

Once Flo starts talking, her mood changed from only seconds ago, I stand and join my younger siblings at the coffee table, where they have begun to fight over the puzzle pieces. Pompeii is holding the box far above Siena's head, taunting her with it, while she punches him again and again, demanding he give her the box.

Sorting out the problem takes longer than I want, but the two soon are working together in sulky silence. The puzzle box is on the table, in-between the two of them.

Roman flips on the TV, scrolling through channels and shows currently streaming, switching back and forth from a serial fiction show and a documentary on deep sea diving. The volume is down low, thankfully, so my ears aren't bleeding, but it's still distracting and soon everyone turns to watch. I don't think this is what Mom had in mind when she told us to come hang out with Grandma and Grandpa Pope.

I glance over at them. They both look slightly like my mother: glasses and a strong jaw, but the similarities end there.

Grandpa has a bald head, so bald that the sunshine streaming through the many windows makes his head shine blindingly. He has a cleft chin and a big nose. He is short and stocky, his build thickset and broad. He is, undoubtedly, an old man. He's strong enough to survive for the next twenty years or so, however, and I know he probably will. He is kind, too, and never turns away the chance to make one of us laugh, even if the joke is terrible and we only laugh to humor him. He enjoys gardening, something I find strange for a man who doesn't like vegetables and is allergic to pollen. I have often wondered why he and Grandma don't move to someplace where the pollen content is much lower.

Grandma has auburn hair like Mom and the rest of us besides

Roman, but her hair is losing its color. It's streaked with grey and white, though if anyone tells her that she will argue strongly against the fact. She has our dark green eyes and sharp, pointed nose. She is short like Grandpa, but her temper is worse than Florence's, so I would never call her *puny*. She loves gardening, just like Grandpa, but she is more into flowers than vegetables or fruit trees and bushes. She always has dirt under her fingernails, no matter where she is or how long she's been away from her garden. She is talkative and eager to uncover the latest gossip, even if it's Virginian gossip and not Floridian gossip. She also has tiny feet.

I tear my gaze away from Grandma and Grandpa Pope when a loud crash startles the somewhat-peaceful air. I discover Pompeii and Siena have finally snapped and are fighting louder than before, throwing puzzle pieces at one another and tossing the box far across the room. The pieces in the box spill out everywhere, raining down on me and Florence and our grandparents. I laugh, since I think it's funny, but Mom shoots me a hard glare and I quickly shut my mouth.

"Clean up the puzzle," Mom says wearily.

Pompeii grabs Siena's arm. "It's her fault! She should have to clean up!"

"You threw the box!" Siena snarls.

"Be quiet," Mom says harshly, and the two kids fall silent. "You both have to pick up the pieces," she continues. "Together. And if I hear a single complaint, you'll go straight to your bedrooms for the next hour. *And*, you'll miss ice cream tonight."

Pompeii and Siena scowl but do as they are told. I help them, which makes Roman scoff, gaze still on the TV.

"Perfect child," he mutters as I collect the pieces around him.

I ignore him, knowing he only wants to spite me. Well, it won't work. I'm too experienced with situations like these to forget myself and go for him. This happens all the time.

All the pieces are returned to the box—at least, I *hope* it's all the pieces—and Siena moves to sit by Flo on the floor to listen in on her stories about the boys she's gone out with. I begin putting the puzzle together, joined by a sulking Pompeii, and I'm glad I'm not being bored by Flo like Grandpa is. He catches my eye and mouths, *Help me*. I grin and motion him over to the table, where he can join us.

Before Grandpa gets up, Mom's phone rings. I look up at her, noticing her pale face. She seems to struggle with something, the ringing phone in her hand. Finally, she declines the call.

"Who was it?" I ask.

She hesitates, then says, "Nobody."

The phone rings, again. Annoyed, Mom declines, again. I stare at her while she does so, curious to know who is calling and why she doesn't want to talk to them. She is usually chatty and enjoys a good conversation. The caller must be a person she isn't in the mood to talk with or it's a machine wanting to know her political status.

Her phone rings for a third time. Mom huffs and turns down the dialer tone. She sees me watching her and shrugs. "Nobody I want to talk to right now," she explains.

I slowly return to the puzzle, not completely believing her. Who would call three times in a row, within the minute, that she doesn't want to talk with? Is it someone from work? No—she'd answer immediately if it was one of her customers.

A text dings. Mom groans. "Why won't they give up?" she mutters, quickly reading through the text.

I stare at her, see her face drain of color, see her body slump down in her seat, see her drop her phone in her lap.

Bad news. Bad, bad news. That much is evident.

I'm on my feet in an instant, picking up her phone and scanning the text. I don't normally read Mom's texts—they're personal—but I feel like this is important.

What shocks me in the name. It's from Melissa Ferrari, my

223

grandma. The next thing that shocks me is the text itself. The more I read, the more I feel like doing exactly what Mom is. A horrible darkness has filled me. I can't believe this is true.

It *can't* be true.

"Venice?" Flo is at my elbow, worried. "Venice, what is it?"

I can't answer. My heart is in my throat, blocking any words from leaving my mouth.

The text is false. There's no way this has happened. I refuse to believe it. It must be a prank or a trick Grandma Ferrari is playing on us. She loves pranks and any kind of joke like this.

She's just joking.

But I feel it. I feel it deep inside of me, that Grandma Ferrari isn't making a joke. It's real.

"Venice?"

I take a shuddering breath, unclogging my throat. "Ferrari family," I begin, reading the text out loud, "I regret to inform you that this morning at six a.m. we received the news that yesterday Angelo Ferrari was killed in a car accident."

TWENTY-SIX

Funnily enough, my first thought after reading that text is *I need to tell Nate.* He is the only one here outside of my family that knows about Dad and how he is a disappointing father. Nate knows Dad is lousy. Nate knows I wish Dad was a better dad. Nate knows how much it hurts for me to live without having any clue what my dad is doing, where he is, and if he even misses his wife or any of his five children.

My next thought is more somber.

Dad is dead.

My dad is dead. The dad we haven't seen for six years. He's dead.

Florence goes white. She grabs my arm, needing something to steady her as she stumbles at the painful news. "No..." she moans quietly, and I'm sure I'm the only one who hears.

"Dad?" Siena says in a deathly whisper. "*Dad*?"

I nod slowly, not meeting anyone's gaze. I resume reading the text. "The accident involved two cars including Angelo's. The second car was an oil truck that promptly exploded, setting fire to everything around it. The heat was so intense it melted both cars and a patch of the road. Neither body..." my voice falters. I take a deep breath before continuing. "Neither of the two drivers' bodies was recovered. They were melted into the pavement by the heat."

Flo squeezes my arm tighter. I start to lose feeling in that limb.

"The funeral will be a private affair," I say, trembling slightly. "You are, of course, welcome. But it is not required. The funeral will be held in two days' time in California. There is no body to bury. We will simply place a headstone in the designated space and bury an empty coffin."

Utter silence greets me after I finish speaking. I set Mom's phone in her lap; she makes no move to pick it up again.

Flo suddenly bursts into tears. She wraps her arms around me and sobs into my shoulder, no doubt smearing make-up all over my shirt. I don't care. I hug her back, resting my cheek on her head.

I feel terrible. But I don't feel like crying.

There is no body to bury.

How had Dad melted? Is that even possible? Who was the person that hit Dad? Or did *Dad* hit the oil truck?

Neither of the two drivers' bodies were recovered.

Both of them melted into the road. Because of the fire. Because of the oil. Because of the heat.

Angelo Ferrari was killed.

Killed. Not died.

It doesn't make any difference if he died or if he was killed. It's the same. He's still dead.

My siblings all look at me blankly. Grandma and Grandpa Pope are trying to console Mom, who is sobbing as hard as Florence. I've never seen Mom cry before, and this alone makes me the most unsettled. What are we going to do now? There isn't any chance of Dad arriving out of the blue and declaring how he has been an idiot for the past six years and wants to be forgiven and become part of our family again. As much as I want it to happen, I know I'm not going to see him and he's not going to surprise us with the announcement I've been hoping to hear for six years.

And now Dad is dead.

"It was him," Flo chokes out, startling us all. We haven't said anything for nearly ten minutes—we're in numb shock, just staring at each other and not speaking—so when Flo admits something about Dad, everyone turns their attention to her.

"What?" I ask, pushing her back to arm's-length.

Flo is a mess. Her face is blotchy and red, her make-up smeared over her cheeks, her mascara bleeding into her skin.

"It was him," she says around another sob. "D-dad. You all thought it was Kent, b-but I was writing to Dad."

I reel back. "What?" I repeat.

"I've b-been writing to him," says Flo. Her thin voice dips and wavers as she continues. "Ever s-since we arrived in Virginia, we've corresponded weekly. I g-got his address from Grandma Ferrari before we left California. And Dad replied a week after I sent him a letter. But he sighed it Michael Bublé and n-not Angelo Ferrari."

"Oh." I stare at her for a moment, then look over at Siena, who is listening without interest. Her face is white and it seems like she might start crying any second, too. "Siena," I say.

She doesn't react. Her posture is slumped. As I watch her, a tear slips out of her eye and trails down her cheek.

The sorrow around me is suffocating. I try taking a deep breath, but that does nothing and soon I need fresh air or I'll burst. I have to get away from my family for a little while. I have to be on my own for a few minutes or a few seconds, it doesn't matter. I just need and have to get away from the pale, unsteady expressions. The dripping tears. The muffled sobs. The faint whimpers.

I pat Florence on the back, then quit the living room, heading upstairs for the seclusiveness of my bedroom. No one tries to stop me as I quietly slip up the staircase. No one calls me back as I wander down the carpeted hallway. No one yells for my return as I enter my bedroom and softly close the door behind me.

I cross the room and snatch my phone off my bedside table. I don't have Nate's contact, I realize. That's rather stupid, since we're working together on a school project. Why don't I have his number? And now how am I going to reach out to him?

I scroll through my texts, stopping when Mandy's name pops up. I quickly send her a text asking for Nate's home address, hoping that she knows where he lives. If not, I'll just have to get his number. I feel like I need to tell someone about my dad, and Nate is the only person who understands the difficulty in our relationship.

Dropping my phone on my bed, I begin pacing. Part of me thinks that it is incredibly stupid that Dad is dead. The other part of me *knows* that it's incredibly stupid.

There is no body to bury.

Because Dad melted. Into the road. Dissolved into a puddle of bones and human flesh and *nothing* at all.

I'm still pacing when my phone chimes. I dart over to my bed, seeing the reply Mandy has sent is short and simple: *Sure thing, Vennie! Can I call you that? Here's his address.* Underneath her text is a link, which I tap on. It sends me to a map. I spend several minutes trying to figure out how it works and if this is actually Nate's address or the directions to the nearest video game store, and after I find my house nearby, I accept that it's his literal address. It's farther down the street from where we live, towards where I always see him go after school or whenever we meet.

I turn in a full circle, looking for my shoes. I find them underneath my bed; Flo probably put them there if she thought they were "invading her space", as she so kindly tells me. I tie the laces, only concentrating on the task at hand and nothing else. I don't want my mind to wander to the different possibilities concerning Dad's death. I don't want to come up with theories that involve Dad being...I shake my head angrily, refusing to go any further. I will *not*. Dad is dead, and that's that. I'm not going to ever see him again. He is never going to see us again.

And that's the end of the matter.

There is no body to bury.

My teeth clench.

I need to distract myself, and walking a few minutes to where

Nate lives will hopefully be a distraction enough. Except, I *will* be walking with no companion but my thoughts.

Maybe that's not such a good idea.

With a last glance at my bedroom, I grab my phone and head down the hallway. My shoes make virtually no noise on the carpeted floor; neither on the bamboo staircase.

My family is still in the living room, still in numb shock, still not speaking to anyone. Roman has his head in his hands. Pompeii is putting together the puzzle, not even checking to see which piece goes where, just snapping on different pieces. Siena is staring out the window, arms folded tightly across her chest. She looks more angry than sad. It's no wonder—she knew Dad the least of all of us. She was only three years old when he divorced Mom and ultimately left us behind. Flo is sitting on the couch in Grandma Pope's vacated spot, not moving. An occasional tear slips down her face. She makes no move to brush them away.

Mom is still being comforted by her parents. The three of them aren't saying anything, just grouped close to each other. Grandma and Grandpa Pope seem like they want to say something but are too scared to.

Grandma glances over at me when I stop in the doorway. She attempts a small, sad smile, one I don't feel like returning. Her eyebrow shoots up as she takes in the fact that I'm wearing my shoes, and it's quite clear I'm about to go somewhere.

I don't answer her silent question. Instead, I cross the room to Mom and take her phone from her lap, where I had put it after reading that fateful text from Grandma Ferrari. I turn on the phone, ignoring the curious looks the Popes are giving me, and slowly walk out of the living room with the phone in my hand. I raise it to my ear as soon as I've entered the deathly quiet kitchen.

Grandma Ferrari picks up on the first ring. "Hello? Linda?"

"This is Venice." I peer over my shoulder, decide I'm too loud for the hushed house.

"Venice." Grandma Ferrari sounds torn between heartbreak and grief. "Hi, Venice. How are you taking the news?"

"Not very well." I open the back door and step outside, welcoming the dull sunlight and the chattering of birds in the trees around me and the faint buzz of insects. "How much do you know about the accident, Grandma? Can you please tell me everything? I want to know."

"Of course, dear." Grandma Ferrari's voice dips. She hiccups. "Angelo was in Kentucky. That's what the officer said when he told me about what had happened. I wanted to know why my son was in Kentucky, but the officer had no idea why."

I don't say a word. Why *was* Dad in Kentucky? I thought he lived in North Dakota, or one of the states that starts with an "N."

"And then I wanted to know about the truck driver," Grandma Ferrari says, her voice wavering slightly. "The officer told me that according to the street cameras that caught the accident on film, the truck driver was the one who hit Angelo's car. And it seemed like it wasn't actually an accident. The truck could have swerved to miss Angelo, but he just plowed on, causing an explosion and the death of my son."

"It wasn't actually an accident?" I repeat. "How?"

"The street was rather wide," says Grandma Ferrari. "Angelo was on the correct side of the road. The truck came roaring around a bend and just...hit Angelo. Smashed right into him. And the oil in the truck caught fire and burned everything around them, including their cars and their...bodies. I saw a video and it was *horrible*."

"Can you send that video to me?"

She pauses. "Of course. It's black-and-white, though. But there are also a few pictures of the accident. And eyewitnesses. I talked to a lady who had seen it from her apartment window, and she said the explosion lit up the whole area. It was like it was day."

"Then that means the accident was caused during the evening or night? Do you know what time?"

"The woman I talked to said it was almost ten. She had just gotten home from the grocery store, disappointed it had closed at nine so she wasn't able to get a last-minute item for the strawberry shortcake she was making for her niece who was visiting early the next morning—"

I interrupt her. When Grandma is nervous, she tends to ramble. "How many eyewitnesses were there?"

"Oh, about two or three." Grandma Ferrari sounds tense. It would have been polite to listen through her rambling, but I'm not feeling in the best of moods right now and don't care for manners. "She was the only one that called me, though. Said she got my number from the police after they found me to tell me the news about...about Angelo. And she talked to me for over an hour, telling me how sorry she was that she hadn't been able to do anything, but I told her she couldn't have, anyway. How could she have? The truck wouldn't have stopped if she jumped out in the road and yelled at the driver to slow down."

I bite the inside of my cheek and look around our small backyard. This is not how I had expected our conversation to go.

"You're right," I say finally, knowing Grandma Ferrari wanted a response. "I appreciate you for explaining this to me. Your text was so brief and didn't have much information concerning Dad's death. What else do you know that might...enlighten me?"

"Well," Grandma Ferrari begins, then stops. She lets out a long breath of air. I hear it through the phone's speaker. "The officer told me that he and his team researched the truck driver and found out he wasn't registered. The company of truckers said that that certain oil truck had been stolen a week or so before from their agency in Kentucky. They weren't pleased to learn their truck was destroyed."

"Wait, wait." I run a hand through my hair, bunching some in my fist. "The oil truck was *stolen*? Do they know who stole it?"

"I'm not a detective. I don't know all the details about his accident. I only know what the officer told me, and they're sparse."

"Sorry." I hesitate, then decide to press her. "Do you—do you think you could find out? Like, ask the officer? I have plenty of questions that I'd love to be answered."

Grandma takes a while to reply. "Maybe," she says after a long minute of me listening to the warbling static-filled silence. "I don't know, Venice. Maybe."

"Thank you."

She attempts lightheartedness as she says, "Are you coming to the funeral in two days? I know it's sudden, but without a...body...to prepare, it won't take as long."

"I have no clue if we're coming or not," I say, unconsciously looking back at the quiet house behind me. "Mom might. She'll probably want to, you know, say goodbye. But as for Florence and Roman and the two younger kids...they won't like the long flight. And I don't think Siena would go anyway. You know she isn't acquainted with Dad. And—our other grandparents are visiting right now, so my siblings might prefer to stay instead of going out to California."

"I see. What about you?"

I pull at the hair in my fist. "I think I'll stay, too."

Grandma Ferrari sounds surprised as she asks why.

"I—" I hesitate again. I can't all very well tell her that I don't want to fly to California for a funeral belonging to the dad who ignored my existence for the last six or so years.

Yet he *had* remembered my fifteenth birthday.

Well, sort of remembered.

"Venice?"

I echo her sigh from before. "I'm not sure I could handle a funeral," I say instead of what I was thinking seconds ago. "Funerals are depressing and so *hard*."

"I know." Grandma's voice softens as she speaks. "And it's even harder if you're a mother burying her son."

We sit in silence for another moment, both lost in our own

thoughts. Then she gently says, "I have to go. Your grandfather is helping me plan the…funeral, and he's complaining how I'm being lazy and all that crap. He's only teasing."

"Yeah." I chew on my bottom lip. "Talk to you later."

"You too. I love you."

She hangs up before I can answer, and I'm left with Mom's phone pressed to my ear and a load of sorrow in my heart.

TWENTY-SEVEN

I ignore the fierce wind as it battles against me, whipping my hair around my face as I walk.

Though I'm not really walking. I'm stomping.

Stomping angrily for a long space of time requires a lot of leg strength, I realize when my legs start to tire after only a minute of stomping down the sidewalk.

But I feel the need to stomp. I'm furious and have to force that fury out of myself, and stomping releases massive amounts.

It also keeps my mind on my feet and my achy soreness instead of the pit of despair in my heart. I throb with pain *every single time* Dad's name resurfaces in my thoughts, reminding me how I'm never going to see him ever again.

Despite the pain of loss, I feel something else, too. Something I can't begin to describe. Something...off. I have an itchy spot in the middle of my back in a spot I can't reach, and it's driving me insane. But it also tells me that there is *something* just out of my reach and waiting to be discovered. I'm trying to ignore the itch and the *something*, but it's near impossible. They both keep popping back up.

My tired legs give up stomping after only two minutes. I have to satisfy myself with long, angry strides instead, and they don't do much to stop my thoughts from wandering. I choose to concentrate on the sidewalk. Gritty pieces of concrete. Cracks every few feet.

Wasn't actually an accident.

I growl at my brain. "Shut up," I snarl, even though I'm talking to an organ, not a person.

There isn't anyone on the sidewalk. I'm the only one outside. I pass quiet houses that remind me of my own quiet house, which reminds me of *why* it's quiet, which reminds me about Dad, which reminds me that I'm not supposed to be thinking about this.

Sighing in exasperation, I try to focus on the ground, but I can't. It's almost pointless to try, really. I know I'm going to return to those painful, unwanted thoughts.

Dad is dead.

Dead.

I shudder, wrapping my arms around myself. I'm glad I got out of my house when I did. I wouldn't have been able to stand another minute in the terrible silence, watching my siblings and mom and grandparents struggle to hide their pain and sorrow at the dreary news of Dad's death. I had to clear my head.

I have to tell someone about this.

And it has to be the only person who understands.

Nate.

But as I walk towards his house, a sense of uneasy, discomfort swells inside of me. A thousand discouraging thoughts flit through me, each one more demoralizing than the other. I almost want to turn around and go back home to the suffocating sorrow. My mind whispers that I can share this unhappy information with Nate tomorrow when we're walking to school. But I doubt I will be going to school in the next few days. This is the only chance I'm going to have to tell him about Dad for the next week or so. I don't know how long we'll be out of school, but if Mom wants to attend the funeral and if we are all moping around the house for the next bit, then I'm certain school won't be a requirement.

So I have to do this now. Even though I've never been to Nate's house and I don't know what it looks like and I don't really think he wants me to be anywhere near it, especially since he lives with his...*unpredictable* grandpa that he doesn't want anyone knowing much about. What is wrong with his grandpa? There's no way Nate will tell me—he's too secretive and claims he doesn't wish for me to be mixed up in his troubles.

Coming upon a street that branches off, I stop by the sign and check my directions to see if I need to turn or if I'm supposed to continue down the street I'm already on.

I am forced to close one of my eyes, the one my broken lens is covering. I can barely read the map with the cracked glass. With all the drama today, I forgot to ask Flo if I can borrow a pair of hers.

After confirming I'm to stay on this street, I shove my phone in my back pocket and resume walking. With each step I take, I grow more and more uncertain about what I'm doing. Why *am* I doing this, anyway? Why should I bother Nate with this unfortunate occurrence? This is *my* business. This is *my* problem. Dealing with a dead father is *my* dilemma. Not Nate's. I should leave him alone.

But he made it clear to me that he's interested in my family because he doesn't have one of his own. Won't he appreciate being the first person I tell about Dad? Won't he, I don't know, feel...flattered?

That's absurd. I don't need to flatter Nate. He's my friend.

My palms begin to sweat. I wipe them on my jeans, nervous about what I'm doing and *why* I am. Should I continue any further? Should I not have even asked for Nate's address?

"Stop," I mutter to myself. "It won't do any good to be second-guessing yourself."

I sneak a quick peek at the directions again, then glance back up. I need to turn left at the next street, where I'll enter a cul-de-sac. Nate's house is at the far end. But I'm still really close to his house. The walk went faster than I'd thought I would. Only twenty-six minutes since I'd left, according to the clock on my phone.

Twenty-six minutes. I wonder if it's this short for Nate to arrive home after school or our meetings. He probably has plenty to think about while he walks.

A sudden bout of nerves spring up when I spot the street sign ahead. I'm barely away from my destination.

Do I really want to bother Nate?

Will he actually care or will he pretend otherwise?

Am I making the right choice going to his house, or will he get mad at me for invading his private space? He has made it known that he doesn't like talking about his family and personal life, and when you go to someone's home you learn plenty about them. I might even meet his grandpa.

Another question pops into my head.

Does Nate ever feel nervous when he walks up to my house, knowing he'll have to knock on my door and maybe face my crazy siblings?

Have to face me?

My shoes crunch on gravel as I turn onto Nate's street. My heart is beating hard inside my chest, thumping thumping thumping. I can hardly breathe as I make my way down the road, passing far-spaced houses that look old and run-down and are crumbling. Broken windows provide a more *abandoned* look and feel, which does nothing to soothe my nerves. These houses all seem like bases for gangs or high school drop-outs that don't care for their life and spend their time doing things they shouldn't.

If Nate lives here, it's no wonder he walks to school. He doesn't want anyone to see how poor this neighborhood is.

Is that even why he walks to school?

Giving myself a slight shake, I keep my head down, eyes on my shoes as I continue towards where the directions say I need to go. Only when I pass a cluster of evergreen trees do I look up, and I find myself awed by the dark green color. I love evergreens. There are plenty of them in Virginia, which is nice—all the other trees are momentarily stripped of their green leaves during the winter season. I can't wait until spring when the leaves grow back and everything is green again.

I pull out my phone and search for the number for Nate's house. *1651.* I glance around for the correct house and, finding the mailbox with the same number, decide that must be it. I start down the gravel driveway, my shoes surprisingly quiet. Trees line the driveway, hiding the house from sight until I round a bend and find myself facing another broken, run-down, crumbling building.

It's old, yes. Filthy white siding in great need of a powerwash. Filthy light green shutters that don't look green at all but brown. Overgrown hedges. Tall grass that has died long ago and is now a light shade of brown. Weeds growing along the side of the house and all along the driveway. Rickety wooden steps leading up to a rickety wooden porch. No completely-shattered windows, thank the trees, but the house is not one I'd envision Nate living in.

He deserves better.

Then again, he might not even live here. Before I left I didn't confirm with him that this is his address, seeing as I stupidly don't have his contact. This could be just a random house in the middle of Virginia where a moneyless tramp lives.

Swallowing hard, I tentatively walk up to the porch, not trusting the creaky steps enough to support my weight. It would be *very* embarrassing to step on one and have it give way underneath me. That would make me feel both humiliated and overweight.

I place my foot on the corner of the stair. It creaks violently but holds, and I breathe a sigh of relief. I carefully step up onto the next stair, and the next, until I'm on the porch and safely on both feet. The floorboards on the porch don't creak, which is somehow ominous for me—I feel like they should, especially after the stairs.

I swallow again. The porch is small and cramped, but I'm the only thing on it. There are two small, rectangular windows besides the door—they are both covered by a dusty-looking lace curtain I'm sure has expired long ago and needs to be thrown away. The door itself is a faded blue color, the paint peeling. I fear if I knock hard enough the wood will give way and crash out of its rusted hinges.

Raising a hand, I prepare to knock.

But a noise from inside stops me. It sounds like a dull *thud*, of someone dropping a heavy item. I have heard that noise before, of course—my siblings throw things all the time—but this thump is followed by a muffled voice as someone responds.

I stand frozen to the porch, unsure of what I should do next. The best idea is to go home. I can talk to Nate in a week or so, whenever we decide to go back to school.

Another crash from inside. An angry yell not long after, one I can't hear—one I probably shouldn't hear.

I teeter on doubt and awkwardness. Knowing it's incredibly rude, I press my ear to the door and listen to the intelligible voices. There is the angry voice and the familiar soft voice.

"...git them now!"

"I told you," says the much calmer voice. "The store isn't open today. You will have to wait until tomorrow."

Muttering. A loud string of expletives that shock me to where I stand on the porch. "Need them now!" yells the angry voice.

"You still have one left," Nate says gently. "Would you like me to get it from the fridge?"

More muttering. I can't hear what the man is saying.

"No, I'm not using this as an excuse to slip away," says Nate. He is barely louder than his grandpa—at least, I *think* he's talking to his grandpa—but his tone is clear and enunciated. I hear everything he says. "Seriously, Gramps. Would you like me to get it for you?"

Mutter, mutter. Doesn't the man know how to speak?

"Yes, I know you can walk. I was only suggesting—" A loud clatter abruptly cuts off Nate's words. I hear him grunt. "Put down your cane, please. It hurts when you hit me."

"Of course!" screams the crazy grandpa. "Of *course* it hurts. Ain't that its job? Ta hurt?"

I clench my fists, not knowing if I should knock and interrupt this or if the better option is to run away and forget this ever happened.

"Gramps, please. I don't want to have to take it from you."

"Ain't gonna do that," mutters the old man. "Nope, nope. You deserve ta be taken away, kid. Far away."

A pause. Nate says something too soft for my ears. I'm not able to hear it. Then his grandpa throws another piece of furniture—it *sounds* like furniture, anyway—and Nate raises his voice. "Gramps, Stop. You're going to tire soon and crash. Remember"—he grunts again—"last time you collapsed outside, I had to carry you back in? You don't want that—" He is drowned out by a shrill cry and the shattering of glass.

I fall back from the door, my face white. What is going *on* with Nate and his grandpa? I wish I could see, but the two windows by the door are blocked by those yellowed lace curtains.

I spot a window to my left, just around the porch. I lean over the flimsy rail and try to peer inside. I know I'm being a snoop and I'm eavesdropping on a personal, private situation, but this is clearly an emergency.

Is this what he's hiding from the world?

The window is dusty and has a crack running over a corner. I lean farther out and peek through the glass, seeing into a dim room. A horrible green couch is in the center of the room, and on it sits a massive dog that is curled tightly into a ball. If it is trying to make itself smaller, it's failing. That dog can in no wise be *small*. I can't see the dog's snout, but I'm sure it's attempting to hide from something or someone.

Nate is standing on the opposite side of the room, his back to me. He's facing a short, white-haired man that is holding a long cane in his hand. The man shifts slightly, revealing a portion of his face, and I can't help but cringe at the sight. He has a tangled, matted beard that falls past his shoulders. Bits and pieces of food are stuck in the hair. He is stubby and small in build; there is no doubt that he can handle the cane he's holding, however. His arms are thin but taut as he glares at Nate.

"Ain't done remembering yet, kid?" The old man swings the cane at Nate, who steps out of the way to avoid it. It misses him, thankfully, but his horrid grandpa hasn't given up. He swings wildly, catching Nate on the arm. The force behind the blow is shocking, and I watch as he stumbles back, away from the dangerous cane.

"Gramps," Nate says through gritted teeth, "please put down the cane."

"Nuh-uh." He shakes his shaggy head. "I gotta git my drink first, 'afore I set this baby down to bed. Git me my drink, boy!" He cracks the cane on Nate's shoulder, the noise making me flinch back from the window. Tripping over my feet, I catch my balance in time to return to the dusty, cracked window and hear Nate reply.

"I'll get you your drink," he says, his voice laced with pain, "if you give me the cane."

His grandpa chortles loudly, whipping it around to smack Nate again.

Nate grabs the end of the cane, yanking it out of his grandpa's grip. The old man lurches forward, cursing and wheezing, and falls onto the floor with an almighty groan.

"Ya killed my knees!" howls the old man.

Nate is breathing heavily. I see him rub his sore shoulder with an ungloved hand, which makes me stare harder. I've rarely seen him without his gloves on. He must not wear them at home, where he doesn't have to hide all his scars.

"Git me up now!" his grandpa demands.

Nate tosses the cane onto the couch, right next to the big dog, who lifts its head and stares at the stick of polished wood with resignation. Then it bends forward, takes the cane in its mouth, and begins to gnaw on it. Splinters drop onto the cushions.

"Gimme that back!"

The old man is on his feet again, waving his hands wildly. "That's my third cane, boy! Ya fed it to the dog!"

"I told you not to hit me," Nate replies, both hard and gentle.

His grandpa growls low in his throat. "Using the smarts on me, eh?" he says roughly. He grabs an empty beer bottle from the floor and throws it at Nate.

I have to stifle a gasp of alarm. What grandpa would do this? Hurt their own grandson?

The beer bottle misses Nate by a mile, crashing into the wall near where I'm looking through the window. I duck out of sight, hoping neither has seen me, and I spend a moment on the porch, breathing deeply through my nose. More shattering noises come from inside the house, so many I start to think that Nate's grandpa has an endless supply of beer bottles to throw at him. I can't believe the horrible old man would even *threaten* Nate with one—he must not know how great of a person Nate is. He must not love Nate like a grandpa should.

It's no wonder Nate doesn't like talking about his grandpa. I suddenly feel really bad for pressing him for information.

"Gramps," says Nate's voice from through the crack in the window, "you need to calm down. Why don't you—*ouch*—sit by Mercury and let me go get your dri—Hey, watch it! Those are glass shards!"

"Ya can't tell me what ta do, kid."

I peer back into the window, first noticing the dog is cowering behind Nate with its tail tucked between its legs, and second spotting bright red blood running down Nate's arm. Just looking at him bleeding makes me enraged, even more so than I already am.

Spilled so easily, yet so precious.

Nate has his hands out in front of him, palms up. "Gramps, take a deep breath. Deep breath. Come on."

"I ain't gonna!"

Another beer bottle explodes, raining glass pieces down on

Nate. He takes no heed of them, despite many of them slicing into his skin. Blood drips onto the wooden floor.

"Deep breath, Gramps."

The old man draws in a shuddering breath. "I ain't gonna," he says again, not realizing he'd just done what Nate wants him to. "I ain't gonna and you can't make me."

"Deep breath."

He inhales sharply, then exhales.

Barely a minute later, Nate's grandpa is calm and willing to obey. He sinks down on the couch, mumbling something quietly. The dog—I think Nate had called it Mercury—doesn't move when Nate motions it forward. It's as if the dog is scared of the grandpa. Smart dog.

"Come on, boy," Nate says soothingly. "Go sit."

The dog whimpers, pressing his body to Nate's legs.

"Mercury." Nate never loses the patient tone of voice. "Go on. Sit. Gramps is better now."

"Ya gonna git my drink?" says his grandpa by way of reply.

Nate pats the dog's head. "Yes, Gramps. In a second. I need to get Mercury back on the couch."

"Bah!" says his grandpa. "Stupid dog."

Mercury whines, almost in agreement. Nate hooks a finger under the thin red collar around the dog's neck and gently pulls Mercury forward in the direction of the couch, all the while speaking soft words of comfort. Mercury finally jumps onto a cushion, the farthest one from Nate's grandpa, and Nate releases a sigh of relief.

He turns and leaves the room, probably off to retrieve the last bottle of beer for his grandpa. Why he would give that old man another weapon, I don't know, but maybe the alcohol dulls his temper.

I step back from the window, all thoughts of telling Nate about Dad gone. I can share the news on a different day. But right now, I don't want to bother him any more than he already is, and the images and horror of what I've just seen are too fresh in my mind for me to be able to face him. When he told me he doesn't like talking about his grandpa, I'd imagined it to be because of some health problem like pancreatic cancer that he doesn't want people knowing about. Not...this.

I'm careful not to make any sound as I creep down the rickety stairs and onto the overgrown, dead grass. Hugging my arms to myself, I walk up the driveway—slightly faster than normal—and hope no one has seen me snooping. In normal circumstances, I would never even *dream* of peering through someone's windows, and I am starting to wish I hadn't. It's what I get for being nosy. It's what I get for wanting to know more about Nate and his grandpa and his life.

It's what I get for coming here in the first place.

This was a terrible idea.

I speed up suddenly terrified that I'll be seen, but when I reach the bend in the driveway, I risk a final glance back at the house. The sight of it freezes me to the gravel road, and a small gasp escapes my mouth. I can't believe I hadn't seen this before. I don't know how I hadn't.

The aura of the entire house is a twisting, snaking black that weaves in and out of the partially-cracked windows and through the overgrown hedges that border the front yard. The black river of *darkness* floods even the air, reaching up past the crooked roof and the stained brick chimney. The whole house just *radiates* cruelty and hidden wickedness.

I turn and run away.

TWENTY-EIGHT

I almost regret returning home to the deathly still atmosphere. Home to the reminders of Dad's accident. Home to the quiet stares from my grandma as she tries to guess what is on my mind. What a weekend this has been! All my sorrowing thoughts for myself are conflicting madly with my concern for Nate and his situation.

I sit at the kitchen table with my grandparents, hoping to forget what I'd just witnessed but failing miserably. In fact, I can't get it out of my head. Every time I close my eyes I see it all over again. The thick cane slamming down on Nate's unprotected shoulder. The glass shards cutting into his skin as he slowly gets his grandpa to chill out and relax, take his mind off abusing his grandson. It is more horrifying than thinking about Dad, so I'm stuck between the two of them.

Grandma finally breaks the silence, and for it, I'm glad. "Where did you go off to?" she asks.

"Just out." I rest my chin on my palms. "I needed to clear my head."

She watches me for a moment, then says, "Did it work?"

"No." I cover my face with my hands. "It didn't help at all. If anything, my walk made everything worse."

Grandma gives me a sympathetic look and doesn't speak again. I wish she had continued, asking me questions and keeping my thoughts from straying to either Dad or Nate.

I twist my ring around my finger, over and over and over. I resist looking at it—the ring reminds me of Dad and the blue stone reminds me of Nate's eyes. Maybe I should take it off. I fidget in my chair, tap my toes on the floor, shift restlessly. I don't try to meet Grandma Pope's gaze. She'll just pity me. Maybe I should let her pity me?

Grandpa Pope arrives in the kitchen doorway, arms folded. "Linda is up in her room," he says to the suffocating silence. "Venice, she wants to see you as soon as you're able."

I sit up straighter in my chair. "Why? Is she all right?"

"She's fine," says Grandpa. "Well, as fine as one can be after learning their ex-husband is dead."

I nod once, then get up and move to exit the kitchen. Grandpa gives my arm a squeeze as I walk past him, muttering, "Be good to your mother, will you? She is taking the news really hard."

I nod again and slip past Grandpa.

Of *course* Mom is taking the news hard. She still loves Dad, even if he does not feel the same way. And now that he's dead, she can't ever see him again and try to patch up some of the holes they made in their hearts and lives. Being separated from each other is one thing, but for one to be dead—never to be seen ever again—is another thing.

The word rings hollow in my ears.

Dead.

My phone chimes, startling me so badly I nearly trip over my shoes. That loud *ding!* seems even more pronounced in this horribly quiet air.

I pull out my phone, seeing Grandma Ferrari has sent me a video and a few pictures. Are these the ones of the accident, the ones she talked about that I wanted to see?

Excited, I go to open them, but stop. I need to visit Mom first. Before I look at the pictures, I can talk to Mom and hopefully cheer her up.

But how can I cheer her up if *I* don't feel cheerful at all?

I can't pretend. She'll know I'm faking.

Shaking my head, I tromp up the staircase and onto the carpeted hallway. Mom's bedroom door is closed, and after I knock softly I hear her thin voice call out, "Come in."

I open the door, not surprised to be greeted by pitch-black darkness. Mom rarely leaves the lights on.

"Hey, Venice." She's lying on her bed, her body almost lost in the mounds of pillows around her.

I shut the door softly and cross the room, sitting down on the corner of her mattress. "Hey, Mom. How are you feeling?"

"Terrible. How should I feel?"

I tug at my fingers. "I don't know, Mom. Have you...told anyone about Dad yet?"

She shifts. "No. No one. Have you?"

I shake my head, then realize she probably can't see it and say, "Nope. I was going to but decided against it."

"Oh." Mom's hand bumps mine, and she folds her fingers over it. "Venice, how are your siblings? Are they—the news—your father..." She draws in a shuddering breath. "I'm never going to see Angelo again. *Ever*, Venice. Ever again. Never never never."

I apply pressure on her hand. "Don't say that, Mom."

"Why?" She sounds shocked.

I hesitate. "Don't discourage yourself," I say after a while. "Don't make yourself even more depressed."

"But I can't help it," Mom moans. "He's all I ever think about."

My heart stops beating momentarily. "What?"

"Angelo." Mom's voice cracks over his name. "Whenever I have a minute of silence I'm always thinking about him. About what I did wrong that made him hate me so much. I thought we were happy together. I thought he—he loved me."

I bite my lip, scrambling to find something to say. But Mom goes on, not letting me speak.

"And whenever I see a picture that he's in, with all you kids gathered around him, looking like a happy family, my heart just *aches* for another moment like that. A joyful, content moment when we all get along and no one is fighting or screaming or arguing like your siblings do pretty much every spare second of their life—" Mom exhales deeply. "I've always wondered, Venice, what it would be like to have our family together again, and even for always and eternity."

"I've wondered that too," I say, extracting my teeth from my bottom lip. "I think we'll have to deal with what we have now, though."

Mom hiccups. "What do you mean?"

"I mean..." I give her hand a squeeze. "I mean, we're already a family, minus Dad. But Grandma and Grandpa Pope are here, and we all have each other, so we can appreciate that for now."

"You're right." She shudders again. "You're right."

We sit in companionable silence until I ask, "Are you going to the funeral in two days?"

"I-I don't know," says Mom. She sounds miserable. "A funeral will only make things worse for me. But I should be there for Melissa. She would want me, right?"

"Yes," I say forcefully. "Grandma Ferrari definitely would love seeing you. She loves you very much."

Mom sniffles. "Thank you, Venice. I might go to California. Except I was *just* over there a month ago, before we moved here. And it costs a lot for a plane ticket, especially if I'm to buy one for a flight tomorrow, and I'm not absolutely sure that I'm ready to face Grandma Ferrari. I've always had a hard time talking to her after I got divorced. I felt awkward whenever I was around her. You know, because of Angelo. And now he's *dead*, and I can't attend his funeral! That would about kill me. And I'd feel bad for leaving my parents here and going to California—"

"Mom."

She goes still, rambling ceasing instantly. She gets her rambling from her mom.

"You should go," I say, staring at her in the darkness. I'm not positive if I'm even looking into her eyes, but I'm close enough. She can't tell anyway. It's too dark. "Mom," I say again. "Don't worry about Grandma and Grandpa Pope. They'll understand. They're going back to Florida in a few days. And I know you can face Grandma Ferrari. She's a considerate person. She is going through the same trial as you are."

"Angelo…" Mom whispers, forlorn. She's so broken, so lonely, and I wish I could do better to help her.

My heart is cracking bit by bit at her words and conflicted emotions bleeding out into the room. "Yes," I agree. "Dad. Grandma Ferrari and you both feel his loss deeply."

"Poor Melissa. She's so compassionate and understanding. I'm embarrassed that I ran away from her and Grandpa Ferrari. I just couldn't stand to be near all those memories of Angelo. Earlier today—Venice, when she called me, I immediately thought it was to tell me I needed to come back. She has done that before. But I can't leave Virginia, and I like it here, and I think going to California won't help at all."

My head spins with this new information. Grandma Ferrari wants us to move back to California? She has been begging Mom to? This must be why Mom didn't want to talk to her this morning. She didn't want to have a hard conversation.

"Going to California, even for his funeral, will give you an opportunity to do *something*," I say, pushing my thoughts aside. "So you won't be stuck at home being sad."

Silence from Mom.

"I *would* go with you," I say, but I don't exactly mean it. "But I have to stay and keep my siblings in check. You can go, though. And you should. You can have a nice long talk with Grandma Ferrari, face-to-face. Tell her you're going to keep living here. Tell her you're done with California for the time being. You need to stop living in the past, Mom. Dad's gone."

She shudders. "Gone…"

"You shouldn't be scared of Grandma and Grandpa Ferrari," I say. "They're both kind and understanding people. They know the trouble and pain and regret you have suffered because of Dad's decision. It's not their fault he quit on you. It's his. So you shouldn't be embarrassed to see them."

"I know. It's just so *hard*."

"Mom." I give her a squeeze. "You're strong. You can do it. And you know that this…this will really give you the chance to say goodbye."

The silence between us stretches paper-thin as I wait for her response. The dark around me seems to press down on me. I wonder how she can stand to be in a pitch-black room after learning about a death. I know I would prefer being out in the sunshine. But look what good my walk did me.

Mom tightens her grip on my hand. "I might go," she says softly, more to herself than to me. "California. And the funeral. Angelo…"

"Would you like me to help you find a flight?" I ask, hoping for something to take her mind off Dad and to also get her out of bed. She can't be in here all day.

She sighs, releasing my hand. "I don't know, Venice. Maybe. Come back in an hour or so. I'll tell you my decision then."

"Okay."

I hop off the bed and make my way to the bedroom door, fumbling blindly for the handle. "Mom," I say, pulling the door open, "I love you. You know that, right?"

"Right," Mom confirms. "I love you too, Venice."

Then I close the door and leave her alone to her unhappy thoughts and her depressed self.

*****

The afternoon bleeds into evening. Nothing has changed around our house except for a rare sighting of a ten year-old girl as she searches the kitchen for some food to eat. Siena doesn't talk to me or Grandma and Grandpa Pope—she just walks out of the kitchen again clutching a protein bar to her chest and her head hung low.

None of my other siblings are seen. I'm the only one not hiding out in my room, I'm the only one making sure I'm properly fed and I'm the only one keeping our grandparents company. I'll admit, I am too nervous to brave Flo, so I stay in the kitchen and don't go up to my bedroom.

Grandma starts to cook something that smells wonderful and also makes wonderful frying noises that are music to my ears. It's better than the faint sobs we occasionally hear from somewhere upstairs. After a short moment, Grandpa gets up from the kitchen counter and helps his wife with the food, whistling a soft tune that reminds me of both Nate and Mr. Castro, which reminds me that I have a report due in a few weeks. Well, six weeks. That's not for a while.

Have we really only lived in Virginia for a month? It has seemed like such a long time. My birthday, two days ago, feels like *years* ago.

My thoughts circulate back to Nate and yesterday. He'd come up with that bizarre theory about my ring and the SUV driver wanting it, the orange-red haired man. Does that man really want something from me? He has roared past me in his car three different times. On my first day of school when I was walking home with Nate. On the day Marc came over for dinner. And yesterday, when the car was inches away from squishing me flat...I owe everything to Nate. If he hadn't pushed me out the way, Dad wouldn't be the only dead member of our family.

I shiver, wrapping my arms around myself. I don't want to think about this right now, but my mind keeps returning to the subject of Dad and his sudden death. His unexpected death.

There is no body to bury.

Biting my lip, I reach into my pocket and pull out my phone. I turn it on, remembering the pictures and video Grandma Ferrari sent me detailing the accident.

Do I really want to examine the pictures and watch the video? Do I really want to see Dad die?

Making a split-second decision, I stand up and leave the room, entering the dim tranquility of the basement where I'll be alone. Roman's bedroom is just down the hall, but he's currently outside in the backyard, throwing rocks as hard as he can at whatever living thing flashes by him. I told him not to hit our neighbors—however, I don't know if he listened to me or even heard me tell him that.

I sink onto the couch, my eyes on my phone. The picture showing must be one a witness took—it's colored and in amazing quality. It's an after shot, after the crash and the explosion and the fire. A pool of melted asphalt, leaking across the road, is the only sad remains of Dad. It is dark outside, with the yellow glow of lampposts and the flashing red-and-blue lights of the police cars. A few dark forms of the cops are grouped around the puddle of asphalt, most likely scratching their heads at how the road had simply grown too hot and melted.

Swiping to the side on my screen, another picture reveals itself. This one is of a blaze—a pile of flaming metal and leather and plastic. I can't even make out either of the cars.

The next picture is of the beginning, before the fire had flared up brightly and blindingly hot. I see Dad's car—a small, smashed, crumpled car with a large, heavy eighteen-wheeler truck stuck in its front. Both vehicles are on fire; in fact, the truck is slowly melting, the red cabin scorched black. Dad's car is almost lost in the inferno.

It's the last picture. The one after it is the video—the one Grandma Ferrari saw and told me was *horrible*. She'd also said it was black-and-white, the result of the accident happening at night without the sunlight to turn things colorful.

Swallowing, I tap on the video.

I immediately realize Grandma Ferrari was wrong. The video isn't black-and-white; it has a greenish hue that, for some reason, reminds me of slimy frogs. The camera angle is cast down at the all-too-familiar street, with an all-too-familiar car sitting in a turn lane, waiting for the stoplight to switch to green. No other vehicles are on the road except for Dad's. No one is walking by on the sidewalks adjoining the street—the eyewitnesses watched the accident from inside buildings around the road. Everything is quiet and peaceful, but that might be because there's no audio to the video. Someone out of the shot of the camera could be screaming right now and I would never know it.

All of a sudden, a dark shape appears, coming fast and hard down the road towards Dad. I can't see Dad inside his car, and I wonder if he knew he was going to die for the split second before the truck slammed into him and everything caught fire. I wonder if Dad felt bad he had neglected his family. I wonder if he tried to repent for all the pain he caused in those few moments before his death.

I get an itchy feeling again—the same I'd had when I was on my way to Nate's house a few hours ago. The spot on my back where I can't reach.

Why has it returned?

And why won't it go away?

I bite my lip, watching the video. The truck takes form, going far above the speed limit for such a small road. Both Dad and the truck are on the same side, both facing each other, both not making any move to swerve out of the way and avoid a head-on collision. My teeth sink deeper and deeper into my bottom lip as I wait, my entire body tense but prepared for the accident when it happens.

The truck is swinging around the street madly, like the driver has lost all control of the wheel and can only close his eyes tight and hope for a fast and painless death. But no matter how wildly the truck is driving, it has made its destination very clear—Dad. After every wide swing to the right or to the left, the truck always is still heading for Dad's car.

Just as the truck is about to ram into Dad, the view of the camera changes to another camera, this one angling on the other side of Dad's car, the other side of the street, the other side of the truck. The screen is still the same shade of green, and it's not very clear, quality-wise and color-wise. Some of the shapes around the street are blurry. Across the road, I see the shadowy figure of a man waiting underneath a lamppost. He isn't doing anything. His features are impossible to make out in the dim light, but I imagine he either doesn't care for Dad's life or he's not paying attention to the disaster about to occur. I tear my gaze from him and realize the truck has straightened out; it's no longer swinging out of control. All it is doing now is heading right for Dad, not bothering to jerk around. And why didn't Dad move his car? Or jump out at least?

I pause the video as the truck is feet away from Dad—right in the middle of the intersection—and peer closer at my phone screen. I can't see anyone in Dad's car. From this view, I should be able to see him. The camera—it's on a stop light, most likely—is trained down at Dad. It should be showing him through his windshield, but I can't see him. There isn't even a dark form in the driver's seat.

Playing the video again, I watch in horror as the truck slams into Dad's car, shoving it farther down the left turn lane. The truck immediately comes to a complete stop—strange for a vehicle that was speeding out of control—and promptly explodes in a brilliant flash of white light. Again, there is no noise. It's only the video.

But the video is enough. It's enough proof to me that Dad is, in fact, dead.

Dead.

And I'm never going to see him again.

I force my teeth out of my lip and replay the video. I watch it over and over until I don't flinch when Dad's car explodes. I watch it over and over until the pain and sorrow of his loss is gone, replaced by gnawing worry and concern that I'm missing something. The itch just below my shoulder blades doesn't go away. An intangible feeling floods into me, taunting me as I try to work out what is bothering me so badly like this.

Then it hits me. So hard I drop my phone in my lap, the video still playing, not even halfway through yet.

I don't believe Dad is dead.

I don't *think* Dad is dead.

I know Dad isn't dead.

TWENTY-NINE

Mom leaves for California the next morning. She doesn't say a word, just walks out of the house with a suitcase in her hand and the car keys in her other. She said her goodbyes to us the night before, smothering us with love and affection like she hasn't in years. She had varying degrees of reception and reciprocation, but this morning everything is still and cold. Pompeii and Siena call another goodbye from the doorway, and I'm glad at least they were here; Roman and Flo are notably absent, despite my attempts to bring them out.

I watch Mom walk down the driveway, a load of something that is *not* sorrow weighing down my heart. Mom's head is hung low, and her usual snappy outfit is wrinkled and creased in many places. She's dejected, Dad's loss pulling her into the depths of despair. I can tell by the way she stumbles over to the car, fumbling to get the door open. I'd offered to drive her to the airport, but she protested that I didn't have my license yet. Plus, she told me she doesn't want any of us to be crashed into like Dad.

Understandable.

I haven't said anything about my new realization. I don't know who to tell; Grandma and Grandpa Pope will think I'm just refusing the truth, and my siblings can't talk to me, and Mom is going to California. If I tell her, she'll probably say I'm wishing for something that isn't true. That it's just blind hope. That Dad is dead, no matter what we want. That I need to stop coming up with daydreams—I'm sixteen now and have to accept Fate, even if I don't want to.

So I keep it to myself. I don't say a word as Mom gets in the car and slowly drives off, not looking back, never looking back. I'm concerned about her—she really should have let me drive her to the airport—and I fervently hope everything goes well for her, that she doesn't run into any trouble. Literally and figuratively.

The morning chill soon starts to get me, and I enter the house, closing the door softly behind me. Grandpa and Grandpa Pope are still downstairs in the guest room and won't be awake for a while—they had a hard time falling asleep after what had happened—and I know that for now, I'm the only one up and about. Pompeii and Siena have returned to their rooms. Normally, Flo is up first, but today I haven't heard a single slight noise from our room. Roman is downstairs, too, and he hasn't shown his face for the past twelve hours. He easily got bored of throwing rocks at living things and returned inside, only to flop down on his bed and ignore my calls that dinner was ready.

Pompeii and Siena came down again, thankfully, faces tear-streaked and eyes red. We ate in silence, not talking, not trusting ourselves enough to without bursting into tears. Well, in Pompeii and Siena's case; I haven't shed one tear over Dad. Grandma Pope has, Grandpa Pope hasn't. I don't think he's ever forgiven Dad for abandoning his daughter and their children.

Siena's tears are for Mom. She told me herself. She's never seen Mom so broken, and she's angry that Mom cares this much about someone who hadn't given us a second thought in years.

Sighing to myself, I press my forehead against the cold door and wait for Nate to show up for our walk to school. It'll be good to escape all the pain and unexpressed feelings in this deathly quiet house. I transfer my own pain and frustration into worry for Nate. I will ask him about his grandpa, not caring if he goes mute; I'll force an answer out of him. I'll take off his gloves as proof of the abuse.

Nate can't deny how he got those cuts then, if I reveal how torn up his hands are, evidence of being cut by glass shards.

I wait by the door for nearly an hour, and as the minutes tick by I get more and more anxious that Nate isn't coming. Right now, when I need him the most, he isn't coming.

At half-past eight, I give up and slide down the wall, landing in a heap on the floor. Why did he have to choose today not to come? Why did he have to skip school or forget about me or whatever happened today? The day I need his company and his smile and his dimples desperately.

I drop my head into my hands, running my fingers through my hair. I know I look like a mess, inside and out. It's probably best Nate didn't come today. Who knows what I would have said or how I would have said it. My emotions are tumbling around and around, certain ones jumping out at me.

Shock. I'm shocked to learn that Dad died, only to determine that maybe he isn't dead, that he is still alive, and that only I believe this. I'm shocked that Nate's grandpa abuses him and Nate does nothing to stop him from throwing beer bottles at him, causing him to be cut up. I'm shocked that Nate hasn't come for me—is it because of yesterday? Is he not going to school today because he's too hurt and too worried people will find out?

Concern. I'm concerned about my family, Mom and Florence especially. Mom has taken Dad's death too seriously. It's been six years since Dad left. And Mom had moved on to Marc. Bleh. Why is she so distraught? Also, Flo rarely shows this much sorrow for someone, but maybe it's since Dad corresponded regularly with her and none of us. She's closer to him than any of us. I am concerned for Nate, concerned about how long his grandpa has treated him like what I saw yesterday. I'm concerned, again, for Mom, who is traveling by herself to California to Dad's funeral—a funeral that I feel strongly probably does *not* need to happen.

Anger. I'm angry at Dad for not reaching out to us and telling us that he is still alive, that the car accident was a hoax and he's healthy and on his way to come visit us soon. I'm angry with the truck that crashed into Dad's car, making everyone believe Dad is dead. I'm angry that I can't prove it and that my theory will be laughed at or dismissed or misunderstood as a delusion of grief. But the more I think about it, the surer I become. I don't think the driver of the truck is dead, either. He staged his death and he staged Dad's. That much was clear by the empty front seats and the *no body to be buried*.

Confusion. I'm confused by the whole thing. What is the charade about? *Why* would someone want Dad dead, or at least presumed dead? Did the thief/driver even know Dad? If so, what is their connection? What kind of trouble is Dad in and, if he's not dead, where is he now?

Plenty of other emotions are swirling around inside of me, too many for me to name. I just stay there on the floor, my back pressed to the wall, my eyes closed, my breaths ragged and drawn-out. A thousand thoughts join in with my emotions, twisting into a bewildering tangle; I can barely distinguish the two.

After a while, my emotions leak out and I'm left worn and tired and still in the same spot on the floor by the front door, waiting for someone I know will not come.

Afternoon is blank and seemingly endless. I don't remember much that goes on except for watching Grandma Pope's favorite TV show for a couple of hours until I'm so hungry I return to the kitchen and moodily whip up a meal that's more of a snack than lunch. While I'm throwing things together, Flo comes down and grabs a handful of random food items before leaving just as fast as she arrived. I want to ask how she's doing, but by the way her face sags and she walks with a droop, I know my twin is not doing well at all. I ask anyway, to show I care, and she hesitates, but she doesn't respond as she heads back upstairs.

My phone chimes, a welcome distraction from my thoughts. I wearily fish the device from my pocket and see Mandy has texted me, wanting to know where I am and why I'm not in school.

I'm too exhausted to answer. I don't want to tell her about all our current problems, but I'm so touched by her concern for me that I almost start crying. Still, I don't reply. I can't talk to her yet.

Eating what I've made is a mistake. It's tasteless and I don't know exactly what I unconsciously mixed up, and after three bites I shove the bowl away and thump my head against the kitchen counter. I'm drained—but it's only because of the suffocating silence around me and my siblings' refusal to talk to me or to our grandparents, who are starting to get bored with me. I catch Grandpa sneaking leftover ice cream from my birthday, and instead of taking the ice cream back, I dig a spoon from the silverware drawer and join him. It doesn't help much, but at least I can say I've eaten *something* today. Not eating is another thing Grandma is appalled by.

The afternoon bleeds into evening, which bleeds into night, which bleeds into day again. I wait by the door for Nate, who doesn't come again. I watch TV with Grandma again, not seeing my siblings once except for Siena. She shows up downstairs and rests against me, staring at the television, not comprehending the show.

By the third day after Mom left, Grandma and Grandpa Pope are ready to go back to Florida, but not before they sit us down and they do their best to tell us it's time to stop moping and to get back to our lives. As they drive away we wave goodbye and blow kisses and try to be grateful grandkids, and the effort really does seem to help lift the gloom. Heading back into the house, we talk quietly about going back to school at the beginning of the next week and about trying to get the house back in order for when Mom gets home. I think everyone is exhausted from the strain of shock and grief and is ready to focus on something else.

As for me, I am surprised at how nervous I am to face Mandy

and Elijah and all my teachers at school. I'm not very good at hiding my emotions and I don't know if I can handle any well-intentioned questions. Unless those questions are asked by Nate. I only want to talk to him. But I'm too scared to go to his house for a second time. I'm scared I'll be seen by Nate's crazy grandpa. I'm scared *I* will see Nate being hurt. I'm scared of everything about that place—the aura, the owner of the house, the neighbors. Well, not *everything*. I'm not scared of Nate.

Except that one time he got mad at me for asking about his family. Then I had been scared of him.

Nate will be at school. But why hasn't he stopped by here? Did he see me at his house? Is he angry with me? These thoughts don't help me want to go back to school.

Closing my eyes, I lean on the door frame, wishing I was somewhere else. I wonder when Mom will come home. I wonder if I should have gone with her to California.

But maybe going with Mom wouldn't have been an escape, anyway. She's just as heartbroken as my siblings, possibly even more so.

My phone dings. Is it Mom? Is it Mandy? Why didn't I ever give Nate my number? Because that's who I want the text to be from.

Before I can get my phone out of my pocket to see who texted me, my phone dings again, sounding impatient. To my surprise, it's Grandma Ferrari, not Nate or Mandy or Mom. She has sent me more pictures of Dad's accident.

Curiosity replacing my disappointment, I open a picture.

It's taken from behind Dad's car, just after the oil truck crashed into him. I can see Dad's license plate, see the numbers and letters. I zoom in on the screen, trying to read it.

Instead, I notice the blue-and-orange colors of the plate. Frowning, I shift my position on the floor and search up what the different state license plates look like and which one matches Dad's. I scroll through the *M* states for what seems like an hour before coming across the *N*'s. Those take just as long, and right when I'm about to pass out from exhaustion and the strain I'm putting on my eyes, I spot it. The familiar blue-and-orange colored plate with a small brown shape in the corner. A bison.

The license plate is from North Dakota.

I shiver violently. This picture must be how the police were able to track down Dad, find out who he is and where he lives and who his family is. So Dad really had been living in North Dakota for some time, until he mysteriously decided to go to Kentucky and fake his death.

I've looked over that video so many times that I'm absolutely sure no one was in those vehicles. Not only could I not see Dad in the driver's seat, but Dad's car had sat in that left turn lane for nearly a whole minute while he could have turned onto the next street. And the truck—with all its fancy maneuvering—suddenly straightens out and crushes Dad's car. Why did the driver stop his twisting and swerving, his *attempts* to avoid a collision?

My theory is that somehow, the driver managed to change the street camera to a different one, cutting out the three seconds it takes for him to jump out of his truck and cross the street, hiding in the shadows. And maybe some of his buddies nabbed Dad before the truck even showed up ahead of Dad's car. There are too many little *why*'s to make me believe Dad is dead.

I should tell my siblings. I should tell them that Dad isn't actually dead, and I can show them the video and point out all the things I discovered. I take a deep breath and am just about to call for everyone to meet up in the living room when my phone rings.

Answering the call, I say, "Hello?"

"Venice! Thank goodness you finally answered!"

I start. "Mom? What's wrong?"

She sighs, long and loud. "The funeral was fine. It was so sad and I bawled the entire time with Grandma Ferrari. Since there isn't a body, we put a picture of Angelo in the coffin and used that."

"Oh." I tuck a strand of auburn hair behind my ear. "How are Grandma and Grandpa Ferrari?"

Mom sighs again. "Fine. We're all fine. Just...fine."

"What else is up? Anything new?"

"I have to go up to North Dakota and look through Angelo's stuff," Mom says, her voice tired. "I don't want to, but his parents convinced me that I should. So I'm going to be gone for a few more days, maybe another week."

"A week?" I echo. "That long? Why?"

"I don't know, Venice. I wish I could come back sooner. Don't get into any trouble, you hear me?"

"You know that's impossible in our family."

There's a hint of a laugh in her voice as she replies, "I know."

Wanting to hear that faint hope of joy, I say, "Remember the time Pompeii held Siena's favorite picture book hostage?"

"And threatened to burn it unless she gave him back his breath mints that she had stolen?" Mom is so close to laughing, but then I hear a distant voice say something over the phone. After a moment, Mom returns. "I have to go now," she mumbles. "Make sure you tell the kids I won't be back for a week. I'll see you guys next Friday. Go to school every day and don't take thirty-minute showers, okay? I promise I'll call you whenever I can. Goodbye, Venice. I love you. Say hi to my parents for me, will you?" And, before I can tell her that Grandma and Grandpa Pope are back in Florida or that I love her too, she hangs up, leaving me disappointed and, more than ever, lonely.

THIRTY

"**Out! Get out of bed** right now, or I'll dump some ice water on you! Yes, I know how uncomfortable that is, Venice. Come on." My twin grabs my warm and precious blankets and heaves them off of me and onto the cold floor of our bedroom. "Hurry up, Venice. We all agreed that we have to go to school today. I already got Siena and Pompeii up."

I'm too weak and groggy and am completely convinced I am dreaming. Especially that last part. Flo got the younger kids out of bed? Flo is trying to help me follow through on something?

"I think they thought I was you coming to wake them, until I ripped their covers off of them and they knew it was me."

Shaking the bewilderment from my sleepy head I sit up and rub my eyes. "Um, thanks Flo." It's almost a question.

"That's the spirit!" she says cheerfully, throwing my blankets at my face. "I'm going to wake up Roman. If you're asleep again when I come back, then I won't be as merciful."

Blessed Hallelujah! I don't have to wake Roman! I am dreaming or I'm in the Twilight Zone, but I don't care which one it is, I'm going with it.

Suddenly, I'm inexplicably curious to watch how she handles Roman.

I skip down the stairs and hurry to the basement, hoping I haven't missed it. It will be tough getting Roman to cooperate, which, I think, is why Flo grabbed her spray bottle full of water on the way out of our room.

The basement is cold and dark. So is Roman's bedroom. I catch up to Flo as soon as she flicks on the light switch. His room is flooded with bright white light that illuminates a Roman-shaped lump on his bed. He grunts something at us, sounding annoyed and, as I'd guessed, grumpy. As a reply, Flo squirts his ear with the spray bottle.

He lets out an inhumane screech, sitting up abruptly. "What was *that*?" he yells, spotting us loitering, and laughing, in the doorway, spray bottle in Flo's hand.

"You needed to wake up." Flo shrugs. "I think we succeeded. Back to school. Back to life." Her tone has gotten unexpectedly gentle. "Come on, Roman, you know we need to move on."

He collapses on his bed, muttering under his breath, but I can tell he's not angry, just annoyed. "Alright, I'll get up. Now leave."

"Sure thing. But just to make sure…" Flo squirts him again, this time in the face, and then bolts out of the room, pushing me out with her in her haste. She is laughing hysterically, and I can't help but laugh, too. Roman roars in outrage, only to slam the door shut behind us.

Our laughter starts to peter out as we hurry upstairs. Flo turns to me and says seriously, "Now don't take a fifteen-minute shower. I barely went over ten today. I promise."

I nod slowly, confused as to why she's telling me this. "Alright," I say. "Uh, good job. Thanks."

Flo smiles brightly, showing off most of her sparkling white teeth. "I know, it's crazy," she says, shrugging her shoulders. "I usually take forever and ever and it makes Mom mad, so when she comes back you can tell her that I took a super short shower. M'kay?"

"Um…" I blink. "Sure." Yeah, definitely the Twilight Zone.

I examine her carefully now. Her dark purple lipstick goes

perfectly well with what she's wearing: long black pants and a crisp white blouse, brown leather ankle boots and a thin jean jacket—the one Marc gave her for her birthday. Her earrings are giant golden hoops Dad sent her a few years ago. A thin gold-chain necklace is around her neck, completing the outfit. Her make-up is perfectly, artistically, put on: dark purple eye-shadow to match her lipstick, faint hints of red blush on her cheeks, eyelashes curled with mascara. To top it off, her fingernails are painted dark purple.

I wonder how long it took her. Her hair isn't even dry yet. Then again, her blow-dryer is losing its gumption and is starting to die.

I examine her for a quick second, then hand her my ring. "Here," I say. "It will go well with your outfit."

"Oh." Surprised, she slides it on her fourth finger.

"You look really great," I say, meaning it.

Flo's smile widens. "Thanks," she says, slightly shyly. "I've had enough of crying and sorrow. It feels good to try to get back to normal. Not that I'm trying to impress anyone. Most of the boys at school are already taken or just jerks, so why should I work so hard to make myself look good if no one will notice?" Her smile turns into a smirk. "The only unclaimed boy I have my eye on won't acknowledge my existence. He's too busy looking at my older sister."

I frown. "What?"

Flo laughs, moving around me. "Never mind, Venice. You must be blind to not know who I mean."

I stare after her, still puzzled why she's acting this way. Teasing me is normal, but could there be some truth to what she's saying? Wait, and is she *jealous* that Nate doesn't pay attention to her, or was that just her way of trying to point out that he only pays attention to me?

It's surprising that he isn't attracted to her.

It's also a relief.

Blowing out a puff of air, I quickly set myself to getting ready for the day. I've given up hope that Nate will stop by. I guess I'm grateful because then I don't have to make excuses and I don't have to face the awkwardness of knowing his secret. But I think I'm more disappointed than grateful.

In no time I make my way downstairs to find my other three siblings in the kitchen, all shouting at each other while fixing their different breakfasts. They all look up at me when I enter, and as one they all fall silent and watch me carefully.

"Good morning everyone," I say, tone lilting towards caution. "Is everything okay? Well, under the circumstances?"

"What is up with Florence?" Roman asks. "She's acting weird, like she's you or something."

As if on cue we hear Florence from the other room shouting in a sing-song voice, "Roman, our bus will be here in ten minutes. Venice, will you be going to get the younger kids to their buses?"

Roman makes a gesture indicating that she's proved his point.

"Okay." I scratch my forearm where my cut from last week has scabbed over and become itchy. "Yeah, of course. Pompeii"—his head snaps up at his name—"are you ready for school?"

"I guess," he says in a thoughtful tone of voice. He's still sad.

"Siena? How about you?"

"My oatmeal is cold," she complains. "And Pompeii used the last of the milk, so I had to use water."

I bite my lip to prevent laughter. "That's too bad," I say. "I can buy some more milk today. Do we need anything else?"

"Soda," says Roman. "And candy and cake and cookies—"

"You want to get sick? Because eating those things will do that to you." I smirk at him. "By the way, if I buy soda, then you have to eat dinner tonight. And I'm making chicken-noodle soup."

Roman glares at me. "I hate that soup. I hate *all* soups."

"It's your decision, not mine."

He groans. "Whatever. Don't get soda. I'm not going to eat chicken-noodle soup even for a reward."

Flo appears in the kitchen doorway, arms crossed tightly. "We have to go soon," she says. "Why are you all in here chatting? We've got to move along, people! Hurry up!"

Grumbling and complaining—well, Siena is complaining—my siblings go back to eating breakfast. They are all dressed for the day and look better than I've seen all week. At least they're preparing for school. I hadn't even hoped that I'd get them all out of bed and off to school. Florence really came through, today.

"So," my twin says, standing at my elbow, "you aren't planning on school today for yourself, are you?"

Another surprise. She's unusually astute today. I peer at her through my broken glasses; I've got to get some new ones. "Yes," I say. "I'm not going to school today. I have to clean the house and go shopping for more food and do a bunch of other stuff. Boring stuff. I wish I was attending school, but with all this…" I wave a hand at our kitchen; the piles of dirty plates in the sink, the stained floors, the filthy countertops, the sticky fingerprints on the walls. "Despite all of Grandma and Grandpa Pope's efforts, it is in desperate need of a deep-cleaning."

"True," says Flo, looking around. She then meets my gaze. "He'll miss you, though."

My frown returns. She works hard not to smile but fails, and after a moment she starts laughing.

"It's the truth!" she says, knocking her shoulder against mine. "For some random reason, he and those other geeks you hang out with actually like you. I don't know how, but they do."

I roll my eyes. She's back to her normal critical self. "Thanks."

"Any day, sister," says Florence. She pats my arm and drifts by, yelling at our younger siblings to hurry up and eat before they all miss the bus and have to walk to school.

That reminds me of Nate, and I glance back at the front door, wondering why he hasn't stopped by in eight days.

*****

Twenty minutes later, the house is quiet and I'm all by myself. I spend the first few hours cleaning up like I said I'd needed to do, and the time flies by so quickly I'm amazed it's almost one in the afternoon when I finally finish the whole middle floor. I won't clean the basement or the third floor—they are slightly better than the ground floor was—and I leave the bedrooms for their inhabitants to clean. They aren't my responsibility.

After a brief lunch, I wheel my bike out of the garage—having to pump up the tires since I haven't ridden it for over two months—and ride to the tiny shoppette down the street opposite our school. The food there is overpriced and I grimace at the sight of my near-empty wallet after paying for my items. I really need to get a job, and soon.

The trip home is harder than the trip to the store. I hang the bags on my handlebars—hurting inside at the plastic—and I am terrified they will break and the food will become inedible and I will have spent my money for nothing. I am lucky, thank the trees, that I arrive home with nothing broken or lost or anything unfortunate.

I unload the groceries then, exhausted, flop down on the bamboo floor by the front door and close my eyes. I rest my back against the wall by the door and release a sigh.

"I want to sleep," I murmur. "I want..."

Suddenly, something in the kitchen shatters. I leap to my feet, startled and now wide-awake and alert.

"You idiot," I hear a voice whisper. "You knocked that jar over. Now she probably knows we're here."

"You just announced that to the world!" exclaims another in a loud whisper.

I freeze where I stand, my heart pounding. My fingers twitch, and I reach for my phone before I comprehend what the men have said.

She. Are they talking about me?

"Whatever." The first voice—he sounds like a Rupert, so that's what I'll call him in my mind—is impatient. "You take the downstairs. I'll search upstairs. If you find her, remember the plan. Sleepy Gumption doesn't want us to kidnap her. We just want it."

"I know." The second man—I'll call him Quentin—is shuffling towards the downstairs. "I know the plan."

"Hurry," says Rupert.

I hold my breath, edge towards the living room. It leads into the kitchen, so maybe I can sneak around these men and escape, then call the police and have them arrested. What are Rupert and Quentin doing in my house, anyway? And are they talking about *me*? Who is Sleepy Gumption? What do they want? What is *it*? They don't mean my ring, do they? That's what Nate said they were after—at least, what the SUV driver was wanting. Are these men working for the driver? Is the driver Sleepy Gumption? And what kind of name is *Sleepy Gumption*?

I peer around the corner, spotting a man dressed in dark clothes standing on the other side of the kitchen, rummaging through our cabinets; probably looking for something to eat. As I watch, Rupert takes a granola bar, glares at it, and throws it over his shoulder in my general direction. I stifle a gasp and duck out of the way.

"There's nothing but crap in these cabinets," Rupert complains. "Organic pretzels? Seriously?"

My eyes flick over to the door, which is far behind Rupert and to the right. I can make it if I run fast enough. I glance back at the front door, wondering if I should use that, but I nix the idea almost immediately. That door has really squeaky hinges and if I go out that way, it'll give away my position. Rupert and Quentin will be after me in an instant.

Rupert continues to bemoan the fact that *nothing* in the kitchen is edible. Quentin is somewhere downstairs, hunting for me. I'm hiding in the doorway to the kitchen, watching Rupert and waiting for my chance to escape. All I need is for him to leave.

Right on cue, he wanders out of the kitchen, down the hallway towards the utility room and Mom's office. I hesitate only a moment before darting out of the living room, making my way to the back door.

It's a mistake. Quentin has just arrived at the top of the stairs in time to see me yank open the back door and slip outside. He shouts something, telling Rupert that I'm right here, and I fumble to lock the door behind me. Quentin is soon banging on the wooden frame, yelling curses at me. I catch a glimpse of his face: pale skin, soft blonde hair, dark brown eyes filled with malice. My heartbeat quickens, then I'm turning and running for the fence separating our yard and our neighbor's.

I quickly call the police while I'm running. I'm scared the men—whoever they are—will catch up to me before I get help.

Splintered sounds from behind me announce that Quentin has succeeded in kicking the door open. I hear him screaming at Rupert to grab me before I can escape. Footsteps beat a steady tattoo on the grass far behind, and I'm more scared than a minute ago.

I reach the chain-link fence and scramble over, the whole thing wobbling under my weight. My feet hit the ground, and I'm running again, this time through a small cluster of trees that border our neighbor's property. She's a kindly old woman and doesn't mind it when we climb the trees here. In my desperation, I allow myself to reason that she is most likely fine with me tearing through her sort-of yard since she's so nice.

Labored breathing. Rupert is catching up to me.

I finish my jumbled call and shove my phone in my pocket, praying I'll have enough time to reach my neighbor's house and that Rupert and Quentin will be too worried to jeopardize their mission to follow me inside.

A hand grabs my arm, yanking me around. I instinctively jab my fingers into Rupert's eyes—a weak spot—and he howls, releasing me. I'm up and running before he can grab me again.

My neighbor's house looms up in front of me. I burst out of the trees and rush up her deck, banging on her back door with my fist. I'm breathing hard, fast and unsteady; my heart is beating so quickly I'm sure it'll never calm down.

I glance back at Rupert and Quentin. I can see them through the trees, the men angrily puffing as they hurry to find me. Rupert has a hand covering his left eye.

Returning to the door, I knock again, louder. I'm nervous and terrified and *what is taking her so long?*

Desperately, I try the doorknob and discover it's locked, which is when I realize all her lights are off and her house is quieter than normal.

"Seriously?" I mutter, turning away. She *had* to choose this day to be gone? The very day when I need her help the most? What is it with people sticking me up this past week?

Rupert and Quentin are almost at the deck. I vault over the side, landing awkwardly on the grass. I get up and head for my neighbor's garage, which I hope isn't locked.

But my luck is out today. All I get in return is the loss of a few precious seconds.

I dive into the trees again, Rupert and Quentin following me. I'm tired and don't know if I'll last much longer. Fortunately for me, my hunters are also growing exhausted. Quentin is lagging behind; he probably isn't used to his prey giving him a serious workout, and Rupert is hurting, eyes wounded from when I'd poked him.

Skidding around several pine trees, I curse my luck—again—as none of the trees have leaves I can hide in, and the ones with leaves, a.k.a. pine needles, have branches too high for me to reach. I can't climb a tree to hide from the men chasing me.

"Stop!" Quentin huffs, coming up next to me.

I jolt, ready to flee, but he latches onto my arm and prevents me from getting away.

"Stop," he repeats, and I struggle to get out of his grasp.

Rupert appears at my side, grabbing my other arm. "What part of stop do you not understand?" he rasps.

I try to yank myself free, but it's pointless. They're too strong. "What do you want?" I force out, hating myself for having paused and given them the chance of capturing me. My only hope is the police now. I really, really, hope they arrive soon. If not, then...I shudder and try not to think about what these men might do to me.

"Where is it?" hisses Rupert.

"Where's what? The library? It's down the street a little ways, right before the school—"

Rupert smacks my head sharply. "Idiot girl," he snarls.

"Listen, Rupert," I say, my eyes watering at the hard blow. "I don't know what you're talking about—"

"Did you just call me *Rupert*?"

I stifle a hysterical giggle. Beside me, Quentin looks humored. His mouth is curving up at the ends. If that man wasn't accosting me, I would probably get right along with him.

"Where is it?" Rupert gives me a shake, like doing that will loosen up my brain and make me instantly know what he wants.

I get even cheekier, trying to buy some time. "Rupert, how am I supposed to know what you want if you don't tell me what it is? Do you want some ice cream? I think we might have some left—"

Another sharp slap silences me.

"The gem," he says, dragging me in the direction of my house. "Where is the gem?"

"What gem?"

Rupert laughs caustically. "My, aren't you stupid!"

I frown. "That's not very nice."

"Rupert," adds Quentin.

"Ugh!" Rupert yanks me from Quentin's grasp and continues our trekking through the trees. "My name isn't Rupert."

"Then what is it?" I ask curiously.

He throws me a nasty look. "I'm not going to tell you."

I shrug one shoulder. "Okay, Rupert." I'm stalling for time so the police can arrive, aiming for nonchalance even though my knees are trembling violently and my heartbeat is fierce. I'm terrified of what these men might do to me—they say they want my ring's stone, the gem—but they can overpower me as easily as before.

Rupert doesn't say anything until we've entered the backyard and are facing the house. He backs me up against the doorway to the kitchen, and I see how Quentin has, luckily, only kicked open the door without breaking pieces of the frame.

"Give it to us," Rupert snarls, pushing me into the house.

The kitchen is still clean—my gorgeous job is only spoiled by the organic snacks littering the floor, the dirt the men tracked in and the broken jar of cinnamon sticks Quentin knocked over.

"Give you what?" I ask, pulling free. I sit down on a stool at the counter and frown at the men who have invaded my home.

Rupert growls low in the back of his throat. "Stop acting like an idiot," he says. "Give us the stone. The one in your ring."

I unconsciously cover my right hand with my left, even though I'm not currently wearing my ring. Nate was right. But my ring isn't there. I sent it to school with Florence. I'm suddenly very glad I did.

"I don't have a ring," I say. "I'm only sixteen. I'm not ready to get married yet. Plus, my mom would be really mad—"

Rupert slaps me again and groans, spinning away from me to face Quentin. "Why is she like this?" he complains. "Malaise Tone said she was smarter than she looks, but I think he was lying!"

"What kind of name is *Malaise Tone*?" I ask.

Rupert sneers at me. "What kind of name is *Rupert*?"

"I don't know," I say readily. "Ask your mom." Then I pause. "Or your dad. Whoever named you."

"For that last time," he growls, "my name is *not* Rupert."

I shrug. "Okay, okay. Sorry. I keep forgetting because I don't know your actual name. You can't blame me for not knowing it— you're the one who won't tell me."

Rupert sighs loudly, turning his back on me. "Cook," he says to Quentin, "I think you need to loosen this girl's tongue. She knows where the ring and the stone are, but she's keeping it from us, and it's really irritating me. She needs to be cracked."

As he's talking, my eyes flick over to the clock on the oven. It's one twenty-eight. I called the police about four minutes ago.

When will they be here?

"So," says Quentin, positioning himself in front of me. "You came up with names for both of us, right?"

"That's right, Quentin," I say, worried what will come next.

He grins, his teeth yellow. I grimace. "Then you won't be offended if I tell you the name I came up with for you?" he says.

"Um…" I tug at the hem of my T-shirt. "Depends."

"I was thinking," he begins, but Rupert interrupts him.

"Hurry up! We haven't got all day!"

Quentin shoots him a nasty look, then returns to me. "I was thinking," he repeats, "that you're a Mary."

I clap my hands together, trying to act perky and obnoxious. "Well, that is funny!" I squeal. "I have an aunt whose name is Mary!" It's a lie. Mom and Dad are both only children. "Aunt Mary is really nice," I continue, stalling. "She is my dad's sister, and she visits whenever he does. But"—here I pause to scowl at Rupert and Quentin—"you guys killed my dad, didn't you?"

Quentin is surprised. He scoffs, smiles, and then smirks. "I *personally* didn't," he says.

"Stop talking!" Rupert slams his fist into Quentin's shoulder. "You're being a bigger idiot than she is! Stop talking, Cook!"

"Hey, hey, break it up," I say, sliding off my stool. Against my better judgment, I sort of like Quentin. He's a fool enough to fall for my playacting. And he's rather funny.

Rupert rounds on me, furious. He grabs me by my throat and shoves me up against the counter. "Where is it?" he yells.

I tug at his hands, trying to pull them away so I can breathe.

He's choking me, and I can't respond to his question unless he lets go of me.

"Stop!" Quentin drags Rupert away, and I collapse to the floor, sucking in huge lungfuls of air. I rub my collarbone, my bruised neck, fingers trembling. "You can't get an answer out of her if she's dead!" Quentin says harshly, pushing Rupert in the chest. "And Sleepy Gumption told us to leave her alive! Malaise Tone agreed, too, though Hubris Jargon said he wanted to kill her himself."

"You're such an idiot!" Rupert screams, going for me again, and I squeak and scramble backwards, my shattered glasses dangling off my nose, glad I hadn't gotten them fixed yet.

He grabs the front of my shirt and pulls me to my feet, roughly shaking me over and over. "Where is it?" he bellows into my face. "Give it to me!"

I cough, his disgusting breath clogging up my lungs. "Give you what?" I ask weakly.

"AGH!" Rupert slams me down, my head hitting the edge of the counter. "YOU ANSWER ME RIGHT NOW!" he roars.

I drop to the floor, landing in a heap. My arms curl around my head, which is throbbing painfully. I feel a massive headache coming on.

"Stop it," says Quentin, pulling on Rupert's arm. "Stop it. She doesn't know anything. You don't need to keep hurting her. Sleepy Gumption won't like it at all."

Rupert turns on his companion, punching him again. "You're giving away too much information!"

I squeeze my eyes shut, wishing the pain would go away. I can barely even think. And all my thoughts are of escape. I need to get out of here. I need to find the police and have Rupert and Quentin arrested. I need to find Flo and my other siblings and my ring. Why do they want my ring? I need to hide it where no one can find it. I need to keep it safe.

But...if I give them my ring, will they leave me alone? Will they never try to run me over again? Will they stop breaking into my house and hurting me? Will they walk away and never come back?

I lift my head, my vision dim.

A pathway to freedom, to the door, to my escape, is directly in front of me. I weakly raise a hand, slowly drag myself to my feet. Neither Quentin nor Rupert pay any attention to me. They're too busy arguing about me, their eyes on each other, their fists on each other.

I take one step, then another, then a third, then a fourth. My freedom is so close, so close. I am almost there.

I am in the hallway when they notice I'm not in the kitchen any more. They both blame one another, then rush after me.

Panicked, I dive for the front door, turn the knob, and abruptly come face-to-face with two men dressed in police attire. Three cars sit in my driveway and against the curb. More cops are heading up our front lawn.

"Thank the trees!" I gasp out, fixing my glasses more firmly on my nose. "Quick! They're in the hallway!"

I jump to the side, let the two cops run in. Quentin and Rupert are nabbed before they can even protest, and I watch as the police load them into one of the cars.

After answering what seems like hundreds of questions about the two men who broke in, and still playing my dumb act—I don't give them any real answers—the cops finally leave with a promise to keep me informed about Rupert and Quentin. Of course, those aren't their actual names, and I'm very curious about who they are and who they work for and why they want my ring and what they'll do with it.

The afternoon passes with me fearfully looking out the window every two seconds. I lock the doors and the windows and stay huddled in my bedroom, breathing heavily. My head throbs where I'd hit the counter—second time I've smacked my head in the past week and a half—and my glasses have a new crack. Unfortunately, it's in the frame this time, so they keep slipping down my face and my good lens popped out once. My heart is still beating fast, and I doubt it will slow down anytime soon. Each car that goes by startles me so badly I end up hiding in the basement with the TV on in an attempt to distract me.

Instead, my mind wanders to snatches of what I've heard and learned and come up with.

In the café two Saturdays ago, Nate said the SUV driver wanted my ring. If the driver is Sleepy Gumption or Malaise Tone or whatever the other weird name was, then I'll know for certain that he wants my ring. But why? And it wasn't so much the ring, it was specifically the *stone*. The *gem.* That's what Rupert had called it.

Earlier, in the kitchen, they had talked about Sleepy Gumption not wanting me dead. Does he know who I am? And the other two—Malaise Tone and Hubris Jargon—what names are those? They are obviously code names. And I don't know who Rupert and Quentin are, but they seemed to know plenty about *me*. It's scary, unnerving, and uncomfortable.

And when I had mentioned Dad...Quentin had said he hadn't *personally* killed Dad. But that means he knows who did, right? Yet I don't think Dad is dead. Do they know he's not dead? Did the weirdly-named men kidnap him for the ring?

Which brings me back to: *Why do they want my ring?* It's old-looking and the two clear stones that used to be set in next to the blue stone were lost before I got the ring from Dad. I'd just assumed he went to a local thrift store and looked through the used jewelry. But I value my ring because it reminds me of Dad. I love it, no matter how dumpy it is. I don't care that the metal is slowly turning grey as the gold plating has slowly washed away. I don't care that it's missing two of its three stones. I don't care that it's cheap and trashy and *nothing* like the exquisite rings Florence has. But it's got to be more valuable that I ever expected.

I squeeze my fingers so hard they turn white. As soon as Flo comes home from school, I'm going to take my ring back and hide it where I will forget it's there and no one will find it. I don't know why, but I can't let those men get it. They can't.

Not after they almost ran me over when I was innocently crossing the road to get to the café.

Not after they killed Dad to get it or, hopefully, faked his death.

Not after they broke into my house, scared me half to death, and nearly killed me.

My resolve strengthened, I pick up my phone, hesitate, and call Mom. I have to tell her what happened.

She answers on the second ring. "Venice? What's wrong?"

My tongue is stuck to the roof of my mouth, but I'm able to force out the words, "Mom—some men broke into the house while I was home and scared me out of my wits. The police came and they're in jail now but I'm still terrified."

"*What?*"

I barely tell her anything, just that two men snuck in and freaked me out, but didn't hurt me—I have to lie there—and I called the police and they took away the criminals. Mom is utterly flabbergasted, and a little hysterical, but I understand—I'm growing unsteady, too. She grills me about every detail; it's hard for me to invent answers that won't reveal the truth.

"They're gone now, and I was alone because I stayed home from school to clean the house and go shopping, and then all of a sudden there were voices in the kitchen, and I called the police instantly, and hid, and when the cops came, they were able to arrest both of the burglars, and..."

"I can't believe this happened while I was gone!" cries Mom, anguished. "I'm flying home immediately! I'm never leaving you all again!"

Just the thought of being reunited with her brings me relief. I know I can always count on her to comfort me and to keep me safe. "Oh, Mom, I'll be so glad to see you."

"I bet you're scared out of your skin! Venice…"

"Yeah, I know it's irrational, but I'm still scared." It's true. I'm trembling. Like, violently. I know it's not over. There are others out there who still want the ring. "Even though the men are gone, I keep imagining I hear voices and footsteps around the house."

"They're in custody, right?" Mom's voice is unsteady.

"The police took them away like an hour ago—I was just too astounded to call you, and now everything's haunting me, and should I tell Flo and the others when they come back from school? They'll probably find out soon enough, whether from me or our neighbors. What do I do, Mom?"

"Let's calm down first." She inhales, exhales, and I copy her. After a minute of silence, she says, "Tell them when you want. Warn them. Be careful how you tell Siena. How could this have happened when I was gone? I'm so sorry, Venice."

I take a deep breath. "I'm better now," I say, though it isn't strictly true.

"You said they didn't hurt you?"

"I'm fine."

"Okay." Mom breathes out. "Okay. They're gone, you're safe." She's saying this to reassure herself and me, and I appreciate it. "I'm trying to get a flight home, but the earliest is Thursday, arriving in the afternoon…Why aren't there any other options? Ugh!"

"I'll be going to school tomorrow," I say. "I'm not going to stay here alone again."

"I understand. Stick close to your siblings, will you? You're a great older sister, and I trust you, but if you're okay with it I'm going to have Ms. Mehaine check on you guys often, too, or I can get Marc to—"

"Ms. Mehaine will be perfect," I say quickly, even though she's currently out of town, as I'd discovered earlier. "Thanks, Mom."

"Of course. You're doing fine? No trauma?"

"I'm definitely traumatized," I say. "But I'll recover. Eventually."

My hands aren't shaking as much as before. Hearing her voice has soothed me. Behold the power of mothers. "I love you so much."

"I love you, too, Venice. Call me whenever you want. I'll be here. I'm going to call the police and get an update on everything. And I'll see you in just a few days."

"Thank the trees."

We talk for a long time, sorting through the different things troubling both her and me—I keep back everything concerning my ring and those strange names—and I'm feeling much better when she finally hangs up.

My movie has long ended, and I play another, not paying attention to it at all. My mind is elsewhere. I don't want to tell my siblings what happened to me while they were at school, but they'll figure it out eventually, and I want them to hear it from me instead of someone else.

Presently, Flo comes skipping downstairs, giggling hysterically.

"Venice," she calls, startling me so badly I drop the TV remote. "Venice, I thought you were Mom's perfect child, but getting home to a big mess in the kitchen and finding you down here watching TV is proof you're not!"

I jerk upwards, blinking at my twin sister in the dim light.

"But who cares?" Flo launches herself onto the couch next to me, beaming from ear to ear. "Venice, you will *not* believe what happened today at school. It was amazing! Today is the best day of the entire year!"

"Did you finally pass a math test with a hundred percent score?" I ask, knowing that's not what she's overjoyed about.

"No, silly!" Florence collapses against me. "I talked to *him*. He actually hunted me down because he wanted to talk to me! But the reason was lame. He only wanted to find out where you were and why you weren't at school. As I told you, he missed you."

"Flo," I say, irritated, "will you *please* call him by name?"

She nudges me with her elbow. "Whatever. *Nate* hunted me

down to talk to me about you, and I think your ring brought me luck since he introduced me to this other hot guy who is friends with all you geeks—and he's not as hot as Nate, but he's pretty cute."

Curious, I ask, "What's his name?"

"Sam. He is super tall and he has nice hair and he's a good kisser, but his breath *stinks*. I mean, his looks make up for it—"

I interrupt her. "Wait, you already kissed him? And is this Sam, Elijah's cousin?"

"Who's Elijah?"

I roll my eyes, sinking deeper into the couch. "He's just one of my friends. I doubt you talked to him."

"Yeah, probably. Is he the blond one that keeps staring at the dark-haired girl like he's terrified of her?"

I smile. "Yes," I say. "That's him."

"Oh, I thought maybe he likes her, because he's constantly looking over at her and he's got this look in his eyes—" Flo suddenly stops. "Venice? Are you alright?"

"Hmm?" I glance up at her drowsily. "Y-yeah."

She purses her lips. "You're acting really strange, and you have an enormous bruise on your head. Did something happen today?"

I rest my head on her shoulder. "I'm just tired. Cleaning up the kitchen was exhausting."

"Yet you somehow forgot to sweep. And there's that broken jar of cinnamon sticks. What happened? I can be as pushy as you."

Groaning, I rub my eyes and straighten, annoyed that I can't erase all the evidence of someone breaking into my house. "I *did* forget," I say irritably. "Oh, I have such a big headache I can barely breathe."

Florence takes my hand, standing up and pulling me to my feet. "Come on," she says. "I can cheer you up. Let's go read that book Marc gave you—the one by that random old poetic dude."

"Shakespeare wasn't random or old," I say, turning off the TV. I allow her to tug me upstairs. "However, he was poetic."

"Not very good at it, though." Flo sighs. "I can't make heads or tails of what he means by what he says. I have to read the one play about the two lovers who both kill themselves since they can't be together because their parents hate each other, and none of it makes sense to me. I mean, I would *never* kill myself for a guy I like, and I don't want his parents to detest me, so like, I'd probably just look for someone who's more perfect and our ending won't be as dramatic as death. But that stupid play is hurting my brain while I try to understand everything."

I sort through what she's said. "You mean *Romeo and Juliet*?"

"Is that what it's called?" Flo and I emerge in the kitchen, and I blink in the bright sunlight. It's a whole lot brighter up here than downstairs.

Roman is examining the snacks Rupert had thrown around the kitchen. He looks up when I come in. "Did you make this mess?"

I begin to shake my head, then stop myself. "Uh, no. It was some magical dwarves that only eat food that isn't organic, so they wrecked the kitchen in search of unhealthy snacks. They couldn't find any and left. They didn't even clean up after themselves."

Flo bursts out laughing. Roman rolls his eyes.

"Is that why you locked the front door?" my twin asks. "I had to use my key to get in."

"Yup." I squeeze her hand. "I didn't want the dwarves to come back."

Roman scoffs. "Those poor dwarves. They didn't eat any of this food. They must be *starving* since they only eat unhealthy stuff like soda."

I lift an eyebrow. "Then I guess they missed the fridge."

"What?" He stares at me. "Wait, wait." His confused expression clears, and he grins. "You didn't, did you?"

"You have to eat soup tonight," I reply, and he groans.

"I knew there was a price!" he complains. "I knew it!"

"What are you talking about?" Flo asks, confused.

I mirror Roman's grin from before. "I bought him soda, but he can only drink it if he eats dinner tonight which, coincidentally, is chicken-noodle soup."

"Oh." Flo lets a small giggle slip out. She's certainly in a happy mood. "Will you not get your soda then, Roman? Since you have sworn never to eat soup again?"

"I didn't *swear* it," he mumbles.

At that moment, Pompeii and Siena come bursting into the house, yelling at each other for whatever they had done, until I interrupt, and everyone gives me their attention, something that is so surprising I'm left speechless for a moment. Then Flo prompts, "Yes?" and I find the courage to continue.

"Guys..." I begin. "While you were gone—"

"Those magic dwarves cleaned the kitchen for us and then ruined it again because they were bored?" asks Roman.

I frown at him. He laughs.

"No." I draw in a breath. "While you were gone, there were two men that broke in and..."

It's as far as I get before I'm interrupted again. "Someone came here? As in, our *house*? And *broke* in?" asks Florence, skeptically.

"You're lying," says Siena absentmindedly.

"I'm not. I called the police and they're gone now, in jail or whatever. Just ask the neighbors—they saw the cops over here, and they know something happened, only you don't need to tell them details. Okay? You don't need to say anything to them."

My siblings look unimpressed.

"I like the dwarves story better," says Florence.

"What's for dinner?" asks Pompeii, and just like that the subject of those men shifts to something totally different.

It's actually...relieving.

THIRTY-ONE

I'm a bundle of nerves the next morning. I have reclaimed my ring from Flo and wait for her to leave our bedroom before sticking it in the bottom of her jewelry box among her discarded pieces. I don't think she will see it in there, and even if she does she'll throw it out at me and tell me not to put it with her jewelry. Because Flo has decided she likes me for the time being, she lets me use an old pair of her glasses, some with grey-steel rims and both lenses smooth, with no cracks at all. I prefer *my* glasses, but I *do* need a pair of fixed ones. And my siblings still don't believe I had those men arrested. I honestly don't know why.

I don't manage to get everyone ready with enough time to spare for me to walk to school and I have to take the bus. It smells really bad and I can barely concentrate on *anything* with all the loud chatter swelling up around me. Flo sits by me, which helps calm me down slightly, but when the school comes into view I start all up again. I'm terrified to face Mandy—I've ignored her calls and texts for the past week and a half; I'm terrified to face Elijah—I'm positive he will bug me for not answering Mandy's calls and texts; and I am terrified to face Nate—I need to tell him everything that's happened, but at the same time I'm sure each time I look at him, I will flinch and remember his grandpa hurting him.

The bus stops with a halt, and after waiting nearly an hour—or so it seems to me—I step off and quickly glance around for my friends before setting off for the school building. I don't see anyone I know except a few kids from my different classes, and I've never had a conversation with them about things that don't relate to homework or that certain class subject.

I walk out of my homeroom and am almost spotted by Mandy, who is with Elijah—they are standing near a group of kids and don't even look my way. I breathe a sigh of relief and disappear down the hallway so I don't have to face them quite yet.

I am eternally grateful that none of my morning classes are with Nate or Mandy or Elijah.

But at the same time, I'm sad. I've missed my friends a lot. I wonder if they just talked about boring stuff without me—Mandy once told me that my contribution to the discussion was highly sought for. I remind myself that Sam, Elijah's cousin, is visiting; he probably spiced things up a bit unless he was too busy making out with my sister to pay attention to his cousin and his cousin's friends.

By lunch, my heart is pounding and I feel faint. I overhear someone telling her boyfriend or brother or just plain friend—I don't know which one—that today is a half-day since one of the floors in the school is getting repainted so the principal cut the school day short. That does nothing to soothe my nerves, knowing I'm going home sooner than later.

The cafeteria is crowded, but not as much as usual. Most kids have already left; lunch isn't mandatory today. We're all leaving early anyway, might as well do it now. I spot Flo talking to her friends and give her a small wave which she returns, surprisingly. I guess she's still acting nice towards me, and thinking that sends a rivet of warmth running down my spine. I make a mental note to be more kind to her.

I sit down at the table I always eat at and wait for my friends to arrive. I'm the first here and wonder if they've skipped lunch today and gone straight to Elijah's house to play video games or, in Nate's case, watch them play video games.

Then I hear someone scream—actually *scream*—my name, and I know they haven't left yet.

Mandy wraps me in her typical bear-hug, squeezing me so hard my ribs creak and my lungs can't draw in oxygen. Kids all around us are staring at me and at Mandy, but I suddenly don't care and hug my best friend back. I really *have* missed her.

"Where have you *been?*" Mandy screeches, pushing me away. "Nine days, Venice! *Nine!* You haven't answered my texts or called me back or let me know that you were still alive—"

I grin tiredly, listening to her ramble on and on about how I should be ashamed for ignoring her and that my mom should ground me—oh, wait, then I can't hang out with my friends, so don't get grounded even though I deserve it.

Elijah slides onto the seat next to me, cutting across Mandy. "Hey, Venice. What's up?"

"Not too much," I lie, trying to keep my focus on him and not on Nate, who has just sat down across the table from me.

"Then, if you haven't been busy," says Elijah, "how come we haven't seen you in..." he thinks hard. "How long was it? Oh, yes. Nine days. Nine whole days, according to Mandy."

I stiffen, shifting my gaze to a spot over his shoulder. "I've..."

Another kid sits down, on the other side of Nate. He looks like Elijah: the same blond hair and beginnings of a mustache, the light hazel eyes and mischievous glint. But the similarities end there. While Elijah is more plain and simple, which I find more attractive—not that I'm saying I'm attracted to *him*—this kid is ruggedly handsome. He also has an air of confidence around him that Elijah does not.

"Hey," he says in a deep voice that is noticeably quieter and less startling than Elijah's. And he winks at me.

Oh no. He thinks I'm my sister. I blush because he thinks he's made out with me, and give Sam a tight smile—he *has* to be Sam—then risk a glance at Nate. He seems slightly confused, and his eyes are narrowed as he stares thoughtfully at me. My blush deepens and I tear my gaze away.

"This is my cousin, Sam, but it appears you two already know each other?" Elijah is saying, motioning towards the blond kid who so closely resembles him but does not at the same time.

"Nice to meet you, Sam," I say, not completely looking at him. "I'm Venice Ferrari."

He frowns. "Venice?

Elijah has caught on, slaps him on the back and says, "She has a twin sister."

"So, Venice," interrupts Mandy. "What took you so long to come back? Were you sick or something?"

I shake my head, eyes on my lap. "No." My response is barely a whisper.

"Then what?"

My shoulders unfold slightly. "Last Sunday..." I take a deep breath. "Last Sunday, we received the news that my dad was killed in a car accident, and it really shook up our family."

I feel Elijah and Mandy exchange glances. Sam isn't paying attention to us at all. Nate continues to stare at me.

"Oh," Mandy says awkwardly but sympathetically. "I'm sorry."

"It's okay," I reply. She doesn't need to be sorry for something she didn't cause. And anyway, Dad is still alive.

"Why didn't you tell me earlier?" Mandy pleads.

I blink at her. "Um, because I didn't really..." I scrunch up my nose and try to invent an excuse on the spot. "You just—I didn't—" I pause, then attempt another answer. "My grandparents were over, and I spent all my free time with them while my siblings were off doing...whatever they were doing. And I just—I forgot to tell anyone."

"Oh," Mandy says again. "Did you have to go to the funeral?"

I straighten. "No, actually. It was in California, and only my mom went. I had to stay home and make sure my siblings didn't burn down the house or murder someone on accident or purpose. Plus, there was no body to bury, so I felt like I didn't need to attend a funeral for an empty coffin."

Both Mandy and Elijah gape at me. "What happened to his body?" Elijah asks finally.

I pull a thoughtful expression. "It melted. Into the road. After his car and the truck that hit him exploded."

Heavy silence falls over us. My friends are probably confused why what I'm saying is so sarcastic. Elijah and Mandy seem to have run out of questions, and Nate hasn't said anything yet.

"Why was the funeral in California?" asks Sam.

I turn to him, and now I'm confused. "What?"

He patiently explains, "You said that your dad's funeral was in California. It's all the way across the country. Why wasn't it here?"

"My mom and dad are divorced," I explain. "Dad's parents live in California and they decided to have the funeral there, close to them. But my dad was killed in Kentucky and he lives in North Dakota."

"Venice, why didn't your sister tell us when we asked her?" says Mandy. "She only said that..." She thinks hard, and I'm almost scared to learn what Florence had told my friends. "There was this nonsense about..." she turns to Nate, who is sitting next to her. "Didn't she say something stupid about Venice being momentarily incapacitated?"

Nate opens his mouth to answer, but at that very moment Flo herself flaunts up to us, her eyes fixed hungrily on Sam.

"Hello," she says, scooting onto my seat to smush against me.

Elijah and Mandy both jerk around, surprised to see her at our table. Nate doesn't move his attention from me.

"Hello, Florence," I say, ignoring Nate the best I can.

My twin is in her popularity mode and doesn't seem to realize we were having a serious conversation on a topic she can't handle without bursting into tears.

"I had a question," she says, turning to address me.

Suspicion overtaking my curiosity, I fix my gaze on her and say, "What?"

She's smiling to herself. "Remember last week when you came back from wherever with your glasses cracked and you yelled at Marc for being there with Mom?"

I close my eyes. So much for her acting nice. She's back to her normal self, embarrassing me in front of others.

"And how after dinner, when Marc left, you and Mom had a big fight?"

My eyelids flick open. "It wasn't a fight," I say. "We were working through some things."

Flo laughs sarcastically. "Well, you know how I heard the part when you were talking about Marc and how his aura is off?"

"Oh, you heard that? Well, it's not scientific, just something I'm interested in." I'm trying to change the subject because I'm not sure where this is headed, but with the mood she's in I don't want it to end in embarrassment for me.

"I was wondering," she says, teeth all showing, "since you're so *good* at distinguishing auras, you can figure mine out?"

I stare at her, exhaustion seeping into me. "Excuse me?"

"What's my aura?" she asks.

I inhale deeply, my eyes darting to the side to see Mandy is hiding a smirk at Flo's words. Nate has an interested look on his face. Sam is bored with the conversation but seems to be amused to see us sitting side by side. Elijah is eating his food and pretending not to listen to what we're talking about.

"Red," I say after a while, knowing everyone—but Elijah and Sam—are waiting for an answer.

"Red?" Florence repeats. "What does that mean?"

I hesitate. To me, red signifies anger and exasperation at everyone and everything. But I can't very well explain that to her with my friends—and Sam—listening.

"It's not all red," I say, pulling my backpack onto my lap. "You have some white in there, too. And a hint of blue."

Flo waits.

My friends wait.

Sighing, I continue. "Red is for…passion," I decide, rummaging around in my backpack so I don't have to meet anyone's gaze. "You have a hot, quick temper and you won't back down from a fight. The white is because you are…" Again, I hesitate. White, in my opinion, is beauty. Will it seem weird to call my sister beautiful with my friends all watching? "White is for your charm," I say. "You're charming and smart"—here I wince internally—"and you're great at convincing old people that they need to sell their cars to you since they're going to die soon."

Flo gasps, smacking me on the arm. "That was once! And it was Grandma and Grandpa Ferrari! They were going to give me their car anyway. I just said they should do it five months earlier. It's too bad the car died before I got it."

"Mh-hm," I say, finding my lunch at the very bottom of my backpack.

Elijah speaks up. "You have your license?" he asks.

"Of course not," says Flo. She sounds affronted.

"Then why did you want a car?"

Flo blinks at him over my shoulder. "Um," she says, and I'm surprised to hear she's uncomfortable.

"Blue," I say, returning to the discussion on her aura, "because you're sad about Dad. You don't normally have blue in the mix, but right now you do. It's not as much as last week; however, there is still a hint."

Flo switches her attention to me. "Is that all?"

I nod, drop my bag at my feet. "Yes. You need anything else?"

"I do," says Mandy. "I want to know what my aura is. Learning about your sister was fun, but I want to learn mine."

Hers is easy.

"Sunshine yellow," I say automatically. "You're happy all the time. Today especially."

She beams at me. "Yes, I am. What else?"

I stare at her for half a second before saying, "Purple. There's something you regret." I tap my bottom lip with a finger. "Mandy, did you prank Elijah again and now wish you hadn't?"

She shakes her head as Elijah glares. "No," she says, but he doesn't look satisfied. "No," she repeats. "It's...something else."

"Oh-kay," he says slowly, eyes still on her. "Venice, what's my aura?"

"The exact same as Mandy's," I respond without checking. "Bright yellow with a shade of purple. You also regret something."

Elijah isn't surprised like I'd thought he would be. He just shrugs one shoulder and doesn't admit or deny that he regrets anything. I study them both through my lashes, wondering if it was a time when he told her how he felt about her and she didn't return the confession, making them regret ever having that conversation.

"What's Nate's aura?" Mandy asks after no one speaks for a while.

I finally look across the table at him, and instantly images of his grandpa abusing him flash through my mind. I grit my teeth, willing them to go away, and clear my head.

"Let's see..."

Since I have been refusing to spare only a quick glance at him, I now notice several things. His dark hair is incredibly messy, as if he hasn't combed it in a week or even *heard* of a comb. His expression is patient and understanding, but there's a hint of annoyance buried deep inside of him. The corners of his mouth are curled up in a small smile, not enough to show off his dimples, and it somehow disappoints me.

"Well?" Mandy says.

I blink, my eyes unfocusing. I realize I've been staring at Nate for longer than necessary, and my cheeks flush pink. Returning my gaze to him, I search for his aura but can't find it. He's impossible to read. The only thing he is letting show is pale grey and swirls of a familiar black that cling to him. The grey represents exhaustion—it's weighing him down. Now that I see it, a few more things come to my attention: his eyes seem darker than ever, his slight smile a touch strained, his wild hair a result of not spending sufficient time looking after his well-being.

The faint black swirls aren't his. They're from his house, which leaks that color of wickedness. They are a constant reminder of his grandpa and how he has been mistreated and how his parents deserted him so early after he was born.

"I can't tell," I say slowly.

Mandy huffs in irritation. "Seriously, Venice? Nothing? Not even a tiny spot?"

Nate's sad smile widens a bit, almost mocking but not.

I sigh and try again. Reading auras may sound strange—and it's normally me just staring at someone until I can see something in their eyes or I know about an occurrence in their past that results in a change of how they act and speak. I tend to understand auras more if I've known the person for quite a while and can determine more about them.

With Nate, I know he's disappointed in his family and he doesn't like them to be brought up. He could have hidden sorrow, but if he does, then he hides it *really* well. He has a small portion of yellow, and it's not the same as Elijah and Mandy—where they have sunshine-bright, Nate's is faded optimism. He still has hope that his parents will reclaim him, maybe, or hope in a positive relationship somewhere else.

He also has a distant speck of lavender, meaning there is someone who scares him.

His grandpa.

"Nate is scared of spiders," I say instead. "No, wait." I stop and study him a third time. "Sorry, I got that wrong. I meant to say that he is scared of the library closing down and destroying his chance of ever finishing all the books in there."

Nate's grin is genuine as Mandy and Elijah laugh. "How'd you guess?" he whispers to me.

I shrug, my eyes dropping to my food. I think I'm getting sick of having the same meal every day for lunch: a peanut butter and honey sandwich.

Beside me, Flo is annoyed that Sam hasn't paid any attention to her. She gets to her feet and heads back to her table without saying goodbye to me or to anyone. She doesn't even wink at Sam, who looked at her *once* during the time she was sitting next to me. I wonder if they are ashamed to see each other.

A second later, Sam wanders away from us, heading in the direction of a blonde girl I spotted him smiling at.

Elijah watches his cousin go. "I know a bunch of girls think he's hot," he says, "but what I don't understand is how he *never* stays with one girl. Does he think he's too good for them? Or do girls not like how he truly is, just how he acts towards them?"

"No," I say, remembering what Flo had told me yesterday. "It's because he has bad breath."

My friends gape at me.

"How do you know that?" Elijah asks in a strangled tone. "Venice, have you been making out with my cousin?"

"What?" I ask, horrified. I suddenly realize how bad my words sounded. "I have *not* kissed Sam," I say firmly. "Florence has, and she told me about it yesterday. She said she never wanted to kiss him again unless he starts using mouthwash."

Elijah's clouded expression clears. "Ah," he says. "That makes sense."

"He isn't even very hot," Mandy mutters.

I have a sudden inspiration. "Hey, Elijah," I say. "Could you and Nate switch places? I have to show Nate something and I'm too lazy to get up and kick Mandy out of her seat."

Elijah rolls his eyes, but I detect uncertainty flickering in his aura. I bite back a grin.

"Fine," he says, standing up. "Nate, my man, we gotta listen to what the woman commands. Otherwise she'll go around telling people how you're terrified of the library and that I'm a video game addict."

"Can't have that happening," Nate replies.

A second later, he's next to me, way too close for my taste. I swallow hard and make a show of digging through my backpack, searching for whatever I am supposed to give to him. I can feel him watching me and know he has an idea of what I'm doing.

I am grateful that Elijah continues from where Mandy left off.

"You don't think Sam is hot?" he says, shocked. "But—he's like the most dreamy guy in this entire school!"

Mandy shrugs. "Not really."

"What?" I cut in. "You have your eye on someone else?"

Nate winces at my subtlety.

"If she does," Elijah says, teasing, "it's probably me."

"Yup," says Mandy.

We all go still, Elijah the most. At my side, Nate is grinning broadly and failing to hide it. I am watching Mandy, seeing her carefully look Elijah in the eye as she explains.

"Of course it's you," she says. "Who else?"

They stare at each other for a long, hard minute. I don't move, don't dare to breathe, don't want to disrupt this moment of truth as Elijah and Mandy simply sit there, acting as if no one is around them, that they are all alone to eye one another flirtatiously.

Then Elijah slowly narrows his eyes, hesitating. "Me?" he repeats. "You've got to be joking."

"I'm not," Mandy says honestly.

Another minute goes by. Elijah finally makes the first move, grabbing her by the shoulders and pressing a kiss against her mouth. She gasps, probably not having expected that, then wraps her arms around his neck and kisses him back. They are oblivious to the fact that they have an audience.

"Let's give them some privacy," Nate whispers in my ear, and I nod my agreement.

We silently stand up and leave the cafeteria, Nate leading. I resist peering back at Elijah and Mandy—who are most likely still kissing—and something that feels like disappointment washes over me when Nate and I are out in the crowded hallway.

He glances around, then stops by the cafeteria doors in an empty part of the hallway. He never moves his attention from me.

"So," he says. "About your dad."

I blink. I hadn't thought the start of our conversation would be that. "Yes? What about him?"

"You don't believe he's dead," says Nate.

Again, I'm astounded. "Does it really show?"

His lips curve into a grin. "Not very much. But I recognized it when you were talking. I like to try to read people, too. You know something that you hope is proof against the accident."

"For starters, it wasn't an accident. The driver purposely faked my dad's death. Secondly, his body was never found, and I'm using that also as evidence. Thirdly, both cars were empty when they crashed together and exploded. I've seen the video."

Nate nods. "Those are good reasons. What does the rest of your family think about it?"

"I haven't told anyone," I admit. "You're the first. Though you guessed it. I didn't tell you."

"How did you learn about the details of the accident?"

I reach into my back pocket and pull out my phone. "My grandma, Dad's mom, sent me a video of the wreck. She seems to believe, along with every other person who heard the news, that Dad is dead. She must not have looked at the video very carefully."

"How did she get the video of it?" Nate asks, taking my phone from me.

I pause. "I don't know," I say. "Probably from the police. It was filmed from a street camera."

"And where did you say he was? Kentucky?"

"Yeah."

Nate is silent for a moment as he watches the video. He is standing so close to me that it starts to make me uncomfortable. I can see the light blue color of his eyes, the ragged ends of his dark brown hair, the thin white scar on his neck that disappears down the collar of his shirt.

Which is when I realize he isn't wearing his jacket.

My eyes roam down the length of his body, taking in the long-sleeves that hide the evidence of abuse from prying eyes such as mine. I know I shouldn't stare at him like this, but I can't help it. I've never seen him in any shirt that isn't covered by his jacket.

"I see what you mean," he says, and I scramble to remember what we are talking about.

Dad. The accident. Not Nate.

"Yeah?" I say again, this time more a question than agreement.

Nate nods at the screen. "You're right. It really looks like no one is in either vehicle. And the oil truck is so suspicious-looking, I'd be surprised if the police haven't investigated the driver and who was currently registered under that truck."

"My grandma said they traced the truck back to an agency," I say. "It was stolen. The truck had been taken a few days before."

"And did anyone dive deeper?" Nate asks, replaying the video.

I shake my head. "Not that I've heard of, no."

Nate doesn't respond—he's engrossed in watching Dad's faked death—and I spare the time to study him again. The ends of his dark eyelashes curve upwards, and they are so long they almost brush against the skin below his eyebrows.

"Have you considered," he says, "that this video might not be from a street camera but a night-vision one that was planted just for the purpose of catching this *accident* on video?"

"Uh…" I force myself to look down at my feet, away from his face. "No, I actually haven't. Why?"

Nate sounds thoughtful as he explains. "Well, this camera is in a strange place for one to be. A random stoplight in a random town in a random state? And it even changes to a different view right before the truck hits your dad's car. What are the chances of there being *two* cameras on the same street, both mere feet from each other?"

Now that he says that, it makes sense.

"You bring up a good point," I acknowledge, and he gives me a tight-lipped smile.

"Another thing." He returns his attention to my phone. "The truck. Right after the camera switches to the other shot of the street, the truck stops its crazy maneuvering."

"I think that's when the driver hopped out," I say. "See? He's over here, on the other side of the road?"

He bends his head, the tips of his hair grazing my cheek as he gets a better look at the dark man standing on the sidewalk, admiring his handiwork. I grit my teeth at him. Stupid man.

"Hm." Nate straightens, nodding his head. "Yes, I thought he was rather suspicious. He isn't doing anything."

"Whoever came up with this plan didn't do it very well," I say seriously, my heart slowing considerably now that he is not as close.

Nate hands me my phone. "I agree. There are too many coincidences and not enough believable footage. Now, if the driver had chosen a different street, one with more cars and more eyewitnesses, then it might have been credible. And the truck driver—he really needs a name other than *the truck driver*—took forever to crash into your dad's car. Why wait so long to show up? And why was your dad just waiting in that turn lane? He totally could have gotten out of the way in time."

"Blessed Hallelujah!" I exclaim. "You understand as well as I do. All these questions I have, you have them, too."

He frowns, his eyelashes sweeping downwards as he slowly blinks at me. "Venice, did you just say *Blessed Hallelujah*?"

I blush. "It's one of my sister's favorite sayings."

"Siena, right? Not Florence?"

I nod. "I can't imagine Flo saying something like that. She's too...refined." I choke over the word, and Nate grins.

"Anyway," he says, going back to the discussion on Dad, "I want to know if the witnesses contacted you or your grandma. There *are* eyewitnesses, am I correct?"

"Yes," I confirm. "There was a kooky cake lady and some others that I can't remember."

"Kooky cake lady?"

My grin matches his. "Yeah. She went on this spiel about the strawberry shortcake she couldn't make because the store she went to was closed that late at night, and she had arrived at her apartment when she witnessed the crash. She got my grandma's number from the police when they did, and she contacted my grandma immediately."

"Ah." Nate is understanding. "I see. Man, now I'm hungry for some cake. You don't have any with you, do you, Venice?"

"Sadly, no." I shove my phone in my pocket. "I wasn't told to bring any to school today. So, the truck driver—"

"He really needs a name," Nate interrupts, but I don't mind it. "We can't just keep calling him *the truck driver*."

"I know."

We're quiet for a moment as we think about it.

I hesitate, then say, "Hubris Jargon."

299

THIRTY-TWO

The second I say his name, bizarre as it is, I can't help but shiver. Nate looks amused for barely a second before he notices my discomfort at the name. He anxiously scans my face.

"Hey, Venice, are you all right?"

I swallow hard. That name has triggered a memory: I remember the stink of Rupert's breath as he dragged me back inside to interrogate me about my ring. I won't forget that easily.

Nate grabs me by my shoulders, tugging me closer to him. "Venice? What's wrong? Who is Hubris Jargon?"

"He…" I close my eyes. "I don't know Just—yesterday, two men broke into my house while I was there. They…I…anyway, it scared me out of my wits. They mentioned three weird, coded names, Hubris Jargon among them. I have reason to believe that he is the truck driver, the driver who almost hit me, and the one who staged Dad's death."

Nate gapes at me. "What? Start over again. Yesterday, two men broke into your house and they…"

I rip myself free and turn away from him, hiding my face in my hands. I am shaking, trembling, as I breathe in heavily and breathe out raggedly. I am worried and nervous because I don't wish for Nate to become involved in this. He doesn't deserve it. He is already hurt, beaten, scorned. He doesn't need any more violence in his life than he has already.

"Venice. Please tell me."

I ignore him. My head is throbbing, a reminder of my injuries yesterday. I don't know what I was thinking. I can't tell Nate!

He moves so I'm facing him again. He slides his hands around mine, pulling them away and forcing me to look up at him. His expression is one of gentleness and concern, and it melts me.

"Venice," he begins, but I'm suddenly not paying attention— I've noticed he isn't wearing gloves, either. How had I not noticed?

I flip his hands over, focusing on his right wrist. There is that scar I saw a few weeks ago, the one that runs over the curve of his wrist and disappears down his sleeve. It must have been one he got from cut glass. The only other thing capable of slicing that deep and that long is a knife, and if Nate is smart he'll keep knives out of his grandpa's reach.

"What are you doing?" Nate asks, attempting to pull away.

I squeeze his hands tighter, finding more tiny white scars dotting his wrists and fingers and palms and the backs of his hands. Most are small, some are long and thin, others are almost invisible. Abandoning his left hand, I turn completely to his right, tracing a finger down the first scar I'd seen. It soon vanishes into his sleeve, and when I go to push the cuff up to see how long this scar is, Nate stops me.

"What are you doing?" he repeats, taking a step back. He bumps against the wall.

If this were any different exchange, I'd be embarrassed to have touched him like that. Instead, I'm only furious. Not at Nate but at all that he is suffering.

"Where did you get all those scars?" I demand, though I already know. I'm giving him a chance to tell me about his grandpa.

He shakes his head, not saying anything.

"This isn't another excuse about cutting yourself, is it?" I say, never losing my hard tone of voice.

Nate shakes his head again. He still remains mute.

Huffing, I cross my arms and turn away from him. I don't want to tell him that I spied on him and witnessed his grandpa abusing him; I want Nate to tell *me* about it. He has to come clean. He has to admit that he isn't safe living with his grandpa.

"We're doing it again."

My head tilts slightly at the sound of his voice. "Hm?"

"We're refusing to tell one another something the other wants to know." Nate is smiling faintly, but it doesn't reach his eyes. "I want to know about what happened to you yesterday, and you want to know about my scars." He shrugs. "We're at a stalemate."

I glare up at him. "I'll tell you if you tell me."

Something that looks like disappointment flashes across his face before he composes himself. "Then I guess I'll never learn about those two men who broke into your house."

I sigh, long and loud, tearing my gaze away from him. I let it roam over the crowded hallway filled with happy, chattering kids who don't have problems like mine. Dangerous problems. Exasperating problems. Why can't I be like them—the thing I'm concerned about most being if or if not I failed the most recent history test, not if someone is going to *actually* run me over today or break into my house and kill me?

"This one was my fault."

I refix my gaze on Nate, wondering what he's talking about. He is pointing to the white scar on his neck, the one that is usually hidden by the collar of his jacket.

"I was getting a book down from my shelf," he continues. "I didn't realize I had an empty picture frame up there, so when I took out some books, it fell and sliced into me. The corner was very sharp." His grin is more genuine now. "And I thought that the cut would scab over, but I kept peeling it off and the cut never healed completely. I was left with a scar. I have a feeling most of my scrapes turn into scars."

I hold his gaze for a second, then say, "I was sitting by my front door when I heard someone break a jar in my kitchen. Two men started talking about a female, and after a short moment I assumed they meant me. They said their boss, a man by the name of Sleepy Gumption, wanted *it*."

Nate and I have a staring contest until he folds back the left cuff of his sleeve and shows me yet another scar. "I got this from my dog when he was excited over playing fetch and accidentally scratched me in his rush to get off my lap and out the door."

"I tried to run away," I say, watching Nate carefully. I don't know if he is lying to me or telling the truth. "The two men caught up to me and dragged me back inside my house, where they interrogated me about my ring and its stone. I played dumb and didn't give anything away, and for it heard some very interesting information."

Nate's eyes are shining with respect and admiration. He holds up his palm and touches a tiny white scar. "This one is from Mandy when she poked me with an incredibly sharp hairpin."

"I called the police," I say, resisting the urge to smile, "and after nearly ten minutes they showed up and arrested the two men. I asked the police to contact me about who the men are and who they're working for, but I have not heard anything so far."

Instead of finding a fourth scar that wasn't given to him by his grandpa like I thought he would, Nate reaches up and touches my temple, his fingers as warm as I'd imagined. "Did they hurt you?" he asks.

"Not really," I reply, my chest suddenly tight.

"How so?"

I hold still as he brushes away a strand of my hair. "One of the men just slammed me down on the edge of the counter."

"And the other man?" Nate tilts my head so he can examine whatever mark is there. "Did he do anything to you?"

"Besides joke with me and stop his companion from strangling me, no."

Nate *hms.* "Are you sure?"

"Well, he grabbed my arm and managed to keep hold of me long enough for his buddy to catch up to us. Other than that, Quentin was fine. He was very humorous."

"Quentin?"

I push Nate's hand away. "Just what I call him. He *does* have to have a name, right?"

"Of course." Nate steps back, bumping against the wall again. "You've got a red mark on the side of your head."

My fingers fly up to touch it. "Better than no head at all."

He doesn't smile. "What was the interesting information you heard them talking about?"

"Oh, just a bunch of names, Hubris Jargon among them. Apparently, he really wants to kill me. So I'm guessing he's the driver who almost ran me over and he's the truck driver who staged my dad's death."

Nate frowns. "And it doesn't bother you that someone wants to kill you?"

"Of course it does!" I exclaim. "I've been jumpy all day. And I'm worried that they'll ransack my house again, this time with my siblings home, and they will find out that people are faking our dad's death and are hunting me down because they want me dead. Or rather, they want my ring, and Hubris Jargon wants to kill me."

Nate takes my hands in his, holding them up to eye-level. "I had noticed that you weren't wearing your ring. Is that because of yesterday?"

"Yes." I speak carefully and steadily to disguise the anxiety building up in me. I'm not used to feeling this way. I've never been touched like this, and definitely not by someone like Nate. "Also, Nate...I called my mom and told her that those men broke in."

His gaze jumps up to mine. "How much does she know?"

"Oh, barely anything. Just that they freaked me out and I called the police and they're in jail or whatever—she thinks they're simple thieves that had the misfortune of thinking to rob place when someone was home."

"So she doesn't know anything else?"

I shake my head. "I mainly called her so she could hear the story firsthand from me, and also to be comforted, you know? I was shaking like mad and I was terrified they would somehow come back—" I shiver, and Nate gives my hands a squeeze. "Anyway." I clear my throat. "She's not aware of the whole shebang, only a bit about those men. Nothing about my ring and Dad and the man who tried to run me over."

"Okay. I suppose that won't give anything away, though she might watch you more closely. Are you going to call the police and tell them?"

I shake my head. "I don't know. Should I? I just feel like it's a bad idea to, that they won't listen to me."

"Two men forced their way inside your house," Nate says seriously. "A car nearly hit you on purpose. There's someone stalking you, finding out things about you such as where you live and where you're currently at and what you're currently doing."

I squeeze my eyes shut. "This is all so complicated."

"You mentioned the boss was named Sleepy Gumption," says Nate. "That *has* to be a code name. There's no way a mother would call her son that, no matter how terrible a mom she was."

I give a pathetic smile. "Yes. There was also a man named Malaise Tone, and the way Quentin talked about him made it seem like he personally knew me. But I've never met anyone who went by that code name or anyone with anything close to it."

"What is *Malaise Tone* spelled backwards? Or do you think it's an anagram or something like that?"

"I don't know, Nate. I-I don't really want to think about it. I just wish it weren't happening and that I could just be a normal kid again." I'm annoyed at myself for being so pathetic, but I seriously want to discuss a different topic.

Nate lets go of my hands, moving farther away from me. I almost call him back—I desperately need his warmth.

But I don't speak.

"Alright." He seems capable of handling disappointment. He is more into solving this mystery than I am. "Alright," he repeats. "We will have to talk sometime, though. But now we should get back to Mandy and Elijah. They've got to have stopped kissing."

I open my eyes, finding him standing by the cafeteria doors. I nod. "Okay," I say, trailing after him. "But they might be passed out from lack of oxygen if they've kissed as long as we've talked."

"You can breathe while you're making out with someone," Nate says, his grin back in place.

"Not if you're either Mandy or Elijah."

He laughs, and the sound breaks up any remaining tension. I envy him for being able to do that. "Very true," he agrees.

We're almost at the table when I stop him by putting my hand on his arm. He jolts and, embarrassed, I retract my hand. "I just remembered something about last week," I say, working hard not to blush. "Nate, why didn't you come by my house?"

"Oh." He shifts his weight to his other foot. "Your mom's car was gone, but that other one was still there—your grandparents', I'm guessing—and I didn't want to disturb you guys."

"They left days ago," I say. "You could have come then."

Nate hesitates. "Your house was too quiet. I knew something was wrong. I didn't think you wanted me to bother you."

I look away from him. He doesn't know how I'd wished for the opposite.

"Shall we get back?" he asks uncomfortably.

I nod, and he leads me around the near-empty tables towards the far end of the room where Mandy and Elijah are sitting, talking. They're also holding hands, and the sight is relieving.

"Hey," Mandy says as Nate and I come closer.

I cock my head, seeing there is something different about her.

Her cheeks are flushed with adrenaline, her stance more relaxed, her dark brown eyes dancing with excitement.

Then I realize it's her aura. She still has the yellow of happiness, but now it is joined by soft pink that fills every nook and cranny inside of her. I glance over at Elijah and see he has the same thing.

"Done finally?" Nate asks.

Mandy rolls her eyes. "Yes, blah blah blah. What were you guys doing? Not the same as us, were you?"

I look affronted at the very idea. "Excuse me!" I say, scoffing. "You're the ones who have been dodging each other's confessions for nearly an entire lifetime."

"And what does that have to do with you and Nate?" Elijah asks, smirking a little. He's annoying.

I copy Mandy's eye-rolling and glance away. Elijah laughs while Nate looks uncomfortable and quickly changes the subject.

"Since it's a half-day," he says, "are you guys planning anything for the afternoon?"

Mandy shrugs. "I thought we were going to do what we normally do. Go to Elijah's and play video games."

"I love how I'm the normal," says Elijah, smiling sloppily at her.

She smiles back, and right then it's only them at the table, staring into each other's eyes. Nate coughs politely and they snap around, both going different shades of red.

"Is it settled?" he wants to know. "Are we going to Elijah's?"

"Only if Venice comes," Mandy says quickly, grabbing onto my arm. "You have to come. It's the law. Plus, I command you. And what I say has to be followed."

"Mh-hm," Elijah agrees.

I gently extract my arm from Mandy's death grip and say, "I might. But I need to find out what my siblings are doing this afternoon. And I can't stay for very long."

"That's all right," says Mandy, beaming. "You'll probably end up on the couch, reading. With Nate."

I cross my arms. "Then should I bring a book?"

"No need," says Nate. "I've got plenty to spare. Elijah's mom is an avid reader, and she has three full bookshelves down by the TV."

"Great." I sit, hauling my backpack up onto my lap. "On the subject of books, I have something for you, Nate..." I shift through my bag, trying to find what I'd put in there over a week ago, while my friends watch, curious.

I pull a familiar hard-cover book from the depths of my bag, already grinning to myself, and hand it to him.

Nate takes one look at the title and starts to laugh. Mandy and Elijah look confused until he shows them, and they both groan.

"Seriously?" Mandy says. "Shakespeare?"

I shrug. "I got it from someone I don't like, so I'm just regifting it to Nate, who will actually read it."

He is already flipping through the pages, seemingly interested. Or maybe he's pretending to be so I'm not offended. I'm not. I won't ever be. "I haven't read this one yet," he says. "*The Merchant of Venice*. Looks like someone was making a play on your name."

"That's what Florence said when I showed her the book." I zip up my bag. "I got that for my birthday, so if there's a note or anything in it, feel free to burn it."

Nate sends me an indescribable look. Elijah and Mandy aren't paying any attention to our conversation—they are back to gazing at each other in a highly uncomfortable way for eyewitnesses.

"Was it Marc?" Nate asks, closing the book softly.

My eyebrows shoot up. "Well, aren't you good at reading me," I say dryly.

He shrugs. "I would compare you to a book, but that might offend you and I can't have that happening."

"Whatever." I slouch in my seat, glancing around the slowly-emptying cafeteria. "Yes, it was Marc. He keeps trying to charm me into liking him, but I never have and probably never will. Not after what he did to my mom."

It pops out of my mouth before I can swallow it, and Nate immediately seizes the opportunity to learn something more.

"What did he do to your mom?"

Luckily, the bell rings and everyone stands up and begins to clear away their things. I'm glad I don't have to answer, but being saved by the bell gives me the chance to ask myself why this has become such a sticking point with me.

I'm such a hypocrite. Wanting him to give me answers to my questions is also what he wants, but from me. We either don't trust or feel the need to burden each other with this information we're keeping to ourselves. I have the upper hand, however, because I was nosy and spied on Nate and know about his grandpa while Nate doesn't know much about Marc or Mom or all the crazy things that happened.

"It's none of your concern," I finally say. "It's my personal business, and you have no right to be bothered by it."

Except I stuck my nose in his own personal business.

I really am a hypocrite.

"And what if I want to make it my concern because I care about you? Because you're my friend," Nate quickly amends. "What if we didn't keep secrets and just told each other everything the other wants to know, even if we don't want to?"

My head turns upwards slightly, and I must admit that I'm intrigued by the idea. "Maybe."

He sighs again and goes to answer, but unfortunately Mandy cuts across him.

"Are you two ready to go?"

I scowl at my lap. She chose *just* the right moment to interrupt us. I wish I could've ventured farther into that conversation with Nate. Our whole debate is now disappearing faster than free ice cream up for grabs at my house.

"Yeah," says Nate, moving closer towards Mandy. He seems afraid that I'm going to smack him for not ignoring Mandy and continuing his offer. He must not know I wouldn't hit him for anything. I don't need to remind him of his abusive grandpa.

I climb to my feet, bringing my backpack up with me. "I only need to talk to my sister and tell her where I'm going. And I should tell Roman, too. I'll also need to find out if they're doing anything."

"Okay." Mandy beams at me, her hand still curled around Elijah's. "See you outside in two minutes?"

I grimace. "Better make it five."

The sun is warm and brilliantly bright, and from the moment I step outside of the school building, I start to sweat. It's really nice out, too warm for not even two weeks into February. My friends are waiting for me by the bus that goes to Mandy and Elijah's neighborhood, and after plenty of talking, I am able to convince them that we should walk. Nate is fine with it—he walks nearly everywhere—and Mandy enjoys holding Elijah's hand, so we are soon heading towards Elijah's house by foot. While we walk, Mandy talks about the most random things, from how her chemistry teacher doesn't understand that *chemistry* means *blowing up things in class* to how Elijah needs to cut his fingernails.

Eventually, she makes me tell every little thing about me, and I quickly tire of the game.

"What's your hidden talent?" Mandy asks fifteen minutes into our trip.

I shrug. "Don't have one."

"You've *got* to," she says, shocked. "Mine is chemistry. That's why I love my teacher so much. She lets me blow up things for every single experiment."

"I didn't know chemistry was about destruction," I say.

Mandy snorts and tosses her shoulder-length hair. "It's not. Well, maybe a tiny bit. But my teacher has a soft spot for me and lets me suggest what fun things we can do in class. Once I convinced her that baking soda volcanoes are how kids survive high school, and the next class we made volcanoes and wrecked the classroom."

I smile. "Must have been quite a sight."

"Oh, it was," Elijah says. "You should have seen it. There was baking soda and red stuff all over the walls."

"The red substance was my blood," Mandy explains. "I wanted lava, and my teacher said we couldn't bring strawberry syrup or ketchup to class, so I used red food coloring and turned my water this pinkish color, and it was a terrible color so I added my own blood, and my teacher said I had to go to the nurse, but I didn't want to, so instead I ran off and found Elijah and Nate in the library and managed to evade my teacher and the school nurse for the rest of the day."

I blink, suddenly very dizzy. What she said has gone over my head. I didn't even catch the gist of it.

"Um," I begin, "how cool."

Nate smirks at me, and I ignore him.

"So," says Mandy, and I get the feeling that it's her favorite word. "Venice. Do you play an instrument?"

"Nope."

"Do you have a pet?"

"Nope. Unless you count my younger sister, and she would hate to be described as a *pet*."

Mandy rolls her eyes. "Is this the first time you've moved?"

"The first time my family has moved, yes. Since my mom is a realtor, we often help her clients pack up, especially the night before they're due to leave. We're really good at boxing."

"Is *that* how you moved in so fast?" Mandy looks impressed. "You guys just waltzed into this town and came to school like, a week later."

"Seventeen days," I correct. "We arrived, took two and a half weeks to unpack, *then* went to school. Mom thought we shouldn't be wasting time getting to know the neighborhood if we were going to be living there for the next few years or however long Mom is planning on staying here. Anyway, we're used to packing and unpacking quickly."

"But you sold and bought your house in how long?" Mandy asks. "I mean, doesn't it normally take a while?"

I nod. "Yes. With Mom, however, she'd already sold our house and bought another a week before telling us we were moving. And she'd given away a lot of our stuff, sorted through other things, and boxed up some. I thought she was just getting rid of a few belongings."

"I think your family set a world record for how fast you moved in."

Grinning, I say, "I doubt it. My mom has moved people faster than us."

Mandy shrugs. "Whatever you say. Do you play any sports?"

I stifle a snort of laughter. "Do I look like I play a sport? No, I don't, and no, I can't. My balance is terrible, my aim worse."

"Uh…" She thinks hard for a second. "I'm out of questions. Elijah, Nate, do you have any?"

Elijah looks over her head at me. "Have you ever played a video game before? Any kind of video game?"

I hesitate, knowing I'm a lost cause here. "Board games and video games aren't the same thing, right?"

"Wow, you're hopeless," says Elijah.

I smile at him. "Thanks. You don't know how much that means to me. I really appreciate it."

He groans. "This is pointless. I don't even know why you're my friend. You don't play video games, never have, probably never will. I probably can only tolerate you because Mandy can."

"Oh, shut up," she says. She turns to me. "He's just joking."

"I gathered that," I respond.

Nate hasn't said anything during the fifteen minutes we've been walking and talking, and I occasionally sneak glances up at him. He seems interested in our conversation, but after a moment I see him take *The Merchant of Venice* out of his backpack and resume reading. I nearly laugh, wondering if he's only reading it because I gave him the book and he doesn't want to disappoint me.

Mandy chatters on, asking me questions that are bizarre and hysterical to answer. She claims she wants to know me better, but by the way her eyes shine I figure she just likes coming up with strange questions that someone will give a reply to.

"What's your favorite way to die?"

"Favorite?" I give her a sharp look. "How would I know? I've never died before."

She flaps her free hand at me. "How would you like to die?"

"Get sucked into the vacuum of space," I say.

Nate makes a small noise, and I'm unconsciously drawn to him, raising an eyebrow in question. His nose is still buried in my book, but he seems to be partly present in this world and the other. He can probably understand every single word there and here.

"You want to die from oxygen deprivation?" he asks.

"At least I'll be in outer space," I say self-consciously. "That's better than drowning or being choked to death or inhaling too much smoke or however else you can die from lack of oxygen."

"You'll probably freeze to death faster," Nate points out.

"Psh." I scoff. "I'll wear a coat."

Mandy sighs deeply, bringing my attention back to her. "When you're done geeking out, Venice," she says, "I would like to know what your favorite thing to do is."

"You don't already know?" I give her a curious look. "It's all you and Elijah tease me about."

"Reading," she guesses, and I nod. "Well," she says, "I'm about to change your mind. You will soon realize how fun video games are. They are how I survive being a teenager."

"I thought that was blowing up stuff," I say.

She huffs. "No, that's how I survive high school. There's a big difference, Venice. You need to come to your senses and admit that reading is boring and hurts your brain—if you even *have* one; like, Elijah doesn't, which is why he's a video game addict and Nate's a bookworm—and it's a waste of time, too. How much of what you read do you remember?"

"Quite a bit, surprisingly. I like re-reading books, and after a few times, it commits to memory."

She groans. "Well yes, but you're cheating. Gosh, Venice. Hey, you never replied to me and agreed to let me call you Vennie."

"I think that's why I didn't reply."

Elijah snorts. "Vennie? What kind of nickname is that?"

"Ask Mandy, not me," I respond. "She's the one that came up with it. And I am totally against it. Sorry, Mandy, but I'd appreciate it if you called me by my real name."

"What if Vennie becomes your real name?" she protests.

I roll my eyes. "No," I say firmly. "It's Venice and will always be Venice. That's what my mom named me."

"Your siblings don't have any nicknames, do they?"

I shake my head. "No. We call Florence Flo, but other than that we are a nickname-free family."

"How sad," says Mandy. "Yet how lucky. My brothers call me all sorts of annoying names that trigger me."

"Oh, we call each other names all the time," I say, hiding a smile. "You guys should hear Siena, my little sister, go after Roman, my younger brother. It is hilarious. She also criticizes our other brother, Pompeii, and those two get into really big fights."

"Are they the ones that are constantly breaking things?" Nate asks. "It seems like whenever I stop by your house is when your younger siblings feel the need to drop something."

I shrug. "Yeah, I guess. And there's plenty of shouting."

"Ah, yes." Nate doesn't even look up from his book while he's talking. "I hear the arguments, too."

"Does it ever embarrass you?" Mandy puts in.

"Occasionally." I roll out my aching shoulders. My backpack is really heavy and I wish I could have sent it home instead of having to drag it with me to my afternoon adventures at Elijah's house.

"I think Venice is immune to embarrassment," says Elijah. "I mean, she gives people books as gifts. I'd be embarrassed at that, but Venice acted all suave when she gave Nate a book of poetry, no less. Wink wink."

My forehead crinkles into a frown. "Suave?"

"That's my favorite word." Elijah grins.

"I have never heard you use that word before," Mandy admits. "But I hear my parents use it to define my brothers. Isn't it typically used for a man?"

Elijah makes an *I-don't-know* noise in the back of his throat. "Who cares, really? Venice doesn't mind."

"Despite the fact that I'm *not* a man," I say, and Nate laughs.

"Thank goodness for that," he says, causing me to blush.

Mandy and Elijah don't seem to notice; they are arguing about the word *suave*, trying to figure out if Elijah should ever call me that again and if it really is his favorite word. Their arguing is the same as ever, despite that major leap forward in their relationship.

I risk a glance over at Nate and see he is smiling at either the book or me, I don't know, but his dimples are showing and it's hard not to concentrate on not tripping over my feet. I hurriedly return my gaze to my shoes, shifting the weight of my backpack to one shoulder as I do so. I should have sent it home with Roman—who actually isn't going home but to the skate park even though he doesn't know how to ride a skateboard—and I immediately dismiss the thought. Both Roman and Florence aren't heading home, so it'd have been pointless to give them my backpack.

We come up to a break in the sidewalk where we have to cross the street, and I hesitate while the others plow on ahead. I have a vision of stepping off the sidewalk onto the road and a black SUV instantly coming rushing towards me, determined to squish me flat.

Nate realizes I'm not following and returns to my side. "What is it?" he asks even though he already knows.

"The cars..." I gesture limply around us.

"I know," he says. "Don't worry. That SUV won't try to hit you if you are with someone else."

My brows draw together. "But what if he doesn't care?"

"You'll be fine," Nate promises.

I still don't move. Mandy and Elijah are on the other side, both not aware that the two of us aren't with them. They are in the middle of an argument, having moved on from *suave* and now tackling *debonair.*

"Would you like me to carry you?" Nate asks, grinning brightly.

I give him a horrified look. "I think I'd rather risk becoming road-kill," I reply. "It's a much faster way to die of embarrassment."

"Elijah believes you are immune to embarrassment," says Nate. He holds out his hand. "Come on. We can run. Less chance of getting hit by that SUV who is determined to kill you."

I stare at his hand, ungloved and disfigured by dozens of white scars, and I accept.

We reach the other side without incident.

And he doesn't let go of me.

And I don't let go of him.

THIRTY-THREE

Three days later I come back from school, having taken the bus with Flo and Roman, to find Mom's car in the driveway. Excitement courses through me, and I rush inside with my two siblings to discover Mom in the kitchen with an apron tied around her waist.

"Hey, kids," she says, accepting a hug from the three of us at the same time. She lingers longer on me, and she's the one who pulls back to look me right in the face. "Venice, are you all right?"

I nod. "Yeah. Better than I was a few days ago."

"What?" asks Flo, lost. She seems a little...It can't be jealousy? How could she be jealous of me?

"You haven't had any other experiences?" says Mom worriedly.

"No, thankfully. It was just that one time. And the police haven't called me and told me anything yet."

"I didn't get very far when I called them, either. One of these days I'll go investigate. Right now, we just need to focus on keeping you and the others safe. Okay?"

"Okay."

"Wait, wait." Roman steps forward. "Did two guys *actually* break in?"

I resist the temptation to roll my eyes. "Yes. I honestly can't believe none of you thought I was telling the truth."

"It sounded a bit far-fetched," he argues. "One minute you blame it on dwarves, the next minute its home invaders."

Mom's smiling, and it's on the weak side. "Venice—seriously, tell me how you're feeling about this. Two men break in, almost kill you—or try to—and you call the police and have the robbers taken away, leaving you home alone again. Are you still terrified?"

"Oh, yes," I say instantly, and it's the truth. "I'm so glad you're back. I'm safer when you're here."

Her smile increases a little. "That's good you feel safe with me. You aren't too traumatized by that experience that you'll have to see a therapist to help you out or anything, right?"

Ignoring Roman's smirk, I say, "I'm much better now. And I hope I won't see those men ever again." I want to say I *know* I won't see them again, but that might not be true. I'm not completely sure of what my future holds, and that annoys me. I wish I could tell how this whole mystery-thing will come to an end, and if Nate ever turns in his grandpa...Anyway.

Mom hugs us again, and I step back first, noting her sparkling gold aura and the twinkle in her eyes and the way she already smells like cinnamon, her favorite freshener, and she's only been here for an hour.

"You're happy," I observe.

"And you got new glasses," she replies, giving Flo an extra squeeze before stepping back and returning to the stove. Something is sizzling in a pan. "So, how were you kids while I was gone, besides the drama with Venice and those robbers? I noticed someone broke the jar of cinnamon sticks I keep by the sink."

"That was Venice," Florence says quickly.

Mom's eyebrows rise. "Really? Good for her."

I grin. "I didn't mean to," I say. "Just, cleaning up my siblings' dirty dishes that overcrowded the sink tends to make me knock things over." Even though Quentin had broken it.

Flo sticks out her tongue at me. I shrug. She basically asked for it. She and the others didn't ever do their chores.

"How was Dad's funeral?" I ask.

Mom doesn't move. "Fine," she says finally. "Your grandma was really shaken up. It's hard burying your son."

"But there wasn't a body to bury," says Florence.

"I know," says Mom. "It was still heartbreaking."

"What did you do up in North Dakota?" I inquire, changing the subject to something only slightly different.

Mom sighs. "We looked through your father's things. I brought a couple of picture frames he had up on his walls. They're all of you guys. Our family, back when we were happy."

"Oh." I don't know what else to say, and we all fall silent. Roman gets up from the table a moment later and disappears downstairs into his bedroom, and I wish I could do the same.

Mom turns around, suddenly smiling broadly. "Venice, do you remember on your first day of school, when I left that note?"

Confused, I only nod.

"Do you remember what I said?"

"For me not to trip and Flo to be nice and for Roman to let Siena into the bathroom while he's attempting to shave his non-existent facial hair," I recall, wondering where this is going.

Mom rolls her eyes. "Other than that?"

"Uh..." I think hard. Had she said something about Pompeii? "No, Mom, I don't remember."

She heaves a disappointed sigh. "I told you about Stephen Goldbeck," she says. "I was helping him move into the high-class neighborhood on the other side of town. He's an uber-rich man, and today he invited me and you to this big fancy party he's throwing to get to know his neighbors and for them to get to know him. I was invited since I was his realtor, and you are invited because—"

"She's the perfect child of the family," Flo interrupts.

Mom stutters to a halt. "No," she says, appalled. "No, that's not why. She's invited because she's, well, now that I think about it, why did he specifically ask for you?" She's kind of talking to herself.

"Really? One of your clients, who doesn't know any of us, specifically invites *Venice* to a party?" Flo snaps. "You expect me to believe that? Mom, you know Venice is socially awkward and not used to big, fancy parties, yet you still choose her! Why not me? Why can't you take me instead? I know how parties work! Why won't you take me, Mom?" She's practically pleading and I actually feel sorry for her, despite that jab about me being social awkward.

"This is exactly why," Mom says wearily. "You've had your share of fun, and now it is Venice's turn."

Flo scoffs. "She's just your favorite daughter, that's why. All your pathetic excuses aren't convincing me, Mom. I know you love her the most. I know she's your favorite."

"Florence," Mom says sternly, "you are talking nonsense."

My twin tosses her hair. "How come you never say that to Venice? How come you never get mad at her for anything? See, Mom? This is proof that you are biased!"

I'm not paying attention to their argument. All I can think about is going to a party for boring adults and not fitting in. I don't want to go. Why would I go, anyway? I'm totally with Florence on this one.

"She's your favorite!" Flo yells, pointing her finger at me.

Well, except for that part.

Mom holds up a spatula, the one she is using to cook whatever is in the pan on the stove. "Florence Ferrari, calm down. You are overreacting for an incredibly stupid reason."

Flo scowls, bristling. She opens her mouth to continue arguing, so I clutch my temples and walk away—far, far away from her and Mom and whatever this *party* thing is. I don't like parties. Eighth grade killed all the fun for the parties in my life.

I'm halfway up the stairs when Mom calls, "It's a formal party! Make sure to wear something nice! And we need to leave before six, all right? That's in three hours!"

I don't respond. I don't want to. Because I'm not going.

I won't.

Flo catches up to me, grabbing my arm and dragging me into our room the second before she explodes.

"I'm tired of all this!" she yells, slamming the door shut and blocking my path of escape. "I'm tired of you being treated like you're this special kid that is Mom's favorite and you get everything you want and I am treated like the rebellious, difficult child!"

My shoulders lock. I don't say anything. I have to hear her out. And once she calms down, I can tell her that she can go to the party instead of me. It's what she wants.

"Mom obviously loves you the most!" Flo snarls, jabbing her finger into my throat. I cough and step away from her, rubbing the spot she poked. "You act like Mom's little angel," Flo continues, "doing everything Mom does and everything she wants us to do because you know you'll get on her good side and be able to get anything out of her!"

I cough once more, inhale a shaky breath. I still don't speak.

"You're allowed to go off wherever you like, and I am stuck here with my stupid babysitting or my stupid 'you're grounded for making out with Gerard Simmons yesterday when the teacher told you to stop' punishment. I *never* get to do what I want! I *never* get to leave everything behind and run around town with an incredibly handsome boy who won't look my way once! I never even *get* what I want, whereas you're constantly earning privileges I won't receive because Mom is biased!"

I try to understand what my twin is hurling my way, but most of it is lost in her shouting, turning almost unintelligible. She's saying something about Nate? And bias?

"You have all this freedom!" Flo's voice is rising higher and higher with each word she yells. Or says. Either one, she's getting louder every second. "Mom let you get your driver's license back in California—"

"Permit," I cut in. "It was my driver's permit. I wasn't old enough to get my license."

She glares at me like I'm crazy. "What's the difference?" she howls. "You still could drive! Mom wouldn't let me even *touch* the steering wheel! She's convinced that I'll crash if I attempt to drive!"

I give a careless shrug. It's true.

"Why should only you deserve these benefits?" She whirls away from me, running a hand through her hair. "Why am I deprived of them? Why can't I be left alone to do as I wish like you can?"

I gape at her. Does she really believe I'm allowed to do whatever I want?

"It's so frustrating, Venice!" Florence yells, spinning around to face me again. "You're constantly being complimented on how you work so well with our younger siblings, but never once has Mom complimented *me*. And she is always telling you how you're so grown up and so nice and so thoughtful and so everything, but she never tells me that! The only things she says to me are *Try to remember next time* and *Grow up, Florence* and *Why are you like this, Florence?* and *Why can't you be more like your older sister, Florence?* I'm being treated like trash, Venice!"

"You're just looking at your life negatively," I say, but she ignores me. She's working herself up and won't calm down anytime soon.

"All the younger kids love you!" she says. "Siena goes to you for help or if she wants to share a joke or have a laugh with someone. She never has and never will come up to me for anything except complaints!"

She's using the word *never* way too much.

"It's the exact same with Pompeii," Flo goes on. "When he would like to go someplace—namely, the *library*—he always seeks you out, not me! It's not like I would refuse to seize an opportunity to flirt with whatever boy might be there!"

She's also using the word *always* a lot. And does she even know what she's saying?

"Pompeii follows you around like a love-sick puppy," Florence snarls. "And I sometimes think he doesn't know I exist! It's like there are only four kids in the family!"

I interrupt her. "Florence, do you know what you're talking about?"

"And don't get me started on Roman!" she yells, ignoring me. Her voice is rising higher and higher as she gets more worked up. "He actually listens to you, whether it's to get out of bed or out of the bathroom, and he does what you ask him to! And you reward him for being a moody teenager by buying soda when Mom isn't here! Why are you giving *him* benefits when *I* am the one working in the sidelines, trying to get everyone to school, trying to make sure we're alright after Dad's death, trying to cheer you up when you are in a depressed mood—"

"Florence, stop. Please. What you're saying—"

She keeps ignoring me. "I do *one* thing Mom doesn't like, and immediately I should be grounded and punished and lectured, but if *you*, Venice, copy what I did or do something close to it, you're just brushed off to the side with barely a reprimand! Like that day you came home right before dark and Mom didn't know where you were—"

"Because you decided not to tell her," I put in.

Flo scoffs. "You shouldn't have told me where you were going. You know I only remember important details."

"That *was* important!" I protest, throwing out my hands. "It was important to Mom!"

Rolling her eyes, Florence picks up from where we left off. "When you got back from the library"—my mouth falls open at her recollection—"Mom said how you shouldn't tell me anything and that I am unreliable, and that I'm a pathetic excuse for a daughter and you should never trust me again because all I do is let everyone down!"

My jaw has dropped lower and lower with each word she says.

Unreliable? Pathetic excuse for a daughter? Never trust? Let down? Mom had said nothing like that! She had told me Florence isn't to be trusted with critical information, but she hadn't insulted my sister. Florence must be making this up to force me to become sympathetic towards her. She's been stewing in some serious negative self-talk.

"And—and Mom said how I was fighting with her for no reason except I wasn't! I wanted her attention, but she wouldn't give it to me since she was too busy yelling at me to tell her where you were!" Flo's eyes are beginning to fill up with tears, but I don't know if they're tears of sorrow or tears of anger. Maybe both. "And when I said I didn't remember where you were, she told me that if you're hurt or lying in a ditch somewhere, it's all my fault for not listening!"

I stare at her, dumbfounded. "*What?*"

"I tried to remember!" she cries. "It wasn't until Mom heard you come into the house that I did, and that you were at the library. But by that time Mom was already talking to you and I couldn't help but listen in on what you two were saying."

"And...what were we saying?" I ask slowly.

Flo buries her face in her hands. "That I'm Mom's torment. That I'm why she is so tired and downhearted and I'm some kind of monster that you have to rescue Mom from."

I dimly recall this conversation. I'd felt guilty for not letting Mom know that I was at the library, but it was unfortunate that my phone had died and I hadn't bothered contacting her through any other mean besides passing the information on to Flo.

"So that's all I am," Florence says, looking up at me. Her hair is ragged and losing its curls. "I'm just a monster."

"That isn't true," I say firmly, taking her by the shoulders. "You're my twin sister. You're *our* sister, and Mom's daughter. She worries about you, which is why she acts strangely to you. She's scared that whatever she says will drive you away, so she says what comes out of her mouth and sometimes it isn't nice. I know how you feel, Florence, because I get the same treatment you get, just from a different person." I shake her a little, forcing her to meet my gaze and see how serious I am right now. "You treat me harshly," I say. "You don't care for what I do, and in your mind that makes you think you can be *my* torment."

Flo bristles. She opens her mouth to speak, but I beat her to it.

"You're constantly mocking me," I say sadly. "Whether it's about boys or how I don't have many friends or the fact that I'm weird and your complete opposite, you mock me. So what if I'm different than you? Nobody is the same, Florence, and definitely not us. Yes, we're twins, and we look alike, but we do not act the same."

She sucks in a deep breath, ready to yell more criticism, and I hurriedly keep talking to prevent her.

"You embarrass me in front of others," I say quickly. "When we first went to the library, and we met Nate, you made it seem like I was a young kid who needed supervision. You purposely said things to make the situation really uncomfortable for both me and for Nate. Why? Why do you do these things to me?"

She rips herself free of my grasp. "Because you're this perfect child and I'm looked down on for *everything*, and *everything* is my fault, and you should know what it feels like to be insulted and ignored and blamed like me!"

"What does that have to do with Nate?" I ask, my brow creasing into a heavy frown.

She is momentarily lost for words. I use it to my advantage.

"Florence, it sometimes seems like you hate me," I say. "Yet other times you're cheerful and try to make me happy. I don't get it. I truly don't."

My twin looks away from me. "It's because I'm jealous," she whispers. "I'm jealous that Mom pays you attention and she doesn't criticize how you dress and how you act and what kind of person you are. But she always does to me. She gets mad that I'm not wearing the clothes she wants me to wear and I use the make-up she doesn't want me to use and I'm acting the way she doesn't want me to act. It's like she's controlling my life, and I don't want her to. I am the person I am. She can't control me. That's why I'm not like you, Venice. Because I don't want to lead the life that you do, with all that weird environmental crap Mom goes on and on about. I have my own views on certain things, Venice. I'm not going to—to *follow* Mom's beliefs if I don't share the same feelings!"

"She's our mom," I say. "She's allowed to teach us how she does. And we should respect her for it."

Florence scoffs and folds her arms. "She can't force her beliefs on me."

"No," I agree, "she can't. And I don't think she wants to. But you should respect her."

"Respect," Flo says disgustedly. "You've said that a lot before, Venice. How can I respect Mom if she doesn't respect me?"

I scramble to find a reply. "Look. Florence. Mom is scared of you. She is scared that every conversation you have with her will turn into an all-out argument. And she doesn't like that. She hates having to punish you. She hates having to yell at you."

"Then why does she do it, hm?"

"Because you're pretty much making her."

Florence looks affronted. "Excuse me?"

"Mom hates having to punish you or yell at you," I say slowly and clearly, enunciate each word carefully. "But you don't give her the option of being patient and kind to you, because you're too busy working yourself up and yelling at her."

My twin raises an eyebrow. "Yet this doesn't explain why she treats you like royalty."

"She doesn't," I reply, slightly confused. Is that how Flo has looked at my life over the past years? "Flo, Mom doesn't treat me the way you think she does. *She* respects *me*, and *I* respect *her*, and we get along well since we're not stopping to complain every step of the way. Mom also tolerates me better because I take her opinions into consideration and go through with them. I don't whine about how walking to school is such a bother. It isn't. I don't care what I wear, as long as it fits me and is rather"—I grimace at Flo's low-cut tank top—"modest. For me. "

She tosses her hair over her shoulder. "Mom has *no* sense of fashion. The clothes she wears for work are ridiculous! A long skirt and plain blouse? Is she *trying* to age faster? She does realize we're in the twenty-first century, not the nineteenth, right?"

"Your views are different from hers," I say soothingly. I don't want her to get riled up again. "As I've said. You shouldn't make fun of how she dresses, and maybe if you stop she'll come to appreciate it and be nicer to you."

"And maybe if she doesn't make fun of how *I* dress," says Flo, "then I'll be nicer to her."

I let out a sigh of relief. "And about before," I continue, moving on from this part of our shout-out, "I do *not* get all that I want. If I did, we would still be in California, Dad would still be with us, and we would still be a happy family with no contention. Instead, we're thousands of miles away from our grandparents, Dad is…gone, and we're a miserable family who can't get along."

Flo's eyebrows inch up again. "Really."

"Really," I confirm. "Siena can't go an hour without shouting at someone or starting a fight or getting in trouble. She's constantly seeking out Pompeii only so she can make him retaliate and begin a feud. And if Pompeii isn't off reading, then he's fighting with Siena! And Roman is becoming more and more a depressed teenager by the minute. He barely gets out of bed and out the door when I wake him up for school in the morning. He's moody and sullen and argumentative. Just like everyone else in this family."

"And what about me?" Flo asks sarcastically.

I falter in the middle of my rant. "You…" I let out another sigh, this one not of relief, and turn away from her so I don't have to face her and see the angry expression she's not bothering to hide, but I immediately whirl around again. I have to say this to her face. "You, Florence, are...hard. It is very hard to talk to you, whether you're in a good mood or a bad one. I don't ever *want* to talk—I'm afraid you'll attack me for something or find fault in me. Whether it's my choice of friends or my relationship with Mom or my sense of fashion or how our family members treat me...I know you'll gladly point out my flaws or mock me for who I am."

Florence is silent for a moment, then she says in a meek voice, "I'm sorry. I didn't realize I was being so...mean. It's just how my friends are—what they talk about. They look down on kids who act differently, who dress differently, who are...*very* different in general. It's pretty much all we talk about. How Sophie Jackson is wearing a nerd sweater with guacamole stains on the fuzzy sleeves; how Bennie Taylor needs new shoes—his are just *horrible* and never should have been made or bought; how you and the geeks you hang with are weird and loud and should shut up, especially the dark-haired girl who has a big mouth."

"Mandy?" I frown. "Florence, you're insulting my friends."

She gives me a pained look. "I know! And I don't mean to! It's just natural for me! I wish I wasn't like this, and I blame it on my stupid bloated ego that forced me to turn into this selfish jerk of a sister and daughter and friend!"

I can't help but wrap my arms around her and hug her. "Flo, it's never too late to change."

She presses her face into my shoulder—she's shorter than me by a bit, another noticeable difference between us. "Thanks. I see why Mom comes to you for help. You're understanding and can handle my rage and frustration without faltering."

"Oh, I've faltered," I say. "On Tuesday, three days ago, when I was telling you your aura, I felt like an idiot."

"That was the whole reason I came over to your table," Flo says unhappily. "I wanted to make you embarrassed. I don't even know why. The day started out fine, but during lunch one of the kids I sit with said how you weren't too bad to look at, and it randomly made me jealous."

I wrinkle my nose. The thought that Flo's "friends" were checking me out isn't a comfortable one.

"So I got up and remembered when I'd heard you talking about auras, and I decided that I could shame you by asking you about them, but it didn't work. Your friend—Mandy, did you say?—was interested, and so was Nate and the other boy, the one who's scared of Mandy and is Sam's cousin."

"Elijah," I supply.

Florence nods. "Yes, him. And I actually *was* a tiny bit curious what my aura was, I just didn't let it show. How do they work, exactly?"

"They're not very easy to explain," I say, stepping back slightly so we aren't hugging any more. "Everyone has an energy field that surrounds them. Some of the energy is tangible enough for me to perceive, especially if it's relating to how the person is currently feeling."

"So..." she begins, "you basically read people? You read their emotions?"

"Yes," I say. "It helps when you know them and past choices or events in their lives."

Flo ponders this, then says, "How'd you read Nate?"

"He was hard," I admit. "I know almost nothing about him. He doesn't like sharing information about his personal life, while Mandy and Elijah told me everything and managed to get me to tell them everything about *me*. With Nate, he gets really quiet when I ask about his family and won't answer my questions. Pretty much all I know about him is that he lives with his grandpa, he hasn't seen his parents in over a decade, and he doubts they'll ever come back. Yet he still has some hope."

She's quiet again. "Then what was that whole thing about him concerned the library will shut down?"

I laugh. "It's an inside joke," I tell her. "Mandy and Elijah are *always* teasing him for enjoying books more than video games. You should hear them go on and on about how shooting virtual people and bad-mouthing the other players is way better than reading Shakespeare."

"I'm going to have to agree," Flo says grimly.

I laugh again. What's everyone's problem with Shakespeare? Honestly, it isn't *that* bad.

"Your friends seem really nice," she continues. "Having fun like that. I don't think I've ever laughed with mine during lunch or in the hallways or all the places I go. We're just...critics. Posh kids who think they're higher than anyone else. The only thing we care about is our reputation and our popularity and that people are looking at us because we're beautiful."

"Flo," I say, "that is the stupidest thing I've ever heard you say. And I don't think you should include yourself with those kids. Sure, you like being the popular girl, and you like it when boys look at you, but you care about other things besides your reputation. Right?"

"Sure," she says unconvincingly. "I care about chocolate."

I snort with suppressed laughter. "Yeah?"

"Yeah. I ate yours, the ones Marc gave you, since I knew you wouldn't touch them. You even gave away the book he gave you. I saw you hand it over to Nate at lunch a few days ago."

"Talking about Marc...you said you overheard the conversation Mom and I were having that day before we learned about Dad?"

Flo hardens. "Yes." Her voice is clipped and curt.

"I'm sorry you heard it," I reply, really meaning it. "I'm sorry you believe you are some kind of monster that plagues Mom. I'm sorry you had to hear about your invisible struggles, the ones you barely recognize that Mom does and shares with me. I'm sorry you feel mistreated and misjudged and that everything fair to me is unfair to you. I'm sorry the younger kids don't want to talk to you like they do to me."

Flo stares at me. "Venice?" she says, it sounding both like a question and a statement. "Why are you like this?"

"Excuse me?"

She forces a strained smile. "Why are you so forgiving? And so...nice and strong and capable of managing to be kind to me, even when in return I'm not to you?"

I blink slowly, unsure of what to say. "Um," I start, and scratch that idea. "I am not what you think I am, Florence. I'm not perfect. I'm not very good at keeping my temper in check. I got mad at Mom for continuing to talk and hang out with Marc. I get mad at you all the time!"

Flo's smile is now more of a grin. "Venice," she says, taking my hands in hers, "stop. You're getting uncomfortable because I complimented you. So accept the compliment and stop trying to convince me that you're not what I know you are."

I flush pink, abashed at her gentle reprimand. The thought I pushed away sneaks back to my mind. This time I'm brave enough to say it. "Flo, I want to be good to you because I love you, and I want so badly for us to be friends." As I say it I can't help it, but tears form in my eyes. I quickly brush them away and get back to the beginning of all of this drama. "So, about the party later this evening..."

Her smile withers slightly.

"You can go instead of me," I say. "I don't want to go. You can. You have way more experience with adults and fancy parties and dressing up and all that stuff I don't...understand. Or care about."

She hesitates. "Venice—"

"It wouldn't be a waste for you," I say. "What's-his-face uber-rich guy, the one Mom helped, would enjoy your company and your charm more than my awkwardness and uncertainty. See, Florence?

It would all be so much better if you went. And Mom would definitely not be ashamed to have brought someone who knew how these things—"

"Venice!"

I stop mid-sentence. "Uh, yeah?"

"I don't want to go any more," Flo says, squeezing my hands. "Honestly. I want you to go."

My horrified expression makes her laugh.

"Come on," she says, tugging me towards her closet. "We've got two and a half hours to make you look presentable."

THIRTY-FOUR

I now understand why it takes Florence so long to choose what to wear for the day. Her closet is jam-packed with all sorts of clothing I am embarrassed to even imagine on a real person let alone ever consider wearing myself. None of her dresses look like something I'd walk around in public, and after a lot of debate she tosses most aside. She's convinced that I have to wear a dress, and when I tell her that I can just pull on a skirt and blouse, her eyes go wide and she almost starts to yell at me. Then she catches herself and quietly suggests we go through *my* things and decide out of those.

I don't have many dresses. I don't need them. The most formal event I've gone to was Roman's middle school graduation, and Mom let me attend in jeans and a silk top. She was grumpy that day and didn't care how I dressed. Plus, she hates Roman's principal—the woman refused to get rid of the vending machines and drinking fountains. Mom protested that vending machines wasted plastic with the individually-wrapped contents, and she said how the drinking fountains used way too much water that most kids didn't drink but watched it go down the drain.

Anyway, my point is that I don't feel the need to have twenty dresses—like Florence does—if I'm never going to wear them, and all they're doing is sitting in my closet collecting dust. We don't go to church, we aren't invited to many fancy parties, we don't participate in formal outings. We're a boring family.

Sometimes we're boring. Occasionally. Whenever Siena isn't threatening to stab Roman or Pompeii with Mom's kitchen knives. Or if we aren't fighting and throwing and breaking things.

Maybe we aren't boring, just dangerous.

"Venice. Venice!"

I blink, my eyes focusing on Florence, who is glaring at me. Her hand is fisted on her hip. She's not mad at me—we're past that—she's simply annoyed. I think. I hope she's only annoyed.

"Hello? Are you still awake?"

"Oh, yeah." I give myself a slight shake. "Sorry. I was lost in my thoughts. You know how often that happens to me. I don't mean to, but I just...It's an unpreventable action."

"Well, stop. We have to keep trying." Flo throws a dark blue dress at me. "Try that one."

I hold it out to arm's-length. "Too many holes," I reply. "Why would you put so many holes in the bodice?"

"Those aren't holes," says Flo, moving to stand next to me. "They're...oh, goodness, those *are* holes. You're right. What fashion designer makes their dresses with those in the front?"

I cock my head. "To some it might look stylish. To others, you'd have to put on an undershirt."

"Hm." Flo takes it from me and hangs it up in her closet. Technically it's *our* closet, but all of her clothes barely fit in, and there was absolutely no space for mine. I had to be fine with the dresser.

"Why can't I wear a blouse and skirt?" I ask for the umpteenth time.

She rolls her eyes at me. "No, Venice. I refuse to allow you to look like a total dork. You have to wear a dress."

"But all of yours are either too fancy for me, or too"—I wrinkle my nose at the navy-blue one—"showy for me."

Flo snorts, giving me another dress, this one yellow. "They are *not* showy."

Then she examines them more closely. "Okay, maybe a bit too short for you. I mean, they fall just past your knees."

"I'm too tall for them," I say, scanning the yellow dress. It's cute, yes, and I think yellow is a good color when the right shade, but it's strapless and I'm not a big fan of those.

It's also the middle of February.

"You won't like that one," says Flo. "Or that. Oh, this might work." She holds up a red dress that falls to her ankles. It'll be a bit shorter on me, but it's long enough that I'll be comfortable in it.

I study it for a moment. The neckline is high, the sleeves reaching to my elbows, the garment itself not too tight.

"Maybe," I say, trading the yellow one for it. "I like the color."

The dress has a flowered pattern of red and black, and I'm rather fond of the two colors when together.

"Try it on," Flo instructs.

"Do you think it'll even fit me?" I ask.

She sighs. "It'd better. You have to leave in an hour, and I'm running out of dresses. And I'm really tired. You're an exhausting, picky dresser."

I shrug carelessly. "I've got my own sense of fashion."

"You're too modest for me," says Flo, pushing me out of the room. "Hurry up and change!"

Laughing, I exit our room and head for the bathroom. Once in the small space, I slip into the dress and examine myself in the mirror hanging above the sink. The dress clashes crazily with my auburn hair, and for a second I'm worried Florence will diss the dress, but then I smirk at my reflection.

"If I like it," I say, "then that's that."

As soon as I return from the bathroom, Flo shrieks and wraps me in a hug. I startle at the contact, and she squeezes my waist tighter to prevent me from pulling away.

"You look great!" she exclaims. "Now all you need is your hair done!"

I give her a pained look as she finally backs off. "Florence, my hair is fine. I don't need to get it all fancy-ified."

She groans. "Venice, your hair is a mess. When did you last brush it?"

"Probably yesterday. Or maybe this morning, after I showered." I frown at her. "Why?"

Flo bites her lip, already picking through the hair products at her bureau. "If anyone sees you like this, Venice, you're going to be really embarrassed. Your hair is a tangle of knots."

"Well, I'm not constantly fixing it up," I say, gathering a handful of it in my fist. "You might be right, Flo. It is rather...tangled."

She whirls around, grabs me by the shoulders and forces me onto the stool she always sits on while doing her morning make-up. "Stay still, sister," she commands, ignoring my squeak of protest. "This may hurt, but I know you're strong."

And before I can argue, she drags a brush down my hair.

I yelp. "Florence! Be careful!"

She grunts, picking at the snarls. "I know, I know. Goodness, Venice. When you told me you brushed it this morning I thought you really *had.* But this is a four-day ignorant hairstyle!"

"Sorry!" I reach for the brush. "Let me, Flo. It'll hurt less."

"It'll look worse," she retorts.

I sulk in my seat, sharp pains tugging at me each time she combs out a knot. I glare at myself in the small mirror placed on her bureau, annoyed that I *could* be preventing this pain if Flo would give me the brush. But she seems to be enjoying herself, and I don't have the heart to snap at her, especially after all the progress we've made this afternoon.

"Done," she announces a few torturous minutes later, finally handing me the brush.

The handle is warm where she's been holding it for the past few minutes, and I curl my lip at the hateful thing that can inflict plenty of pain for just doing its job.

"What about make-up?" Flo asks, opening and closing the drawers around me as she looks for whatever she's looking for.

"What about it?"

She briefly makes eye contact with me, and I see she's quite exasperated at my response. "Would you so kindly allow me to create the finishing touches on my masterpiece?" she says, far too sarcastically. "You've got your hair brushed—not up in a hairdo, unfortunately—and you're dressed up, but your face is as plain as the day you were born."

I scowl while she laughs.

"What?" Flo starts stacking up the different products she uses. "I'm just telling the truth."

"I don't need make-up," I say. "I'm fine without it."

She pouts. "I know I'm a great cosmetologist," she says, "but it'd be nice if you would let me practice on you."

"Practice?" I wrinkle my brow.

Releasing a heavy sigh, Flo puts away the things she'd brought out, then straightens and settles her hands on my shoulders. "Venice, you've got to at least wear *something* cosmetic," she says. "Eye-shadow? I have silver that will go really well with your dress. You don't need mascara—your eyelashes are naturally dark, but you could use some blush..." She pinches my cheek. "You are as pale as a ghost."

"I am not!" I swat her hand away. "I get more sun than you."

"What else?" she murmurs, more to herself than to me. "There's another that I'm forgetting..." She suddenly snaps her fingers. "Lipstick! Come on, you've got to have some lipstick."

I meet her gaze in the mirror, and my expression must be one of resignation because she squeals with excitement and hugs me again.

"Yes! And you can use your bright red kind! The one Mom bought me that I gave to you!"

"The plant-based lipstick?" I wearily gesture towards the small shelf above my bedside table. "It's up there. Somewhere. In the black tube. I think it's by my gondola."

Florence spends a quick second searching for it, and when she finds the tube she returns to me. "Can I put it on you?" she asks with almost enough energy as Siena does when she pleads.

"Sure," I say, giving in.

Barely a moment later, I'm sporting fiery red lipstick that makes me seem like I've just drunk either a gallon of blood or a gallon of cherry Kool-Aid. Flo nods her head in agreement, pleased with her job, and I just grimace. I hope the lipstick doesn't stain my teeth.

"Only things left are your hair and your shoes," she says, tugging at a lock of my freshly-brushed hair. "Will you let me do something with it?"

"Depends," I reply. "You won't cut it, right?"

She looks horrified. "Why would I do that? I love your hair! It's so curly and long and it has a nice color."

"Oh." I'm slightly baffled by her compliments. "Thanks."

"Please please please let me," she begs. "I promise you can take it out if you don't like it."

I prepare myself for whatever comes next. "Okay. Bring it on."

The hour I have left to prepare passes all too quickly. One minute I'm talking with Florence about the difference between plant-based lipstick and lipstick made with pigment and parabens, the next Mom's telling me that we have to leave in three minutes, once she finishes whatever important phone call she has to make.

"Let's see…" Flo quickly looks me over, searching for something we either forgot or got wrong. She tugs at the hem of my dress, applies a fresh layer of lipstick across my mouth, and checks my hair to make sure the fancy up-braid she gave me is still intact. "I think you're ready to tackle them all," she says, grinning.

"Am I to go without shoes?" I ask, wiggling my bare toes.

She gasps. "Holy Mother Earth! I forgot about shoes!" She

yanks open the closet door, ignoring my smirk at her new usage of my language, and starts sorting through the piles and piles of shoes.

"Can't I wear my tennis shoes?"

She gasps again. "Don't you dare, Venice. That would ruin my entire outfit. And it'd make you look dorkish."

"You said that about everything I wanted," I point out.

"Because it's true!" She backs away from the closet, tapping a finger against her lips. Her eyes catch on something out of the window, and she stares at it for half a second before dashing out of the room. "Keep looking for my black ankle boots!" she yells.

I blink. "Um…" Her sudden departure has startled me.

Going to the closet, I'm digging through her shoes when Mom yells my name.

"Venice! We've got to go!"

"I'm coming!" I yell back, trying to find the shoes Flo told me to.

I soon give up and leave my room. "Florence!" I call, hoping that wherever she went off to, she can still hear me. "Flo! Where are those shoes? I have to leave right now!"

Her voice, faintly coming from the living room or the kitchen, answers me. "Check in the coat room by the front door!"

Sighing, I go down the stairs as quickly as possible, focusing on my feet and hoping I don't trip on the hem of my dress. I'm lucky it isn't too long, otherwise I'm sure I'd be flat on my face.

I whirl around the banister and turn down the hallway, almost crashing into someone in my haste.

"Sorry!" I say apologetically.

Then my heart momentarily stops beating as I realize who it is and that I'm currently dressed up like Florence.

"Nate? What are you doing here?"

He's having a hard time fighting back a huge grin. "I don't mean to intrude," he says, taking in my appearance, "but Mandy sent these with me to bring to you. She's convinced you need them more than she does."

He holds out a bag full of books. I take it from him, partly out of curiosity and partly so I don't have to look him in the eye.

"I'm sure she could find a use for these," I say, hoping we remain on this topic and not the reason why I'm dressed like this. "They must not be on mastering the art of video game controllers, otherwise I'm positive she'd have them memorized."

"That she would," Nate agrees. Then he raises an eyebrow. "Are you going somewhere?"

I wince. "Yes," I say. "A work party with my mom that some rich guy invited us to."

"Ah. That explains why you look...why you're dressed up."

I force down a blush. "Yes," I say again.

Thank the trees, Mom puts a grateful end to this awkward conversation by poking her head out of the kitchen doorway and saying, "Venice, we have to—Oh, hello." She gives Nate a curious look. "Who is this?"

I wince again.

So much for being saved from embarrassment.

"Mom," I say, "this is my friend Nate. Nate, this is my mom."

She smiles at him as he says, "Good evening, Mrs. Ferrari. I've noted how you both are dressed up. Going to the same party?"

"That we are," Mom confirms. She raises her eyebrows at me. "I heard you needed your shoes. Would you like me to get Florence to find them while you see to your guest?"

"Sure," I say haltingly.

Nate speaks up. "No, I don't need to be a bother. I've got to head back home for dinner anyway. I won't take up any more of your time."

I walk him to the door, placing the bag of books on the bottom step of the staircase as I pass it. I think I'll look through them and select one I want to take to the party in case I get bored.

"Venice." Nate stops in the doorway, half in and half out. His voice has dropped lower. "We should meet up somewhere and discuss the…strange things that have been happening to you. It'll help if we get all that out in the open to sort through. "

I rub my face, careful not to smear my lipstick. "I know. I just—I don't want to be always thinking about it…"

"Bring your ring," he says quietly. "I have no idea why so many people are searching for it and why they want it, but you're the current owner and it's our only clue."

"Okay," I agree slowly, not fully in on the plan.

Nate gives me a small smile. "When and where?"

"The library," I say reluctantly. "I'm sick of the café. And I'm free tomorrow—it's Saturday and I rarely do anything then—so whenever you're ready we can…meet."

"How about eleven?"

"Eleven-thirty."

His smile widens into a grin, showing off his nice teeth and his two dimples. I almost wince a third time. "See you then," he says, leaving the doorway and stepping on the porch. Then he calls over his shoulder, "You look really great, Venice."

And he's gone.

My cheeks burning red, I close the door and press my forehead against the cold metal. I can't believe he just said that.

"Venice, are you ready to go?" Mom yells from the kitchen.

I turn around, my insides squirming with nerves and the fact that Nate said I looked nice, and the fact that he knew I wasn't Flo, and the fact that I'm meeting up with him tomorrow at eleven thirty and we'll be talking about my ring and the danger it's put me in. Still, I'll be with Nate, and that isn't necessarily bad, right?

"I need my shoes!" I yell back.

Flo comes running down the stairs, holding a pair of black ankle boots in her hand. "Here!" she says breathlessly, shoving them at me. "They will go perfectly with your dress."

"I need socks, too."

She gestures to the boots. "I put a pair in the left boot."

I sit down and start pulling on the socks. "Thanks, Florence. Where were these boots?"

She sounds almost...sheepish...as she says, "Under my bed."

"Wait." I pause. "Did you *know* they were? Did you make me come down when Nate was here?"

Flo lets a giggle slip out of her mouth. "So what?" she says. "It worked, didn't it?"

"Florence!" I throw one of the socks at her. "That was very embarrassing! Why did you do it?"

"Oh come on," she says, giving me the sock. "Girls like looking beautiful, especially when there's a boy around, and you were looking beautiful and there was a boy around. It all worked out perfectly!"

I scowl. "Is *extreme mortification* part of that plan?"

"Stop being so awkward, Venice," Flo chides. "Embrace your femininity! You are a woman!"

"I'm sixteen and don't care for femininity," I retort, tugging up the zippers on my boots. I stand up, the two-inch heels causing me to tower over my twin more than usual.

"Psh." Flo scans me quickly, then nods. "Good. You're ready."

Mom appears behind Florence, smiling broadly. "You look amazing," she says. "Great job, Flo."

My twin is stunned, though she tries not to show it. I smirk. She isn't used to being paid a compliment by Mom. It's normally a complaint on how the fashion isn't acceptable.

"Let's go," Mom says, shouldering her purse. "Flo, the kids are allowed to watch a movie with you, but it *has* to be appropriate. I don't want Siena getting any more ideas, all right?"

Flo flashes me a grin. "I got it," she acknowledges.

"Dinner is on the table," Mom continues, not having caught the quick grin. "You all have to eat some if you want to watch TV."

"Okay."

Mom anxiously opens the recently-closed door. "You know my

phone number, and Ms. Mehaine's, and you just go over to her house if there's any trouble or danger."

"I know, Mom!" Flo shoves her out the door. "Go have fun!"

"Thank you," I mutter as I pass her. "Thanks for everything, Flo. You have fun, too."

She snorts, holding open the screen door with one hand as I walk out. "I doubt I'll be as bored as you," she says. "Oh, wait. You'll want a book to read, right?"

Before I can ask her what she's doing, she has disappeared back into the house, the screen door swinging shut. I see her digging through the bag of books Mandy gave me, and a moment later Flo comes back outside with a soft-cover book.

"Here," she says, pressing it into my hand.

I take it, not recognizing the title. "Thanks again," I say.

She rolls her eyes. "Go on!"

"I am!" I hurry down the driveway, unconsciously glancing around to see if Nate is walking in the direction of his house; I don't spot him, and for some reason I'm both relieved and disappointed.

"You have to tell me everything when you get back!" Florence calls from the doorway.

I raise the book over my head as a reply, then reach the car and yank open the passenger side door right as Mom's phone rings.

"Gah!" She digs through her purse, finds it, and answers. "Hello? Oh, hey, Marc."

I go still as he responds.

"That's funny!" Mom says. "I was just about to go out with Venice. No, I'm sorry I won't be able to today. Yes, it's a bummer. I'll see you Monday, right? Will you stop by the Vales?"

Sighing, I take the keys from her, shove her into the passenger seat, and walk around the car to the other side. I slide in, first putting on my seatbelt before starting the engine. Mom seems grateful that I'm willing to drive, and she prattles on with Marc not realizing that I have no idea how to get to our destination.

Slowly, carefully, I leave our neighborhood and wait at the stop sign for a second while trying to decide if I should turn left or right. Going right would be to pass the library, high school, and café. Left would be towards Pompeii and Siena's school.

"Mom," I interrupt. "How do I get to Goldbeck's?"

She takes a second to reply. "Um...left."

I follow her directions for the next ten minutes until she hangs up from her call and says, "Why don't you use your phone? I forwarded the email to you detailing the party invitation, and it had his address on it."

"I didn't bring my phone," I say, checking the rear-view mirror to make sure I can change lanes right here without slamming into another car. "I only brought a book."

Mom scoffs, picking up the book. "I've never seen this before."

"I got it barely a few minutes ago."

Her voice turns softer, sweeter. "From Nate?"

I groan, easing the brakes so the car comes to a complete stop in front of a red light. "Yes."

"He seems like a good kid," Mom says, flipping through the pages in my new book. "It's a mystery why Flo hasn't wrapped him around her finger yet. You'd think she would, given he's so cute."

I want to start yelling in aggravation. I would if I wasn't driving.

Why do they have to keep talking about Nate like this?

"She's already tried," I say, hating myself for continuing this conversation. "Nate isn't her type."

Mom bats her eyelashes at me. "Are you?"

I close my mouth.

"Hm." She turns another page in my book, then lets out a small gasp of surprise. "Why is your ring in here?"

"What?" I quickly glance over at her and, sure enough, my ring is sitting innocently on the middle of the page, glinting gold in the dying sunlight.

THIRTY-FIVE

"I didn't put that there," I say, astonished. "Florence must have."

"It's a good thing she did," says Mom. "You almost forgot it. Here, put it on. I think it'll go well with your outfit."

"Silver would be better," I argue, gripping the steering wheel tighter so I don't have to accept my ring from her.

Mom snorts. "Venice, you should wear it. It's the last thing Dad ever gave you, and you should honor his memory. It's all you have of him now."

I open my mouth to tell her that no, it's *not* all that I have of him, but right then something catches my eye. I look to my left and spot a massive black SUV weaving in and out of traffic, heading straight for us.

Panicked, I shoot forward the second the stop light changes to green. I quickly change lanes, attempting to hide myself from Hubris Jargon and his monstrous SUV.

"Venice!" Mom grips her seatbelt. "What are you doing? Do you want to get us killed?"

I ignore her, concentrating only on the SUV. "Stop freaking out," I mutter under my breath. "It might not even be him. It could be a different SUV out for a Friday evening drive."

"What?" Mom asks, squeezing her seatbelt harder.

"Nothing," I say louder, moving around a slow Honda. "Mom, you know we are going to be late unless I speed up."

"It doesn't matter if we're late!" she cries. "It matters if we're alive!"

I go back to ignoring her.

Paranoid, I glance back at the SUV. It's closer to me—I can almost see into the front seat. Then I really will be able to decide if it is Hubris Jargon or not.

"Venice!" Mom squeals.

I slam on the brakes, stopping right before a red light. The SUV comes up behind us, dark and brooding and threatening. I look at it through the rear-view mirror and catch a flash of bright orange, which immediately arouses my suspicion that this is, in fact, the man and his car who just about ran me down.

The light turns green. I quickly scan the onslaught of cars around us as I keep driving, trying to find a way to escape Hubris Jargon and his powerful SUV. If he crashes into us...I shudder. Our car will be destroyed, along with us.

"Venice," Mom says through gritted teeth, "do you want to end up like your father?"

"That's harsh, Mom," I reply absentmindedly, spotting a chance to get out of this mess.

Barely ten feet from us is a car—same brand, color, model—as ours. If I can trick Hubris Jargon into following *that* car, I might be able to shake him off our tail and prevent a massive collision.

I move into the same lane as the car. The driver doesn't seem to notice I am using it as bait, and for that I thank them. Behind me, Hubris Jargon is determined to trail after us, copying every move I make and once forcing me to stay in the opposite lane as the other Hybrid. He must have recognized my pathetic attempt to get away.

"You missed the turn!" Mom says helpfully.

"Hm?" I anxiously tap my fingers against the steering wheel, sending nervous looks back at the SUV, who has managed to get in the middle of a crowded section of the road and can't escape. Hubris Jargon keeps blowing his horn, which does a wondrous job of attracting attention to him, and I somehow slip in front of the other Hybrid, then stay with it for the next few streets and turns. Once it goes down a different road, I pull through a busy intersection and am lost amid the traffic.

I finally breathe a sigh of relief, sagging against my seat.

"What was *that*?" Mom demands. "Were you not wanting to go to the party, Venice? Is that why you brought us into the middle of traffic? You do know it's rush hour, right? This is when everyone is coming back from their jobs in and are clogging up the streets!"

"I know," I say, maneuvering around an eighteen-wheeler.

She crosses her arms. "I can't believe you did this. You nearly killed us four times, Venice!"

"Sorry. I was hoping we would nearly get killed five times."

"That isn't funny." She takes a deep breath. "Explain yourself right now, or we're turning around and going home right now."

"Fine with me."

Mom waits until we have a clear road ahead of us before saying, "Venice, pull over."

I obey, moving into the closest gas station. Once the car has stopped, Mom gets out of her seat and marches around the car to my side. She yanks open the door.

"I'm driving now," she says. "You shouldn't even be on the roads! You're as terrifying a driver as Florence! You are *definitely* grounded until you explain yourself."

"If I'm grounded," I say, sliding onto the passenger seat, "then how can I go to this party? And how can I do my homework with Nate at the library tomorrow?"

Mom gets in, slamming shut the door. She clicks in her seatbelt. "Now is not the time to be talking like that," she says, pulling out of the gas station. "I think you should be ashamed of yourself, Venice. I always thought you were cautious and careful, but that colorful driving is not to be accepted! I don't know if I can let you drive anymore."

"Well, I can't exactly promise this to be an once-in-a-lifetime experience."

She is getting frustrated. I should shut my mouth.

I do.

"Venice," she says as she cautiously and carefully merges with the other cars, "I need you to tell me why you did that."

My mouth remains shut.

"Venice, if you don't tell me, then I'll call Nate's parents and say you aren't allowed to meet with him tomorrow."

"His parents deserted him."

Mom is silent for a moment, then sighs heavily. "That's not the point. I'm saying, you are going to lose privileges if you don't come clean."

I don't speak.

"Am I going to have to force you to come to all of the Goldbeck parties?" Mom threatens.

"Fine!" I say quickly.

She allows herself a small smile of triumph as she flips a U-turn, heading back to the street I missed.

"Did you see the black SUV back there?" I ask.

"What SUV?"

I open my book and take my ring from the pages, staring at the tiny piece of jewelry that has complicated my life so badly. "There was this huge SUV," I say softly, putting the ring onto my finger. "It came up really close to us, so close that I thought it was going to crash into us. So I panicked. I maybe went a bit crazy. Sorry about that. I didn't mean to scare you, I just wanted to get as far away from the SUV as I could."

Mom hesitates, then says, "I understand, Venice. Those cars can be pretty intimidating, especially if you're in a small car like this one. But that isn't an excuse to start madly tearing down the road."

"Sorry," I mutter, hoping to sound chastened.

She sighs again. "I won't say that it's okay," she continues, "since it *isn't*, but I will forgive you. You're a young, inexperienced driver and another big car frightened you. It's going to happen a lot, Venice. You'll be scared you're about to get into a wreck, and after your father died it has been harder for even me to drive my car. I am reminded of that terrible day."

"Mom…" I begin, wanting to tell her that Dad isn't dead, wanting to tell her that I am sick of lying, wanting to tell her that I'm being hunted for my ring, wanting to tell her that those men broke into our house not to rob her but to rob me, wanting to tell her *everything*—yet I pause. I'm not sure she will believe me.

"I really am sorry," I say instead, internally cursing my cowardly self. "I hope I didn't make us extra late."

She gives me a tight-lipped smile. "We're lucky Mr. Goldbeck lives close to us, otherwise we definitely would be late."

"Yeah," I say, hiding the strain in my voice. "Lucky."

Mom changes the subject, and we're talking about how SUVs emit plenty of carbon dioxide when we arrive at the Goldbeck mansion. It is a lavish building, fancily decorated with red and pink balloons and streamers. Mom grimaces at the sight of all the balloons and whispers how she wishes she had been part of the decoration crew—she would have used biodegradable balloons.

A parking valet takes the car keys from Mom, giving us in return a slip of paper to show where our car will be put, and after thanking the kid, she leads me up to the front door. I don't pay any attention to the white-stoned fountain in the center of Goldbeck's yard, or the gold trim that runs along the sides of every window and door, or the butler who answers the door and shows us through winding corridors all furnished lavishly. I clutch my book to my side, concentrating on Mom's impressed expression and forcing myself not to copy it. The polite thing to do would be to at least *fake* awe, but I have a strange feeling that Goldbeck's ornaments are for show, like he set out all these fancy, expensive things to rub it in other peoples' faces.

349

The butler opens a tall door and waves us into an enormous room full of exquisitely dressed, happily chattering rich people. I wrinkle my nose as the heat of too many bodies in one room hits me, and I am looking for a cool, dark corner to hide in and read when a stubby man in a perfectly-tailored tuxedo comes waddling up to us.

"Linda Pope!" he bellows, pumping Mom's hand energetically. "It's great to see you!"

"Good evening, Mr. Goldbeck," Mom says, smiling.

He waves it away. "I thought I told you to call me Stephen," he says, his voice lilting towards bluster.

"Very well, Stephen," concedes Mom. She motions to me. "This is Venice, my oldest daughter."

"Hello!" Mr. Goldbeck says cheerily.

I give a timid wave, the dim metal of my ring catching in the bright light.

"Well, don't stand there in the doorway!" says Mr. Goldbeck, pulling us farther into the room. He takes us over to a tiny woman talking with a group of old gossiping ladies, but the old women all vanish when Goldbeck arrives, leaving the tiny woman alone.

"This is my wife, Rebecca," Goldbeck introduces.

"Good evening," she says in a thin voice. She is the exact opposite from her husband. Where he is more on the cubby side, she is toothpick-thin, her bony figure sharp and brittle. In my opinion, Goldbeck is soft and squishy; his wife is hard and firm.

She has iron-grey hair wrapped around the crown of her head in a braid. Her eyes are narrow and harsh; she reminds me of a vulture ready to tear apart anyone she sees as weak. She carries herself with an air of dignity, like she knows she is better than everyone else and wants them to know it, too. The woman is made of steel—I doubt anything will snap her in half. She can face a monstrous storm and survive.

However, her aura reeks of greed. She has to have whatever

she wants *right now or else*. She's been pampered her entire life and is used to making everyone bow to her every whim.

Her husband is no different. His aura is also pure greed.

What is it with rich people and greed?

"...moved in all right," Mom is saying, and I pull myself out of La-La Land so that I don't seem impolite and bored with this conversation. "I really love what you've done with the place," she continues. "All these fancy decorations! If I may ask, what's with the red-and-pink theme?"

"My dear!" Goldbeck says affectionately, patting her on the shoulder. "Do you not know it is Valentine's Day?"

Oh, no.

Mom goes cold. "I did not remember," she says bluntly.

The Goldbecks don't notice. "I am a lover of red," says Rebecca Goldbeck. "This color suits me very well."

"Yes, it does," Goldbeck chuckles, squeezing his massive arm around her tiny waist.

I nearly gag. I busy myself with tapping a finger against the cover of my book, wondering what it's about. I haven't read the introduction yet. I really hope it isn't difficult to read, but I am glad I at least have a distraction if this party gets dull.

"You look familiar," says Rebecca, peering up at me.

I blink. "Uh...I look a lot like my mom."

She doesn't appreciate my snarky response, though I wasn't intending for it to be snarky.

"Yes, you do," she says, sniffing in disdain.

I nervously brush a loose strand of hair behind my ear, worried about the glare she's giving me.

"That's a nice ring," she says suddenly.

I freeze, my hand automatically falling to my side and out of sight. "Thank you," I say tersely.

"May I see it?" she asks.

I hesitate long enough for Mom to come to her senses and

gesture for me to obey the woman's wishes. I reluctantly hold out my hand, and Rebecca Goldbeck seizes it eagerly, her sharp fingernails digging painfully into my soft skin.

"Gold goes well," she murmurs.

I swallow as her aura is washed over with even more greed.

"I happen to have a large jewelry collection," she says, moving to slide off my ring.

I quickly stop her. "That's interesting," I say, but I'm lying. I don't care if she has a collection—there is no way I will let her take my ring from me. I am too cautious, especially after the past month.

"My wife certainly *does* have a large collection," Goldbeck says, chuckling. He sounds like he's finding this whole exchange extremely humorous. "Each year, I give her a new ring. She loves them, you see. Rebecca, my dear, how many do you have?"

She lifts her chin. "Nearly four hundred."

I hide my hand behind my back so she can't take it from me. "That's...interesting," I repeat.

"May I see yours again?" she asks me.

I don't want to let her, but Mom is giving me a hard look. Slowly, I lift my hand and show Rebecca Goldbeck my ring.

"I don't have one like this," she muses. "I'll give you fifty dollars for it."

My jaw drops a little. "Excuse me?"

Rebecca Goldbeck gestures to my hand, which I have safely returned to my side. "I will pay you fifty dollars for your ring," she says. "I really like it, and I wish to add it to my collection."

"Er—" I don't know what to say. No thanks? This is one of my only connections to my "dead" dad? I've been very cautious about my ring ever since I was almost killed for it?

"Her father gave it to her," Mom cuts in. "Before he died."

Something flicks across Rebecca's smooth face. Something like...pride? Understanding? Uncertainty? All the emotions blend together until I can't untangle them and I'm left wondering what is going on in her mind right now. She's hard to read other than the obvious greed.

"I'm sorry," says Mrs. Goldbeck. "Death is a tragedy."

Yet she doesn't sound remotely sorry.

Goldbeck speaks up. "Rebecca, since Miss Venice has shown interest in rings, why don't you take her to your room and let her see them? Maybe she will change her mind and want to add to your collection."

My blood freezes over. I have no desire to go *anywhere* with Goldbeck's creepy wife.

Thank the trees Mom refuses.

"Actually, I was just about to take Venice to the backyard," says Mom. "She loves evergreen trees, and you have a whole forest of them out there."

Rebecca Goldbeck hardens slightly as her husband laughs, the sound a bit forced in my ears. She reaches over and grabs my wrist as I start to walk away with Mom, and she whispers, "I'll give you two hundred. Two hundred dollars for your ring."

"I—" I gently extract myself from her death grip. "That's an extraordinary offer, but I will have to decline. My ring isn't for sale."

She grows desperate. "Five hundred. One thousand! I need that in my collection!"

"Mrs. Goldbeck. If you want to get a vintage ring like mine, then just go to a nearby second-hand store and search through the jewelry. There are tons of rings that are much better than mine."

Rebecca is disgusted. "I would *never* go to a second-hand store!" she says, repulsed.

"I'm truly sorry."

But I'm not. I smile thinly, and hurry after Mom. My mind is buzzing with that recent exchange, and I tell myself I need to keep a closer watch on my ring in case Rebecca Goldbeck or one of her employees tries to steal it.

*****

After I explore the forest of evergreens, I sit underneath a yellow lantern and begin my book. To my surprise, it's both hilarious and engaging, and I wonder why Mandy gave it to me. I know she isn't a fan of reading, but this book is a great way to pass time.

When it gets darker, and I finish my book, I return inside and try to find Mom. She's talking to Stephen Goldbeck again, and his wife isn't in sight, so I feel safe going up to them. Rebecca is terrifying.

"Hello!" Goldbeck chirps when he spots me.

I smile nervously, not showing any of my teeth.

Mom gives my hand a squeeze. "Enjoying yourself?" she asks.

I nod slowly. "Yeah."

But it's a lie. I'm not enjoying myself. I wish I had a friend here—I'd settle for Flo, even—because reading can get lonely. And after my discussion with Rebecca Goldbeck, I've been wanting to go home more than ever. I'm worried she'll pop up and offer two million dollars for my junky ring and Mom will make me sell it.

"There aren't many things I'd planned for a young teenager to do," says Mr. Goldbeck. "And I'm sorry. This is more of an adult party than a wild one those youngsters throw nowadays."

I nod again, opting not to say anything.

"We have refreshments," he continues, waving a hand towards the far end of the gigantic room. I can barely make out a long table with a bright pink tablecloth. That must be the refreshment table. "There are all sorts of people here," Goldbeck goes on. "Mostly my neighbors and a few friends who helped with my move—including your brilliant mother—but I don't think there is anyone your age. I'm very sorry, Miss Venice."

"It's...alright," I reply hesitantly. "Um, do you have a library?"

Goldbeck blinks at me while Mom places a hand over her mouth to cover a smile.

"Library?" he echoes. "My dear, neither my wife nor I read very much. We do not have a library."

I pout, disappointed. I'm done with my book and need a new one to read, otherwise I'll have to—*ugh*—mingle with the other guests and strike up a conversation with whatever rich snobby person I decide to talk to. And I hate having to seek out entertainment. Why couldn't he just have a library with a few books? I wouldn't even mind boring ones about tree bark. I give Mom a pleading look. We've been here quite a while.

Mom gets the hint and starts to make her goodbyes. But Goldbeck is having none of it. He insists that there are a few people he wants her to meet, potential lucrative clients he calls them.

"In the meantime, there are plenty of people I'm sure you would enjoy talking with, Venice," he says. "Why, Moira Zane, the woman over there, is exceptionally chatty. I'm sure you would have fun with her."

I gulp and look in the direction he's gesturing to. I see a stout woman in a horrible turquoise dress talking loudly to a man in a tuxedo I recognize as the butler. The two are in the middle of an argument, but the instant Goldbeck says her name, the woman turns to us.

"Hello," she says in a nasally voice, wandering up to stand by my side. "It's great to see you looking so sharp, Stephen. When was the last time you even dressed in clothes other than your pajamas?"

I like the woman straight away. She reminds me of Florence.

"Oh, Moira," says Goldbeck, chuckling his regular laugh. It comes right from his belly, building up as it forces its way out of his mouth. "Aren't you the life of the party!"

Moira tosses her hair. Now that she's next to me, I notice several things about her. She isn't old, but she isn't young, either. She's shorter than me by a lot, and I'm definitely thinner; her nose is sharp, as is her jaw, yet at the same time they are fleshy. Her black hair is curled in giant ringlets that drape over her shoulders, and she keeps pushing them back, then pulling them forward again. Her face is painted thoroughly with make-up; I doubt this is what she really looks like. Her eyes are a rich amber color, which I find to be curious. I've never met anyone with amber eyes before.

Moira's aura is rather like Flo's, too. Blindingly white beauty. Fierce red that bubbles and boils inside of her. But she also has bronze deep down, and I feel compassion for her.

She isn't liked because of how loud and obnoxious she is.

"I try to be fun," she replies. "If I'm not, then everything is simply boring. I am what generates the entertainment."

Goldbeck laughs while Mom manages a strained smile.

I study Moira again, liking what I see. She's got to be barely younger than Mom.

"Unfortunately"—she sighs dramatically—"there is not much I can do to make things enjoyable. Too many people, too many opinions, too many options."

"At least you try," I say, unsure of what we're talking about.

Moira eyes me with interest. "Hello," she says. "Who are you?"

"Venice Ferrari."

A grin spreads across her face, revealing her slightly-crooked teeth. I think they fit right in with how her personality works. "I love your name," she says. "I haven't heard that one before."

"I hear it a lot," I say, matching her grin. "Whenever I get in trouble."

She throws back her head and laughs loudly, the sound booming and very obnoxious.

But I don't mind. Not at all.

"You don't seem like a kid who gets in trouble all the time," she says once she has calmed down sufficiently. "You remind me of my goody-goody little cousin. No offence."

It's my turn to laugh. "Don't worry," I say. "My siblings tell me that too."

While we've been talking, Mom and Goldbeck have snuck away, either to descend on those lucrative clients or because they can't stand Moira's boisterous character.

"What are your sibling's names?" Moira asks, smirking. "Not Rome and Milan and Sardinia?"

"Not quite," I say. "But close. I have a brother by the name of Roman."

She nods energetically in understanding. "Ah. What about Bologna? And Naples? Maybe Verona?"

I shake my head.

"Florence?"

"Yes." I grin. "She's my twin sister."

We play this guessing game for the next few minutes until Moira learns all their names, and that's when she tells me that she lived in Italy for eighteen years while her father worked for some cruise company. It sends a spark of jealousy rushing down my spine. I've always wanted to go to the city I was named after, but we've never gotten the chance.

Moira is thirty-nine, I discover after subtly asking her age. She doesn't feel embarrassed to be acting like a rowdy teenager—in fact, I realize she *wants* to be a teenager again, not an accountable adult. She is immature and has a bad mouth, making me horrified and uncomfortable at the things she tells me about.

I notice people give us a wide berth, like they can't even *glance* at Moira without being disgusted, and it frustrates me. Sure, Moira is…childish…but that isn't an excuse to be rude.

We've been talking for nearly twenty minutes when she links her arm with mine and drags me out into the backyard, where we take a stroll around the massive flower garden. I don't understand how the Goldbecks got flowers to bloom in the middle of February until Moira explains they bought hundreds of flowers to be planted in the ground just for this one day. Soon, they will wither and die, leaving behind brown stalks and brown petals and a big mess for the servants to clean up. It makes me respect the Goldbecks less than I already do.

Moira points out different twinkling stars, telling me how her mother was very interested in astronomy and taught her how to identify the dozens of constellations in the night sky. I don't even need to feign attentiveness—she is an amazing tour guide to the mystery that is outer space. She talks clearly, shares fascinating information, and never ignores my questions, despite how idiotic they sound.

We're heading back to the crowded house when she stops me by putting her hand on my arm.

"Venice—"

I pause, looking over at her. "Yes?"

"I would like to thank you," she says gruffly. "You stuck around and were able to tolerate my…nauseating self."

My brow creases in a frown. "You aren't nauseating."

She lets out a short bark of laughter. "Ah, Venice. I wish everyone was like you. Unfortunately, not many are. Your mother must be so lucky to have you as her daughter."

I blush pink at her compliment. "Thank you."

Moira sighs. "Will you ever come over and visit? I live just down the street from Stephen. My house is the cute one with stone lions out front. It's the smallest building in this whole neighborhood."

"I…might," I reply uncertainly. "I'd like to. My mom—"

"Doesn't like me," Moira finishes for me, though it's not what I was going to say. "I understand why," she says. "Most adults don't think I'm a good influence on the younger generation."

"I think you're a great friend," I say, meaning it. She may be strange and inappropriate at times, but when I look past all that, I know she's fun to talk to and hang out with. She kept me from being bored for the past hour and a bit. I haven't been tempted to reread my book once since I met her.

"Thank you, Venice," she says, giving me a small hug. "I know you're only saying that to make me feel good, but thanks anyway."

"I do mean it," I say, but she's already walking away, back into the house and to her freedom. I wish I could escape with her instead of joining with the boring adults and such. Maybe Mom is finally ready to go.

Wandering inside the ballroom again, I politely push my way through the crowds of chatting snobs, heading for the refreshment table. I should get a drink, if they have a fruit punch or lemonade or something. Hopefully it isn't all alcoholic. I wonder if Mom has had a drink since the day she came home drunk. She hadn't exactly *promised* she wouldn't touch alcohol, and I hope she remembers that she's supposed to be an accountable adult.

Suddenly I stop mid-step, awkwardly catching my balance on some random man to my left. The sight before me is unbelievable.

Standing next to the refreshment table is a tall man wearing sunglasses despite being indoors and eight fifteen in the evening. He is talking on his phone and smoking a cigarette, which earns him disapproving looks from passing guests.

He also has bright orange hair.

Hubris Jargon?

THIRTY-SIX

My fingernails dig into the old man's shoulder. He grunts in pain and turns to me, ready to yell a reprimand, but I'm already gone, rushing off to find Mom or Stephen Goldbeck. I need to borrow a phone and call the police. Hubris Jargon is here at the party, standing so casually by the refreshment table, as if he isn't scared to be recognized and spotted and arrested. What is that man *thinking*?

He must have followed us here, even after I'd thought I'd done a good job of losing him in the traffic.

I shove through the crowd, searching for Goldbeck amid the sea of tuxedo-clad men and cocktail-dressed women. Finding the host of the party should *not* be this hard, especially if he's the center of attention and in the middle of things. And where is Mom?

Desperation drives me into a deeper hunt, and just when I'm about to give up and return to spy on Hubris Jargon, I spot Stephen Goldbeck standing in a group of puffed-up people dressed in fancy, lavish outfits. They are tittering at something Goldbeck has just said, and I don't bother finding out what or if it even *was* funny or if their laughing was purely sycophantic.

"Excuse me," I say, finally reaching Goldbeck.

He looks up, confused, but his face clears when he sees me. "Miss Venice! How do you like the party so far? Did my wife find you to show you her ring collection?"

"Oh, it's fine, and no," I say, and get to my point. "Do you know where my mother is?"

His confused expression returns. "I'm not sure. Whatever is troubling you? Can I help?"

"There's someone here," I explain desperately, waving a hand towards the refreshment table. "He almost hit me with his car a few weeks ago. The witnesses say he purposely wanted to run me down."

Shock takes over the confusion. "Miss Venice!" he exclaims with a nervous laugh, and guides me away from the small crowd. "Are you sure about all of this? Did you file a report with the authorities? How do you know who was the driver?"

His questions irritate me, but they do make me realize my claims sound ridiculous. "Well, no," I say, "I didn't file a report. But I'm fairly certain he's here. I'll show you. Actually, maybe you could tell me his name."

He lays his hand on my arm, making me jump. "Miss Venice," he whispers so only I hear, "you are overreacting. I'm sure you're imagining things. I can assure you that no one in this building would do you harm. You are safe, Miss Venice. You're perfectly safe. No need to worry."

"But the man..." I start to say.

Goldbeck interrupts me. "I can tell you're upset. I'll go find your mom. In the meantime, why don't you go locate Rebecca and have her show you her rings? She has taken to you and has decided she likes you. And it's definitely a good thing to be on her good side."

I jerk away from him and wander across the room, annoyed that he doesn't believe me. I scan my vicinity for Mom. *She* will believe me. Will she?

All of a sudden, Mom is at my shoulder, saying, "Hi, Venice. Are you ready to go home? I think we've been here long enough, and I'm starting to get a bit tired. And if you have that meeting at the library tomorrow morning, you might want to sleep well tonight."

"Mom can I..." my voice trails away as I notice Hubris Jargon isn't by the refreshment table any more. He has disappeared into the crowd, lost and out of sight. I wish I could have worked up the courage to face him—there is no way he would have hurt me in front of all these people. Plus, plenty of the men around me look capable of pounding Hubris Jargon into pulp. I would have been perfectly fine, and I could have gotten Jargon arrested and taken out of my life forever. Maybe I am overreacting. When I stop to listen to my thoughts I do sound kind of crazy.

"Can you what?" Mom asks, waiting for me to finish. "You don't want to stay any longer, do you?"

I slowly shake my head, my eyes on the bright pink tablecloth. "No, we can go. I've been ready to go for a long time."

"Yes, of course," Mom says, smiling softly. "And you're not grounded. You were really patient with that loud-mouthed woman back there. She was a bit like Florence, don't you agree?"

I nod. "So I'm not grounded?" I ask, wanting clarification.

"You have to meet with Nate, don't you? Can't stick him up." Mom's grin widens. "Yes, you're not grounded, Venice. But you are *not* allowed to drive until you can master your fear of big cars. Okay?"

"Okay," I agree.

"Good girl." She gives me a one-armed hug, and I lean into her. "Did you enjoy yourself?"

"Talking to Moira was fun. And I finished my book."

She laughs. "Of course you did. Goodness, when you asked Stephen about his non-existent library, I almost died."

I grin, glad I'd created a brief moment of joy for her.

"His wife is a big strange, isn't she?"

"Yeah, especially since she offered to buy my ring for a thousand dollars. I wonder what she sees in it." I glance down at it to hide the lie on my face. I know that she wants it. For what, that is what I would like to know.

"She's quite pinched," agrees Mom. "But they seem to love each other very much."

Her voice takes on a tinge of melancholy. She's probably thinking about Dad, confused why he gave up on her and left her.

We hesitate for a while, just standing there. I'm clutching my book against my side.

"I wonder if Stephen will be insulted if we don't say goodbye to him or to his wife," Mom muses, breaking the silence.

"You take care of that. I have to check something out first, okay? I'll meet up with you out front in less than a minute."

Before Mom can object, I'm walking towards the refreshment table, disappointment burrowing deep inside of me at the sight of no orange hair. I had seen him, been close enough for him to see *me*, and if Goldbeck would have believed me, Hubris Jargon might have been identified and detained. And I'd be able to tell Nate that no one wanted me dead.

The only evidence that Jargon was here is the lingering stench of his cigarette smoke.

"And the other people? What did they look like? What were their dresses like? Were there any hot boys?"

"The people were all old and snobby," I say, undoing the small braid that wrapped around the crown of my head. "And some women wore really tight dresses that were just *horrible* on their old bodies. And no, there weren't any hot boys. I think I was the youngest there."

Flo groans, thumping her head against the wall. "Ugh, that party sounds so *boring*. How did you even survive?"

"I read," I say, pull my hair down my shoulders. "And talked."

"You made a new friend?"

I hesitate. "You could call her that," I say after a while. "Moira was very...interesting. She knew a lot about stars and such. And she was pretty funny. She reminded me of you."

"Was she fashionable?"

I snort, grab Flo's brush and drag it through my hair. "In her own way, yes. She wore this poufy, gigantic turquoise dress that clashed terribly with her amber eyes. Oh, did I tell you she had amber eyes? They were really pretty."

"How old was she?"

"Only a few years younger than Mom." I tug at a snarl. "Moira probably was the second-youngest person there."

Flo stretches an arm over her head, leaning more heavily against the wall. "I'm glad you went, though. You got to experience boring adults. Were you awkward at all?"

"Only when Goldbeck's creepy wife offered to buy my ring for a thousand dollars," I reply, locking gazes with my twin in the mirror. "Flo, why did you slip my ring into my book?"

She grins. "You forgot it. You left it in my jewelry box, and I thought it was needed to complete your outfit, so I cleverly sent it with you."

"It got me into a load of trouble," I mutter. "But thanks."

Flo sighs, flopping down on her bed. "A thousand dollars! Seriously? Why didn't you take it?" Suddenly, she remembers, and I don't need to answer her question. "You're lucky you didn't have to be here to watch the younger kids. Siena was a nightmare! She wouldn't let me choose the movie *I* wanted to see, because she said we couldn't watch big people movies, that we had to watch this stupid cartoon with terrible animation. And Pompeii talked the *entire* time about useless facts relating to the movie, and Roman was being his normal annoying self. I would have preferred sitting in a dark corner reading instead of having to babysit our siblings."

I laugh, even though it isn't very funny. "Flo, your cartoon sounds more interesting than the party."

"It was *not*," Flo scoffs. "It was about this dog—but I thought he was a fox at first—and then..." her voice trails away in my mind as I unintentionally block her out.

Rebecca Goldbeck had been eager to get my ring. Hubris Jargon had been at the party. Could Rebecca have invited him? Was she Hubris Jargon? Or had he just followed us to the mansion and snuck in? Either way, I now know what he looks like and how he acts, not just that he has orange hair and wants to kill me. He is tall, smokes cigarettes, and might know Rebecca Goldbeck. Stephen Goldbeck obviously doesn't know the man, otherwise he would have told me who he was and tried to reassure me, right? I grudgingly admit that I could have been more explanatory and less forceful. Maybe then Goldbeck would've given me the man's real name.

Except...I don't think he was invited.

I stare at my reflection in the mirror, my dark green eyes reminding me of the evergreens I'd explored at Goldbeck's house. I look tired and weary and frightened, and I am. I'm tired of all this tension and stress that is keeping me from being safe. No matter where I am, it seems like Hubris Jargon can find me. I'm weary of hiding my ring and pushing it out of sight from anyone wanting it. I'm frightened that one day, when I'm off on my own, Hubris Jargon will come out of nowhere and kill me and steal my ring and walk away without regret.

But one good thing has come out of tonight.

I fall asleep with my head in Flo's lap listening to her prattling on about something as she gently strokes my loosened hair.

THIRTY-SEVEN

I don't sleep very well. My mind is whirling with all that has happened to me over the past two months—it seems like all my problems started when we left California and came here. The first day of school, two and a half weeks after we moved in, Hubris Jargon had driven past me for the first time. Two days later, when Marc was coming over for dinner, Hubris Jargon had gone by again, this time soaking me with rainwater from the road. And then the day after my birthday Hubris Jargon almost ran me down. I don't know if he purposely missed me or if Nate is the reason I'm still alive—couldn't Jargon have hit both of us if he wanted?

The Monday before I went to school again, Rupert and Quentin had come into my house, hurt me, and gotten arrested. It's been five days since then, but I haven't heard anything from the police about who those men are and why they broke in and who they're working for. Maybe the police haven't figured it out yet. And Mom hasn't made any headway with them either.

And now yesterday, Rebecca Goldbeck offered to buy my ring. Was it only because she likes how it looks? Or is she working for Jargon, is he working for her, or is she, him? Maybe they're not connected at all? I need to stop jumping to conclusions, but I am currently suspicious about *everyone*.

Including someone who had Jargon at her house for her party.

Unless she didn't know him, like Goldbeck didn't.

Unless Jargon snuck in without an invitation or their consent.

Groaning into my pillow, I ease onto my back and stare up at the ceiling. I hear Florence confabulating with one of her friends on the phone, their voices loud and animated.

"...club, but she didn't even look at me!" Flo sighs dramatically, swooning against her bed. "And when I called her name, she looked back at me for like, *one* second, and then continued on into the classroom. So I don't know if she broke up with him or not."

I roll my eyes.

There's a pause while Flo's friend replies; then Flo answers.

"No," she says. "His face is kind of lopsided. And his top lip is so wonky! I don't understand how other girls like him."

I check the time on my phone. Ten forty-seven. Yikes. I need to get ready for the day—I'm meeting with Nate at the library in less than fifty minutes. I'm glad Mom ungrounded me, as I would hate to have to turn him down, especially since I have plenty to tell him. And I really do crave his opinion on the things that are troubling me. He's the only one who knows most of my problems.

I think I'm ready to open up to him all the way.

Mom is in the kitchen when I wander down, and I spare a quick moment to study her. She seems happy—her aura is a bright and bubbly green—but she is moving slowly, like there is something weighing her down that she doesn't want to have to think about. I guess it's related to Dad; however, I don't know for sure.

"Venice!" Pompeii appears at my shoulder. He's getting taller, inch by inch, and might one day tower over me. I snort in disgust at the thought. "Venice," he repeats. "I heard that you were going to the library later this morning."

"Yes, I am," I confirm.

A grin stretches across his face. "Can I come with you?"

Horror strikes a chord in my heart. "Uh…" To say no would be mean and rude. But to say yes would result in him stalking me as I work with Nate. I do *not* want him there.

367

"Please?" Pompeii begs. "It's the *library*, Venice."

I bite my lip. "I don't know."

Mom catches my eye. "Venice," she says, "you should take him. Did you know it's supposed to be seventy degrees this afternoon? Getting out of the house will do Pompeii good."

I still hesitate.

"Either you take him or you get to do all the line-dry laundry instead of going to the library," Mom threatens, pointing a finger at me. She's smiling, however, and I know she's joking.

"Okay," I agree reluctantly. "Fine. You can come, Pompeii. But you can't say a single word."

He blinks at me, his innocence not convincing. "What would I even say?" he asks sweetly, batting his eyelashes.

I groan and turn away from him, almost crashing into Siena.

"Are you guys going to the library?" she says loudly, not bothering to keep her voice down despite the fact that we're inside and barely a foot away from each other. "I want to go! Mom, tell Venice that she has to take me too, not only Pompeii."

Mom mouths *I'm sorry* at me before nodding to Siena. "Of course," she says.

Dread seeps into me. "Seriously, Mom?"

"I'm sorry!" she says, spreading out her hands in front of her. "But this is a rare opportunity for me to be Pompeii- and Siena-free. I can't pass it up. You're going to have to take them both."

"If they say *anything*," I begin, "then I'm sending them home instantly. All right?"

Mom twists her lips to the side, thinking. "All right," she says finally. "This isn't my fault, Venice. You're the one who scheduled a meeting at the library. If you had picked a different setting, then I wouldn't have forced you to take the kids."

"Really?" I deadpan.

Mom shrugs her shoulders, returning to the stove and whatever breakfast she's cooking.

I look down at my younger siblings, who are smirking to each other, and wonder how I already have managed to screw up my morning. With Pompeii and Siena at the library—and I know they're going to spy on me—how will I converse with Nate about all the things relating to my ring? How will I even be able to talk without worrying that the kids are listening in on our conversation? I guess we'll actually have to work on our orangutan report.

"Venice," says Siena, "when are we leaving?"

I sigh. "Forty minutes. And if you guys are late or taking forever to come out, then I will leave without you. Got it?"

Pompeii and Siena give identical nods, identical grins on their faces.

And that's how, forty minutes later, I ended up walking to the library with my two youngest siblings behind me, happily chatting about whatever books they want to check out. I try to block them from my mind, but they have such *loud* voices it's impossible to ignore them. We attract a lot of attention from other people outside on this beautiful morning, and it's even harder to ignore the frowns they cast on us. It's not my fault that I had to be saddled with the two loudest, most annoying kids known to date. At the same time I feel protective of them and mumble to myself how adults are so impatient with the energy of childhood.

Straightening out my tight shoulders, I determine that this is the longest journey to the library that I have ever taken. I want to hurry up and arrive, so I can desert my siblings and find Nate and enjoy myself much more. But the library is still five minutes away.

Pompeii and Siena are now talking about cars. It's one of their favorite subjects, and I normally don't mind listening to what they have to say. Today, however, they aren't just talking, they're yelling at each other over which model of whatever car is better. And everyone we pass by can hear their conversation. I get really embarrassed—because no matter what Elijah believes, I am *not* immune to embarrassment—when we walk by an old lady fixing up the dead bushes lining her driveway, and she overhears Siena calling Pompeii a stupid dumbhead who doesn't know what one plus one is. The old lady frowns at me, and I hurriedly switch my gaze to the far end of the street where the library will soon appear.

"I'm not the stupid one!" Pompeii exclaims loudly, shoving Siena violently. "You are! You can't tell the difference between cheese and *queso!*"

"Because they're the same thing!" Siena retorts, shoving him back with equal force.

"No, they're not!" He dodges her hands. "One's in Spanish! Even a baby knows that!"

I groan to myself, amazed that I'd chosen their company over line-drying the laundry. Now I regret ever giving in and letting them come with me. I know it's going to be worse at the library, when I'm with Nate. I have a feeling Siena will keep bothering us, and Pompeii might meander over just to have a staring contest with Nate while I awkwardly tell him to leave us alone and get back to his biographies.

Thank the trees, the library comes into sight. I'm glad it's on our side of the street—I now have paranoia crossing the road—and I notice there are quite a few cars in the parking lot. Today must be busier than usual.

I don't see Nate as I hold the door open for my siblings, but once we are inside and Pompeii rushes off into the non-fiction section and Siena heads towards the juvenile fiction books, I search for my friend. For a moment, I can't find him, but then I spot him sitting at a small table near the graphic novels on the far side of the room. He isn't wearing his jacket or gloves, which is surprising, and his elbow-length sleeves show off pale white scars that trail up and around his arms.

For some reason, the sight of him makes my heartbeat speed up. Is it because of yesterday, when he complimented me on how I looked? Did he even mean it, or was he just teasing?

Nervously, I lick my lips and steel myself. It's just Nate. He's my friend. I don't need to be jittery when I see him. But he's pretty much the first boy I've hung out with and talked to and been friends with. I don't exactly know where our relationship is going; I hope I don't somehow destroy everything between us.

Because I think I *might* like him a tiny bit.

I take a deep breath to calm my nerves, then walk up to him and claim the chair by his. He is resting his chin on his palm, his eyes closed, almost like he's asleep. He doesn't stir when I sit down next to him, and I spare a quick moment to study him.

He's obviously handsome—I don't need Florence to tell me that. He has a nice mouth with perfectly curved lips that I force myself not to stare at. As I have noticed before, his eyelashes are long and dark, curling upwards at the ends. His messy hair is growing longer and more untamed; several strands reach to his cheeks.

"When did you get here?"

Nate jolts awake, startled at my voice. His head comes up; he looks around and sees me sitting to his immediate left. "Oh," he says. "You're here. Sorry, I was really tired and just fell asleep waiting for you…"

"What time did you come?" I ask, smiling at his sheepishness.

He shrugs, his chin falling back onto his palm. "When the library opened a little bit ago."

"You've been here for an hour and a half?"

He shrugs again, his eyes slipping shut.

"Are you going to sleep this entire time?"

He grunts. "Nah. How was that party you went to last night? Was it wild? Did you end up reading?"

"It was…interesting," I say. "I've got plenty to tell you."

And I tell him everything. I tell him about Hubris Jargon following me while I was driving to Goldbeck's mansion. I tell him about Rebecca Goldbeck offering to buy my ring for one thousand dollars when she got desperate that I was refusing. I tell him about spotting Jargon by the refreshment table. And I tell him about how Goldbeck didn't believe me or help me.

When I finish, Nate is wide awake. He raises his eyebrows in amazement, staring sideways at me. "That *is* plenty," he agrees. "You saw Jargon twice? In the car and at the party?"

"Yeah." I sigh and bury my hands in my tangled hair that I forgot to brush this morning. "It frightened me, but now I'm kicking myself for not acting. I could have confronted him in front of everyone, called him out. There were hundreds of people around me. Jargon couldn't've hurt me. At the very least I could have discreetly asked Goldbeck who he was."

"I'm glad you didn't confront him," says Nate. "Purposely putting yourself in danger is not how we're going to figure this out. We need to find a safer approach. Did you bring your ring?"

I pull it out of my back pocket. "Here."

Nate takes it, revealing his scarred hand, and turns the ring over and over in his fingers. "This doesn't look unique," he murmurs. "Why do so many people want it?"

"Could they be confusing it with another ring?" I ask.

Nate hesitates, then shakes his head. "Not likely. Didn't those men who broke into your house say they wanted your ring? And the gem inside it? I don't think they would get it wrong, especially since someone is obviously stalking you and your family."

"Why do they want my ring?" I take it from him and study it critically. The thing doesn't look special. The clear blue stone set in the middle, the one that reminds me of Nate's eyes, is cut in a rectangular and isn't very big. It's not some precious stone worth millions of dollars, is it?

"We should write down all the questions we can think of," says Nate. He shifts and rummages around in his pockets for a moment, then holds a blank and crinkled piece of paper and an ink pen out to me.

"I have to write them?" I ask incredulously. This is the second time he has made me do the work. I'm not complaining—I'm simply surprised that he immediately assumes that I will do it.

He blinks at me. "Um...no, not if you don't want to. I mean, you don't *have* to. I just thought—Well, you probably have better handwriting than me. Mine is terrible."

I hold his gaze for an entire minute, trying to find out why he's so reluctant to write down a few things, but he's impossible to read other than the faint wisps of exhaustion floating around in his aura.

Finally, he sets down the paper and begins to write. "First question," he says, "is the most obvious one. Why is your ring so wanted?"

"M-hm," I confirm. I can't see what he's writing—his hand is blocking the inky words.

"Second question," Nate continues, moving to another line of the paper, "is *who* wants your ring? And since we know their aliases, we can have those be the answer."

I stare at the paper. His calligraphy is fine, better than a lot I've seen, and just as I'm about to tell him that, he sighs and sets the pen down on the table with a soft *clink*.

"So you brought your younger siblings to the library," he says.

I assume an innocent look. "Hm?"

Nate grins. "Your little sister is watching us. She's over in the graphic novel section." He gives Siena a smile and a little wave. She responds by squinting up her eyes and giving him the two-finger *I'm watching you* signal. He replies with a salute.

"Oh, yeah, I guess that is my sister," I say nonchalantly. "And she's unsuccessfully attempting to spy on us."

Nate's grin widens as Siena's gaze snaps to me. She glares at me. I smirk by way of reply.

She wanders up to us, abandoning her spying. "Hey, Venice," she says casually, handing me a thin picture book. "I found this and remembered your report."

It's on orangutans. "Thanks, Siena," I say, flipping open the book. The spine crackles with the sound of being either recently-printed or rarely ever read by anyone.

Siena is still standing there, and when I raise my eyebrows at her, she goes red and stumbles away, muttering about something under her breath.

"Your sisters are funny," Nate observes.

I cast a frown on him.

"And so are you," he adds, and I roll my eyes.

"Can we please concentrate on these questions and try to avoid as many interruptions as possible?"

"Okay, okay." He returns to the paper, picking up his pen again. "What should the next one be?"

We spend the next hour or so compiling questions and answers that are only half-solved and that create more questions. We are disrupted twice, once by Pompeii and once by Siena, but other than that we're left alone. The questions, now that they're out in the open, only serve to confuse me more than before.

"My dad's death is part of this all," I say, running a finger down the edge of the paper. "He was killed the day Jargon almost turned me into road-kill. That was a fun weekend," I add sarcastically.

"Wait. That was at about nine in the morning, right? When we were walking to the Rainy Afternoon and Jargon drove by."

I nod cautiously. "Yes."

"And your dad died later that night." Nate frowns. "Do you think Jargon could have left Virginia immediately, driven over to Kentucky, and crashed into your dad's car?"

"I suppose that could have happened." But it doesn't seem plausible even if it is possible.

He picks up his pen, already writing down the times. "A trip to Kentucky from here is about seven and a half hours, depending on the traffic and where in Kentucky you're going. Do you know what town your dad was in?"

"No."

He sighs. "It'd help if people shared this information with you."

"I can ask my grandma. She should know."

Nate shakes his head. "No, it's all right. Don't bother her." He continues to write, then leans back in his chair and points to the paper. "It's possible that Jargon left Virginia after his failed attempt to kill you and went to Kentucky to fake your dad's death. But it's also possible that more people are involved in this."

"Shush." I nudge him with my elbow. "Pompeii is right there."

Nate winces, leaning slightly away from me. "You could give me a bruise if you stab me anymore."

"Sorry." I meet Pompeii's gaze and give him a *go away* look that he ignores or pretends not to see. Instead of drifting off to a different aisle, he comes up to us.

"Venice," he says, taking no regard of Nate, "when are we going home?"

I stare at my younger brother. "You can't tell me you're already bored and want to return home. It's only been an hour."

Pompeii shrugs. "I've read all of the biographies in the library's system, and now there's nothing else left to read."

"What about the history books?" I suggest. "Or the other non-fictions. Or maybe you could try to read some young adult novels."

"Those are fantasy. There isn't anything worth learning there."

I take off my glasses, clean the lenses on the corner of my shirt, and put them back on. It's a sign that I'm growing exasperated. "Pompeii, there are plenty of books in here for you to read that have interesting facts worth learning. You need find them."

"But I've already looked through every book."

"Impossible. Go bother Siena. You always love that."

He rolls his eyes. "I did that a minute ago. She hit me and told me to eat a breath mint."

"Then walk home. If you want to go home, you can. You don't have to wait for me."

Pompeii hesitates. "Okay." He turns around and walks away.

I groan and bury my face in my hands. "I am *never* going to bring him and Siena back here again."

"Oh they're fine. Why did you bring them, anyway?" Nate asks. He sounds like he's about to laugh and, knowing him, he probably will. I'm glad he finds them amusing and not annoying.

"So I wouldn't have to line-dry the laundry."

He lets the laughter slip out now. Ha. Guessed it. "Ah, that makes sense."

"Anyway, we have twelve questions. And they all include either Hubris Jargon or my ring."

"And Sleepy Gumption and Malaise Tone." Nate taps the pen against the latter's name. "I searched up the definitions of these words, and they're very strange and don't make any sense at all. Malaise is a general feeling of discomfort, illness, or uneasiness whose exact cause is difficult to identify. Gumption is shrewd or spirited initiative and resourcefulness. Hubris is excessive pride or self-confidence—"

"That suits his personality really well," I mumble.

Nate grins. "Yes, it does. If that's him. And jargon is special words or expressions that are used by a particular profession or group and are difficult for others to understand."

"His *name* is hard to understand. Knowing the definitions doesn't make all of their weird code names or aliases any stranger. And every single word is a noun except for sleepy, which is an adjective. But...Sleepy *Gumption*? Aren't those contradictory?"

"Yes," Nate murmurs, writing that down next to his name. "Venice—I have a question."

"Shoot."

"How do we know that these three men are actually men? Do you think Malaise Tone might be a woman?"

I shake my head. "I thought the same thing after Goldbeck's party. I wondered if Rebecca could be one of the three coded people. But I remembered that Malaise Tone is a man. Quentin said so. The same for Hubris Jargon. But I don't know about Sleepy Gumption. The only things I heard about him—or her—were that he—or she—wanted my ring's stone and for me to be left alive."

"Then Sleepy Gumption doesn't have an ill will," Nate observes, copying down everything I'd just told him.

I look around while he's writing, trying to spot Siena wherever she is so I can feel comforted that she isn't listening in on our conversation and also that she's safe. I don't see her, which instantly makes me nervous; then I spot her outside of the library walking towards home with Pompeii. She didn't even tell me she was going back. She should have. I hope they make it home without killing each other.

"Okay," Nate says, holding up the paper. "Here's everything we have so far. Correct me if I'm wrong. So—four or more people want your ring's stone, for what reason is unknown to us except Rebecca Goldbeck seems to need it for her collection."

"And that gold goes well," I say. "She mumbled that to herself."

Nate inclines his head. "All right. I can add that, too." He grabs his pen and jolts down the quick note. "She likes the ring, thinks it goes well with whatever she means by that. Her only known connections are with Hubris Jargon, who showed up at her party. Venice, do you think she might be Sleepy Gumption?"

I bite my lip. "I don't know. But you can definitely add her to the list of suspicious people."

"Right. Next, we have Rupert and Quentin. We know Sleepy Gumption was the one who employed them to get your ring, but we don't know anything about them: what their real names are, if they personally know Gumption, if they know what he or she wants with your ring. The police haven't gotten back to you with their information, which means they either don't have any crime evidence against Rupert and Quentin or they are nobodies unwilling to spill the beans on their employer."

"M-hm."

"Sleepy Gumption doesn't want you dead. He or she—I'm just going to say he's male; there's less confusion that way—seems sensible despite the fact that he is fine with sending men to hurt you and force an answer out of you. Gumption might know you, or have spied on you, but is unwilling to cross a certain line.

"Hubris Jargon wants to kill you the most. He almost did when you were crossing the road. What makes me wonder is why he didn't hop out of his car and steal your ring as it was lying on the pavement. Maybe it was because he didn't want so many witnesses to see him do it."

"Maybe. He doesn't seem like someone who would care, though. I think he knew you would get to it first and then once we knew he wanted it, it would be even harder to get."

"He chased you down yesterday when you were driving to the party. He was probably just trying to intimidate you that time. Did you catch his license plate number? I memorized it then forgot it."

"I was too busy trying to dodge him to check."

"And that's a perfectly acceptable excuse." Nate grins, showing off his two dimples, and I wince inwardly. "You saw him later, at the party, standing next to the refreshment table. He was smoking and seemed to be at complete ease, like he was supposed to be there or something. He knew he could smoke inside the house, and no one was kicking him out, so maybe he *does* know Rebecca Goldbeck."

"Or he's used to getting his way."

"His frustration at not gaining ownership of your ring is proof."

I'm unable to prevent a smile from blossoming. Nate has the uncanny knack of making me smile.

"Last of all is Malaise Tone. The way Quentin talked about him gave me the idea that he knows you. Or maybe he's spent the longest time stalking you and your family, and knows every little thing about you guys. He's most likely the informant that reports back to Gumption and Jargon."

I frown, my smile gone instantly. Hopefully, Nate can bring it back later on. "I don't like that. I don't like having someone always watching me."

"It's scary, isn't it? I understand how you feel. I'm constantly worried someone has followed me home and is spying on me—ever since Keller Jacobs did, I'm paranoid there's a snoop behind me."

I raise my eyebrows in shock. I had *not* expected him to say that. He rarely admits things like this that will make me nosy. And, well, I have been that snoop, and I have seen what he wants no one to see.

"Anyway," Nate says, clearing his throat, "this leaves your dad. Do you think he knows all three of those…men? Do you think he purposely gave you the ring to keep it from them?"

"I have no clue," I admit honestly.

Nate runs a hand through his hair, messing it up even more than it already is. "If he's not dead, where the heck is your dad? Did Jargon kidnap him and is he holding him somewhere? Here, in Virginia, or someplace else? And *what* was your dad doing in Kentucky?"

"I don't know, I don't know, I don't know, and…I don't know."

He sighs in aggravation. "This is so confusing," he says, setting the paper down on the table. "We barely have any information. Just three weird names with weird meanings."

I close my eyes and lean back against my chair. "Yeah."

We're silent for a moment until Nate says, "Elijah wants me to come over, and Mandy demands that you come with me. She isn't really giving you a choice."

"That's fine."

"And…we should probably leave soon. You know how excited Mandy can be when she's meeting up with you."

I open my eyes. "Soon like right now?"

Nate grins tiredly. He nods.

"Ugh…" I slouch down, not wanting to leave the library quite yet, to leave our discussion, to leave and join up with the others so Nate and I are no longer alone.

He bends over the paper, writing again. His hand moves slowly and cautiously, as if he's uncertain about what he's jotting down, and I watch him as he does it. The back of his hand is dotted with thin, long white scars that are evidence of abuse. I am mesmerized by the careful way he uses the pen; he told me his handwriting wasn't very good, but is that because he's...I am suddenly aware that he's using his left hand.

"Nate," I say, startling him, "are you left-handed?"

He pauses. "Um," he begins, then stops. "Sort of," he says finally. "I guess I am. Both. I'm ambidextrous."

"That's cool," I say. "Do you favor your left?"

Again, he hesitates to find an answer. "No."

I blink at him. "No?"

"My right hand is my dominant," he explains. "I tend to use it more often. But sometimes I use my left. Like whenever I get a paper-cut on my thumb"—he is smiling now—"and it hurts to write, so I just...switch hands. It's really nice. And you're the first to notice."

"How often do you get a paper-cut?" I ask.

His smile is more a smirk. "You won't believe it. I owe it all to my excessive reading."

"I've never gotten a paper-cut from *reading*," I say.

Nate shrugs, looking uncomfortable.

"Well..." I say slowly when he doesn't speak, "should we go?"

THIRTY-EIGHT

The walk is long and uneventful. We don't say much other than reminding each other that we still need to do our presentation on orangutans, which I have forgotten in all the confusion during the past few weeks. The sun is bright and warm, which instantly makes me glad I'm walking to Elijah's house and not stuck at home doing the laundry. Suffering an hour with my two youngest siblings was definitely worth it—and Mom can't complain to me that I didn't even watch them. I won't be back home for the next few hours while I'm at Elijah's.

Plenty of people are out and about, taking walks and riding bikes and playing in their yards. Kids rush past us on skateboards and rollerblades, talking loudly to one another and ignoring the pained looks from the adults outside. I smile, happy I'm with Nate, who is much better company than Siena or Pompeii—not nearly as argumentative.

We're only a few minutes away from Elijah's house when I notice Nate is frowning to himself. He looks around as we pass a public park, and I wonder what he's currently thinking.

"What's wrong?" I ask.

He startles, glancing down at me before returning his gaze to the park. "I was just thinking about…if I remembered to do certain things."

"Like what?"

He brushes his hair out of his eyes. "Um...just certain things I needed to do before leaving for the library."

I'm about to tell him that he's being so very *clear* when I stop myself. He doesn't need my sarcasm, and his responsibilities include taking care of his difficult grandpa.

"It's really nice out," I say instead. "What do you normally do on days like these?"

"Random stuff. I read. I hang out with Elijah and Mandy."

"Do you ever bring your dog to their houses?"

He goes still. "What?"

I take his left arm, pushing up his sleeve just enough to reveal the scar he had told me was given by his dog. I tap a finger against his skin. "This one," I say. "You said your dog scratched you when he was overexcited to play fetch with you."

Nate stares down at me. "I did?"

"Yes." I don't entirely believe what he'd told me about those scars, and I have a feeling he invented those excuses. He must have forgotten them.

"I-I guess I did," he says slowly.

I drop his arm so things don't get too awkward, but he's looking at me in a way that makes this situation uncomfortable anyway. I wish he'd stop. There is such an intense look in his eyes that it is causing my insides to squirm with unease.

"What kind of dog do you have?" I prompt.

He doesn't move his gaze from me. "Newfoundland."

My discomfort is growing rapidly as he keeps staring at me. "Um," I say, pushing up the bridge of my glasses, "what kind of dog is that? That breed doesn't sound familiar to me."

"Mercury is big, fluffy, and brown." Nate finally looks away, and I can breathe again. "He slobbers a lot," he continues, "and shreds up pretty much every tennis ball I buy for him. He sheds all over the place, and I'm always finding his hair in my food."

I manage a weak smile. "That's the downside of having pets."

"It's fine, really," Nate disagrees, but somewhat gently. "It's a small price to pay for a best friend."

We're quiet again, and I'm remembering seeing Mercury cowering behind Nate as his grandpa is throwing glass shards at him. The dog must be used to it, and he knows Nate's grandpa is bad, but he doesn't do anything to stop him from hurting his owner. There's not much he can do anyway.

"Do you like dogs, Venice?"

I take a moment to answer. "I don't really know," I say. "The only dog I've known was my grandma's old terrier, and he was extremely annoying. He never stopped barking."

"I guess that can be a reason to dislike dogs," Nate says. "Mercury doesn't ever bark unless something's wrong."

"And how often is that?" I ask carefully.

He gives me an irritated look and doesn't reply, and I'm left wondering if his dog is trained not to bark at danger, otherwise he would constantly be doing it.

The silence between us is stretching thin when I say, "Why is it so hot out today? It's the middle of February."

"We have wacky weather here," Nate says. "It's supposed to hail tomorrow."

I frown as the scenery around us changes from the busy street to the even busier neighborhood Elijah and Mandy live in. "Hail? Tomorrow? But it's seventy degrees right now!"

"As I just said, we have wacky weather here."

"Obviously. I'll need to tell my mom she has to get all the laundry done today if it's going to be icy tomorrow."

"She'll probably want your help to make things go faster," Nate teases.

I pull a horrified look. "Then in that case, I won't say a word."

He barely manages a short laugh, and I feel bad that I caused him hurt by asking about his dog. I really need to help Nate, no matter if he doesn't want my help, and I'm thinking about ways to help him feel like he can open up to me when we reach Elijah's house.

It's small and cramped, and the first time I saw it I immediately felt self-conscious that my house is obviously the biggest and nicest of all my friends'. Well, I haven't seen Mandy's house yet. I learned that Elijah has twelve siblings, half of them younger and half older than him. Only eight are living there now, nine if you count Sam, Elijah's cousin, who is staying with them while his dad is deployed, and I haven't seen him since last week. Mrs. Jenkins, Elijah's mom, must be a saint, and a very patient one at that.

Elijah's dad is an all-time trucker, and he's often traveling. However, he loves his job and wouldn't trade it for the world, Elijah told me, but his family all wishes they saw him more often.

The front yard is littered with bikes, skateboards, and toys. The grass has brown spots where it died, along with plenty of weeds that would make Mom wince. I loved the house the instant I saw it, and it's what reminds me of a poor-but-happy family.

With a loud *bang!* the front door is flung open, and two little kids come streaming out of the house, both yelling Nate's name. I don't remember who they are, but Nate does, and he scoops them into his arms while happily returning the greeting.

"Oliver! You're bigger than you were three days ago!" Nate keeps his arm around the boy's shoulder; the little girl clings to his leg. "Aubrey, you know I can't carry you all the way inside."

Aubrey frowns. She looks just like the other five kids I was introduced to—and forgot—with long, stringy blonde hair and wide eyes and a mischievous expression. If she had the beginnings of a mustache, she'd be the feminine version of Elijah.

"You always carry me," she says, squeezing Nate's leg tighter.

He takes a step, dragging her along, and she shrieks with delight while her brother—Oliver, who is mini Elijah except for the facial hair—complains about how his toy truck got stepped on and broken. I smile as I watch the three of them, all grinning but for

Oliver, and I understand why Nate likes these kids so much. He doesn't want to be like his grandpa, so he treats little kids gently and pays them attention and makes them feel good inside. They are pleased that someone older jokes around with them, and I am suddenly feeling the need to get to know Elijah's siblings—and maybe appreciate mine more, too. I wonder if they like it when I chill with them.

"I lost a tooth!" Aubrey interrupts, still clinging to Nate. "Mommy said I have a bunch more to lose, but I think this is the only one I will *ever* take out. It hurt too much."

"Really?" Nate leads the way up to the front door, which is wide open, and I trail after him, my smile deepening.

"Yes!" Aubrey nods her head vigorously. "Elijah tied it to the toaster and dropped it on the floor. Mommy wasn't very happy 'bout that, but at least it took my tooth out."

Oliver tugs at Nate's hand. "Nate, are you going to help fix my truck?"

Nate waves the little boy inside the house, waits for me to slip in after him, then follows us and closes the door. Aubrey finally relaxes her grip on his leg and slides onto the floor.

"Let's take a look at your broken truck, Oliver," Nate invites, and the little boy beams.

I examine the entryway while Oliver replies. Shoes are stacked along the wall, mounds and mounds of them. Doorways to our left and right reveal a living room and dining room. Both are full of stuff—just *stuff*—that makes me sorry for Mrs. Jenkins, who must be in over her head here trying to clean up after everyone. I know the basement is just past the kitchen, inside the family room, and I can hear Elijah and Mandy's voices shouting at their video game far below us.

Mrs. Jenkins appears in the living room doorway, her tired but happy face split in a grin. "Nate, Venice," she says. "It's so good to see you."

"You too," I reply, and it's the truth. Mrs. Jenkins is probably the nicest woman I have ever met.

Nate gives her a smile in return, but his isn't as tired as hers. "Oliver was telling me about his truck," he says, to which Mrs. Jenkins responds with a drawn-out groan.

"Yes, yes." She rubs her forehead, her other hand beckoning Aubrey forwards. "It's all he ever talks about."

Stomping up the stairs announces that Mandy is coming. Presently, she comes into view, delight lighting up her face. She wraps me in her typical bear-hug, making my ribs creak, then pulls away and grabs my hand. "You're finally here!" she says breathlessly. "Good! Now, come on. The downstairs awaits!"

I am dragged away from Nate, who is asking Mrs. Jenkins if he can do anything to help fix Oliver's truck, and I want to stay with him instead of watching Mandy and Elijah play video games. However, I allow myself to be taken to the basement, where Elijah is standing in front of the TV, controller in hand, wearing his gaming headset. He's yelling things into the microphone but stops when Mandy and I arrive.

"Well, you took your swell time, Venice," he says, then goes back to his game.

Mandy lets go of me, and I turn in a full circle while trying to decide where to sit. There's an old, stained couch pushed up against the far wall, beanbags all over the floor, and an ancient-looking armchair placed by the bookshelf that holds Mrs. Jenkins's books. I select one before sinking down onto the couch, eyes on my friends.

Elijah continues to speak into the microphone, saying how he's going to kill everyone and that his girlfriend is better than anyone in the game and that they should all go cry to their mommies. Mandy is beaming at Elijah, soaking up all the compliments he's paying her by telling the other players that she's the best gamer in the world and that she'll whip their butts. I can't hear the responses, but after a minute Elijah takes off the headset and gives it to Mandy, along with the controller.

I watch her destroy anyone who gets in her path for a few minutes, then open my book and start to read. It's hard to concentrate with both Elijah and Mandy yelling, but I manage to reach the second chapter and remember what the book is about. It's a mystery—Mrs. Jenkins is partial to mysteries—and it reminds me horribly of my own life. The car chase in the first chapter is similar to when Hubris Jargon was stalking me on the way to Goldbeck's Valentine's Day party.

It sends a shiver down my spine; not the chase part but the party. As soon as Goldbeck had mentioned it was Valentine's Day, Mom had gone cold, though only I had noticed.

Mom met Dad on Valentine's Day. She was in a local card shop, trying to find a good card made from recycled paper that she could send to her mom who, despite her determination to receive only email instead paper mail, loves getting cards. She puts them up on her bulletin board so she can look at them every day.

Anyway, Mom picked a card Grandma Pope might like, and went to buy it at the counter. Dad, who worked there at the time, started a discussion about the card she had selected: one with the Colosseum. He explained how he had lived in Italy for a few years, that he was Italian, and they talked for hours. He got her phone number and they stayed in touch for the next year before deciding to get married.

I've always thought they had a good marriage. I've always thought that the first few years were bliss for Mom. I never thought Dad would scorn Mom's beliefs, or that he would have five kids with her then desert her, leaving her to support the family alone. I never thought we'd have so much trouble showing love and affection for each other. And yet, here we are.

Then again, I was ten when my parents got divorced. I was innocent to the hardships of the world. I didn't know anything—

well, I didn't know *much*—about the disappointments and misfortunes that come with divorce and unhappy marriages.

But what if Dad still loves Mom? I know she loves him. I *think* she loves him. What if she just loves the idea of a happy family but knows that we weren't that even with Dad? What if Dad hadn't left us? Would we be a happy family, or would we continue to struggle to communicate and appreciate each other? Would I still be stuck in this mess of rings and code names and faked deaths? Would my reaction to his *death* have been different if I'd known Dad for sixteen years, not ten?

I sigh to myself and turn the page in my book. Chapter three. The heroine has just gotten a mysterious phone call from someone telling her to stop investigating the crime, otherwise she'll get hurt. I haven't been called yet, only almost run over and had two men break into my house, but maybe one day Hubris Jargon or Sleepy Gumption will call me and tell me to give them my ring or I'll suffer.

Faux trumpets blast out of the TV's speakers, startling me. I look up from my book to see Mandy hugging Elijah and screaming happily while the TV screen flashes *YOU WIN!!!!* in gold letters. I wonder how often they win, and if they freak out every time.

Returning to my book, I grip the pages and force myself to read and not let my thoughts wander. I should probably swap this out for a different one, so I don't draw parallels to my own circumstances. It all started when we moved to Virginia! Would these not have happened to me if we'd stayed in California? Would Dad never have been kidnapped, with everyone—but me—thinking him dead?

"Are you even reading?"

I jerk, sending the book flying. Nate laughs and picks it up, handing it to me while I blush furiously.

"Don't do that!" I complain. "You startled me so badly."

He sinks gracefully onto the couch next to me, rather too close for my taste, but I swallow and try hard to ignore how his shoulder and arm and hand and hip and thigh are pressed against mine.

"Wasn't that my point?" he asks, teasing.

I hold my book closer to my face so I can block him out. It's really hard to.

"Well, are you going to answer my question?"

"What question?" I mumble, inhaling deeply. I love the smell of old books, and this book definitely smells old.

Nate makes an exasperated noise. "Are you even reading?"

"I'm *trying*," I say viciously. "But this annoying boy keeps asking annoying questions and I can't concentrate."

He laughs. "What page are you on?"

"Thirty-four."

"What?" Nate sounds shocked. "Only thirty-four? I thought you would be halfway through the book by now."

I finally look up at him, and this time I'm the one who's exasperated. "Nate, you were gone for barely ten minutes. I can't read half of this book in such a short space of time."

He doesn't seem convinced. "Really. Well, I'm not even sure you're actually reading. You have a faraway look in your eyes. You're too busy thinking about something else."

"Yes." I sigh and close the book—it's pointless to continue. I don't want to anyway, now that Nate's here.

He nudges me with his elbow. "Are you going to tell me what?"

"You already know," I reply. "My dad. I can't decide if I should tell Mom or my siblings about him not being dead. They took the news really hard, and this might cheer them up. But at the same time..." I sigh again. "I don't know, Nate. Do you think I should?"

"No," he answers immediately.

I meet his gaze, surprised by the instant response. "Why?"

"You're going to get your dad back soon," Nate promises. "Once we figure all this out, you'll be able to bring your dad home and *then* your family will learn he's alive. Surprising them then is better than right now."

My shoulders droop, and I lean slightly away from him. I don't want to be pressed up against him like that. "You're right," I admit, "if we figure it out. But we have so little to go on!"

"Hey." He touches my hand. "Don't sound so forlorn. Somehow or other this is going to play itself out, and I'm betting you'll see your dad soon enough. At least you know you want to see your dad. I don't want to see mine. He's made it clear how he feels about me. That he doesn't give me a single thought."

I give him a curious look. He's opening up! I try to keep my excitement contained, wanting more than that sorry confession.

"Funny thing is," Nate goes on, shocking me further, "my dad lives about an hour from here. He works in D.C. as some rich businessman for some Fortune 500 company I don't care about. But I haven't seen him since I was…three years old? Four? I can't remember exactly."

This is the most he has ever told me about his dad. I wait patiently, hoping he'll keep talking.

"He's rather like your dad," Nate says suddenly. "He *could* stop by and see me, but he decides not to. He *could* send me something for Christmas or my birthday, but he decides not to. He *could* come help me and my grandpa, but he hasn't yet." Nate smiles ruefully; however, it doesn't contain any of his usual warmth and light and optimism. "So I make do with what I have, just like you."

We are nothing alike, I want to say. Instead, I bite my tongue and nod faintly. I don't trust myself to talk.

"Anyway…" He gets up and crosses the room to the bookshelf, needing something to take his mind off his dad and what he's just admitted to me. I watch him sort through the books, and my heart cracks little by little until all I want to do is wrap my arms around him and hold him until his problems go away forever.

When he comes back, he sits farther away from me than before, which for some reason disappoints me. He opens his book and starts to read, ignoring me completely.

I don't know what to do now. I try to continue my mystery, but it only serves to make me more depressed, so I focus on Mandy and Elijah's video game. None of it is sensical to me, just violent. Jumping around shooting virtual people, animated blood spilling everywhere, guns firing a steady tattoo.

My head hurts after a while. I wonder how long it'll take me to ask when I can leave. I'm not walking home alone—Nate will have to come with me—and I'm terrified Jargon will swoop down on me and kidnap or kill me.

I finally work up the nerve to peer over Nate's arm at the book he selected. "Are you into psychology?"

He looks over at me, his face devoid of expression. "A little," he says. "Mrs. Jenkins wanted to be a psychologist, but she became a mom instead, although she argues that she's had to become a psychologist after all with so many different personalities in the family. She has all of these books around her house to keep her training sharp. I have no idea how she finds the time to read."

"And you're reading them, too?"

He nods. "They're really interesting. Some are textbooks, and those are hard to get through, but it's worth it."

"I could imagine you as a psychopath, Nate," Mandy says, sitting on my other side of the couch. "Going around murdering people. You're a violent, unstable person."

Nate smiles and shakes his head.

"Pretty sure Nate is the *only* person in this room that won't turn out to be a psychopath," I say. "He's more likely to become a *psychologist*. Or maybe even a librarian."

She frowns. "Yeah? What about me? What am I going to be?"

"Everyone knows you'll be a mad scientist," I reply, making her laugh, along with Nate. Elijah is oblivious to the whole exchange.

"And you, Venice?" Nate asks. "What will you become?"

I shrug. "A realtor, like my mom, so I'm not stuck at an old folk's home with dozens of creepy old people."

"I'm positive you won't end up there," says Mandy. "But you

might. You're good at listening to someone blab on and on about the most *random* things. I mean, I do it all the time!"

Both Nate and I nod our agreement. Elijah takes his headset off and comes over to us, shouting, "What are you guys talking about?"

I grimace. He really has got to stop yelling.

"What we'll become when we grow up," Mandy explains.

"Oh." Elijah grins. "I'mma be a programmer, and I'll hack all the video games on this planet so I automatically win. And I'll make the annoying guys who can't handle my fame be forced to wear mustaches like mine so that they look *just* like me, and the avatars are all going to be me, and every time someone dies I get their stuff, even if they just fall too hard on the ground and go *splat...*"

"He certainly has big dreams," I mutter to Nate.

"This is the first that I have heard of him saying he's wanting to be a programmer," Nate mutters back.

Elijah rambles on until the next round in his game starts—then he returns to it with Mandy, who is saying that it's now *her* turn to crush all the weak and pathetic players.

And I'm left with Nate. He starts reading again like nothing has happened, and I sink deeper into the couch while trying to come up with another conversation starter. Why has it become awkward for me to talk to him?

After waiting four, five, six, seven minutes, I give up. I look over at him, watching him read his book. Before, at the library, I thought he was wearing an elbow-length shirt, but now that I'm closer, I realize the shirt is too small for him and that's why it shows so much of his forearms. I notice how the sleeves are fraying, how the shirt is too tight on him and reveals every detail of his arms, which are, in fact, well-defined.

I blush a dark red and look away. Nate is obviously stronger than his old, thin grandpa. He could easily fight back and stop him. But Nate isn't like that. He would never hurt his grandpa, even though his grandpa is hurting *him*.

Is that what Keller Jacobs had seen? Had he followed Nate home and seen him getting abused by his grandpa? Is that why Nate doesn't like him anymore, despite their being best friends once? Holy Mother Earth, if that's what happens to people who know his secret, I pray he will never know that I do.

I try not to stare at Nate. I really do. But he's like a magnet, drawing my gaze to him despite all my attempts to keep my eyes on my book or the TV or anything, just not him. I finally give in and turn to him, tracing a finger over the nearest scar to me. He startles, not having expected me to do that, and I pull his left arm onto my lap so I can examine the scars better.

"Venice—"

My fingers run over a long scar that disappears up his sleeve, farther up his arm. "How did you get this one?"

"Venice, what are you doing?"

I ignore him. "This looks like it's from a knife cut. And it's so long...Where and how did you get it?"

He ignores me, trying to pull free. I don't let him and continue studying the scar. It has to be at least a foot long, from the middle of his forearm up to his shoulder. Or maybe it's longer or shorter. I can't see—his sleeve is covering it—and Nate won't let me push the sleeve up higher than it already is. He again attempts to extract himself from my grip, but I squeeze his arm tighter.

"Nate," I say, "these aren't usual scars. They're from something different than dog claws and picture frames. This one"—my finger trails across his skin, following the white scar—"is a knife wound, or a sharp object that can cut deep enough."

He holds very, very still as I brush along his skin, all the way to his upper arm and underneath his sleeve until I find where the scar finally stops.

"You'd better talk, or I'll continue my survey."

Nate stares at me, his light blue eyes never wavering from my face. I'm not looking at him; I'm concentrating on the other long scars running down his arm. I know his right arm is just like his left, and it depresses me.

Suddenly, Mandy shows up, talking excitedly about how she killed all the players and won faster than Elijah, beating his record for the second time in three weeks, and she doesn't seem to notice what Nate and I were in the middle of.

"Mandy, look at this," I say, lifting up Nate's arm.

He manages to rip free of me, pulling up his sleeve while tucking his arm behind his back. He shoots me a glare.

"Look at what?" Mandy asks. "You touching Nate? That was weird. You guys aren't…"

I give her a sharp look that quite plainly says *shut up*. She wisely chooses to not continue.

"Venice, I was wondering…" she begins, "if you would like to come over to my house. It's just down the street from here. I have to grab something, and my parents are home, so it'd be nice to not face them alone. They're kinda intimidating."

I don't want to go to her house. I want to stay here and force an answer out of Nate However, I remind myself to be patient with him and myself. Besides, I think I have better luck with the hit-and-run confrontation. It's better than a standoff. He's one of the most stubborn people I've met, and I live with a bunch of them. To be honest, I must admit that I'm pretty stubborn, too.

"Okay," I agree reluctantly.

Mandy's face splits into a wide grin. "Thanks, Venice. Hey, Elijah, Venice and I are going to grab something from home. We'll be right back."

"I'll get my shoes." I stand up and walk away from Nate, not bothering to even wave goodbye.

THIRTY-NINE

Mandy's house is barely a minute's walk from Elijah's. Of course, that means she won't give up the opportunity to talk about things, all sorts of things, that make no sense to me. I think she's just blabbing on and on to keep my thoughts from wandering to Nate or the scars or *why* won't he just tell me what's going on with him? Why does he pointedly make up excuses that are so far from the truth I don't even bother believing?

Great. I've managed to block out Mandy, focusing only on Nate and his impossibly stubborn self.

"...don't eat gluten, and we have *no* bread in the house." Mandy twirls a lock of her dark hair around her finger as she talks. "My mom thinks it isn't good for you, but whenever I'm at Elijah's— which is *all the time*—his mom like, force-feeds me her delicious homemade bread. It's so addictive, Venice! You really need to try some."

"Okay."

"And the dinners she makes!" Mandy is beaming. "Oh my goodness, you will not believe how great they are. Sometimes, Nate helps her, you know, because he's like that, but I think it's since he's bored and wants to do something other than watch me and Elijah whip those nerds at our video game."

"Huh."

"I once met Elijah's dad," Mandy continues, leading me up the paved driveway that belongs to her house. "He was really nice. He gave me this cool keychain and said it held the spirit of a demented soul, but I didn't believe him. My mom found it in my room and said it was junk, so of course I took it from her and said it was my most prized possession and how *dare* she call my most prized possession junk."

"Hm."

Mandy yanks open the front door and shoves me inside. "Don't worry about taking off your shoes. We only have hardwood floors. Mom says they are better than carpet, that sweeping is better than vacuuming, and that puke is easier to clean off the hardwood floors than cleaning it off carpet. It's the only thing I agree with her on. See, my older brother, Zac, is severely allergic to my perfume, and he throws up each time he comes to visit, and my mom told me to dump out all my perfume, but it's the only thing Elijah buys for me, so I told her no, and she got *really* mad at me. I still have the perfume, and I wear it all the time to irritate her and infuriate Zac and all that good stuff."

Still talking, she takes me upstairs and into her bedroom, which is brightly lit with the afternoon sun. I can see the dust particles floating around in the air, drifting throughout the room before settling down on the floor or any of her furniture.

"Okay, all I need to grab is my…" Mandy hesitates, looking all around her. "I, uh, can't really remember." She turns back to face me. "Venice, are you all right?"

I blink. "Um…"

"You've been more quiet than usual since your dad's death," she says, her voice low. "I worry about you, Venice. You rarely text me, and you're always hanging out with Nate and not me or Elijah…There's something going on between the two of you that you won't tell me."

I don't know how to reply to that.

"It's not anything…serious, is it?"

I shake my head, stop myself. "What do you mean by *serious*?" I demand. She can't be referring to...Well, I honestly don't want to continue this train of thought.

She shrugs uncomfortably. "Back there, at Elijah's, you had Nate's arm in your lap."

"Because I was examining his scars!" I bury my hands in my auburn curls. "Mandy, have you ever seen how his hands and arms are covered in all sorts of scars?"

"No. I never stare at him."

I heave a frustrated sigh. "How often does he wear gloves?"

"Oh, all the time." She frowns at me. "I guess all the time. I don't know if he does in the summer—he's always out working and can't spare a single moment with us, but I don't think..." She suddenly stops, and her frown deepens into a scowl. "Why?"

"I told you," I say, tugging at my hair. "His hands are dotted with tiny white scars. He wears gloves to hide them."

She looks surprised, her anger gone. "I've never noticed."

"How long have you known him?"

Mandy takes a second to answer, her brow creased with deep consideration as she counts back the years. "Since third grade," she decides. "That was when Nate started talking to me in the hallways outside of class. Then he introduced me to Elijah—I had seen him on the bus but never talked to him before—and we all became good friends."

"Did you know that he's ambidextrous?"

Again, she's surprised. "No."

"What's his last name?"

"I-I don't know." Mandy tries to think of it. "I know he told me once, or I saw it or I heard someone call him by his last name, but for as long as I've known, everyone calls him Nate."

"Is that short for something?"

Mandy gives me a sharp look. "Why are you asking all these questions?"

I fall back on her bed, exhaustion seeping into me. "Mandy, have you ever been to his house?"

"No." She sits next to me, the mattress sagging underneath her weight. "I have never needed to."

"Then how'd you give me his address?"

Her posture stiffens. "My mom," she says with a slight sneer. "She makes it her business to know everything about my friends. She's on the parent committee for the school board, and she has access to all the information about Nate. And you. And Elijah. I just had to bribe her with some of her favorite candies to get her to give me Nate's address. I always keep a small stash in case bribery is my only chance of getting something from her."

"Do you know how to access his form?" I ask.

Mandy gestures to the desk beside her bed. "My computer."

I get off the bed and stand before the desk, taking in the chunky computer that looks like it's seen better days. It is obviously quite old; her brothers probably used this before her.

"Here." Mandy signs in, the computer taking *forever* to load, and spends a minute shuffling around her storage for Nate's form. I know I shouldn't be snooping on him, but he seriously needs help. He can't let his grandpa abuse him for the rest of his life, or at least the rest of his life with his grandpa. And I don't even know Nate's last name.

"Aha. Found it."

Mandy clicks on a folder, and it opens up to reveal a page detailing all of Nate's information.

Just then, a high-pitched voice from downstairs yells Mandy's name. She groans and slouches out of the chair, heading for her door. "That's my mom," she says. "I'll go talk to her while you…" she waves a hand at the computer and doesn't finish.

I'm in front of the computer before I hear her footsteps on the stairs. At the top of the page is Nate's full name, looking strange and foreign.

Nathaniel Wilson.

He either doesn't have a middle name or it isn't listed here. But I like his name as it is. Just Nate. It sounds better than *Nathaniel*. In my ears, at least. It makes him seem humble—he *is* humble—and simple.

It suits him perfectly.

No wonder he has people call him Nate.

I scroll down farther, finding information about his parents. His dad has the most, including a link to his Facebook page and, curious, I click on it.

Less than four minutes later, it finally loads. There is a huge picture of a slightly-familiar man. He has short dark brown hair, the opposite of Nate's messy hairstyle, and dull blue eyes that are nothing like Nate's shining ones. His dad looks like him, but they are so different. His dad—Robert Wilson—in the picture is standing next to two men who are both half a foot taller than him. He's either very short, unlike Nate, or the men he's with are giants.

Another difference is Robert Wilson's expression. His face is smooth and serene, giving away no emotions, and in that picture he looks like a dull, lifeless person, or that he's hiding his emotions. On the contrary, Nate is constantly—well, normally—smiling, and his eyes shine bright. He laughs easily, while his dad seems rather serious.

Robert Wilson's Facebook page is long. It lists his business, how he works for a bank in D.C., how he wants to move to a smaller house, how he drives his fancy sports car to work every weekday, how his wife has been dead for twelve years last week. I read through a post commemorating her death.

My beloved Jeannie died twelve years ago today, says the post. It's dated the thirteenth of February. *We did not have the happiest of marriages,* the article continues. *Jeannie didn't want children, but I wanted one to carry on my name. We disagreed on silly things like diapers and milk bottles, but in the end I won and we had a son.*

However, not long after, my poor Jeannie said she couldn't do the mom thing and left me with the baby. She moved in with her parents, and we kept in touch until the unfortunate day of her death four years later, when she was driving home from the gym and was killed by a drunk driver. The accident hurt me; I still loved my wife; I miss her more each day.

I pause in the middle of the article, my eyebrows rising as I keep scrolling down and down. Robert Wilson has published twenty minutes of reading. He must truly miss his wife—but does he miss Nate? He just mentioned him as "the baby" and "a son", never saying Nate's name.

I find a picture of a younger Robert Wilson standing next to a tall woman, his arm around her shoulders, and I immediately know this is Nate's mom. She looks like him—same smile, same perfect teeth; she even has a dimple in her left cheek. Her name is posted underneath: *Jeannie Wilson.* This was posted a year before she quit on her husband and son, but I don't think Nate was born then. There isn't anything that introduces Nate as their son, or that they were planning on having a baby.

Maybe she's already had him.

There are comments below the picture, calling them a cute couple and so happy and young-looking, and several questions if the Wilsons are thinking about expanding their family.

I close the Facebook page, disappointed in what I've seen. Nate's dad is obviously obsessed with his dead wife—why keep up a picture and post and all the comments for more than sixteen years?—and that whole article on her was slightly creepy.

Mandy comes back into the room. "Hey," she says, peering at the screen. "Did you find anything?"

"Yeah." I close the file on Nate, too, and am greeted by her bright lock screen—pink bubbles floating up to the top—and shut off the computer. "I found out some stuff. Nothing much about Nate, just his dad. And mom. It was...depressing."

She waits for me to continue. When I don't, she says, "What?"

"His mom died when he was four," I say. "And his dad got rid of him around that time. I wonder if Nate's dad couldn't handle the loss of his wife *and* having to care for a kid, so he sent Nate to live with his grandpa. I think the grandpa is Nate's dad's dad, not his mom's dad, since his mom lived with her parents for a bit and didn't have Nate with her."

"Hm." Mandy sits down on her bed and doesn't speak.

I sigh and run a hand through my hair. "How did things go with your mom? What did she need?"

"Oh, just wanted to show off the dirt I tracked in," Mandy says carelessly, waving towards the downstairs. "I told her it was my brother, but then she reminded me that he's currently in Colorado. And then *I* said that maybe he snuck over here just to spread dirt across the floor and blame me for doing it, but my mom said that wasn't probable. She has *no* imagination. Or sense of humor."

I hide a smirk. Mandy has cheered me up a little. "I must say," I admit, "it's hard to believe that your brother from Colorado came all the way here to get you in trouble."

"Dylan has done it before," she says seriously. And she proceeds to tell me about the time her oldest brother showed up at their house a day early and no one was home, so he toilet-papered the only tree in the front yard, then disappeared. When Mandy came home from school and her parents from work, they blamed Mandy for trashing the tree. Dylan's plan would have been successful if their next-door neighbor hadn't ratted out on him.

I almost blank out during her story. My brain is numb by the time she has finished, and I have to blink a few times to clear the thin film of drowsiness that has blanketed my mind.

"Serves him right," I say.

Mandy nods in agreement. "Oh, yeah. My parents were *so* mad at Dylan, and they made him clean up all the toilet paper and buy them a new roll. It was the best day of my life."

"I thought the best day of your life was when you blew up your chemistry classroom."

She smiles at the memory. "I have a lot of good days." She hesitates, then asks, "Did you read any of those books I sent you?"

I nod. "Finished one yesterday. Thank you, by the way."

"You're absolutely welcome. I wasn't reading them."

We're quiet for a moment, me sitting at her desk, she on her bed. We are simply soaking up each other's company, enjoying the silent friendship. I feel myself start to nod off, and I give a small shake to stay awake. I don't want to seem rude by falling asleep.

Mandy notices anyway. "I'm done here," she says, standing up. "We can head back to Elijah's, if you'd like. I think Mrs. Jenkins will probably start to make dinner soon, and she has the most *delicious* pork chops you could ever *dream* of tasting."

"You said the same thing about her bread," I say, following my best friend out of her room.

"That's because Mrs. Jenkins is a stellar cook."

We exit her house and walk two minutes over to Elijah's. I'm not entirely ready to face Nate again, especially since I researched his family, but this has made me more determined than ever to help him. And even if he thinks he doesn't need my help—he is far too thoughtful to want to saddle me with his problems—living with his abusive old grandpa is *not* healthy. Nate should know that.

And I'm going to do whatever it takes to make that clear to him if he does *not* know that.

True to his word, there is a hailstorm the next morning.

FORTY

In the weeks that follow, I don't get the chance to put my plan in action. I try to think up ways that can help me reveal the source of Nate's scars, but the only ideas I come up with are taking off his gloves when he's still bleeding or knocking on his door during one of his grandpa's violent episodes. Each time I attempt to get Nate alone, it seems like he knows what I'm doing and is able to thrust us in with other people. For more than two weeks, Nate dodges me. He stops coming by my house on Mondays to walk with me to school. Twice it happened but he just said Mondays are rough and he can't come.

I notice he moves carefully on the Tuesdays and Wednesdays, which leads me to believe that he is still recuperating from his grandpa's attacks that most likely happen on Sundays, and on Mondays he has to stay at home. But we don't talk about any of that, and we don't talk about my ring or my dad either. Or our report. I'm starting to doubt we'll finish it.

Some days it rains, some days it's cloudy, some days it's sunny yet cold, and some days it's sunny and warm. On one of those days Mom and I plant daffodils in front of our house—Mom tells me that they won't bloom this year, but the next; we're supposed to plant the bulbs in the fall instead of the spring. Since we moved here in mid-winter and didn't invest any time in our flower garden until now, we'll have to wait a while to see them bloom.

Nothing goes bad for me during these weeks. No cars try to hit me, no creepy old women offer to buy my ring, no intimidating SUVs trail after us when we're driving places. I start to worry—why haven't I seen Jargon in almost a month?—and I also begin to worry about my family. They haven't been targeted yet, just me and Dad, but someday it might happen and I'll be the only one who knows what's going on. I haven't told Mom or Florence or anyone besides Nate about all the strange, dangerous, threatening things that have been happening to me. I don't want Mom to be overly concerned, I don't want Florence to freak out, I don't want to be stuck inside all day, not allowed to leave by fear of death, and I don't want to be pitied.

I know I'm scared. I'm terrified, actually. I really don't think ending up like Dad—kidnapped, presumed dead—will help Mom's metal stability. She has tried to seem happy and bouncy, but she's only that when talking to Marc or visiting with him. I grudgingly admit to myself that I'm *slightly* grateful to him distracting her from the shock and sorrow—ours and hers.

A.k.a. Dad's *"death."*

My relationship with Florence has strengthened considerably. She wakes me up every morning by cheerfully or crabbily calling out good morning. Her moods change quickly, however, and she's soon either extremely happy or bad-tempered. Still, she doesn't criticize me like she used to, and it's one thing I will never miss.

My other siblings are normal—that is to say, they're constantly fighting and arguing with one another about whatever they can pick a fight over; it's one of their talents—and Roman becomes more and more withdrawn from our conversations, more and more dark. He rarely speaks, even when I come back from the store holding a case of his favorite soda. He is starting to worry me, to be honest. I try to talk to him and he shuns me. I try to cheer him up, and he yells at me to go away. I try to bring him things that might help him return to his usual self. Nothing works; Mom tells me that it's just how moody teenagers work, but I don't remember me or Flo ever being like Roman is now. I wonder if it's Dad's death or Dad's absence which happened long before his death.

Pompeii forces me to take him to the library twice a week, which is fine with me; I'm scared to walk alone someplace. Just because Hubris Jargon and Sleepy Gumption haven't bothered me in three weeks doesn't mean they aren't still stalking me. Pompeii occasionally drags me out to climb the trees in our backyard or rollerblade with him to prevent me from becoming sullen like Roman. I appreciate my youngest brother's attempts at helping me, and it makes me love him even more. If he would just *stop* fighting with Siena, then things among my two youngest siblings will be closer to perfect than ever, and it would make Mom happier.

Siena talks as loudly as she can; she doesn't seem to notice that no matter how loudly she talks, Mom won't pay her any attention if she's on the phone with one of her clients or with Marc. Siena gets grumpy often, only cheering up when Florence and I watch her favorite TV show with her. She sometimes joins me and Pompeii during our frequent visits to the library, but other than school, she doesn't leave the house much, not even to go outside and play.

To calm myself, I sit out on the patio and stare at the trees while enjoying the breeze that blows through our backyard. The leaves are starting to bud; it makes me excited to learn that our bare, grey trees will soon be covered with brilliant green leaves.

But it still doesn't keep my mind from wandering.

We have lived here for about two months. Time has gone by slowly; to me, it seems we've been in Virginia for *ages*.

But I still love it here, despite the new holes in my friendships and the cold weather, my moody, argumentative siblings, and all the danger I've gotten into by simply being the owner of my ring.

One Monday morning, I awake to see Pompeii's grinning face. Of course, he is blurry—I'm not wearing my glasses—and once I put them on I can see him more clearly.

"Venice," he says, beaming, "you won't believe it."

I sit up; it's pointless to try to fall back asleep. "What?"

"We don't have school today," he says. "It's a holiday, so we can go to the library."

I groan. "Seriously?"

"Hey." He frowns playfully at me. "I read all the books I checked out last Saturday. I need some new ones. Wanna come?"

"Why don't you bug Florence into taking you?" I mumble.

Pompeii scoffs. "Nah, she's already gone. She went all-day shopping with her friends. And Mom can't take me. She's got to go figure out a problem that someone's having. And Roman can't take me since he's being stupid right now, so you're the only one."

"And what if I have plans for the day?"

"You don't."

I glare at him. "Oh, really?"

"Yeah." He nods energetically. "I know so because you didn't realize we had school off today, and you thought it was just a normal boring Monday, and you didn't set up anything to do"— here he winks at me—"except for being the great sister you are and going to the library. It only has to be for an hour."

"What if the library is closed? You said it's a holiday."

He rolls his eyes. "I'm sure it'll be open. I checked the website."

"You did not."

He pretends to be offended. "Are you accusing me of lying?"

I laugh. I can't help it. "Okay, okay, you win. We aren't leaving until I eat breakfast first, though. And you need to see if Siena or Roman wants to tag along."

Pompeii wrinkles his nose. "Roman?"

"Yes." I slide out of bed. "Roman. He should get out more often. And here's a chance for him to say yes. He probably won't, but at least you extend the invitation." Then I pause, scanning my youngest brother's face, and say forcefully, "Right?"

"Right," he says grudgingly.

"Good. We can go in twenty minutes." I check the time on my phone. It's only nine o'clock. "Scratch that," I say. "The library doesn't open until ten, so we'll have to leave in an hour. Is that okay?"

Pompeii shrugs. "Whenever is fine, as long as we actually go."

I ruffle his hair because he lets me, then I exit my bedroom and head for downstairs. Siena is in the kitchen, moodily toasting—or rather, *burning*—two slices of bread that she'd shoved in the new toaster we bought. She's muttering under her breath but stops when I walk in, and she rearranges her expression into one of innocence.

"Good morning!" she says chipperly.

I eye her with suspicion. "Good morning to you, too. Is everything alright?"

"Um…" she looks over her shoulder at the toaster. "Yes."

I sigh. "Are you sure, Siena?"

"What?" she asks, outraged. "I gave you an answer. You should be satisfied that I even replied."

"You're right." I open the fridge, weighing my options on what to eat. "I just noticed that something is burning in the toaster and you seem to be rather upset. Did you put Roman's shoes in there?"

Siena grumbles to herself but softens. "I *was* making toast for Mom, but then she said she wasn't hungry, so I wasted two slices of bread for someone who didn't even want them. And she was rushing out the door! She could have stopped and grabbed them on her way out! But no. She *had* to brush me aside and storm out like her hair was on fire."

"And…why did you put the toasted bread back in the toaster?"

My littlest sister hesitates. "Well," she begins, "since no one was going to eat them, I decided to experiment and see how long it takes for toasted bread to turn into burnt bread."

"You're wasting food, Siena," I say, not knowing whether to laugh or to reprimand her for doing this.

She widens her eyes. "I told *you* that," she says. "And it was Mom who wasted it."

I choke on a snort of suppressed laughter and extract myself from the cool fridge, a carton of almond milk in my hand. "Yes, you're right," I acknowledge. "How's your experiment going?"

Siena glances back at the toaster, where a trail of black smoke is rising up. "I think it's going perfectly."

"Great." I pull a box of bran cereal from the cabinet. "Siena, do you know when Mom is getting back from work today?"

"She's probably gonna visit Marc before coming home," says Siena. "She'll be gone for a while. Which means..." She yanks her blackened bread out of the toaster and throws it at the kitchen wall. "We can do whatever we want! Mom's gone all day!"

Having ducked to miss the flying bread, I straighten and say, "Pompeii and I are going to the library. You should come, too."

"Er..." Siena wipes her hands on her jeans. "I don't know. I'm not really in the mood to wander around a building full of books and snoring old people, and it's so nice outside and we don't have school..."

"You can't stay here with Roman."

She frowns at me. "Why?"

I grab a bowl from the cabinet and a spoon from the silverware drawer. "I can't believe you just asked *why*," I say incredulously. "Why can't you stay here with Roman? Because he's unfit to watch out for you. He'd let a car run you over."

"True." Siena slouches.

"Which is why you need to come to the library," I say, pouring cereal into my bowl. "You'll be safer with me."

Siena groans. She crosses the room and picks up her bread. "But, Venice," she complains, "I was going to paint the walls after my toaster experiment. I can't paint my trees if I'm at the library."

"You've filled all the walls with your trees," I say.

It's true. The kitchen walls are all decorated with the trees

Siena paints—it is her favorite thing to do. She didn't even ask Mom if she could, just simply assumed Mom would let her since she did back home in California.

Mom wasn't pleased to see her new, clean, white walls covered in brilliant green leaves and brown branches and brown trunks. I thought Siena's art was adorable.

Siena beams at me. "That's why I'll paint the hallway."

I have to bite back an explosive laugh. "Yeah, that will make Mom especially happy."

"It's like having a forest in our house," my sister says, ignoring me. "But the trees all look *so* much better because I painted them."

"Way to be humble," I mutter.

Siena doesn't seem to hear me. She keeps talking, going on and on about her trees and the leaves and all her tiny little details that make the pictures complete. I start eating my cereal, watching her talk animatedly, waving her hands at the walls. She retrieves her jar of paint brushes from off the fridge and shows them all to me, explaining how she uses *this one* to add the strokes to the bark to make it look realistic, and *this one* is her favorite, because it's so big and can get the tree trunks painted in seconds. I'm glad she has reasons not to have to be babysat by me at the library, but I know she's still going to have to come with us. Just because things have been quiet for a few weeks doesn't mean the danger has passed.

Pompeii arrives, telling me over Siena's monologue on trees that Roman has refused my offer of coming along to the library. I'm not surprised, but I'm pleased Pompeii asked him.

We spend the next hour and a half in the kitchen, talking, and I manage to convince Siena that she has to come. She still doesn't want to. As soon as I promise her ice cream at the Rainy Afternoon café, however, she cheers up and agrees wholeheartedly. Pompeii whines until I tell him he can get some, too.

After changing into different clothes that don't look like I've slept in them, I lead my siblings out of the house and down the street. I have a flash of déjà vu, remembering that I'd told myself never to take Pompeii and Siena to the library again, and I have a fun time laughing at my thoughts. Today, our trip isn't quite as embarrassing. My siblings are chatting easily with each other—they don't want to irritate me and lose their ice cream bonus, I suppose. I'm happy because of it.

The library is closed when we arrive, which bums Pompeii out. He'd been really excited to come.

"I thought you said you checked the website, Pompeii! Today is some sort of holiday I've never heard of," I say, reading a sign on the library door. "I think it's just an excuse to take the day off of work. The same goes for school."

Pompeii sighs. "There goes reading," he says sadly.

"We can still get ice cream, right?" Siena pipes up. "Cafés don't close on holidays, do they?"

"I don't think so," I reply slowly.

"Then let's go!" Siena grabs my hand and starts pulling me down the sidewalk. "Where is the café?"

"Past my high school."

Pompeii trails after us, disappointment etched across his face. "We didn't get to go inside," he says glumly. "Why couldn't the library be open on a day when we didn't have school?"

"We don't have school on Saturdays," I point out, "and the library is open then."

He sighs again. "I was *so* looking forward to reading those fantastical young adult books you told me about," he deadpans.

I almost believe him until I see the smile tugging at the corners of his lips. "You are one weird brother," I say. "You know that, right, Pompeii? You are the weirdest brother ever."

"So are you," he replies.

Siena laughs, dragging me towards my high school. "Venice isn't even our brother," she says.

"Tell that to Pompeii," I respond.

410

We continue our journey, Siena arguing—but *gently*—with Pompeii about what flavor of ice cream they should get. I don't bother telling them that the Rainy Afternoon only has vanilla to go with their delicious apple pie Mom told me about last week. She goes there nearly every other day with Marc to try everything on the menu, and the hot chocolate and pies are what she loves most.

Passing the high school, I stare at the empty parking lot that is usually filled with dozens and dozens of cars. The sidewalks are blank—no one is around here—and the school seems rather...sad. I wonder what all of the students are doing right now. The boys are probably playing video games or sleeping or at the skate park or hanging out with their girlfriends. The girls are probably at the mall, shopping with Florence or shopping *like* Florence. If my sister had invited me, I might have actually considered her invitation. I don't have anything to do today besides bribe my youngest siblings to get outside. I'm not planning on hanging out at Elijah or Mandy's houses. She hasn't texted me anyway. And Nate hasn't stopped by to see if I wanted to work on our report or try to crack the mystery of my ring.

So I'm all alone today.

Well, not *alone*. I have Pompeii and Siena.

But they don't really count.

We reach the street where I was almost run over a month ago. I have to take a deep breath and triple-check for cars before bolting across with Siena at my heels. Pompeii walks slowly, and in that time, I'm so nervous for him that I'm tempted to pick him up and carry him over to speed him up. When he *finally* arrives, Siena pretty much drags us into the café. She is chattering loudly, asking me questions about the café and if I can make the employees turn off the jazz music because it *sucks*.

I wearily order two vanilla ice creams, and the woman working behind the register gives me a strange look that I'm not getting anything besides that.

She must not get this order a lot.

I make my siblings sit down before they can eat the ice cream—I know they will get it all over the place if I don't put them in one spot. I go to sit down next to Siena, who is slightly annoyed that the only option was vanilla, when my phone chimes, ringing almost immediately after; it's startlingly loud in this dim, quiet café.

Quickly answering the call before checking my texts, I find it's Mom. I go outside to talk to her so I won't disturb anyone with our conversation.

"Hey, Mom," I say.

"Where are you?"

I frown at her panicked tone of voice. "Uh, I'm at the café. With Pompeii and Siena. I bought them some ice cream because the library was closed."

"Venice!" Mom complains. "It's ten thirty in the morning! You shouldn't be buying them sugary things! They'll be horribly grumpy for the rest of the day because they didn't have anything healthy for breakfast!"

"Sorry."

She sighs. "Anyway, what time do you think you'll be back?"

"I don't know. Why?"

"I'm at home right now," she says. "I just returned from my client's house and found all of my kids except for Roman gone. Flo told me she was going shopping, but I didn't know about you and the other two."

"Sorry," I say again. "I didn't think you would be back this early. Pompeii said you were hanging out with Marc."

"I'm not—"

"Oh, wait," I interrupt. "Siena said you were. Not Pompeii. I was talking with her in the kitchen, with the whole toaster experiment, and Pompeii was downstairs asking Roman if he wanted to come with us to the library. It's hard to remember who tells me what."

"What toaster experiment was Siena doing?" Mom asks.

I hesitate. "Um…it was either that or she said she would paint trees in the hallway, too."

"Then thank you for stopping her," says Mom. "Anyway, you need to bring the kids home soon. I want to take them to the thrift store and get them some spring clothes."

"Okay." I peer at my siblings through the café door. Siena is laughing at Pompeii, who has white ice cream on his nose.

"Would you like to come, too?" Mom offers. "I haven't taken you shopping in a long time."

I take a moment to answer. I'm not really sure I want to go with her. All my shopping experiences result in me awkwardly following Mom around while she pulls clothes off the racks and tells me to try it on. "Um…" I begin, "I don't know…"

Mom sounds like she's smiling when she replies. "I understand. You're probably busy later today, visiting your friends. You need to introduce them all to me someday. I've only met Nate, and if your other two friends are as nice as him, then you've made better friends than Florence has during her entire life. By what you tell me, they seem great."

"Yeah," I agree haltingly. "Mandy and Elijah are nice."

Mom clears her throat. "Okay, could you bring the kids home in the next hour or so? Tell them I'm not only taking them shopping, but we can get dinner on the way home."

"Just how long are you going to take?" I ask, horrified at the thought of looking at clothes all day. And she's really shooting big here—she knows Pompeii and Siena can't go long without fighting, and if they're bored and hangry, it'll make things worse. Poor Mom. She's not going to enjoy this.

"Oh, only a few hours," Mom says. "We might stop by some other places to pick up a couple of things I need."

I grimace. "All right. I'll go tell them."

"Thank you, Venice. See you soon."

"You too." I hang up and check to see who had texted me. It's

413

Grandma Ferrari, sending yet another picture. I tap on it, not really wanting to see the fire that consumed Dad's car, but when the picture loads, I see it's of Dad. Not of his totaled car.

We don't have many pictures of Dad in our house. I know Florence has one of him on her bedside table, but it was taken right after the two of us were born and is outdated. Mom has one of him that's more recent; I have yet to look at it. I don't really want to.

This picture must have been shot years after he left us. He is standing all alone in front of a highway sign promoting organic, milk-free, fat-free cheese that's made at the factory off the next exit. Dad has his hands in his pockets, smiling at the camera or whoever took this, and he looks like he's happy but not completely. His hair is short; so dark it's almost black, and I wonder if he dyes it. It's too dark to be natural. There's no way he doesn't have any grey or white hairs. His eyes are deep brown, just like Roman's, and seeing them drives a stake of pain into my heart.

Dad is tall—perhaps not as tall as Nate, but close; I can't exactly tell—and his head reaches the bottom of the sign. He seems happy, peaceful, calm, content. However, there is something else in his expression that causes me to study him closer.

His smile is strained, his eyes tired, his stance slightly slumped. He's going through a hard time in life.

Suddenly furious at him for everything he has put our family through over the past years, I shove my phone in my pocket then turn to open the café door and rejoin my siblings.

But…

I pause. The reflection in the glass door is showing me someone across the street. Someone who looks painfully familiar, especially after scanning that photo just seconds ago.

I whirl around. Not fifty feet from me, walking briskly, is Dad.

FORTY-ONE

I gasp loudly. I can't believe it.

Dad?

It's definitely him. I can tell by his almost-black hair and broad shoulders and tall height.

What is he *doing* in Virginia?

"Dad!" I yell.

He doesn't even glance around at the sudden shout. He continues to head towards the shops past the Rainy Afternoon, widening his stride so he will reach his destination faster.

I run after him, staying parallel with him. I'm too afraid to cross the street. "Dad!" I call.

When he doesn't reply or look over at me, I shout his actual name. He still ignores me, moving more quickly. He doesn't break into a run, just walks swiftly in the direction of a tall brick building. I call his name again; nothing. He seems completely ignorant.

Or maybe he *can* hear me, but he doesn't want to talk to me.

I stop, watching Dad arrive at the brick building. He pushes past a *No Trespassing* sign, ignoring that too, and disappears inside.

Is this where Sleepy Gumption and Hubris Jargon are hiding out?

I *would* follow Dad, but I can't leave Pompeii and Siena.

Immediately, I start talking myself out of what I just witnessed. I only *thought* I saw Dad because I'd just been studying that picture

Grandma Ferrari sent me. Besides, if he was being held somewhere like I thought he was why would he be free and walking around? And why wouldn't he respond when I called his name? Because it wasn't him. It couldn't have been. He had to have heard me and seen me. But for all my rationalization, another part of me says something else. *I saw my dad and this proves he isn't dead and he's barely thirty minutes away from our house.*

Carefully, I study the brick building, growing more and more glad that I didn't plunge in headlong after Dad. The building is old—very, very old—and is in great need of repair. The windows, few as they are, are all cracked or totally gone; the sign above the rusted metal door reads *Paint Manufactory: Buy your paint for less!* in peeling letters. There are several posters stuck up around the shop, saying trespassing can result in a two thousand-dollar fine. It doesn't make any sense to me—why would you put up those warnings if you ran a business?

The building doesn't look to have been used in years, however. Some of the bricks are covered in dark ivy that is clinging to them, growing higher and covering one of the open windows. A chain-link fence surrounds the premises, keeping out everyone but Dad, who had just shoved by the gate and continued on.

It looks abandoned.

But Dad, or someone who looks very much like him, just went in, so I know there is something going on in this place. I just need to find out what.

Or do I? Do I need to go looking for trouble?

But maybe I can get my dad back in the process.

During our walk home, Pompeii and Siena are moping about their shopping trip and how it's a waste of time. Pompeii is outraged that Mom is making him pick out clothes to buy when he could be outside, playing with the next-door neighbor. Siena complains that she has plenty of clothes and doesn't need any more.

I'm quiet, not saying anything, keeping to my thoughts and theories and far too many questions. Dad's sudden appearance and disappearance has shocked me to silence. What is he doing in Virginia? Why would he go to that abandoned building? Could he be part of this whole attempt to get my ring?

And what is the chance that he walked by just as I was on the sidewalk in front of the café? Did he want me to see him? Should I have crossed the street and gotten into his face so he *actually* saw me? Should I call the police and tell them someone is inside the building that clearly states no one is allowed to occupy?

My mind is still swimming with these thoughts once we arrive home. Mom greets us warmly, telling Pompeii and Siena to keep their shoes on; they have to leave in a few minutes.

She gives me a big hug. "Hey, Venice," she says. "How were the little devils?"

"Hm?" I pull myself out of my thoughts. "Oh, they were fine. It was slightly disappointing when the library was closed, but other than that everything went fine."

She eyes me, her brow creased in a frown. "What's wrong?"

"Nothing!" I say, maybe too quickly. "Nothing. I'm just…tired. Pompeii woke me up early this morning."

He snorts. "I did not!"

Mom smiles a little. "And what are you going to do while we're gone, Venice?" she asks innocently.

"I don't know."

But I do. I do know what I'm doing the instant Mom's car drives away, and I'm free to do whatever I want with no one knowing.

"Really?" Mom isn't convinced. "Well, the fridge needs cleaning out, and I didn't prepare a frozen dinner for you and your siblings, so you'll have to eat leftovers—"

I manage a small smile to match hers. "Yeah?"

"Mom, are we going soon?" Siena whines. "I want to go *right now* so we can get this over with. You're taking forever."

Mom sighs. "Yes, we're leaving. Go get in the car."

Pompeii and Siena are out the door in a second, fighting over who gets to sit in the front seat.

Mom and I watch them, Mom releasing another sigh. "They are going to be a handful," she murmurs. "I wonder why I'm even doing this. Half of the morning and the entire afternoon with them? This is going to kill me dead, Venice."

I take her hand and give her a squeeze. "Yes, it is. But you'll have fun."

"Maybe," she says darkly. She hugs me again, then shoulders her purse and steps out onto the porch.

"By the way," I call after her, "you owe me six bucks for their ice cream."

She scoffs. "That's coming out of your wallet, Venice! I wasn't the one who bribed them out for a walk!"

I grin ruefully. "Whatever you say."

"See you later," Mom says, walking down the driveway. "And you have to tell me what you did when I get back!"

"Then you owe me six dollars!"

Her only response is waving her hand over her head, not even bothering to turn around. She reaches the car and slides in, and a second later it pulls away from the curb and drives off.

I stare after them for one minute, making sure they haven't forgotten anything and have to come back to retrieve it, and when that minute is up, I run up to my room. I toss my phone onto my bed—I won't be needing it—and return to the ground floor.

The wide-open door taunts me. The screen has clicked shut, preventing the air from getting out or bugs from coming in.

I suck in a deep breath. "No matter what it takes," I mutter to myself. "No matter what."

Then I push open the door and walk out.

The sun is high in the sky—it's about eleven in the morning—and it's mildly hot outside. It's not enough for me to break a sweat, which is extremely relieving, and I appreciate the slight breeze that ruffles through my hair and keeps me from becoming too warm.

I'm not exactly looking forward to arriving at my destination. I don't even want to go.

But it's for the best.

I have to do this.

Holding my head high, I continue my brisk journey down the sidewalk, remembering how last time I had been stomping. I'd been angry at hearing about Dad's death. And now, a month later, I'm angry again; however, this time there is something I can do about it. Dad walked out of my life years ago leaving me with so many unanswered questions. Since then, those questions have haunted me, mocked me, even, because Dad never came around long enough for me to ask him. Now I know his absence was his answer, that he didn't care enough to be a part of my life. He messed up the last six years of my life and even now, when he's supposed to be dead, he's still messing it up, his behavior still generating questions I can't answer. My thoughts are coming faster and stronger as I let my anger take a spin. I'm working myself up really well. I have to, because I need the courage to follow through on my decision.

If I've learned anything from Dad's leaving and neglect, it's that I don't ever want to abandon someone I care about. I never want to be so wrapped up in myself, or anything, for that matter, that I don't even acknowledge my own daughter when I pass her on the street. I had called out to him, and he completely ignored me. It was as if I didn't exist for him. Even if it wasn't really my dad that I saw, I am grateful for the resolve it has given me, clear and strong and possessive, taking control of my mind and body. I don't know exactly what my feelings are for Nate, but I know that I cannot, I will not, abandon him, not while I know his pain.

I remember how the past three weeks have been hard on me. I remember how school has turned from the highlight of my day to something I dread. I remember how I don't talk during lunch because I'm too busy scowling at my food to lock gazes with anyone and participate in the conversation. I remember how walking to school has been awkward and frustrating. And I am ashamed.

This whole time I've allowed myself to think it's all because Nate can't accept the fact that he needs my help. But today I see that I don't deserve his trust. This whole time I've been convinced that in order for me to help him he needed to do the one thing he didn't want to do. I could have been helping him in so many other ways, but—and this thought hurts me—I selfishly added to his pain. What he needed was someone to distract him, to make him laugh, to remind him that there is joy to be had in life. Instead I've been intrusive, demanding, and sulky. This time when I confront him, I won't insist he open up to me. It's my turn to be vulnerable and to take a risk. He may not feel the same about me, but I value his friendship too much for me to watch it waste away. I have to tell him that I care, that I am here for him, and that I know his secret.

I turn down his street, ignoring the dumpy houses and the unseen people watching me. I shine like a beacon in the bright sunlight—having red hair instantly makes me easy to spot—and there's no doubt that Nate's creepy criminal neighbors are staring at me.

Passing the evergreens that hide Nate's house from view, I start down his driveway. It's a Monday, so hopefully that means he's still recovering from the violent attacks his grandpa inflicts on Sundays.

Unless I'm totally wrong...

What if Nate's at Elijah's house? What if he isn't even here? What if I come in contact with his scary grandpa, who decides I need the same treatment as Nate gets?

I stop halfway down the driveway, close my eyes, and take a deep breath. If Nate isn't here, then I will immediately turn around and run for home so I don't have to face his grandpa.

The crunch of gravel startles me. I snap my eyes open and see a gigantic dog trotting towards me, a tennis ball in his mouth. He has long, glossy, dark brown fur that looks recently cleaned and brushed. His tail is wagging madly, his droopy ears flattened back against his head. A red collar is placed around his shaggy neck.

"Hello, Mercury," I say, tentatively holding a hand out for him to sniff; I'm a little afraid he'll bite it clean off.

Mercury takes in a deep whiff, then sneezes all over my hand. I grimace and wipe it on my jeans. The dog nudges my leg, so I stroke his soft head for a moment; then he steps back and drops the tennis ball onto the gravel driveway.

I scrunch my nose, eyeing his slobbery, wet ball with distaste. "I am *not* going to throw that for you," I say. "Sorry."

The dog seems to understand. He picks up the tennis ball and lopes down the driveway, towards Nate's house. I hesitate, then follow after the dog. I am nervous, and even more so when I reach the end of the line of trees and can see the sad building Nate calls home.

Mercury has walked up to the porch, where Nate himself is sitting. My heartbeat speeds up.

"Hey," Nate says, talking to the dog. He hasn't noticed me. "Oh, don't put that in my lap..." He goes to throw the ball but stops. "What is..." he begins, thinking hard, and I don't know what he's observing until he lifts his head and looks directly at me.

I hold still.

Nate stands up. "Venice? What are *you* doing here?"

I gulp and don't answer. I want to say it all but I can't. Where did that resolve go? My mouth is refusing to open, my tongue not cooperating with me. I hadn't expected our meeting to be pleasant, but he clearly doesn't want to see me. My heart is pounding in my chest and panic clouds my judgment. I've already lost my chance. My selfishness has pushed him away. Was the awkwardness of the past three weeks Nate's way of rejecting me, just like my dad?

Dad.

Remembering this morning lights the fire in me again. No. Nate is not like Dad and neither am I. I can do this.

"What are you doing here?" he repeats.

I bite my lip. "Um…" Maybe I can't do this.

Just my luck—he's wearing his gloves and jacket, which means his wounds are still healing. There is no other reason to be dressed like that.

Mercury comes back up to me when it becomes clear to him that Nate won't throw his ball. Mercury nudges my fingers again, wanting me to pet him, but I'm too scared.

"Venice?"

I swallow hard. "I-I have to tell you something."

Nate holds my gaze for a moment, then steps off the porch and comes up to me. I can tell he's upset, but I notice he's trying to control his expression, and that gives me courage. It must be embarrassing for him, that I'm seeing his run-down old house and intruding on the part of his life that he works so hard to hide from everyone.

"What do you have to tell me?" he asks, less demanding. He now sounds patient.

He's back to normal. Thank the trees. My heart starts to slow down.

How does he do that? I wish I could restrain my temper and stop myself from exploding into anger.

"Well…" I hesitate awkwardly, not able to meet his eyes. I peer over his shoulder at his house, recognizing the black swirls snaking in and out and all around the building. They aren't coming *from* the house, rather the person inside. Nate's grandpa generates so much evil and abuse and malice that it fills his entire house.

Nate sighs. "Come on," he says, jerking his head to the right.

I stare at him. "What?"

He releases another long sigh and grabs my hand, pulling me towards the grove of evergreen trees far to my right. I stumble after him, wondering what on Holy Mother Earth he's doing and where we're going. Mercury follows us, which calms me—Nate's dog is so gently attentive that his presence makes this intimidating situation seem almost normal.

Nate leads me through the trees, pushing past low-hanging branches and moving around thorn bushes. We walk for a while in heavy silence—until Nate stops.

"Just past here," he says, "is my favorite place. It's better than the library, even."

He's in a humorous mood. What a relief. Maybe I'll be able to go through with it after all.

"What is it?" I ask curiously.

Nate tugs me out of the tree-line, and I find myself in a small clearing. The evergreens are more prominent here, catching my eye easily. Bright sunlight fills the entire area, lighting it up brilliantly. A small pond is set in the middle of the glade, the sun glinting off the still brown water. All along the bank tall reeds are growing, thick and green and full of life. The grass, a lush green color that looks healthy and alive, is trimmed short, unlike the overgrown front yard back at Nate's house. Birds chirp from branches around us, calling to one another, shattering the silence between us and replacing it with joyful song.

"I spend almost all of my time here," Nate explains, bringing me back to the surface. "It's the only place I can find total peace. Mercury likes swimming in the pond, which is probably why it's brown, and we can just...hang out for hours."

"It's beautiful," I say. "This whole place."

He smiles at me. "I try to make it beautiful. Instead of taking care of my front yard, I garden this. I've planted some seeds over there"—he gestures to a spot far to my left where I can see a couple of wooden boxes that form a miniature garden—"and once they grow, I won't have to suffer the wilted vegetables they sell at the market."

I manage a soft smile that doesn't quite match his.

"My tulips and daffodils aren't blooming quite yet, but they're growing," Nate continues, pulling me over to the box gardens. There are tulip leaves poking out of the ground. "I planted rocket larkspur this year," he says, eyes on his flowers. "I haven't tried them before, and I hope they come out soon. They're supposed to bloom in summer since I seeded them this early in the springtime."

"I didn't know you were into flowers," I say, unable to keep the admiration from my voice.

He just grins at me. "Yep," he says. "They're great. Easy to plant and look after. And I have an unlimited water source right over there." He throws out an arm at the pond.

"So, you garden vegetables and you garden flowers," I observe. "What else do you do that I don't know about?"

Nate and I wander over to the pond while he tells me about his great view of the stars from this grove—right above us we can see the brilliant blue sky that reminds me of his eyes. Mercury comes bounding up to us, and Nate has to stop him from launching himself into the pond.

"I washed him yesterday," Nate says, holding his dog back by his collar. "I don't want to have to clean him again."

"The pond seems like a good way to get filthy," I agree.

Nate distracts Mercury by tossing his tennis ball away from the pond. We watch the dog gallop after it, tearing up the grass in his haste to retrieve his favorite toy.

"How can you pick that up?" I ask as Mercury returns, dropping the soggy ball at Nate's feet. Bits of grass are stuck to it.

He throws it again, and I notice he does it with his left hand. He's holding onto me with his right. "It's not gross when I'm wearing gloves," he says. "It's another reason why I wear them."

I smile, though it doesn't reach my eyes.

Nate sits down, pulling me with him. We sit on the grass by the pond, Nate tossing Mercury's tennis ball every time he comes back.

When I wonder out loud why the dog continues to play fetch even when he's doing the same thing over and over again—getting the ball to bring it back, only to have it thrown—Nate laughs and tells me he has no clue why. Late morning changes to early afternoon as we continue to talk, him still holding my hand. I occasionally loosen my grip in case he wants to break away, but he doesn't and just tightens his hold.

I ask about Mercury, learning Nate got him from a neighbor that moved out of his neighborhood a year ago. Mercury is barely four years old, and it cheers Nate to know his best friend still has plenty of time to share with him. We talk about all sorts of things that help me understand Nate more. Of course, he won't tell me anything relating to his parents or his grandpa, but I manage to learn interesting facts about him nonetheless.

It feels weird holding his gloved hand. I'm not touching his skin, only the coarse material. I wonder if it is hurting him, if the cuts on his hands ache when I apply pressure, if he will let go of me sometime.

He doesn't.

Time passes comfortably, the warm sun making me drowsy. I release him and fall back on the soft grass, taking off my glasses before throwing an arm over my face. I am tired—all the adrenaline from my emotional walk this morning having run its course. Maybe I'll put off my confession for some other time. I'm such a coward.

"You're tired," Nate observes.

How do I tell him I'm exhausted with the burden of his secret? "My brother forced me to go to the library this morning, but when we got there, it was closed." *Chicken*.

"That's unfortunate," he says. I hear him petting Mercury, and the dog's tail thumping on the ground, his panting almost inaudible as he slowly cools down.

I hear Mercury scramble to his feet, and suddenly before I can do anything about it he's sitting on top of me. All the breath leaves my lungs as his massive weight settles on me, impossibly solid and suffocatingly heavy. He sticks his nose in my neck, wiping cold drool across my skin. I shriek and try to push him off me, but he is too big and hefty.

Nate is laughing as he drags his dog away; I am not. My ribs are sore, my chest is sore, and I feel like Mandy has given me one of her bear-hugs—four times her strength.

"Sorry about that," Nate says, still laughing quietly.

I struggle to sit up before Mercury can flatten me again, but I ache too much. I give up and fall back on the grass. "Mercury wiped his *slobber* on my neck," I grumble.

"Sorry about that, too."

I take a deep breath, ignoring the slight pain it causes, and close my eyes. I am now tired and sore. And still a coward.

"You know..." Nate begins, then stops himself.

"Know what?" I ask, not moving an inch.

He shifts on the grass. "The sunlight is making you look like your head is on fire."

I reach up and pat my hair, eyes closed. "No fire."

He picks up one of my curls. "Yeah, but your hair is really red. It reminds me of the tulips I grow." His gloved finger trails down my cheek while I hold very, very still. "And your eyes are the same color as the evergreens around here. Have you ever noticed that?"

"Yes," I admit, hoping the anxiety will stay out of my voice. "When I was at Goldbeck's party, I toured his forest of evergreens and saw the similarities."

"I like that shade of green," says Nate. His finger travels to my neck, where he brushes away the curls on my skin. "It's the color of life. The tree leaves, the grass, the evergreen boughs, your eyes..."

I swallow, glad I don't have to look at him. I would probably not survive this moment if I did.

"Oh, look, I found where Mercury drooled on you," Nate says suddenly, either changing the subject on purpose or just voicing the discovery for my benefit. "You have bits of grass on your neck, too. It's not only slobber."

"That's disgusting."

His fingers brush away the grass, which serves to make me more stressed; one, because he's touching me, and two, because I know why he's wearing gloves. "He *is* a dog."

We stay there for some time, me laying on the grass, Nate still sitting at my side. He continues to play with my hair, occasionally brushing across my cheek and neck, and the affectionate gesture reassures me that he must care, too. I thought he was mad at me. Those past three weeks are proof of his annoyance, when he avoided me and refused to talk to me alone and wouldn't even look at me during lunch or out walk to school or during our classes together. Yet now here we are, alone. And he's touching me.

Almost...tenderly.

The silence between us isn't strained, astonishingly. It's more companionable. And I don't want to do anything that might ruin this moment. What if I drift off to sleep?

Nate's fingers trace down my arm and across my palm, to fit our hands together, but he pulls back a half-second later and rubs his thumb over the hollow of my wrist. My entire body is quivering almost invisibly, and it's impossible to relax. He has his stupid gloves on, though, and I'm sadly reminded of what I came here to do.

With a quiet sigh, I open my eyes and slide on my glasses, gaze sharpening on his face. He doesn't seem embarrassed at all by his behavior. I am reminded of the Saturday he had stopped talking to me, when I had blatantly examined the scars on his arm.

He retracts his hand, watching me with unveiled curiosity, the look forcing me to fight another blush.

"Anyway..." Nate lets out a puff of air, suddenly breaking the still atmosphere that has sheltered us for the past few hours. "Are you going to lay on the grass all afternoon?"

"If you'll let me," I reply, keeping my gaze on him. I can see the dejected slump of his shoulders, the exhaustion weaving through his aura. An overwhelming sense of awe comes over me as I reflect on the kind, considerate person Nate has become despite all of the hardship he's endured in his life.

I wonder how much longer he can bear all this stress, all this pressure that has settled over him. I want him to know that I am willing to help him bear it, all of it. If I can just say the words...

He doesn't look at me as he responds. "It's okay with me. Stay here as long as you like."

I would love to. Except I came here to do something, not to be lazy. Shoving down my disappointment, I manage to sit up without hurting too much, and he immediately notices I'm struggling due to the hug his dog gave me. Nate takes my hands in his and pulls me up to my feet, smiling softly, the drowsy feel around us dispersing quickly.

"You said you had something to tell me?"

FORTY-TWO

I open my mouth to speak, then stop. I frown and start again. "Yes," I say carefully. I'm glad the topic has changed, but I'm also not eager to confess what I know about him and how long I've known it, and why I feel compelled to tell him. In fact, the more I stall, the more I start to panic again, terrified that when Nate knows I know and how I found out, he will cast me aside like he did Keller Jacobs. It's a huge risk; and even bigger now that I know I care for him, but it's precisely because I care for him that I *have* to tell him.

"Well, what is it?"

I take a deep breath and decide to tell him the really long round-about way. "Do you remember how earlier today, I told you about bribing Pompeii and Siena out of the house?"

Nate lists his head, messy hair falling over his eyes. "No," he says. "Bribe?"

"Yeah. I promised them I'd buy them ice cream at the Rainy Afternoon if they—well, if Siena—would come to the library with me. And Pompeii. So, of *course* Siena agreed, and we walked all the way to the library only to find that it was—"

"Closed," Nate finishes. "Since it's a holiday."

I nod. "Yes. My siblings were really disappointed—" I pause and correct myself. "*Pompeii* was really disappointed, and after getting dragged down to the café, he cheered up. It was rather painful crossing the street for me."

"I can imagine. No cars hit you? Or tried to, for that matter?"

I shake my head. "I wasn't almost killed, otherwise I would have told you a *long* time ago."

"Then what happened? I'm dying to know."

I let out a breath of air. "I bought my siblings some ice cream, and the lady who took my order looked at me weird, like she doesn't get that very often—which she probably doesn't. I went to sit down with Pompeii and Siena, but my mom called me, wanting to know where we were, and I moved out of the store so I wouldn't be disturbing anyone."

"Yeah, you do things like that," Nate interrupts.

I frown at him, not knowing if that was a compliment or a criticism. He sounds sincere. "After talking to my mom," I continue, "I was about to return to my siblings when I saw…" My voice falters. I don't know if I can go on.

Nate laces our fingers together, tugging me slightly closer to him. "You saw what?"

"I saw…" I swallow. "I think I saw my dad."

He isn't as surprised as I'd expected him to be. He just smiles broadly, both dimples flashing this time. "And?"

"I called his name," I say, thinking back on the moment. "I started to run after him, but he completely ignored me. He didn't even look my way. It must not have been him, but there's just something that keeps compelling me to believe it was him." I tell him about the picture my grandmother had sent. "I was looking at it minutes before I saw him. So maybe I just convinced myself it was same person. But I *know* he heard me. Even if it wasn't him, any normal person would have looked around at the yelling girl that was chasing him down. He didn't even flinch. I stopped calling after him when he entered that old, run-down building over there."

"What old, run-down building?"

I scrunch up my nose. My glasses slip down a hair. "This…paint manufactory place. Brick building. Chain-link fence surrounding it. It seems abandoned, but I watched my dad go in it. He didn't pay any attention to my calls or the *No Trespassing* signs posted around the premises."

"Wow. Your instincts tell you it was him?"

"Yes," I say. "I know it doesn't make any sense. He's supposed to be dead. And what would he be doing here of all places?"

Nate hesitates. "His family is here. Would that be enough to bring him?"

"I don't know." I sigh. "I want to believe that. But the truth is, he hasn't visited us in years. I wish he would've at least glanced at me. It would have been…well, it would have made a big difference."

"Honestly, I'm surprised you didn't jump the fence and follow him with your propensity to honor the impulse."

Now he's back to teasing me.

"Oh, I really wanted to, but I couldn't just run off and leave my siblings wondering where I was!"

"That's so like you. No thought of danger to yourself, but you make sure to keep track of everyone else."

"About that. Seeing my dad wasn't the only thing I wanted to talk to you about, Nate." I look down. I don't know if I can face him quite yet. Here goes.

"What is it, Venice?" He takes a step closer to me. He can see I'm struggling, and he reaches for my hand again. Even through those ever-present gloves his touch strengthens me.

I take a deep breath. "You're right. I do like to keep track of the people I care about and I try my best to keep them safe. My dad abandoned that role long ago, and it's hurt me for a long time. But I won't do that. I won't do it to my mom, to my family, and…" my voice falters. He claims my other hand and I finally look up into his eyes. "And I won't do it to you. I know who is important to me."

My glasses sit on my nose at an awkward angle. I wish I could fix them, but Nate is holding onto both of my hands and I don't exactly want to let go of him. He must notice my dilemma because he slowly releases one of my hands and tenderly adjusts my glasses so they sit correctly.

"Brave Venice. You don't need to worry about me." He smiles and tucks a stray strand of hair behind my ear, and his exposed fingertips brush my cheek and neck, kicking my pulse to a canter.

I take his hand again this time, and I hold both firmly in my own. "What if I want to? What if we do what you suggested a while ago—no more secrets between us. We tell each other everything. *Everything.*"

He stiffens a little, struggling to find words to say.

"What if..." I start, my palms resting on his forearms, "we begin trusting one another? I've dragged you into my tangled mess of problems and danger. Do I feel guilty? Yes! You don't need my drama and the more you get involved the more danger you face. But having you there for me, Nate, has also made me feel safer and stronger and happier than I've felt in a very long time. I want to be that for you, too.

"What if..." my fingers drift past his elbows, "we admit all of the difficulties in our lives, all of the insecurities, all of the unfortunate occurrences in which someone hurts us, physically and mentally. What if..." my fingers reach his shoulders, "we accept each other's offers of help no matter how vulnerable that makes us or how scared we might be of being rejected yet again?"

Nate holds still while my hands slide behind his neck. His eyes never waver from mine.

I feel his arms curl around my waist, bringing me closer. "What if..." I say, my thumb curving down his jaw, "you let me care about you?"

The last one is a question, not a suggestion.

All I need is his answer.

"Venice..."

"Nate."

My hands slips out of his hair and down to his chest, where I

432

feel his own beating heart galloping madly under my touch. He is tense, his muscles taut, his whole body stiff with the expectation of what might happen next.

But what happens next surprises me.

He leans forward, barely an inch from my face, and my breath catches and I unintentionally grip his shirt, my gaze dropping to his mouth. I fully expect him to close the remaining distance between us; instead, he lets out a soft sigh and steps back slightly, taking my wrists in the process.

Without a word, he rotates my palm upward and places his gloved hand in mine, an invitation.

I hesitate, look up at him, wanting confirmation.

He simply nods.

Slowly, carefully, I peel the glove off, feeling as if the whole world is waiting with bated breath for this critical moment to finally be broached. I keep my head down, staring as I finish removing the glove to reveal his skin.

At first look, nothing seems to be wrong other than the few scars here and there, but when I turn his hand over I see an angry red line trailing across the side of his palm and into the cuff of his jacket sleeve. The sight of his blood, spilled so easily, makes me both temperamental and depressed.

"Nate," I say cautiously, and he interrupts.

"How much do you know?" It's asked curiously, rather than in an accusative tone.

I let his glove drop to the grass and begin rolling up his jacket sleeve, uncovering more cuts as I do. I'm not sure how to answer, if I should tell him.

Of course I should. I came here to do this.

"Most of it," I admit.

He doesn't seem surprised. "And...?"

I hold back a sigh. How do I tell him that I spied on him? "The day my dad died, I got your address from Mandy and came over to your house to tell you. You were the first person I thought of after hearing about my dad, and I really wanted to share the news with you." I'm glad I have my eyes on his bleeding wrist and not on his face; it saves me from finding out what his reaction to this is. "Of course," I continue, "when I arrived, your grandpa was having a fit, and…" I pause again, then say, "I heard him. I heard him throwing bottles at you, and I heard you calming him down. I wanted to interrupt, to make your grandpa stop, but I was scared. I was scared that you would be mad at me and not talk to me ever again."

"I…I can promise you that I wouldn't do that."

"You sort of did," I say unhelpfully, risking a glance up at him and discovering that he's far more sad than angry. "The past three weeks, you've stopped talking to me."

He blows out a puff of air. "I'm sorry I did. Those few weeks were the hardest moments of my life. And I'm sorry for doing that to you. I'm sorry I made everything awkward between us. I was just trying to prevent you from finding out about my grandpa and what he does to me. But…you already knew. You knew for over a month, yet you didn't tell me."

"I couldn't." I brush my thumb over his wrist, catching some of the blood on my skin. "I'm sorry too, Nate. I'm sorry I entered your life and turned it on its head—"

"Oh, I'm *glad* you did," he says vehemently, and my cheeks tinge red. "And don't feel like you forced me to admit about my grandpa. That was solely my choice."

I hold his gaze for a hot minute, astounded that I happened to meet someone this incredibly kind and understanding and…I'm ninety-nine point nine percent certain he likes me. He could easily be furious that I intruded on his personal life, that I'm aware of his frequent abuse, that I could spread the word—not that I ever would do that—and put him in the spotlight, something I know he doesn't want. There are plenty of reasons…and he seems content.

Seized by a sudden impulse, I latch onto his shirt and pull him down to my level of height. Before he can speak or my courage desert me, I kiss him.

Nate's arms come around me, closing any distance between us, his uncertainty ebbing away the longer we stand here. I am quite dazed, only comprehending him, not the world, registering the calm sensation of his touch and his gentleness and his friendship and his loyalty.

He abruptly jerks back, retracting his arms as he goes. "I'm getting blood on you," he explains.

"I don't care." I know my cheeks are scarlet.

Without warning, he takes me by the waist again and presses another kiss to my mouth, and my hands slide up his chest and into his hair, and I'm smiling now and I would stay here all afternoon if there weren't other things we have to do, namely divulge all that we have neglected to.

I'm the one who breaks away this time, albeit breathlessly. My head is spinning. "Priorities first, Nate."

FORTY-THREE

"You have to come over to my house," I say, extracting my hands from his hair to grab his. "I can clean up your cuts."

Nate holds up his one gloved hand and taps my lips with a finger. "Venice, don't command me." He looks a bit dazed, too.

I heave a big, exaggerated sigh. "*Please* come to my house."

"Why?"

"So I can fix your hands." I grab his right hand and take off the glove. He has a cut down his palm instead of along the side. No wonder he played fetch with Mercury using his left. His right is more torn and more bloody and probably more painful.

"And why would you want to fix them?"

I groan. "I can't believe you just asked me that." I don't wait for him to reply before continuing. "Nate, your hands are bleeding, they're cut up, and they need to be cleaned and properly bandaged. Past experience has shown me that you don't do anything to your wounds after you receive them. So *please* come over to my house and let me help you."

"And if I tell you I don't need you to?"

"I'll drag you along anyway."

He laughs. "All right. I'll come. But only if there's no one else around. I can't have anyone noticing my hands and connecting the dots like you did. The less who knows about my grandpa and me, the better."

"Roman is the only one there, but he won't bother us," I say. "Mom took the two youngest kids shopping for spring clothes, and Florence is hanging out at the mall with her friends. She won't be back any time soon."

Nate gives me a skeptical look. "You'd better be right."

"Of course I am." I study his hands again. My own are stained red with his blood in some places, like on my palms and fingers, where I've touched the cuts. There are more along his wrists. "Nate, how often do you *actually* clean your cuts?"

He shrugs. "Whenever they seem really bad."

"So, every time?"

His annoyed expression almost causes me to laugh. "No," he says. "They aren't always this bad. Honestly, these aren't the worst I've gotten. You saw one of the most painful ones"—he releases one of my hands and rolls up the sleeve on his jacket, flashing off the now-scarred-over cut I had first noticed more than a month ago—"and this one hurt the most. It took a whole week to heal, and the scab was pure torture. I scratch—Wait." He stops. "You probably don't want to hear this."

"Oh, I do. Keep talking." I drop his other hand and take his arm, pushing the sleeve up higher, revealing his scars and more fresh cuts. I'm glad I am concentrating on his wounds and not his face, seeing as I am sorely tempted to kiss him again. He had tasted so good.

"If I come to your house," he begins slowly, "and no one else is there, can I bring Mercury? He can wait outside."

"As long as he doesn't end up eating all the squirrels."

Nate frowns. "I have never seen Mercury eat a squirrel. He chases them, but he's too slow. The squirrels make it up a tree before Mercury can catch up with them."

"People will think I adopted a bear."

"Mercury doesn't look like a bear."

I raise an eyebrow.

Nate sighs and amends his statement. "Mercury doesn't look a lot like a bear."

"He's big enough to knock down my old neighbor," I say. "The one who lives behind our house. She's going blind and will probably call the police for mistaking Mercury for a wild animal."

Nate is horrified. "She would do that to my dog?"

"Your dog doesn't look much like one," I say, pointing with my free hand at Mercury, who is sprawled out on the grass a few feet from us, snoring loudly. I wonder how Nate can sleep at night with those kinds of noises filling his tiny house.

He glances over at his dog. "You're right. Okay, he can stay here. But I have to put him in the house. He can't stay outside, otherwise he'll follow us back to your place."

"Has he done that before?" I ask, walking up to the dog with him. "Has he followed you?"

"Yeah." Nate bends down, releasing me, and shakes Mercury awake. The dog snorts and whips his head around, glaring up at us. Then he realizes it's his owner who woke him and bounds to his feet, wagging his tail madly. I think I'm relieved he doesn't snore when he's awake.

He pulls on his gloves again, and when he catches me looking, he just shrugs one shoulder. "My hands are protected more if I'm wearing these," he explains.

"I was only curious. You didn't have to defend yourself."

He simply nods.

We emerge from the trees, Nate's house directly in front of us. Mercury lets out a faint whimper as he looks up at Nate, a silent pleading in his eyes. He knows he has to go inside, but he doesn't want to. It breaks my heart to see the sorrowful look in his dark brown eyes.

Maybe I should let him come.

"Go on," says Nate. He grabs Mercury's collar and leads him up the porch to the front door, which he opens and pushes the dog inside. "I'll be back soon," I hear him call softly. "Don't worry. Don't bother Gramps."

I watch as he closes the door and moves over to his gravel driveway. He waves his hand at me. "Are you coming or staying?"

I hurry to catch up with him. I don't want to be here any longer. "I'd rather hang out with you than your grandpa."

"That's both flattering and prejudiced," Nate replies. "You've never met my grandpa, so you can't determine if you would enjoy my company or his more."

"I've seen the result of his actions," I cut in.

Nate glances over at me before returning his gaze to his driveway. "And it's flattering," he continues, "that you chose me over an old man you've never met and have only heard bad things about."

"You really are loyal to him," I compliment him, although I don't understand it. "Defending your grandpa, and all he's done is hurt you."

"Oh, that's not all he's done for me," Nate corrects. "This has only been happening for the last few years or so. He wasn't always like this. I remember some really good times together." He sighs, his hand brushing mine as we walk. I don't know if it was an accident or not. "Am I going to have to tell you my entire life story?"

"Only what you're ready to say, but I'm ready for everything." Except I'm not really looking forward to this—all the pain and loneliness and betrayal and heartbreak. He deserves joy. Shouldn't he at least get *some*?

He sighs again. "Okay. I told you my dad and mom abandoned me at an early age. I was about four when I came to live with my grandpa. At first, he was really nice to me, and I felt loved. We would take drives around town after school or on the weekends, and he would tell me all about the different places and shops and houses, and who lives where, and who is who, and who owns what model car. For a few years, we were happy together. But the day after I turned ten, he invited some of his buddies over to have a drink. Of course, one drink turned into five, and once everyone had left, Gramps randomly got mad at me. He took one of the empty bottles and threw it at me as hard as he could. He missed, but it shattered against the wall and one of the shards, well, a few of them cut me up. "

I listen to this confession, horrified.

"I didn't go to school for the next few days," Nate says. "I hid in my room until my cuts became scabs. But that..." he stops walking, we having arrived at his mailbox, and he closes his eyes as he relives the memory. "That was a mistake. If I had gone out of my room the next day and shown Gramps my bleeding arms, he probably would have never touched a drink again. He probably would have never hurt me again." He shakes his head, opens his eyes, and resumes walking.

I fall in step with him. "What did you find when you finally left your room?" I ask.

"My gramps," Nate answers. "Drunk. On the couch. He couldn't ever hold much liquor, and twenty bottles in half a week is *not* keeping his alcohol limit in check. He started drinking more, up until the point when he wouldn't get off the couch. I didn't know what to do, but I knew what I couldn't do. I couldn't tell anyone."

I gingerly take his hand in mine. Poor ten year-old Nate.

"He used to drive me to school," Nate murmurs, more to himself than to me. "He didn't like me having to walk far to the bus stop. It's..." He looks around us. We're barely a few feet from his mailbox. "At the end of this road. Anyway, I began walking because it got me out of the house earlier and I wanted as little attention paid to me as possible. I went to school and acted like I was a normal kid, just like everyone else. I knew Mandy and Elijah by then, and we were all good friends. I never told them *anything*, though. You, Venice, are the first to know about any of my past."

"I feel honored." And I mean it.

He scoffs. "Great. As I was saying, my grandpa wasn't stable any more. He stopped doing anything. I had to buy and cook food if I wanted to eat. And all Gramps did was watch TV and pay the bills." Nate grins ruefully at the thought, but his smile isn't sincere. His dimples don't even show. "I must say, the only good things that came out of this were I learned how to cook, I learned how to calm down an old drunk man while being hurt yet still hanging in there, and I learned that sometimes, the only way to wake up an old drunk man is a bucket of ice-cold water."

I snort with restrained laughter. "Noted."

"When Gramps got *really* mad," continues Nate, "he would use all his nice empty bottles as ammunition. I started taking them outside and breaking them all, but then I had glass all over the sidewalk, and that wasn't a very smart idea. So I gathered them together and..." He suddenly grabs my hand and whirls me around to face him. "Come on. I want to show you what I did with all the bottles."

"Oh-kay," I say, my voice hiccupping over the word. I hadn't expected this sudden change.

Nate leads me back to his mailbox, but instead of going down the driveway, we plunge straight into the woods. The trees here are oaks and maples that haven't grown their leaves yet—however, on some of the branches I see tiny red buds.

We walk through the forest, Nate talking constantly. The words come out of his mouth in a stream; I have never heard him talk this much. He's usually so quiet. But I think it's because he's eager to finally tell someone about his unfortunate life.

"Grocery shopping was the hardest when I was twelve," he says, moving us around a clump of briars. "All the adults there looked at me funny as I was pushing the cart down the aisle, and when I got to checkout, the cashiers almost always asked where my parents were. Of course, I wouldn't dare tell them, so I'd just shrug and hand them the money for the groceries. I knew where

Gramps's stash of money was, and that's what I used to pay. I don't think he has realized it yet, and it's been four years. Now, of course, I know all about social security and retirement and bank transfers. The people at Gramps' bank love me. They think I'm such a dutiful grandson taking care of my grandpa."

"Wait," I say, as all this is confusing me. "You said he stopped going places when you were ten, but you started shopping two years later?"

Nate shakes his head. "No, I went with Gramps until I was twelve. Oh, I really am confusing you. Sorry. I've never told anyone this, so it's kind of hard to get everything straight. Okay. My grandpa would still go to the store, but he'd only buy beer. I went along to buy the groceries. But two years later, when I was twelve, Gramps stopped going. He stayed home and didn't go out. Shopping was the only thing he left the house for, and after he gave that up, he remained inside always. He hasn't been out around town in years. I sometimes try; I'll tell him we can go take a drive to his favorite sights, but he just shrugs me off. I guess that's sort of good, because I don't trust him to drive and *I* can't legally, but..." he sighs. "All the same, I'd wish he would come out for *some* things."

I squeeze his hand, making him wince, and I am horrified to remember that he's hurt. "Sorry!"

He waves me off. "It's fine. Oh, we're here."

We come to a stop in front of a lone tree. The others around it are far away, almost like they're ashamed to be too close to it. We're in the middle of the forest, surrounded by dead-looking trees on all sides; the thin branches allowing sunlight to filter through and light up the area, which helps create a less depressing, less lonely feel.

The tree before us is small and short. But the branches are thick and strong; tied to each one is an empty beer bottle. There are dozens of green and blue and brown bottles hanging, sunlight glinting off the glass.

"This is…" I can't finish. I don't know what to say.

Nate, standing so close to me I can hear his soft breath, dips his head in a nod. "It's my collection. Pretty soon, I'll have to find either another tree or a different one. This is nearly full, and the sad thing is that these aren't all of the bottles my grandpa goes through. Plenty don't make it this far."

"Because they're broken," I supply. "Over you."

He just nods again.

We stand in silence, examining the tree. Personally, I find it to be a rather beautiful work of art, despite all the pain it has inflicted. Nate is very skilled in a lot of things, like making ugly, wicked things into glittering decorations and making ugly, wicked people seem kind and gentle. Besides the abuse, excessive drinking problem, and neglect, Nate has only said nice things about his grandpa. It just shows what a good person Nate is.

"Let's get back," he says, breaking the silence. "By the time we reach your house, it'll be midnight."

I smile. "My family will all be there by then."

"Except for your dad."

My smile fades slightly at the mention of Dad. "I don't know if I count him as part of our family," I say stiffly.

Nate begins walking—in a different direction from where we came—and says, "Your dad is here, in this town. Don't you think he knows where you live? With all these strange circumstances surrounding your dad, don't you think he might reach out to your family?"

"I'm not sure I want him to." I tromp through the forest, glaring down at my feet so I don't have to look up at Nate. "We've spent six years without Dad. It'll feel weird if he joins our family again. And I'm not saying he will, once we find him or he finds us, but it will be strange talking with him and seeing him. Then again, he might just leave us and go wherever."

Nate opens his mouth to speak, but I do first, cutting him off.

"Anyway, we aren't talking about my dad. We're talking about your grandpa. So you may continue. Please."

"I can't remember what I was saying."

I smile tiredly. "I'll help you remember if you'll tell me where we're going."

"This is just a shortcut to the road," he explains. "So we don't have to go past all my creepy neighbors."

"Oh." I trip over some sort of branch and catch myself before I face-plant onto the ground. "Well, you were saying your grandpa doesn't leave the house anymore."

Nate tightens his grip on my hand—which must be painful for him—and ducks under a low-hanging branch, bringing me with him. "Oh, yeah. I think the last time he went outside was my fourteenth birthday when he chased me out for asking if I could watch something I wanted to on the TV. I went to Elijah's after that and learned how to make Mrs. Jenkins's favorite vegetable stir-fry. It's delicious. And easy to throw together. I got the recipe from her, and I've made it a couple times for my grandpa. He isn't exactly a big fan of vegetables, but the meal is cheap and easy, and I'm going to make it no matter what."

"If you used organic vegetables, then you would be my mom's favorite person in the world."

Nate grins at me. "If I used organic vegetables," he says, "then the meal would be twice as expensive."

I grin back. "Touché."

He clears his throat. "I don't know if you've noticed—I'm sure you have—I don't have any scars or cuts or scrapes on my face. The highest Gramps got were my shoulders."

"Then the one on your neck really was from a picture frame?"

Nate gives me a hurt look. "Did you not believe me?"

"It's rather hard to believe you unless I know the entire story."

"I never lied to you. I just…avoided the truth."

We leave the forest, finding ourselves on the paved road

leading toward my house. He immediately sets off, and I remember how familiar he is with this track. He walks here nearly every day.

"My grandpa knows not to give me wounds on my face," Nate says while we walk. "He's smart like that. He knows if I go to school with blood running down the side of my head, people will realize I'm being mistreated, and then Gramps will get taken away and put in an institute for mentally damaged old folks."

"Your grandpa *does* seem mentally damaged," I comment.

He blows out a puff of air. "Thanks. Yeah, he is. He's definitely messed up in the head. It might be all the alcohol, but it might be old age. He forgets things, like my name and who he is and what's going on, and he has frequent violent and aggressive episodes. I usually trigger him, though I don't mean to. Just saying one word can set him off. It's normally when he runs out of his drink and tells me—well, more like *demands*—to go buy more, but it's a Sunday, and the store doesn't sell alcohol on Sundays."

I blink. "What?"

"The store I go to," says Nate, "is run by a man who believes selling alcohol on Sunday is disrupting the Sabbath. I respect him for being firm and steadfast in his beliefs, but unfortunately Sunday is the one day I wish he wouldn't prohibit the sales."

"Why don't you go to other stores?" I suggest.

"You can't buy any alcoholic drink until you're twenty-one," he says. "The manager of the store I go to knows who I am and that my grandpa is...addicted. He's one of my grandpa's old buddies. He doesn't know about the abuse, but he knows that I have to get Gramps's drinks since Gramps can't. So he lets me buy them and doesn't say a word."

"That's...kind of him, I guess," I say.

"Yes, it is." Nate drags his free hand through his hair, like he needs to do something with his hands instead of staying still. "It's really unfortunate he only sells bottles, not cans. Those would be a lot nicer for Gramps to use against me."

"Nate," I say, so sad at his confession, "why do you buy alcohol for your grandpa if you know it's just going to make him worse?"

He gives me a pained look. "I have to," he says. "He leaves me alone when he's drunk, but when he doesn't have anything left, he flips out and..." Nate gestures to himself. "I get hurt."

I glance at the trees lining the road, despair crashing through me. Poor Nate. He just wants someone to love him.

"Summer is probably the worst time of the year," Nate says. He must be finally voicing thoughts that have been stuck inside of him for years. "During the summer months, I do odd jobs and help out at obscure places all day long, every day. It's one of the only times I can work. The fall and winter and spring, I have to pretend that everything is going fine with me. But I still do *some* jobs. There's a fast-food restaurant down the street that I work at after school on the days Elijah or you don't need me."

Me? Need him? I always need him. Whether it's his dimples or his smile or his laugh or himself, I always need him.

I'm surprised that it's taken this long for me to realize that I like him.

And...does he ever need me?

"...retreat to La-La Land, then it's pointless to continue," Nate is saying, and I quickly pull my head out of the clouds.

"Sorry," I say. "Please, keep talking."

He grins his usual grin, the one that has recently started to make my palms sweat and my heartbeat sped up at the sight of his dimples. "I'd much rather just stare at you."

A pink flush rises to my cheeks. I look away from him. "Don't tease."

He laughs his usual laugh, the one that is so full of joy and light that it's hard to recall how bad of a life he has. "You're easy to tease. You don't freak out when people tease you. And you can't get annoyed with me because I rarely tease."

"You do plenty," I mutter. "Like the day I went to that party."

Nate stops in the middle of the sidewalk, bringing me to an abrupt halt next to him. "You think I was teasing when I said you looked good?"

I shrug carelessly, but inside my heart is pounding even harder.

"Seriously?" He touches two fingers to my chin, tilting my head up to face him. "I wasn't. I meant it. Still do."

I swallow hard. "Then…thank you. I didn't get the chance to say that."

"You're definitely welcome." He doesn't move, his fingers still on my chin, his eyes boring into mine. I really want him to close the distance between us, to kiss me again, and after a moment he leans down and brushes his lips against my forehead. I close my eyes.

But he steps back barely a second later. "I told you about my grandpa," he says. "Tell me about Florence and Marc?"

I sigh and pull away from him, my hand falling back to my side. My eyes are open now. "Florence just delights in making fun of me," I say, resuming our walk in the direction of my house. "She used to mock me for not having any friends, and that I'm awkward, and that I'm never going to…" I quickly glance at Nate before finishing. "Whatever."

"You said 'used to,'" he observes. "She doesn't anymore?"

I shake my head. "No, not after the day of the Goldbeck's party. We had a big argument after she learned I was going to the party and not her, and we talked through a lot of things that helped me understand her views of my life and helped her understand my views of her life. We're better friends now. At least, I hope we still are. I haven't gotten to hang out with her much, and she could have invited me to go to the mall with her today and she didn't." Then I shrug. "But I'm glad she didn't."

A smile plays at his lips, and I realize I'm staring. Flushing, I return my gaze to the sidewalk and my shoes.

"And you've miraculously recovered from all the harsh things she's said to you? All the embarrassing circumstances she's put you through? Like at the library when we first met, how she made it sound like you were a little kid who needed supervision?"

I groan, push my glasses up my nose. "Yes, it was…mortifying. I'm fine now, recovered nicely; her words never really hurt anyway. And at the library…well it didn't help that she tried to flirt with you and you didn't respond. Most boys normally do."

"She was *flirting* with me?" Nate exclaims.

"Uh…yes."

He has a horrified look on his face. "That explains why she got mad. I thought she was just making conversation to draw attention away from you; you were picking up all the books Siena gave you that you couldn't hold. I didn't know Florence was flirting. Oh, that's kind of awkward now."

I shake my head in utter amazement. I can't believe he didn't recognize it. "I agree," I say. "It's uncomfortable to watch her flirt."

"And uncomfortable to be flirted with." Nate's eyes flick over to me for half a second. "Anyway, what about Marc? Will you tell me what he did to your mom and why you don't like him?"

I start. *Will you*, he'd said. Not *you have to*.

What a guy. Better than me.

"Marc is a pathetic loser chasing after my mom," I say simply. "I don't like him, never will. And what he did to Mom…You remember that day at the café? Well, when I got home and Mom hadn't come back yet, I was slightly worried. But hours later, even after Flo arrived home from her date and Mom still hadn't returned, I was really concerned. And the next morning…" I sigh. My hands, both hanging at my sides, swing back and forth in the warm air. "I woke up to hearing Marc's truck roaring down the street. I found Mom on the porch, asleep. She'd passed out after drinking too much."

"That's what it was?" Nate doesn't sound very surprised. "She was drunk because of Marc?"

I nod unhappily. "I hate alcohol."

"So do I." He takes my hand in his, lacing our fingers together.

"And the worst part about my mom being drunk," I continue, "is that she didn't vow never to drink again, or that she'll never see Marc again. A week later, the day my grandparents and Marc were over, the day Hubris Jargon almost killed me, I was…rash. And impulsive. Even though you told me not to. I was blinded by intense dislike and just marched straight inside, yelled at Marc, and was dismissed."

Nate gives me a squeeze, which must hurt him a little. "I understand why now. He made your mom drunk."

"But she could have refused!" I let go of him and bury my face in my hands, coming to a stop for the second time. "Mom could have said she doesn't drink—because she *doesn't*—but she still agreed and ended up drunk!" My shoulders are shaking; it's from fury, not tears.

Nate slides his hands around mine, pulling them away from my face so I am forced to look him in the eye. "Venice. This isn't your fault. Your mom makes her own decisions. You can't protect everyone all the time. But, yeah, it was a jerk move by Marc to leave her on the front porch."

I watch him for a second, and nod. "The next time I saw him, he didn't seem remotely embarrassed."

"Things could have worked out differently, especially in his favor." Nate scans our surroundings; we're getting close to the entrance into my neighborhood. "We're almost to your place."

"And it isn't midnight," I reply.

"No, it's three in the afternoon," he says. "When did you say your mom and Florence would be back?"

We resume walking, not touching each other, inches between us. "Mom's gone all day," I explain. "She won't be home in time for dinner, so she told me she's taking Pompeii and Siena out to eat. And Florence could return in a week, for all I know."

Nate has a slight smirk on his face. "Why would you want to spend a week at the mall?"

449

"She's very different from the...rest...of..." My voice trails away as an enormous black SUV comes up behind us. My heart picks up speed as the car starts to slow.

Nate is closer to the road than me. I grab his hand, ready to drag us into the forest, but he stays firm, steady, and instead pulls me toward him.

"It isn't him," he whispers, not glancing at the SUV .

"How do you know?" I whisper back.

He waits for the SUV to pass us before replying. "They have a license plate on their front and back," he says. "Jargon's doesn't have one on the front, but he does on the rear. Unlike this car."

I relax slightly. "I'm just really terrified whenever I see cars like those."

"Has anyone bothered you for the past few weeks?"

"No." I shake my head. "I've been left alone. No men breaking into my house, no one trying to run me down, no threatening phone calls or texts or any other sort of message."

"Have you gotten one before?"

I shake my head again, having to hide a smile. "Not a single one," I confess. "But in those mystery books Mrs. Jenkins likes, the detective always gets some."

"Oh." Nate leads me down my street. I can see my house.

"Blessed Hallelujah," I mutter. It's been such a long day, and it's only half over. I still have to show Nate how to properly clean his cuts—if there's one thing he's bad at, it's bandaging his wounds. Putting on gloves and a jacket hides them, but doesn't help heal them.

"Are you sure no one's home?" he asks nervously.

I give him an exasperated look. "Roman is," I say. "But he's downstairs. He won't bother us. I think. I hope."

Nate groans. "Great."

"Roman is in a depressed mood right now," I say, crossing the street to my house, Nate at my side. "He never comes up for dinner and he doesn't come up when Mom yells for him to. He simply watches TV all day and eats his stash of snacks and junk food he hoards down there."

"Does he ever randomly decide to pop into the kitchen?"

I open the screen door, then the front door. "Yes, he does. But we can hear him stomping up the stairs and know he's coming. You'll be fine, Nate. I promise. And even if Roman sees anything, he won't understand."

Nate sighs. "Okay, okay."

We slip inside, and before going to the kitchen, I dart upstairs to check and make sure my ring is still where I've hidden it—in-between the pages of my favorite book. To my relief, I find the ring. I shove my book back into its place on my tiny shelf, then go back down to Nate.

He's examining the hallway, where Siena has painted one tree just outside of the kitchen. "What's this?" he asks when I come up to him.

"Siena has a fascination with trees," I say. "She's really good at painting them, too. Unfortunately, she likes painting big trees, so she does her art on the walls. There are more in the kitchen."

"I see," Nate says, following me into the brightly-lit room. The afternoon sun bleeds through the windows, which aren't covered by the curtains like usual. "Oh, that's where the smell comes from," he says suddenly, the odd declaration startling me.

"What smell?"

He gestures at me. "Your kitchen smells like cinnamon. And so do you."

I frown. I've never realized I smell like Mom's favorite perfume. Maybe I'm so used to the fragrance that I can't smell it as Nate can. I wonder if others also smell it.

"You taste like cinnamon, too," he says.

I blush and turn away from him. My eyes fall upon a pile of wrappers scattered across the floor and counters. Roman has been here recently, not bothering to clean up after himself. There are also empty soda cans—I think I won't buy him any more soda—littered around the kitchen, as if Roman had gone into a rage and thrown them. And one isn't empty, but has spilled all over the floor.

I march over to the basement door and yank it open, glad for a distraction. I don't think I can face Nate after what he had said.

"Roman Ferrari!" I yell into the depths of the cold downstairs. "What is this mess up here?"

He takes a moment to answer, his voice faint. "Go away!"

I slam the door shut, disgusted. "What a lazy slob," I mutter.

"Your kitchen isn't normally like this?" Nate asks, stepping over the line of spilled soda as he comes closer to me.

"No." I'm appalled by the idea. "Of course not."

He shrugs. "Just wondering."

"All right, let's see your hands," I say, holding out my own. He takes off his gloves before placing his hands in mine, fresh blood beading here and there on his wounds.

I lead Nate over to the kitchen sink, where I examine the cuts in the light of the sun streaming through the window above. "What do you do to your cuts after you get them?"

Nate looks sheepish. "Um…nothing."

I groan. "Shouldn't you at least clean and bandage them?"

"I've never bought bandages."

My stare turns horrified. "Never? How come?"

"I don't want people seeing me buy bandages and somehow connecting that to my grandpa."

"Nate, bandages are a normal thing to buy. No one will get suspicious if you are seen getting some." I rinse his hands in the sink, watching the water turn pink as the blood is slowly washed off. When they are clean, I study the cuts again, noting how they seem less severe than before.

Mom keeps the First-Aid kit in our kitchen. Since we get scrapes and cuts pretty much every time we go outside, it's nice to have the

First-Aid kit on hand. I've cleaned and bandaged so many injuries my hands move without me paying much attention to what I'm doing and if I'm doing it correctly.

With Nate, I concentrate on making sure I carefully clean each cut with antiseptic before wrapping his hands in bandages. He watches me the entire time, standing right next to me, and answers the questions I ask him. I learn about Keller Jacobs, how they were friends until the day he followed Nate home and saw how his grandpa abused him. Nate spotted Keller and ran out to confront him, saying how Keller could *never* tell anyone what he saw or Nate would get him in trouble for trespassing on private land. I'm glad Nate didn't say that to me when I went over earlier today.

I learn about his family, how he doesn't know if his other grandparents, his mom's parents, even care about him. They haven't been in contact with him, just like his dad. He tells me that his dad sometimes calls his grandpa, and they talk for a little while, but his dad never asks to speak with him. It's very depressing, the way Nate talks like he knows his dad pretends he doesn't exist. Of course, I can relate, and having such knowledge of the hurt that comes from neglect has me wishing no one had to suffer it, and especially not someone like Nate.

He persuades me to talk about my family, and I tell him that I have no aunts or uncles or cousins since neither of my parents have siblings. Nate finds this unfortunate—he seems to think the more family you have, the better—but I'm fine with not having any extended family. Makes Christmas a whole lot easier.

I finish with his hands and have him take off his jacket so I can clean his arms. He has one major cut on his left arm, one that would heal faster if stitched up, but other than that, he's as fine as one can be who is cut so often.

"You saw how I did it?" I ask him when I'm done.

Nate nods. "Clean, then bandage. Problem is, I don't have any bandages. And I'm not going to buy any."

I sigh, exasperated by his distrust. "No one will be suspicious to see you buying some."

"I don't take chances."

"You did today." I collect the two remaining rolls of bandaging. "You took a chance by not sending me away when I showed up at your house, and look how that ended up for you."

He dips his head in recognition. "True."

"Do you have any other cuts?"

Nate hesitates. "I don't think so."

"Any on your shoulders or your back? Chest? Where does your grandpa hit you other than your hands and arms?"

He shifts his weight. "Um...I probably am cut on my chest, but I'm not taking my shirt off in your kitchen."

A pink flush rises to my cheeks. "You'll dress them at home?"

"I don't have..." he starts to say, but I thrust the two rolls of bandages at him, and say, "All right, take these. We can get some more at the store when we go."

Nate hesitates again, then accepts them. He shoves the rolls in his jacket pockets. "Thank you." He slides into his jacket, puts his gloves on, and looks like he's merely cold, not that he's hiding anything from the world. "Thank you," he repeats "For...everything you did for me today."

"You're welcome."

We stand in the kitchen, surrounded by Roman's mess; *my* mess of First-Aid equipment is back in its spot. The sink has been rinsed, washing away any trace of blood. There isn't any evidence of what we've been doing.

We stand there for a few minutes, just watching each other. I keep waiting for him to move forward, to touch me, to maybe even kiss me, but Nate stays where he is. I guess after all we've been through today, it feels natural to reach out and touch him, but I'm too scared to be the one making the first move, especially since I did earlier.

The front door suddenly bangs open, then slams shut. Nate flinches and exchanges a quick glance with me. I shrug. He's fine now that he's covered.

"Venice?" calls Flo's voice. "Venice, are you home?"

"In the kitchen," I call back.

Nate gives me a horrified look. "I don't want her to see me!" he says in a harsh whisper.

It's too late. Flo has already walked in, startled to find I'm not alone. "Oh, hello, Nate," she says. She's holding several shopping bags in her hands, and I can practically hear the bursting closet upstairs groan at the added collection of clothes. "Fancy seeing you here."

He smiles, though it's quite strained and doesn't reveal either dimple. "Hello, Florence. How was shopping?"

"Fun, as always." She flashes me a smirk. I roll my eyes. "How have you been? I haven't seen you stop by in forever."

"I've been…busy," Nate replies. He sounds stiff. I wonder if it's because I told him Florence tried to flirt with him. "And, uh, I've actually got to go now. I should be starting dinner soon."

"Okay." Flo winks at me, then sets down her shopping bags on the kitchen counter. She begins searching the cabinets for a snack to eat.

I walk with Nate to the front door, both of us ignoring Florence when she calls after us how it was nice to see Nate.

"You're not going to tell anyone about me, are you?" he asks quietly.

I'm outraged. "Of course not. Why would I? It's your secret. I'm not going to tell anyone, even Mandy or Elijah. But you know you're going to have to someday, right?"

"Maybe." Nate steps out onto the porch, looking frustrated. "I just don't want their pity. Everyone who knew would look at my life with pity because I have a grandpa that treats me awfully. You were very understanding earlier today, Venice. I know you don't like the idea of me living with my grandpa, but you tried to understand. And that really makes me glad."

I push up the bridge of my glasses, feeling embarrassed at his praise. "I *am* trying," I say. "You've made it clear you don't want pity. Help and support are what I offer."

He opens his mouth to say something, then changes his mind and simply nods once.

For a moment, I think he's going to reach out to me, but he just turns his back on me and walks away without saying goodbye. It breaks my heart to see him looking so dejected. I'm not sure today eased his burden. If anything, me knowing about him is making him more stressed.

I watch him disappear around the corner, then I retreat inside. I don't want to face Flo, but she comes up to me anyway.

"What was *that*?" she asks in a whisper. "What was he doing here while you two were all alone?"

I push past her. "We weren't alone. Roman is here."

"Okay…" She follows me into the kitchen, making it clear she wanted more information.

"I was helping him with something," I reply shortly.

She raises an eyebrow in question, but I that's all I'm going to give her.

"Venice." Flo sighs. "I'm just concerned about your safety. This is the first time you've shown interest in a boy, and I have the most experience with boys in our family."

"I don't need your advice," I snap. Then I immediately soften my tone, thinking I was too harsh. "But I really do appreciate your concern, Flo. I'm all right. We're not…He's a really good friend."

But that isn't exactly true.

"Just be warned," Flo says, a worried look on her face. "Broken hearts are the hardest to heal."

FORTY-FOUR

Dinner is a quiet affair. It's just Flo and me, and my twin is too busy on her phone to talk to me. I pick at my food, thinking about the day, trying to make sense of everything, and frankly replaying the moments with Nate. I focus on the table, noting the stained, chipped, and scratched wood on the surface. This has lasted us forever. I'm surprised Mom hasn't bought a new one, but she's a use-it-until-it-breaks person. This is the same table we used to sit around as a family years ago...with Dad.

Roman comes upstairs for two minutes, grabbing a handful of crackers before heading outside into the dwindling sunlight. The sun sets in an hour, but dusk has already fallen and it's steadily growing darker out there. I can see Roman for barely a minute until he disappears into the miniature forest behind our house.

Mom and the two younger kids will be home in half an hour, she said in a text message to me, but they might take longer since Siena took off her shoes and left them at the restaurant and Mom has to go back and get them.

I've almost finished my dinner when Flo puts down her phone and gives me a purposeful look.

"What did you do this afternoon, Venice?" she asks. "Besides hanging out with Nate alone."

I noiselessly set down my fork. "I took the kids to the library this morning."

"What fun," Flo says sarcastically. "So you didn't do anything worthwhile? We didn't have school today!"

I shrug. "I didn't plan on doing anything. I didn't know today was a holiday until Pompeii woke me up and told me, then dragged me out to the library."

"Well, I wanted to invite you, but I thought you were doing something." Her tone has changed. It's softer and kinder and it melts me.

"Flo, it actually means a lot to me to hear you say that," I say, sincerely touched at her attempt to include me.

"You're rarely ever on your phone," says Flo randomly.

I push up my glasses. "I don't need it for much."

Flo gasps dramatically, clutching a hand over her heart. "You did *not* just say that. Phones are what help me survive! I'd have died ten years ago if I didn't have a phone!"

"You didn't have one ten years ago," I cut in.

She rolls her eyes. "That's not the point," she says. "What I'm telling you is, teenage girls *live* because of their phones. That's how we communicate with the hot boys around us. That's how we plan parties and outings and trips and fun times. You won't be included if you're not always texting or sending emails or making phone calls. You won't understand conversations if you're not scrolling through social media all the time and reading all the posts and memes."

"My friends don't talk about things like those," I say.

"If you want to make more friends, then you need to." Florence closes her eyes, like she's pretending to be exasperated with me. "You're not really the out-going sort," she says, "You're too shy. But if you ever do want to meet someone new, you're going to have a hard time, especially since you know almost nothing in the teenage world. You don't go to parties—"

"I did last month."

Flo snaps open her eyes and gawks at me. "That was a boring old people party. I'm talking about the crazy teenage parties that are put on while the host's parents are gone and the music blasts the house, and you make out with hot boys in quiet corners—"

"You're right," I say, interrupting her. "I don't do that. Because I don't like that kind of stuff."

"But it's fun!" she protests.

"For you."

"I'm sure you would like it if you came to one," Florence says encouragingly. "My best friend Ana is throwing a wild party during spring break in three weeks, and she said she wanted me to bring you because she wants to meet you. I think it would be great if you came, Venice. You could meet all my friends! And I promise not to embarrass you again."

I hold her gaze for an entire minute. The only sounds in the house are our breaths, the wind blowing against the house and making it creak—it has suddenly gotten fiercely windy outside—and the distant *thud* while Roman does whatever he's doing. Probably throwing something.

"You still don't want to come?" She sounds a little wounded.

I shake my head. "Sorry to disappoint, Flo, but I'm not party material. I'm sure I'd get really bored an hour into the party."

She sighs. "That's too bad."

"Tell your friend—tell Ana that if she wants to meet me, I'm available at lunchtime," I say, standing up. I grab my plate and move to the sink, washing my things just like I'd cleaned Nate's cuts.

"Venice."

I turn and raise my eyebrows. "Yes, Flo?"

She hesitates, then says, "Just so you know, you're not a lame sister. You're actually pretty cool. And though my friends might think otherwise because you chill with weirdos, I know I'll always think you're…an excellent person. Despite you not doing the same things as I do."

I blink at her in shock. Those are the nicest things she has *ever* told me.

"You're welcome," she says, a faint smirk settling over her face. She gets up from the table and leaves, ever-present phone in her hand.

Our argument the day of Goldbeck's party has strengthened our relationship.

Ever since she learned my view of her world, and I learned her view of mine, we've been getting along much better. Sometimes, at school, she will pass me in the hallway and call out a greeting or give my hand a squeeze as she walks by.

I'm better friends with all my siblings now except Roman, who seems determined to refuse any kindness I offer. He's going through a hard time in life, and I'm sure it's worse because Dad isn't around and Roman is the oldest boy in our family and Mom doesn't pay much attention to him, but he doesn't try very hard to get on our good side.

Talking about Roman...

I glance out the window as I dry off my dishes. I can't see him in the forest. I can hear him hitting something with whatever he is flinging at it. He's probably using the trees as targets.

I wipe my hands on my jeans and exit the kitchen, entering the cool dusk outside. It's not cold enough to go hunt for a jacket, but I still find myself shivering slightly as I cross the yard to reach the forest. I have to climb over the chain-link fence separating our lawn from the trees, and doing it brings back memories of when I'd scrambled over it while Rupert and Quentin were chasing after me. I shudder again, this time not from the cold, and land on my feet on the other side of the fence.

I find Roman standing in the middle of the woods, where the light is almost completely blotted out. I can barely see.

"Hey," I say.

Roman doesn't budge. "Piss off."

"What's wrong?" I ask, ignoring him. He only says things like that to us nowadays. He rarely communicates with us in acceptable language. Mom isn't happy with his new vocabulary. She blames it on his friends.

"Go away."

I don't. I stay there, goosebumps prickling my arms. I'm cold but refuse to let it get to myself.

Roman picks up a rock from a pile on the ground and hurls it at the nearest tree. It hits the bark and bounces off, only chipping away a small piece of wood.

This is what he's been doing for days?

He throws another rock. "Stupid," he mutters, not clarifying what or who is stupid.

I step up next to him and select a rock. When he throws his, I mirror the action, though his rock hits the tree and mine doesn't even reach it. I'm not good at throwing.

"Don't bend your elbow when you draw back your arm," he instructs. "Keep it straight until you release."

I obey, and my second rock strikes the tree, though it is only a glancing blow.

"Let go before your hand comes level with your shoulder," he continues. "Your rocks are going lower and not as far because you're holding onto it for too long."

Thunk. My third rock hits a tree I wasn't aiming for. I grin while Roman laughs at my lack of skill.

"Here, watch me." He slides a large, smooth rock onto his palm, turning it over and over in his hand. He draws back his arm, then hurls the rock with all his strength at the target tree. I notice he releases it while his arm is still in the air above his shoulder.

The rock slams into the tree, driving a deep gash into the bark before it drops to the forest floor.

"Good shot," I compliment. Poor tree, I think.

Roman grins back at me. He seems to be in a better mood than just two seconds ago. "Lots of practice," he explains. "Now. You try."

I follow his instructions, and in the steadily-darkening outside, we work on perfecting my aim. My arm is soon sore and quickly it's too dark to see, but I don't want to go in yet, because I'm slowly getting onto Roman's good side and he might open up to me. So I turn on the flashlight on my phone and use it to light up the area around us.

"We've got to go collect them all," Roman says, gesturing to the rocks that are scattered around the forest. "There should be twenty-three of them. I counted them."

"Okay." I help him retrieve the rocks, and once we have them all, Roman goes back to throwing them.

"Did you know that Marc stopped by today?"

He says it like it's a passing thought, careless and by-the-way.

"Marc came over today?" I repeat, shocked. "What for?"

Roman shrugs. "I was in the kitchen getting a snack when I heard footsteps upstairs. I didn't think anyone was home, so I called out, and Marc walked down and said Mom had asked him to get something for a client of hers that she'd left at home. He had totally missed it on the coffee table in the living room. He's going blind."

"Why did Mom need him to rummage through our house to find something for her client? That's really weird."

"It was some puzzles that she doesn't want Siena and Pompeii fighting over and losing the pieces too. And Marc said he was doing something for her so she didn't have to." Roman shrugs. "I thought it was nice of him. He's an altruistic kind of guy."

Did Roman just use the word altruistic? I roll my eyes. I would never call Marc that.

"Unlike Dad ever was," he continues. "And it's pathetic how this stupid drama has happened because of Dad. Mom forcing us to move here, Mom falling for Marc, Mom getting drunk and, finally, Dad dying. I think living in Virginia has been bad luck." He flings another stone. "Venice, do you think Dad would still be alive if we hadn't moved here?"

I hesitate. "Um…" The sudden change from Marc to Dad, and that Roman is talking like this, has unsettled my mind.

"Actually, I shouldn't ask you." He scoffs. "Out of everyone, you were the least sad about Dad's death. You got up and left right after you read the text from Grandma Ferrari. You just walked away from us all. Are you even sad?"

I purse my lips. Should I tell him?

"Dad's the whole reason our family split up," Roman continues. "Florence started her little rebellion against Mom, Pompeii and Siena fought—and still do—every day over ridiculous things like pouring salt on the slugs that show up after a rainstorm. And you…" he turns and stares at me in the dim light. "You stayed the same, I guess. Very, *very* bossy."

"Thank you."

Roman smirks. Then it slides off his face as he remembers what we are talking about. "Sometimes," he says, "I wonder if Dad is alive. His death seemed really abrupt."

I swallow. "Roman…"

"Yeah?"

"That's why I haven't been sad," I say, wrapping a curl of my hair around my finger. I need something to do with my hands. "I don't believe that Dad is dead, and I think have proof—"

"Venice! Roman! Mom's home!"

Flo's yell startles both of us. He and I exchange looks, then he takes a step closer to me and whispers, "What do you mean?"

"Grandma Ferrari sent me a video of the accident," I whisper back to him. "After I watched it, and showed it to…someone else, we agreed that Dad isn't dead. There's no way he is."

Roman is having quite a hard time absorbing this information. "But…I want to see the video. And can you tell me everything about the accident? I want to see for myself."

"Of course. I'll send you the video."

"Venice! Roman!" This time it's Mom that is calling for us.

We share another long look.

"Don't tell anyone my suspicions, all right?" I say. "This is a serious matter. Mom or Florence can't find out and...either get their hopes up or totally shut me down."

Roman nods. "Got it. I won't tell anyone."

I breathe a sigh of relief. "Thank you."

We walk back together—he jumps the fence while I take a second longer to climb over—and don't say a word. But I feel his energy has changed from anger and depression to hope. He walks with more purpose than his usual slouch; his shoulders are rolled back, his stride long and firm.

"There you are," says Mom's voice.

I look up from the ground and see her in the doorway to the kitchen, her arms crossed. The yellow light surrounding her makes her form seem dark, but her bright hair glints red and ruins the effect.

"Hey, Mom," I say, and Roman mumbles the greeting, too.

She ushers us inside the warm kitchen, closing the door behind us. "What were you doing out there in the cold?"

Roman freezes. I don't think he wants Mom to know that he has been throwing rocks at the trees.

I answer for him. "Talking."

"Well," Mom says slowly, looking between us, "I'm glad you were talking. Sorry I interrupted."

"It's alright," I say simply, though I wish she hadn't interrupted. I was finally telling one of my siblings about Dad.

Mom uncrosses her arms. She's exhausted. "Did you guys have some dinner?"

"I had leftovers," I say.

Roman mumbles something. He sure is in a mumbling mood.

"There's some ravioli, Roman," Mom says invitingly, pointing to the fridge. "It's better for you than those cans of soda. I think you spilled some on the floor, because it's terribly sticky."

I grimace. I guess I'd missed a spot when cleaning up after Nate had left.

"Whatever," Roman mutters, moving towards the fridge. He's faking his exasperation. I can see in his aura that he's sparkling with excitement. He's wondering about Dad.

"Why did you have Marc come over?" I ask Mom carefully, not wanting her to get offended.

She blinks. "Oh. He came today? I was expecting him to stop by when I was here. Well…You see, he lives near this old client of mine, and I offered the woman some of our puzzles that we don't use any more, and instead of me having to drive them out to her, Marc said he could do it the next time he stopped by. I wonder why he came by when I was gone." She dismisses his visit with a shrug. "What did you do while we were gone, Venice?"

Remembering our conversation before she'd left, I hold out my hand and say, "That'll be six dollars."

She gapes at me for half a second. Then her expression clears as she, too, recalls our brief talk. "Should I go ask Florence, then?" she wonders. "Flo will be happy to tell me anything concerning you and a certain…person."

I scowl. Why did she immediately assume I was with Nate? But—if she asks Florence, my twin will definitely confirm that I was.

"Florence has nothing to tell you," I say stubbornly, hoping I can reach my twin first and beg her not to spill any information about my afternoon and Nate and me.

"What, do you?" asks Mom.

I sigh heavily. "Fine. Yes, I hung out with my friend. Was I not supposed to? Should I have stayed home instead and knitted you a nice sweater?"

Mom smiles, her exhaustion slipping away for a second at my sarcasm. "Venice," she says, hugging me so tightly my glasses dig into my face, "I'm glad you have friends you can hang out with."

I hug her for a minute longer, then gently back away. I fix my glasses. They probably have left indents in my flesh where the bridge pressed into my nose.

"All though," Mom continues, "I wouldn't mind a nice, knitted sweater."

"I don't know how to knit."

She pouts. "How disappointing."

As we both grin at each other, I feel that, just for this quick moment in our lives, I have succeeded in making Mom happy.

When I enter my room that night, ready to crash, Flo is waiting for me. She closes the door behind me and pushes me down on my bed, her hard glare so serious I worry about what she's going to tell me.

But then her expression crumbles, replaced by a wide smile that shows off all her teeth. I'm immediately even more wary.

"Venice," she whispers, "will you *please* tell me about you and Nate and what you did today?"

I frown at her.

"Please," she begs. "This is the first time you've so much as talked to a boy. I need to know so I can tease you."

"Why should I tell you if you're going to tease me?"

Flo grabs my hands, squeezing them. "Venice. I'm your sister. It's my job to tease you. You have teased me all my life about boys—"

"I'm sure I'm the only one who hasn't, actually," I cut in, but she decides to ignore me.

"Venice, please. I'm begging you. Please. I want to know about you guys and what's going on. You don't have to say anything about today, just your...relationship. If you have one. *Please*, Venice. I want to know." She gives me such a pleading look that I give up and sigh in resignation. I can't believe she got me so easily.

"What do you want to know?" I ask grudgingly. "There isn't much."

She sits next to me on the bed. "Um…Has he ever told you that he likes you?"

"Sort of."

"Do you think he likes you?"

"I don't know."

"Do you like him?"

I take a moment to answer, thinking it through. Yes, of course I like him, but should I let Flo know that? "Yeah, I do."

My twin's grin widens. "Has he ever told you he thinks you're beautiful?"

I squirm on my bed. I really can't believe I got myself into this mess. Why did I? "Not in those exact words."

She lets loose a squeal of excitement, hugging me around the middle so fiercely I can barely breathe. "When did he say that? Oh—I'll bet it was the day of that boring party you went to!"

"Yes," I admit wryly. "The same day you tricked me into going downstairs when he was over—"

"But look how it paid off!" she protests.

I roll my eyes. "Extreme mortification," I say. "It was extremely mortifying when he said…that."

Florence is giggling madly, her arms still around me. "What else has he told you?"

"Nothing of *that* sort," I reply.

"How disappointing." She leans back slightly. "Has he ever flirted with you?"

I pull a face, ready to make some disgusted response, but I stop myself as I remember earlier today. Did that count as flirting? He told me flirting was uncomfortable. Though it was Flo's flirting, not mine…I've never flirted with him before.

I think.

"Hello?" Flo waves her hand in front of my face. "You going to continue?"

I shake my head to clear myself of my thoughts. "Uh…I don't

think Nate has ever flirted with me. And if he has, then I didn't recognize it."

"How lame." Flo sighs deeply. "Have you gone on any dates?"

"Educational."

She groans. "That's even more lame. Educational dates are officially the worst. There isn't any making out."

I hide a smile, though what she's said causes my heartbeat to increase.

"Wait." Flo locks gazes with me, her eyes holding an unspoken question. I don't want her to voice it, but she does. "Has he kissed you?"

I bite my lip and don't answer.

Pointless; she immediately knows what my silence means.

Florence literally screams, hugging me tight again. My ribs creak, and I'm reminded of Mandy's powerful bear-hugs, similar to the one Flo is giving me now. I try to push my sister away, but she squeezes tighter while words spill out of her mouth in a jumble of happiness.

"I am *so* jealous!" Flo finally releases me, falling back on my bed. "It's so unfair that the only boy I want is obsessed with you."

"Stop saying things like that," I say, growing embarrassed. It's annoying to hear her speaking this way about Nate.

She raises an eyebrow at me. "Why? Can't handle the truth?"

I take a deep breath, my ribs sore from her embrace. "Flo, you don't even know Nate personally. Why do you talk about him like that? Like—like you're engrossed with only his looks and have to have him otherwise everything is unfair?"

"I don't talk about him like that," she says. I give her a sharp look, and she corrects her statement. "Okay, I guess I do. But he's a handsome boy, and I'm attracted to handsome boys—"

"This is why your relationships don't last long, Florence," I say earnestly. "Because you only care about how they look, not how they act or what they are like. The boys you pick—sure, they're undoubtedly attractive, but they're shallow and only care for what *you* look like."

"And Nate isn't like that?" Flo asks sarcastically.

I blink. "You really don't know him at all."

She releases a pent-up breath. Her shoulders slump and she drops the "popular girl" posture. "Venice…You're right about my boyfriends. I only choose them for their looks. I don't pay attention to their personality and what they're like. I mostly just care if they're a good kisser or not. There have been some boys who were *terrible*, so I dumped them before we were even officially together, and I didn't even get to know like, his favorite color. Or whatever crap we're supposed to know about each other if we're a…a couple."

"Favorite color?" I give myself a shake, waking my mind again. "That's not what I meant. It's just—Flo, please don't take offence at this, but I'm pretty sure that your different relationships with different boys have gone wrong because of how you operate. You choose popular boys, the ones girls fawn over at school, and only be with them to make others jealous and you seem more popular."

Flo sits up, opens her mouth to contradict me, then stops. She slowly nods her head. "Yeah," she says in a small voice. "It's true."

"Have you ever considered renouncing your popularity?" I ask, a hint of amusement in my voice.

She looks over at me. "I-I actually have," she admits quietly. "Whenever I see you laughing with your friends at lunch, I wonder what it would be like to not always have people staring at me, judging me, sizing me up, and me caring. I wonder what it would be like to just be myself. To not constantly be worrying that my lipstick has stained my teeth—because that's a big concern to me. To not be forced to laugh at the terrible jokes Harrison Miller tells because if I don't, he might get offended and make me sit somewhere else. You have it easy, Venice. You don't have to bear the stress that I do. You can just be yourself."

"You can, too," I say. I take her hand and give her a squeeze. "Flo, you can't let other kids control your life. You can be free like me. You can choose your friends, not faking friendship with the popular kids so people look at you and think, *Wow, she's popular.*"

"Venice..." she growls in the back of her throat, sounding like Siena. "You really don't understand how I survive because of my popularity. I want to give it up sometimes, but then I remember just how much fun I have and that kids look at me and think I'm beautiful and have it all."

"But, Flo," I say. "You don't need random kids telling you you're beautiful to believe it."

She stares at me, long and hard, then nods. "You're right."

"Sure, you have fun with your friends," I continue. "But it comes with a price, right? You're not allowed to act how you want to act—you have to act like them. You have to be like them so they don't kick you out of their clan. You have to say similar things to what they say, otherwise they look down on you. It's ridiculous, Flo. They're limiting your abilities. They're forcing you to be a person you're not. What if you set the tone? What if you lead out on changing the way you view and treat other people?"

She's quiet as she takes this in. Her aura has lost some of the brilliant red of her passion—it's now a rose color that shows how she's working hard to keep her temper in check, to keep the mean things from spilling out like they used to. She's managed to take hold of some serious self-control. She has changed so much from the Florence she was when we first arrived here in Virginia.

I think it has helped her. Not knowing as many people; not frequently going places with her no-good boyfriend Kent who didn't care at all for her; not spending her time trying to ruin Mom's life instead of making her own life more fulfilling.

Virginia has helped me a lot, despite the danger and all that. I have friends who enjoy my company and like me. My twin doesn't hate my guts any more. I feel more comfortable, more relaxed, here, but only when I'm safe and not being hunted. I'm glad we aren't still in California, because I would never have met Nate.

Or Mandy or Elijah, for that matter.

But mostly Nate. I wouldn't have been able to help him—well, sort of help him—and I wouldn't have been able to realize that there are really good people out in this world that are mistreated and beaten and scorned but still get up and continue on with life and don't complain once.

"Venice…" Flo sucks in a deep breath. "You're right. Again. Like you so often are. I don't need the popular kids controlling my life. I can choose to do what I want to do, who I want to be friends with, what I want to say. And I don't have to care about what people think of me. I'm my own self. I'm not some girl who can easily be manipulated by a handsome face."

I smile. "Good. It makes me happy to hear that."

She gives me another hug, and I squeeze her back, and we sit there for a moment before she mumbles, "Did you mess with my jewelry box?"

"Um…no. Why?"

"I was putting away the things I bought earlier at the mall and I noticed someone had ruffled up my jewelry. I don't mind if Siena wants to borrow a bracelet or something, but she needs to be more respectful of my belongings."

We sit in silence for a few minutes, and I find I'm tired, ready to actually go to bed.

"I miss having nightly talks with you," I tell Flo.

She smiles. "Yeah, well now you don't have to sit and listen to me blab on and on about boys. You can contribute. And this doesn't mean that I'm not allowed to flirt with Nate, does it?"

She does mean it.

I hope she doesn't.

I scowl at her and she laughs, hugging me a fourth time. "Just teasing you!" she says. "Just teasing."

471

"You'd better be," I reply.

"Don't worry." She pulls back an inch and sees the look in my eyes. Understanding passes between us. "We both know he never gives me a second glance. He's yours."

I push her away, playfully. "That's not what I meant."

"Then what did you mean?" She giggles, nudging me in the side with her elbow. "That I'm not allowed to steal him from you? What if I do? Will you hate me for the rest of eternity?"

"No." I roll my eyes.

Flo stops giggling. "Wait, really?"

I nudge her back. "Because it's never going to happen."

She raises an elegant eyebrow. "Yeah, right. You know when he said you were beautiful?"

"He didn't say that *exactly*," I say, hedging.

She tosses her hair. "Whatever. Anyway, since he said that you are beautiful, that means he thinks I am beautiful, too."

I stare at her.

"We're identical!" she says.

I groan and throw my pillow at her. "Go away, Florence."

Laughing, she leaves our room.

FORTY-FIVE

The next morning is rushed. I wake up late, having been exhausted when I finally went to bed. I get up ten minutes before I have to leave for school, and Flo is hogging the bathroom and Roman is using the other, so I have to sneak into Mom's bedroom to use the one in there. She's still asleep—she was up late talking to Grandma Ferrari on the phone, who doesn't mind the three hour difference as much as Mom.

My breakfast is hurried; I barely manage to pack the lunch I probably won't eat when the clock reaches seven-thirty. I have to go, or I'll be late for school and late for Nate.

Will he come by today? I hope he does.

I quickly pack my backpack, hesitating at the reminder of my ring. It's been hiding in my favorite book for the last three weeks while Hubris Jargon and Sleepy Gumption have left me alone, but should I take it with me? Just to keep it safe?

Then I nix the idea. My ring has been safe here at home for three weeks; why should this week be any different?

I lace my shoes, tying them as tight as I can. I hate loose laces. They unravel and I trip over them and somehow shove my sandwich up someone's nose. I smirk at the memory; it doesn't bother me anymore. Sure, it's embarrassing, but I'm no longer in California. And I'm glad I'm not.

Changing my smirk to a soft smile, I swing my backpack onto

my shoulder and head downstairs. I pass Flo as she finally leaves the bathroom—she gives me a bright smile in return—and I'm glad our relationship is secure. I haven't forgotten all the mean things she has said to me, but I'm not thinking back on them or wondering if they're true. I know they aren't. They still sting a little, some of them, but I have learned to forgive her.

Arriving at the front door, I peer outside to see if Nate is coming up to our house. The sidewalks are bare and empty. The sun is gradually rising above the treetops, but the sun seems sleepy and is taking forever. No one is out and about yet, except for a few cars on the road.

I'm worried as I check the time. Nate is a few minutes late. He's rarely late.

I don't expect the crushing disappointment that hits me when another thought ignites.

He might not be coming today.

I glance out the window again, at the empty sidewalks, empty yards, empty street.

But it isn't empty...

A huge black SUV comes rolling down the street, moving quite leisurely, seeming either unsure where it's going or too lazy to speed up and reach its destination. I shrink back behind the safety of my door, but peek out to see how the SUV doesn't have a license plate on the front. And there's a flash of brilliant orange through the windshield.

I hold my breath as the SUV drives by carelessly, threatening me. My heart is beating a steady tattoo in my chest as I wait until the coast is clear, until Hubris Jargon is gone.

With a roar of the engine, the SUV vanishes around the bend in our street, out of my view.

I let out my breath, unpeel myself from the door.

So much for them leaving me alone.

I look outside again, finally spotting a familiar lone figure coming towards me from the opposite direction of the SUV, hands in his jacket pockets. My heart aches at the sight of him.

"I'm leaving now!" I yell into the quiet house.

I have to force myself not to run up to Nate and throw my arms around him. Instead, I calmly walk down to the end of my driveway and pretend like this is any normal day where we're simply walking to school together.

He looks the same as he did yesterday: tired, stressed out, worried. Yet he still manages a smile. "Good morning, Venice," he says, the sound of his voice making my palms start to sweat. I focus on his messy hair instead of his beautiful clear blue eyes.

"Good morning," I say. I'm so happy to see him that I even forget about the SUV for a moment.

Nate returns my smile so warmly that I'm brave enough to loop my arm through his, and it feels so natural.

Then I remember. "D-did you see him? Did you see Hubris Jargon as he drove past?"

"No." He's shocked. "When was this?"

"J-just a second ago." I squeeze my eyes shut. "He drove by and slowed down when he passed my house. I'm certain he knew I'd be out walking or at least watching. I'm so glad you're with me. What if he comes back around?"

He is quiet for a little while, taking this in. "Do you think your dad is mixed up in all of this? It seems like something has happened to get things going again."

I bite my lip and stare down at the sidewalk, not trusting myself to speak. It's been quiet these last few weeks. I'd allowed myself to believe the danger had passed.

"Come on." His gloved hand covers mine in the crook of his arm. "Let's stay aware, but not dwell on it. We've got to get to school, and that's what we should be worrying about right now."

A half-smile curves at my lips. "Yeah."

We walk in the direction of where Jargon disappeared, and I

expect him to be waiting for us when we come round the bend. However, there's no one on the street, no one at the stop sign, no one lingering on the road, ready to threaten me or demand my ring.

There's silence between us as we walk, and it isn't until we're out of sight of my neighborhood and we're surrounded by the looming trees to both our left and right when I stop and disengage from Nate, tugging his glove off one of his hands.

"You changed the bandaging," I note.

"I thought it would make you glad."

"M-hm." I unwrap the bandage, finding his hand in better condition than yesterday. The cut down his palm isn't bleeding, but a quick movement might open it again.

"I can't decide," Nate says, continuing to speak in his cheerful tone, "which stage is the most painful. If they hurt the most right after I get them, if they hurt the most the day after, or if they hurt the most two days after, when they're terribly stiff."

"That isn't funny at all, Nate."

He frowns at me. "What's wrong with you? You normally laugh at every pathetic thing I say."

"I can't laugh at your pain," I say tenderly. I take his other hand and examine it, too.

He nods slowly. "Well, I'll have to be more clever with my jokes, then. "

"Good luck with that," I say, teasing, and he assumes a hurt look that provokes a pale smile from me. I bandage his hands again and let him pull on his gloves before continuing on.

I don't grip his hand tightly, knowing it will be painful for him, but he holds onto me like everything is normal and he isn't hurting right now. It feels weird to be holding onto his gloved hand. I want to be touching his real hand—though he's wearing bandages underneath his glove, so I won't even be feeling his actual skin.

"Do you know how to knit?" I ask randomly.

Nate shakes his head. "Um...no."

"That's too bad." I pretend to pout. "I don't, and my mom was hoping for a nice, knitted sweater, so I wanted to make her one. Unfortunately, no one I know will teach me how."

"How many people have you asked?"

I let a smile surface. "Just you. I'll need to ask around if I really do want to knit that sweater for her."

We walk on, not talking. The school building is just ahead of us; I can hear kids chatting excitedly. Some are on the sidewalks, merging with the crowds near the doors—Nate and I aren't the only ones who walk to school, though we probably come the farthest.

That reminds me that I still have more questions for him.

"About lunch," I say, startling him with yet another bizarre statement. "You rarely eat anything."

Nate nods. "Yes. I don't exactly eat lunch."

"It is probably the most-skipped meal of the day."

He gives me a curious look. "But you don't eat breakfast."

I frown. "What?"

"When I come to your house," he says, "your kitchen is a hive of activity while all of your siblings make their lunches. And you sometimes don't get to eat anything because it's too crowded or they're arguing so loudly I can hear them outside, and it must be worse for you."

"Yeah, it is." I smirk. "Yesterday, I went down to get something to eat right before I took the younger kids to the library, and Siena was double-toasting two pieces of bread that Mom didn't want."

"Double-toasting?"

My smirk turns into a big grin. "Burning," I clarify. "Scorching. Toasting until the bread turns black."

"Ah."

We cross the street to the school, and I first check to make sure there aren't any SUVs preparing to hit me before darting across with Nate.

"You never told me," I say as we join up with the other kids, "why you don't eat lunch. Is it because you don't have enough food?"

"Pretty much." Nate squeezes around a group of kids, wincing as one of his cuts is bumped. "I don't buy snacks. Or lunch things. I'm more focused on fresh fruits and vegetables and meats and grains. Occasionally, I'll get a box of protein bars, but Mandy ends up eating them—I somehow can't unwrap the dang things while wearing these fingerless gloves. I think they're too slippery?"

I shouldn't laugh, but I do anyway. "That's really sad."

"Not for Mandy."

I laugh again and Nate grins at me. And this time I let myself notice how incredibly handsome he is, and how his lips really are perfectly curved, and his dimples are adorable, and he's been blessed with an amazing personality, even though he has suffered pain and abandonment his entire life.

I'm sure we could have stayed there forever, just staring at each other, but someone yells my name and the moment between us is broken. I turn to the source of the sound, immediately being tackled as Mandy slams into me with her usual bear-hug.

"You're finally here!" she says, crushing me with her powerful upper-arm strength.

"Hi, Mandy," I gasp out.

Mandy backs away, thankfully, and beams at me. "Venice, guess what I did with Elijah yesterday."

"You played video games," I say, and feel Nate smile.

She shakes her head vigorously, her dark shoulder-length hair flying around her face.

"You visited the arcade?"

"No."

"Then I don't know what."

Nate speaks up. "You went on a picnic and made out the entire time, so your food was eaten by ants."

Mandy giggles hysterically in reply. "I *wish.* No, we cleaned up his house while his mom was out on a date with his dad—who came back on Saturday and is here for like a *week*—and we made a huge mess in the kitchen because I wanted to make this cake and Elijah let me."

"And *then* we made out," Elijah finishes for her, appearing at her side.

I laugh as she blushes. "Sounds like fun," I comment. "I babysat my two youngest siblings yesterday."

"And I worked on my garden," says Nate.

"How boring," Mandy says. "You guys should have been over at Elijah's with us. That was *so* awesome. And we didn't even play a single minute of video games."

"You finally figured out that there are far more entertaining things?" I tease.

She scowls at me. "Oh, be quiet. I'm not saying I won't play—" Her five-minute alarm on her phone suddenly goes off, startling all of us. "Dang!" she shrieks. "I *hate* this thing!" There has to be a backstory to it, one she hasn't disclosed yet. I should ask. "Time to go," she says. "See you all at lunch."

"Bye."

Elijah echoes my farewell, but I have already slipped away through the huge crowd of kids who don't seem like they want to go inside quite yet. I don't blame them. The sun has finally risen, filling the day with bright light that falls over everything around us, bathing it in yellow light. It's going to be a beautiful day.

"Wait—Venice."

I'll definitely wait. "Yeah?"

He pushes open the door into the school—I wonder if it hurts—and waves me in. "Today is the first time you have seen Jargon since the Valentine's Day party, right?"

"Correct." I weave through the packed hallways, spotting Flo talking to a tall boy near a row of lockers. I hope he's a nice boy. He's watching her, every move she makes, listening to every word she says, seemingly completely engrossed in her. He isn't familiar—I've never seen him. I don't think he's a popular boy.

"Who's that?" I ask, abruptly changing the subject. "Nate, do you know the boy Florence is talking to?"

Nate looks over my head at them. "Uh...Bradley something. I think. He's really quiet. Doesn't talk to many people. I'm surprised Florence is with him. She's not into people like him."

I nod. "Thank you. I just wanted to know if he was nice."

"He is. I think." Nate shrugs. "I've only exchanged brief words with him."

I catch Flo's eye and smile at her. She smiles back, and it's not strained or her look-at-me-I'm-beautiful smile. It's her natural one, if slightly nervous. Huh. This is a lot different from other times I've seen her talking to boys.

"Sorry," I tell Nate. "Go on. You were saying?"

He trails after me as I make my way to my homeroom. I have three minutes to get there, otherwise I'll be late. "I know I said we should let school distract us from worrying too much about those guys who want your ring, but we should be watchful. They might make another move soon."

"Right."

"Will you be extra careful?"

I stop outside my homeroom door and frown at him. "I am always careful," I say. At his obvious disbelieving expression, I add, "Normally."

"Venice—"

"Nate, I've been thinking," I interrupt. "What if I give them my ring? Won't all the danger stop then?"

He blinks. "Then you'd be giving them what they want."

"I love my ring," I say, "because my dad sent it to me for my birthday. And it reminds me of him. But he probably gave it to me on purpose, maybe to keep it from Sleepy Gumption or Hubris Jargon? If he knew people were after it, why would he put me in danger like that? What if I'm cherishing a gift from a father who only gave it to me to get throw those jerks off his own trail?"

"This is a new twist. Listen, maybe your dad sent you the ring because he knew you would keep it safe. I mean, he could have sent it to Florence, right? But he didn't. He sent it to you."

I go to respond, but the bell rings.

"You're going to be late to class," I say, glancing over at my homeroom behind me. "You need to go. We can continue later."

He dips his head, then turns to walk away.

"Nate."

He stops immediately and faces me, like he thought I would call him back. I reach forwards and press my fingers into his cheeks where his dimples show up when he smiles. "Did you know," I say, willing myself not to blush at the slightly-confused, slightly-concerned look he's giving me, "that your dimples make you look adorable?"

Then, surprised at my own impulsivity, I back away and quickly vanish inside the classroom.

FORTY-SIX

I have a hard time during my morning classes. I want everything to speed up and for it suddenly to be lunch.

Then I can see Nate.

As soon as the bell rings, I'm out of my classroom and heading for the cafeteria. Mandy appears at my elbow, already talking about something I missed the first half of.

"...and I told them I don't like anatomy, because chemistry is *so* much better, so they got offended and told our mom. And of *course* she had to agree with my stupid brothers—she's biased—but I think blowing up things is tons more fun than studying the human body." Mandy gags. "Bleh. You look at the pictures of all those thingies that live inside of you, and then you're like, ew, I never want to see those again, but it's too late; the pictures are like, imprinted in your mind. Get what I'm saying?"

"Uh, yeah. Sure."

"Have you *seen* the pictures of human bodies? The ones where it reveals your veins and organs and other gross things like that? Well, why do they always have to be of men? It's disgusting!"

I blink, not hearing half of what she's telling me. She talks too fast, doesn't pause to take a breath, and uses too many words so everything confuses me. I heard *human bodies, veins,* and *men.* That's all. But I love every minute of it.

"And then Dylan was like, chemistry sucks even though he's big into math, but I know he only said that since he flunked. He didn't turn in any assignments, yet he *still* got a perfect score, because Mom's on the parent-school-council thingy, and she bullied Dylan's chemistry teacher into changing his grades. That's cheating, I know, but none of the teachers or the principal objected. Now, when she did the same thing for Zac, who also failed chemistry—and also likes math—I got really mad and decided I was going to be really good at chem and show her that she doesn't have to change the scores if the student actually *tries*. And I have top grades. So I showed her."

I blink again. Picking through the new information I've just received, I say, "Is that why you like chem so much?"

"Yeah." She drags me into the cafeteria. "Because my brothers hate it and are terrible at it. I wanted to be good at something my idiotic no-good brothers weren't, so I worked really hard and succeeded. And I loved chem in the process. It was good for me. And then Nate started inviting me over to Elijah's house whenever he went, and I got really good at killing the video game players who suck—so pretty much everyone—and I developed a new skill. So I'm glad I'm nothing like my brothers. They'd never touch a video game to save their lives."

I think I'm correct. *So* is her favorite word.

"Mom corrupted them," Mandy continues, leading me around the tables towards our usual one. "She refused to allow any sort of video game in our house, so I'm really happy that Elijah let me borrow his when I go to his place. And that's all the time. Like, every day. Or whenever I can. And we don't always play games the entire time—like yesterday. We made that cake."

"And that giant mess," I reply, surprised I was able to squeeze something in.

Mandy nods energetically. "Oh, yeah. Big mess. You should have seen it, Venice. There was flour all over the counters and floor and microwave and oven and whatever other appliance is in the kitchen. I threw some flour at Elijah, and we had a really big flour-fight, which resulted in us both being covered in it. We looked like snowmen. In March!"

I smile. "I hope you took pictures! Sounds fun, Mandy."

"Oh, it was. And after was even better." Her voice drops. "You know, when we like, went outside and made out."

I bite my lip to prevent a laugh.

"I've always wanted to," she says in a more normal tone. "Ever since the day we had this party at his house for his sister's birthday. It was a few years ago. Two, I think. Anyway, Elijah's mom played some music, and we started to dance, but Elijah barely talked to me the entire time. And I think we might have gotten together then if he'd just opened his mouth and told me he liked me right then."

"You guys were fourteen."

"So what?" Mandy pulls me around another packed table. I catch a quick glimpse of Elijah's blond hair before someone shifts and he's out of my sight. "Anyway," Mandy says again, "I stormed away from him during the second song, because I was mad at him for not talking to me, and I regret that more than anything I've ever done."

"Aha!" I snap my fingers. "That's what it was! I knew you and Elijah both regretted the same thing, and I was right!"

She nods. "Yeah. It was that day. After that, we weren't great friends. Nate kept us all together. We probably would've gone our separate ways if he had left us alone. But I couldn't leave *Nate*— we're like, his only friends, and he deserves to have some. He's like, the nicest person in the world besides Mrs. Jenkins."

"Mm," I agree, finally spotting our table. Nate and Elijah are there, talking, but I'm sure it's Nate listening to Elijah talk, kind of like how it is with me and Mandy.

"You took your swell time," says Elijah, looking up when we approach.

"Mandy was geeking out about her love for chemistry," I reply.

"Oh." Elijah smirks. "No wonder you're late."

Mandy releases me and smacks him on the head. He yelps and turns to face her, scowling. He opens his mouth to speak, or to protest, but she grabs the front of his shirt and kisses him before he can say anything.

I roll my eyes and sit down next to Nate, who is grinning at our friends.

"It's worse when they win at their game," he whispers in my ear, his mouth so close his breath tickles my skin.

"How so?" I whisper back, firmly avoiding looking at him.

I feel his lips brush my cheek as he replies. "They do this until the round starts."

"Poor you." I open my backpack and dig through it, still not looking at him, but I don't move away from him. "I don't watch them. I'm too busy reading Mrs. Jenkins's mysteries."

"Getting any ideas?" He doesn't move away from me, either.

"Self-sacrifice." I find my lunch and place it on the table. "I can give myself up and have the bad guys torture me until the police come and arrest them all."

"That's a terrible idea."

I smile. "I can bait them. Leave my ring out for them to see, and when they come to steal it, have the police nab 'em then."

"That isn't as bad."

Mandy and Elijah finally break apart, and Nate pulls back a few inches so it doesn't look like we were too close.

"If I told you I was in love with you," says Mandy, her hands curled into Elijah's shirt, "would you believe me?"

I bury my face in my hands.

Elijah grunts.

"Okay," Mandy says. "I'm in love with you."

"Guys." Nate picks a grape from my lunch and throws it at Elijah, hitting him on the face and rebounding. I snatch it up before it can bounce onto the floor and become gross. "Not during lunch," Nate says. "Please."

Mandy sighs and releases Elijah, sinking down on the seat by him. "Why not?"

"It's extremely uncomfortable," Nate replies.

I hand Elijah the grape Nate had thrown. "You get to eat this as penance," I say.

He takes it and pops it into his mouth without paying attention to what he's doing. "You just ruined a perfect moment, Nate," he says after swallowing.

"I got here first," Nate points out. "If you want to…smooch, then *you* can leave."

Elijah groans. "Whatever."

I can't help but laugh, and so does everyone else.

"Nate," says Mandy, "since you're talking to us this week, can you tell us about those scars Venice mentioned?"

The abrupt change in subject and the new subject itself causes me to go still, so still. Nate stiffens and turns to me, questioning. I take a deep breath. "I told her a few weeks ago," I explain. "That day at Elijah's, remember?"

He looks at Mandy and Elijah, who are waiting expectantly. "Ah, it's a really long story, Mandy," he says nonchalantly. "Maybe later, and in a less public place."

Hidden from their view, I slip my hand into his. He needs to— he *should*—seize this opportunity to come clean and tell Mandy and Elijah why he hides underneath gloves and a jacket, why he only walks to school, why he rarely talks about his grandpa.

But he doesn't speak.

"You should tell them," I whisper. Mandy and Elijah—bless their short attention spans—are conversing about something else. They are easily distracted. But they are also good friends and they are willing to be patient. I also think they're hoping to resume what Nate interrupted; I see, out of the corner of my eye, Elijah put his arm around her waist.

"Nate." I return my gaze to him. "Please."

He hesitates. It's clear he doesn't want to discuss this in front of Mandy and Elijah. I'm done with my lunch anyway so I get up, and he comes along with me.

"We'll be right back, okay?" I tell Mandy, and she briefly catches my eye to nod before resuming her stare-fest with Elijah.

I snag my lunch off the table and pull Nate towards the trash cans near the back of the room. After making sure we're out of earshot, I turn to him and give him an expectant look.

"I-I can't tell them," he whispers. "Not right now. I just have this feeling that I should wait for a better time. But I promise I will tell them."

"I know you don't want your grandpa to get in trouble," I say quietly, dumping my uneaten, disgusting-looking honey-and-peanut-butter sandwich into the trash. I'm not in the mood for it any more. "But telling your best friends will help you. And you can trust them not to tell anyone."

"Have you ever known Mandy to keep something in?" His attempt to lighten things up helps ease the tension a little.

I gently retake his hand. "You aren't unloved, Nate. There are plenty of people who care about you. Mandy and Elijah do. Do you know what she was telling me earlier? She said that when she was fourteen, she and Elijah had a falling out and probably wouldn't have been friends if you hadn't kept all of you guys together. She said she couldn't leave you behind because you're her friend. So she stuck it out. She stayed with you and Elijah. She didn't go off and find new friends." I give him a small squeeze, not enough for it to hurt, just enough for him to get my point. "You can trust them. They're your friends."

Nate glances down at me. He has almost no emotion on his face—I can see exhaustion and strain. He's having a hard time fighting this battle. He wants to give in, but he doesn't know if it's a prudent idea.

"I promise to give it some thought. Just not right now, okay?"

I breathe in deeply. I relent, but I'm disappointed. "Okay."

He manages a weak smile, and that's when I notice the faint lavender streaks in his aura have become more pronounced. That makes me frown.

"Nate," I say suddenly but slowly, focusing in on that lavender, "you're afraid of something else, aren't you?" I'm still studying him, trying to figure it out. "It's not just what might happen if people know your secret. It's something else." I used to think he was scared of his grandpa, but the past few days have shown me that he only pities and cares for the old man.

His eyebrows lift. "You don't know? You, Venice, the master of emotion-reading, can't tell what scares me?"

He's teasing. I think.

I shake my head, curious.

"It's you," he admits quietly, and now *my* eyebrows rise up. "I was terrified that you would find out about..." His voice, low as it is, falters. He cuts a quick glance around us, making sure we're still far from anyone's prying ears. "And when you did find out, I realized I had hoped you would," he continues. "For six years, I tried to keep this a secret, and it wasn't until you entered my life that I thought maybe...well, anyway. Venice, did you know you can be quite convincing sometimes? I'm not used to letting someone have that kind of influence over me."

That's a nice way to put it. My siblings call it bossy. But my heart is pounding as he tells me more; we're slowly coming back to our table, and Mandy is giggling at what Elijah just said.

"My life would have gone on, normal in its own way, if I hadn't met you." Nate holds my gaze, anguish clear in his eyes. "I need time. I can't all of a sudden decide to tell everyone about something I've lived with my whole life. It's more complicated than all that."

How does he do that? I'm so certain I'm right about something, and then Nate patiently explains the way he sees things and now I'm ashamed of my assumptions.

"It must be so hard for you, Nate. Thank you for helping me to understand," I say repentantly. "Take your time. I suppose I just had it in my head that since you told me, you'd let the others know. I'm sorry. I was insensitive and irrational."

We've made it back to the table as I say these last words, and Elijah abruptly breaks away from Mandy to stare me down. "I can't believe you just said that," he says, glaring at me.

I freeze, thinking he has heard our conversation. Plus, I don't think I've ever seen Elijah angry. "What?"

"You said a curse word, Venice."

Did I? What did I say? At my blank look, he takes pity on me. "You said *irrational*," he explains. "I thought I said any reference to math is not acceptable at our table."

Ten whole seconds pass with me just staring at him. I have no idea what to do. I'm so relieved he hasn't overheard what Nate and I were talking about, only the last word.

And then I bark out a laugh, not being able to prevent it. I slam my emptied container on the tabletop and clutch my stomach, shaking with uncontrollable laughter. What Elijah said wasn't even very funny.

My friends all join in, even Nate.

"That was terrible!" Mandy cries joyfully, slapping Elijah across the back.

"No it wasn't!" He hugs her in reply, and they both hold each other while laughing their heads off. We're loud and obnoxious; I can feel the dozens of pairs of eyes belonging to the other kids in the cafeteria trained on us as we all make raucous noises.

"That seriously was terrible," I say, regaining control of myself. I run my hands through my curly hair, reminded, once again, that I haven't brushed it in quite a while.

"All my jokes are hilarious," Elijah protests, pulling away from Mandy. He keeps his arm around her, however, and she doesn't seem to mind. "And you liked that one. You laughed the loudest."

My cheeks feel hot as I take my seat. "Did you make that up on the spot? And since when do you pay attention to math? How did you remember irrational even is a mathematical concept?"

"I sucked at Algebra," he says, shrugging. "My mom had to help me. And when moms help with math, you tend to remember things better."

"That, and Mrs. Jenkins is an ace at math," Mandy puts in.

Elijah nods. "You're right."

I shake my head, bemused. I truly do have the weirdest friends, and I'm glad.

"Oh my gosh," Mandy says suddenly. "We have nine minutes left to eat. I didn't even get my food out! Why has the time gone by so fast?"

"You were making out for ten minutes," Nate says, having sat at my side.

She rolls her eyes. "It was eight and a half."

The nine minutes pass mostly in silence as they eat—of course, the kids all around us are loud, dispelling any quietness—and I am filled with love and appreciation for my friends. I don't have any remaining lunch since I got rid of it, and Nate didn't pack anything, per usual. But now I know why.

Mandy's alarm rings, startling us all. She groans and turns it off. "Are we doing anything this afternoon?" she asks as we pack up.

"I'm unavailable," Nate says quietly.

"Venice?" she pleads.

"Depends. If it's video games and Nate's not there, I'll have to pass."

"Guess it'll be just me and Mandy. Yes!" Elijah is using his loud voice again. "But seriously, Mandy, we should consider expanding our interests so Nate and Venice want to hang out with us more."

"Elijah, you would be willing to give up video games for Nate and Venice? Oh my gosh you are so hot right now." She looks like she's about to kiss him again, so I quickly gather up my belongings and get to my feet, Nate coming with me. I wave at Mandy, who waves back. "I'll see you later," I say, and turn and walk towards the exit.

I'm lost in my thoughts as Nate and I leave together, and I don't notice my twin until she's right in front of me.

"Venice!" she whispers, as if she doesn't want anyone hearing what she's about to say, though Nate's at my side. She cuts him a quick look before facing me again. "Venice, I think I'm in love. Like, actually. For the first time in my life."

"That's…awesome." Florence has never sought me out like this in public. I'm rather flattered. And she's clearly excited.

"His name is Bradley, and he's the nicest boy I have *ever* met." Flo latches onto my arm. "And guess what!"

"What?"

"He isn't a popular kid." She beams at me. "He's this quiet boy who rarely speaks, but he's really nice and he listens to everything I say. I met him on the bus this morning. I could have chosen to sit with this one girl, but then I saw him and remembered what you'd told me yesterday, and I decided that I wanted to get to know some of the less popular kids. The kids who blend in. Kinda like you."

I nod, encouraging her on.

"And I ate lunch with him," she continues. "Instead of hanging with my other friends who just criticize others, I talked with Bradley and learned all this stuff about him. Even his favorite color!"

At this, I smile, and I'm pretty sure Nate is smiling, too.

"I think I really truly like him." Flo glances over her shoulder. "Oh, he's in the hallway waiting for me. I've got to go. We have the same class after this. I never noticed, but it turns out our schedules are very similar! Destiny, I know." She grins. "I am destined to like him."

Then she skips away.

I watch her meet up with Bradley, who gives her a shy smile, and they look like they actually do like each other. I am so pleased for her. I wonder if Nate would ever look at me like that in public. He is much too bashful, but, then again, so am I.

"You were right," I tell Nate. "His name *is* Bradley."

"I have a class with him. It must be the only one Florence isn't in, because she has never shown up." He takes my hand, beginning to walk again. I guess he's not too shy to hold my hand in public. And I find that I'm not too shy to let him.

I look up at him. His hair keeps falling over his eyes. "You need a haircut," I say.

He frowns playfully, blinking madly and catching his lashes in his hair. "No, I don't."

"You can barely see."

"I can see just fine. Perfectly, actually."

I roll my eyes and look away from him. "So," I say, hoping to continue our friendly-talk, "how is Mercury?"

"Good." Nate twists around a group of kids congregated in the middle of the hallway. "He eats a lot, drools a lot, sleeps a lot." He shrugs. "The usual. I think he misses you because I found him sniffing the cinnamon I keep in the kitchen."

"How does that have anything to do with me?"

"You smell like cinnamon, remember?"

"Ah." Understanding dawns on me. "Well, it's really sweet that he knows what I smell like. And completely adorable."

Nate's smile is back.

"How is your grandpa?"

"He's...doing the same as always," Nate says quietly. "He didn't even look up from the TV when I left. But he ate plenty of dinner yesterday. All of it and more."

I push up my glasses. "That's good."

"And he only drank one bottle this morning. That I know of."

"Hey—Nathaniel!"

A boy rudely shoves me to the side so he can face Nate. I gag as the stench of cigarette smoke fills the air around us.

"You get your grandpa arrested yet?" the boy sneers.

Nate ignores him, first turning to me to make sure I'm not hurt—I'm not, I was able to catch my balance to not hit the floor—before facing Keller Jacobs again. At least, I *think* it's Keller. He's the only one that knows about Nate's grandpa, and the stink coming off him is faintly familiar. Months ago, when I'd first met him, I hadn't seen what he looked like because the room had no light. But now I know his features.

He's thin, short, and has a pinched face that reminds me of a rat. I hope he isn't a rat—he needs to keep Nate's secret.

"What do you want, Keller?" Nate asks calmly.

Keller Jacobs smirks. "Just wanna know if you're still a coward, Nathaniel. If you're still too scared to turn in your grandpa."

"I still am," Nate replies, then grabs my hand and pulls me away. "Sorry," he murmurs as we put as much distance between us and Keller as possible. "I wish he would leave me alone."

I stumble over my laces—which have, unfortunately, irritatingly come undone—and nearly trip. "Nate, slow down."

"Sorry," he says again, slowing.

I shake him off. "It's fine, fine." I crouch and begin tying up my shoes. "He certainly is an unpleasant boy."

"Unpleasant, indeed." Nate sighs and runs his hand through his messy hair. "You know what," he says, "you're right, Venice. I *do* need a haircut."

I laugh, and all the remaining tension in my stomach loosens up. I don't know if he changed the subject on purpose, or if he just voiced that admittance to cheer me up. "Florence would love to give you a trim," I say, pulling the laces tight. "And she's excellent at it, too."

"I'm good." Nate shivers. "The idea of being at her mercy with scissors and a razor is unnerving."

Grinning, I finish with my shoes and straighten out. "She would love it."

He shivers again. "No thanks."

"You're seriously the only boy I've known to refuse her," I say, not making any move to continue on our way to class.

"I've got my reasons," he says, holding my gaze.

I will myself not to blush, but I do anyway. "I don't like it when you tease me."

"Who says I'm teasing?"

My blush deepens. I open my mouth to reply when yet another boy comes up to us, this time addressing me. Or rather, who he thinks I am.

"Florence," he says, "you stood me up last night."

I blink. "I'm not Florence. I'm her twin sister. Venice. Florence is..." I scan the hallway, not seeing her. No wonder. She's hanging out with Bradley. "I'm not sure what class she has right now. She didn't mention any plans last night to me."

The boy gapes at me for a moment, then snaps his mouth shut and whirls away.

"Ugh." I stomp my foot. "I *hate* when people mistake me for my sister."

Nate lists his head. "You just stomped your foot."

"I'm angry."

"Obviously." He takes my hand and begins walking towards class. "How often do people think you're Florence?"

I heave a sigh. "All the time."

"Seems pretty annoying, yet fun. If I had an identical twin, I would use him to my advantage." Nate grins at me, his dimples showing. "Confuse and trick people, pretend to be my twin..."

I shrug my shoulders. "I guess it can be fun. At least you can tell us apart."

His grin reappears at full force. "Probably because I stare at you more than I stare at Florence."

"What is it with you today?" I ask, shocked. He's very...bold.

He pulls me to a stop outside the biology classroom. "What?

Am I not allowed to tease you, especially after this morning? Being open with you is surprisingly liberating."

I plunge into the room, a smile tugging at the corners of my mouth. I am prepared for the darkness that fills the classroom—I am *not* prepared for the empty room and empty seats all around me. I pause, Nate crashing into me at my sudden halt.

"Are we using this room today?" I ask.

He nods, his hair brushing against my forehead and cheek. "Yeah. I'm pretty sure."

I check the time on my phone, the dim light of my small screen blinding in the dark. "We have four minutes until class is supposed to start. Where is everyone?"

Right as those words come out of my mouth, a flood of kids stream in, all talking noisily with one another. Nate puts his hands on my hips and gently pushes me towards the chairs farthest from the windows, farthest from the door, farthest from the light.

"Mr. Castro is usually late," he says in my ear. "So we probably have six or seven minutes until class begins."

"Speaking about class…" I twist out of his hold and claim one of the chairs in front of me. "When are we going to finish our report on orangutans? We have two weeks left."

Nate sits next to me, drops his backpack on the floor with little ceremony. "We've been too busy keeping you alive."

I snort. "I'll be dead if I don't turn in this assignment."

He grins, and I only know he does because I'm watching his mouth. "You think Mr. Castro might hunt down and make his students extinct if they don't do what they're required to?" He pretends to think about it. "I guess that's one way to make sure you have no failing students. Just get rid of them and leave the others."

I give him a playful shove. "How much have we done, again?"

"The outline." Nate nudges my glasses up my nose—they're slipping down a little. "And that's all."

I groan. "Great."

"I wonder when is Mr. Castro will get here," Nate muses quietly, his soft breath touching my face.

"I don't know." I look around and can barely discern the dark shapes of the other kids who are taking their seats or fighting over Mr. Castro's seat in the center of the room. No one is near us; they all seem to want to sit by the door or the covered windows, close to some light. I don't mind the dark, I don't mind not being seen, and I don't mind being left alone with Nate.

"He's going to be tardy." Nate is still talking quietly, as if he doesn't want any of the other kids to hear us. Pointless. They're all too far away.

I face him again, having a hard time distinguishing his features. "We could count him absent." I tip forward and press my lips to the spot on his right cheek where I think one of his dimples forms.

Nate stiffens, and I instantly freeze, worried I'd done something he didn't appreciate. Then he slips his arm around my waist, pulling me slightly closer. He turns his head so his mouth brushes mine.

All the heat coming from him unfreezes me within a fraction of a second. I lean into him, my hands sliding into his hair.

"Venice."

I don't pull away. "Mm?"

"What if I told you that Mr. Castro has an enforced no-kissing-in-class policy?"

"Class hasn't started yet."

"True enough." He still breaks away, rests his forehead against mine. "I really do like you."

I disentangle my fingers and move my hands to his neck. His skin is so soft, just like his hair. "I like you, too."

"Thank the trees."

I finally put some short distance between us, humor spreading through my entire body. "I've never heard you say that before."

He laughs. "You said it a long time ago. I never forgot. Why do you say it?"

"It's just my language," I reply.

"Blessed Hallelujah is part of your language." He kisses the tip of my nose. "Same with Holy Mother Earth."

I smile as his lips brush my cheek. "You remember them all."

"They're bizarre," he says, "which make you unique. I have to say, you have a much cleaner mouth than my grandpa does."

"Nate, are you actually unavailable this afternoon, or did you just say that?"

"Sorry. I *am* unavailable, regrettably. I have to teach myself how to knit."

I laugh and kiss him on the mouth because I can. "Great. Then you can mentor me."

"Seriously, though, I have work." He pulls back, taking away his hands and his warmth and his comfort.

I retract my hands from his neck. "What if Hubris Jargon starts things up again?"

"That's always on my mind. Venice, please be careful." Nate shifts in his chair so he's facing the class, not me anymore. I see why he's doing this now. There is a familiarly-shaped figure in the middle of the room, talking with several kids. On the man's head is his signature fedora. I still don't know what Mr. Castro looks like in the light—I have only seen him in the dark.

"I promise I'll be more careful. And you *will* stop by my house tomorrow morning for school, right?"

"Of course." He sounds surprised by the question.

I breathe a sigh of relief. "And you'll change the bandages on your hands and arms?"

"Of course."

"And you'll tell Mandy and Elijah...You'll tell them everything in the next few of days?"

Nate reluctantly replies, "When the time is right, of course."

Mr. Castro claps his hands, ending the swelling chatter. "Hello, everyone!" he says cheerfully, and several of the kids yell it back at him, earning a wave from him. "How many of you are done with your reports?"

A collective groan rises up, dispelling the cheerfulness of their earlier greetings. I smile.

"None of you?" Mr. Castro sounds disappointed, but I'm sure he's faking it. He's probably so used to getting this response. "Tanya and Caleb! What about you two?"

There's a pause, then a girl answers. "It turns out aardvarks are really hard to research."

My smile widens.

"I wondered who had chosen them," Nate whispers in my ear.

Mr. Castro spins around, searching for someone else he can pick on. I don't know how he can recognize any of his students in the dark, but he manages to and asks several other teams how they're progressing on the assignment. Much to his chagrin, not a single student has finished their report. It makes me glad to hear Nate and I aren't the only ones not finding enough time to sit down and write a ten-page essay.

"You guys are really letting me down," says Castro, shuffling through a sheaf of papers in his briefcase. "All right. I'll be the generous teacher I am and give you an extra week." He pauses, expectant, and isn't disappointed to hear a couple kids cheer half-heartedly. I wonder how often he does this and if it's each time. "So—not this Tuesday, but the next. The week before spring break. Can you all finish before then? I'm talking specifically to you, Keller. Nate isn't your partner this time and won't do your report for you."

I feel the temperature in the classroom spike. Beside me, Nate stiffens. He doesn't appreciate Mr. Castro calling him out like that. And I don't think Keller does, either.

"Why did he say that?" I whisper to Nate as Keller yells back at Mr. Castro saying he's perfectly capable of completing assignments within the given time.

Nate sighs. "Because I've done that more than once."

498

I stare down at my lap in the darkness, not listening or paying attention to Mr. Castro as he talks on, ignorant of the tension he has just created.

Taking a deep breath, I look up into the gentle darkness of the classroom, hoping I'll be able to focus. I tried to play it off casually with Nate, but try as I might, I honestly can't suppress the feeling that something bad is about to happen.

FORTY-SEVEN

My week passes with significant change. For one, Roman doesn't keep to the basement; he comes to family meals and joins in on the conversations. He has watched the video of Dad's staged death over and over, agreeing with me that it seems unlikely Dad is dead. However, Roman had to have me point out all the indifferences before he admitted to believing in the improbable. I haven't told him that I thought I saw Dad here, in Virginia.

Secondly, Flo is in a good mood constantly, and it surprises me how just the way she acts affects the atmosphere of our family. She is head over heels in love with Bradley, despite having known him only for a few days, and she tells me each night how she can't understand why he tolerates her. She also tells me about all the long talks they have—how he listens to what she has to say without criticizing her opinions. He sounds like a good person, someone rather like Nate, and I hope that Florence can find joy in their relationship instead of betrayal or heartbreak. I haven't forgotten what she told me that afternoon in our kitchen: broken hearts are the hardest to heal.

Thirdly, my walks to and from school are extremely enjoyable. Nate and I have plenty to talk about, and yes, we *do* work a little on our presentation, but we're normally busy brainstorming on what to do if Sleepy Gumption or Hubris Jargon resurface. Nate seems to think that they will be making their move soon; they have left me alone for too long. I agree because I still can't shake the feeling that it will all come to a head soon.

I grow stressed about leaving my ring at home, especially after Hubris Jargon drove by threateningly. What if Siena and Pompeii are there next time someone comes looking for it?

Anyway, I start taking my ring to school with me. I leave it in-between page one hundred seventy-one and page one hundred seventy-two of my most favorite book, and I check it frequently—a.k.a. every time I have a second to dig through my backpack and make sure it's there—and each time, it is. I know I'm paranoid, but I can't help it. I'm not taking any chances, and even keeping it at my house in a spot they will probably miss doesn't soothe my nerves. They know where I live; any time they want, they can storm my house and hold us all hostage until I hand over my ring. And constantly having it with me at school may be a bad idea, but I seriously believe Hubris Jargon won't just march into the building, locate me, drag me out of my class, and demand my ring. He would not risk being caught.

Nate, despite his promise, hasn't told Mandy and Elijah about his home life. I tell myself I can't remind him whenever I have the chance, that I have to be patient with him, but I really start to doubt he ever will. I won't tell his secret since it's his and I would *never* betray him like that. I can't do that to him.

Sunday morning, it's Mom who wakes me up, not my siblings. She is trying to convince Florence to start a garden with her, but Flo is protesting that it's too early for a garden—plus, she planned a fun day with Bradley and won't postpone it for the world.

So, naturally, Mom turns to me next.

"Venice," she says, not noticing that I'm still half-asleep, "will you plant a garden with me?"

I fumble for my glasses, my hand not finding them on my bedside table. "What time is it?" I grab at cold metal and discover my glasses. I slip them on. Mom's face is suddenly sharpened, so I can see her excited, encouraging expression.

"It's only seven." She beams at me. "Will you help me?"

I groan and sink deeper into my pillow. "Mom! It's seven in the morning! On Sunday!"

"Sorry, I'm just ready to start a garden. We can actually plant things here and have them grow! Like tomatoes!"

My deep sigh of annoyance doesn't dissuade her.

"Come on, Venice." She tugs at my arm. "You can help me pick out different seeds. Do you like beans? I was thinking we could do the ones that grow up and around a pole. Aren't those more fun than the bushes? I think so. And we can plant carrots and corn and zucchini. What about peppers? Siena hates them, so I thought we wouldn't do those…"

Her voice trails away as I slip into La-La Land, more drowsy than thoughtful this time. I don't want to get out of my warm bed to go shopping for seeds, and I doubt any stores have the organic heirloom seeds Mom uses. And we'll have to buy fertilizer—our compost hasn't broken down enough to work. And, personally, I think it's too early to be starting a garden. It's only halfway through March. Today is the fifteenth.

I smile in my sleepy state, wondering if Nate has read the Shakespearian play about Julius Caesar, and if the Ides of March mean anything to him. Certainly is a strange day.

"Venice? Are you even listening to me?"

I snap open my eyes, smile vanishing instantly as I remember I'm not supposed to be lost in my thoughts right now. "Er—yeah," I say quickly, my groggy mind scrambling to figure out what Mom has just told me. I wasn't paying attention, and I have no clue.

"She was daydreaming," Flo says from where she's sitting on her bed. I can't see her from my position, but I'm positive she's on her phone, texting Bradley, and adding small comments on this conversation we're having. "I think," Florence continues, "that

Venice was not just daydreaming randomly, but daydreaming about a specific person."

I sit up, my head spinning because I did so too fast, and throw my pillow at my twin. She shrieks with laughter and ducks to avoid it, phone in hand.

"Guessed it!" she says, tossing my pillow back at me. "I saw that smile on your face, Venice! I knew what you were thinking!"

I throw my pillow again, because she just gave it back to me. "Florence!"

"Girls!" Mom grabs the pillow before Flo can use it. "Calm down. We're talking about a garden, not boys."

Flo gives me a saucy look, but it's humored, not flippant.

"Since you're such a help with teasing Venice," says Mom, "you, Florence, can watch the kids while Venice and I gather up all the necessary things for our garden."

My twin groans. "But Siena doesn't listen to anything I say! And Bradley was going to take me to the movie theater where he works occasionally."

"At what time?" Mom asks, raising an eyebrow. She hasn't met Bradley yet, so she doesn't know what he's like. I think she has envisioned him in her mind as one of Flo's regular crushes.

Flo pauses, then answers. "Uh...three fifteen."

"Venice and I will be back by then."

I hold up my hands at this. "Mom," I say, "I didn't agree to helping you yet. Could you please wait a moment and give me a chance to think this over?"

"Sure." Mom crosses her arms, watching me expectantly. Her eyebrow is still cocked.

I grab my phone from off my bedside table, annoyed to find I hadn't plugged it in last night. The battery is almost dead. I haven't received any texts from Mandy or Nate so I assume they are either still asleep or haven't yet concocted a plan to meet up at Elijah's and play video games/read this afternoon.

"Looks like I'm free," I say, sinking back down on my bed. My pillow isn't there—Mom is holding it—and my sheet is cold where it usually sits. My neck aches at this angle. "But Mom, isn't it too early to start a garden?"

She huffs and drops my pillow on my face. I push it off and arrange it so my head is resting on it. "That's what Flo said. And no, it's not too early. I researched it. We're going to get some grow lights to start our seedlings."

I check the temperatures for the next week, grimacing at the freezing rain that's expected. "Did you look at the weather report?"

"It's constantly changing."

With no answer for that, I try another flaw in her plan. "Where will we find enough room to plant a garden?"

"Well," Mom begins, "we will start with the tiny pots. I have the equipment in the garage. And we'll put the seeds in there. Once they grow, we'll move the plants outside, into these bamboo boxes I bought. You'll see them if you go out in the backyard, Venice. They're impossible to miss."

"Okay," I say slowly. "Where are we getting the seeds?"

Mom replies instantly. "I searched up the kinds I was hoping we could get, and they are all at a local store. Apparently, the owner only sells heirloom seeds, and those are the ones I want."

"What do we do about fertilizer?"

"Oh, I already got that." Mom's cheeks tinge pink, rather like mine do each time Nate teases me, and I know why she's blushing. She must have gotten the fertilizer with Marc.

"And all the tools?" I ask, ignoring her blush.

Her cheeks redden. "I have those, too. They're all out in the garage. We got them yesterday while you all were off hanging out with friends."

Flo must not be paying enough attention to notice Mom's not-so-subtle explanation of her day, because she says, "We? Who did you go with to the garden shops?"

"Marc." Mom shoots me a quick look before returning her gaze to Flo. "It turns out he's done a garden and knows how to help me."

"Why doesn't he?" I ask bluntly, fiddling with something on my phone so I don't have to see her hard expression. "If he's so helpful, and such a good gardener, why doesn't he do it with you? And why didn't you get the seeds and grow lights yesterday?"

"Because I want my kids do this with me." Mom's voice has gone cold. She knows I have an intense dislike for Marc. Thank the trees I haven't seen him face-to-face since the day Hubris Jargon almost killed me. Whenever Marc comes over for dinner or just to visit Mom, I'm always at Elijah's or Mandy's or up in my room, doing everything I can to ignore the laughter and chatter floating up from below. I've successfully avoided Marc, and though it makes Mom annoyed, I'm glad I have.

I turn off my phone. "I'll help you," I say, sensing the silence between us has stretched thin.

"Thank you." Mom doesn't sound very grateful.

"When do we go?"

She sighs. "In an hour or so. You need to eat something and brush your hair and...I don't know...do whatever you do." She turns and walks out of our room without another word.

"Ouch," says Flo.

I sit up and glare at my twin. "It was our fault she got icy with me. You're the one who forced her to mention Marc."

"Woah!" Flo glances up from her phone, surprise written across her face. "You're spiteful this morning, sis. What's wrong?"

I shake my head. "Did I not just tell you?"

"Mean," she mutters to herself, going back to her phone. "Time to change the subject, if I may. Do you think Bradley likes me? I mean, I quite obviously like him, but does he return the feelings? I don't know. And I don't want to make a fool of myself by offering love that he won't accept. But if he *does* like me, could we be together or would that ruin—"

I get up abruptly and leave, not able to handle her blather. I normally can with ease, but today I'm in a terrible mood and can't suffer through it. What wonders the mere mention of Marc can do to me.

I bump into Siena in the hallway. She starts grumbling about not watching where I go, and even in my fury I notice she's sleepy.

"Mom wake you up, too?"

She nods, her glasses sliding down her nose. "Screaming on and on about a stupid garden."

"Did she wake the others?"

"I don't know." Siena sighs. "I wanted to sleep in—it's Sunday, for crying out loud—but Mom had plans for me. I have to paint her indoor boxes, the ones she's using to grow her plants."

"Paint?"

"Must you ask so many questions, Venice?" she says wearily. "Yes, paint. With a little brush and the colored liquid that you spread over a surface to make it smooth or a different shade—"

I close my eyes. Is she being sarcastic because of her lack of sleep? It's very annoying and my temper is heating up again.

"I have to paint designs on the wood," says Siena, ignoring the plain look of exasperation on my face. "Tiny trees and tomatoes and corn and all the other vegetables Mom's growing."

Mom's voice comes from her room. "It's bamboo, not wood!"

"Eh, same thing." Siena pushes past me—I still have my eyes closed—and I hear her tromping down the stairs, thumping her feet on the bamboo steps as hard as she can.

I take a deep breath, calming myself. I take another breath, then follow after my littlest sister, who is now in the kitchen, yelling at Pompeii for eating the last of the cereal. Pompeii also is tired; he must have been forced out of bed, too. The only kid missing is Roman, and I doubt he would have gotten up despite Mom's best attempts.

"You're an idiot!" Siena yells, throwing the empty cereal box at

Pompeii. "You *had* to eat it all, you greedy pig! Did you not stop to think that someone else might want some?"

"I got here first!" Pompeii blocks the box with his arm, sending it flying back at Siena.

She gives a caustic laugh, stomping the cardboard flat. "I hate you!"

"Stop it, you two," I snap as Pompeii opens his mouth to return the hate. "When are you going to grow up?"

He sneers at me, not answering.

"What job did Mom assign you, Pompeii?" I ask, sitting down at the counter next to him.

"I'm the DJ," he replies through a mouthful of cereal. "I have to play all the lame songs that Mom likes. Did you know she told me I couldn't do any of my favorites? I think she shouldn't be entitled to force me to play the crappy songs I hate."

"Stop using that word."

"What? Crappy?"

I nearly roll my eyes, but instead manage a tired grin. "No. Hate. And you know I meant that."

"Guess what *hate* rhymes with," says Siena.

I do roll my eyes now. My siblings have all been teasing me mercilessly since last Tuesday, as if they've guessed something has changed in my friendship with Nate, and they make fun of me because of it. Which is why I have been very careful to not reveal anything.

"Fate," says Pompeii. "Fate rhymes with hate."

Siena copies my eye roll, but hers is more sarcastic. "Good job, Pompeii. You actually rhymed a word. What else?"

"Date," I put in.

She flutters her eyelashes at me in a horrible imitation of Flo. "According to Flo, you've gone on some dates."

"Plate!" Pompeii says loudly.

"Shut up!" she snarls, grabbing a silicone plate from a cabinet.

507

"You're both being stupid." She Frisbees the plate at Pompeii; it hits his head and bounces off, falling to the floor.

Pompeii lets out an enraged roar and moves to lunge at Siena, but I hold him back. "Calm!" I command. "Be calm."

He shrugs me off, livid. "How come *she* is allowed to hit me, but I can't?"

"She's immature!"

"Thank you." Siena dips into a graceful bow. "I just *love* being insulted. It's something I cannot live without."

I sigh wearily. Her sarcasm is choking me. "Siena—"

"Don't even," she warns.

Maybe that's for the best, then.

Moving towards the pantry, I pull the door open and dig through the items inside, attempting to decide what I want to eat for breakfast. While I do so, I block out my arguing siblings and try to focus on my thoughts. Mom wants to plant a garden. We've never had a garden before, and I'm sure she doesn't know how to. Marc may be able to help her, but I won't if he's going to be there.

Loud stomping up the basement staircase announces Roman's arrival seconds before he bursts out. He looks to be in a good mood, better than Pompeii or Siena, and he gives me a big grin. His glasses are crookedly set on his nose, his hair tousled from sleep, his clothes rumpled and wrinkled like he'd slept in them.

"Guess what," he says, moving to stand next to me.

I raise my eyebrows. "What?"

He inches closer to me, dropping his voice so our siblings don't hear. "So, I finally texted Grandma Ferrari about Dad's accident, and she managed to give me the chance to talk to the police chief over the tiny town in Kentucky where Dad's death was staged."

"You did?" I exclaim, keeping my voice low. "What'd he say?"

"Well, I pointed out all the things you'd told me, and he agreed that the accident seemed intentional. He said that he and his troops hadn't been able to look through and investigate it because they're currently swamped with these random robberies on restaurants, but he wants to divulge Dad's accident."

To tell the truth, I am impressed with Roman's determination to get this mystery surrounding our Dad's death solved. I don't think I would have had the guts to call the police chief.

"I asked him about the street cameras," Roman continues, still quietly, "and the chief said they aren't his. They don't exist there, at that stop light. The only time there ever were cameras there were the two that caught Dad's faked death on film."

"I think the truck driver was the one who owned the cameras."

"And the chief agreed," says Roman. "He said the video, the one with Dad, just appeared out of the blue on their security footage of different streets. After the accident, after the chief told Grandma Ferrari about Dad, he went to that street to examine those cameras, and there weren't any."

"Which means the bad guys who planted them took them."

Roman nods. "Venice, do you have any idea why people would want Dad dead? And who?"

I hesitate. I haven't told him about Hubris Jargon or my ring. "Nothing credible, really."

"It has to be someone who thinks Dad has something they want," says my brother, giving me a serious look. "Someone who would go through all this trouble to make people believe Dad is dead, just to get Dad alone. My only hypothesis is that Dad has or knows where something they want is."

"Yeah." I bite my lip.

His serious expression turns slightly curious. "Do you know of anything someone might want from Dad?"

Should I tell him? Should I tell him that three people are stalking me, waiting for the right moment to strike, and they are the same men who plotted Dad's whole accident? And that they want my ring, the ring Dad gave me? And that Dad himself is here, in our town, barely a twenty-minute's walk away?

Thank the trees, my twin sister saves me. Sort of.

"Venice!" Flo comes skipping into the kitchen, hair swinging madly, a grin on her face. She spots me by the pantry and grabs my arm. "Venice, your phone rang a minute ago. I didn't answer it because that seems rude, but it was Nate."

There is immediate silence in the kitchen. Siena and Pompeii, who I have successfully blotted out from my mind and are still arguing, suddenly stop to glance over at me. Roman, standing at my side, smirks. And Flo is beaming.

"Oh," Pompeii says, breaking the silence. "That's what hate rhymes with. Nate."

I resist rolling my eyes. It's harder than I thought. "Thanks, Flo," I say, keeping the sarcasm out of my tone. "Everyone in this room needed to hear that."

She smiles wider, flashing her brilliant white teeth. "Here's your phone," she says, shoving it into my hands.

I fumble with it for a moment, not having expected that, and give her a lightly-exasperated look. "Roman," I say, turning towards him, "I'll talk to you later."

"Much later," he replies, his smirk growing.

I leave the kitchen, shaking my head to myself. Sometimes, it's a real pain having siblings.

FORTY-EIGHT

"Here, take this." Mom shoves a packet of carrot seeds at me. "These are great vegetables. Good for your eyesight, too."

I take it, placing it in the shopping basket dangling on my arm. "That's the eighth type of seed you've chosen," I say, peering down at the stack. "How many others do you want?"

"Four more." Mom rifles through the shelf of seeds. "That's a nice number, right? Twelve different plants?"

I shrug. "I guess."

"Do you like beets? Or turnips?" Mom holds up the packets. "I've never eaten either, so I don't know if we should get some."

"Siena will complain if we do."

Mom scoffs. "Siena complains about everything."

"True." I examine the beets, marveling at how weirdly they are shaped. "I don't think we will eat them," I decide. "The beets or the turnips. We should just stick with basic garden vegetables."

"We've gotten all the basics." Mom places the packets back on the shelf and grabs the basket from me, digging around at the eight plants she has picked. "Carrots, potatoes, tomatoes, bell peppers, corn, beans, cucumber, and squash. Does that seem like a lot?"

"No."

Mom purses her lips. "It does to me. But it feels like I'm missing something. What?"

"I don't know."

"We have plenty of good vegetables," she murmurs to herself, completely ignoring me. "What else is there to plant?"

I watch her look through the other seeds, my mind elsewhere. It's only ten in the morning, but I feel exhausted and ready to crash. My morning has been crazy—whether it was Flo, teasing me; or Roman, wanting to know if I have any suspicions about Dad's accident that I'm not sharing with him; or Pompeii, grumbling on and on how the library is closed on Sunday; or Mom dragging me along to a tiny corner store on the other side of our neighborhood; or Mandy, begging me to come over and watch her and Elijah play video games since Nate can't make it, I've constantly been busy. That's what Nate had called me to tell me—he's tied up with his grandpa and can't make it over to Elijah's, in case I was wondering.

There's a part of me that is glad Nate can't go—it gives me an excuse to decline too—but there's also a part of me that wishes I could be over with my friends instead of at a store picking out seeds for our garden.

"Radishes?" Mom wrinkles her nose. "Do you guys like those?"

I shrug again. I've been doing that every time she asks me a question. "I don't know if I've eaten them before."

"How sad." She puts the packet back. "I feel like such a bad mom. I'm not feeding my kids enough vegetables!"

"We get plenty," I say hurriedly. "It's just the more...obscure ones that we don't eat. Like radishes."

Mom pulls out a packet of lettuce seeds. "Lettuce?"

I reach around her and select another. "Basil."

"That's a good herb," she agrees. "Put it in the basket."

I drop it in. "Are we getting any other types of tomatoes? You have the regular kinds, but do you want cherry tomatoes? Or these, Roma? Early Girl?"

"How boring." Mom shakes her head. "We don't need more tomatoes. We've got enough."

"Whatever you say."

She bites her lip, scanning the shelf. "I don't know what else we should plant."

"Might I make a suggestion?"

Both Mom and I jump at the voice: loud and sudden and unexpected. There is an old, dark-skinned man standing behind us, his expression one of polite interest. He is wearing a faded blue button-down shirt, a nametag pinned above his left breast pocket. *Charles Hill, Manager.* He has dark copper eyes, brown but holding hints of sunlight. His hair is shock-white, standing out against his near-black complexion. He is smiling at both of us. He has a very warm aura, one of golden relaxed gentleness.

"Hello," he says. "I couldn't help overhear you ladies talking about planting seeds." He has a faint accent, one I can't place, but his English is crisp and perfectly understandable.

"Oh!" Mom gives Charles Hill a small smile. "Yes, please. I'm open to any suggestions."

"Are you looking only for vegetables?"

"No, not really."

He leans forward and snags a packet of seeds. "Cantaloupe," he says, holding it up. "Excellent melon. You should try."

"Cantaloupe." Mom turns her gaze to me. "Venice, do you think we could plant these?"

"Sure." I push up my glasses, which have slid down my nose due to sweat. This store is suffocatingly hot. "I like melons."

"That's a yes." Mom accepts the packet from Charles Hill and places it in our basket, taking it from me. Then she looks back at him. "You're the manager of this cute little corner store?"

Charles Hill dips his head. "That I am."

"Well, thank you for selling heirloom seeds." Mom grins. "I tried to get some at another store, but they didn't have any. And I thought these seeds were pretty popular."

I roll my eyes to myself and glance around, bored with this conversation. I spot the cold foods section across the aisle from us, and wonder if it would be strange to stick my head in and cool down. I notice a piece of blue paper taped to the refrigerators farthest from me, the ones that hold the alcohol and power drinks.

Curious, I drift towards them and read the paper. *The purchase of alcoholic drinks is prohibited on the Sabbath Day.*

I blink. Is this the same store Nate comes to when he has to buy drinks for his grandpa? And is Charles Hill the man who once was friends with Bob Wilson?

"Venice! What are you doing?"

I snap around. Mom has come to collect me, the manager trailing after her while pretending to not look interested. He sees me standing before the blue paper and smiles.

"I saw this sign," I say, pointing. "A friend of mine mentioned a store where alcoholic drinks weren't sold on Sundays." It surprises me that I'm this bold, that I'm speaking like this. I don't normally voice my thoughts out loud. And never to someone I've met barely a minute ago.

Mom scans the sign. "How...intriguing."

"My friend said it was because the manager didn't think it was right to sell these liquors on the Sabbath," I continue, keeping my gaze on Charles Hill. "I didn't realize this was that shop, and that you, Mr. Hill, are that man."

"It is indeed." The man's smile has grown. "And please, call me Charles. I would much rather hear that name." Then he cocks his head. "I must say, who is this friend of yours who seems to know me so well?"

I wince internally. "Nate Wilson."

Charles Hill's smile widens even more, showing off crease lines on his face. Mom may call them wrinkles, but I think smiling lines show how kindly and friendly someone is.

"I know who you are talking about," says Charles. "Nate comes here often. He brings his dog."

"You let Mercury inside your shop?" I ask, surprised.

Charles is also surprised. "You know his dog?"

"Venice is kind of like Nate's girlfriend," Mom puts in, not wanting to be left out of the discussion.

I blush scarlet. "Mom!" I complain. "I am *not*. We're friends. And if you ever say that again, I won't do the garden with you!"

"I would not like to be the reason for your feud," Charles speaks up, "and the loss of a helper, so I will change the subject. Are you prepared to plant a garden so early in the year, when frosts still linger and may kill off all your seedlings?"

Mom answers, but I'm lost in my mind again and don't hear it. She doesn't usually tease me, and saying something like that—in front of someone else!—has shocked me. It also gets me thinking thoughts I'm not sure I want to develop.

Am I his girlfriend? I've kissed him twice, and he's kissed me twice, so does that mean we're...together? We haven't talked about anything like this. Do we need to?

I shake myself free of these thoughts and realize Mom and Charles have moved to another part of the store, away from the cool refrigerators. Mom is talking energetically, waving her hands in the air, the basket balancing on her arm. She seems eager to explain her plans for the garden, and Charles seems eager to listen, but I'm positive it's because he's a kind old man who is able to sit through long talks while feigning interest. He also adds in small comments about how she can improve her garden, which does nothing to persuade me that it's a perfect time to plant. I still think, despite Nate having a garden, that now is too early.

But I *am* grumpy this morning.

The very second Mom opens the front door, Florence comes rushing up, her eyes wide. "Thank the trees you're here!" she says, practically dragging us inside. "Siena is being a problematic child and needs someone with proper authority to tell her to stop! She won't listen to me!"

"What's she doing?" Mom asks, unconcerned.

"Pouring her paint on Pompeii!"

I clap a hand over my mouth to stifle my laughter. Florence will definitely *not* appreciate it.

Mom sighs, sets down the bag of seeds, and hurries off to save Pompeii.

Flo grabs my arm. "Venice, I don't know how you're able to babysit them. I thought it would be easy, but these little devils couldn't stay in one spot for longer than two minutes! And Roman was hogging the TV, so I told Siena to go paint her boxes, and look how that turned out!"

I smile.

"And my friends were calling me nonstop, so I was constantly talking with one or the other—"

"Are they your real friends?" I interrupt.

She nods. "Yes. Ana, and Bradley, and this other girl who once said she liked my hair. I found her again, and talked to her, and we're instant friends. Is that how you became friends with Mandy and Elijah and Nate?"

"I met Nate at the library. Mandy and Elijah I met at school. They've been friends with Nate for years, and once I started talking to them, they liked me, I guess."

"For some strange reason," Flo puts in, then grins at me.

I roll my eyes. "Thanks, sis."

"Come on." She loops her arm through mine. "Can you help me decide what I should wear this afternoon when Bradley comes?"

"Flo, hold on." I'm hopping up and down as she pulls me up the stairs while I try to take off my shoes. "What kind of date is this? A fun, hang-out-as-friends date? Or a dark-corner-kissy date?"

Flo makes a face, partly in irritation and partly in distress. "I don't know. We haven't kissed yet, so probably not the second one. We're still just friends."

"Okay." I push open our bedroom door, and we stumble in. Flo is still holding onto my arm, and it's pulling me off-balance. "Then don't wear anything sexy. Just a T-shirt and jeans."

My sister wrinkles her forehead. "I don't have any T-shirts."

"What about this one?" I release her and dig through her closet, finding a solid-colored T-shirt buried in the tangle of tank tops and jeans and the other chic clothes that are shoved in here. "Try it."

Flo grabs the shirt. "Ew."

"What?"

"I can't wear this," she says, throwing it back at me. "It's not my style. How could you trade silk for cotton?"

"You have silk shirts?" I shake my head. How bizarre my twin is.

"How about my camisole?" Flo plucks a white camisole from the closet. "Or is this too sexy?"

I frown at it. "Don't you think it's too cold outside for that?"

"We're never going to get something picked out." She drops the camisole. "I'd just better not be late for Bradley."

With a quick glance at my phone, I say, "You have three hours."

"Ugh!" Flo tosses her hair. "Whatever. Just help me, Venice. I helped you when you went to that party, so you can help me with this. You know what clothes are…appropriate for a less popular boy to see on me. I shouldn't wear designer, right?"

My mind is whirling. "Um…no?"

"Great, thanks, Venice. You're being an excellent help."

"I told you, a T-shirt and jeans will be perfect. It's super casual and easy." I pick up the forgotten shirt. "Why don't you wear this?"

Flo glares at it for a moment, then grudgingly shrugs. "Okay, fine. I guess something simple will suffice. But I will curse you if Bradley dumps me for not being beautiful enough."

I blink at her. "I doubt he'll dump you for that reason. Plus, you don't need alluring clothes to make boys like you."

"I suppose." She gives me a hard look. "You're a good example of that."

517

My irritated expression causes her to laugh, and she hugs me tightly. "You are so easy to tease, Venice!" she says. "It's totally your fault that you leave yourself open for these taunts!"

"It's also your fault!" I shoot back, hugging her with one arm. "All of you shouldn't tease me. Even Mom did today. At the store. In front of someone else!"

Flo stifles a giggle. "Did that person know who Mom was talking about?"

"Yes." I push her away so she can continue her preparations for her date in three hours. "It was mortifying."

"You always use that word when Nate is involved."

I sigh. "Let's not talk about him right now."

"Why?" Florence's anxious expression makes me even more uncomfortable. "You guys aren't…Everything's good with you two, right?"

I cross my arms, annoyed. Can they not lay off me for even one *minute*? "It's all right," I say. "We're just talking about you and Bradley, not me and Nate. You are the one with a date tonight, not me. So let's concentrate on you. Have you ever gone out with him?"

"No." Flo bites her lip. "That's why I'm nervous. For the first time, Venice, I'm nervous to go on a date with a boy."

"Bradley seems nice. Why do you like him?"

"Well…" she plays with the T-shirt, hands needing something to touch and move around with while she talks. "He's a great listener. He can handle my impertinence. He likes movies, and so do I. He skateboards sometimes, and once we—meaning me and a couple of his buddies—went to the skate park and I watched all of them do flips and things around the set."

"Cool."

"I know, right? And after that, we went to this really cute ice cream shop that sold sarsaparilla that didn't actually contain sarsaparilla. Bradley paid for mine, and it was really sweet of him."

I smile. I'm glad to hear my sister gush about a boy she actually likes, not one she's using just to become more popular or spite a girl she doesn't like.

"Mom doesn't know Bradley," Flo continues, "and she thinks he's one of the other boys I was infatuated with. But Bradley is much different from any of them. I haven't flirted with him once. I'm too scared, and—Venice, I'm seriously scared that when I talk to him, I'll say something stupid or offensive that will make him not want to hang out with me. Every single time I see him, I get super nervous and my heartbeat speeds up, and my palms sweat, and I think that I'm about to faint."

My smile widens. "Has this ever happened before?"

"No…" Flo thinks hard. "I don't—I don't think so. Not with Kent, or Ethan, or Sam—"

"Okay, I get the idea," I interrupt, not wanting to hear her long list of ex-boyfriends.

She tugs at a loose thread on the sleeve of her T-shirt, and I pull away her hand before she unravels the entire shirt. "Venice, I can't believe I'm coming to you for advice about boys, but can you tell me how not to act like an idiot in front of Bradley?"

"Advice?" I twist my lips to one side. "Um, just be yourself, but your positive, encouraging self. If you try too hard to get someone's attention, it's…cringy, I guess. And it gives people—well, *some* people something to talk about. behind your back."

"Do people do this at school?" Flo asks, appalled.

I slowly nod. "I've heard a couple kids talking. I'm sure they were just the ex-girlfriends of the boys you robbed from them."

"Oh." She looks stunned, like I'd hit her over the head with a shovel. "I never knew I was a source of gossip among all those sore losers."

Exasperated, I take off my glasses and clean the lenses on the corner of my shirt before sliding them back on. "Flo, this is why kids talk about you. You're not afraid to insult them."

"Do you talk about me to your friends?" she asks innocently.

"Of course not. At least, not like…that."

She chews on her bottom lip. "But others do. Because I'm who I am. Truthfully, I'm surprised Bradley can stand me, unlike some."

"Do your relationships not last long since you're…blunt?"

She gives a short bark of laughter. "Yes! Boys tire of me easily, it seems. I have such bad luck staying with one boy for a while. Kent was probably the longest I was in a relationship with."

"And even then, he wasn't being faithful."

"Yeah." Flo finally sets down the T-shirt, now rumpled more than ever. "For a bit, I thought I could forget the betrayal by finding a new boyfriend, but nothing could erase the pain. I was a bad sister for the past few years, and I'm sorry because of it. I'm trying to be better, and I think I'm doing an okay job, but I don't know for sure."

"You're doing excellent." I take her hand and give her a slight squeeze. "You're an awesome twin sister."

She smiles, a hint sadly. "We should see if we can communicate telepathically. You know, because twins seem to have a connection that regular people don't? Wouldn't it be cool if we could?"

I match her exact smile. "Yes. Then we can plot all sorts of fun mischief without anyone hearing or finding out, and they wouldn't know until it's too late."

"Ah, to dream…"

I hug her tightly. "I hope you have fun tonight. Be safe. Don't do anything you'll regret later. And don't eat too much popcorn."

She snorts. "Stop worrying about me, Venice."

"I'm allowed to worry about you. I'm your older sister."

"By eight minutes!"

We both smile at this. Flo has always complained that I should control the younger kids since I'm the oldest, and that the eight minutes between us means I have to have more chores and responsibilities than her. She rarely finds fault with me being older except when it comes to the privileges.

"All right." Flo steps back. "I have to go check on my bread. I made some while Siena was painting, and as you know, bread is the only thing I can bake with a good result." She flashes me a rueful grin. "See ya." She turns and skips out of the room, nearly bowling Mom over as she comes walking up the hallway.

"You're happy," Mom observes. "And is that your bread on the stove? It has risen."

Flo nods. "That's mine! And I'm going to do it right now!"

"Did you do that?" Mom asks me as she steps in.

"We've been working on our relationship."

She looks impressed. "You know, Venice, you have a way with people." Before I can reply, she continues. "I've gotten two calls from a woman named Moira Zane, wondering if you want to meet up with her and do something, like an afternoon at the spa or shopping. Do you know who she is?"

"I met her at Goldbeck's party," I say. "She was the big, loud woman who was kind of like Flo."

Mom's mouth curves into an O. "Okay. So, do you want to meet with her?"

I shrug. I haven't seen Moira since the party, and she was great fun, so maybe. "Are you comfortable with that?"

"I don't know!" Mom looks amused. "I trust you, Venice."

"Why don't you give me her number," I say. "Then I can call her and figure something out without you having to be involved. It'll be less stressful for you."

"Okay." Mom pulls out her phone and takes a moment to send me Moira's phone number. "Emailed it," she announces.

"Email?"

She grins. "What, should I have texted?"

Shaking my head, I say, "No. But Flo was teasing me the other day for not checking my email enough, so you using it just reminded me of that. And I probably *should* check my email often—I missed the one my high school sent out about school being cancelled last Monday."

"M-hm." Mom backs out of my room, waving a hand. "I have to go. I need to prepare my little pots for planting. Are you going to help me?"

"In a minute."

"Great. See you soon."

I mumble a reply, already going through my emails. I have hundreds of unread messages from school, advertisements, Mom, and all sorts of others. I can't find the one Mom just sent me, so I search up her name.

Fifty-six emails, all unread, from her over the past few months pop up. I grimace, laughing internally that I haven't been paying attention to my inbox.

Discovering the most recent, I tap it and scan the email. "Your weirdo old lady friend," I mutter to myself. "Blah blah blah strange person, blah blah blah afternoon out at the mall, blah...Finally, her number. Mom didn't need to say so much."

I add Moira's number to my contact lists—which has about four people on it now—and go through Mom's other emails. I find one she forwarded me, one detailing Goldbeck's party invitation and, curious, I select it. It's been a month and I'm finally reading it.

My heart suddenly skips a beat. My mouth falls open. I can't believe what I'm seeing.

It could totally be a coincidence.

But it makes *so much* sense.

And if it's true...Oh, Mother Earth save us.

My fingers trembling so hard I can barely do anything on my phone, I close the email and dial Nate's number. My heart is now pounding in my ears, my blood pulsing, every inch of me quaking.

"Hello? Could you hold on a minute while I—Oh. Oops. Um, can I call you back, Venice?"

I breathe out heavily. "Uh, sure, just—real quickly."

"Thanks." Nate hangs up, and during the next couple or so minutes, I pace my bedroom with a load of anxiety weighing me down. I have to tell him, I need him to hurry up so I can tell him, and *what is taking him so long?!* Yes, today is Sunday and he might be patching up wounds from earlier—I really hope that's not the case—but does he need to take so long to hurry up and finish what he's doing?

After what seems like a year, he calls me. I answer instantly.

"Sorry!" he says, almost too cheerfully. "My bacon was about to burn, and my grandpa can't stand burnt bacon, so I'm sorry for taking a while to get back to you. What's up?"

Bacon? I want to scream. He couldn't talk because of *bacon*?

"Venice?"

"I found something," I say in a rush. "I was looking through my emails, and I saw the one about Goldbeck's party, so I read it, and you won't believe what I found."

"What?"

"His name." I'm still pacing. "At the corner of the invitation, it had his two initials. They're S and G, Nate. Stephen Goldbeck. But they can also be Sleepy Gumption."

There's silence on his side for so long I start to think he has hung up to fry more bacon for his grandpa. Then he speaks. "You were at his house, and he knew you had the ring, and you were in even more danger there than we thought?"

"Yes!" I am trembling worse than before. "And it all makes sense now. I had wondered why I, specifically, was invited to the party, yet no other kids my age were. And Rebecca wanted to buy my ring, and Hubris Jargon was at the party because he *knew* we were going to be there, and I talked to Sleepy Gumption, Nate! I talked to the man who wants my ring! I talked to the man who conspired in my dad's faked death, and I thought he was nice, even! I can't believe it."

"This is…unsettling." Nate sounds hard and determined. "You could have been hurt. I suppose they were trying to get the ring the gentle way."

"Do you think Malaise Tone was there, too?" I ask worriedly.

"Maybe. But—Venice, you talked to Gumption! You were *right there* and he acted all innocent and perfectly normal. It was his creepy wife who was the one asking about your ring. No wonder we didn't suspect him. Goldbeck seemed like a regular rich guy."

I grip my phone tighter. "That's why he tried to talk me down when I saw Jargon. They're buddies."

"Do you think Rebecca Goldbeck is Malaise Tone? She wants your ring, too."

"Malaise Tone is a male. Her name doesn't fit, anyway."

Nate's silent. When he speaks, his voice is more controlled. "You're right. Whose name does? Venice, do you know anyone with the initials M and T?"

I open my mouth to say no when Mom suddenly appears in the doorway to my bedroom, her hands on her hips. She raises her eyebrows to see me on the phone, and she whispers, "Venice, don't get mad at me, but I was just going to er, *warn you* that Marc is coming over for dinner tonight. You can stay up in your bedroom if you want, or go over to a friend's house, instead of seeing him. Okay? Just please don't march into the dining room and start yelling at him for random reasons. Thanks!" She disappears as fast as she'd come, but I barely notice.

"Venice?"

My mouth is still open. My throat is dry, so I wet it. "Nate," I say, "I think Malaise Tone is Marc."

FORTY-NINE

Silence on his end. I keep talking, pieces of the puzzles falling into place as I do. "That's why Marc was interested in my ring that day he came over for dinner so long ago. That's why he's been over at our house so often. That's why he likes Mom and our family. And that's why Flo's jewelry box was rifled that day Roman found Marc in the house. Because I have what he wants! I have the ring."

"Venice. You have come in contact with *all three* of them. Everything is a lot closer than we thought. Do you realize how much danger you are in?"

"Marc is how they know so much about me," I go on, ignoring Nate. "He's learning my information and passing it on to Jargon and Gumption. He's how they know where I live, what I do during the day, what—whatever else goes on in my life. And getting Mom drunk! He probably did it so he could ask her questions without her remembering. Questions about Dad, and me, and my ring, if he was bold enough. How did I not see this? It's so obvious!"

"Venice—"

"He's coming over for dinner tonight," I say, cutting him off, "and I don't know what I should do. Call the police? Tell them that Marc is a psychopath who wants a piece of jewelry I own? Tell them that Marc was in on the plan to kill my dad?"

"Venice! Just listen for a moment."

I fall silent.

"Stay away from him," says Nate. "Don't face him. That would be incredibly stupid, no offence intended. You're smart and you know that doing something impulsive like that could be the trigger they are waiting for."

"I want that man in jail!" I force myself to keep my voice down, but I really want to yell. "I want them to stop bothering me, I want to know what truly happened to my dad, and I want them to leave me and my family alone." A new thought suddenly takes hold of me. "What if I destroy the ring? I can have Roman help me smash it. Then I can present Marc with the pulverized remnants."

"Woah, Venice, you might want to think that through."

"Should I tell my family? Should I tell them that Marc wants my ring, and that Dad isn't dead, and my ring has gotten me into sp much trouble? And do you think that they're all working together? Should I sell my ring to Rebecca Goldbeck?" I'm almost breathless thinking of ways to get out of this insanity. Is holding on to my ring really worth it?

"Venice, slow down. Listen, I want all of this to end and I want you and your family to be safe. But you're forgetting one critical piece. It's possible they have your dad."

This realization brings my racing thoughts to a hard stop. If they have Dad and if I destroy my ring...well, I don't think they'll fake it the next time he dies.

"The more you provoke Marc, the more suspicious he will become, and that might force them into ramping up their efforts to get your ring. It would put you in more danger."

I spin off one heel, my pacing not helping calm my temper. "I'm already in plenty of danger, Nate. What's a little more?"

"There's a big difference. Believe me, Venice. I know. There's a difference between threatening danger and physical danger. Right now, you've been relatively safe. You're surrounded by your family; you're rarely alone. Until now Jargon and Marc haven't been bold enough to burst in and force the ring from you. But if Jargon or

Marc or Goldbeck know that you're onto them, that you know who they are and what they want, there are more risks they'll be willing to take. If they kidnap you, there is nothing stopping them from hurting or killing you, and maybe your dad, too."

"But I don't know *why* they want my ring!" A sudden though makes me gasp. "And I've totally forgotten! You were with me twice when Jargon drove by! And you stopped him from hitting me that day. You're also a target, Nate. They could come after you."

"If they did, I think I could handle it. I'm no stranger to pain."

He's trying to make light of it, but emotional pain strikes my heart at his words. "Has—has your grandpa hurt you today?"

There's a very pregnant pause. "It's Sunday. Of course he has."

"Nate! You're not doing anything to prevent that."

"I-I know." He sounds like he should be doing something, but he doesn't want to. And I know he doesn't. "Anyway, we're talking about you and your problems, not mine."

"You're the one actually being hurt!"

"It's fine. I'm fine. Today wasn't as bad as some days. I didn't need to bandage the cuts. Gramps is calm now. He asked for lunch, even, and he only does that if he's doing better."

He sounds tender and hopeful and somehow that breaks my heart more and more. "Is there no other solution to this problem? Can you not avoid your grandpa on Sundays until he's asleep or something?"

"I've tried plenty of different solutions. Now, are we going to discuss what is happening to you, or should I hang up and let you deal with it?"

I flinch visibly, but he can't see. He is rarely this unkind.

"I'm sorry, Venice." He realizes he's been harsh. "I didn't mean it to come out like that. I'm just—I'm getting really frustrated that you understand my dilemma occasionally, but other times you're mad at me for not fighting back against my grandpa. He's a poor, senile old man, Venice, and I could snap him in half if I wanted to."

"You would never do that. Because you're not like that. But doing nothing—not avoiding him on Sundays after *years* of days like this—There has to be a better way of taking care of yourself, Nate."

His voice is level when he speaks, though I'm sure I'm making him angry. "Venice, let's not talk about me."

"I would rather! I don't want to have to figure out my own problems."

"You're shouting at me," he says quietly.

"Of course I'm shouting. You won't listen to me." I spin around, pulling at my hair in frustration. Why won't he listen? "All this nonsense about no one in your family caring about you has gotten to your head. You really believe it. You really do believe that if your grandpa is taken away, then you won't have any family members left to love you. But I think you should call your dad. Or your other grandparents. Maybe if they knew the kind of help you and your grandpa needed they would be more involved. You said your dad only lives an hour or so from here. So ask him to meet up with you sometime. Tell him his father needs help that you can't give him. Help him remember that he wanted a son, and he has one."

There is silence for a moment, and he says, "I could try. Though I doubt he would care."

"You won't know that unless you talk to him."

"Venice." He is still speaking softly, and I suddenly recognize he is using the tone of voice he adopts when he attempts to placate his grandpa, and it's a bit embarrassing. "Stop. Please. I told you once that it hurts to talk about my family, and it still does, despite you knowing about them. It really does hurt me to tell you that my dad is never going to want to get to know me. If he had, he would've called me years ago."

I take in a deep, controlled breath, trying to calm myself down. "Maybe he deserves a second chance? If not for you, maybe you could reach out to your dad for your grandfather's sake."

"Maybe. I said I might try. I do need time, though, and I would appreciate it if you could give me that time. You, on the other hand, may be running out of time."

He's right. I should be patient. But I'm so worried about him and the pain he suffers, and the abandonment, and I want to help him.

Except...I can't control him. He gets to decide for himself.

"All right." I wearily sink down on my bed, tired from my fast pacing. I feel bad for giving him that push when he doesn't want it. "I'm sorry. I'm trying to force you to do something that you should do in your own time."

Nate laughs, but it has a hollow ring to it. "I understand. You don't want me to suffer any more, or to suffer alone. The truth is, Venice, I'm not alone—I have you, Elijah, Mandy, Mercury...and none of you hurt me except the few occasions when words do, or when Mandy accidentally pokes me with an astonishingly sharp hairpin—"

"Did she really?"

"Yeah. I showed you the scar, remember? I'm surprised I got one, truthfully."

Our conversation has switched, and I feel way more relieved talking about the ridiculous things Mandy does—except I'm still undecided about Nate's dislike for fixing what needs to be fixed.

"So." He sounds worried. "Do you think Goldbeck knows you know that he wants your ring?"

I shrug, then remember he can't see it. "No, not really. I mean, he probably thinks he's too smart for me to figure out."

"Well, he's wrong," says Nate. "The only problem is keeping him away from you and your family." He's also in danger—Jargon probably doesn't like him, especially since he prevented me from becoming road-kill.

"Hey, Nate?"

"Yeah?"

"Thanks for dealing with my impatience. Thanks for continuing to help me sort through these unfortunate circumstances. You're always ready to help me figure out this obnoxious mystery my dad caused."

Nate laughs. It almost sounds true. "You're definitely welcome. I enjoy spending the time with you, even when you get frustrated. I'm most willing to help you—except the rare occasion we fight over *my* problems. And thank *you* for understanding."

"I try. Everyone has problems, and though I'm kind of someone who likes dealing with those problems, I know you want to do this on your own." A sudden slight noise alerts me, and I look up to see Flo standing in the open doorway, her jaw hanging low in surprise, and when she sees she has my attention, she blushes.

I freeze. My blood runs cold. How much has she heard? Does she know enough to piece together that Dad isn't dead? That I'm being hunted?

"Sorry," she whispers, looking scared.

I get up, march over to her, close the door in her face—rude, I know, but I am too nervous to care. My heart is pounding furiously. This is bad. Very bad. I don't know if I have the emotional capacity to try to explain everything to Florence.

"Venice? Did you hang up?"

"N-no."

He sounds concerned as he asks, "What's wrong?"

"Florence was…" My throat is dry. I have to wet it before trying to speak again. "Florence was just outside my room. I don't know if she heard…"

"Oh." He's even more concerned. "If she learns about your dad, or Jargon, then things will certainly come to a head, and fast."

"Florence would definitely tell Mom, and Mom would go to the police. Maybe it's for the best, Nate." I'm trembling, both from my fury and my anxiety. "I had better go talk to her. And, Nate—I'm sorry for yelling at you. I just really want you to be safe, and living with your grandpa isn't safe at all. And I want you to be happy."

"Venice, since we met I can't remember ever feeling happier. Don't bother worrying about me. Worry about yourself. And your family. Maybe it's a good think Florence overheard. Your mom…she probably should know."

"Minutes ago, you were telling me not to say anything."

"I've changed my mind."

I sigh deeply and sit down on my bed, my ear hurting from where I have pressed my phone against it. "Nate…"

"Yes?"

"I miss you."

"Miss me or miss my dimples?"

"Your pathetic attempts to make me laugh."

He laughs again, more smoothly. "Okay, you win."

I don't have anything else left to say. I am tired and annoyed at myself for getting frustrated with Nate when it wasn't my job to.

"Let me know how it goes with Florence."

"Okay. I'll call you later." I hang up and take a deep breath. I just want to crawl in bed and forget everything that's happening. But…I've made Nate happier than he has ever been? I vacillate between elation at knowing I've brought some happiness into his life and despair that I keep pressing him about his family situation and causing him pain. If only that was where my problems ended.

Shaking my head to clear myself of all doubt and worry and my remaining fury, I drop my phone on my bed and leave my room. I have to find Florence and ask her how much of our conversation she heard. I really hope it wasn't enough for her to suspect anything that's going on.

I meet up with Pompeii in the hallway. He's sitting on the floor by the edge of the staircase, scrolling through his playlist on his tablet. His headphones are around his neck.

"Hey," he says, not looking up at me. "Why were you yelling?"

I roll my eyes and step around him. "Why do you have to sit right in front of the stairs?"

"Touché."

I stomp down the stairs, exhaustion flooding through my entire body. I don't know if I'll be able to stay awake while planting those seeds. I wonder if this is how Nate feels, 24/7.

Reaching the end of the staircase, I whirl around the banister and progress into the kitchen, which smells strongly of Flo's fresh bread. The oven is on, so the bread pans must be inside. Flo herself is in the room, and she blushes when she sees me.

"Hey," she says. "I'm super sorry I was eavesdropping on your conversation with Nate. I didn't mean to. Mom had just told me that Marc was coming over for dinner, so I was thinking about asking if you wanted to go with Bradley and me to the theaters tonight to get you away from him."

First off, she's apologizing to me and she means it. It's enough tenderness to put my fear in check. And she's inviting me out with her? I'm baffled by the offer. "That would be...nice."

I think I'm really starting to like my sister. But I have to know what she heard. I take her arm, shoot a look over my shoulder and, after checking to make sure we're alone, I say quietly, "Florence, how much did you hear?"

She shuffles her feet, looking supremely awkward. "Um, just a pinch. There was something about obnoxious mysteries, and Dad, and problems."

"What about Dad?"

"Uh..." she nervously pushes her glasses up. "He caused some obnoxious mystery."

I relax somewhat. She doesn't know he's still alive.

"Now, I don't mean to intrude," she says, "what is this about Dad? Why were you talking about him to Nate? And what mystery did he cause?"

I shake my head. "Nothing. It's...nothing."

Flo senses there definitely isn't nothing and that I don't want to share what. "I get it, you don't want to tell me. You can't trust me with critical information." She is defensive and bitter, but she's also genuinely hurt that I won't tell her.

I start to protest, but she says maturely, "No, it's okay. I don't blame you. But I hope that one day we can trust each other. Are you—and Nate—Is everything fine?"

"Yeah." I bit my lip. "We're fine."

"So…do you want to come with me? And Bradley?"

"Are you sure he won't mind if I do?"

"He won't. He's sweet like that." Flo smiles. "And I want to see if he can tell the difference between us. I don't think he has talked to you, or you, him. Of course, he knows I have a twin sister, but he hasn't seen the both of us side-by-side."

"You want to trick him?"

"I want to test him," she corrects. "See if he can figure out which of us is which."

I shrug. "Okay. I'll come. Beats having to stay up in my room all evening. I don't want to talk to Marc or even see his ugly face."

Flo giggles. "All right. I'll text Bradley and tell him we'll have a chaperone. And do you want to invite Nate?"

For the first time in a long time, Flo dresses like me. She wears a T-shirt and jeans, leaves her hair down, and doesn't put on even a hint of make-up. She looks exactly like me—and it's not just the clothes—and we have a laugh over it while standing in front of the bathroom mirror.

"No one is going to know which one of us is which," Flo says, taking out her dangly earrings and trading them for simple studs. They are the only jewelry she has decided to wear, and she looks less weighed-down without all her other pieces. She's really pretty without too much of anything.

"Good thing we know who we are," I say.

She scoffs, then smiles at my reflection. "Are you sure about that? We are identical. It's easy to get switched around."

"We're not identical." I pat the top of her head, and she swats me away. "I happen to be a couple inches taller than you, Florence. Anyone who knows that will easily tell the difference between us."

She pouts. "I should put on heels."

"Discreet heels."

"I don't know what that word means," she says, batting her eyelashes, and I have to roll my eyes at her feigned ignorance.

"You're so stuck-up," I say.

Flo laughs and links her arm through mine. "Whatever you say, sister dear. Come on. We've got to go test Mom."

"She'll know who we are," I argue good-naturedly, allowing her to pull me out of the bathroom.

"Psh." She leads me down the stairs—I'm wearing shoes and she isn't, and she slips a little on the bottom step—and we meet up with Mom in the living room. She's talking to Roman, who doesn't look happy in the slightest, and she does a double take when we come down.

Regaining control of her surprise, she says, "Well, it looks like Venice was cloned."

"From birth," I reply.

My twin is working hard not to grin. It would give us away if she did. Mom knows I rarely smile with my teeth showing—every time she takes a picture of me, she tells me I have to smile and show my teeth—and Flo definitely flashes hers.

"You're both going tonight?" Mom asks.

I nod. "Bradley was fine with it."

She narrows her eyes, calculating. "Hm. You *could* be Florence, since you talk like she does, especially when Bradley is concerned, but you're too tall to be Flo. I say you're Venice."

"Which one of us are you talking to?" Flo challenges.

Mom hesitates, then points to me.

"Ah. Good guess." I smile at her, not showing my teeth, and she instantly knows she was right.

"What time is Bradley getting here?" asks Mom.

Flo answers immediately. "About two minutes."

"You need shoes, Flo," I put in, and she snorts.

"And now you sound like me, Venice." She disengages from me and skips over to the hallway closet to dig through the shoes, though I don't think she puts her shoes there.

"You're not going to dress alike often, are you?"

I turn back to Mom. "Er—no? This is an once-in-a-lifetime experience. But it also might not. I don't know if Flo will want to wear T-shirts and jeans and sneakers for the rest of her life."

"I don't!" she calls from the hallway.

"Good." Mom breathes an exaggerated sigh of relief. "If I really *did* have a pair of identical twins, it would drive me crazy."

"Maybe I should dress like Flo," I muse.

Florence's scoff can be heard from where Mom and I stand. "I won't share my clothes with you, Venice."

"Thank the trees." Mom grins at me. "I can't have two of you like that."

"Hey!" My twin appears next to me, holding an old pair of my tennis shoes. "That is *very* offensive!"

"Bradley's here!" Roman yells, preventing Flo from continuing, and there's a violent flurry of movement as she bends down and quickly laces up my shoes, and Mom darts to look out the window to catch a glimpse of Bradley before he comes to the door, and I pull my phone out of my pocket to check the time. He has arrived at exactly three-fifteen.

A knock sounds on the door. Mom pivots and barges a way to the door, Flo hurrying after her. I take my time, but the second before Mom opens up the door, I link my arm through Flo's.

"Ready?" I whisper.

She grins at me. "As ever."

A second later, Mom is talking to Bradley, who is polite and gracious; he has a constant smile on his face as he talks or listens to what Mom is saying. He spots Florence and me, and his smile takes on more of a sheepish look.

"Hello," Flo says, wiggling her fingers at him.

"Hello, Florence," he says, addressing her directly. "This is your older twin sister?"

"Yes." She is obviously pleased he recognized her. Then again, she'd spoken first when I would not have. "Venice, this is Bradley. Bradley, this is Venice."

I give him a small wave. "Hi."

"Nice to meet you. And it's fun that you get to come with us."

Mom is surprised at how he acts. She hadn't expected him to be this way, so different from Flo's other dates.

"Should we get going?" asks my twin.

"Yes." Bradley steps back from the doorway so we can come out onto the porch. He then turns to Mom. "Mrs. Ferrari," he says, not using her maiden name as some might, "when would you like your daughters back? The movie doesn't start until half-past four, and it ends at six. And I was thinking maybe we would get some dinner, too."

"Ten is a good time," says Mom, even though ten-thirty is our curfew. "I'm having a visitor over, and he leaves around that time, so it'll be nice to have all the family back then."

Bradley nods. "All right. Ten it is."

I've studied him while he and Mom were conversing, and I find that I really think he's a kind person, having never talked to him before. He's tall, not as tall as Nate—I'm sure Nate is the tallest kid I know or have seen—and he has sandy-brown hair that is cut short. His eyes are light hazel, but at the same time have a slight shade of green. His build is wiry—he is strong and tough, yet gentle at heart. He constantly has a small smile on his face, and he looks so dang innocent, like he won't break Florence's heart just because he's too considerate.

All in all, he's the only boy I've ever approved of for my sister.

"Venice, you're lost in your thoughts again." Flo gives my arm a small, slight squeeze, shaking me free from La-La Land.

"Sorry." I push up my glasses. "Are we going now?"

She beams. "Yes."

"Goodbye," Mom says, moving to close the door. "Have fun. Don't return home late."

"We won't," Flo calls over her shoulder as the three of us make our way off the porch and out onto the driveway. Bradley's car is parked there, instead of at the curb, because Mom *always* parks hers by our mailbox. I don't know why, but she prefers the curb to our driveway.

"Legally, since I haven't had my license for over a year," Bradley says in a soft voice as we reach his car, "I'm not allowed to drive two people I'm not related to, so we'll have to be discreet."

I nudge Flo at his usage of one of my favorite words. She grins at me in reply.

"We're breaking the law? Awesome."

Bradley smiles at her, and it's the same sort of smile Elijah and Mandy give each other at lunch when Nate and I are watching them with discomfort at how awkward it is for us.

"I call shotgun!" Flo says, breaking away from me to slap the car door first.

I resist the urge to roll my eyes. "You don't need to fight me for a seat, Flo," I say.

"You're such a pacifist," she replies good-naturedly.

Bradley opens the door for Flo, then the backseat door for me, and I thank him with some surprise because of it. He also closes them, which is an act of thoughtfulness.

As he settles in the car, Flo turns on the radio and flips through different channels. Brief clips of all sorts of music greet my ears.

"What do you like?" she asks.

Bradley backs out of the driveway carefully, and it is how I would imagine him driving. He is a careful and cautious driver. Mom would approve of him, like how she disapproved of *my* careless and wild driving.

"I like all kinds of music," he says, slowly easing past Mom's car.

"Pop?" Flo hesitates on a certain station, and after a second of silence from us, she changes it. "Classical?" Instrumental music, soft and gentle, fills the car. It reminds me of Nate.

"My little brother likes classical a lot," says Bradley, leaving our neighborhood. I glance around, unable to stop myself, for Jargon, but we're alone. The street is empty.

"My little brother likes rock." Flo changes the station again, and we hear the kind of music Pompeii listens to all the time: screaming guitars and screaming men and screaming everything.

Bradley smiles at the song, at her, I don't know. "I've heard this one before. It's pretty good."

"Then rock it is."

I look out the window as they talk about their favorite songs, and I feel rather comforted. We're meeting Nate at the theater and tomorrow I have a spa date with Moira that I'm not entirely looking forward to—I'm not big into the spa, but Moira is cool.

And I almost feel like a normal teenager having a normal high school experience—except that I'm in incessant danger.

But my family is happy. Flo is happy. Roman is too. And Mom. As for Siena and Pompeii? They're happy fighting with each other.

I have to force back a stupid grin.

FIFTY

TO: Hubris Jargon, Malaise Tone
FROM: Sleepy Gumption
SUBJECT:
TIME: 10:32 p.m.
DATE: Wednesday, March 18

I am done waiting. We will do it now.

FIFTY-ONE

My week is really, really hard. I have to take the bus to school with Roman and Flo—Mom isn't pleased about that—but at least I'm able to use the excuse that it's too cold out to walk. At the movies, Nate had told me how his grandpa had sobered up a little and was even in a good mood, wanting to clean himself up and get out of the house a bit. So Nate was planning to miss school and ride out the good moment while it lasted.

I'm surprised at how much his presence makes an impact on my school experience. Especially after last week, I've really come to depend on his "pathetic attempts to make me laugh" and yes, his dimples. Biology isn't as fun without him sitting next to me, ready to share something he finds amusing; lunch isn't as fun without him there, his quiet presence comforting; and my trips to and from school are boring and bleak. The bus is shockingly loud—I put in earbuds to block out most of the noise—and none of my friends ride on the same one as me. Although Florence shares a seat with me, she talks with her buddies the whole time, and I'm left alone. I don't mind it, though; I'm glad she has good friends.

To make matters worse, after Sunday afternoon at the theater, I haven't had a real conversation with Nate. He's texted me updates on his grandpa, all amazingly positive, but it feels like forever since we talked. I don't know if it's because I offended him or something, but being cut off from him is really bringing me down.

I'm not threatened by Jargon or Marc, even though when we came back from the movies Marc had still been here, talking to Mom. I had avoided eye contact, hurried up to my room, and checked on my ring to make sure it was in my book. Thank the trees it was. I know I've put it in a random place that won't be discovered easily, but I'm still paranoid that someone *will*. Especially after Marc rifled through Flo's jewelry in search of it. Knowing me, he might guess where it is.

Roman doesn't approach me again with questions about Dad. I'm impressed that he called the chief of police over the town in Kentucky to talk about the weird accident, and I'm impressed that he actually got an answer and some new information. I don't want to start a conversation centered around this topic that could lead to him finding out everything I know, so I don't approach *him*.

Mom's garden, starting out in the garage, isn't working as well as she had hoped. She won't give up, of course, and Siena has already painted the four bamboo boxes, decorating them with tiny colorful vegetables and a random unicorn. She told me it was in honor of Chuck the Unicorn, the one from the show we watched when Mom was getting drunk at Marc's, and I'm surprised that she remembers that show. I've forgotten it. All I can recall from that horrible night was my anxiety that Mom wasn't back yet and Flo was nice to me and my siblings all fell asleep in the living room while we waited for Mom.

I wonder every day if I should call the police or tell Mom about everything going on. I wonder if I should tell her that Dad is alive, that he's here, in our town. I wonder if I should tell her someone wants my ring badly enough to kill me, and has tried to before. I wonder if I should tell her that one of the reasons I don't like Marc is because he's working with the man who kidnapped Dad and nearly ran me over.

But I don't say anything. I'm worried she will freak out and force me to stay in the house. I'm worried she won't believe me and think me only to be saying this to make her turn against Marc. She knows I don't like him. And after I told her about his aura being off, she doesn't take my distrust towards him seriously.

On a more happy note, Flo is much happier and therefore much kinder to us all. She is cheerful to everyone—more than I am these days—and she can talk to Mom and Roman without arguing. She doesn't say things that are offensive just to spite one of us. Florence stops caring about her image, stops caring about being popular, stops caring about having everyone look at her. All in all, she's a much different person from the stuck-up chic girl she was just two months ago, and we get along way better.

At school during the week, Mandy and Elijah seem surprised to see me all by myself when I'm outside after getting off the bus. I'm usually with Nate. Mandy asks me every day if I know what's going on with him, and I pass along the updates he gives me.

Elijah keeps the conversations alive, but it's only because he rambles on about his hilarious siblings and if he should get a tattoo secretly; apparently, his mom is very against tattoos—especially when her sixteen year-old son wants one. And I agree with Mrs. Jenkins, not saying anything to Elijah's face, of course, but Mandy thinks if he gets one, it'll make him more macho than he already is.

Thursday morning dawns like all the other mornings: cold, cloudy, cheerless. I almost want to stay in bed, where it's warm, but Flo is digging around in our room and making a lot of noise.

"Why do you have to be so loud?" I mumble, pulling my blanket over my head. No doubt I'm tangling my hair even worse than it already is.

Flo's voice answers. She's in a cheerful mood, as always. "Don't mind me! I'm just trying to find those shirts Grandma Pope bought for us. They are in here somewhere..."

I groan and sit up, my blanket tumbling down to my hips. I reach for my glasses on my bedside table and slide them on. "The dark green ones with a white heart? The ones promoting saving the environment?"

"Yes." Flo escapes from the closet. "I gave you mine since I was never going to wear it. I used to hate T-shirts."

"And now you're okay with them?"

"I like to diversify my style. It keeps things interesting."

"T-shirts can get addictive. Pretty soon you won't want to wear anything else."

She giggles. "I'm sure I'll always want pants and socks, too."

I roll my eyes. "Yeah, yeah. The shirts should be in my second drawer."

"Why do you put your clothes in a drawer?" asks Flo, moving to the dresser.

"Because you hog the closet."

She giggles again, rummaging through the drawer where I put my shirts. They get wrinkled in there if I don't fold them, and I never do, so they're wrinkled.

"Found it." Flo pulls the two identical shirts out, then separates them and tosses me one. "You should wear that today."

"Mom won't like it."

She snorts, already changing out of her pajama top. "It's been a while since I've done something that Mom doesn't like. This one is harmless. She will be able to tell us apart. You *are* taller than me."

"Ha! You admit it."

Flo pulls on the shirt. "I never denied it." After fixing her hair, she stands in front of the mirror and admires her reflection. "I really do look like you," she says.

"And is that a good thing or a bad thing?" I ask, giving up on sleeping and getting out of bed.

"A good thing, of course." She disentangles her glasses from a curl where they had gotten stuck. "I wouldn't tell myself I look horrible."

I shake my head, amused.

Sudden loud voices sound from downstairs, quickly followed by laughter. Florence sighs. "They're having fun without me," she says. "I'm going to join them. See you later! Make sure you wear that shirt, or I will force you into it. I know I'm not big into saving the environment, but it will totally be fun if we actually start acting like identical twins."

"Fun," I echo. "Yeah."

She frowns at me, then leaves the room, her hair swinging.

I cross the room and close the door, cutting off some of the loud voices from down below. I quickly change into jeans and the green T-shirt Flo wants me to wear, though I haven't worn it before and it's wrinkled. A lot. It also is slightly too small for me and doesn't quite reach my hips. I'm not usually for shirts that fall too short; I'm rather self-conscious of showing off my skin. Florence doesn't have a problem with it—she likes it when people look at her—but I don't.

My hair proves to be hard to brush. I give up after a minute and simply stare at myself in the mirror. I should ask Mom to cut it shorter. It falls almost to my waist. My curls are crazy and explosive and springy, near impossible to brush.

I shake my head and grab a pair of socks from my bottom drawer. I shove them in my pocket, then pick up my backpack and place my phone inside. I haven't received any texts.

Slinging my backpack over my shoulder, I open the bedroom door and go out into the hallway. My family is still talking loudly, and it sounds like all of them are awake. They must have no respect for the one person in the house who was trying to sleep.

I step down the stairs quietly, not drawing any attention to myself. I can't see my family—they're all in the living room—and when I come off the stairs and around the wall separating the staircase from the living room, I stop in my tracks.

Roman and Pompeii are sitting on the floor next to the coffee table. Siena is on the couch, chin on her palms, elbows on her knees. Mom is standing, laughing at something that was just shared, something I missed. And sitting by Siena, a notebook in his lap and a pen in his left hand is—

My heart skips a beat.

"...trees are the hardest, with all the leaves and how the trunk sometimes is too fat or too skinny," Nate is saying. He has his eyes on Siena; he doesn't see me in the doorway. "I admire that you've chosen a difficult picture to draw. My trees always turn into an unrecognizable mess of ink or lead, but yours are excellent."

I cross my arms and lean against the door frame, watching Siena dive into an explanation on how her different paint brushes help with the strokes and details. Nate seems interested, but that might only be because he's like that, and he still hasn't noticed me. I am quite glad to see him, and suddenly stressed that I certainly hadn't planned on walking.

Mom finally spots me while Nate and Siena are discussing the branches, Nate drawing what she is saying. I never thought he was an artist on paper, and I haven't seen him draw before, only write. And he's using his left hand to draw, which means his right aches. But he isn't wearing gloves or a jacket. His scars are in plain sight. Has my family seen them? Have they asked any questions about them?

"Venice!" says Mom, claiming my attention. Nate looks up at the sound of my name and gives me a smile.

"Venice," Mom says again, and I meet her gaze. She frowns at me. "Wait—you *are* Venice, right?"

I nod. "Of course. I'm not in the middle of an identity crisis."

"You sure sound like Florence," Pompeii speaks up.

I throw him a saucy look and toss my hair over my shoulder in perfect imitation of how my twin does it.

Roman laughs. "I thought Mom told you there couldn't be two of you. Yet here you are, Venice, acting like Florence."

"How do you know I'm Venice?" I challenge.

545

He grins at me. "Flo wouldn't stare at Nate as long as you did."

I roll my eyes and step away from the door frame. "I'm going to go make my lunch."

"Good morning to you, too," Nate laughs.

I don't bother replying. I walk down the hallway and into the kitchen, first finding Flo at the cutting board, making a sandwich, and next spotting tiny snowflakes drifting down outside. I move to the kitchen window and look out, watching the snow.

"It's March," Flo says, "and it's snowing. Sort of."

"At least we finally get some." I stare at the snow for another moment, then turn around and wait for Flo to finish with her lunch so I can make my own. "Siena has been looking forward to having it snow. She wants to shove some in Pompeii's face."

"Ah, typical siblings." Flo smiles at me. "She hasn't noticed yet that it's snowing. She's busy being obnoxious about her trees."

"Nate doesn't mind. And how long has he been here, anyway? I woke up like five minutes ago."

Flo places her sandwich in a container and snaps it closed. "I don't know. He was in the living room when I went down."

"Oh." I go to slice bread, but she shoves the container at me.

"I made you lunch. Now hurry up and get ready. He's waiting for you, and even though he would wait for you until the end of the world, it's impolite to make him late."

"Thanks, Florence." I cram the sandwich in my backpack and rummage around in the cabinets for something to eat for breakfast. My stomach grumbles, announcing that I am *starving*, and Florence smirks.

She pulls the bag of trail mix out of the pantry and pours a handful onto her palm. "I don't understand how you can eat this," she says as I snag the bag from her and drop the entire thing into my backpack after sealing it. "I mean, look how gross it is. There isn't any chocolate."

"Pompeii and Siena cherry-picked them all out." I take my

water bottle out of my backpack pocket and clean it out in the sink before refilling it. "Chocolate lasts barely a minute in our house."

"Mom doesn't like chocolate."

I screw on my bottle lid and shake off a few loose drops of water. "She's weird. We all know that."

Flo laughs. "Very true."

"Do you know of anything else I can bring?" I ask, glancing throughout the airy kitchen. We don't have any fresh fruits—Mom hasn't been to the store in a week—and there isn't much food left. We're all out of snacks, despite them being organic and tasting like wheat germ.

"No." Flo pats my arm. "Guess you'll just have to starve."

I grin at her. "I'm not *that* hungry."

"Venice! You have to leave soon!"

Mom's shout startles both of us. Florence matches my grin and pushes me towards the living room, where Nate is waiting. "Have fun," she says in a soft whisper. She scoops my backpack off the floor and hands it to me, surprised at the weight of it. "What do you have in here? Books?"

"Exactly." I snatch up my water bottle and slide it back into its pocket. "I'm lonely without my books."

She just rolls her eyes and gives me another push.

I laugh to myself and leave the kitchen, stopping by the closet to collect my shoes and coat before progressing into the entryway. Nate is still drawing, with Siena watching, and Mom is talking to Pompeii and Roman. The boys look bored with the conversation. And they probably are. Mom is explaining—in detail—how her garden-in-the-garage is harder than she thought.

I sit down on the third step on the staircase and pull on my socks, then my shoes, and lace them tightly. I try to work quickly.

"You do your boughs that way?" asks Siena. "I always thought that took a lot more time."

"You're the expert," says Nate. "I wouldn't know."

I hide a smile and stand up. "Siena," I say, "did you see the snow outside?"

She glances over her shoulder out the window. "It's only the flakes," she replies, sounding disgruntled. "There has to be an inch or so before I can make a snowball."

And shove it down Pompeii's pants.

"It wasn't supposed to snow today," Mom puts in, giving up on talking to the boys.

"The weather report is constantly changing," I add.

She frowns at me—I'd used one of her excuses for planting a garden this early. I smile in reply, and she looks away from me. "You're going to be late if you take any longer."

"I'm ready," I say, pulling on my coat.

Nate hands the notebook and pen to Siena, who immediately rips out the page and holds it up. His picture is really good; the tree is an evergreen that instantly makes me suspicious, and I narrow my eyes at him. He shrugs and picks up his backpack from off the floor where it had sat by his feet.

"It's official," Siena says, shaking the paper. "Nate is my favorite person in the world."

"Gee, thanks," Mom mutters.

Nate grins at my sister. "I've never officially been someone's favorite before. What are the perks?"

"I won't pour my paint on you, throw a plate at you, or soak your clothes in vegetable oil."

"Those are great perks," Nate says without a trace of sarcasm.

"Wait." Pompeii shoots up, anger spreading across his face. "You were the one who drenched my clothes in oil?"

I back towards the door, motioning for Nate to follow. We should leave right now, or we will suffer the consequences of being caught in the crossfire. Siena and Pompeii are swelling up, both preparing themselves for an intense shout-out, and it certainly will be explosive.

"Venice." Mom catches my eye. "Make sure you come home directly after school. I don't have work today and I want to do something with the whole family."

I twist the doorknob and pull open the door a second before Siena starts to shout. I stumble out of the house, laughing, and Nate is right behind me. He closes the door, and we make our way down the driveway, both laughing hard.

"They're always like that, right?" Nate asks.

I nod. "Always. I didn't know about the oil thing, but I did see Siena hit Pompeii with a plate, and Florence was babysitting them when Siena poured her paint on him."

"Your siblings are awesome."

"I'm not sure that's the correct word to use to describe them. Difficult is one. Annoying is another."

"Perhaps, but they are entertaining too, you must admit."

"Very true. Nate, why didn't you text me this morning or call? I would have been ready for you. In fact, I haven't heard from you since early yesterday."

Nate raises an eyebrow. "Yes, well, I have some bad news. The reason I haven't talked to you since then is because after what I thought was some real progress, my grandpa became suddenly and surprisingly violent. I haven't seen a rage like this one in a long time. I actually had to step out of the house for a while with Mercury. I was worried he'd hurt himself so we stayed nearby. When I went back in I found that he'd smashed both my phone and my laptop into tiny little bits."

My mouth falls open.

He reaches over and nudges my chin up, closing my mouth. His fingers are warm, despite the cold air all around us. "He's never done anything like that. And I'd worked hard to save up money for them." He shrugs.

"I'm sorry, Nate. I'm just so glad it wasn't you he pulverized. Why did he wreck them?" I'm horrified.

"Probably because I wasn't there," he admits. "But that's why it seemed like I fell off the edge of the world."

"Glad *that* didn't happen," I mutter.

He ignores me. "My grandpa was in a terrible mood," he goes on. "After those couple of days of peace, I had some real hope that he was ready to regain control on his life. But he totally flipped out. It took forever to calm him down—"

"Where did he hurt you?" I interrupt.

Nate throws me an irritated look. And that's when I notice he has a long cut running down the center of his right cheek and over his jaw, where it disappears into his neck. Unable to stop myself, I lift a hand and trace a finger down the cut.

"I thought you said he didn't hit you on the face."

"He missed."

I drop my hand and shake my head. "That's just horrible, Nate. Anywhere else?"

"Oh, only a few scratches on my arms. And my ankles. And one shard sliced right through my shirt."

"Are things a little better now?" I ask bluntly. "You're able to come to school today."

He flinches. "Gramps hurt himself. It calmed him, surprisingly, and I was able to leave the house early this morning without waking him. I was hoping...well, I just wanted to see you." He smiles softly, and it makes me overcome my temper and thankfully let it slip away. I don't want to be angry with him, and I smile back at him, his warm fingers threading through mine.

"But this morning..." He hesitates. "I left the house really early, before he'd woken up, because I *had* to go over to your place and make sure you were still safe and you needed an explanation as to why I was..." he waves his free hand in the air and doesn't finish.

I don't speak. I don't want to say the wrong thing, but I'm so frustrated that this kind of thing has been going on so long.

"Of course, I arrived there half an hour early," Nate continues.

"You weren't even awake. And your siblings and mom kept me company. Siena was very entertaining. She made me draw a bunch of different things for her, namely trees."

"I didn't know you were an artist like that."

"I don't normally draw. I'm not very good. But Siena wanted me to, and she was rather demanding, so I did."

"Siena is *extremely* demanding," I say. "She pretty much gets whatever she wants and more. Also, I noticed you used your left hand to draw. Is your other hurt?"

"Actually, no." Nate shakes his head. "Siena was sitting on my right, so I decided using my left hand would make things easier. She wouldn't bump my arm while I was drawing if she sat away from it."

"Smart."

We walk in silence. I feel like I have so many things I want to say to him, but whenever I open my mouth, I change my mind, willing myself to be patient and understanding. I have some serious opinions about his situation.

"Did anything interesting happen to you?" he asks. "While I was cut off from existence."

"Um…" I push up my glasses. "Nothing much. I haven't been bothered. I've taken special care to ride the bus and constantly be surrounded by people when I'm outside. And I haven't seen Jargon since a week ago."

Nate squeezes my hand. "That's good."

"Oh, did I tell you that I showed Roman the sketchy video of my dad's crash?"

"Wait." He pulls me to a stop and frowns at me. "Roman? You shared this with your brother? No, you didn't tell me."

"I was going to," I say, starting to walk again. I tell him about trying to connect with Roman, his suspicions, and my decision to tell him. I catch him up on what Roman learned from the police chief in Kentucky. "But I didn't tell him anything about the ring and about seeing Dad. We were interrupted and I never really had a chance or an inclination to tell him the rest. It was nice to let him know, though."

"Did you end up telling your mom, too? Maybe it's time we both try to get professionals involved in helping us."

"What are you saying? Should we go to the police? Do we have enough evidence? And what do you mean, both of us?"

He takes a minute to answer me. "Venice, I think I'm starting to convince myself that the best solution is sending my grandpa to a care center where employees are trained to look after old folks with mental problems and substance abuse. Except, I'm not sure I have the proper authority to do it right. I don't want my grandpa in some state corrections facility so, as much as I don't want to ask, I'll need help from my dad..." he sighs. "I don't exactly know what is best for my grandpa."

"If you sent him in," I say slowly, "and didn't tell anyone it was because of the abuse—"

"But it's not only the abuse," he cuts in. "He really *is* suffering from mental illness."

"Yes. What I'm saying is, your grandpa has tons of reasons to be admitted into a mental health facility. The people around here won't think you're doing it for your own safety—they'll understand your grandpa needs professional help."

"Precisely. I'm just worried about Keller. He'll realize I sent in my grandpa because of how he treats me, and I'm stressed Keller will spread the word. After all, there's nothing keeping him back."

"How were you guys even friends?"

Nate smiles. "Same way you and I became friends. He moved in, didn't know anyone, didn't know who to talk to. He never hung out with us during lunch. I think he didn't like Mandy, but we had some of the same classes and always talked then. We were okay friends until he started noticing all my scars and how I walked to school and never mentioned my grandpa. Then he was rude about it, followed me home, and discovered the answers."

"If he followed you, what were the chances of your grandpa picking that moment to hurt you?"

"Oh, Gramps was in a terrible mood," Nate explains. "Had been all week. It was unfortunate Keller chose then to spy on me."

"Why do you think he hasn't ratted you out?"

He takes a minute to reply, and in that time a school bus rumbles past us, the one that is carrying my siblings. I resist the urge to wave at the tinted windows.

"I have no idea," Nate says finally. "I don't know why Keller hasn't told anyone about my grandpa. And last Tuesday, when he rudely pushed you over and asked if I'd gotten my grandpa arrested, he said so in front of you, which leads me to believe he thinks you know everything. And you do."

"Do I?"

Nate looks down at me, not amused, and I hide a smile. "You should *not* be doubting that," he says. "You figured out most, and I told you the rest."

"Oh!" I say, suddenly remembering something from Sunday. "When I went to buy seeds with my mom, we went to the store where Charles Hill is the manager."

"Charles? Oh, yeah. He's really nice."

"We talked about you. He said you bring Mercury with you."

Nate swings our hands back and forth, needing to release some of his nervous energy. "Yeah, I do. Pretty much every time I go to that store, I take Mercury with me. He needs to get away from my grandpa as often as possible."

"Has he ever been hurt?"

Nate hesitates. Up ahead, I can see the high school. Kids are swarming the sidewalks, all laughing and chatting noisily. The snow must be creating some excitement, though it's only flakes and they are rather weak. I think it might stop soon.

"Once," admits Nate. "There was glass all over the place, and Mercury cut himself. But it wasn't my grandpa's fault. Well, it sort of was, since he'd been the one to break the bottles and spread glass everywhere, but he didn't *personally* cut Mercury."

"You should bring him over to my house. Dogs are pretty much the only thing Pompeii isn't scared of, and he really likes them."

"Last time I asked if I could take him with me, you said no. That Mercury looks too much like a bear."

"He does!"

Nate shakes his head in disagreement, though he's smiling. He looks out into the road—we're almost to the school—and opens his mouth to say something, but he suddenly jerks to a stop, his smile fading.

"What's wrong?"

He turns to me, his eyes dark. "Jargon's coming up the street."

I flinch. I peer behind him and see that so-familiar black SUV hesitating at a stop sign, waiting for the road to clear so he can come after me. "Do you think he has seen me?"

"I don't know." Nate grabs my coat hood and pulls it over my head, covering my hair. He turns his back to the road, keeping me hidden from view, angling himself so there's an impossibly-slight chance of keeping Jargon from catching sight of me.

I turn my head down, try to calm my racing heart. I hear that awful roar of the SUV's engine coming up the street towards us. I wonder if it's really Jargon and if he *has* seen me and if he's here to take me in front of witnesses.

Nate shifts again, and I admire that he has the courage to have his back on our enemy. "It really is him," he whispers, and my heart just about stops beating.

I expect to hear the car slow down when it passes us, but it continues on at a roar, leaving only horrible exhaust behind.

Ten whole seconds pass until Nate sighs and steps back. He looks angry yet tranquil at the same time.

"He saw you," he says quietly. "He knew it was you."

"How do you know?"

Nate gives me a sad half-smile that doesn't contain any of his usual light. "Venice, he only had eyes for you. His attention was trained on you as he drove by. He's getting impatient, and he most likely would have taken you if I hadn't been with you. This just shows you can't ever be alone outside."

I shiver, and it isn't because I'm cold. I shove back my hood—the only thing it does is mess up my hair even more—and try to assume a hopeful but knowledgeable expression. "Nate. He hasn't gotten me yet."

"He will someday." He takes my hand, resumes our walk. "You just be extra careful, okay? I don't want you to get hurt."

"I can assure you, I don't want to, either," I say.

"Which means you aren't going to take risks, right?"

"Of course."

Nate frowns at me. "The way you said that made it sound like you definitely *are* going to take risks, not the other way around."

I watch as we come closer to the school, where the buses are unloading all of the students. "I won't endanger my life on purpose, I promise. Though, I think coming here"—I gesture to the building in front of us—"contradicts that promise."

"What do you mean?"

"Every time I meet up with Mandy, it's dangerous. One of these days, she is seriously going to break my ribs."

"Her hugs aren't *that* powerful."

I have successfully, intentionally, moved the subject on to something else, something I would rather discuss. "Really? Because every single one has just about cracked them."

"I guess I'll have to see for myself. She last hugged me a few years ago on my birthday."

"Sad. I should get her to update your chart."

"Thank you for caring, Venice. I think Mandy will probably be too busy with Elijah to remember that she is due on nearly breaking my ribs."

My heart has slowed considerably, and I internally thank Nate for keeping this conversation away from Jargon. "I'm glad they were able to realize that they were meant for each other."

"Remember when I said you would be a better matchmaker than me? And you disagreed? Well, look what you caused in just a few months. You pretty much brought them together. I've known them for *years*, and I haven't ever tried to do anything to make them recognize they would be a perfect couple. They're both video game addicts and have insanely short attention spans..."

"And enjoy geeking out about things they like."

"Namely, video games."

I laugh, and Nate smiles and leads me across the street to the school, both of us frequently checking to make sure no cars are coming. Once we merge with the other kids, Nate changes from the talkative person he is when we're alone to the more quiet person he is publicly. Unobtrusively, we look around for Mandy and Elijah, who must be somewhere out here. They always wait outside for us after getting off their bus, no matter the weather.

"What time is it?" I ask Nate and we push our way through the crowd.

He takes a moment to answer. "Eight. Exactly. We have three minutes until we have to be in our homerooms."

"Mandy and Elijah might already be there."

"I'm sure he would use anything as an excuse to hang around here instead of being in class."

I smile, because it's the complete truth, and that's when I hear someone yell my name, followed shortly by Nate's.

He startles as Mandy appears out of nowhere and throws her arms around him, squeezing him tightly. I smirk. It's his turn to suffer the wrath of her incredible upper-arm strength. And we had just been talking about this.

Nate awkwardly pats her head—he's at least a foot taller than her—just as Elijah arrives.

"Why are you hugging my girlfriend, Nate?" asks Elijah.

"Can't...breathe," Nate chokes out.

Mandy finally steps back, beaming up at him. "You're here! We all thought you had gotten eaten by a tiger or something!"

"Tigers don't live in Virginia," he says, grimacing as he moves farther away from her, rather gingerly.

"My cousin got eaten by a tiger in Virginia," says Mandy.

I grin. I've missed her a lot, and I saw her yesterday.

"He worked at the zoo," she continues. "We all told him not to try to train the tiger when she was hungry, but did he listen? No. And look how that ended up for him."

I exchange a look with Nate. He has a hand pressed to his ribs and a half-smile on his face.

"It's a true story!" she says, sensing our disbelief. Then she lets a sheepish grin spread across her face. "Except for the true part."

We all laugh at the exact moment the bell rings.

"Yes!" Elijah pumps his fist. "Fourth day in a row! I'm late."

"Is this what happens when I'm gone?" Nate asks me. "Elijah is purposely late to his homeroom? And no one stops him?"

"Apparently," I reply.

"Since we're already late," says Mandy, "why don't you tell me if you're our friend Venice or her creepy twin sister who suddenly looks just like you? When I got here, there was a girl identical to you talking to these kids, and you never talk to random people."

"I'm Venice," I confirm. "Florence has discovered that T-shirts and jeans are a valid and comfortable style. Plus she wants to play up the identical twin thing today. Frankly, I'm flattered."

Mandy folds her arms over her chest and gives me a suspicious look. "The two of you *never* gave me a hard time distinguishing who was who. I always knew how to tell the difference between you and Florence. Others couldn't, but I could. However, now I can't. And it doesn't help that you're wearing the same shirt as your twin was."

I glance down at my dark green T-shirt. "That was her point."

"Good thing you have a different coat than she does," says Elijah. "If not, I wouldn't be able to tell if you were our best friend or our mortal enemy."

Mandy jabs her elbow into his side, and he grunts. "That was rude, Elijah," she scolds. "Don't talk about Florence like that, and especially not in front of her sister!"

I shake my head as the two start arguing. "I have to get to class," I tell Nate. "See you at lunch."

"That seems like such a long time away," he says, walking with me into the school building. I don't know where he has to go, but he'll be even later if he goes with me to my homeroom.

"Just because you skipped school the past three days doesn't mean you can't handle a couple of hours by yourself," I tease.

"I didn't skip school. And it's not that I'll be alone. I often am. It's that I'll have to give my teachers a believable and significant explanation as to why I've been gone for the past three days. I'll have to say my grandpa was sick, and then they might ask more questions—"

"Okay, okay, I get it." I give him a gentle shove. "Go on. I'll see you at lunch."

He stops and stares at me for one long, blissful minute, then nods and disappears down another hallway. I hurry off to my class, hoping I'm not too late and that I won't get in more trouble.

FIFTY-TWO

Nate and I are the first to our table at lunch. Mandy and Elijah show up about a half second later, both complaining about the extra homework they have and how their teachers are biased and have favorites in class and never give those kids more work.

"Totally unfair that the kids who come early don't get make-up work," says Nate.

Mandy rolls her eyes. "I know! Ugh. None of my teachers like me."

"And it's all because of your mom," says Elijah, sitting down next to Nate. "And that day you brought a squirrel into each of your classes. Remember how much fun that was?"

She claims the empty seat by me. "Greatest day of my life."

"Squirrels?" I ask, still in the dark.

Nate takes pity on me. "Elijah bet Mandy she couldn't catch a squirrel, but she caught three and brought them here, to class, and released one per class she had in the morning. No one knew where the squirrels came from, so she didn't get in trouble."

"What did your teachers do with the squirrel problem? Did they have to put the rodents back outside?"

"Well..." Mandy pulls out her lunch and sets it on the table. "The squirrels managed to escape the classrooms, since someone happened to be seated near the door and opened it"—she flashes me a grin—"and all my rodent friends ran out into the hallway. The principal called animal control and had this huge search conducted throughout the school, wanting to find where the squirrels had come in, and he never suspected that it might have been a student, not an open window."

"How come you always have interesting events in your life?" I ask. "I feel so dull compared to you."

She pats my arm. "Don't worry. You're not dull."

"Thanks."

"Having a twin must be fun," she continues. "And you're the oldest kid in your family, so your siblings aren't all grown up and obnoxious and the worst people ever."

"No, they're young and obnoxious," I say.

Nate makes noise that sounds like he agrees. "Occasionally," he says. "They aren't terrible."

"My little sister is only angelic in front of others who aren't her family," I reply, opening my backpack and sifting through the items inside for the sandwich Flo made for me.

"Your family sounds like mine," comments Elijah.

At this, Nate, who is surprisingly talkative right now, turns to Elijah and says, "Your siblings are just great, Elijah. Remember when Oliver threw up all over Mateo? He did it on accident. And he even *apologized* afterward."

"And in my family," I cut in, "my sister would purposely do it."

"Has she?" asks Mandy.

I think about it. "Yes. Twice on me, three times on Roman, and too many times to count on Pompeii."

"And you're not talking about Florence, right?"

I laugh at that. "No. My littlest sister. Siena."

"I should meet her one day," says Mandy. "We can collaborate. And then we will plan world domination and rule the galaxy. *And*, we'll banish older brothers."

"Only if they're annoying," Elijah puts in. "Because I'm an older brother."

Mandy gives him a long, hard look. "Maybe," she says finally.

I lean forward and whisper to Nate, "Remind me to never let Mandy meet Siena."

"Noted," he whispers back.

Elijah, with his short attention span, has grown bored of this conversation and is now dumping out his entire backpack in search of his lunch. He talks all the while. "My mom always forgets to send good food with me, and it's a pain, since she gives me gross stuff that she says is good for my body, but I think she's only saying that because she wants me to eat the leftovers that have been in the fridge too long. I mean, look at this! It's ancient meatloaf." He holds up a container. "I can't eat this for lunch. I'll get food poisoning and die, and that would be a horrible way to die. Not dramatic at all. And I don't even have a tattoo yet."

Nate snags the container from Elijah and peels back the lid. "Mandy, when did Mrs. Jenkins make meatloaf?"

"Uh, yesterday, I think," she replies.

"See? Ancient." Elijah huffs. "I *hate* meatloaf."

"I'll eat it." Nate sets the container down in front of him. "Do you have a fork? Actually, why would I want a fork from you? It has probably been up your nose."

"I did that with a butter knife," Elijah corrects. "It tickled."

I grimace. I can't believe we're seriously having a conversation like this. And that Elijah is talking about sticking a butter knife up his nose and no one seems to care.

"Here, Nate, I have a fork." Mandy throws a plastic fork at him. The handle is snapped in half.

"Where did you get this?" he asks suspiciously.

"Definitely not the floor."

He shrugs. "Okay." Without further ado, he begins eating. I notice he uses his right hand instead of his left.

I finally find my lunch and take out my sandwich. Mandy is talking to Elijah about her favorite most-embarrassing moment in her life, which completely confuses me. Why would she have a favorite most-embarrassing moment?

Then again, why would she not?

The first bite I take is strange. I peel the bread slices apart and groan, the sound attracting everyone's attention.

"What's up?" asks Mandy.

"Florence made this for me," I say, "and she forgot the honey. It's just plain peanut butter."

"How sad," Mandy sympathizes. "You said she made it? Even the bread?"

I nod absentmindedly, smushing my sandwich back together. "It's the only thing she can bake."

"I can't bake or cook anything. I once burned water."

I take another bite, preventing me from replying. Which is fine, since Elijah is talking. "My mom is good at cooking," he says. "But the meals she makes are disgusting."

"Only because you don't like them," says Nate.

"I don't like them, because I never eat them. You always eat everything."

"Because you don't eat it."

"Because you're eating it!"

"I think we get the idea," Mandy interrupts, and I internally thank her for it.

My sandwich, despite missing its key ingredient, is delicious, and I finish it after barely a minute. I was starving. I hadn't had breakfast. "How often do you have dinner at the Jenkins'?" I ask Nate.

"Whenever I can." He gives the empty container back to Elijah. "Thanks for not wanting your lunch, Elijah."

"Thanks for eating it. Now my mom will think I did."

"You're welcome."

I shake my head and exchange an amused look with Mandy. We both don't get it. *Boys,* she mouths, and I grin.

"So, Nate," she says, turning to him, "I didn't ask this earlier, since I didn't want to make us even later than we already were, but where were you the past few days?"

He shifts in his seat, nervous. "My grandpa was sick. I had to take care of him. Turns out he's a really difficult patient."

"Oh." Mandy frowns. "I feel like a terrible friend, Nate. I didn't even know you were ambidextrous until Venice told me forever ago. And I had no clue about your scars, either."

Elijah looks lost. "What scars? Nate's ambidextrous?"

I hold Nate's gaze for barely a second before he extends his right arm and shows off the scars covering it. Mandy leans forward for a closer look. Elijah raises his eyebrows in surprise, but his surprise doesn't last long—it quickly becomes awe.

"Those are so cool!" he exclaims. "Dude, I want scars like those. They're kinda like tattoos."

Nate is visibly startled. "Oh...thanks, I guess?"

"How did you get them?" asks Mandy, leaving her seat to walk around the table. She takes his arm in her hands and examines his scars, just as I had done weeks ago.

"Uh..." Nate's eyes flick over to me. I nod, urging him on. "Each one was a different story," he says. "Some were my fault. Others weren't. But it seems like every cut I get takes forever to heal and ends up a scar. I'm amazed that I have so many."

"Yeah." Mandy drops his arm and picks up his other. "This one's the same."

"Not exactly." He is obviously uncomfortable. He doesn't like her touching him. He didn't when I had, either.

Elijah clears his throat. "Nate," he says, "why is my girlfriend touching you so often today?"

Mandy shoots him a nasty look and lets go of Nate. "You're just jealous."

"I want to know why!" Elijah protests.

"Sounds like jealousy to me," says Mandy, returning to her

seat. "Nate, you never told me how you got your scars. I'm guessing Venice knows, given the fact she hasn't asked any questions, but you aren't saying anything. Would you like to tell us about your scars?"

Nate hesitates. "Um…"

A sudden and loud noise startles us all. Mandy reaches into her backpack and pulls out her phone, turns off the five-minute alarm. She keeps her gaze pinned on Nate, waiting for an answer.

"I—" he stops. "I can't explain right now. It won't make sense, and it'll take too long, and we don't have enough time."

"Okay." Mandy looks disappointed. "In your own due time."

She's more patient than I am.

"That reminds me," says Elijah, snapping his fingers. "Nate, my mom wants you to come over to my house and babysit my little siblings while she takes me to get my license."

"Mandy's not available?" Nate says.

"I'm a terrible babysitter. Plus my mom has me in therapy this afternoon." Mandy shrugs carelessly.

Nate stares at me for a moment, then says slowly, "I'm busy. I can't."

"Dude, it's my license!"

"Nate, you can help out," I say, getting to my feet. "You're not doing anything this afternoon."

"Is that code for something?" Mandy inquires. "You two are staring at each other strangely. I feel like I'm missing something."

"You're right, Venice," he says, ignoring her. But it's all he says.

I sling my backpack over my shoulder. "I'll see you guys after school." I turn on my heel and walk away, leaving my friends in audible confusion. As I pass tables in the cafeteria, several kids call out to me, mistaking me for my twin. But this time, I can't blame them. Florence and I dressed similarly and now look identical. It'll be easy for someone to think I'm my sister.

I haven't seen her today except once in the hallways, where

she was with Bradley and another girl I didn't know or recognize. I'm guessing it was either Ana or the one girl who said she liked Flo's hair.

Nate catches up to me just as I have left the cafeteria. He grabs my arm and swings me around to face him. "Venice," he says, "you know if you walk home by yourself, Jargon is going to kidnap you. This morning is proof."

"If I take the bus, he won't." I put my hands on his shoulders and stare right into his light blue eyes. "Nate. I'll be fine."

"Do you have the ring?"

I nod. "It's in my bag."

"Venice..." he sighs and unexpectedly wraps his arms around me, burying his face in my hair.

I freeze. He never touches me like this in public.

He pulls away a moment later, grinning at the look of shock on my face. "I'm sorry," he says. "But I had to do that. Anyway, I'm suspicious about your sudden desire for me to go babysit Elijah's siblings and leave you alone to be captured."

"Suspicious?" I repeat, stepping back so I bump up against the wall. "How are you suspicious? I think you should go hang out with Elijah's little siblings because they have missed you."

"That doesn't explain why you're so inclined to force me to go."

I cross my arms over my chest. "I'm not *forcing* you. I just want you to stay away from your grandpa as long as possible. Being at the Jenkins' will give you an excuse to delay."

"Aha! I knew there was a reason." Nate looks over his shoulder at someone or something, then back at me. "Venice, if I go, you should come with me."

"I can't." I grimace. "My mom needs me back. She wants to do that family thing together, remember?"

Nate frowns. "Okay. I'll walk you home first."

"I'll take the bus."

"Do you promise?"

"Are you saying you think I'm doing this on purpose? That I *want* to be kidnapped by Jargon? Because I'm not. I don't." I glare at Nate. "I wouldn't send you away just so I can get captured and taken to that brick building where my dad is, and have everything be solved or put to an end. Although, the solving and ending part sounds nice. But the other part doesn't, so don't worry."

Nate isn't persuaded. He copies me, folding his arms over his chest, and matches my glare, though his holds more concern than annoyance. "If you get kidnapped—"

"I won't!" I interrupt, not voicing *I hope*.

"If you get kidnapped," he continues, "then I will have to write our report and present it to the class next week."

Instead of getting annoyed like I should, I gasp and say, "Next week? That soon? We haven't finished it yet."

He can't prevent a smile from blossoming, dimples appearing, the cut on his cheek stretching. "Yes, that soon. And we'd better work on it"—he leans forward so he is inches away from me— "today. After school."

I duck around him and march down the hallway, hiding a stupid grin. Nate follows me, laughing to himself.

"Come on. Admit it. You'd rather research orangutans than be kidnapped."

"Stop using that word," I reply irritably. "It sounds bad and ridiculous."

"Of course it sounds bad. It means something bad."

"Captured is much better," I say, pushing through the crowd of kids in my way.

He makes a disagreeing noise. "There's really no difference."

I scoff, and he studies me for a long minute. Then he shrugs. "If I didn't know better, I'd say you were Florence. But you don't look anything like her."

I grin at him. "You really do stare at me too often."

"Is a bad thing?" Nate stops in front of our biology classroom.

"Venice, I don't think I'm going to go to the Jenkins'. You need someone with you when you're walking home."

"Nate." I take his other hand. "I will be *fine*."

"Didn't I tell you I don't believe that?"

I roll my eyes. "Seriously, Nate."

"Seriously?" He raises his eyebrows. "You shouldn't ever be alone. Jargon is constantly watching you, waiting for a chance to swoop down and nab you. And I don't want that to happen."

My exasperated expression does not dissuade him.

"What would I do," he whispers, "if the one time I'm not with you, you get taken?"

"You would call the police," I answer promptly.

Nate sighs. "All right. Fine. You win. If you are kidnapped and murdered tonight, don't say I didn't tell you not to walk alone."

FIFTY-THREE

Right after school ends, Elijah and Mandy descend upon me and Nate, the both of them arguing loudly. I catch the words *lovely, disgusting, fool,* and *arbitrary.* What the context of their argument is, I have no idea. It really is incredible that they can fight so amiably over the simplest things.

The snow hasn't stopped, surprisingly. The ground is covered in a thin layer of white, just enough for Siena to make a snowball or shove Pompeii's face into it. She will be thrilled when she leaves school this afternoon. The flakes are still whirling around, thicker and bigger, sticking in my hair and melting on my glasses. I have to wipe the lenses off every few minutes, smearing tiny water droplets across the glass.

"I still don't think this is a good idea," Nate says to me in a low voice so our squabbling friends won't overhear. I don't think they could even if they were right next to us.

"I'll be fine. They need you today."

He gives me a disgruntled look. "I haven't seen *you* for the past few days. Just remember, Venice, if you disappear from existence and it's my entire fault because I wasn't with you, I'll be the one in therapy, not Mandy."

I shoot him a nasty look. "I'll call you when I get home, let you know that I haven't disappeared."

"My grandpa smashed my phone."

criminals? Rupert, one of those unknown men who broke into my house, had said something along the lines of Sleepy Gumption being the boss. And Stephen Goldbeck seems to like being on top, above everyone, number one.

I haven't seen all of Jargon yet, just his orange hair sticking out in front of the headrest. He looks so ridiculous that I have to suppress a giggle. I think I am going slightly hysterical. The pending danger of what will happen to me is threatening, taunting, and I am more scared of the future than the present. These men won't hurt me until they have what they want. And right now, I am the one with it.

"We're here." Jargon screeches to a halt, throwing me forward. I catch myself on the filthy floor of the car, my backpack tumbling off my lap and onto the ground next to me. I snatch it up quickly, press it against me.

Jargon leaves the car only to open the door in front of me. He grabs my arm and drags me out, his grip furious and cruel. I stumble after him, bag in hand, trying to keep my feet underneath me.

We are at the back of the brick building I saw Dad go into. The courtyard around us is empty and forlorn, paint cans stacked up everywhere. Jargon, from somewhere behind me, smacks the back of my head and I immediately drop my gaze to my shoes, my head smarting with the blow. I feel the start of a headache coming on. Concentrating on my feet, I notice the cracks in the concrete floor. Weeds are growing there. The weeds are green; some are brown; some are squashed like people have walked here often and have trampled them each time. Snow blankets the concrete, footprints visible in certain places. The flakes aren't drifting down as heavily as minutes ago, but they're still coming.

Goldbeck pulls me into the factory. We climb up a winding staircase—it is dark and musty and I can barely breathe—for what seems like hours. Finally, he stops in front of a rusted metal door and shoves it open.

We're in a brightly-lit room. The windows aren't blocked, which allows the watery sunlight to stream in. A jumble of furniture and heaps of trash fill the area, creating an obstacle course just to reach the other wall. There are even more paint cans, old and gross, on the floor. I spot a sleeping bag rolled out across the hard concrete floor far to my left, right underneath one of the windows. I wonder who has to sleep there. It doesn't look very comfortable. I would hate to have to sleep in this harsh building. Shouldn't Goldbeck let his buddies hang at his place? His mansion has plenty of space to accommodate three extra people.

Marc is standing in the center of the room, casually holding a gun in his hand. I remember him, on the first day I'd met him, saying something about how he was a special forces officer working for the government, and that he knew how to shoot a gun. I hadn't imagined his "special force" to be a band of criminals.

Sitting against the wall on the far side of the room is Dad. His clothes are dirty and rumpled, as if he has been in them for the past few weeks. And I'm sure he has. His hair is wildly curly, he is in desperate need of a shave, and his face is smeared with dirt or dust or some sort of filth. His eyes are on his lap when I walk in, but he snaps up his head at the sound of Goldbeck's voice as Goldbeck speaks to Jargon in a low undertone.

I'm not paying attention to the two men. I'm staring at Dad.

His jaw drops at the sight of me.

And he says one word, one single word, that instantly breaks through my determination not to show emotion.

"Florence?"

FIFTY-FOUR

The men surrounding me jolt at this. Marc swings towards me, gun leveled at my head in case I try to run away, as if this is my fault that I was mistaken for my sister and why would I run, anyway? I wouldn't get far enough away before they caught up with me.

I flinch so badly at Dad's voice that I drop my backpack. I snatch it up and press it tightly to my chest, shaking with anger.

I want to yell.

I want to scream.

I want to march over to Dad and demand why he can't tell the difference between me and my twin. He's our dad. He should know that I am clearly not Florence. I am Venice. I am *his* eldest daughter. He sent the ring to *me*. And he should know that.

But I don't move. I still don't speak.

"Florence?" Marc repeats. Everyone has gone deathly quiet. "What do you mean, Florence?"

Dad pulls himself to his feet. I was right. He isn't as tall as Nate. "That's my daughter," he says in a hoarse whisper, pointing at me. "What is my daughter doing here?"

Marc ignores him and turns to Jargon, who is standing directly behind me.

I still haven't seen his face, only smelled his stink. And felt his strength. On the day of Goldbeck's party, I hadn't caught a good glimpse of Jargon, just his orange hair and skinny build.

I wonder what he looks like.

"Florence?" Marc says again. "This should be Venice. Don't tell me you got the wrong girl, Jones."

Jones?

No one is paying attention to Dad, so when he briefly winks at me, I am the only one who sees. What does that wink mean?

"We grabbed the one walking home alone," Goldbeck puts in. "I've never seen her twin walking. She always takes the bus. And this one"—he jabs his fat thumb into my back, sending me a few steps forward—"walks home with that one kid. He didn't go with her today, so Jones and I seized the golden opportunity."

"I can't tell the difference," Hubris Jargon—who has to be this Jones character—rasps out. "It's the girl."

"She's a girl," corrects Marc. He latches onto my arm and pulls me closer, and I flinch again. "Which one are you?" he asks roughly, shaking me. My headache has gotten worse.

Deciding to be brave, I yank my arm out of his grasp and snarl, "You're such a despicable person, Marc. My mom trusted you! We all liked you! And now you have my dad—who is supposed to be *dead*—and why do you want my sister so badly?"

I stump them for a good minute. Then Goldbeck says, "Are you Florence?"

"What does it look like, you idiot?" I'm trying to sound like Flo, say things she would say, but would she even be acting like this is such a situation? "Of *course* I'm Florence. Ugh! I *hate* when people can't tell that I am *obviously* not Venice. I mean like, she's like all weird and stuff, and we are like, *so* different but it's like we're completely identical."

"You *are*," says Marc, leaning towards me. "You...could be Venice." He isn't one hundred percent certain.

"Could be?!" I shriek. "Honestly, Marc, I thought you knew me! I was the one who would talk to you, anyway. Venice always ran away from you. And that reminds me...who even *are* you? Why am I here? Why is my dad here? What do you want with my sister?" My voice takes on a tinge of protectiveness, though I don't know if Flo would talk like this.

The three men exchange glances. Silence descends on the room like the snow drifting onto the ground outside.

Then an eruption of voices and angry discussions has me shying away from them, making my way towards Dad with my backpack clutched tighter to my chest. If they get my bag, they'll for certain know I'm Venice. My homework and favorite books are in there, along with my ring, and the rest of the contents aren't things Flo would ever have.

Dad grabs my arm, and I drop my backpack and hug him tightly, shaking slightly.

"Venice," he whispers in my ear, his whiskers tickling. "Venice, are you all right? Did they hurt you?"

"I'm fine. And I'm Florence, remember?" I pull back a touch, send him an almost-invisible wink. Raising my voice, I ask, "Dad? We thought you were dead! What are you doing here with these guys? Why did they kidnap me? What is going on here?"

He sighs. A quick glance over my head has him confirming that the three criminals are still arguing. "Do you have it?" He speaks in a low tone.

"Yeah. It's in my backpack." I scoop up the bag and go to dig around inside for it, because I'm going to either bury it in this mess of a room or throw it out the window so they can't get it, but a whiff of cigarette makes me aware that Jargon is behind me.

"If we got the wrong one," he hisses, "then we get to dispose of you."

Dad slides in front of me. "No, you don't."

My heartbeat patters. One thing I know, they wouldn't need me or Dad any more, and there is no way they would ever just simply set us free. I wish I was braver. I wish I could lie better. I wish I was more convincing.

"Are we going to have to go get Venice from her *house*?" ask Goldbeck. "I can't kidnap her if she's surrounded by people."

"We could ransom her," Jargon suggests, leering at me. "One twin for the other, otherwise we kill *both* Ferrari and...whatever this girl's name is. Petunia."

I suppress a snort. Petunia? Seriously? Florence sounds nothing like that. And his plan stinks. Really sucks. No one would ever follow through with that deal. Unless it would spare *one* life...

"No." Marc shoves Jargon aside and squints at my face. "We don't know for a certain that we have the wrong girl."

Warning bells peel in my head. What can I do?

"Check her bag," says Goldbeck, attempting to take it from me. I cling even tighter to it.

Jargon huffs, releasing a puff of cigarette smoke. "Just get it."

"She's too quiet," says Marc. He leans down and stares right at me, as if he can determine just who I am by looking straight into my soul. "You're not Florence," he says slowly. "Florence is constantly loud and annoying."

I rip my arm out of his grasp and step away from him, towards Dad. I hold onto my backpack with all my strength.

Marc lifts his gun and wags it at me. I freeze. I have no doubt he can shoot and hit what he is aiming for. "Tell us who you are," he says. "Or I'll put two bullets through your pretty head."

I glare at him for a full ten seconds, not saying anything. I don't know if I can speak; my courage has deserted me as fast as it came.

"Right, then." Marc's finger curls around the trigger.

Will he shoot me? No, I don't think so. Not until they are sure they can get the ring from me.

"Tyron," Goldbeck warns. "Don't kill her."

"I already claimed her death, anyway," says Jargon. "I get to kill her. Tyron, give me the gun. I get to shoot her."

Marc throws both of them murderous looks. He turns back to me. "I'll give you ten seconds," he says, swinging the gun so it is now pointing at Dad, far behind me. I feel Dad stiffening. "Ten," says Marc. "Nine. Eight."

I take a deep breath.

"Six, five, four…"

"I'm Venice," I say, fast. I am glad my voice doesn't crack. "And Goldbeck is right, Marc. There's no need to shoot me or my dad."

All three men standing before me laugh. They seem relieved that I finally confessed. Jargon moves closer, and I pay attention to his features now. He looks like a rat—which reminds me of Keller Jacobs. His nose is thin and long, pointed and narrow. His chin is sharp, jutting out farther than most chins do. His brilliant hair sticks straight up.

He has a cigarette between two fingers. "Your daddy once begged us to kill him," Jargon says, smirking. "Why would we give up that opportunity?"

"Venice," Marc interrupts, "where is your ring?"

I go still. Take another deep breath. "The ring you three have been trying to steal from me for the past few months? The ring my dad gave to me for my fifteenth birthday? The ring you are willing to kill me to get? The ring that has done nothing but cause trouble for me?"

"Yes," hisses Jargon. He steps closer to me, and I flinch away. He grins nastily. "Where is it?"

"Stephen!" The rusty door is dramatically thrown open, and in enters Rebecca Goldbeck. She doesn't seem surprised to see me, just gives me a curl of her lip and faces her husband. "Stephen, I broke a nail moving one of those paint cans. Can't you have one of these men do it instead of me? How about Ferrari? He hasn't done anything to repay our hospitality."

I resist rolling my eyes at how ridiculous this woman is.

"Rebecca, dear," says Goldbeck, sounding exasperated, "we are right in the middle of doing something. Could you please come back later?"

She scoffs. "You don't seem to be busy."

"We're getting your ring," Goldbeck replies, gesturing towards me. "She has it. Remember Venice Pope?"

"Ferrari," I automatically correct. "My name is Venice Ferrari."

Rebecca twirls a strand of iron-grey hair around her finger. "I do like that ring," she says softly to herself. "Gold goes well with us, doesn't it, darling?"

"Yes, dear," Goldbeck agrees wearily. "Why don't you go back home and wait for me? I won't be long."

She marches across the room and settles into an ancient-looking chair. "I think I'll stay here," she says, stroking the velvet arm rest. She ignores the annoyed looks on Marc and Jargon and Goldbeck's faces. "This way, I'll get my ring even sooner."

"Yes, the ring." Marc trains the gun on me. "Venice, give it to us."

"What if I don't have it?" I ask nervously, eyeing the gun.

He growls low in the back of his throat. "Jones, grab her bag. It's probably in there."

Jargon snags my backpack from me before I can protest. Now armorless, I step away from the men, away from Marc's gun, and move closer to Dad. He hasn't said anything in a while. He has only said a few words when he tricked them into believing I was Flo.

"Ha!" Marc pulls out *The Merchant of Venice*, courtesy of Nate from a few weeks ago. "This proves she's Venice. I gave this to her." He starts flipping through the pages, noticing the yellow highlights Nate colored. "It looks like you really enjoyed this book. How often did you read this?"

"I read one paragraph," I say, eyes on Marc's gun. "I gave the book to my friend, and he was the one who liked it."

Marc snorts and tosses the book over his shoulder. It drops to the floor in a heap, the pages bent. "Of course. Inconsiderate girl." He notices how I am mere inches away from Dad and raises his gun, making me freeze. "Don't go any farther," he warns.

"Venice," Dad says quietly, "are they going to find it?"

"It's really all your fault," I say casually, sitting on the top of a random nearby desk. I watch the three men before us dig through my backpack in search of my ring. They throw most of what they find, which enrages me, especially when they do so with my books. Unknowingly, Jargon tosses my favorite one—the book containing my ring, in-between the pages one hundred seventy and one hundred seventy-one—across the room without pausing to check to see if my ring was indeed in there.

I hold my breath as I watch the book fly. My ring slips out from the pages somewhere during its flight, dropping into the mess of furniture and other obscure things in this room.

No one except me sees the ring.

Or so I thought.

Rebecca Goldbeck jumps out of her chair and hurries over to the general place where my ring had fallen. She daintily pokes at the jumbled collection of things with her foot, annoyed that she'll have to get down on her hands and knees to find the tiny piece of jewelry.

"Stephen!" she calls.

Her husband, too busy with trashing my belongings, says, "Not now, dear."

"Stephen!" she says again. "The ring is over here."

All three of them release my backpack to hurry up to Rebecca. They ask excited questions, even Marc.

"Dad," I begin, "why do they want my ring so badly? What is the deal with it, anyway?" My anger is starting to overcome my fear, or maybe my fear is feeding the anger. Either way, Dad seems to be more concerned about the ring than me or even himself. And that understanding draws up years of unexpressed resentment.

He has a pained look on his face. "I didn't mean for you to get hurt. I knew I could trust you with keeping that ring safe. I hoped you wouldn't have to get caught up in all this violence. I'm sorry."

"I'm sorry," I repeat slowly. "I've been waiting to hear those words from you for a long time. But I never expected them to be about a ring."

"Venice, please." He reaches out a hand, like he wants to touch me, but I am too far away. His hand drops back to his side. "I thought that since I was estranged from my family, they would never trace the ring to you. You kept it safe for an entire year."

I look away from him, watching our captors sift through the debris where my ring fell. I am angry—angry at Dad, angry at myself, angry at the ring, angry at the four people who want the ring and are willing to hurt me for it. I am also scared—scared for Dad, scared for myself, scared that Goldbeck will give in and let Jargon kill either me or Dad. Despite being furious at Dad for leaving us six years ago and for giving me that ring, I don't want him to die. I am rather relieved to see him again, and he even after all these years he somehow knew me as Venice.

"Where is it?" Marc demands, shifting a stack of papers.

Rebecca stands above the three men, searching for the glint of gold that will give away the spot where my ring is hiding in. "It's somewhere around here!" she squeals greedily. "Find it! It's mine! I want it."

"Get in line, woman," Jargon snarls, shoving aside a paint can. "There are plenty of people who get it first."

Get it first? What does that mean?

"Dad," I say softly, startling him.

He sits down, leaning against the cold wall. "Yeah?"

"Please tell me what they want with my ring."

Dad sighs. "That's a long story. Even I don't know all of it. See, a long time ago, me and my friend Harry worked for this old rich guy who had passed his business on to his grandson. But the grandson was a disappointment so he liquidated his share of the company and started a new company, which is where Harry and I came in the story. The old boss must have been going senile, though, because he would wander around the warehouse handcuffed to a briefcase with one hand and carrying a gun with the other. He didn't trust the bank or his grandson. One time he pulled me and Harry aside and showed us what was inside—millions, Venice! Tens, maybe even hundreds of millions! And he told me and Harry that he wanted us to take it when he died and to keep it away from his grandson."

I sigh. I think I know where this is going.

I'm already disgusted with this story only because it is glaringly clear what is most important to Dad, and it's not me or my family.

"The codger was brilliant in his paranoia. The briefcase was rigged with this little mechanism that initiated a chemical reaction that would cause the cash to burst into flames if the briefcase was forced open. The only way to open it was by key," continues Dad. "And the only key was a ring his grandmother wore when she got married. Yes, Venice, your ring."

My despair at this situation, at Dad's confession, at the truth, is steadily growing. Jargon has tired of watching the Goldbecks search for the ring and returns to my backpack tearing it apart and rifling every possible compartment.

Dad goes on in a lower tone, "The old man started sleeping at the warehouse. He knew he was dying. One night he called me and Harry to his bedside. He gave me the ring and Harry the briefcase, then laughed his head off until he kicked the bucket. At the time all I could think about was our unbelievable luck, but now I understand his sick, cruel, joke. Harry laughed right along with him, because he had no intention of sharing the money with me.

"We couldn't use the briefcase without the ring, or the ring without the briefcase. I wasn't going to give up the key. I basically ignored Harry for the next couple of years, wouldn't talk to him, wouldn't meet up with him. He couldn't contact me since I blocked him, and for that I was grateful. Anyway, about ten, eleven years later, he somehow found me living in California with my family, and he practically forced me to join him for a drink at the local pub."

My disproval matches my despair. I don't want him to go on. He's telling me what a terrible, shallow person he was and still is, it appears.

"I had kind of forgotten the ring by this time," he muses. "I had it with me pretty much every single day, and unfortunately Harry caught me when it was snugly fit in my pocket. He had the briefcase with him—he told me he had been looking for me everywhere, and had practically planned this chance meeting in the streets—and he dragged me into the pub and sat me down and firmly told me to give him the ring."

"Did you?"

He shakes his head, appalled. "No. Of course not. I told him he was stupid to believe I would ever do that, and he got angry. He threatened to kill me if I wouldn't hand over the key. I said the ring might not even unlock the briefcase, that our old boss might have been pranking us or something. I asked him if he was willing to share the money, arguing that half of it was better than none of it. He threatened me with a knife and made for me to leave the pub with him. So I started a brawl and things got really confusing, but I got away, snatching the briefcase on the way out."

I stare at him. "Why?"

"Harry couldn't get the money out, no matter what he tried, and I had the key to unlock it! All that cash would be mine. So I went home. I opened it and counted the money—fifty million in cash and checks—I was rich! Your mother never knew anything about it. She still doesn't."

I glance over at the men searching for my ring, and find Jargon glaring at the two of us. He sneers. "Shut your trap!" he calls. "Just be quiet, Ferrari. Same goes for your daughter."

Dad ignores him. "It didn't take long for Harry to discover where I lived, so I left. It took forever to divorce your mother, but once I was free, I went off to the eastern states, changed my name and identity, and passed a few months there. I spent some of the

584

money and had a nice, luxurious time. Of course, Harry had to spoil that. Somehow he found me again and kidnapped me. He tortured and threatened me, trashed my place looking for everything, but I'd stashed it in my house *very* well, and all of his rampaging couldn't reveal where it was—and I refused to tell him. Eventually, I was able to escape and went home, packed up, and moved yet again."

I'm still back at the "so I left" part of his story. Was it really that easy to walk away from a wife and five kids? And for what? To not have to share fifty million dollars? He's a hypocrite; willing to share it with Harry, but not with us?

"Shut up!" Jargon yells again, stalking towards us. If he hadn't said it, I think I might have.

I'm suddenly really worried for Dad's safety. He could have been killed years ago. People have been killed over far less. Is this whole thing really just about money? Well, lots and lots of money.

"I evaded him for a while, finally settling in North Dakota. I was there for only a few months when my mom gave your sister my address—and she started writing letters to me, and I knew that communicating with Florence might give my position away, but I responded to her anyway. I was tired of running. What was the benefit of having millions of dollars if I was always looking over my shoulder? When Harry showed up again, I decided to be done with it all. I took out a nice chunk of the cash and kept that. Then I made a deal with Harry that I'd give him the briefcase and ring if he'd just leave me alone. I gave him a duplicate ring that I'd had made and shipped the real key off to you."

I can't believe this man is my father. I have no compassion for Harry, but I can definitely see why he hates my dad so much.

"Anyway"—he doesn't sound remorseful at all—"it didn't take long for Harry to realize he didn't have the right ring. He located me once again, and this time it was when I was driving to Virginia to see you guys. I'd led a lonely life, and I missed you all, and I wanted to pop in just for a couple minutes."

A couple minutes. After six whole *years*?

And out of the blue like that. Had he assumed that we would welcome him with open arms?

"Harry was surprisingly smart and resourceful," he says, like it's an afterthought. "He managed to continually figure out where I was. I didn't think that was in his capabilities, but I guess it is."

"Shut up, Ferrari!" Jargon screams, stalking towards us.

"I mean, he found the exact road I was on in the exact region of Kentucky," Dad goes on. "And he found all of you. Maybe he's not as much of an idiot as I thought."

Jargon shoves me aside, and I fall awkwardly on the ground, hands splayed out to catch myself. I feel a jolt run through my body, a painful jolt, and I hope I won't have to use my wrist too much in the near future.

"Not another word, Ferrari," he snarls, grabbing Dad by the front of his shirt and hauling him to his feet. "I'm giving you this one chance."

"What's the problem with telling her?" Dad shoots back, seemingly not caring about how Jargon has the upper hand in this situation. "If she's going to die, can't she know why?"

Jargon hesitates. Then he shakes his head. My heart sinks. "She doesn't need to know anything," he says in a hoarse whisper. He stinks of cigarette smoke; it comes off his breath and his clothes. "She's a stupid little girl. She doesn't need to know anything."

"Oh, come on," I say, slowly rising to my knees. "I know plenty. I know how you have ridiculous code names like Hubris Jargon and Sleepy Gumption and Malaise Tone. I know how you faked my dad's death in order to bring him to this town and interrogate him about my ring. I know how you nearly ran me over months ago. I know how you followed me to Goldbeck's party. I know how you tried to steal my ring by sending two men over to my house—who failed, by the way—and ended up spilling most of your secrets. I know how Marc and Goldbeck are members of your gang. I know how you all have been watching me for weeks. I know how you all want my ring to unlock this briefcase."

Silence. Marc and Goldbeck have stopped digging through the junk where my ring landed. Jargon is staring at me in shock. He must have seriously thought I was stupid.

"She didn't say anything about me," sniffles Rebecca.

Marc shoots her a look. She shuts up.

"Well," Goldbeck says finally. "I think Venice has earned the right to know the rest of the story."

Jargon turns back to Dad. With a snarl, he drops him onto the ground. Dad grunts, catching himself before he face-plants. Jargon storms past me, back to the two other men, to continue the search for my ring.

"Harry wanted to kill me, especially since he knew you had the ring, but he wanted to gloat when he got the ring so he staged my death, hoping that could get him closer to the ring."

"Wait," I interrupt. "Harry. What's his last name?"

Dad's eyes flick over to Jargon. "Jones."

I sit down on the desk again, hating how the legs tremble. How sturdy is this thing?

I had guessed as much. And it doesn't exactly surprise me that Dad and Jargon—Harry Jones—used to be best friends.

Then again, nothing surprises me now.

"He blew up my car and took me here, where I realized a full-scale crime was going on. He had even hired several men to trail my family and see if any of you had the ring. Funny, isn't it? That Harry wasn't willing to split the money with me but he's okay splitting it with three others."

"But not you, Ferrari," Jargon sneers. "Once we get the key, there's more revenge to come."

"He almost ran me over," I add.

"I heard," says Dad. "That was what Harry was bragging about on the drive here from Kentucky."

I look at him.

He doesn't seem concerned.

"They were all gleeful to have the briefcase in their hands," he continues. "All they needed was the ring, and you kept that from them for a long time. So good job, Venice."

"Thanks," I say coldly.

Dad rubs his beard. "It's too bad you brought the ring with you. Everything is over now. The chase is over. The game is over."

"And you lost," says Jargon smugly. "I won."

"The money doesn't belong to you!" Dad bursts out. "Any of you! None of you deserve it!"

"Then who does?" snaps Jargon. "You?"

Dad falls silent. He should know that he most certainly doesn't deserve it, either, and that what he spent wasn't his, and that he's a criminal, too.

Jargon spits out his cigarette, sending it flying across the room. "Thought so," he says, and returns to look for my ring. His cigarette lands on a pile of trash and, as I watch, part of the paper in that pile turns black. A faint trail of smoke rises up.

I stand and move over there, watching the lit cigarette slowly catch the trash on fire. Making up my mind to stomp it out, I do so with satisfaction. I could have let it burn, but if I did, this building would be in danger and so would I. Does Jargon want to set this floor on fire? There are plenty of things that will easily ignite.

"Venice." Dad's tone is sharp. "Venice, come back here."

I look over my shoulder. Marc has given up searching and is now pointing his gun at me. I wonder if he will ever pull the trigger this afternoon. He sure likes threatening people with his gun.

I quickly return to my seat and plop down on the desk. "So you left us for money."

Dad sighs. "Yes," he mumbles. "It was a tough decision, quitting on you to save those fifty million dollars from falling into the wrong hands. If Harry had only been willing to share from the start we would have both been living in luxury now. Things would have been so much better."

"You ruined our lives over money?" I exclaim. "You messed up everything because of money?"

"I'm sorry!" Dad looks disappointed in himself. He should be. "I didn't mean for anything bad to happen while I was gone—"

"No, it's not that!" I curl my hands into fists. "Your choice to leave us was what ruined everything. Mom went through a long depression phase that lasted six years. Florence was constantly horrible to me and the rest of us. Roman couldn't find a single nice thing to say to us. And Pompeii and Siena grew up without a dad! We all did! Siena was only a few years old when you left. She doesn't remember you."

Dad stares down at his lap. "I'm sorry," he says again. "I did it to keep you all safe."

"Really? Don't you think giving up the ring would have kept us safer and happier?" I huff.

"Venice—"

I cross one leg over the other. "Whatever, Dad." I don't know if I want to talk to him further. I thought he was repenting for what he's done, but he is clearly oblivious to the fact that he was the one to mess up, not Harry or me or Mom or whomever else he's trying to blame. "Honestly, why were you coming here after you gave up the briefcase?"

Dad hesitates. "I wanted to visit you guys, check in on you. I thought I'd get the ring and throw it in the ocean, far from Harry. I was done with it. It didn't bring me any joy."

"The ocean?" I demand, uncrossing my legs. "Seriously? Do you *want* to make Mom mad?"

He manages a faint smile, almost hidden beneath his facial hair. "She was always talking about how only idiotic people litter in the ocean. I'm an idiotic person, that's for sure."

At least he admitted that.

"Goldbeck, do you have it yet?" Marc calls sharply, attracting my attention. He still has his gun trained on me.

Shouldn't his arm be getting tired by now?

"I can't...find it," pants Goldbeck. "Rebecca, are you sure that it landed over here?"

His wife cleans her fingernails as she speaks. "Yes. It fell out of the book and dropped around this area. It's unfortunate how that silly ring chose to bury itself in this tangled mess."

"Hurry up and get it!" snaps Jargon. "Otherwise I'll tell Tyron to shoot someone."

"I'll do it with pleasure," says Marc.

I glare at him. Nate was wrong. Marc really does want me dead. He has no pity for me. Which is perfectly all right with me. I don't need his pity. I don't need anyone's pity.

"Come on, Goldbeck," says Jargon. "Find it."

"Can't I kill the girl?" asks Marc. "We know the ring is here. She doesn't need to stay alive."

"No one is going to die!" yells Goldbeck.

"No one'll miss her if she dies," Marc muses, his finger curling around the trigger.

I do the most infuriating thing I can think of—I turn my back on him and peer down at Dad. "How did you know we moved here?"

"My mom told me."

"Oh."

Dad gives me a small smile. "I'm sorry I wasn't able to make it over before Harry faked my death. I was sitting at this stop light, waiting for it to be my turn, when he roared up in this gigantic SUV and pulled me from my car. Then he slammed this oil truck into my car and exploded everything." He shrugs. "Oh well. Tell me what you all have been up to over the past few years. I've only heard snatches from Harry's conversations with Goldbeck and Tyron."

I explain how Siena is a talented painter, and Pompeii enjoys biographies, and Roman is growing up, maturing, and Florence and I act like identical twins. I tell him about the adventures I've been having, and a bit about my friends, and I mention in passing how Nate had been the one to save me from Jargon.

Dad doesn't speak again, so I look back at Marc and Marc's gun. He gives me a nasty smile.

"I never liked you," he says.

"That's funny," I reply. "I never liked you, either. Especially after you got my mom drunk. And she acted as if nothing shocking had happened. I must admit, I'm rather glad you're evil, so now the police can haul you off to jail and get you out of my life. It will be nicer without you, too."

Marc stares at me for a split second, then bursts out laughing. He bangs the butt of his gun on his knee, which isn't a smart idea, and points his finger at me as he chuckles. "You're one spiteful girl!" he says.

"Thank you...I guess."

"Your mom is much better than you," he goes on. "But she got obnoxious really quickly. All she could talk about was how her kids were stressing her out because they were off on their own and weren't speaking to her and all that—" he makes a gagging noise. "Ugh! So obnoxious."

"Then you had to go and get her drunk!"

Marc smirks. "That was easy. She got tempted real easily. But she wouldn't tell me anything I didn't know about your ring. I asked her all these different questions, and she had no clue what I wanted to know."

"*That's* why you made her drunk? So you could ask her about my ring and she wouldn't remember your conversation when she sobered?" I'm utterly disgusted. "You really are a terrible person." I already knew that; it's been a known fact since I ever met him, but it's nice telling him that to his face.

He barks out a laugh again. "That was definitely the highlight of my adventures working with Jones and Goldbeck. Everything else was horrible. Like when Goldbeck forced us to use these pathetic cryptonyms that make absolutely no sense. It was to communicate with one another without anyone finding us out." He squints at me. "Except you did. But only because those idiotic greenies who broke into your house spilled everything. They didn't know much. Just our code names and the fact that I knew you and your family."

I quickly gather up all this new information, storing it safely in my mind. A lot of things make sense to me now. He seems talkative enough. I try for more.

"So how did you and Goldbeck get involved in this?"

"Goldbeck put me on the job."

"Yeah, without consulting me, so Tyron's share is coming out of Goldbeck's," adds Jargon, bitterly.

"Something snapped when Harry realized I'd given him a fake ring," Dad explains, sitting next to me on the desk. "He realized he needed help, so he went to Goldbeck and told him all about the money. The Goldbecks had run up some debt, so they were excited about the money. They staged a move and planned that party to meet up and see if they could buy the ring from you. You stubborn girl, you refused."

"Yeah, well, it used to mean something to me."

"Goldbeck brought Marc on. Harry wasn't happy about it, but Goldbeck said they needed someone who could cozy up to the family. And Harry told me they knew they were close to getting the money the day Tyron noticed you wore the ring on your pinky. He and Harry hadn't had any success in spotting your ring so far, but that day he did and told Goldbeck about it. Tyron kept a closer eye on you and your ring, noting down everything you did and where you went. Regular stalker, is he not?" Dad grins at me, and I can't help but smile back, even though I'm still mad at him. "I was outraged that a man was stalking my daughter," he continues. "I mean, you are sixteen years old, Venice. You shouldn't have men watching every move you make."

"I wholeheartedly agree with you."

He nods. "When Harry told me that he tried to run you down, that was when I knew I'd been a fool to think they wouldn't come after you, ring or no ring. I'm so sorry I put you in danger, Venice. I can't believe how grown up you are now. I don't know what I would have done if I'd been the cause of your death." He begins to sound wistful here, and my heartstrings are pulled tight. It's nice that he's developing a conscience, but he may yet be the cause of my death.

I run a hand through my hair, dragging it away from my face. As more and more of this story unfolds, I grow more and more angry and depressed. "What about those two fools who broke into my house?"

"The thieves' grapevine," says Marc carelessly. "It's how Jones found Goldbeck. And those two idiots were expendable and clearly incompetent."

That's the truth. But they were scary, too.

"I always suspected you were a criminal in disguise," I say, trying to keep him talking. "You felt off. What made you get into bad stuff?"

"Following the rules is boring," he says. "Abiding by my own law is so much better."

"Ruining your life is better than having a successful one?"

"Oh, just shoot her," rasps Jargon. "She's annoying me."

Marc wags his gun at me. "Venice, would you like me to shoot you?"

"Depends," I say as calmly as I can. "Try not to hit my nose. It's my favorite feature."

His eyebrows go up. Jargon snorts.

"All right," Marc says slowly, raising the gun again. He points it at me, his finger once more curling around the trigger. I notice his hand is shaking just a tiny bit, almost imperceptibly.

Maybe he doesn't actually want to kill me.

Hopefully.

"Fire the gun, blast you!" yells Jargon. "We don't need her any more, and I want Ferrari to see her die."

I glance over at Goldbeck. He has his head buried in the jumble of things. His body wriggles as he searches for my ring. He won't be of any help.

"Kill her!" Jargon commands.

Marc takes a deep breath.

"I found it!" Goldbeck exclaims.

Marc jerks.

He pulls the trigger.

FIFTY-FIVE

I instinctively dive to the floor. Dad yells something I can't hear. My ears are ringing. I can't hear anything.

What happened?

Am I dead?

No.

I feel a sharp pain in my left palm. I can't see. I can only feel. And I feel all sorts of things. I feel hungry. I didn't eat much for lunch, just that peanut butter sandwich Florence made for me. The trail mix had been forgotten at the bottom of my bag. It's probably somewhere in this room, where it was thrown while the three men were digging through my bag.

I feel angry. I am angry at Dad for caring more about the ring and the money in the briefcase than his family. I am angry at Marc for firing his gun. I am angry that he didn't listen to Goldbeck.

My body hurts. I feel pain in my palm, my leg, my head.

But I'm still alive.

I groan and roll over so I am on my back. I try to open my eyes, and when I do, everything is blurry. Where are my glasses? I hope they aren't broken. That would make me even angrier.

My fingers find a wooden post. A desk leg. I use it to sit myself up, wincing at the waves of pain crashing over me. I scramble to find my glasses, needing my sight, and remain blind.

Where am I again? And why is my hand throbbing?

Oh, yes. That brick building Dad went into last Monday. That brick building with the men who want my ring.

What time is it?

I have no idea.

"Venice!" Someone warm grabs my arm, and I can only see dark hair and my first thought is that it's Nate, that I'm finally safe, that the police are here and have rounded up the criminals.

"Venice!" the voice says again, and I am quite disappointed to realize that the person grasping me is Dad, not Nate.

I yank myself free, which does wonders to my head, and notice that there is a red spot in my vision. I hold my hand up to my face, squinting at it, and see I am bleeding. How am I bleeding? And why does this hand hurt so much when that tiny wound shouldn't ache this badly?

Dad presses something into my other hand, and I am grateful that it is my glasses. I slide them on, Dad's face sharpening now that I have my sight back. I see he is deathly pale. A flash of déjà vu reminds me of how Nate had crouched in front of me after he had saved me from almost being run down.

"What happened?" I cough out, wiping the blood off my palm and onto my jeans. I must have sliced it open on some random paint can when I fell.

Dad heaves a relieved sigh. "Tyron missed. He hit the window instead. You would have gotten hit if you had stayed where you were sitting, though. I'm glad you ducked."

"My hand hurts," I blurt out, unable to not state the obvious.

"Venice, do you think you can get up?" Dad suggests quietly.

"They have it."

"Have what?" I ask, my voice slurring as Dad takes my arm and hauls me to my feet. My head pounds worse than before, and I sway in his grip. He is the only thing keeping me up.

"The ring." Dad helps me sit down on the desk. "They have your ring. And the briefcase."

"Does that mean we're out of time?"

He hesitates.

And that is all the answer I need.

It's only a matter of time before they have Marc shoot again. And next time he won't miss.

They have both things, the briefcase and the key. The money is theirs. And Dad and I are just extra baggage

"Open it," Jargon is saying excitedly, handing Goldbeck a small black briefcase. Goldbeck has the ring in his hand.

Goldbeck sucks in a quick breath, then inserts the stone into a hole in the briefcase that I can't see from my position. A soft *click!* sounds, and all four greedy criminals gasp.

I stare at the people, see their reactions. Rebecca is interested now, licking her lips. Her husband, standing next to her, has also been overcome by greed. He is even rubbing his hands together. Marc is still holding his gun, but for once it is pointed down at the ground. Marc himself is staring at the contents of the briefcase, a wicked grin curving at the corners of his mouth. Jargon is on the other side of Rebecca, another lit cigarette dangling from his lips. He puffs, releasing a cloud of smoke, eyes on the briefcase.

We sit in silence for a moment, watching Jargon and Goldbeck dig through the briefcase while Rebecca and Marc stare hungrily. Rebecca is holding my ring in her fist.

Finally, I say, "Dad, why did you ignore me when I yelled at you that one morning? I said your name several times, loud enough for you to hear me, but you didn't even react and just continued to walk on into this building."

"They were watching me. I was only allowed a short walk outside once a day, and that happened to be while you were across the street—just my luck, eh?—and if I had paid attention to you, they probably would have kidnapped you then instead of now."

"Did they not see me?" I ask incredulously.

"No. None of them mentioned it when I came back. They were

arguing over something. But I'm surprised, really. Your callings were pretty obvious."

I slouch. "Well, I'm glad they *somehow* didn't see me. "

"Yeah, so am I. I'm sorry I messed everything up for you and the family, Venice. This is all my fault."

Yes. It is. I can't erase the choices he made and the years of dysfunction and discord we've had to wade through, and I can't forget that the one gift I received from my father happened to be a double-crossing trick that has only brought me danger. But now, at the end, I find that I'm quite forgiving. I pity him. Sure, he lived it up for a while on the cash, but he's also missed so much that could have brought him love and peace. And to be constantly looking over your shoulder, hunted down...well, I've had a taste of that and I do understand how he's feeling.

I rest my chin on my right palm. "Dad," I say, "do you still love us, even after those horrible things you did to show that you clearly didn't care?"

He gives me a hurt look, but I have to know. "Venice, of course I still loved you guys. I just—I was greedy and couldn't give up that much money. If you had gotten fifty million dollars, would you want to hand it off to someone who clearly didn't deserve it?"

"You didn't deserve it, either. You should have left it."

"Then Harry would have claimed it."

I scoff. "And you would still have a family."

Dad flinches a little. He opens his mouth to speak, hesitates, and closes without a word. He looks broken, frustrated with himself and me and the situation at hand. The poor, foolish man. He threw away everything for nothing.

I fix my attention on the criminals who helped assist in Dad's ruin. Jargon is messing with the money.

"How much is there?" asks Marc.

It takes a surprisingly long time to count all of the cash. Finally, Jargon exchanges looks with Goldbeck and answers. "There's forty-three million dollars. I promised Goldbeck twelve. I get the rest," he says gruffly.

"Hold on," says Marc, pointing his gun at Jargon. "What about my share?"

He scoffs, unconcerned about the gun. "That's not my concern. Goldbeck brought you on, ask him. It's not coming out of my share."

"Boys!" Goldbeck steps between the arguing men. "Calm down, boys. Let's sort this out like the civil people we are."

I snort loudly.

Everyone ignores me except Rebecca. She comes drifting over as the other three criminals try to figure out who should get how much.

"I hate all three of them," she sniffs.

My eyebrows rise in surprise; I had not expected that to be the start of our conversation. "Even your husband?"

Rebecca pulls a disgusted expression. "Ew, yes, I hate him. His name is the worst possible. Why would I want to be called Rebecca Goldbeck? If anyone gave me a nickname—let's say, Becky—then I would be Becky Goldbeck. Isn't that name just awful?"

I hadn't liked her at that party, and I still don't like her now. But I'm grateful for some comic relief. She is something else, that's for sure. "Okay," I agree disinterestedly.

"But I finally have this ring," she says, twirling my ring around her fingers. "It looks better if I'm wearing it, but it's tiny. My fingers don't fit. I think I'll have to take it to the jewelers and get the band expanded."

She already has plans for my ring?

"Another thing wrong with this lot," she continues, gesturing languidly at the arguing men. "They all have those fancy code names they call each other by, and I don't have one. I was thinking Regal something, and I'm not going to use *Gumption*—that's a horrible name—but there aren't any good words that start with G."

"Grace," I suggest. "You could be Regal Grace."

Rebecca thinks about it for a moment. "I like it," she says. "It fits me. It fits perfectly."

I opt not to comment. I am starting to worry a little. She is clearly unstable.

"Say, if you weren't currently our prisoner, then I'd probably take you shopping," Rebecca says suddenly. "These clothes you're wearing...they're just *horrible*. What kind of coat is this? And your shirt—my dear, how can you choose to wear *that*?"

I don't know if it's the tension or what, but I can't help it. I burst out laughing at the ridiculous thought of me shopping with Rebecca Goldbeck.

"And your pants...What are those called?"

"Jeans."

"Yes! Jeans!" Rebecca nods energetically. "How can you fit in those? They are so thin. There is barely any space for your legs to squeeze in. And I have seen kids wearing the jeans with all those rips and tears and holes in them, and I can't imagine that being comfortable."

My teeth sink deeper into my bottom lip. It's all I can do to stop myself from bursting into a fit of giggles. The stress is definitely getting to me.

I have been kidnapped, threatened, and shot at, and now I'm talking to one of my captors about *ripped jeans*?

"Kids these days have no sense of fashion," says Rebecca. "I obviously do; you can tell from my excellent wardrobe"—she fluffs her skirt—"but so many others don't. For example, you, Venice dear, have no sense of style.

I shrug. I don't trust myself to speak.

"Oh! I just had the *best* idea ever!" Rebecca claps her hands together a few times, like she's an excited little kid who was given the privilege of an ice cream cone. "Stephen, darling, what if we took Venice with us? I have always wanted a daughter!"

My blood runs cold. I'm not in a laughing mood any more.

Take me with them? Holy Mother Earth, she *is* insane.

I exchange a look with Dad, whose face is pale again. He has a frightened look in his eyes.

"What do you mean, dear?" Goldbeck asks wearily, pausing the argument so he can listen to his wife.

"Instead of killing Venice, we should take her with us when we leave!"

Goldbeck's expression is horrified.

"We can go shopping every day!" says Rebecca, hugging onto my arm. "We can take her to France and Italy and go to Venice, the city she was named after!"

I am only interested in this last bit—I have always wanted to go to Venice. And at least I'd be alive.

"Dear," Goldbeck begins, "I don't think we should bring Venice. She isn't a toy. She is a person. We cannot simply *take* her."

"You did earlier this afternoon," retorts his wife, clinging tighter to my arm. Her fingernails imprint tiny crescents in my flesh, all of her nails except the one she broke while moving paint cans. "You kidnapped her earlier," she goes on haughtily. "Why can't we just elongate her capture? And this is better than killing her!"

Goldbeck looks extremely tired. "Dear," he says again, "no one is going to be killed."

"I wouldn't be so sure," Jargon mumbles.

"We are not taking her with us," Goldbeck says firmly, wisely ignoring Jargon. "And that's that. Rebecca dear, why don't you come back over here and get your share of the money?"

She huffs and tosses her iron-grey curls. "No. I'm not going anywhere until you let me keep Venice."

And so another argument starts.

"Jones and Tryon are ready to kill her and Ferrari as soon as you let them!" Rebecca snaps. "They're going to do it! Venice will stay alive if I can have her as my daughter! I won't be lonely, I won't follow you around everywhere like I have to—"

Goldbeck seems to be leaning in her favor at this. He must not enjoy her company, especially when he's doing business.

"—and Venice already likes me!" protests Rebecca, giving my arm a hard squeeze. I grimace as her fingernails dig even deeper into my flesh. "We will have so much fun together. I won't be bored. I won't constantly be spending your money on parties if I have Venice."

Goldbeck likes this, too.

My heart sinks.

"I'll go on trips around the world with her instead of making you come with me!" She's eager now, more eager than before. "You're always complaining about having to come with me, but if Venice does, not you, then you'll be free to do whatever."

"Venice is not a toy," he says again. "She won't be forced to go with you."

Rebecca wilts, because even she can recognize that I don't want to go.

"Hold on," rasps Jargon, tossing his second lit cigarette onto the floor. He grinds it under his boot. "Where do I get to sign up for her? I want the girl. I want to kill her."

He really is malicious. What's his problem with me, anyway?

I voice the question out loud.

Jargon sneers at me. "You were born to be murdered by me," he says. "I've been waiting. Ever since that day your daddy took my briefcase, I wanted to kill his precious little family—"

"We aren't that little," I interrupt. "There's seven of us."

Dad is surprised to be included. Truthfully, I don't know why I did; it just popped out.

"The more, the merrier!" exclaims Jargon. "Seven! That will be fun. I can do all different types of deaths. Have any of you ever suffocated in mud? What about being strung up by your ankles?"

I scowl at him. "You're going to Hell when you die," I spit.

He laughs raucously. "I knew that! But now I'll go to Hell a rich man." He lights another cigarette and sucks in for half a second, closing this conversation. I turn my back on him and face Goldbeck, who will decide my future.

"I don't know, Rebecca," he says slowly. "Jones and Tyron obviously want to kill her, and *I* don't want her dead. I don't want her blood on my hands. So I guess you can have her."

Rebecca squeals with excitement and wraps her arms around me, giving me a brief and boney hug. I am stiff, my heart thumping madly, my eyes swimming with sudden unpreventable tears.

I don't want to be a pet.

Though I suppose it's better than death. Right?

I am a human being. I am a girl with most of my life ahead of me. I want to get my driver's license. I want to fall in love and get married and have a family of my own. I want to go to college. I haven't done anything remotely exciting besides all this drama.

I haven't said goodbye to my family.

"No."

We all look at Marc. He is cleaning his gun with the corner of his shirt, the action careless but threatening.

"No?" Goldbeck repeats.

"No." Marc finishes cleaning his gun and cocks it, pointing it at me. "You're not getting her. I do."

"Why do you all want to kill me?" I burst out. "You have your money. Take it! Go off and never come back."

Marc scoffs. He goes to respond, but Goldbeck cuts in.

"Exactly. Jones, Tyron, what do you have against Venice? Why are you both so determined to end her life?"

"I want her no-good, double-crossing dad to see her brains splattered across the room and to know it was his fault," rasps Jargon.

"And I get to be the one to do it," says Marc. "She's annoying." But there is something he's hiding, something I'm curious about, and he clearly won't tell us what it is.

I hop off the desk, plant my hands on my hips. I'm glad I'm taller than two of the five people besides me here. "I can't believe my family liked you," I say to Marc. "I can't believe my *mom* liked you. Because here you are, wanting to kill me, and I was the only one who suspected you to be rotten. And you are. You are very, very rotten."

He smirks. "I am a criminal," he says. "Of course I'm rotten."

"Venice." Rebecca Goldbeck—man, she really does have an unfortunate name—jumps down next to me and puts her hand on my shoulder. "Venice, I don't think it's wise to be insulting the man who would like to kill you."

I shrug her off. "If you're going to be the one to end my life, Marc," I say, "then how are you going to do it? Shoot me? That's a rather boring way to go, no offence. Jargon had more interesting methods."

"There's plenty of paint around here," hisses Jargon. "You could drown her in that."

Goldbeck holds up his hands. "Venice is *not* dying," he says. "She will go with my wife. And that's the end of this discussion. Tyron, you and Jones will either collect your payment right now or never."

"Can't we do that back at the house?" suggests his wife, gliding over to the briefcase. "I have treats."

My stomach rumbles at the mention of food.

"Good. I'm starving." Jargon flicks some ash off his cigarette. "Goldbeck, are you *sure* we can't kill this girl?"

"No," he says sharply. "She is to remain alive. Don't mention that again, or I will cut your payment in half."

I settle back down on the desk, watching them converse. I am confused as to who is the leader, the boss, in this gang. Is it Goldbeck, the richest, who is the spokesperson and determines what happens? Is it Jargon, the one who started all this? Is it Marc, the gunman, who seems to think he can get whatever he wants?

"Dad," I say quietly.

He has sat at my side for the past ten minutes while everyone argued over my future—and not said or done anything, I realize—and now that they have moved on to the money, he has relaxed somewhat.

"Yes, Venice?"

"Who is the ringleader?"

Dad is surprised by my question. "Goldbeck," he answers. "Harry found the briefcase, started this whole thing, but he couldn't have finished without Goldbeck's help. He didn't have enough money for a car or all the technology used to stage my death and make it seem real. Harry isn't the best of commanders. Goldbeck is capable of keeping everything together and making decisions."

I wipe my palm on my jeans again, rubbing off most of the blood. I think I was cut on the corner of the paint can that is below this desk. There are paint cans everywhere. "What time is it?"

"Um…almost four in the afternoon."

I left school at three-fifteen. I have about twenty minutes to stall until the police get here.

How can I stall?

FIFTY-SIX

It turns out that I don't have to stall for very long. Rebecca drags on and on about different things, wasting time when she could be doing this on her way home, her way to safety. She complains about the paint cans, the junk around us, the cold temperature in this room, the broken window that Marc created by shooting a bullet through when he was meaning to hit me. The snowstorm outside is still there, swirling down and covering everything in a white sheet.

I stand near the window, leaning against the wall and sending frequent looks out at the street below. I wonder when the police will get here. Soon, I hope. I haven't told Dad that Nate is my backup; I don't want word to get out that the cops are coming.

Dad doesn't talk, just huddles on the desk, trying to keep warm. He is cold, I know, but there is nothing I can do besides offer my coat, which is slightly too small and doesn't make that much of a difference. He gives me a smile; I pretend that I'm not cold and go back to the window.

The minutes slowly trickle by and I begin to allow myself to hope that I might make it out alive after all. After ten minutes, Jargon stomps out his third cigarette and starts another.

Another five pass when Marc gets angry with Rebecca and threatens to kill her with his gun.

Finally Goldbeck yells that he is leaving, and I am to go with him and Rebecca. It sends a shiver of fear running down my spine. I don't want to go anywhere with him or his wife. I want to go home. If we leave here, will Nate be able to find me? Will he know to send the police to the Goldbecks? Would the police even believe him?

Marc and Jargon stall for me this time, arguing about how they have to kill me and Dad, that we know way too much about them.

They're right. I'll go straight to the police.

So we have to die. Is it an understatement to say the realization is incredibly depressing?

Blocking out their fight, I turn to the window and concentrate on the road below me. The snow melts as soon as it touches the asphalt, leaving it wet and dark because of it. An occasional car will drive by, disappearing down the street or stopping in front of one of the shops around this part of town. An occasional pedestrian will walk down the sidewalk, never glancing up at this building as they pass by.

I grip the windowsill, willing the police to suddenly show up. They have to get here soon.

They *have to*.

Otherwise I'll be a slave to Rebecca Goldbeck and Dad will actually be dead and I'll never see Mom or my siblings or Nate again. Will Florence feel…anything…if I am killed by Marc despite Goldbeck's orders? Will my twin sense that I am dead through our supposed connection?

I try to shift through my emotions to find one that isn't what I am feeling right now, one that might belong to Florence that I can sense because we have some sort of link that others don't, but I can't come up with anything. I don't know what Flo is thinking.

With a sigh of defeat, I peer back out the window. A sudden gust of wind rushes in through the hole in the glass, and I shiver in the cold, hugging my arms around my body in an attempt to get warm.

"Get away from the window!" shouts Marc.

"Venice, you can have your coat back," Dad says gently.

I glance over at Dad and shake my head. "No, you keep it. I'm good."

"You're freezing."

Wow. He actually cares, unlike the past six years when he really didn't.

"I said get away from the window!" Marc moves toward me threateningly.

I look down at the street once more, then step back and return to sit on the desk with Dad. I don't move fast enough, because Jargon comes over, grabs me by the hair, and throws me on the floor. He turns and slams his fist into Dad's face, then kicks him in the gut for good measure. He's anxious to have this over with.

I slam into a stack of paint cans that come crashing down on top of me. I curl into a ball, covering my head as the heavy cans rain down, one smacking me on the shoulder. The cans clatter across the floor, rolling around in different directions and knocking over other things. Miraculously, none burst open, and I thank the trees that I didn't get drenched with rancid paint. My hands, shoulder, and sides have suffered the blow; I'm sure I will have bruises all over the place after this.

"Venice!" Dad crawls over to me, moving paint cans out of the way, helping me sit up among the wreckage. "Are you all right?"

Again, I'm surprised he cares.

I grumble something under my breath, slowly unraveling my body from the fetal position I was in. "What idiot thought it would be a smart idea to throw me into a stack of paint cans?"

Jargon laughs, his stink of cigarette smoke overwhelming me despite him being feet away from me. "You're welcome."

Dad helps me to my feet, and we're shuffled towards Goldbeck and Marc and Rebecca. "Be strong," Dad whispers in my ear as we slowly make our way across the room.

"I'm fine," I mumble, rubbing my forehead with a cold hand.

"What was *that*?" Goldbeck demands when Jargon shoves Dad and me forwards.

Jargon huffs, releasing more smoke. "I was having fun."

"You're damaging my treasure," whimpers Rebecca Goldbeck, and I shoot her a glare she doesn't acknowledge.

"Do you *want* everyone to know we're in here?" Goldbeck says in a harsh whisper. "Jones, you can't just go about hurting people as you please! I won't be implicated in more of this mess. No one gets hurt, you understand?"

"You'll be implicated for sure if you left them go, Goldbeck. I know how this works. The only way to walk away clean is to make them disappear." Marc is calm, authoritative, convincing. "Ferrari is already dead. That's been taken care of. No one will come looking for him, unless she lives. You think you'll be able to keep her from ratting on us all? Drop the naïve act, Goldbeck. If you want to live to be able to spend this money, they both have to disappear forever, and you know it."

"That's the most logical thing I've heard all day," says Jargon, cruelly waving his cigarette in my face. He goes to burn me with the butt, and I shy away from him, and he laughs.

I slowly walk around a table in the room to rejoin Dad, and I finally catch a glimpse of the briefcase. It's small, yet overflowing with stacks of money. As I pass it, I bend down for a closer look, and spot a bit of white paper sticking out. Frowning, I pick it up, and Marc and Jargon screech and lunge at me, but Rebecca is closer and she gets to me first, tugging on my arm as she pulls me toward her. Her pull sends pain shooting up my shoulder—and I shift slightly off to the side, shoving the paper in my jeans pocket. I can still see the briefcase. The lid is open; Jargon and Marc make sure I haven't taken anything, but no one wants to risk shutting it again since there is only one way to open it safely.

"We're wasting time," Jargon curses. Angrily, he lets loose more smoke. "I'm tired of taking orders from you Goldbeck."

I stare at his lit cigarette, then down at the money. An idea begins to take root in my mind.

"Fine, we'll leave," Goldbeck is saying. "But I refuse to be an accomplice. You wait until we're gone, long gone before you do anything. And if the police come after me asking about my role in it, I'll have no trouble turning you in."

This threat seems to make the others pause. I keep my eyes on Jargon. He occasionally knocks off ash or sucks in a draft. He has already gone through three cigarettes in the past hour; why won't he hurry up and finish this one? I need it.

"I can handle the girl. We leave the country tonight. I'm sorry, Venice, but I'm going to have to bind your hands and legs. Marc, take care of it. Rebecca," Goldbeck says hurriedly, not wanting to start yet another argument, "pull the car around the back. It's time to go." He goes to get his share of the cash from the briefcase, and Marc cocks his gun and points in at Goldbeck.

"Hold on now," he sneers. "I'll tie her up, but no one's touching the briefcase without me watching. And where's the ring? It stays on the table until the money's gone."

Rebecca whimpers, but Goldbeck commands, "Do as he says, dear. You'll get it back."

Marc has his gun trained on her now. She places the ring next to the briefcase then steps back from the table and from Marc and his gun.

"Just make the girl divide up the money if you don't trust us, Tyron," Jargon rasps, tossing his cigarette at me. He laughs with delight as I jump back to avoid it. In a stroke of brilliance, I pretend to stumble and fall, and when I land I make sure to secretly pick up the smoking butt.

Goldbeck sighs. "Venice, get up and divide the money. Ten for me and two for Tyron. The rest goes to Jones."

Marc opens his mouth to argue, but I have already approached the table, trembling like mad. I hide the cigarette from view, not reassured that I have my back to Marc; he's angry enough that he could—

I hear him click his tongue. "Venice," he says in a terrifyingly controlled voice, "you heard him. Set out two million."

Carefully, I count out two million dollars with one hand, then place it on the tabletop where he can see it.

Marc comes up to the table and his money. Instead of going for it, he reaches for the ring and, slowly, delicately, examines what has brought so much trouble to all of us. My spine stiffens. To my right, Jargon has gone ridged; Goldbeck is fidgeting uncomfortably. When Marc puts the ring in his pocket, both Jargon and Goldbeck flinch, and he points his gun at Jargon, then at the Goldbecks, then at Dad, then at me.

"Now," he says, "shut the briefcase, Venice, and step back from the table."

I hesitate, looking to Goldbeck for confirmation. Jargon growls, guttural and feral.

"Do it!" Marc commands.

As fast as I can, I drop the smoldering cigarette in the briefcase and close the lid.

"What's all this about, Marc? We've worked together in the past. I've helped you out of a couple of scrapes before." Goldbeck is smooth and calm.

"Yes, Stephen, which is why I'm sure you will be more than happy to walk away with the portion you were so generously willing to give me." He takes the two million from the table and tosses it at Goldbeck's feet. I've backed away by now and have rejoined Dad. He may not be much of a dad, but he's all I have right now.

Jargon has taken a few steps toward Marc, but Marc's gun is keeping everyone at bay. "I'll be taking what is rightfully mine, now, thank you." He grabs the briefcase from the table and starts backing towards the doorway.

"What do you mean it's rightfully yours? It's mine! This was my heist all along!" Jargon is furious, his entire body tense and poised to attack. His face is redder than his flaming orange hair.

"This briefcase belonged to *my* grandpa, you idiots! You robbed me of my inheritance!"

Utter silence follows his outburst.

"*What?*" Jargon finally asks.

"Sherman Wilhiker was *my* grandpa!" says Marc, snarling. "The senile old man played us all for fools. He gave me his company but cashed everything out. Before I knew what had happened, the company bottomed out and he died, leaving few traces of the whereabouts of his fortune. But I finally caught up with you."

"You're lying," says Dad. "I never heard him talking about you."

"Oh really?" Marc sneers. "Never mentioned his daughter, Beth Tyron, and her son?"

"Wilhiker said that his grandson's name was Marc," speaks up Jargon.

"Precisely. So if you'll all excuse me, we've spent far too long together." To our surprise, Marc puts the briefcase down, only to pull a can of gasoline from behind an old shelf unit. Comprehension dawns on all of us as he begins to douse the floor around him, sliding the briefcase behind him with his foot, walking backwards to the stairwell.

Rebecca Goldbeck screams. Marc stops pouring the gasoline to aims the gun at her. Her scream turns to a whimper.

Goldbeck says confidently, "Come, dear. We're finished here." Taking no heed of the gun, Goldbeck guides his wife toward Marc and the exit. "I know how Marc works and he knows how I work. We'll be fine."

"Stop right there!" Marc shouts, and they do stop. "I'll let you go, Goldbeck, but you do it on my terms, not yours."

"Of course, Marc, whatever you say."

Marc grabs the gas can and works to empty it, the Goldbecks waiting patiently for permission to leave. Dad and I have slowly moved closer to the window, our only hope of escaping the inferno to come. As the last few drops fall from the can, Jargon realizes the moment is now or never.

With an inhuman screech he lunges at Marc, who is tossing aside the gas can to pick up the briefcase.

Marc wasn't kidding when he bragged about being a good shot.

Jargon is hit in the shoulder and then in the chest. He falls to the ground, a gargled gasp escaping his mouth. I stare, horrified, as his blood begins to stain the floor, spreading out underneath him in a sweep of dark red. He jerks once, twice, and falls silent.

Dad looks utterly disgusted, yet at the same time...forlorn. No wonder. He just watched his former best friend die.

I just watched a man die.

My hand rises to my mouth as I switch my gaze to Marc, who does not seem remorseful at all. Goldbeck is using this moment to scurry past Jargon's body and the gasoline and Marc to the doorway without his wife, but something stops him from making his escape. I follow his gaze to the briefcase. Soft tendrils of smoke are gently wafting through the seam, barely perceptible.

I pray that Goldbeck doesn't say anything, that Marc just lights the match and leaves so that Dad and I can figure how to get out of here alive. I have a feeling we have a better chance of survival as long as Marc thinks he's leaving with the money.

Marc is fiddling with the matches when Goldbeck says, "Tyron, why is the briefcase smoking?"

I close my eyes against the rising panic, holding onto my fraying courage with everything I have in me.

"What are you talking about?" he snaps, suspicious it's some sort of ruse to distract him. But he can see it, too, and he rummages through his pocket for the ring.

I slowly back away, putting as much distance between me and Marc as possible. I have a pretty good idea of what he will do when he finds his money has turned to ash.

I reach the farthest window just as Marc manages to fit the key and raise the lid. Everyone—Marc, Dad, Rebecca, and Goldbeck—gasp loudly. I think that is proof enough that my plan worked.

Knowing I have only a split second before they point me out, I glance out the window at the street. The snow is still drifting down lazily.

And pulling up against the curb are three police cars.

I breathe a sigh of relief. But even now, they could be too late.

"What is this?" Marc exclaims. "Where is the money? Why are there only ashes?" He is sputtering with rage. He frantically paws through the pile of ashes, searching for any leftover money left intact. Instead, he finds a blackened cigarette.

Immediately, all eyes are on me. I spot Dad through the mess of obstacles in this room, and I see he has his mouth open in shock. He must not have expected me to play such a bold move.

"You burned the money," Marc says in a murderous whisper.

He fires off two shots, shattering the unbroken window behind me. I drop to the floor, with glass raining down on me, but other than a few cuts, I am fine. I don't have any bullets in me. I seek cover behind a blocky desk that is shoved up around plenty of other strange things to give me a neat hiding place. My heart is pounding. I know he's coming for me.

Another round of gunshots sounds. I hear the bullets crash through the rotten wood of the desk and feel one graze my arm. I clap a hand to the spot—warm blood trickles through my fingers—and I have to work hard to bite back a scream. The bullet only scratched me, and the cut isn't very deep, but it still stings.

"She's just a child, Marc!" I wish it was Dad defending me, but it's Goldbeck. "Let's leave before things get worse."

"Come on out!" Marc calls gently. "Come out, Venice."

I can hear him reloading his gun while he gets closer and closer to me. I'm sure if I survive, this moment will linger in my mind.

I am breathing hard. I don't know what to do. The police should know we are up here—the gunshots were a dead giveaway—and *why* are they taking so long?

I hear soft footsteps to my left. Casting a nervous look around me, I find there is a paint can underneath the desk. I snatch it up—it is half full—and hurl it in his direction. Marc dodges the paint can and instantly has me by the hair.

I hear a soft click, feel cold metal press against the back of my head.

"Don't move," Marc commands. "I will shoot you. But I want to hurt you first."

I freeze, anxiety crashing through me. It clashes with despair—I was *so close* to my freedom—and I have the most embarrassing urge to cry. The last time I cried was years ago and it didn't solve anything. I haven't cried since.

He roughly shoves me with enough hatred and malice to send me crashing down, and I slam my head into the desk I was just hiding behind.

I lie in a heap on the floor waiting for the next blow, my heart beating so fiercely it hurts. My palm and head and shoulder ache tremendously, but the scratch on my arm from Marc's bullet stings the sharpest. Will a gunshot at this range kill me instantly?

All I can think is *I'm going to die I'm going to die I'm going to die and the police will be too late.*

I wish I had listened to Nate earlier. I wish he was here with me, lending his help and strength. I wish I could talk to him one last time.

I wish I had told Mom about this trouble earlier, so she would understand when I turned up dead. I wish I'd told my family how much I love them.

"I am really going to enjoy this," Marc sneers.

The Goldbecks have deserted me. Figures.

And where is Dad?

He can't leave me like this.

"So am I," says another voice, and there is a loud clatter, a thud, a groan, then scuffling noises.

I slowly look up.

Dad is struggling with Marc. Keeping the gun pointed at the ceiling, their faces red and their breath coming in short gasps. The metal briefcase is on the ground—Dad must have hit Marc with it—and the ash from the money and checks is spilling across the floor. I watch them fight, not knowing what to do, if I should intervene or if that would just make things worse.

Marc punches Dad in the gut, and he stumbles back, clutching his stomach; he must be in a lot of pain. Marc slowly points the gun at me, and I freeze all over again, looking Death right in the face.

"Say goodbye," he whispers, and pulls the trigger.

FIFTY–SEVEN

I don't remember much of what happens afterword. All I can recall are brief, hazy flashes—the blood arching across the floor, the stunned look on Marc's fury-struck face, the wide-eyed surprise of Dad's realization of what he had done. I remember feeling faint, light-headed, angry. I remember several police officers storming up the stairs and grabbing Marc and Jargon's body and the Goldbecks and leading them away. I remember staring down at Dad and trying to ask him if he can see me when his eyes are glazed over.

I remember the cops telling me that I have to move, that they needed to get his body off the floor. I remember watching from the second floor of the brick building as the criminals were loaded up.

Marc argues at first, protesting innocence, but after one of the officers finds something about he has been involved in numerous petty crimes, Marc goes quiet and asks to contact his lawyer. Rebecca is the hardest—her husband obeys the police's commands without resistance—but she refuses to get in the car for fear of having her skirt stained. There is nothing on the seat that will cause a stain, and I think she's just furious because she was arrested.

I also reclaimed my ring. I found it near the doorway lying in a pool of gasoline.

I remember gathering my things and shoving them in my backpack, and casting the room one last look before numbly wandering down the stairs and into the cold, snowy outside where a kind police officer by the name of Bromwell greets me with silent support. My phone is cracked, all my belongings either trashed or unrecognizable to me anymore. I remember feeling angry and sad and broken and exhausted.

I remember curious shoppers stopping to stare at the flashing police lights, and I'll bet they are wondering what has happened here. Several people walk across the road to come to find out; the cops don't share much other than the building was being used for criminal activity.

It's only five in the afternoon, yet so much has gone on during the past hour and forty minutes. I think I'm ready for a long nap.

My arm and palm are cleaned and bandaged, though I barely feel the pain any more. My head is reeling whether from all that's happened or from all the banging around I suffered. Probably both.

I can't believe it.

I'm free.

Hubris Jargon and Malaise Tone and Sleepy Gumption will never bother me again.

Never.

I'm free.

I can cross the street without worrying that someone in their intimidating SUV is about to try to run me down. I can walk to and from school without looking over my shoulder, stressed out that I am being hunted. I can live my life in peace.

And I thank the trees for it.

I list the good things that have come out of this horrendous afternoon. 1) I was reunited with my dad; 2) everything was solved or came to a conclusion; 3) all the people after me are arrested; and 4) my ring really is worthless now.

It had one responsibility: unlocking that briefcase. I destroyed what was inside, so now the key is pointless. It isn't needed.

It feels awfully good to have it back on my pinky and to know it's junk now.

I know I should be freaking out that I was kidnapped and threatened and shot at and *hit*, but all I want to do is meet up with my family again, thank Nate for saving me, and sleep for a really long time.

I know I should also be mad at myself for sending forty-one million dollars up in flames, but no one needs that money. It only caused problems for me and Dad and the people who wanted it.

I let my mind wander to everything but the one thing I don't want to face. I didn't stop Marc from shooting Dad. I stood by helplessly and watched it happen. I'm the reason my dad is dead.

I remember the last words Dad had said, the last words I had heard past all the fuzzy buzzing in my head.

Forgive me.

I'd already forgiven him.

An ambulance comes and takes his body away, and I remember the lights and sirens, but they don't make sense to my weary mind. I dimly remember his body is still wearing my coat, that now I'm freezing in the cold outside while he takes my warmth farther and farther away.

The cold feels good. It's...refreshing. The snow that has covered the ground gives me the faith that I can have a new beginning, that I still have my family, that I'm still alive. The police insist on driving me to the hospital to check and see if I'm alright, and they question me about the incident the whole ride there, and I do my best but I don't think I'm making much sense, because they eventually stop asking questions and let me rest.

It hurts. It hurts a lot. I wish I had known Dad better. I wish he hadn't been so shallow and chosen money over family. In a way, though, he had prevented us from harm by leading Jargon away from us, and I'm grateful to him for that, but I wish he hadn't started it all in the first place. He didn't need that money. He could have let Jargon keep it.

Jargon. He's dead, too, now.

The nice officer, Bromwell, understands my predicament more than the others. He's familiar with me—miraculously, he is one of the men that responded to my call for help the day Rupert and Quentin broke into my house.

Bromwell is solicitous and protective. I ask him if my family knows where I am and what's happened and he tells me he spoke with Mom himself and that another officer was dispatched to bring her to the hospital to meet us. I like Bromwell. I'm glad he was the one to tell Mom. He has a way of making people feel safe.

Mom is at the hospital when I get there and, characteristically, she is frantic over everything. Bromwell smoothly manages to calm her fears and explains all he knows while the doctors check my injuries. I'm grateful the officer is doing the talking. I'm starting to feel rather numb. I overhear the doctors say something about how I'm in mental shock and that it's normal and that I need rest and care.

I catch snippets of what Officer Bromwell is telling Mom. He doesn't know it all, only what happened at the paint-manufacturer place, but he tells her about Dad, and I'm glad because I don't know how I could possibly break that news. Mom takes it rather stoically on the outside, but horror and sorrow crash through her aura. She has already grieved for Dad, when he first left and each year after that, and then most recently when he died the first time. The sorrow in her aura is less for Dad or for herself. It's for me. It's now that I let the tears flow steady and silently. Mom has always given so much for her family, for me.

Finally, Officer Bromwell gifts me a veggie burger and sweet potato fries from the vegan deli across the street and tells me I'm free to go home. He helps me and Mom into the car and I quickly snuggle up to Mom and lay my head on her shoulder.

Neither of us says much as Officer Bromwell drives us home, but the warmth and safety of Mom's embrace and the kind officer's protection threatens to bring on more tears.

I'm saved by the ringing of my smashed up phone as Mandy calls me. I can't believe it still works.

"Venice! You picked up finally! After therapy when Elijah and I were at his house, Nate got us worried about you with his nagging that I call you and make sure you had gotten home. Did you make it home? Can you tell me why he was like that? Why didn't you pick up the last hundred times I called? Did you know you made us all worry?"

"I'm okay now, Mandy. Thanks for checking up on me. It means a lot." It feels good to say that I'm okay even though I'm not. "I just ran into something...uncomfortable."

"Girl, you will be the death of me someday." She sighs. "Glad to know you're all right. What happened?"

"It's a really long story." I bite my lip as the memories from this afternoon flood through my mind.

"Venice, are you sure you're all right? You sound like you're about to burst into tears."

As soon as she says that, I have to fight back the tears again. I hope this crying thing doesn't become a habit. "I'm...really shaken up. That's all. I promise I'll tell you all about it later."

"Wait, what? Venice? Does this have to do with what Nate was panicking about? Hello? Venice?"

"Yeah, I'm still here, but I do need to go. Look, I'm okay now, I really am. I'll call you tomorrow and we'll talk, okay?"

"Of course. And I'm here for you, Venice. If you need anything, please call me."

"I will. And thank you, Mandy. You're a really great friend." She hangs up and I shove my phone into my backpack, out of sight.

We ride the rest of the way in silence. I can't wait to see my siblings again, and I'm sure Mom and the others are bursting with impatience to hear all the details of what happened. Suddenly, I want to be unburdened, too. I want to clean my slate, to pour out every secret I have kept these long months. They will be stunned to hear about Dad, alive once more but dead again. Roman will take it especially hard.

I wipe a single tear off my cheek. To be reunited with Dad after six years of *nothing*, only to have him taken away from me again, is cruel. I curse the life Marc has lived. I curse Marc himself. I curse his grandpa and the money and my ring and that horrid briefcase and the feud between Jargon and Dad that resulted in all of this destruction. I glance down at my pinky, see the clear blue gem and the worn gold metal and the greenish tint, and I vow never to take it off again. This is my link to Dad. This is how I'll remember him.

I remember sitting on my hands once they get cold, which is when I'm aware of something in my back pocket. I pull out a square, folded piece of white paper and stare at it for a long time before working up the courage to unwrap it. I don't think anyone else had realized this paper was in the briefcase.

The message is short, written in slanted elegant calligraphy that doesn't resemble what I would think an old man's hand would look like. Still, I read what Sherman Wilhiker, Marc's grandpa, wrote.

To the one who deserves it: they will know what to do with it.

He must have meant the money. Well. I know I didn't deserve any of the baggage that came with that man's money, but I sure had to deal with it.

I put the paper back in my pocket.

The only time anything is said during the rest of the ride is when Bromwell pulls up to the curb at my house and his companion says, "Is that a *bear*?"

My head snaps up. I spot my siblings out on my front lawn, talking loudly with one another, a huge brown dog moving among them, tail wagging madly. Mercury swivels in our direction as the police cruiser slows before my house, and he starts to bound forward. Nate suddenly appears—I hadn't seen him; how had I not seen him?—and grabs his dog by the collar to prevent him from leaping out in front of the car.

I throw open the door before Bromwell has completely killed the engine. I step out onto the sidewalk and hug Mercury around the neck as he licks my face energetically, wagging his whole body. I find comfort in his shaggy fur, in his disgusting slobbery kisses. Somehow, I know he understands. Maybe this is why Nate loves dogs so much.

They simply know.

"Venice!" Florence grabs me by my hurt arm and drags me to my feet, making me wince so badly she flinches away. "Venice, where have you been? What were you doing this afternoon? Why did you come home in a *police car*? And what is all this talk about your ring and the Goldbecks and Marc and some maniacal driver who wants you dead?"

I glance over at Nate. I half expect him to smile, but his face is white, and he's staring at the dark stain on the knees of my jeans. The blood stains. From Dad's blood. On the ground.

The world shifts around me. I blink, steady myself on Mercury.

"Venice?" Mom and Nate are instantly on either side of me, holding me up.

I let them guide me inside and onto the couch, out of the cold, and I welcome the warmth.

Bromwell has followed us inside and Mom is asking him to tell everyone what he told her at the hospital. He really does have a calming effect on us all, and he begins explaining everything to my dumbstruck family.

Even sitting, I almost faint, overwhelmed by the pain pounding in my head and the shock still flooding my system, but Florence sees I'm struggling. She sits next to me and pulls me into her arms and holds me tight. I remember that I feel her own pain and loss and I let her into my heart and I don't let go of her because I can finally sense our connection.

I remember that Bromwell doesn't stay long. He asks Mom and me permission to come back tomorrow to ask some questions and take a statement. Naturally, both of us agree. He soon gets back in his car, and he and his buddy drive off with Mom standing on the sidewalk, waving goodbye. From the house we watch her slowly, but resolutely, head back to the house.

My twin goes to her, and I watch them embrace, both erupting in simultaneous sobs. But their tears are tinged with happiness. They are healing their relationship and it's beautiful to see. Those blasted tears come back to my own eyes.

Siena, Pompeii, and Roman are all talking quietly amongst themselves, sorting through the different things Bromwell said, trying to grasp the truth that yes, Dad was alive when everyone thought he was dead, and now he really is dead, and that's that.

I look down at my feet, noticing my backpack on the floor near my leg, and I mentally thank Bromwell for bringing that in for me. I would have forgotten it.

Now that Florence has left my side, Nate comes closer to me, and I turn to him and fall into his arms, willing the strength to reenter my body. I want to cry this time.

Yet I don't.

"Venice," Nate says softly, and I shake my head against him. I can't. Not at this moment, not right now, not when I'm depleted. And he understands what I can and can't do, and he simply holds me tighter.

I vow that I will do the same for him. No more demands. Just love and support.

I understand his fears better now. Being reunited with my dad was painful. I learned some hurtful things about him that I wish I'd never known. But there was also beauty to be found. It's a risk, and I hope he can find some joy with his own father, even if it comes at price.

My head lifts off his chest, and I look straight into his eyes. "Nate," I say in a broken voice, "you still have time. Maybe you'll succeed where I have failed."

He brushes a thumb down my cheek. I know I'm crying now. He doesn't speak at all, simply nods, and I am satisfied with that. His hold around me is safe and warm. I'm so glad I have him, so glad he's alive, so glad he's nothing like my dad, willing to trade the people he loves for glittering emptiness.

I don't know how he can choose to be cheerful after all the heartbreak he goes through nearly every day. I don't know how he can still want to talk to me and help me and like me after how hard I am on him for not helping himself. I don't know how he can find joy in things I would skip over, in things no one would ever think could provide light.

I don't know how, but I want him to teach me.

Hours later, after everything has been explained and my entire family knows about my recent adventures, Mom finally finds her voice. She asks question upon question, squeezing me and Nate dry of every little detail. It is a huge relief to get it off my back.

And when we finish, my family's reactions are priceless.

Florence is shocked and disgusted and horrified. She gives me another hug and tells me she's so so *so* sorry for not understanding why I had been acting a little jumpy since Dad's accident.

Roman is awed. He thinks it's incredibly awesome that I faced down three criminals and succeeded. He tells me that he's going to brag to all his friends, around the neighborhood and at school, that his older sister arrested six crooks, was shot in the arm, and burned forty-three million dollars with a cigarette butt.

Pompeii has pretty much the same reaction. He and Roman don't know just how scared I was, how I wish I could forget all that has happened to me, how I never want to be involved with anything like this again.

Siena is alternately awed and terrified, particularly fascinated with the part Rebecca Goldbeck played. She keeps asking me why Rebecca wanted me as a pet and what that means and why she thought her skirt might get stained in a police car. But I can tell my story has frightened her. She has never been this clingy to Mom before, and I notice Mom seems to enjoy the extra affection.

My voice is ragged by the time I wrap up all the loose ends, and Mercury hops up onto the couch the instant I close my mouth.

When we first came inside, no one had noticed that Mercury had followed us in. It wasn't until Nate got up to get me a drink of water that we noticed him following Nate into the kitchen. Despite his size, Mercury hasn't shattered anything so far. He's better behaved than my siblings.

Mercury places his gigantic head in my lap and smiles up at me, drool soaking into my pants. I stroke his fur, slowly losing feeling in my legs as his tremendous weight sinks into me.

I'm sitting on the couch with Nate, so close my aching shoulder is pressed against his. My right arm, the one that was grazed by Marc's bullet, stings every time Nate shifts and applies the slightest bit of pressure on my skin. I don't say anything, however. I don't want him to leave.

The others are grouped around us, pestering us with questions, so many questions. Nate answers the ones he can, and I'm so grateful for him. I am more tired than ever.

Everyone is numb, shocked that Dad is dead *again*, but they handle it much better than the first time they learned about him. Mom is more sad that he didn't exactly love her, that he preferred money over her, than the fact that he's gone. I get that—I'm hurt because of that, too. I wish—

I stop myself.

Enough wishing. It's already happened.

But in the end Dad did give his life to save mine, and I do my best to make sure my family knows that, and also that he hoped we would forgive him.

I'm exhausted. I take off my glasses and set them on Mercury's back—I know that is a terrible idea but there is nowhere else to put them—and I rest my head on Nate's shoulder. He isn't completely comfortable with me doing this in front of my family, but they are all talking amongst themselves and are ignoring us. Nate leans against me; I hear his heart beating and his quiet breath. I am safe with him.

I must have fallen asleep because the next thing I know Nate and I are the only ones in the living room besides Mercury the bear-dog. I hear soft voices coming from the kitchen.

"You're awake," Nate notes.

"Mm..." I mindlessly run my fingers up and down his arm, tracing along the paths of his different scars. I can't see—my glasses are off and the lights are low—but I can feel his soft skin and I know I really love touching him. If he is uncomfortable with this, then he keeps it to himself and doesn't object. He says nothing as my fingers drift across his palm, then back up his arm to the very fringe of his T-shirt sleeve. He says nothing as I go down, my fingertips so light they barely even brush against his skin.

My eyes close. My cheek is pressed into his shoulder. My legs have lost all feeling because of Mercury's hefty head. I try to move, but my legs won't budge an inch. They're trapped.

I sigh softly. I don't want Nate to leave, though I do know he probably needs to go soon. After calling me a few times from the Jenkins' and getting no answer, he waited until Mandy returned from her therapy and had her watch the kids and continue to try to contact me. He hurried to his own home and collected Mercury, checked on his drunk grandpa, then returned here. Finding me absent, he called the police using Roman's phone. My brother was so excited about that.

My hand rests on Nate's arm for a moment while I start to fall asleep again. He nudges me, and I snap awake, head coming up.

"I should go," he whispers.

I scramble to find my glasses and slide them on. "Can't you stay for a few more minutes?"

"Venice." He leans so close I think he's going to kiss me, but he doesn't. "I have to get back to my grandpa. I haven't taken care of him all day."

Disappointment fills my soul. I stare down at his arm, tainted by dozens of white scars, and wish he was less responsible. I know I'm being rather selfish, but I want him here with me for as long as possible. I'm paranoid of losing Nate, and I know he's not safe at home.

"Don't worry." He pushes a stray auburn curl off my neck. My skin burns where he touches me, except it's a good kind of burn. "You inspired me to be brave," he says quietly.

I am confused about what he has said, and I open my mouth to ask what he meant by that when he drops a soft kiss on my cheek. I instantly forget my question. He pulls back and stands up, taking away his warmth and comfort and strength.

Nate and I stop by the kitchen so he can say his goodbyes to the others. Pompeii waves Mercury over, and he and Siena take turns showering the dog with attention and ear-scratches.

Mom thanks him for staying calm throughout the whole thing while I was gone and no one knew what was happening to me. Flo thanks him for keeping me from dying. Roman thanks him for using *his* phone to call the police because that was awesome and totally worthy of bragging. Pompeii thanks him for bringing Mercury and could he please bring him again sometime. Siena tells him that he has to draw her some more pictures.

Nate looks like he's going to laugh when my three younger siblings say these things to him. He replies with a "you're welcome" to everyone except Siena; instead, he promises her that he will draw more for her the next time he sees her. It satisfies her.

Once they all say goodbye, my family returns to wondering what's going to change in life from now on.

I walk Nate to the door, careful not to swing my hurting arm. Mercury gets to the door first, and he looks back at me, wanting to go out. I quickly set him free, and Nate smiles at that, tired and happy all the same.

"It's pitch-black out here," I say, stepping onto the porch with him. The sun went down over an hour ago. "It's also freezing."

"This is the perfect temperature," he replies, breathing in deeply. I know he likes this weather, where he can wear *T-shirts*.

I close the door behind us, cutting off any heat coming from inside. Beside me, the porch light flickers. Mom rarely uses it, and I doubt she has changed the bulb from the one that was in there when we moved in. The porch is covered in a halo of dim yellow-orange light, just enough to illuminate everything within a five-foot radius.

We stand side-by-side for a minute, watching Mercury's dark form sniffing my yard. He occasionally rolls around in the snow, and I feel bad for Nate, who will have to deal with a soaking-wet dog on his walk home.

"Would you like a ride back?" I ask him. "So you don't have to walk in the dark."

He shakes his head. "We'll be fine."

I shrug. "Your choice."

There is silence between us again, the only sound Mercury's paws on the crusted snow. I am growing colder and colder by the moment; I'm wearing short-sleeves and my shirt is slightly too small. As I'd noticed before, the hem falls barely over the top of my jeans. I don't like too-short shirts. I think I'll put this one away and not wear it again.

Nate takes my left hand, examining the bandage on my palm. "How did you get this?"

"Fell over."

He gives me an annoyed look, though it holds concern and a faint trace of what could be humor.

"I was getting out of the way of Marc's gun," I explain. "I dove off a desk and sliced my palm on a paint can."

"Marc deserved to be taken away."

"I agree wholeheartedly."

Nate moves, releasing my hand and going to my arm. "I feel like such a child. We joked about those men wanting to kill you, but today was no joke. Why did we think we could handle this alone? Marc killed two men today, and if he'd had his way he would have killed you, too. Can you forgive me for leaving you alone?"

"I've thought it over a thousand times, Nate. They were getting desperate. If you had been with me they may have hurt you, too. If you hadn't called the police things would have turned out very differently. You saved my life again."

"You must have lightning-fast reflexes to dodge a bullet like that."

"Nah, I think it was Marc's terrible aim."

Nate shakes his head in wonder as he wraps my arm up. "I can't believe you just went through that horrible experience, and you're still joking about it. Especially since your dad..." He doesn't finish.

"There are plenty of jokes I can tell from this afternoon." My gaze is distant as I stare out across my yard. "I talked with Rebecca Goldbeck about ripped jeans. She insulted my sense of fashion."

"No." Nate fakes a gasp of horror. "She didn't go *that* far."

I punch him, forgetting that my arm is wounded, and suck back a grunt of pain.

"What? I'm just trying to make conversation."

I chew on my bottom lip, thinking through what had happened. "Nate, I burned forty-three million dollars. Should I not have? I did it and my dad died because of me."

He's quiet. "It's not your fault," he says finally. "Marc was going to kill you and your dad and even Jargon anyway. That place would have gone up in flames in no time. You would've been trapped up there. And your dad could have chosen not to defend you and jump in the way of the bullet. He could have let you die and done nothing. It's not your fault, Venice."

"But—"

"It *isn't*," he says fiercely. Then he's soft again. "It isn't. Trust me and don't blame yourself. Remember his last words? It was an act of love, Venice. For all the pain and trauma and danger he caused you, he loved you."

I bite my lip against tears and nod. "Well, I turned that much money into ash…"

"It was paper."

"That's what I mean." I sigh, putting away thoughts of Dad. "My grandma is going to be furious that I sent that paper up in flames instead of recycling it."

Nate groans. "Seriously?"

"Just teasing." I grin at him, though it isn't sincere, and he grins back, quite sincerely, and I'm suddenly reminded of lunch when Mandy and Elijah look at each other like this in front of me, making everything awkward. I'm glad no one else is out here. I'm glad it's just me and him.

"I should probably head home." Nate moves his attention to his dog, who has stuck his head in a nearby bush, and the moment between us is broken.

"Are you sure you want to walk in the dark?"

He nods once. "Yeah. I'll be fine."

"Okay." I wait for him to say something, but he doesn't.

Mercury trots up to us, a baseball in his mouth. Nate takes it from him and throws it far to the right, using his left hand. I wonder why he uses his left when his right is dominant.

"Did you name your dog?" I ask suddenly.

Nate seems surprised by such a random question. "Oh…yes. His first owner called him Dog, which is an ironic name since Mercury just happens to be a dog—"

I frown at him. He is rarely sarcastic.

"—so once I got him, I gave him a real name." Nate slips his hand into my uninjured one and pulls me off the porch. He points to the night sky, which is clear; hundreds of twinkling stars shine down on us. "I named him after my favorite planet."

"I think my favorite planet is Earth."

"How boring."

I smile, because I can't help it, and we stand right there for a while until he speaks again.

"Are you going to be all right after...everything?"

I sigh. "Yeah. I just—it'll take a while to process."

"I know what it feels like to lose a parent, one who hasn't paid you any attention for *years*—and it's probably harder than losing one you've known forever. It's hard either way, but when you reflect on how many memories you could have created with that person, and how you won't ever be able to now that they're gone...Well, it's difficult."

"What do you mean?" I ask, puzzled.

"This week...when my grandpa was mostly sane, he told me that...that my mom is dead, has been for twelve years, and that my dad changed after the accident, and all this other stuff. It made sense, why she at least hadn't yet contacted me. I wish I had known sooner. Gramps wasn't very delicate about telling me this."

I look down at my feet. I'm glad I didn't have to be the one to let him know that his mom is dead.

"So I get how you feel." He sounds rueful.

He's suffered more than I could imagine.

I turn to him and he wraps his arms around my waist, holding me tightly. "I don't know what I would do without you," I mutter.

He rests his chin on my head. "You wouldn't have anyone to yell at."

"That's cruel, Nate." I'm comforted by his words—the ones that came from his heart, not the pathetic attempt to make me laugh—and I'm comforted by the knowledge that I can always go to him and he'll help me.

"All right. I should go. You need to get back to your family."

"They won't miss me for a few more minutes."

Nate looks down at me. I can barely see him, but I'm sure he's wearing a mocking frown. "Venice, of *course* they will miss you. Your mom was going crazy earlier when you didn't show up after an hour, and once I told her all about your ring, she was even more freaked out. She will definitely notice if you are gone for too long."

"It's been only a couple minutes."

He isn't satisfied with my excuse. "Whatever you say." He looks back at his friend, who is now digging a hole in Mom's flower bed. "Mercury! Get out of that, you silly dog."

Mercury sneezes in reply and ignores Nate's command to stop.

"Nate." I give him a squeeze; try to keep him with me just a few minutes longer. "I'm grateful that you called the police and saved me from becoming extinct like the orangutans will be since we haven't written our report and given Mr. Castro a good reason not to kill them."

"If that's your way of saying thank you, then you're welcome."

I let myself smile, and it feels really nice.

"Venice." He slides a hand behind my neck and tilts my face up. His expression is hidden in the dark. "When will I see you again?"

My answer is barely a whisper. "Tomorrow, please. Even if it's just for a few minutes. I have to talk to the police, but I want to try to get back to normal life as soon as possible. I'll for sure be at school on Tuesday for our report. I won't desert you."

He laughs quietly, joylessly. "Well, I'm counting on you never deserting me. And as for the report, we'll face the consequences together. We haven't finished the presentation or essay."

"Mr. Castro will understand."

"He *is* a fair teacher." Nate holds my gaze for the fraction of a second, then softly kisses me on the mouth. My eyelids slip shut.

I tighten my grip around his shoulders, holding him close to me. My entire system is buzzing with delight. I love the feel of him. I wonder if this is why Flo has kissed so many boys so many times: to experience this rush of exhilaration. Then again, does she even feel this way? Or is it just me?

Nate's fingers brush the skin of my bare waist—this stupid shirt had risen an inch or so when I reached my arms around his neck—and I flinch so badly that he moves his hand to the small of my back instead. It both surprises me and is a relief.

He gently pulls me closer. His movements are always gentle, and even more so when he's with me. He breaks away, much to my disappointment, and presses his face in my hair, his arms encircled about my waist keeping me right here with him.

We stand there for several moments—I am warm all the way through—until Mercury comes up to us and sits on our feet. I laugh silently and step back from Nate, having a hard time with Mercury preventing me from going anywhere, and pat the dog on his wet head.

"You can go home now," I tell him. I am overflowing with joy; I hope this feeling won't go away. It has washed me clean of sorrow and depression for the time being, and it's helping me heal.

Nate checks to make sure Mercury doesn't have that random baseball in his mouth before moving farther away from me, taking the dog with him. He is halfway down the driveway when he calls, "I'll see you tomorrow?"

"Tomorrow and the next day and the next," I confirm.

He doesn't say anything else to me, and a second later he and Mercury blend into the night and disappear from my sight. I am left in the semi-darkness, a soft smile on my face.

I can't stop myself from lifting a hand and lightly touching my fingertips to my lips.

Tomorrow suddenly seems like an awfully long time away.

FIFTY-EIGHT

During the next four days, everything changes. Mom keeps us close, not that I mind, and we're always doing things together and strengthening our trust and love and friendships. My siblings work in harmony and unity for the first time in a long time, and I like to say that Dad was the reason for this, that Dad made us realize how bittersweet life is and that we should always live it the best we can, with strong relationships and a solid foundation at home. I don't mind walking down the hallway to my bedroom and having my siblings genuinely ask if I'm doing all right today. I don't mind the group hugs Mom frequently announces, and after a few times we start calling for them ourselves.

We're not a perfect family. We still have our ups and downs. But during the following days after that horrible afternoon, things are almost...flawless. Maybe it's my view on Pompeii and Siena's arguments—finding humor and laughter instead of annoyance. Maybe it's my better understanding of how Florence is feeling and her understanding of how I'm feeling. Maybe it's the long talks I have with Roman, discussing different points of the crime I busted. Maybe it's the dreaming with Mom, planning fun activities that will bring our family back together.

She certainly keeps a closer eye on me. I can't go to the library unless I have three people with me, which seems like a lot given the fact Pompeii and Siena are the only ones in our family that enjoy taking a trip there. I luck out when Flo and Roman agree to come with me, and Mom is perfectly fine with that. She even joins us, and though I'm really going to meet Nate there, I have a good time with my siblings, helping Florence find novels I enjoyed, helping Pompeii select the interesting-looking fantasy young adult fictions that he said he would read because he wants to make me smile.

Officer Bromwell and a team of investigators return to collect my statement. I'm ready to talk, and I tell them everything I know. They have tons and tons of questions and the session goes pretty long. Mom offers the officers refreshments, all the organic snacks that she likes to buy that none of us like to eat. The officers either politely decline or take a couple of bites and then leave the rest on the plate.

Except for Bromwell. He goes on and on about the health benefits of those particular vitamins or nutrients or minerals that the snacks contain. He and Mom share their favorite brands with each other and their preferred grocery stores, and it cracks me up. I'm thrilled because I really like Officer Bromwell, and I think Mom does, too.

Marc is already forgotten. Mom gave me a blank look once when I ask her if she was mad at herself for falling for him.

Now that no one is after me and my ring, I wear it every day. I am disappointed to find that the stone has become loose—I'm worried that it will fall out. I love the stone. I love that shade of blue.

Our neighbors, one-by-one, knock on our door and ask with some interest why there was so much police activity that Thursday afternoon and evening. Mom doesn't really want to tell anyone about what had happened, but I do. I want everyone who will listen to know.

So I tell them. And my siblings join in, and gradually Mom does, too. Word spreads fast in this neighborhood; soon we are getting calls and visits from people that live here that we don't even know.

The old woman who lives behind us, Ms. Mehaine, bakes cookies and brings them over so she can tell me she's so so *so* sorry that she wasn't home when Rupert and Quentin chased me. It's all right, I reply, because the men were arrested anyway. It annoys me that Roman and Pompeii and Siena eat all the cookies before I can get one. But then it makes me smile, and they know they succeeded.

I have a long talk with Mandy over the phone. She is utterly shocked to hear about what happened, and she screams in my ear for an hour, going on and on how she should have known because she would have been a great help. She is obviously disgruntled that I let Nate know and not her. She tells everything to Elijah, who spreads the word to his family, who spreads the word to neighbors, and pretty quickly my adventures are common knowledge.

Mom doesn't like the publicity, but I don't mind it. I am glad people aren't left in the dark. I'm glad plenty of citizens in this town know that the Goldbecks were evil, that my ring caused all this trouble.

Grandma and Grandpa Ferrari have a four-hour talk with Mom, which beats my conversation with Mandy by about two and a half hours. Dad's parents are shocked to discover their son was alive throughout the past month or so until last Thursday. Grandpa tells Mom that she will have to somehow send Dad's body to California, where they can actually bury it where the grave is. That hurts Mom, the whole conversation, and I try to comfort her, and she tells me she appreciates it, but I know she's steadily breaking.

On Monday morning, we get a call from a woman who says she is Beth Tryon, Marc's mother. She explains how her father had been the head of the company Dad and Jargon—Harry Jones—worked for, and that she was truthfully glad that the money was gone. She sounds disappointed in her son for turning to criminal activity when he hadn't gotten what he wanted, and I soon hand the phone to Mom and have her talk to Mrs. Tyron because I know I won't say very nice things to console her.

My life is surprisingly better now that I'm not carrying around such a big, dangerous secret. I promise myself that I won't keep any more secrets from Mom and my siblings and anyone, but that fails almost immediately once I realize I am still holding onto Nate's. But it's not my secret. I hope he comes clean.

He stops by every day for a few minutes. It's pure torture that it's so short and I can't decide if I'd rather he not come at all or if I should just love the few minutes that I get with him. He's up to something, something he hasn't opened up to me about it yet. *You inspired me to be brave,* he'd said. What does that mean?

But I've learned to be patient with him.

Two months ago, I totally would have kept the secret of my adventures only to my family and myself and Nate. However, now I have changed. I still don't like being in the spotlight, and this experience definitely has put me there, but for some reason I don't regret my decision to let people know about Thursday. And I'm not bragging, going around saying how amazing I was that I faced down four criminals and beat them to the *dust*—I would never do that— yet I am unremorseful because of my choice. There's nothing wrong with letting people understand why the police were at the brick building last week. And yes, every time I say my dad died for me, it hurts worse than ever, but the more I say it the more I believe it and the more I forgive him. He left us for money. And he gave his life for me in the end, repaying the debt he owed us. He's still causing plenty of pain and abandonment, but we've mostly forgiven him. I have. Florence has. It's just Mom.

And I get it. She suffered the greatest out of all of us.

Tuesday dawns sunny and bright, perfect weather for walking. Outside, it's only a little chilly, but I won't mind it. Mom worries about me walking to school and even just attending it. She argues that we have spring break next week—why don't I just go back after that?

To my surprise, my siblings agree with me and say I should go. Roman says I need to be strengthened by my friends as well as my family, and that's when she finally gives in. She tries to drive me, but there's no way I'm passing up walking with Nate.

After promising multiple times that I won't walk alone, Mom grants me permission. I find it strange that I have to convince *her* to let me attend school. I wonder what kid would have to beg their mom to go.

I know that going back to school will make me the center of attention. But I will be with Nate and Mandy and Elijah, and that's a good enough excuse to be there.

Everyone is awake Tuesday morning. Mom makes her delicious waffles, and I remember how we had eaten these on my birthday, the day I was in a horrible mood. The day before Jargon tried to kill me. Two days before we received the fake news that Dad was dead and—

I stop myself. I don't need to rehash all of that.

Florence strikes up conversation while we eat, but most of us are too busy stuffing ourselves full of waffles to talk. I sit across the table from Siena, who is being absolutely adorable and I love her for it. I want to tell her that, but I can't interrupt Flo as she drags on and on about her favorite jam. I call tell Siena at a different time.

"My favorite jam is *shut up, Florence*," says Roman.

"How funny," my twin says dryly.

"I like raspberry," Siena buts in, drizzling maple syrup over her waffle. "My favorite thing to put on waffles, however, is ranch dressing."

Pompeii snorts into his breakfast. He has whipped cream on his face. "You have never eaten ranch on waffles," he says. "That's disgusting, anyway. Why would you want to eat it?"

"I love trying new things," Siena says simply.

I raise my eyebrows in shock. When Pompeii starts picking a fight with her like that, she normally takes the bait and bites back.

She hasn't changed from her usual snappy self, has she?

She seriously has me convinced until she up-ends the bottle of syrup on Pompeii's head.

We all burst out laughing except for Pompeii. He lets loose a high-pitched scream that nearly shatters my eardrums; I clap my hands over my ears and wait for him to finish. He grabs the bottle from Siena and tries to pour it on her, but she is smart and has backed away, out of range. Pompeii throws down the half-empty bottle of syrup and rushes off to clean his hair before the sticky substance soaks into it even more.

I'm glad we can still find joy.

"Ah, a typical day in the Ferrari household," says Mom. "Siena, there are several spots on the table and Pompeii's chair and the floor that now are covered in syrup. I would appreciate it if you cleaned them up."

"Okay!" Siena replies in a chipper tone, and she's sounding totally suspicious.

Mom frowns, wary.

"Venice, would you get me a rag?" Siena asks sweetly. "You're closer to the sink than I am."

I get to my feet, carrying my empty plate with me, and walk to the sink. I have a feeling that Siena is acting like this for a reason. She must have something else planned. I'm glad I have school today.

I grab a wet rag that is draped over the side of the sink and toss it at my littlest sister. "Here, Siena."

She catches it and begins wiping up the syrup, humming softly to herself.

"There is something going on here," says Flo. She is suspicious, just like the rest of us.

"We aren't having ice cream tonight, are we?" asks Roman.

Mom shakes her head.

Siena moves on from the table to Roman, who is in the chair

next to the one Pompeii was sitting in, and she starts to clean his head. He swats her away furiously. He opens his mouth to yell at her, but Mom suddenly breaks down laughing again, interrupting Roman's preparations of war.

We all join in, even Roman.

"Siena, can you *actually* mop up the syrup, please?" Mom says, having a hard time speaking through her laughter.

"But there is some other gross stuff that I have to clean!" she protests, and goes for Roman again.

I smile and wash off my dishes, placing them on a towel to dry off. I return to the table, making sure Siena is doing her job before claiming my seat. "I hope Pompeii doesn't retaliate."

"Knowing him," Flo puts in, "I'm sure he will."

"I doubt he will ever learn not to," Mom agrees. "And Siena won't stop making him angry. Isn't that right, Siena?"

"Yessir!"

Florence goes to say something, probably to correct Siena, when a knock sounds on the front door. All eyes swing over to me, and Roman smirks knowingly. I ignore everyone and shove back from the table.

"I've got to go." I grab my backpack from off the floor by my seat. "See you all later."

"Don't get into any fights!" Flo calls as I walk towards the door.

"Don't make out during class!" Roman yells.

I groan loudly. "You guys are so annoying." I stop to slip on my shoes before opening the front door. It isn't cold enough that I need a coat, but I *could* wear a jacket. I decide not to because I don't want to have to look for it.

Nate stands on the porch, having a difficult time hiding a grin. Something seems to be different about him, and I list my head while trying to work it out. His hair is a mess as always, his light blue eyes dancing as always, his dimples adorable as always. He isn't wearing his jacket or gloves, showing off the long white scars that trail up and around his arms. The cut on his cheek has healed and scarred over, and I have to resist the urge to touch it. One of his hands is wrapped around the strap of his backpack, and he looks incredibly pleased with himself, a peculiar expression for someone as humble as he is.

"Why are you staring at me like my head is cracked open?"

I narrow my eyes, still trying to find what is different.

Then it strikes me.

He isn't exhausted. He constantly has exhaustion buried deep inside of him, but he doesn't now. And the strain, the burden he carries, is gone. It has vanished without a trace. He looks lighter than he ever has.

I slowly close the door behind me, eyes never wavering from his. "Nate," I say, "what happened?"

His grin widens. "Man, you're good." He takes my hand and leads me off the porch, down the driveway, onto the sidewalk before he continues to talk. "I can't believe how fast you recognized something has changed, Venice."

"What are you talking about?"

He hesitates, gathering his thoughts, and I prepare myself for a ten minute speech when he simply says, "I turned my grandpa in."

After making sure there is no one out on the sidewalks, I shriek and throw my arms around Nate, startling him.

"That's awesome!" I cry. Then I rethink what I have just said. "I mean, how are you handling it all?"

I ask it, but the answer is pretty obvious.

He laughs and hugs me back; I step away first. "It's all right, Venice," he says, continuing our walk out of the neighborhood. "I'm not depressed over sending him in. He needed to go. It took all weekend and Monday, so I didn't go to school, but I talked to my dad and convinced him to commit Gramps to this facility for people like him. It's in Delaware, but I did my research and I think this is the best fit for him. It's a good place, with specialists trained to take care of old folks with similar problems to his, and they'll even let us visit him as often as we like."

How he dealt with it just shows he really cares for his grandpa, despite the pain that old man inflicted in his life. "I'm so happy for you, Nate. And you said you talked to your dad?"

He nods. "Yeah. It was really awkward at first. Turns out he was thinking about reaching out to me sometime but he was so ashamed for deserting me that he figured I would hate him and resent him and reject him. He didn't think I would ever want to see him again, which is the opposite, actually. I've been hoping to get to know him my entire life, and it looks like he wishes the same thing, he just couldn't convince himself to face me. He feels supremely guilty for leaving me so long ago."

"I told you!" I poke him with my elbow. "I told you that your dad probably wanted to meet up with you again, and you wouldn't listen. This is great. So great." I am happy—so happy—until what he has said about his grandpa sinks in. "Wait. If you don't have a guardian any more, where will you go? Are you going to live with your dad?"

"That's the best part." Nate grins at me. "My dad—you know he lives like an hour away, right? Anyway, he told me he wanted to downsize, that he was going to start telecommuting and was wondering if I'd consider helping him find a place here."

"And...?"

"He's thinking about moving in."

I hug Nate again—he groans humorously and says, "We don't need two Mandys."

"Oh, be quiet." I pull back and we keep walking. "Your dad might move in here? That's even more awesome."

Nate's grin widens, flashing his dimples. "He'll need a realtor."

"I can definitely help you there."

He slips his hand into mine, and I don't wince even though he has taken my hurt one. My palm is in the process of healing—I still keep a bandage around the skin so it won't get infected when I'm doing things—and it occasionally throbs. The same goes for my arm. I think I will have scars in both places, and that doesn't bother me at all. I like scars.

"Oh—sorry." Nate notices the bandage over my palm and drops my hand, but I grab him again.

"It's all right. My hand doesn't hurt as much."

He gives me a long, hard look. "You're just saying that."

I roll my eyes. "Whatever. Now that your grandpa is gone, where are you staying until your dad moves in?"

"Elijah's. I feel a little bad, since they already have a crowded house, and I have Mercury with me, but Mrs. Jenkins is nice enough to let me stay. She likes my dog. He's a good distraction and watches her kids when she isn't. So I don't feel as bad as I should."

I grin. "And have you told anyone why you're scarred? And not living with your grandpa anymore?"

He shakes his head, and my grin fades a touch. "I want you to be there," he says. "I'm planning on telling Mandy and Elijah today at lunch. I waited until you could be with me to do it."

"That's also great." I sigh happily. "Well, this day has definitely turned out amazing." And it has—I'm utterly pleased that he found the right people to take care of his grandpa, and that he talked to his dad, and that he's hopefully getting his dad back, and that he succeeded where I failed.

Mandy's jaw drops farther and farther down with each word Nate says. Her expression is priceless. Elijah is the same: bewildered, shocked, disgusted, horrified.

When Nate finishes explaining his life, there is total silence.

I give him a small smile to show I'm proud that he finally let someone else know the truth, and he smiles back. He looks immensely relieved; it's good that he has shared his secret to his two best friends who care about him.

Mandy is the first to speak. "*What?*" she splutters. "That's the reason why you have scars, and you hide beneath a jacket and gloves, and—I feel like a really bad friend, Nate. Why did you never tell us?"

"I didn't want you to worry." He shrugs. "You two not knowing anything made it real easy to fake it."

"Well, that isn't healthy!" Mandy explodes.

Kids are looking this way. I am already a source of many stares. I was right—coming back to school after what happened instantly made me the subject of much gossip. I don't mind.

Nate shifts in his seat beside me, nervous that Mandy is yelling. "I know it isn't healthy," he says patiently. "You won't believe how many times Venice told me that."

"When did she know? When did you tell her?"

"She found out on her own."

Mandy huffs. "And you let her know, yet you didn't tell us? Nate, you're really making me feel like a terrible friend. I didn't know about your grandpa, I didn't know about your scars, I didn't know about Venice and all the things she went through until she told me. How can I be a good friend if you two won't let me help?"

"My problems were family related," I say.

"Nate can say the same thing!" Mandy protests, and she has a point. "Do you have any more secrets, Nate? Venice?"

I shake my head. Nate copies me.

"Hm." She frowns at us. "Elijah, what should I do? Beat them up for not telling me these things?"

Elijah hasn't spoken once, and when he does, his voice is strangled. "Wow. I also feel like a bad friend. Nate, my man, how did you suffer through six or more years of abuse without saying anything? You're always there for us if we need you. You're always cheerful and act like nothing is wrong in your life and that you don't have an abusive grandpa who treats you like dirt. Why did you not trust us enough to let us know?"

"This wasn't a matter of trust." Nate sighs. "When I explained why I didn't tell anyone about my grandpa to Venice, I told her that I didn't want any pity. I didn't want my grandpa to get taken, either. He was the only family I had. But Venice kept nagging me"—I scoff—"until I finally decided to be brave and call my dad."

Is that why he said I inspired him to be brave?

"He's thinking about moving here." Nate smiles at his friends.

It cheers me to see him excited. He deserves to be happy. He deserves to have a father, someone who hopefully won't treat him as badly as his angry old grandpa did.

"That's great," says Elijah. "Then you can get out of my house."

I laugh, hoping he meant that as a joke.

"Nate..." Mandy begins, and once she has his full attention, she goes on. "I'm really sorry for not asking about this earlier. I'm sorry you have had to carry this secret around with you for years. And I know you don't want pity, so I'll try not to pity you. But, please, we are your friends because we want to share your burdens and help you shoulder them. You can trust us. We won't say anything to anyone."

"Actually, I don't mind," he replies. "If anyone asks, you can tell them if you want. You don't need to make an announcement, but you also don't have to hide it."

A smile curves up the sides of my mouth. I hadn't expected him to say that, but now that his grandpa isn't here, Nate doesn't need to protect him.

"Well, even though you got your scars from your grandpa," says Elijah, "I like them. They're really cool."

"I like your scars, too," I say, brushing a finger down his arm.

Nate is surprised. "Why?"

"Because they give me an excuse to touch you."

He actually—*actually*—rolls his eyes and looks away. I detect a redness in his cheeks, however, and I think I made him slightly embarrassed that I said that in front of our friends.

"Dude!" Elijah sounds shocked. "She just *flirted* with you."

Mandy is grinning broadly when I meet her eye.

Nate suddenly gets to his feet, watching someone on the far end of the cafeteria. "I'll be right back," he says, and vanishes into the tangled mess of tables and kids. I stare after him, spotting him walking towards a lone boy on the other side of the room.

Keller Jacobs.

"What was *that*?" Mandy whispers, leaning across the table. "You like, totally flirted. I didn't think that was your thing. And if you had been any other girl, I probably would have punched you. It's a good thing I like you."

I shrug. "I can't help it. I'm crazy about that boy."

Mandy and Elijah exchange concerned looks.

"Is this how you and Nate feel when Mandy and I—" Elijah starts, but I cut him off.

"Yes, exactly."

We're talking about bullet wounds and how they are extremely painful when Nate comes back, a thoughtful expression on his face. He is quiet for the rest of lunch, which is fine since Mandy rambles on and on about how she is totally going to brag to everyone that her best friend was shot in the upper arm. Roman was right—I *am* strengthened by my amazing friends and the love and concern and humor they share.

I am disappointed when lunch ends and I have to go to biology. We hadn't finished our report in time, and I'm rather nervous about what Mr. Castro's reaction will be.

I stand up, ready to leave, but Mandy stops me. "Hold on," she says. "I have to show you the awesome shirt I got last week. My mom thinks it's immature, but Elijah got it for me, so it's my favorite shirt ever." She unzips her jacket and reveals a red T-shirt with a chicken on it. The words *When life gives you chickens, make chicken nuggets* are scrawled above the picture.

"That's an awesome shirt," I agree, grinning. "Good job, Elijah."

He matches my grin. "I only go shopping every once in a while, but when I do, I always get the best things."

"Now that you've seen it," Mandy says, "you can leave." She winks at me, and it's worse than the smirk Roman gave me earlier. I turn and walk out of the cafeteria, far from her teasing; I'm already regretting saying what I did about Nate.

As I walk through the hallways with him, kids stare at me. Some come up and talk to me, and I find that I am talkative and energetic to complete strangers—this is definitely a surprising experience. I am asked plenty of questions, all that I answer, and I actually enjoy myself. Nate knows some of the kids—he supplies the names. Most of them express how they were awed by what I did, but one wants to know if I can come to a party she's having, and two freshmen ask for my autograph.

We are finally left alone when Nate and I reach our classroom.

I stop him from entering by placing my hurt hand on his arm. "Nate. What did you talk to Keller about?"

"Told him I turned in my grandpa." He gives me a tiny smile. "I don't think we will ever be friends again, but at least now I won't be worried that he's going to spill my secrets."

"And you're letting everyone know?" I ask. "Back at lunch, you said Mandy could tell anyone she wanted. It seems like you're okay with people knowing."

Nate's smile turns into a grin. "Everyone will know," he agrees. "I just need to put this behind me."

He looks into the classroom—for once, the lights are on, probably because we're giving presentations today and the others need to see—then back at me. "Venice. You ready?"

I take a deep breath. "Heck yeah."

EPILOGUE

I stand on the Bridge of Sighs with my family, staring down at the canal below us. I can't believe I am actually in the city I was named after; this trip is sudden and abrupt. Mom's announcement that we were taking a family trip to Italy over spring break startled us all, and by the way she and Flo look very pleased with themselves, I know they had planned this together.

Mom has forever wanted to go to Italy. She never had the time or the money, but now she does. And she tells me over and over how this trip is far more fun with her family than by herself.

I don't know about that—Siena and Pompeii complained the entire flight here—and walking around Venice with those kids is very hard. Even now, I can hear them arguing behind me, saying how if they could paddle a gondola down the canal, they would be going much faster. I glance over my shoulder at them; I think they are tiring the other people on our tour.

Florence is on my left, talking on her phone. She is speaking to Bradley—he is one of the only kids who can listen to her gush and remember what she says. She catches me looking at her and gives me a tiny wave. She is excited for our next stop: Florence.

Roman is standing next to her, moodily kicking at the white limestone this bridge was made out of. He isn't very happy about leaving so suddenly, but it is mostly because he thinks this will be a boring trip. He doesn't want to look at amazing artwork. He'd rather see ruins—which I understand; Rome is our third stop and we will go there in two days.

Mom is deep in conversation with our tour guide, asking plenty of questions and voicing opinions on the architecture of the bridge. She's excited, and so am I, and I can't help but grin to myself as I watch her wave her hands wildly in the air with her usual gusto.

I glance down at the water again. My fingers unconsciously play with the ring on my pinky. I am incredibly happy. My family is back together again. I have helped each of my siblings find joy in their lives. I have helped Nate realize he can have so much more in life— his dad is already one of Mom's clients, and he's preparing to move into our town.

I have solved a dangerous mystery that put my life on the line, and despite the loss I suffered, I think it was worth it. I was reunited with my dad. I learned he loved me, loved everyone in our family, and regretted his decision for going off with the money instead of staying with us.

A loud laugh startles me. I look back at Mom and see she is laughing her head off at something another tourist has said in the conversation she's leading with the guide. They're all having a good time, especially her.

Virginia really has done our family good. I haven't heard Mom laugh like that in forever.

Facing the water, I lean against the walls of the closed bridge and breathe a soft sigh of relief.

We came to Virginia an unhappy, contentious family. Now we have worked through our problems and assisted each other in solving them. Now, we are a happy, whole family again.

Thank the trees.

THE END